FINAL BEGINNINGS

FINAL
BEGINNINGS

John Edward
and Natasha Stoynoff

P

Princess Books
New York, NY

Copyright © 2004 by John Edward and Natasha Stoynoff

Published in the United States by: Princess Books, a Division of Get Psych'd, Inc., New York, NY.

Distributed in the United States by: Hay House, Inc., P.O. Box 5100, Carlsbad, CA 92018-5100 • *Phone:* (760) 431-7695 or (800) 654-5126 • *Fax:* (760) 431-6948 or (800) 650-5115 • www.hayhouse.com • **Distributed in Australia by:** Hay House Australia Pty. Ltd., 18/36 Ralph St., Alexandria NSW 2015 • *Phone:* 612-9669-4299 • *Fax:* 612-9669-4144 • www.hayhouse.com.au • **Distributed in the United Kingdom by:** Hay House UK, Ltd. • Unit 62, Canalot Studios • 222 Kensal Rd., London W10 5BN • *Phone:* 44-20-8962-1230 • *Fax:* 44-20-8962-1239 • www. hayhouse.co.uk • **Distributed in the Republic of South Africa by:** Hay House SA (Pty), Ltd., P.O. Box 990, Witkoppen 2068 • *Phone/Fax:* 27-11-706-6612 • orders@psdprom.co.za • **Distributed in Canada by:** Raincoast • 9050 Shaughnessy St., Vancouver, B.C. V6P 6E5 • *Phone:* (604) 323-7100 • *Fax:* (604) 323-2600

Design: Summer McStravick

Library of Congress Control Number: 2004115495

Hardcover (1-932128-02-6) and tradepaper (1-932128-09-3) versions of this book were first published by Princess Books in 2004 and have been catalogued by the Library of Congress.

ISBN 13: 978-1-932128-10-9
ISBN 10: 1-932128-10-7

08 07 06 05 4 3 2 1
1st mass-market printing, August 2005

Printed in the United States of America

With love to Vasilly Shamanduroff.

For Isobel, Jim . . . and Blake.

In the not-so-distant future . . .

CHAPTER 1

"THEY'RE CALLING IT 'THE CROWN OF GOD'—*la corona di Dio*," Giovanni said, dipping his oar into the dark water and delicately launching the gondola into the Venetian night.

La corona di Dio. Why does everything sound so much more romantic in Italian? Katherine Haywood mused, studying the shimmering turquoise light reflecting across the harbor. She followed the gondolier's gaze upward to the dazzling display of the aurora borealis illuminating the night sky with a circle of green fire.

Who comes all the way to Italy to see the northern lights? she wondered.

She knew why she'd come—for a desperately needed break, deliberately choosing a destination where she didn't speak the language, wouldn't be recognized, and where no one would stop her in the street asking her to connect them with a dead loved one.

As a psychic medium, easing people's pain over the loss of someone they'd loved had been her work and her life for nearly two decades. But after thousands of readings, Katherine was feeling tired, empty.

She wondered if she'd reached a point of "spiritual burnout." No matter how hard she worked, no matter how much heart she put into it, it never seemed to be enough.

If I could bring everyone's loved ones back from the dead so they'd be standing right in front of them, I would, Katherine thought. *But I'm just the messenger, not a miracle worker. And I'm one exhausted messenger.*

She listened to the soft waves of the lagoon lapping against the gondola, wishing the waters of the ancient city would wash her weariness away.

Katherine had never intended to be a famous psychic; she'd just wanted to use her abilities to help people. But like it or not, the fame had come, and the endless demands on her time and talents had quickly followed.

She hoped that putting an ocean between herself and her home would allow her to escape for a while, to tune out the world around her—and the world above. She needed to figure out how she'd reached this point: on the verge of abandoning what she considered to be her life's work, which she'd always believed was her destiny.

"They say these lights in the sky are being created by the biggest solar storm in nearly 200 years," Giovanni said, sliding his oar against the water. He spoke flawless English, but with a robust Italian accent.

She looked at the man sternly. She'd paid him $300 for the gondola ride—twice the going rate—on the condition that he didn't talk. She'd already read all about the unexpected space storm sweeping over the earth's atmosphere during her transatlantic flight. She didn't need a newscast from a gondolier; she just wanted to slip through the fabled city's watery roadways in peace.

"Some people are frightened by the sky. They say it's the end of the world. But others say it's a miracle, that the Blessed Mother is reaching out to—"

"Excuse me, Giovanni . . ."

"Hey, pretty lady, call me Johnny."

"Yes, all right . . . Johnny. I've just arrived in Italy today after a very long flight. I don't mean to be rude, but I did pay for a silent tour. So please . . . I just want a little quiet time right now to take in the sights. Okay? Thanks for understanding."

"Oh, sure, pretty lady. You don't want me to talk? I won't talk. I shut up like you ask."

In a flash, Katherine could see that the spirit world had no intention of letting her hide out. For a moment, the smiling gondolier wasn't wearing the traditional striped shirt and cap he'd been in when she climbed into the boat. The vision lasted only a second, but it was crystal clear: The man was wearing a Boston Bruins hockey jersey.

He'd approached her earlier on the pier with a grandiose "Ciao, bella donna." He assured her that he was a born-and-bred Venetian and would give the best water tour money could buy. But now she realized that his thick Italian accent and flirty-gondolier attitude were just typical tourist ploys.

She brushed the vision aside, hoping that her spirit guides weren't preparing to bring through all of the gondolier's undoubtedly chatty relatives who'd passed over to the Other Side.

They left the main lagoon, passing beneath a footbridge, and headed toward the heart of the old city.

"Hundreds of years ago, my ancestors named this bridge the Bridge of Sighs," Giovanni explained, "because condemned men sighed as they crossed it on their way to the prison tower." The word *tower* bounced off the tunnel walls and echoed in Katherine's ears like a tolling bell.

"Please, Giovanni . . . some quiet?"

"Oh, pretty lady, call me Johnny!"

"Yes . . . Johnny, now *please* . . ." Katherine said more insistently, "and if you're going to pretend to be a Venetian instead of a Bostonian, you could at least learn the local history. The bridge wasn't named by *your* ancestors, but by the English poet Lord Byron. And the condemned prisoners were led across the bridge to a *dungeon,* not a tower."

"I didn't say *tower* . . . I said *dungeon,*" Giovanni insisted, his Italian accent quickly dissolving. "I've given this tour a thousand times, and I've never said *tower.* And how the heck did you know I was from Boston? I've been doing this for ten years, and you're the first to ever guess."

"I never 'guess.'"

I was sure he said "tower," Katherine thought, as they glided silently though the ancient canals.

Katherine had hoped that this trip to Italy

would recharge her emotional batteries, but already she was feeling worse than when she'd boarded the plane in New York.

I'm just jet-lagged. All I is need a good night's sleep, she decided, suddenly feeling claustrophobic.

As they moved quietly across the water, the walls of the buildings lining the canal seemed to be closing in on her. She tried to focus on the glowing night sky above, but her vision began to blur. A jumble of disconnected images burst through her mind: a handsome, dark-haired gentleman hugging a smiling little girl; a tired young man injecting himself with a strange-looking needle; a picnic basket; and the smoking barrel of a gun. A moment later, the gondola had pulled into the wide passage of the Grand Canal, and the images vanished.

Katherine shivered.

"Giovanni, I apologize—it's not you . . . I'm just suddenly feeling ill. Could you please take me back to the pier? I want to go to my hotel."

"No problem, pretty lady. But I think I've upset you. I'm sorry. Let me make it up to you . . . I'm taking a nice long drive through Tuscany tomorrow and spending the night at our family villa. If you've got no plans, please join me as my guest."

"I don't think so."

"Don't worry," he laughed. "My wife will be with us. And she barely says a word to anyone, especially me . . . so you'll have a quiet ride through the beautiful Tuscan countryside—vineyards, olive groves, beautiful rolling hills. Sounds good, no?"

"Well . . ."

"Tell you what . . . we'll stop by your hotel tomorrow morning, and if you feel like coming along, then come. If you don't, then don't worry about it. Nothing ventured, nothing gained, right?"

Olive groves and vineyards, Katherine considered. *That does sound like the perfect escape.*

"What time?"

"We'll be in front of your hotel at 8 A.M. Where are you staying?"

"The Hotel Pisa."

"Ah, the leaning tower . . . nice place."

Tower, tower, tower . . . the word reverberated through Katherine's mind.

KATHERINE WOKE AT DAWN feeling groggy and irritable. She was on her way outside to get some fresh air when the hotel concierge handed her a fax.

Great, I'm getting faxed, and no one's even supposed to know where I am, she thought. She was about to crumple it up and toss it into the Grand Canal without reading it, but decided to stick it in her purse until she'd found an open café and a triple espresso to wake herself up.

As she walked the cobblestone streets lining the canal, a group of early-rising Italian workmen began whistling and shouting at her.

"Buon giorno, signora bella! Mama mia! Bello dai capelli rossi! You 'av a date with me tonight, please?"

Katherine stood out in any crowd—a well-put-together redhead standing just over six feet tall was hard to miss. She favored well-tailored business suits in public, but today she'd dressed down for her countryside sojourn—jeans and a T-shirt.

"Sorry gentlemen, I'm married," she lied, holding up the wedding band she was still wearing five years after her divorce to ward off unwanted suitors.

"That's, how you say, a pity. Such beauty should never belong to only one man alone," one of them called out, as Katherine slipped into a café.

After drinking her second cup of espresso, she began reading the fax. It was a request from Daniel Dinnick in New York City to be a guest on his radio station later in the week. The invitation was for the top-rated program in the city, so despite its ridiculous name—*The Jungle Hour*—and its particularly odious host, Katherine had appeared on it several times. Since it was widely syndicated, it was a fast and easy way to reach as many people as she could.

The fax was the standard request form: *Please join us on our Friday-morning show. . . .*

But it was odd that Daniel Dinnick, whose father was one of the world's wealthiest men, would send her a personal invitation. Those things were usually handled by booking agents or interns, not billionaires.

And how in heaven's name did he know where to find me? Katherine wondered.

She folded the fax and was about to return it to her purse when she felt a prickly tingle at the back of her neck—a sure sign that she was about to get a message from the Other Side. A moment later, she had an image of herself sitting with her father—who'd been dead five years—in a hospital room. He was shrunken and frail, in pain, lying on a bed with tubes running in and out of his arms. She was holding his hand, kissing his cheek, whispering to him that it was okay to let go . . . that family was waiting for him. The image morphed into another—a young girl receiving a chemo treatment, calling out for her mother but getting no answer.

Then the images were gone. She was back in the café, staring at the water taxis speeding along the Grand Canal. Getting sudden, unexpected images she didn't understand was nothing new to her—their meaning would eventually become clear. The Other Side was trying to tell her something . . . maybe that she was needed somewhere to help someone pass . . . maybe a sick little girl needed her help. She didn't know yet, but sooner or later she would.

She looked at the fax in her hand. *No . . . I'm done with all that,* she told herself.

Media appearances had helped her get her message across, and had hopefully eased the suffering of thousands of grieving people. But what had fame given her in return? A broken marriage, an empty Manhattan apartment, and a loneliness only worsened by being unaccompanied in one of the world's most romantic cities.

She was watching a pair of young lovers leaning against the canal bridge, kissing passionately, and began to rip up the fax when her eyes fell upon a single phrase that made her freeze: *at our new location in the BioWorld Tower.*

Katherine shook her head, looking up at the cloudless Venetian sky.

Come on, what's with all these tower references? She paid for her coffee and headed back to the hotel.

Katherine strolled through the narrow streets, peering into the windows of the shops that were just opening, and savoring the sweet aroma of freshly baked biscotti. A group of Italian school-children walked past, laughing and carefree. It reminded Katherine of her own youth, and the day she'd first realized she was different from other kids, that she straddled two worlds—the world her parents and friends lived in, and the other world, the place where people who had died . . . lived.

She'd been crossing a busy street on the way to school in her Queens neighborhood when she dropped one of her schoolbooks. A strong gust of wind had blown the book into the street, and she'd begun to chase after it when she heard: *Kathy, you forgot to look both ways!*

She turned around, and there was her grand-mother, who'd passed away more than a year before. A moment later, her grandmother vanished.

Katherine shook her head, thinking that her imagination was playing tricks on her, and then turned to retrieve her book, which was being flat-tened by a speeding bus. She jumped back from the curb, realizing how close she'd come to being under that bus herself.

"Thanks, Grams," Katherine said out loud.

You're welcome, my little Kathy, she heard a voice say in her head. In her mind she saw a quick image of a pink rose, and was flooded with the feelings of love she and her grandmother had always shared.

As she grew older, Katherine's ability to receive information from the Other Side, as she began calling it, grew more pronounced. She often knew who was on the phone before anyone answered it, and her best friends knew that if they lost something—a ring, a notebook, or a stuffed animal—she could picture the item in her mind and know where it was.

But on the night of her 13th birthday, she realized both the power—and the burden—of her ability. She was blowing out the candles on her cake and looking at her best friend, Caitlin, smiling at her from across the table. Suddenly, the room grew dark and she heard tires screeching on pavement. There was a flash . . . and a quick, vivid image of Caitlin's mother smashing through a windshield, then lying dead at the side of the road.

The vision vanished as quickly as it had come. Everything was normal again. They were singing "Happy Birthday," and Caitlin was smiling, passing her a big piece of cake. *What do I do now?* Katherine wondered, staring sadly at her friend, who was happily spooning chocolate ice cream onto her plate. *Am I supposed to tell her?*

After the party, Katherine walked Caitlin home and did what she thought was right: She told her about the vision, begging Caitlin to warn her mom not to drive.

"Why do you have to tell me stuff like that?" Caitlin asked, obviously upset by Katherine's words. "I don't want to hear it."

A week later, the accident happened exactly as Katherine had envisioned.

When Caitlin eventually returned to school, she wouldn't talk to Katherine, refusing to even make eye contact with her. Then one day Caitlin cornered her in the girls' bathroom. "What are you, *a freak?!*" she screamed at her supposed best friend. "Why didn't you *stop* it?"

Katherine didn't know what to say—she didn't have an answer. She got sick to her stomach and ran home in tears, shutting herself in her room and lying on her bed for hours, staring at the ceiling and trying to make sense of it all.

"Something's seriously wrong with me, Dad," she told her father when he came to get her for dinner that night and found her crying. She told him what had happened, and how her visions were beginning to terrify her. "Why do I see things like that when no one else does?"

"Don't you worry," he told her, dabbing her eyes with the corner of her pillowcase. "There's nothing wrong with you. You're special. Maybe I never told you this, but my mother was special in the same way." He smiled. "I think it just takes time to know what you're supposed to *do* with your specialness."

WHEN KATHERINE GOT BACK to the hotel, Giovanni and his wife were waiting for her in their Austin Mini.

"This is Vanessa, my beautiful wife," Giovanni said, greeting Katherine.

"Oh my God . . . you're the psychic from TV!" Vanessa shouted in Katherine's face. She turned and punched Giovanni in the arm. "Why didn't you tell me it was Katherine Haywood, you idiot?"

Vanessa turned back to Katherine, saying, "I'm your biggest fan . . . maybe you could talk to my uncle Gino who—"

"Excuse my wife, miss," Giovanni said. "She usually never says anything to anybody. I promise she won't pester you on the trip. I didn't even know you were a celebrity."

"Oh, you must get that all the time. I'm so sorry," Vanessa said, pulling her fingers across her lips. "My mouth is zipped from now on."

"Climb in," Giovanni instructed. "We're taking you to one of the most beautiful old cities in Tuscany—San Gimignano. They call it *la citta delle belle torri.*"

"What does that mean?" Katherine asked.

"The city of beautiful towers. It has more medieval towers than any city in Italy . . . 13 altogether."

The color drained from Katherine's face. She leaned on the roof of the Mini to steady herself and had a sudden mental image of a car bursting into flames and dropping into a river.

That's the East River, Katherine realized, as her head began to pound.

"Are you all right?" Vanessa asked.

"Um . . . I'm fine," Katherine replied, as another image flashed in front of her. This time it was a little girl—she thought it might be her niece, lying on a field of grass with the New York City skyline in the background. The girl was struggling to breathe—an oxygen mask was strapped to her face. She turned and looked at Katherine, her eyes pleading for help.

Katherine felt like she was suffocating. She couldn't catch her breath.

Something's terribly wrong, she thought.

She stepped away from the car and took a few deep breaths.

"I appreciate your offer, Giovanni, I really do," she said, quickly, "but something has come up . . . a family emergency. I wonder if you would be kind enough to wait for me to get my bags from my room and then drive me to the airport? I've got to get back to New York City."

I've got to get back home.

CHAPTER 2

THE PLANE DROPPED HUNDREDS OF FEET IN A FEW SECONDS, sending food plates flying and flight attendants tumbling into the aisle.

"This is your captain speaking, folks. No need for alarm—we've just hit a patch of unexpected turbulence." The pilot's voice was calm and controlled, intended to soothe his jittery passengers, but Katherine picked up on the man's nervousness and fear.

"Um . . . the small problem we're having has to do with this solar storm you might have heard about, the one giving us those beautiful night skies," the captain continued. "It seems to be getting worse, and it's messing up a few of our instruments just the tiniest bit. Nothing to worry about, mind you, but we might be in for a slightly bumpier ride than usual. So stay in your seats with your belts fastened, and we should have you at JFK in just under three hours. Relax and enjoy the rest of the movie."

Before the plane had taken off, Katherine had tried to call home to make sure her niece was all right, but the solar storm had created havoc with the phone lines, and she never got through. Now, she looked at the little overhead movie screen. Bruce Willis was machine-gunning bad guys on top of a skyscraper somewhere.

Another tower, she thought, leaning her head against the cold windowpane, catching scattered glimpses of the blue Atlantic through a broken patchwork of clouds.

Towers, towers, towers.

Whatever the message was, it had gotten her attention.

Her mind drifted back to the day the tower image had first become significant in her life. She'd been 18, still inexperienced and uncertain about her psychic talents. She was driving to the mall to buy supplies for her first day at NYU coming up the following week. She rolled down the car window and was singing along with John Lennon as her favorite Beatles song wafted through the radio speakers: *Juuuliaaaa . . . Juuuliaaaa . . . I sing my song of love . . . to reach you. . . .*

Katherine sped up to beat a yellow traffic light, but it turned red before she got there. She slammed on the brakes, stopping in front of the local community center, where she saw a banner hanging over the front door advertising a psychic fair taking place that day. On impulse, she pulled into the center's parking lot and bought a ticket at the front door for a psychic reading, writing her name in bold strokes on the little slip of paper.

The first thing she saw when she walked into the large gymnasium was a long row of psychics—some working with tarot cards, others using numerology—sitting behind foldout bridge tables. The tarot readers were flipping cards like they were playing solitaire. Katherine was transfixed, watching the cards roll through the readers' fingers, landing on their tablecloths with a loud *snap!*

She'd wandered past a dozen or so card readers, the Beatles tune still echoing in her head: *Juuuuuuliaaaa . . . calls meeeee . . .* when her eyes landed on a sign taped to one of the bridge tables: Julia Asher, Psychic Medium.

Katherine stopped in front of the table, and John Lennon stopped singing in her head.

Okay, assuming there are signs in this world, this has got to be one, Katherine thought. She sat down in front of the woman and handed her the ticket.

The psychic didn't look anything like Katherine had expected—this was no cheap carnival fortune-teller. The woman sitting in front of her was elegant and professional, wearing a simple navy skirt and white blouse, her glossy black hair carefully gathered into a French twist. She had the kind of face that was beautiful without any makeup, and a smile that instantly put Katherine at ease.

The woman looked at Katherine's name scribbled on the slip of paper and grinned.

"Hello, Katherine, my name is Julia . . . and you are the one."

"I beg your pardon?" Katherine asked uncertainly.

"Every time I'm at one of these fairs, or doing a seminar or group reading, I feel that there's one special person I'm supposed to reach," she explained. "Today, *you* are that person. I can feel it. Now . . . can I hold your ring for a moment?"

Katherine slipped her silver thumb ring into Julia's palm.

"What I'm doing is called *psychometry*," the woman said, cupping the ring in her hands. "I'm receiving energy from your ring, and I'm getting that you have a strong psychic connection . . . but you know that already, don't you?"

"Well . . . I've been able to . . . see things," Katherine told her, unsure how much of herself to reveal.

"You have very highly evolved spirit guides— guides working for the higher good of humankind. I think you have an important mission. . . ."

Katherine shifted uncomfortably in her seat. She felt like she was being recruited into some sort of cult, but still . . . she was beginning to instinctively trust this woman.

"There are powerful forces around you, Katherine. You're going to have to deal with a lot of death in your life, but you must remember that even the darkest tunnel can open up onto the brightest of lights."

"What do you mean?" Katherine asked nervously.

"I mean that every ending is also a beginning . . . nothing is final . . . everything is eternal."

"Holy cow," Katherine muttered, stunned by the older woman's intensity.

Julia laughed, handing Katherine back her ring. "Am I freaking you out? I don't usually get quite so heavy on a first reading. But kid, you've got some powerful guides around you."

"Really?"

"No doubt about it . . . and I can tell that this is going to be your life's work. You're a born psychic. In fact, I think you're going to be famous one day—TV, radio, books, the works."

"Are you joking with me?" Katherine asked.

"Nope, but that's all in the future. You've got lots of work to do between now and then, and it's time for you to start learning the tools of your trade. These are called tarot cards," Julia said, shuffling the exotic deck.

For more than half an hour, the psychic turned over card after card and spoke of Katherine's future. She mentioned marriage, divorce, travel—and again, fame and fortune. Then she stopped and looked at Katherine with a serious expression. "This is the most important part of the reading. It will reveal when your true mission in life will begin . . . and it's the reason we're both here today. I need you to ask a question out loud, a question you *really* want answered."

Katherine was silent.

"Cat got your tongue?" Julia smiled.

"It just seems so . . . important. I don't know what to ask."

"I'll ask for you then. Okay?"

"Okay."

Julia closed her eyes and said, "Please give me

one symbol that will let Katherine know when her mission is about to unfold."

Julia turned over the final card, placing it in the center of the table. It was a picture of a tall building with flames shooting out of the windows.

"It's the Tower card," Julia told her.

"LADIES AND GENTLEMEN, we're now beginning our final approach to JFK. Please make sure your tray tables are locked in their upright positions and your seat is brought all the way forward. . . ."

Katherine pulled out of her daydream.

The Tower card, she remembered. Her stomach tightened with remorse as she wondered—for the thousandth time—if she'd already missed out on her mission in life by not somehow stopping the 9/11 tragedy.

She'd been on a plane herself that horrible morning six years ago when the Twin Towers were attacked. Even though she'd had premonitions that something catastrophic was going to happen in New York City, perhaps even involving a plane, the feelings were too vague for her to interpret or act upon.

She knew in her heart that there was nothing she could have done to prevent what had happened—the universe had its own plans that day that didn't involve her. But that didn't stop scores of skeptics and critics from jumping all over her for her "intuitive lapse."

"If you're so psychic, why didn't you see it coming? Why didn't you stop it?" they'd ask accusingly.

She answered them by saying that she was only shown what she was meant to see . . . that no one can see God's bigger plan.

"I need you to put your seat up, Miss," a flight attendant said to Katherine, interrupting her reverie.

She adjusted her seat, looked down at the Manhattan skyline, and smiled, still basking in the memory of her first meeting with Julia—who would later become her mentor and a dear friend for many years.

As well as being a psychic, Julia was also a part-time poetry professor at NYU. They often got together after class to talk about books, philosophy, and, of course, all things psychic.

There had also been the many fun weekends when Julia invited her entire poetry class to visit her Hamptons beach house. Usually it was just the girls who'd show up. They'd get tipsy on wine, and laugh and sing, while Julia tried to get them to listen to her favorite Frank Sinatra tunes on a beat-up old record player.

"Don't you listen to any music from *this* century?" the girls would tease her.

"Hey, don't knock Frankie," Julia would say. "He's seen me through a lot of tough times. And 'Summer Wind' is one of the greatest songs ever written."

Over the years, in her relaxed, no-pressure way, Julia slowly built up Katherine's confidence in her own psychic abilities, and set her on a career path as a professional psychic.

Katherine built a solid reputation as an honest, highly gifted medium. She was so good that

celebrity soon followed, along with all its complications. She was often too busy working to dedicate time to anything else. After a few strained
years of marriage, her husband left her, complaining that she spent more time connecting strangers
with dead people than she did connecting with
him.

Soon after her divorce, Katherine lost Julia as
well. Despite their closeness, her friend had never
told her that she was dying of cancer until the
very end. Julia's passing left a hole in Katherine's
heart that had never quite healed.

Katherine had tried repeatedly to connect
with her mentor on the Other Side, but had never
succeeded. She couldn't understand why—she'd
helped so many others reach lost loved ones, yet
she couldn't do it for herself.

The tires of the 747 bounced off the runway.
As soon as she had disembarked and was inside
the terminal, Katherine called her sister to see if
all was well with her niece.

"No problem here," her sister told her.

Then what the hell am I doing back in New York?
Katherine wondered.

ON THE RIDE HOME, the radio in the taxi was tuned
to WARP, the station owned by the Dinnick family, which aired *The Jungle Hour* every morning.

There's no way I'm going to do that show!
Katherine thought.

But no sooner had the thought passed
through her mind than she heard the nighttime
DJ announce: "Make sure you tune in tomorrow
morning. In our brand-new studio in the Dinnick

BioWorld Tower, you'll hear the psychic of the century, Katherine Haywood, taking calls on *The Jungle Hour,* with your host, Tarzan."

Katherine couldn't believe what she was hearing.

I'll be taking calls? I don't think so . . . I didn't even accept their offer to come on the show! She immediately called her publicist to chew her out.

"Kathy? I'm so sorry, but we had an intern in the office that day, and she must have given out your contact information. I tried to reach you, but the phones were all out." Katherine's publicist apologized profusely.

Katherine hung up and looked out the taxi window. A bus pulled up beside them with a huge billboard on its side, advertising Tower Records.

The tower again, she thought. *That must be why I'm here. Looks like I'll be at BioWorld Tower tomorrow doing their radio show after all. As Julia always said, every show or reading has a purpose . . . someone out there must need my help.*

EARLY THE NEXT MORNING, Katherine was greeted by a young woman as she entered the BioWorld Tower. The building was a post-9/11 phenomenon, hermetically sealed to protect against any kind of poisoned-air attack, with a security desk equipped with a metal detector, x-ray machine, and a device that took a personal DNA sample before allowing anyone to enter.

"Hi, Katherine, I'm Bronwyn, the show's production assistant. Don't worry about any of this crazy security business—it's *so* James Bond, just ridiculous . . . but I guess it's the times we live in, huh? I made sure you got celebrity clearance, so we can skip right through it," Bronwyn said, leading Katherine straight to the studio.

"I've got a confession . . . it could cost me my job, but I've got to tell you," Bronwyn continued. "It was me who faxed you in Italy. I even signed the boss's name to it. I couldn't help it—I dreamed every night for a week that I had to book you on the show today . . . it was the weirdest thing. But I just had to do it . . . so there it is. I don't care if you get me fired, but I always follow my intuition, no matter what. But I'm really, really sorry I wrecked your vacation." Bronwyn guided Katherine into the studio before the psychic had a chance to respond.

A minute later, she'd been fitted with a set of headphones and was sitting across from Tarzan, a tiny bald man with a booming voice, who had somehow become New York City's most popular disc jockey.

"AhhhhEEEEeeee . . . AhhhhEEEEeeeee . . . Ahhhhhhhh!"

Tarzan bellowed his obnoxious trademark, a poor Johnny Weissmuller imitation, into the microphone and through the headphones. Katherine's head began to pound, and she had an instant headache.

Tarzan put his hand over the microphone and whispered apologetically, "Sorry about that, Katherine. You know how New Yorkers love their wacky DJs."

His hand came off the mike and he was right back into character, letting out a few grunting ape sounds before introducing the morning lineup. Katherine thought he sounded ridiculous, but the

Tarzan shtick worked very well for him. His morning show, for reasons Katherine couldn't fathom, had remained at number one in the biggest radio market in the country for years.

"AhhhhEEEEeeee . . . AhhhhEEEEeeeee . . . Ahhhhhhhh!"

Katherine cradled her head in her hands as Tarzan's yodeling cry blasted through her headset.

"Good morning, New York! I'm Tarzan, and we have a treat today for all you jungle animals out there. With me in the tree house is Katherine Haywood, one of the most renowned psychics in the world. She'll be taking calls in just a few minutes, but first a quick update on this weird solar storm that's been giving us the spectacular northern lights the last couple nights.

"Seems that no one was expecting this, and it's playing havoc with communications around the planet . . . get this, some scientists claim that if this storm intensifies, it will top the one way back in September 1859—the worst on record. That one actually *melted* telegraph wires, and set buildings on fire around the world . . . so expect some real communication problems today, folks. . . but hopefully that won't affect our first guest, the lovely Katherine Haywood, from communicating with the Other Side. . . . Good morning, Katherine, good to have you back on the show."

"Thank you, it's good to be here."

"I understand you just came back from a vacation in Italy. Sounds like fun."

"Um . . . it was a very short trip."

"Well, I'm really glad you're here with us, and

I see the call board is lit up like a Christmas tree, so why don't we go right to the phones. Caller one, you're on the air with Katherine Haywood."

"Hi, Katherine, this is Evelyn."

"What can Katherine help you with today?" Tarzan asked. "Money? Work? Love life?"

Katherine began speaking before Evelyn had a chance to respond.

"I'm seeing a man on the Other Side with beautiful blue eyes. . . . I'm feeling a blackness in the pancreas and head. . . . He passed young, maybe early or mid-40s. I feel as if he wants me to tell you he sees what's happening in your life. . . . I think he's trying to tell me about your engagement or possibly a wedding."

There was the sound of gentle sobbing on the other end of the line.

"He's telling me he has Camille with him," Katherine continued. "They will both be at this event . . . I think it's your dad coming through. Does this make sense to you?"

"Oh, yes, absolutely. My dad passed away when he was 44 from stomach and brain cancer . . . and my mom, Camille, passed from a heart attack two months ago . . . and I'm getting married next month!" Evelyn cried into the phone. "Thank you, thank you so much, Katherine."

"Wow . . . right on the money," Tarzan said. "Let's go straight to another caller. Caller number two, what's your name, and what can Katherine help you with today?"

"Hi, Katherine . . . my name is Farah, and I just want you to know I'm such a big fan, and have friends who lost husbands who were New York firefighters when . . . well, you know. They were at one of your seminars, and you were so helpful to them."

"Thank you, that's special work for me, and very kind of you to say. Are you calling with a question about a K-N name . . . Karen, maybe?"

"Yes, exactly. My sister, she—"

"Don't tell me anything. I feel a head trauma . . . but also some fluid in the lungs . . . like she passed by drowning."

"Yes, yes," Farah said. "We found her in the lake near our cabin."

"Was there some police involvement with this . . . like a criminal investigation?"

"Yes, there was an inquest. She was such a strong swimmer that we thought—"

"Maybe she was murdered or committed suicide?"

"Yes, Katherine, that's what has haunted us."

"I'm seeing a cliff and water, and . . . my sense is that she was walking or hiking and slipped. She's showing me that she fell into the water and lost consciousness and drowned."

"That's what the coroner said, but hearing it from you means so much more . . . thank you."

"Wait . . . your sister is showing me pink roses, which means she's sending you her love . . . but I'm also getting . . ."

Katherine's mind flashed with lightning-quick images of car wrecks and washed-out bridges.

"I think she's suggesting that you shouldn't drive today. Were you going somewhere in your car?"

"Just over the Queensboro Bridge into Manhattan to—"

"Whoa," Katherine interjected. "I'm not telling you what to do, but I'm getting a pretty strong sense you may want to get your car checked out or take the subway today."

"Okay, thanks again," Farah said.

"All right," Tarzan broke in. "Caller number three, you're on the air."

"Hi, Katherine, my name is Bob. This might sound silly compared to your other callers, but my dog is really old, and I'm wondering if when pets die—"

"Sorry to interrupt, Bob . . . but . . . are you calling from your car?"

"Yeah, I am . . ."

Katherine kept getting images of car wrecks . . . and then a collapsing tunnel.

"Are you in a tunnel?"

"No, but I was just heading to the Lincoln Tunnel . . ."

"I really don't have a clear fix on who's sending this, but my sense is that someone is telling me you should maybe avoid the tunnel today. If there's an alternate route, maybe you should consider it. . . ."

"Okay, I will . . . but, my question—"

"Is your dog's name Jay or Joe or—"

"Yes, Joe."

"Well, I hear him barking. There are pets on the Other Side, too. So if you're worried you won't be seeing him again, stop worrying. But really, reconsider the tunnel."

"Will do. Thanks again, Katherine."

"Seems like you're getting a lot of traffic reports from the Other Side today, Katherine. Are we seeing a psychic pattern here?" Tarzan asked.

"I'm not sure what that's all about," Katherine said, rubbing her temple, her head still throbbing. "I keep getting these images of . . . well, images of traffic mishaps, let's say."

"Interesting," Tarzan said. "All you animals driving out there better pay extra attention to the road. So, Katherine, let's not stick to local traffic, as we've got listeners out there from coast to coast. Do you have any predictions for next year's Oscars?"

"No, I'm not really picking up on celebrity news today . . . but I'm getting a lot of images of car wrecks, fire—there's a bridge burning somewhere. . . ."

"Really? Some kind of disaster . . . any idea where?"

"I just . . . I'm seeing the Oklahoma City bombing . . . and I'm getting the month of September . . . I don't understand this . . . and they're showing me a helicopter crash . . . and a pair of handcuffs . . . it's all jumbled right now, and . . . I . . . I just don't know yet."

"Okay, well, let's go to our next caller . . . a man from Brooklyn. What's your name, sir, and what can Katherine help you with?"

"Help me? She can't help me at all. I just called to say I think it's disgusting that she pretends—"

"Now hold on, sir, no need to be rude. Miss Haywood has an impeccable—"

Katherine bolted upright in her seat and interrupted, "Caller, do you wear a uniform?" She tried to focus on an image in front of her.

"What did you say?"

"Do you wear a uniform?"

"You know damn well I do. I told your switch-board operator I was—"

"They're showing me that you wear a uni-form—or you used to. I've got someone coming through loud and clear from the Other Side for you. I see a fire engine and a medal . . . a uniform and a gun. Is this making sense to you?"

"Listen, lady, what are you trying to pull? You already know I work for the—"

"Hold on . . . are you going on a red ski lift? Or something like . . . a cave? I see a dark cave. I'm at a loss here . . . do these things mean anything to you?"

"I don't ski, and the only cave I know about is the one you must have crawled out of . . . I called to say that I think your making a living on people's grief is the lowest—"

"I see fire all around you . . . there's smoke, I'm choking—"

"You should choke on your words, lady! You should be ashamed of yourself. Screw you and the broom you flew in on!"

There was the sound of a dial tone.

"Wait . . . Susan is coming through . . . she says it's not your fault . . . leave the gun alone . . . caller? Caller? Are you there?"

Tarzan was silently waving at Katherine to forget the caller. "Why don't we move on—"

"No. That man needs help. Can you trace that call? Get him back on the line!"

"Well, we can't really do that, and we're about to go to a commercial."

"No, don't, please . . . you have to get the man in the uniform back on the line. I need to tell him that Susan . . ." Katherine began coughing. Her head pounded.

"There's smoke . . . so much smoke," she continued. And then she blurted out a warning she couldn't believe she was making on a live broadcast, but it was out of her mouth before she could stop herself.

"Oh my God . . . oh my God! It's an explosion . . . many explosions . . . God, no . . . it looks like another attack. The explosions are going to happen here, in New York. Oh my God, it's going to happen today!"

Someone threw a switch in the control room, and the studio went silent. For a brief moment, there was nothing being broadcast on millions of radios across the country.

Nothing but dead air.

CHAPTER 3

JACK MORGAN OPENED HIS EYES AND WINCED. The familiar searing pain clawed into his hip and sliced toward his shoulder along the length of his spine—the same way it did every morning.

He'd been dreaming of Susan. He could still smell the lilac-scented French soap she loved so much. But now he was here, awake and alone. Gathering his strength, he rolled off the couch and got to his feet. A barely audible moan escaped through his lips.

Enough. Stop complaining, Jack thought, biting the inside of his cheek until he tasted blood.

He hated mornings most—the first minutes of consciousness before he got a grip on his near-constant physical pain and chronic loneliness. Mornings made him feel weak, and he hated weakness.

He pulled the bedding off the couch and stowed it inside the wicker chest, which doubled as a linen closet. He'd been sleeping in the guest room since Susan had gone. He couldn't bear to be in their bedroom, not even for one minute.

He spent an hour forcing himself to do 100 sit-ups and 200 push-ups. It was agony, but it was his routine, and routine was all that kept him going. He put on his uniform—jeans and a white, neatly pressed dress shirt and Army boots—then limped to the small bathroom in the corner to clean up. Few people ever saw him at all these days, but when he was on the job, he made sure he looked presentable and professional.

He was still a cop, and he wanted to feel like one.

Although he was in his 50s, Jack still had a full head of wavy black hair, and even though he cut it himself, it was always neat and regulation short. Now, he washed his face without looking in the mirror—he'd stopped looking long ago, not noticing the deep creases that years of pain had embedded in his face. But the creases hadn't destroyed the naturally boyish expression he'd always worn—and hated—his entire life.

Susan had never tired of kidding him about it. "Stop trying to hide it, sweetie," she'd say, whenever he tried to grow a mustache. "You'll always look like an adorable ten-year-old. What woman wouldn't want to love you to pieces?"

Jack toweled himself off and turned to face the day.

The morning sunlight flooded the guest room. The drapes were usually pulled tight throughout the house all day, but he must have left them open yesterday when he'd cleaned up—he'd washed the place from top to bottom so it would be spotless when he was found.

He was drawing the curtains when he spotted Mrs. Tirella—Mrs. T.—pushing her wire buggy of newspapers down the street. She was 72, but insisted on being called "the paper boy." She walked with the easy gait and reckless speed of a teenager. Her long gray hair was forever tucked beneath an ancient Brooklyn Dodgers ball cap.

Mrs. T. was one of a handful of local small-time criminals Jack had befriended in his Brooklyn neighborhood known as Park Slope. He knew that Mrs. T. spent no more than a dollar's worth of quarters at the newspaper boxes each morning, but she always managed to fill her buggy to the brim with fresh newsprint. Jack didn't mind, and had turned a blind eye to her petty larceny when he'd been walking the beat in Park Slope because he knew Mrs. T. had been dealt a tough hand. She'd been widowed just a few weeks after arriving in the country when her husband had come into some bad luck while walking home after his grave-yard shift as night watchman at the Brooklyn Navy Yard. He'd survived just long enough to tell the tale.

One Christmas, Jack and Susan had Mrs. T. over for turkey dinner. Mrs. T. always brought her own homemade wine because Jack didn't keep any booze in the house. After she'd had a few glasses too many, Mrs. T. told them about her husband's brush with God.

According to her, Vito Tirella was just two blocks from their apartment on 7th Avenue when a DC-8 exploded in a massive fireball so close to him that his eyebrows were singed and the plastic tips of his shoelaces melted.

"He come in the door and told me he seen the souls of dead peoples leaving their bodies and floatin' up to heaven," Mrs. T. had confided to Jack and Susan in a conspiratorial whisper, crossing herself with her right hand and polishing off a tumbler of vino with her left.

"That's why God take him from me. Vito seen too much. After he told me the story . . . he kiss me, kiss the babies, and then—Santa Maria—he drop dead on the floor at my feet. But Capitano Jack, I swear . . . Vito, he still come to me every day to give me strength to go on."

Jack just nodded when Mrs. T. had spun him the yarn about her dead husband, and then he'd taken away her wineglass. He'd never been one for the hereafter. As far as he was concerned, once you were dead, you were dead—period, end of story. But the plane crash in Park Slope, well, that was not only fact, it was one of his most vivid childhood memories.

The jet had gone down on December 16, 1960—two days after his seventh birthday—just a few blocks from his house. It was a Friday morning, and he'd pretended to be sick so he could stay home from school and watch out for his mom, who'd "fallen down the stairs" and hurt herself pretty badly the night before after an argument with his drunken father.

He was lying on his bed watching big drops of freezing rain smack against his window like blobs of paste when the plane roared overhead and disappeared in a ball of fire.

He went up to his rooftop hideout and watched the firefighters carry dozens of body bags away from the site—but he didn't remember seeing any spirits flying around . . . at least he didn't think he had. There was a moment when . . .

Nah . . ., he thought, *that was just a kid's overactive imagination.*

The only one he saw giving up the ghost that day was his mother—she'd fallen down the stairs once too often. Jack figured that the plane crash had made her realize how fragile life was and that she wasn't going to waste hers being brutalized by an alcoholic husband.

He'd watched her from the roof as she walked through the burning neighborhood with a suitcase in her hand. But that was a long time ago, and Jack didn't like to think about it.

Mrs. T. tended to tell a few tall tales when she was on the vino, but she was a good woman who'd raised two boys on her own. And when Susan was out shopping or visiting her mother in the nursing home, she always had the old lady watch over their son, Liam.

Jack watched Mrs. T. make a sale to a couple of early-morning yuppies across the street lounging on the patio of Mimo's Authentic Neapolitan Bistro. He remembered when Mimo's was called Mo's Deli, after its owner, Mohammed Shahmah. Mohammed had discovered that a trendy name change was a perfectly legal way to sell a nickel's worth of coffee and a few drops of steamed milk for $3.50.

This used to be such a nice, affordable family neighborhood, Jack thought, looking at the yuppies whose kind had all but taken over Park Slope.

"*Buon giorno,* Capitano Jack . . . you like I should bring you up a free paper?" Mrs. T. had spotted Jack standing in the second-story window and started waving *The Trumpet,* one of New York's notoriously trashy tabloids, at him.

Jack shook his head silently at the old woman. He hadn't spoken to her or anyone else in the neighborhood for years—he wasn't going to start entertaining visitors now, not today of all days.

"You no take a paper since they put you picture on the front page when Mrs. Susan was . . ."

Mrs. Tirella chopped her sentence so hard Jack heard her dentures clack from the street.

"I'm so sorry, Capitano . . . I got big mouth. I talk too much. Please, I'm so sorry," Mrs. Tirella kept apologizing, but Jack had drawn the drapes.

He limped from the guest room to the long hallway, where the few memories he allowed himself were neatly arranged on the wall in a single row of framed photographs.

He called it "the family gallery." Fifteen photos in all, one for each year of his marriage. There wasn't a single photo from his childhood: no snapshots of his parents, summer holidays, or smiling grandparents. As far as Jack was concerned, his life began when he met his wife.

"We weren't what you'd call a 'Kodak moment' kind of family," Jack had told Susan when asked about the lack of memorabilia. "You've heard of a mean drunk? My old man was mean sober and a murderous bastard after a few drinks. He beat on my mom until she left, then he beat on me until I could beat him back. And that's about all I've got to say about my family."

What amazed Jack was that, despite his contempt for his father, he'd ended up just like him. He'd become a cop and a bitter, mean drunk—until he met Susan and gave up the booze for good.

Jack continued down the hall as he did every morning, pausing before each picture until his legs began to ache so much that he had to move along.

He lifted the first photo off the hook and held it in both hands. The image was of him and Susan huddling together in front of Niagara Falls on their honeymoon. They were wearing rain slickers and we've-just-won-the-lottery smiles. Jack was holding Susan's left wrist toward the camera, and Susan was hamming it up, displaying her ring finger with a dramatic flourish, as though the diamond weighed a pound. But Jack had been so broke when he bought the ring that he'd needed the jeweler's magnifying glass to see what he was getting for a week's pay. It was just a tiny chip of a rock, but in the photo it had caught the rainbow reflection from the falls and was sparkling like a star. Later he tried to buy a bigger diamond, but Susan didn't want one. That was her way.

"Why tamper with perfection," she'd said.

Jack had never figured out what she'd seen in him. The first time they met, Jack was lying facedown, drunk and unconscious on the street outside a Flatbush Avenue dive bar. Susan took pity on him and practically carried him to her apartment, where she let him sleep it off on her couch. The next morning she plopped a hot mug of coffee in front of him and said that he shouldn't treat himself so poorly because "tomorrow will be a better day."

It was the first thing she ever said to him, and she'd repeat it whenever the job or money troubles got him down. She must have said it a million times, and he never tired of it. *Tomorrow will be a better day.*

They were married 12 months later, on the first anniversary of Jack's sobriety.

Jack returned the honeymoon picture to its place and continued down the hall.

The next photo was of Susan, her wedding dress hiked up to her knees and her wild perm of dark hair poking out from the bottom of her American flag motorcycle helmet. She was straddling the seat of Jack's Harley minutes after they'd taken their vows at City Hall. Susan had wanted a church wedding, but Jack refused. He didn't believe in God, and said if heaven and hell existed, they could be found in New York City, just below 14th Street.

The next picture was of the two of them laughing, holding buckets over their heads to catch the rain streaming through the ceiling of the Catskill Mountain cabin they'd rented each summer.

Then there was the picture of Susan in a hospital bed cradling two-hour-old Liam—the boy's pink face wrinkled up like an old man, and Susan grinning ear-to-ear despite enduring 18 hours of labor.

Beside that was the Polaroid of Liam at age nine—his mop of auburn hair exploding in all directions, wearing the flannel cowboy-and-Indian pajamas he'd loved so much. He was posing in front of the Christmas tree they'd chopped down themselves in Connecticut, proudly displaying his new, four-foot-long fire engine with the "authentic" clanging brass bell and extendable ladder.

Jack remembered that Liam had begged him for the truck for nearly a year. The boy had wanted to be a fireman since he'd learned to talk. The last picture on the wall was of Liam in his new uniform just after he'd finished his training with the New York Fire Department.

Jack looked at the pictures but felt nothing.

In the first years after Susan had died, he'd let the images pull him back through time—past the pain to a place where he could briefly relive those happy moments. But he stopped doing that after Liam had left as well.

Now, he studied the images like crime-scene photos, focusing on details: Susan's earrings, Liam's Band-Aid—searching for something that might yield a hidden clue that could explain his ruined life.

At the end of the hall, Jack slid back the lid of his grandfather's rolltop desk and picked up a yellowing, ten-year-old tabloid newspaper with a banner headline that screamed from the past: TOP COP SHOT; WIFE RAPED, MURDERED.

Six words. A simple phrase that, like his marriage, had ended with *murder*. Under the headline, there were two photos vertically dividing the front page. On the left was Jack's NYPD graduation photo; on the right was Susan, but you wouldn't know it. She was just another nameless corpse on a New York street—a red circle soaking through the white sheet covering her body.

Jack didn't have to read the story; he could recite it as easily as rattling off Miranda rights:

> The wife of a New York City police captain was raped and shot dead in Central Park last night as her husband of 15 years, Captain Jack Morgan, lay bleeding and helpless on the ground just three feet away.
>
> Police spokesperson David Kelly said the Morgans were celebrating their 15th wedding anniversary with a carriage ride through the park when they encountered four youths attacking a female jogger.
>
> According to police and witnesses, Captain Morgan jumped from the carriage and went to the jogger's defense. One of the youths pulled a handgun and shot the heroic cop three times: in the leg, hip and back, narrowly missing his spinal cord.
>
> The men, described as white males in their late teens or early 20s, then pulled Mrs. Morgan from the carriage and sexually assaulted her before shooting her through the heart. The suspects were last seen fleeing through the park toward Strawberry Fields.
>
> "It was terrible what those punks done— they were so happy in the carriage, holding hands and kissing like a couple of kids," said hansom cab driver Nicholas Copland.

"I ran after the jogger to see if she was all right, and when I got back there was blood everywhere and the lady was dead."

Captain Morgan remains in Roosevelt hospital in critical condition. The attackers are still at large, but police say they have the name of at least one of the suspects.

Jack traced his finger over the image of Susan's corpse. He couldn't remember anything about that night. He had to piece it together from what he'd been told or what he'd read.

AT FIRST THE PAPERS called Jack a hero; the entire city seemed to empathize with his loss. But the sympathy didn't last. The papers had turned on him before he'd checked out of the hospital. It happened when a priest turned up at his bedside four weeks after the attack, assuring Jack that Susan was "in heaven with God." Even though he was in traction, Jack nearly killed the man, fracturing the priest's skull and breaking his jaw in two places.

The next day's headline read: CRAZY JACK SMACKS PRIEST. The article explained that Jack had been insane with grief when he'd attacked the priest, but the name Crazy Jack stuck. It hadn't helped that an unidentified nurse had been quoted as saying that Jack had spit on the priest while beating him about the head with a bedpan.

Then there was the trial 18 months later. The boys who killed Susan had been caught and convicted of second-degree murder, but Jack refused to go to the courthouse, even for the sentencing.

When a reporter showed up at his house to find out why, Jack said, "Because they're not guilty; they didn't kill her."

It was the last time Jack had ever talked to anyone about Susan's murder, and the last time he landed on a tabloid's front page.

CRAZY JACK CLAIMS COPS GOT IT WRONG; WIFE'S KILLERS INNOCENT!

Jack didn't care. As far as he was concerned, the story was true. *He* was the one who'd taken Susan into the park that night and put her at risk by playing hero. It didn't matter how many low-lifes they locked up—in his mind, his wife's killer was still free. Jack Morgan murdered Susan; there was no doubt about it.

But that was nobody else's business. He hung up the phone when concerned relatives called, and closed the door on consoling neighbors. Jack wouldn't even talk about the murder with Liam, who, after he was grown, stopped by the house every weekend to check up on his dad. They talked about sports and Liam's career, but never about the murder. Then one weekend the visits stopped. Jack never saw his son again.

Due to his injuries, Jack was declared unfit for active duty, but he was years away from retirement. He offered to serve out his time working homicide cold cases from his home. The police chief was only too happy to oblige, and to get Crazy Jack out of the public eye.

His living room was soon crammed with stacks of cardboard boxes filled with files on long-forgotten murders. Jack phoned in his reports at first, but eventually taught himself to use a computer. Once he could communicate over the Internet, he basically never left his house.

That had started ten years ago. It would end at 5 P.M. today, when he would be officially retired from the NYPD.

JACK TOOK A LAST LOOK at the young face staring up at him from the old newspaper, then let the tabloid fall to the floor. On the desk in front of him sat three carefully arranged items: his service revolver and two silver medals.

The first medal arrived in the mail from the Fire Department of New York in the winter of 2001. He slipped it into the front pocket of his jeans without looking at it.

The other medallion was heavier, a commemorative reward from the NYPD for wounds suffered the night Susan was killed. He looked at the Latin words embossed on its face. "*Fidelis Ad Mortem* . . . faithful unto death," he whispered. "Well, I have been." He dropped the medal back on the desk, picked up his service revolver, and carefully walked downstairs.

Jack maneuvered around the neatly stacked corridor of cardboard case files lining his living room before reaching the kitchen and flicking on the radio. He put his gun on top of the counter, thinking of Susan's mantra: *Tomorrow will be a better day.*

Well, for the first time in ten years, tomorrow actually will *be a better day,* Jack thought.

He turned on the radio and began fiddling with the tuner. At first there was just static, then he hit a clear signal.

"AhhhhEEEEeeee . . . AhhhhEEEEeeeee . . . Ahhhhhhhh!"

What the hell is this? Jack wondered, quickly turning down the volume. He was about to tune in to another station when he heard the name of the upcoming guest: psychic Katherine Haywood.

There were three types of people Jack couldn't stomach: reporters, priests, and psychics. He remembered this particular psychic's name from several cold cases he'd worked on . . . the files all said that she'd actually helped find the bodies of the victims, even though the murderers hadn't been found. In all the cases, the officers involved had praised Katherine Haywood as a professional and said that she'd been extremely helpful—both during the investigation and in helping the victims' families cope in the aftermath.

Jack didn't buy it. He thought she had everybody fooled and was probably making a good living from people's suffering. For all he knew, she'd committed the crimes herself for the publicity.

He turned up the radio, grinding his teeth as he listened.

"He's telling me he has Camille with him. They will both be at this event . . . I think it's your dad coming through. Does this make sense to you?"

This is obscene, Jack fumed. *Listen to this grief hustler, leeching off that woman's pain.*

He turned up the radio even louder.

". . . my mom, Camille, passed from a heart attack two months ago . . . and I'm getting married next month. Thank you, thank you so much, Katherine."

Jack picked up the phone, dialed 411, and got the number for WARP. His heart was pounding like a rookie patrolman making his first bust when the receptionist picked up the phone

"Good morning. WARP. How may I direct your call?" the woman asked.

"It's about this so-called psychic you have on the air. I'm a cop, and I know about the missing persons and homicide cases she worked on—"

"Where are you calling from, sir?"

"What? What difference—from Brooklyn, but—"

"Please hold."

"Hold? No. I won't hold. I just want you to know this woman is a phony and a liar, and you people should be ashamed for letting her . . . Hello? Hello?"

". . . a man from Brooklyn . . . what's your name, sir, and what can Katherine help you with?"

"Help me? She can't help me at all. I just called to say I think it's disgusting that she pretends—"

"Now hold on, sir, no need to be rude. Miss Haywood has an impeccable—"

Katherine interrupted, "Caller, do you wear a uniform?"

"What did you say?"

"Do you wear a uniform?"

"You know damn well I do. I told your switch-board operator I was—"

"They're showing me that you wear a uniform—or you used to. I've got someone coming through loud and clear from the Other Side for you. I see a fire engine and a medal . . . a uniform and a gun. Is this making sense to you?"

"Listen, lady, what are you trying to pull? You already know I work for the—"

"Hold on . . . are you going on a red ski lift? Or something like . . . a cave? I see a dark cave. I'm at a loss here . . . do these things mean anything to you?"

"I don't ski, and the only cave I know about is the one you must have crawled out of . . . I called to say that I think your making a living on people's grief is the lowest—"

"I see fire all around you . . . there's smoke, I'm choking—"

"You should choke on your words, lady! You should be ashamed of yourself. Screw you and the broom you flew in on!"

Jack slammed down the receiver.

Of course she'd say she saw a uniform, I told the receptionist I was a cop. Damn phony! I can't believe I let her use me like that.

Jack picked up his gun from the counter and moved as quickly as he could to the living room. He opened the six-cylinder on his .38 and dropped in the single bullet he'd been saving for a decade. He'd been planning to check out at 5 P.M. on the nose—the end of the workday and his career—but the psychic had him so riled up that he couldn't wait one more second to end it all.

He stepped onto the large plastic sheet he'd spread out on the floor after he'd cleaned the house, and planted the muzzle of the .38 into the soft tissue between his chin and Adam's apple. Closing his eyes, he tightened his finger on the trigger . . . then he heard Katherine's shrieking voice echoing from the kitchen.

"Oh my God . . . oh my God! It's an explosion . . . many explosions . . . God, no . . . it looks like another attack. The explosions are going to happen here, in New York. Oh my God, it's going to happen today!"

Jack froze. In an instant, all the emotions he'd repressed for years surged through his body.

"Now you've gone too far, lady!" he yelled in the direction of the kitchen. "You're feeding off the fears of a whole city!"

Jack stumbled to the hall closet, pulling out his leather jacket and helmet. He tucked his gun into his jacket.

"I'm going to put the fear of God into that fraudulent bitch!" he yelled, stepping out of his house with a true purpose for the first time in years.

CHAPTER 4

"WE GOT A FLOATER IN THE EAST RIVER. . . ."

Zoe Crane's fingers froze in mid-stroke, the plastic staccato clacking of her keyboard falling silent.

"Did you copy, Central?"

Zoe cocked an ear toward the police-scanner room on the other side of her cubicle. Her eyes darted to the travel clock by her computer, her hands hovering over the keyboard. She sucked her lower lip between her teeth.

Her *AstroChart* column was due in three hours, and she hadn't even gotten to the earth signs yet. The managing editor was looking for any excuse to crucify her; and handing in late copy would be like donating nails for the cross. But she couldn't help herself. She was a cop reporter through and through, and a hard-news junkie, addicted to the electronic chatter of the police scanner. Besides, a good floater was a guaranteed shot at the front page.

A serious reporter by trade, Zoe had been banished to do horoscopes and fluff pieces for the lifestyles section of the newspaper. She didn't buy any of this zodiac nonsense and usually let Carolyn, her assistant and a true astrology fanatic, write all the horoscopes. But Carolyn had called in sick today, leaving Zoe in a real jam.

"Say again, Harbor Unit 2 . . . was that a 'boater' on the East River?"

"Negative, Central . . . a floater . . . possible 1029. We're a couple hundred yards out, but through the binoculars it looks like a female, faceup in the water and definitely DOA. She's snagged on the rocks at the bottom of the bridge support."

"The Queensboro Bridge—is that affirmative, Harbor 2?"

"Affirmative, Central—Queensboro Bridge, at the support pillar on the Manhattan side of Roosevelt Island."

"Okay. 10-4, Harbor 2 . . . East River floater under the Queensboro Bridge, west side of Roosevelt Island. Check it out and report back."

"10-4, Central . . . but . . . uh . . . we're stationed here as lead security detail for the mayor and governor's arrival . . . Harbor 2, over."

"Copy that, Harbor 2 . . . stand by for instructions."

Under the Queensboro Bridge? That's practically right beneath our office . . . I bet I could see it from the scanner room, Zoe considered.

Her fingers dropped to the keys, her eyes focusing on the planetary-chart cheat sheet Carolyn had taped to the edge of her computer screen. She took a deep breath, exhaled slowly, and began typing.

Sagittarius: You've been too self-indulgent for too long! Dwelling on your problems while ignoring the needs of others has left you spiritually bereft and emotionally stunted. Nourish your soul by doing a good deed or selfless act for someone else—and do it soon! Work also looms large this week—time to think of a career change?

Zoe stopped typing, and started to laugh. *I can't believe how accurate these things can actually be. I'm a Sagittarius, and this prediction is dead on. I really do need a career change, and it doesn't look like I'm going to get it here.*

But if she wanted to keep working at *The New York Daily Trumpet,* she had to bite the bullet and put her name on this fluff, at least until she could get her hands on a *real* news story again. And that wasn't going to happen until either the managing editor dropped dead from a heart attack or some Pulitzer Prize–winning story landed in her lap.

What galled her the most was that she didn't believe a single word of the psychic mumbo jumbo she had to write about.

Zoe stood and stretched, her calf muscles cramping from the workout her boxing trainer had put them through that morning. She actually liked the pain; it meant she was getting stronger, and she hated the thought of ever being at a disadvantage. Besides, the boxing kept her mind sharp, and she needed that, especially this week.

She checked her work calendar, groaning at the heavy load. There were weekly horoscopes due by noon, a feature on the Manhattan Ghost Finders'

Club due by 6 P.M., and a palm-reading class to attend so she could write a scathing article on those phony psychics who were all over Manhattan. Then there was that stack of mail from her "fans" that she had to respond to.

Zoe picked up the first letter from a large stack of envelopes on her desk, and her stomach knotted slightly. The letter had obviously been written by a child. It had no return address, there was a picture of a pony drawn on the envelope in crayon, and it was covered with little paste-on stars. She read the badly misspelled letter:

> *Dear Zoe,*
>   *I love your collimns about horriscopes and read them everyday. I live in a foster home now, but I use to live on a farm and had a pony like this one. If I move to anuther farm, I will get another pony and name it Lucky Stars, like after your collimn.*
>
> *Your big fan,*
> *Cassandra*

Zoe stared at the letter for several minutes. "Cassandra" was Zoe's favorite name. She even used it as the password to log on to her computer.

If I ever have a daughter, if I'd only been able to . . . stop it! That's enough sentiment—the past is the past, she reminded herself, tucking the letter back into the envelope and tossing it into the trash.

A moment later, she pulled it out.

Well, it is kind of sweet, she thought, and pinned it to her bulletin board, next to the picture of her dog, Rewrite, a little border collie she'd had since moving to New York. She'd found him on the street near Columbia University, shivering and half-starved.

"You're a stray just like me," Zoe said, when she took him back to her room. Rewrite was the only thing she'd ever really loved since leaving New Jersey. But he'd gotten old and sick with cancer, and she had to have him put him down just last week.

Don't think about that . . . back to work, what else do I have to do? Oh yeah, I can't forget the ultimate bullshit artist herself! She remembered that in five minutes, celebrity psychic Katherine Haywood would be on the radio.

Exposing the country's best-known and most-respected psychic as a fraud could be a one-way ticket back to serious reporting.

Zoe had already caught a few fraudulent psychics red-handed since being stuck on this beat, but they were your typical fortune-teller types or those 1-900-dial-a-psychics.

No matter how hard she studied Katherine Haywood's style on the radio, on TV, or at seminars, Zoe had never been able to discover how she did it. But she still wasn't about to believe any of it—not until she saw some hard evidence. She was convinced that Katherine had a sophisticated con-artist system going, and sooner or later she'd figure it out. She'd even implied as much in one of her columns, but still didn't have the hard facts she needed to put her out of business.

"Harbor 2 . . . you're cleared to check out your floater. Harbor 3 will cover your security detail. . . ."

"10-4, Central. Proceeding to the bridge pillar."

"And Harbor 2, don't take the body onto the island; transport it to Manhattan by boat—we don't want to ruin the mayor's ribbon cutting at the new BioWorld Center by dragging a corpse in front of the TV cameras."

"Copy that. Will do, Central. We'll hide the stiff from hizzonner and the cameras. Harbor 2 out."

Zoe leaned back in her chair, past the edge of her cubicle, peering at the two night-shift reporters assigned to the scanner room. She called them Sleepy and Dopey, because no matter how loud the police scanners chattered, they kept dozing. Today was no exception: A floater in the river, and they were sleeping in their swivel chairs—two pasty-faced old-timers dreaming their way to retirement.

A floater was a homicide or a suicide—and either could be a huge story. It's right outside their window and they don't even know it's happening. Zoe scowled, picking up her new palmtop computer with the super-zoom camera lens and strolling nonchalantly into the scanner room.

Through the window, Zoe could see that the Queensboro Bridge was busier than usual. She looked down at the East River and across to Roosevelt Island, where a crowd was gathering for the opening of Bioworld's new Supercomputer Re-Creation Center.

Zoe zoomed in on the crowd. There were plenty of cops, a bunch of balloons, what looked like a string quartet, and maybe a dozen or more members of the city council that she recognized. She focused in on the bridge's support pillar and followed it down to the water.

"Bingo . . . thar she blows," she whispered, bringing the NYPD police boat into the crosshairs of the lens. An officer was tossing a hook out toward the shore of the island. Zoe pressed the shutter button, and the camera beeped softly as she followed the rope to the corpse.

That looks weird, she thought, snapping a few more shots before the police scanner kicked to life again.

"Central, this is Harbor 2."

Sleepy and Dopey stirred in their chairs as Zoe slipped by them and back to her cubicle.

"Go ahead, Harbor 2."

"Central, it's negative on the 1029. The floater is a Miss Bloomingdale. She's caught up in some old fishing cable or something. We'll be a while cutting her loose from the bridge piling."

"Okay, copy that, Harbor 2. Let us know when you're done. And boys, do be gentle with her. Central out."

So much for the front page, Zoe concluded. A "Miss Bloomingdale" meant a department-store mannequin.

But it might have been Jimmy Hoffa they found in the river, and those two guys would have slept through it! And these losers are my replacements?

Zoe had come a long way from Trenton, New Jersey. Until a year and a half ago, she'd been the top police reporter in New York City and had broken more crime stories than any other journalist in the city—probably the entire country. And she didn't have to slum around cop bars or sleep with desk sergeants to do it. She'd never once cashed in on her looks to get ahead—she'd left all that behind in Jersey.

She'd seen too many hard-luck cases in New York to whine about being born blonde and beautiful. But the truth was . . . good looks had always been her biggest handicap.

From the age of four, Zoe's adopted mother—the "evil stepmother," Zoe called her—had forced her into one beauty pageant after another. Zoe just wanted to ride her bike and play sports like other kids, but it wasn't to be.

"You got looks, and those looks pay the rent. So stop complainin'. Maybe you'll meet a nice guy," was all her mother would say about it.

Just before her 16th birthday, she did meet a nice guy, a local college boy. He proposed when she told him she was pregnant, and they planned to get married before the baby was born. But Zoe's mother put an end to that. She wanted her daughter to go all the way to Miss America.

"And you ain't gonna do that with a kid," she'd said.

Her mother threatened to have Zoe's boyfriend charged with statutory rape if he didn't disappear. Then she forced Zoe to give up the baby for adoption. Zoe wasn't allowed to see the newborn, and never even knew if she'd given birth to a boy or a girl.

Zoe barely spoke a word to her mother for the next two years.

As soon as she graduated from high school, she cut off her long blonde hair, took the money left over from her pageant winnings, got on a bus for New York City, and said good-bye to Trenton and her mother forever.

She studied journalism at Columbia University and then focused solely on her career. She swore off men forever, and the only release she allowed herself was two hours a day of boxing at a local gym. Her boxing coach, a wiry old Irishman who called himself Wildcat, had been a former featherweight champ. Now he was a part-time night watchman at the city morgue and would occasionally sneak Zoe in after hours so she could study forensic reports. She was determined to be the city's best crime reporter, and figured that learning what crime looked like up close was one of the best ways to get there.

Zoe landed her first real job as a gofer at *The New York Daily Trumpet,* the best-selling tabloid in New York City. She had loftier ambitions, but it was a good place to start. A few years later, she got her big break—covering a drive-by shooting in Spanish Harlem that left three young brothers lying dead in the doorway of their housing complex.

According to police, the kids were caught in the cross fire of rival drug dealers—wrong place, wrong time. Every news organization in the city was vying for an interview with the family, but the police had sealed the block off.

It was Zoe's day off, but she headed uptown anyway just to see what was going on. She was hanging back from the pack of reporters who were surrounding the victims' apartment when she spotted a pizza guy delivering to the neighbor next door.

"Fifty bucks for your pizza and hat," she said.

"This pizza is spoken for, lady, and the hat is property of Tony's Pizzeria—for official company use only," the pizza man said, brushing past Zoe.

"Make it a hundred," Zoe yelled to his back. The pizza man turned and said, "Well, when you put it that way, all I can is say is . . . sold!"

A few minutes later, Zoe was in official pizza-company uniform, standing beside the yellow crime-scene tape, nodding to the patrolman.

"For the family," she said, holding up the pizza box.

"Go ahead," the patrolman said, lifting the tape and letting her pass. "Watch out for those media animals. They'd steal the pizza outta your mouth and the hat off your head if you gave them half a chance."

"Tell me about it," Zoe said, and strolled into the apartment building.

When the grieving parents opened the door—clutching their one surviving child in diapers between them—Zoe called upon her high school Spanish to tell them she worked for *The Trumpet*.

"¡Oh sí! *La Trompeta*," the mother said, looking to Zoe for some kind of justice.

Between her very limited English and Zoe's rusty Spanish, they worked out a deal where Zoe would help find the men who killed their sons if the parents would cooperate with her on a story.

Zoe snatched up every snapshot of the boys, making sure not to leave a single photo for any rival newspaper. Then she sat down and listened as the parents told her how police officers had been taking money to let gangs sell drugs outside the apartment building.

It was her first big story. The front-page headline above the pictures of the dead boys screamed: CROOKED COPS AND DRUG KINGS KILL KIDS!

Half a dozen police officers were arrested, several senior officers were forced to resign, and Zoe was immediately promoted to the police beat over many more senior reporters. Within a year, *New York* magazine had dubbed her "The Queen of Crime" for her relentless investigations of both criminals and cops. At 29, Zoe was at the top of her game . . . but the game had come to an abrupt end.

After being tipped off that an NYPD sergeant on medical leave was peddling drugs near a Bronx schoolyard, Zoe was convinced she had another cop-on-the-take feature. She'd found the sergeant's house and tailed him for weeks until he turned up near a schoolyard of screaming kids. She was half a block away with her camera when the sergeant exchanged packages with a man Zoe recognized as a known drug dealer with mob connections. She snapped a picture of the transaction, and could practically taste the Pulitzer Prize.

Unfortunately, she couldn't get any comment from the police department spokesperson.

Two days before the story ran, the police chief called her at home at midnight and left a message on her answering machine.

"Zoe, I'd appreciate it if you held that story until next week," the chief had asked. "We're running our own investigation, and anything in the papers right now would be a goddamn disaster. I'll explain it to you in a few months."

Yeah, right . . . a few months to cover up another bad cop, Zoe thought. *That story is running tomorrow.*

And it *did* run the next day, right across the front page. Zoe came to work early, half expecting *The New York Times* or *The Washington Post* to be calling her with job offers. But when the phone rang, it was her managing editor summoning her to his glass-enclosed office.

His chubby face was beet red, and she knew she was in serious trouble. "I'm told the police chief called you last night and asked you to hold the story. Is that right?"

"Um . . . someone called, but my answering machine isn't working. Is there . . . a problem?"

"Not really, except that your so-called dirty cop was undercover, investigating a drug ring suspected of funneling money to terrorists. But guess what? He's not doing that anymore, thanks to you. He's not a cop at *all* anymore because his picture is on the front of my goddamned newspaper!"

He stood there, struggling for breath, mopping his face with a Dunkin' Donuts napkin. "I want your resignation on my desk in an hour!" he finally spat.

"I'm not quitting. You want to fire me, then fire me. But you approved the story, and if I go,

I'm taking you with me," Zoe said.

The man's face turned gray. Zoe though he was having a stroke.

"All right, Miss Crane, have it your way. Don't quit. In fact, take the rest of the day off and enjoy yourself. But be here early tomorrow for reassignment. Now get out of my sight."

The next day the receptionist directed Zoe to her cramped new cubicle across from the police-scanner room. There was a self-help paperback on her desk called *Astrology for Absolute Morons*.

The book was signed by the managing editor: *All the best to a "star reporter." Copy is due Fridays— don't be late.*

A clipping from that day's lifestyles section was tucked inside the pages of the book:

> *For amusement purposes only!* The Trumpet *is happy to introduce a new feature in this section called "Your Lucky Stars." This column will keep you abreast of the latest in New Age news, as well as provide your daily horoscope, and a column from Lucky Stars reporter Zoe Crane.*
>
> *"I can't wait to get started," said Zoe. "I've been preparing for this my entire career, and now that I've got the New Age beat, I don't think I'll ever be able to leave. I'm polishing my crystal ball and counting my lucky stars!"*

Zoe sat down hard. She knew that staying on at *The Trumpet* could mean the end of her career as a serious journalist. But quitting would be a sign of weakness—and other papers wouldn't exactly be clamoring to hire her after a major front-page screwup.

She opened *Astrology for Absolute Morons* to page one and started reading. If it hadn't been for her assistant, Carolyn, she would have been completely lost. Fortunately, the young woman was obsessed with anything New Age and threw herself into research on the topic, giving Zoe time to do more investigative stories, like tracking down phony psychics.

"CENTRAL, THIS IS HARBOR 2. There's some weird stuff on this mannequin. . . ."

The scanner was buzzing again.

Zoe looked over to the cop room and saw that Sleepy and Dopey had nodded off again.

"This is Central, Harbor 2, didn't copy that . . . say again."

"There's some weird graffiti or something painted on this dummy—looks like an exploding castle or something."

"Harbor 2, don't waste time on this. Cut it loose, pull it out of the water, and get back to your post. Central out."

"Roger that, Central . . . Harbor 2 out."

Busy day on the river, Zoe thought, returning to her column and beginning to type:

Capricorn: You may have forgotten something . . .

She looked at the clock.

Oh, shoot, talk about forgetting something—I almost missed the subject of next week's column.

She turned on the radio and tuned in to WARP. The static was terrible, but as soon as the reception cleared, she could hear Katherine giving bad news to what seemed to be a very angry caller.

"I see fire all around you . . . there's smoke, I'm choking—"

"You should choke on your words, lady! You should be ashamed of yourself. Screw you and the broom you flew in on!"

Zoe laughed. But seconds later she realized there was nothing funny about what she was hearing: "Oh my God . . . oh my God! It's an explosion . . . many explosions . . . God, no . . . it looks like another attack. The explosions are going to happen here, in New York. Oh my God, it's going to happen today!"

Zoe froze, and her reporter's instincts kicked into high gear. *Holy crap, did she just predict another terrorist attack? And on national radio?*

Zoe reached under her desk for the knapsack she'd had ready ever since 9/11. It was stuffed with everything a reporter would need in the field to handle any dangerous situation—from bandages to a stun gun.

She grabbed her palmtop and ran to the elevator. *Katherine has either gone crazy, or she has some kind of inside information on a possible terrorist attack,* she thought. *Either way, I've got a major story. If I hurry, I can be at the radio station in less than five minutes.*

She was already on the street, halfway to the BioWorld Tower, when the police scanner at her office went off again. But this time no one was listening.

"Central, this is Harbor 2. The wires on this dummy are . . . oh no . . . we've got fire in the hole . . . our gas tank just . . . oh my God, there's a . . ."

There was a sharp burst of static, and then the scanner went silent.

CHAPTER 5

FRANK DELL KICKED THE REAR BUMPER of his old Dodge pickup truck, and the tailgate dropped open with a heavy clang. Leaning forward, he let two 100-pound bags of fertilizer slip from his shoulders onto the truck's bed, sending a cloud of dust in the air and rattling the landscaping tools piled next to the wheel well.

It was still early, and he'd done very little heavy work, but sweat was already streaming into his eyes, and his work shirt was soaked through. He moved across the new lawn toward the company toolshed, avoiding the sun by walking through the shade cast by the bridge directly above him.

Man, she's a hot one—like being back in the freakin' desert. Everybody in the city's going to be cooked by noon . . . must be this solar storm everyone's talking about, he thought, slamming the shed door tight and securing it with a thick titanium padlock.

Frank wiped the sweat from his forehead and looked down the length of the island.

He was a tall man—well over six feet, with the tan complexion and lean, muscular build of someone who'd spent his life working outdoors. Although he was in his early 40s, his body was laced with sinewy muscle, and he moved with the confident energy of a high school athlete.

Frank bent down and stroked the tips of the boat-shaped blades of young Kentucky bluegrass he'd laid six weeks earlier. Roosevelt Island was just over two miles long and not even a thousand feet across. He'd landscaped almost half of it, and it was by far the biggest job he'd ever tackled on his own. But the work came naturally to him. His people had worked miracles—turning parched, arid land in Sicily into rich vineyards—back when their family was still known by the name Delvecchio.

He sucked in a mouthful of air and savored the earthy aroma, taking pride in what he'd accomplished. The lawn stretched north for a mile from the ruins of the old smallpox hospital at the southern tip of the island, all the way up to below the Queensboro Bridge where it engulfed the sparkling new Supercomputer Re-Creation Center, which was scheduled to open that morning.

The landscaping was simple and, Frank thought, elegant: a few strategically placed Japanese rock gardens breaking up the sea of green; a lilac path running down the center; and a hundred cherry trees lining the asphalt walk that circled the lower half of the island. The acres of grass replaced what had been a concrete wasteland of burnt-out hospitals and crumbling laboratories, abandoned and forgotten decades ago. In the center of the lawn was a giant blue rosebush that Conrad Dinnick had personally requested.

Like the tree in the middle of Eden, Frank silently approved.

He knew he was lucky—he'd only been landscaping for six years and, really, should never have landed such a big contract. But he'd gotten a call from a former general now running BioWorld Security, who said that he needed a good man he could trust, and that Frank's Army record was "spectacular." Next thing Frank knew, he had a check for a $30,000 and the promise of $200,000 more when the whole thing was done.

When he wasn't spending time with his daughter, Samantha, he put in 20-hour shifts to finish the job on time and do it well. Not only did he need the money, but he knew that everybody in the city was going to see his work. Roosevelt Island sat smack-dab in the middle of the East River, between Manhattan and Queens, and millions of people saw it every day.

He took a deep breath and smiled. *I didn't botch it—it's gorgeous, and it's a free organic billboard advertising my handiwork to the biggest city in America.*

And God knew, Frank needed the business. The savings account was nearly dry, the advance money was nearly gone, the mortgage was overdue, and his Army pension didn't come close to covering Samantha's medical bills for the more advanced treatments she required.

He sat on the ground and yanked the mud-caked construction boots and worn-out socks from his feet. Before slipping on his sneakers, he sank his feet in the damp, lush green, enjoying the touch of a living thing against his skin after so many years spent in places of dust and death.

Oh Jesus, I'm late. I've gotta get Sam, Frank thought, checking his watch and looking up at the Queensboro Bridge while hearing the relentless honking overhead. It sounded like it was being swarmed by a flock of psychotic Canada geese, which meant that trying to cross it this morning would become a daylong nightmare.

He'd have to take a detour if he was going to get to the clinic on time. Instead of the Queensboro, he'd have to drive north and cross into Manhattan using the Triboro Bridge into East Harlem, before doubling back 40 blocks to the clinic. *That could take an extra freaking hour,* he realized, and jumped into the truck.

"FINISHING UP EARLY, FRANK?" a guard asked, when he reached the checkpoint beside the Supercomputer Re-Creation Center.

The guard leaned out of his sentry box and eyeballed the back of the truck while Frank handed over his DNA-encoded clearance card. The Island was crawling with Conrad Dinnick's brown-shirted, pseudo-cop security force today, and it gave Frank the creeps.

Sure, it's been a long time since I wore a uniform, but at least I earned the right to wear one. But these punks? Frank thought bitterly.

He couldn't stomach the sight of these rent-a-cops marching around saluting each other like a bunch of neo-Nazis. And it seemed as if they were spreading all over the city as BioWorld put up more and more buildings in New York.

"I said, you finishing up early today, Frank?" the guard repeated.

"Huh? Oh yeah, well, I actually finished the main work yesterday. Just had to make sure everything was cool before the ceremony starts this morning. Don't want the sprinklers accidentally going off and raining on the boss's parade."

"I'm sure Mr. Dinnick will appreciate that, Frank. Anyway, the grass looks good. I can't believe you landscaped half the island all by yourself," the guard said, swiping Frank's ID through a small black box and passing it back through the window.

"I guess I don't like handing out paychecks to anyone except myself. Can I go?"

"Just a sec . . . couldn't help noticing some fertilizer, quite a few rolls of sod, a rake, and few shovels in the back of your truck there. Planning on taking them off the island?"

"It's my truck, and it's my stuff. Maybe you didn't notice, but I run a landscaping company. You want to run an inventory on everything in the storage shed, go right ahead. But I don't have time to stick around waiting for it. If anything's missing, call the cops and report me. Okay, pal?"

"No need to be rude, Frank. It's my job to keep track of these things."

"Good job you got there. Now open the gate, *please*," Frank said, not looking at the man.

"Sure, Frank, and you have a nice day now."

Frank gunned the Dodge, leaving a black patch of rubber streaked across the freshly paved road and yelled, "Sieg heil!" as he sped away.

The sleek, stainless steel walls of the Supercomputer Re-Creation Center rose steeply on his right, reflecting the morning light as it soared toward the bottom of the Queensboro Bridge— each wall panel was engraved with a single blue rose.

A catering van was parked in front of the building, its rear door open wide to expose stacks of folding chairs and boxes of plastic-wrapped crystal champagne flutes. A string quartet was setting up on a small stage, and at least a dozen state troopers and Secret Service agents were walking bomb-sniffing dogs around the building's perimeter.

"Goddamn son-of-a-bitch no-good bastard mutts!" Frank yelled. "Those four-legged mongrels better not crap on my new lawn."

A vein over Frank's left eye began to throb, a sure sign that his blood pressure was rising fast. The brief exchange with the security guard had left him seriously aggravated, and he knew that Samantha would pick up on his stress instantly— and that would be even worse for her than if he was a little bit late.

Pulling over to the side of the road, Frank got out of the truck for a minute to do the relaxation exercises Samantha had taught him, the ones from her pain-management sessions. Breathing slowly through his nose, he let the air drop to his belly, and then he exhaled slowly from his mouth, all the while trying to visualize "a happy place." But the air by the water stank of dead fish, and the only thing he could visualize was the skyline of midtown Manhattan on the other side of the river, shimmering in the hazy smog and harsh yellow light of a too-hot New York morning.

A police boat was advancing toward the island from the middle of the river. A fat cop stood on the bow twirling a grappling hook like an overweight cowboy trying to lasso a sea cow.

Frank looked up at the century-old Queensboro Bridge—50,000 tons of intricately laced structural steel, so groovy looking that Simon and Garfunkel had written a song about it.

I can't believe the city actually sold that beautiful hunk of metal just to balance the books, he thought, as the Roosevelt Island tram came sliding alongside the top of the bridge, suspended 250 feet above the river on cables stretching from the island all the way up the wheelhouse on Second Avenue.

If I didn't have the truck, I could just jump on the tram and be in Manhattan in eight minutes, Frank thought, heading back to the Dodge.

He crossed the island and drove north on Main Street to the East Channel bridge leading to Queens. In the rearview mirror he noticed a Lincoln Town Car hard on his tail. A Town Car usually meant NYPD detectives, so he pulled over as a courtesy to let them pass.

As Frank waited for them to go by, he looked at the ruins of the notorious 19th-century lunatic asylum and remembered the day he'd brought Sarah to the island to apartment hunt. They'd been married only a year then, and he'd just finished his last tour in the Gulf. The Army had loaned him to the United Nations for a couple of years, and he'd thought the island would be a convenient and inexpensive place to live.

"It's not exactly teeming with trendy night-spots, but the rents are half what they are across the river, and I can get to the UN in 15 minutes," he'd said to Sarah.

Sarah, as usual, had done her homework and had come prepared with a binder filled with housing prices and local history.

"Nice neighborhood you've picked, Franklin Madison Dell. Just over there is where the city dumped its smallpox victims. Over here was the infamous New York City poorhouse, but that was before they built the penitentiary for the really bad-ass criminals. Here's my favorite quote from a 1930s magazine article: 'Roosevelt Island is the miserable sewer into which New York dumped its pitiful sweepings.' Oh yeah—it used to be called Welfare Island, where they put all the poor folks like us . . . and then there was the insane asylum with a long history of abuse and torture and—"

"Okay, honey, I get the point. We'll buy the house you like in Jersey."

"Thanks, Frank," Sarah had said, reaching for his hand and flattening it against her belly. "Besides, this really isn't the kind of place you want to raise your child, is it?"

"What? You're not . . . ?" Frank had asked in wonderment.

"No, Frank . . . *I'm* not. But *we* are."

THE TOWN CAR PASSED, and Frank followed it through a second checkpoint, across the bridge and into Queens.

Forty-five minutes later, he pulled up in front of the cancer clinic. It was the first time he hadn't held Samantha's hand during a chemo treatment, and he felt awful about it. But what could he do? The money from the contract meant money for more chemo and experimental drugs.

He found her in the waiting room with a nurse.

"How ya doing, slugger?"

"Just peachy keen," Samantha replied.

Frank thanked the nurse and bent to pick Samantha up.

"I'm not crippled, Frank," she said, feebly pushing his arm away. "Just carry my barf bag for me, please."

When they reached the truck, Frank opened the door and waited while Samantha struggled onto the seat. He was gently closing the door behind her when he spotted the Lincoln Town Car parked across the street. He recognized the ripped American flag flapping on the bent antenna, and knew immediately it was the same car he'd followed off the island.

That's strange, he thought, climbing behind the wheel. "So, kiddo, whaddaya say we call it a day and head home? We can pick up *The Lion King* and invite your buddies Ben and Jerry to come over."

Samantha said nothing.

"I know I promised, Sammy, but it's so hot outside and, honest, sweetie, you look . . . well . . . just a little tired."

Samantha did up her seat belt and sat quietly.

"Okay, Sam," Frank said, starting the truck.

"St. Pat's or the mosque?"

"It's Friday. Take me to the mosque."

THE RITUAL MUSLIM CALL TO PRAYER wailed from the towering minaret of Manhattan's largest mosque at Third Avenue and 96th Street. It was the official prayer time, and the plaintive, beckoning cry echoed down the street.

"They're calling me, Franklin. I've got to go."

Frank looked at his 11-year-old daughter pulling impatiently on the passenger door's long silver lever. He knew that she only used his full first name when she was mad at him. He figured she was pissed off because he'd been late getting to the clinic. He didn't blame her; he was pissed at himself.

They'd been going through the same routine every Tuesday and Friday for months: a 45-minute drive from their home across the Hudson River in Newark, then an hour to 90 minutes at the clinic. Afterward, unless Samantha was really sick, they'd stop at St. Patrick's Cathedral so she could say a prayer and light a candle for her mom; or a make a prayer trip to a temple, synagogue, or mosque before taking the tunnel back beneath the river and heading home.

Frank had long ago accepted Samantha's strange fascination with world religions, even though he hadn't set foot in any house of worship since Sarah had been killed. But his daughter insisted that he wait outside wherever and whenever she was struck by the mood to pray. And lately, the mood was striking her more and more often.

He wasn't sure when it had started, but he guessed it had been the second-to-last Christmas Eve that Sarah had been alive. His wife had tried to explain the concept of Santa Claus to Samantha, but, being a Muslim, she had a hard time herself with the story of St. Nick.

"He has a magic moose that pulls him in a big wagon across the sky right around the whole planet, and they stop on rooftops while he jumps down chimneys and puts presents under potted plants for all the girls and boys in the world," Sarah had explained hesitantly, looking at Frank for support, but getting none.

"And Santa Claus is supposed to do this in one night? Fuhgettaboutit!" Samantha had responded, cracking both of them up. Even at five, she'd been precocious, with a wickedly wry sense of humor, an insatiable curiosity, and a phenomenal memory. She never forgot a single detail of anything she heard, no matter how minute or insignificant. She'd dismissed the Santa story out of hand, and for the rest of that Christmas Eve, the three of them had sat around wrapping presents, drinking cocoa, and discussing the many religious beliefs held by people from different cultures.

Frank remembered that after that night, Samantha couldn't get enough of religion. There were mandatory Bible readings at bedtime as well as stories from the Torah and Koran. Later, she insisted on hearing tales from Greek mythology, and was enthralled by the bloody battles waged by the Hindu gods.

Samantha's Beach House Barbie set became a surreal Nativity scene where the baby Jesus had a big brother named Buddha, and Ken and Barbie took everyone to Mecca for picnics. For the next two years, Samantha insisted that her mother accompany her to the mosque every Friday, and that Frank take her to Mass every Sunday. She made both of her parents wait for her outside the temple on Saturdays.

"She's one really weird kid, Sarah. Maybe we should take her to a shrink. Did you ever know any kid who wanted to go to church even once a week, much less two or three times?" Frank had asked Sarah while they waited for Samantha's Bible study class to finish one Sunday afternoon, a month before Sarah left.

"Come on, Frank. She's just curious . . . and so smart it's scary. Do you know that she can recite the names of all the books of the Bible, quote from the Koran, and rattle off the names and special powers of every god on Mount Olympus? She's remarkable, not weird, and she's having fun. I think we should just let her explore. Besides, think of all the money you're saving in ballet lessons."

"That's what I mean. Little girls usually want to be ballerinas, but our kid wants to be Pope or something. I don't even think she really believes half the stuff she reads."

"She's developing her own beliefs, and that's really special—particularly at her age." Sarah had moved close to him and leaned her head against his shoulder.

"You know what she said to me when I tucked her in last night?" she continued. "That she thought different religions are just different languages people speak in heaven, and she had to learn all of them in case God needed to speak to her one day. She calls it 'God language.' Doesn't that break your heart?"

"No, Sarah, what breaks my heart is you going back to that hellhole."

"Please . . . don't start. It's only for two weeks. It's not like there's an oversupply of Arab-speaking aid workers. You know how many orphans are over there now?"

"We've got our own daughter to take care of, and we both served our time. How much more do we have to give?"

"Please, Frank . . ."

"Sarah, I've got a bad feeling about this."

"I promise I'll be extra, extra careful. Besides, I'm going to be with the good guys, remember?"

"Okay . . . okay. Just be back for Easter. Sam's got her heart set on you seeing her in the Sunday-School pageant."

"I promise. Nothing could keep me away."

NOTHING BUT A BLOODTHIRSTY GRUNT WITH AN M16, Frank thought.

At Sarah's funeral, Frank dropped the crucifix his mother had given him into the coffin.

"Daddy, didn't Nonna give that to you? Why are you giving it to Mommy?" Samantha had asked him, as they left the cemetery.

"I don't need it anymore. I don't want it anymore. I don't believe in any of it anymore."

The continuing call to prayer jolted him back to the present. Samantha was sitting beside him, fighting with the door handle.

In the four years since Sarah's death, Frank had tried to make sure that Samantha never missed her prayer sessions. Even sickness hadn't curbed her enthusiasm, and he figured that her passion was good medicine as long as it didn't tire her out too much. So far it hadn't, but watching her wage a losing battle with the door handle made him think that it was time for her to slow down.

"Oh, stop looking so worried, Daddy. I'll get it . . . eventually," Samantha said, looking at her father and hitting the lever with a balled-up fist.

Frank studied her face. The warm olive complexion she'd inherited from her mother had been dulled by the chemo, leaving her looking chalky. The dark circles under her eyes and the red kerchief she wore to hide her vanished dark curls gave her the look of a seasick pirate. But as ill as she was, Frank knew that she could turn on a thousand-watt smile if she was happy. And it didn't take much to please her: a favorite song on the radio, a sweet story about her mother, a dish of Chunky Monkey ice cream. . . .

But she wasn't smiling this morning; she wasn't at all pleased with Frank. And he soon realized that it had nothing to do with his being late.

"Let me help you," he offered, leaning over to open the door.

"I don't need your help."

"I just want to—"

"I know what you want, Daddy, but you can't have it."

"I don't know what you're talking about, Sammy."

"Yes, you do, Daddy."

"I don't."

"You're lying. You promised you would never lie to me, and now you lie all the time. You're a liar, Franklin."

"I'm not . . . I . . . if it's the chemo . . . you know you have to have the treatments."

"Why? They just make me sicker. They make me throw up, and they make me bald."

"I know they do, sweetheart, but you know you need them to get better."

"I'm not stupid, Frank. *I* know I'm not going to get better, and *you* know I'm not going to get better. So stop lying to me, and stop lying to yourself. I'm dying."

"Don't ever say that."

"But it's the truth."

"Don't say it."

"It's true."

Frank stopped talking. He stared at his daughter, who was gazing out the window into the courtyard of the mosque where half a dozen women and girls, their heads and faces covered, were praying quietly.

Frank and Samantha had been fighting her leukemia for two years. It went into remission but always came back. Two weeks ago, Samantha's oncologist told Frank that they'd done everything they could do for her, that even with continued chemo and the newer, more expensive drugs, all they could hope to do now was keep her comfortable. The doctor had said there was little chance she'd survive the year, and suggested that the most humane thing to do would be to end the chemo and let Samantha enjoy the time she had left.

"Very little chance doesn't mean *no* chance," Frank said to the doctor, feeling like he wanted to snap the man's neck in two. Later, he told Samantha that the cancer was going away, but the doctors said it would just take longer than expected. They had to be brave and keep up with the treatments. Samantha had given him a quizzical look and said, "Okay, Daddy, if that's what you think is best."

But today Samantha looked more exhausted than he'd ever seen her, and he wondered if he was doing the best thing for her.

"Listen, Sammy, I know I'm not good at . . . I mean, your mom—"

The call to prayer was playing again.

"It's okay, Daddy, don't worry about it. We'll talk later, all right? But I've got to go."

Samantha gritted her teeth and pulled up on the lever with all her strength. The door popped open. Frank leaned over, placing his hand gently on his daughter's arm before she slipped out of the cab.

"Hold on a second, Sammy. Allah may be great, but he's not in such a great hurry that a little girl can't kiss her father good-bye before prayers."

He wrapped his arms around her, and she pecked him on the cheek before breaking his hug and pulling her small prayer rug from the glove compartment.

"Honestly, Daddy, I'm not going anywhere. I'll be, like, ten feet away, and you can watch me through the fence the whole time. Now I really have to go. And for God's sake, try to fix the door handle before I get back."

Frank laughed. He watched her in the rearview mirror as she entered the mosque's main gate, and then he saw it again: the Lincoln with the bent antenna and ripped flag.

Okay. Twice is a coincidence, three times is a definite tail, Frank thought.

He flipped on the truck's radio for a traffic report to plan his escape route. But what came through the speaker wasn't a traffic update—not by a long shot.

"Oh my God . . . oh my God! It's an explosion . . . many explosions . . . God, no . . . it looks like another attack. The explosions are going to happen here, in New York. Oh my God, it's going to happen today!"

Frank looked through the fence and saw Samantha spreading her prayer mat on the ground. He wasn't exactly sure what he'd just heard on the radio, but it didn't sound good—and he wasn't taking any chances where his daughter was concerned. He grabbed the door handle.

I've got to get her out of here.

CHAPTER 6

CONRAD DINNICK PULLED THE SHARP BLADE of the heavy straight razor away from his throat, glaring at the helicopter hovering in front of his window. He could tell by the color and markings that it wasn't one of his.

I build a multibillion-dollar tower and I have Peeping Toms? For God's sake . . . and today of all days! He placed the razor on the washbasin and pressed one of the many red intercom buttons scattered throughout his rambling penthouse suite at the top of the BioWorld Tower in Manhattan.

"Why is there a news helicopter outside my bedroom window?!" he demanded.

Within seconds, a voice from the building's main security desk piped through the suite's concealed speakers: "Security Chief Wilson here, sir. There seems to be some breaking news in the vicinity—a huge traffic tie-up on the Queensboro Bridge, and police activity on the river just in front of Roosevelt Island."

"Police activity in front of the island? Will this be a problem for the ceremony?" Conrad asked.

"No. No problem at all, sir. The area is secure—just a boating mishap with one of the Harbor Units. Should be cleared up shortly, but the news choppers are swarming around it like flies. I've called the NYPD Aviation Unit, and have been assured the airspace will be cleared momentarily," Wilson reported in a brisk, no-nonsense manner.

A blue and white police helicopter swung into Conrad's view as the security chief finished speaking. Conrad couldn't hear anything on the other side of the UltraPlexi window he'd personally designed to safeguard him from unwanted noise and uninvited bullets. Whatever was silently exchanged between the two aircraft was effective.

"Never mind," Conrad said, leaning on the intercom button again. "It's gone. Put another security detail on the river, and clear my bridge."

"Right away, sir . . . Wilson out."

Conrad returned to his vanity basin and continued shaving with calculated strokes. He was nearing 60, but still looked like he was in his late 40s. A recent *New York Times* profile described him as "the eternally youthful founder of BioWorld Security—a lean, mean, trillion-dollar gene machine." It attributed his vitality to his chore-filled, Iowa farm upbringing; a fastidiously healthy diet; a lifelong avoidance of tobacco, alcohol, and drugs; and a near-monkish aversion to emotional entanglements—except for, the reporter noted, one messy, highly publicized divorce.

When Conrad read the profile, he was amazed by how so-called professional journalists were so often completely ignorant about topics they were paid to write about. Yes, his marriage had ended in divorce and had made headlines because of the size of the settlement, but it wasn't messy in the least. He'd handled the divorce the way he handled everything: with clinical efficiency. He'd simply married the wrong woman—someone who couldn't accept that his work came before anything else, and who was overwhelmed by the responsibilities of motherhood.

She'd become an emotional burden, making constant demands on his time and interfering with his research, so he'd offered her $10 million in exchange for an uncontested divorce, and then she was out of his life forever.

The farm-boy anecdote was also a fabrication. The only chore expected of him was finishing library books before their due dates. As far as his looks were concerned, that wasn't about clean living, it was all about good genes. That fact had been the governing truth of his life since his mother summoned him to her greenhouse on the frigid February afternoon of his eighth birthday.

"Did you know, Connie, that even a simple farmer's wife can play God?" his mother had asked, leaning over a shrub taller than he was. "I'd like to introduce you to Miss Rosa Blanda. She's pretty enough to become Iowa's official state flower. But like lots of pretty things, she's weak, Connie." She cupped one of the plant's soft, pink flowers in her hand and inserted a pair of tweezers in its center.

"All I have to do is borrow a few cells from pretty Miss Rosa, and I can give them to a sturdy, but less beautiful, domestic rose—and I've made a new flower that's both beautiful and strong. My own act of cosmic creation, Connie," she'd explained, dropping the wild rose's pollen into a small glass dish and handing the tweezers to Conrad.

"Here's a blue tulip and a white rose," she'd said. "It's your turn to try, Connie. If a farmer's wife can play God, I don't see why a farmer's son can't, do you?"

Conrad was brought back to the present by the sound of the sliding doors of the suite's private express elevator opening with a hiss of pressurized air, followed quickly by heavy footsteps. A man in his mid-30s who bore a striking resemblance to Conrad lurched into the room, red-faced, breathless, and stumbling over his words.

"Um, uh . . . oh boy. On the radio, on the radio, yeah," the man blurted out, staring at his shoes and sucking air noisily through his mouth.

Conrad looked at him, and, as always, was amazed at the difference in temperament and bearing between his two sons—considering they'd been born identical twins, and it had been utterly impossible to distinguish one from the other physically.

His colleagues at the time had dubbed Conrad "The Godfather" when Michael and Daniel were born because monozygotic—identical—twins were often referred to as God's clones since they shared an identical DNA code.

What were the odds, they'd joked, *of a geneticist specializing in gene replication producing identical twins?* Well, he knew the odds—they were the same as for everyone else—one in 285, not a long shot by any stretch, but long enough to start a whisper campaign that he'd been taking his work home with him.

Conrad also knew that, statistically, the boys should share similar IQs and personality traits. But while the boys *looked* the same, they'd turned out as different as night and day.

From the time he could speak, Michael exuded a natural poise and remarkable self-confidence. By the end of high school, he'd mastered three languages, and eventually became the youngest-ever recipient of a Ph.D. from Stanford's genetics program. He'd joined the family business as a BioWorld Security senior vice president before he turned 26.

Michael had inherited Conrad's passion for science, but his ambition to always be first, combined with a ruthless intellect, had worried his father immensely.

While Conrad was undoubtedly the most daring scientist of *his* generation, he was always deliberate and careful in his experimentation. Michael's approach, however, made his father look like a timid schoolboy. Despite everyone's acknowledgment of his brilliance, Michael seemed driven to outdo Conrad's breakthroughs, and was often extremely reckless in his research, dismissing both safety and ethical issues in his pursuit of results.

That recklessness had caused a major rift between father and son after Conrad discovered that the young man was injecting himself with a large number of stem cells extracted from hundreds of human embryos, which was not only incredibly dangerous, but also illegal.

They fought bitterly—a vicious argument that echoed through the complex. Conrad accused Michael of jeopardizing his government contracts as well as the funds he received to search for cures for a dozen diseases from Alzheimer's to multiple sclerosis.

At first Michael seemed hurt, yelling at his father, "You've never picked on Danny like this! You've always let him do whatever he wanted, no questions asked. All I've done my entire life is try to please you, to show you how much I respected your work, to advance your research . . . but you do nothing but criticize me. Nothing will ever satisfy you unless you can do it yourself and claim the glory as all your own—isn't that right, Dad? So I took a few embryos and used some stem cells for my research. So what? You've made a fortune selling human growth hormone to people afraid of getting old and tired. What's the difference?"

Then Michael laughed in Conrad's face. He lashed out at his father, accusing him of wasting his life trying to "cure" disease—and that the real challenge was to beat death altogether . . . to stop the aging process by preventing human cells from decaying.

"I'm not talking about using Botox to smooth out wrinkles on middle-aged ladies, or developing a new kind of chemotherapy to squeeze a few more years of life into the sick and dying!" Michael screamed. "I'm taking about *real* eternal youth—about conquering death. You've always played at being God, Dad. I'm going to *be* God!"

Conrad had realized at that moment that his son—either through the experimental drugs he'd injected or because of insanely out-of-control ambition—had become unstable, and a dangerous liability to BioWorld.

He banned Michael from setting foot inside the Hoboken research laboratory ever again. It was the last time he'd talked to his son. Six months later, Michael stole a gun from a BioWorld security guard and killed himself.

Conrad tried not to think about it, but it was nearly impossible not to when Daniel was standing in front of him looking exactly like Michael, but acting as though he'd crawled out of a completely different gene pool.

Daniel was sweating profusely, as pathologically shy and as nervous as ever: a flushed-faced stutterer who, despite years of study at Harvard Divinity School, struggled to put a sentence together. He'd dropped out before getting his doctorate, seeming more interested in volunteering as a missionary in every backwater village of the developing world than in getting a real job. It had always irked Conrad that while Michael, despite his obsessiveness, was earning millions of dollars for BioWorld, Daniel was in the African bush handing out Bibles to the poor.

The brothers, although inseparable as children, had been at odds with each other since adolescence. Conrad recalled hearing one of their fierce debates when they were teens: Daniel argued in his hesitant, stammering manner that you didn't use a microscope to find God, that He could be found simply by looking inward at one's own soul. Michael dismissed his argument scornfully, saying that as soon as someone developed a better MRI machine, there'd be scientific proof that the soul was nothing but a collection of hyperactive neurons bouncing around in the brain. Michael taunted Daniel by quoting Francis Crick, the co-discoverer of DNA's double helix.

"Remember what Crick said, Danny boy: 'Your joys and your sorrows, your memories and your ambitions, your sense of personal identity and free will, are in fact no more than the behavior of a vast assembly of nerve cells and their associated molecules.' That, in a nutshell, is the definition of the human soul—the gospel according to DNA."

"The g-g-gospel of DNA, is not the gos-gospel truth. Not God's truth. Everyone has a s-s-soul, Mike . . . even you . . . even Dad," Daniel would stutter back.

After Michael's suicide, Daniel seemed to change. He'd begged for a public-relations job at the BioWorld research center in Hoboken. Conrad gladly gave it to him, hoping it would force the boy to confront his shyness. But he also insisted that Daniel manage his latest acquisition—New York City's leading radio station—so he'd develop business skills to prepare him to take charge of

BioWorld one day. But so far, he'd been completely inept at managing the station.

Looking at his son now, Conrad wondered in despair, *How could he come in here and disturb me while I'm preparing for one of the biggest announcements I've ever made?* Aloud, he demanded, "For God's sake, Daniel, if you've got something to say to me, spit it out! Has it slipped your mind what a critically important day this is for us?"

"No, sir, I haven't forgotten. It's a big d-d-day, sure, I know that all right, but, uh . . . there's a pro-prob-problem on the morning show."

"What kind of problem, Danny?"

"A guest, a psychic. She's saying things, things . . . she's sc-scaring people. We've had complaints . . . the police called and—"

"The *police*. Oh my God, Danny, how could you let this happen? And how did a *psychic* get booked on the show in the first place? You know how I feel about those sorts of quacks. But that doesn't matter right now. For God's sake, I made you station manager, didn't I? Go manage. Start doing your job. I've got the governor and the mayor arriving shortly, so please, no psychics and no police, okay?"

"I think you'd better come down and—"

"No, Danny. I think you'd better take care of this yourself. Now, I have to get ready for the ceremony, so excuse me."

"Okay, sir . . . I'll . . . I'll . . . I'll tell Mr. Wilson . . . tha-tha-tha-," Danny stuttered while crossing over to the control console by the elevator and pushing a blue button, ". . . that I'm . . . um . . . coming down."

"Jesus, Danny, that's not the intercom, it's the damn security door in the basement—it's never supposed to be opened . . . it breaks the building's entire air lock and lets anyone stroll into the Tower. Get away from the console, and go deal with the psychic situation, please?"

What next? Conrad wondered. *First my accountants wake me up to tell me that hundreds of millions, maybe billions, of dollars seems to have been "misplaced." Then Wilson informs me there are problems on the river just before the ceremony, and now my dim-witted son lets me know that the police are complaining about a psychic on my radio station.*

Conrad heard the suite's doors slide shut as Danny left and turned back to the mirror. As he dabbed more shaving cream on his face, he couldn't help but see the faces of his boys in his reflection.

His sons had been so close that they used *cryptophasia*—their own secret twin language—to communicate with each other until they started school. But after their mother had left and their grandmother, who had helped raise them, died . . . the differences that would become so pronounced by adolescence had begun to appear. Michael had always thrived in school, scoring off-the-chart grades from his very first math quiz, while Daniel became more withdrawn, began stuttering, and was reading the Bible more often than his textbooks.

But that was one of the many things about his sons Conrad hadn't known at the time—when they were young, he was far too busy conducting research for other people to worry about raising children. He let his mother and a long line of nannies attend to the child rearing. By the time the boys were teenagers, he was completely dedicated to building his own company and rarely saw them except on scheduled holidays and the occasional birthday.

Conrad finished shaving and wiped his razor clean on a hand towel before studying it in the sunlight flooding through the wraparound floor-to-ceiling windows. Daylight slid along the handle like a bubble of yellow liquid. It was 24-karat, as pure a gold as you could find anywhere on the planet. The chairman of the New York Stock Exchange had presented it to him as a gift the day BioWorld Security went public. The blade was engraved on both sides. On one side, it said: "Remember the Golden Rule of Commerce." On the other side was: "Cut their throat before they cut yours."

"If you think commerce is cutthroat, get a job as a scientist," Conrad had said as he was accepting the gift. "They'll pick your brains, your pockets, and your bones until there's nothing left to pick . . . and then pick some more."

Conrad Dinnick turned his back on pure research decades ago, not intending to use his intellect to make pharmaceutical executives rich. He invested a small inheritance to set up his first lab, and became a maverick pioneer in genetic research.

But he hadn't gone into genetics to get rich—he did it to save his mother's life. She'd been diagnosed with multiple neuronal degeneration just after he graduated from medical school. He was stunned by the diagnosis, knowing that the disease would slowly but surely destroy his mother's keen mind and leave her once-vigorous body a twisted, withered ruin. Doctors believed that the disease was caused by a genetically mutated virus, so Conrad decided to abandon a career in medicine to devote himself to finding the viral gene attacking his mother's brain and nervous system.

He never succeeded, and considered it his greatest failure—at least until Michael's suicide.

While the gene that caused his mother's illness had eluded him, it led him deep into the field of genetic research and unraveling the mysteries of DNA's double helix.

His groundbreaking work had earned him two Nobel Prizes and caught the attention of the Pentagon, and he was asked to advise the President on defending the country against biological attack. His contacts with the government soon brought lucrative contracts to his small but growing company.

Then came the first World Trade Center attack in 1993, and the beginnings of his enormous financial empire. After the bombing, he dedicated his biogenetic and computer research to national defense, developing a screening device capable of analyzing a person's entire genetic profile in a matter of seconds and downloading the information into a central database.

When the World Trade Center was attacked a second time, Conrad quietly sold several hundred Dinnick DNA Samplers to the new Department of Homeland Security—the first of dozens of his patented biotechnical devices purchased by increasingly nervous world governments.

On the fourth anniversary of the 9/11 attacks, one of Conrad's inventions detected a large quantity of aerosol anthrax in a shipping container in Calais, France. When the media reported that the discovery had probably saved hundreds of thousands of lives, the price of BioWorld Security stock quadrupled overnight and kept going up. The profits were staggering, allowing Conrad to build dozens of new research facilities, invest billions in an antiviral drug program, and develop new computer systems to help identify genetic diseases. And all the while, the profits kept pouring in.

This morning he would announce the beginning of Project PAT, BioWorld's most closely guarded, and by far, most revolutionary, venture. PAT was a method of genetic cloning that, with the aid of a massive supercomputer, would soon allow him to create—to actually grow—human organs in a laboratory. It meant that, for a certain price, no one would ever have to wait for a transplant again.

The implications would shock the world: Life expectancy in the Western Hemisphere could increase by 10, perhaps as much as 20 or even 30 years . . . and that was just the beginning. Even *he* didn't know where the research would lead once the project was up and running—the potential for putting an end to scores of genetic diseases in just a few years was within reach.

Conrad looked out of the suite's east window as he slipped into the shirt he'd had made especially for today. From the Tower's 120th floor, he had an unimpeded view of the East River and Roosevelt Island, where the new jewel of his growing empire, The BioWorld Supercomputer Re-Creation Center, or, as he simply called it, The Re-Creation Center, was about to officially open.

The cigar-shaped building stretched for more than 300 feet along the center of the skinny island. The Queensboro Bridge hovered high above, intersecting it in a way that gave the Center—at least from Conrad's bird's-eye view—the look of a giant cross.

He smiled as the morning sun flashed across the solar panels on the building's roof—like a beacon pointing to a new future.

Just as it should, Conrad thought, knowing that inside the center was a revolutionary computer system that had the potential to rewrite every religious, philosophical, and scientific notion humankind had ever held dear.

He'd spent hundreds of billions of dollars to buy both Roosevelt Island and the famous bridge so he could build in the heart of New York—a show of support for a city still sitting at the top of the terrorist hit list.

But after today, maybe, just maybe, terrorism would no longer be such a constant threat. If Project PAT went according to plan, there would be so much less suffering in the world, so much more hope, and so much less to fight about.

He would still make immense profits from the project, but it would also be his way of giving something back.

Soon, Conrad would be joining the mayor and governor to ride the cable car down to the island. He would officially open the Re-Creation Center with a ribbon-cutting ceremony and then reveal to the world the full potential of Project PAT.

He put on his jacket, removed a carefully folded sheet of calligraphy paper from his inside breast pocket, and began to read:

"Gentlemen, ladies, honored guests, scientists, citizens of New York, and people of the world . . ." Conrad put the paper back in his pocket—he didn't need it. He looked into the mirror and rehearsed his speech.

"Two years ago I lost my son Michael, who took his life rather than die a slow, painful death brought on by an incurable disease. Today, thanks in large part to his tireless and daring research, I have the honor and privilege to announce that many who now suffer from so-called incurable diseases need no longer fear death. Today, I am proud to announce that death has been dealt a blow—"

"Excuse me, sir . . ."

"What is it now, Wilson?" Conrad said, turning toward his ceiling speakers.

"There's a woman on the radio claiming the city is about to be attacked by terrorists."

"What? I told Daniel to take care of this."

"Daniel went to the basement to check on the security door he said he accidentally opened from your suite. I would have attended to the matter myself, but I was busy dispatching additional security personnel to the island per your instructions, sir."

"Replay the radio program up here."

"Stand by, sir."

To his dismay, Conrad heard a woman's voice say: *"Oh my God . . . oh my God! It's an explosion . . . many explosions . . . God, no . . . it looks like another attack. . . ."*

A few seconds later, Conrad was tripping over his pants, trying to pull them up as he got into his private elevator. He was certain that the voice he was hearing was either an actress hired by a competitor to undermine his announcement today, or someone in cahoots with a terrorist group trying to steal his work.

He listened to the rest of the broadcast through the elevator speakers as he began the 120-floor descent to the lobby.

"The explosions are going to happen here, in New York. Oh my God, it's going to happen today!"

CHAPTER 7

KATHERINE WAS SUSPENDED IN MIDAIR, stretched out in a hammock, swinging between two poplar trees by the beach house of her dear friend Julia.

She could hear snatches of Julia's favorite Sinatra song drifting on the breeze, and she began singing along to herself.

The summer wind . . . came blowin' in . . . from across the sea . . .

The song stopped abruptly as a voice called out, "Kathy, go find Frankie's place."

Katherine sat up in the hammock, startled. She saw Julia walking toward her.

"This isn't the best time or place for a visit, Katherine," Julia said in her soft, cultivated voice.

"Julia! What am I . . . what are *we* doing here? Am I—?"

"No, Kathy, just sleeping . . . sleeping when you should be up and moving. Remember when I told you that you had a mission in store for you?

Well, it's here. It's time for you to begin your journey."

"What are you talking about, Julia? Why did you bring me here?"

"I didn't bring you here. You came to me, and you have to find the answers. Go find Frankie. Drive to Sinatra. I have to go."

"Wait. I miss you so much," Katherine begged, reaching up to touch Julia's cheek.

"I miss you too, Kathy. But you have work to do. You don't want people looking like *this,* do you?"

Katherine recoiled in horror. Julia's beautiful, delicate face was filling up with open, weeping sores, and it seemed like her face was melting off her bones.

"Drive to Sinatra, or everyone could look like this," Julia said. "Now wake up . . . wake up . . . wake up. . . ."

Katherine opened her eyes, and for some reason she thought she saw an image of Abraham Lincoln above her . . . and then Tarzan's face came into view, and he was yelling: "Wake up, wake up . . . wake up!"

Pain shot through Katherine's skull as her headache returned in full force.

"Are you having some kind of mental breakdown?" Tarzan demanded, shaking his head. "Do you know the trouble we're in?" He was prancing around the room like his feet were on fire.

"What happened? What's going on here?" Katherine asked, slowly getting up off the floor and drawing herself up to her full height. She looked down at Tarzan, who quickly retreated backward a few steps.

"That's a question a lot of people, including the police and the FBI, will be asking *you*, Ms. Haywood."

Katherine whirled around and came face-to-face with a tall, blond man wearing what appeared to be an SS uniform. She rubbed her eyes and steadied herself again. She realized that the man was actually wearing an expensive, well-tailored black suit.

"Okay, please just give me a second," she said, taking a deep breath and surveying the tiny studio. There were several people in the little room, all staring at her like she had six heads.

Bronwyn, the production assistant, came running into the room and gave Katherine a glass of cold water.

"Are you okay, Katherine? You passed out."

"I . . . I think so. I don't really remember anything after the first caller. Maybe I'm still jet-lagged. I've only passed out one other time in my life."

"Well, the phones are jammed. There are a lot of freaked-out people wondering what's going on," said Bronwyn.

"Oh my God! And you don't remember what happened?!" Tarzan pressed Katherine. "Well, let me refresh your memory. You basically announced—*on my show*—that New York City is going to be attacked by terrorists today. Do you know what the FCC could do to me? I could get pulled off the air!"

"Please lower your voice," Katherine said evenly. "My head is hurting. I'm sure it will all come back to me in a few minutes. I apologize if

I've disrupted your show."

"Disrupted?! We had to pull the plug on you. My show was putting out nothing but dead air for 30 seconds—*dead air!* That's the kiss of death in radio."

Katherine was trying to regain her bearings and recall the last few minutes. A second later, the images from her last readings came back to her in a flash: the red ski lift, car wrecks, a burning bridge, a collapsing tunnel . . . a uniform and a gun.

"Look, I'm sorry about what just happened here," she repeated, looking at the apprehensive faces surrounding her. "I'm as upset about it as any of you. The last thing I want to do is frighten anyone during a reading. What I said just came out, and it's—"

"'Sorry' isn't going to cut it here, lady!" Tarzan's voice was rising.

"Please, Tarzan, I'm trying to tell you that what I saw was real. Surely if your producers invited me on your show, they don't think I'm faking all of this, right? Now, I have to figure this out because someone's in trouble. Something bad is going to happen, and it's connected to this place . . . to the man on the phone. If you could just forget the show for a minute and—"

"Forget the show? It's *my* show! I'm Tarzan—"

"Shut up and sit down, Tarzan. She's right—this isn't about you," the tall blond man interjected.

"No, this *is* about me. *The Jungle Hour* has a reputation—"

"If you don't sit down, I *will* make it about you. And trust me, that's something you don't want. Do we understand each other?" the blond man asked menacingly.

Tarzan sat down behind his microphone, and the man turned to Katherine.

"Now, Ms. Haywood, let's have a little chat, shall we? My name is John Wilson. I'm chief of security for all the BioWorld facilities, including the BioWorld Tower. There have been a lot of calls coming in from local, state, and federal law enforcement regarding your statements about a possible attack on New York. Besides panicking thousands of our listeners, your little performance has upset a lot of high-ranking officials from the local police chief to the Department of Homeland Security in Washington," Wilson said.

"'Performance'?" Katherine asked, shaking her head. "You think that was some kind of act I was putting on? I would never deliberately panic people. I'm a professional, and what I said could very well be a warning to—"

"That's all well and good," Wilson interrupted, "and I'm sure your credentials are impeccable. Unfortunately, we're preparing for a rather sensitive, high-security ceremony. You've jeopardized that, and I need to find out why. So if you would please join me and my employers in the security office across the main lobby—"

"What? Are you placing me under arrest?"

"No, although I could. At the moment, I'm leaving that up to the police. I'm merely inviting you to join me in a discussion."

Katherine felt extremely uneasy about this man, but she knew that a line had been crossed, and she had to make things right.

"Okay, as long as you're asking politely, take me to see them. I'll be glad to provide an explanation," Katherine said, hoping she'd be able to clear everything up.

Bronwyn popped her head through the door to say, "We're going back on the air in 30 seconds. You'll have to clear the studio. Are you good to go, Tarzan?"

"I'm a professional—I'm always good to go," Tarzan spat, putting on his headphones and glaring at Katherine as she turned to leave.

He leaned in front of his microphone and was back in character.

"AhhhhEEEEeeee AhhhhEEEEeeee Ahhhhhhhhh! Hello, folks, it's Tarzan swinging back to you in the Jungle. Sorry about that little interruption. That was just a bad joke . . . nothing to worry about. This solar storm is really playing havoc with all our systems, and our guest psychic was feeling under the weather, but I think we've got things sorted out now. So whaddaya say we cool down those solar flares with a hip-hop version of an oldie but goodie—a tune made famous by the hippest cat to ever cross the Lincoln Tunnel, Hoboken's favorite son, Ol' Blue Eyes himself, my man . . . Frankie S."

Katherine stopped in her tracks. "Julia," she whispered, as Tarzan pushed the play button and the familiar words filled the suite.

"The summer wind . . . came blowin' in . . . from across the sea. . . ."

CHAPTER 8

ZOE LOOKED UP, WAY UP. She wasn't usually impressed by buildings, but, as always, the BioWorld Tower wowed her completely.

She'd sprinted the two blocks from her office to the Tower, hoping to get to the psychic before the police or other reporters did, but she couldn't resist pausing for a second to admire the imposing structure.

Talk about your phallic symbols! Zoe joked to herself as she strained her neck to take in the full view.

It was an intimidating skyscraper, even by New York City standards. The cylindrical ebony pillar dominated the Manhattan skyline with its dizzying height, shrouding the surrounding buildings in perpetual shadow. It had been unveiled with great fanfare and, at the time, was hailed as the *Titanic* of architecture: enormous, inspiring, and indestructible.

The Tower's revolutionary "steeltanium" frame was encased in thousands of shatterproof black windows that seemed to suck the sunlight out of the midtown area.

At the ribbon cutting, the Japanese architect had boasted that the Tower was terrorist-proof: "Hermetically sealed, with its own pure air supply, and so strong that a 747 would bounce off it like a tennis ball," although a *New York Times* columnist later wrote that the allusion was in such bad taste that something must have been lost in the translation.

Critics had dubbed Conrad Dinnick the "Prince of Darkness" for his eerie ability to convert human genome research into staggering profits. And they christened his building "The Dark Fortress"—declaring that its lack of charm was surpassed only by its radiant bleakness.

This sucker must run a mile straight up, Zoe observed, mounting the black marble steps leading from York Avenue to the Tower's main entrance.

The massive revolving door was flanked by hand-carved crystalline sculptures of the double helix—the basic structure of DNA and the foundation of Conrad Dinnick's vast fortune.

Inside, the many government offices and science labs were constructed along the perimeter of the circular walls. Each level was stacked atop the next like an upright roll of LifeSavers.

In the center of the building, a vast atrium overflowed with exotic trees, plants, and flowers that Zoe didn't recognize, and was alive with the sound of babbling streams and waterfalls. Sun filtered down through the entire atrium from a massive domed skylight 120 floors overhead.

What is this, the Amazon rain forest? Zoe couldn't believe that she'd worked down the street from the Tower for years and had never been inside. Then again, given her reputation, she wasn't on many of the city's invitation lists.

Zoe approached the main gate cautiously. Some members of Conrad Dinnick's enormous security staff were former NYPD officers, and her exposés on dirty cops had left her few fans on the police force. In general, pretty much everyone considered *The Trumpet*'s reporters to be gutter slime.

"Your business in Dinnick Tower today, Miss?" asked the guard at the security desk.

"New York Department of Environmental Health. I'll be testing for air quality today," Zoe said, offering him a fake photo ID that she'd recently paid a grand for. Since the increase in anthrax attacks, ricin scares, and dirty-bomb threats, a DEH identification card got her past most government and civilian checkpoints.

"There's nothing on the computer about a DEH inspection today, Miss . . . uh . . . Miss . . . " The officer squinted at his computer screen and then back at Zoe's fake ID.

"Merryfield," Zoe said. "Isobel Merryfield. And if you don't mind, it's *Ms*. Please check your new DEH regulation guide: chapter 7, subsection 3. You'll discover that state law grants DEH inspectors immediate and unlimited access to all buildings, structures, and substructures within New York City and surrounding counties."

"I'm familiar with the law, Ms. Merryfield, but I still don't see your name on the computer. You'll have to stick your finger in the Sampler."

"Stick my *what, where?*"

"Your finger in the Sampler, please. I have to code you."

Zoe knew about the Dinnick Sampler, but had never been asked to submit to one. The machines looked like electric pencil sharpeners, and painlessly extracted a microscopic skin sample from the user's forefinger. DNA from the sample was then recorded and downloaded into a global network that scanned for infectious diseases, drug use, and contact with restricted chemicals or pathogens. Despite civil rights protests, the Samplers were becoming more commonplace in airports, government offices, and private businesses.

Welcome to the new world, Zoe thought ruefully. She could see the red neon sign of WARP Radio flickering through the leaves from the other side of the atrium.

"Let's go, Miss. The machine won't bite, and it's a busy day."

Zoe held up her middle finger. "Is this the one you want?"

The officer sighed. "Very original. What is this, your first day on the job? Just insert your finger, please."

Zoe scowled, but then slipped her finger into the opening and felt a tiny jolt, less than a static electricity shock. Five seconds later, a green light flashed, and an electronic female voice announced: "Subject: Unknown. Status: Clean."

"What does that mean? It knows I had a shower this morning?"

"No, *Ms.* Merryfield," said the guard, rolling his eyes. "Clean means you're disease free and haven't handled things that could go boom, and now your genetic code is in the global DNA database. Just place your knapsack on the x-ray belt, and you'll be good to go."

"My bag?"

"Yes, your bag."

"Um . . . there's sensitive testing equipment in here. I'll just carry it through."

"Hand it to me, please. I'll do a physical inspection to make sure there are no—"

Across the atrium, an angry voice from the radio studio was getting louder, echoing through the cavernous atrium.

"You basically announced—*on my show*—that New York City is going to be attacked by terrorists today. Do you know what the FCC could do to me? I could get pulled off the air!"

The guard went pale and he whipped his walkie-talkie from his belt, turning his back to Zoe: "Building alert: possible Code Red. Building alert . . ."

That was Tarzan ranting, Zoe realized. *And no doubt Katherine is at the other end of it. I've gotta get in there.*

She scooped up her bag, slid it across her shoulder, and slipped into the tangle of leaves.

CHAPTER 9

CONRAD DINNICK USED THE 120-FLOOR DESCENT from his penthouse to finish dressing. He was straightening his Italian silk tie when he stepped from the private elevator and saw his son standing in the lobby.

"Danny? What the hell are you doing here? You were supposed to deal with . . . forget about it, just follow me," he snapped, brushing past his son to the Tower's west-side security desk.

"Mr. Dinnick, sir," said the guard, "the main security desk is reporting some trouble in the radio studio. A possible Code Red—"

"I know," Conrad said, sticking his forefinger into a Sampler. The machine's electronic voice stated: "Subject: Dinnick, Conrad. Status: Clean." Conrad walked through the security gate.

"But, sir . . . a possible Code Red. Should we evacuate the—"

"No! Do you want to create a panic? Do nothing until you receive a direct order from Chief

Wilson or myself. Understood?"

"Yes, sir."

Conrad waited for his son to be screened by the Sampler.

"Subject: Dinnick, Daniel. Status: Clean. Subject: Dinnick, Michael. Status: Clean."

Conrad's stomach tightened as the computer announced Michael's name. As identical twins, Daniel and Michael had identical DNA, and the sampler couldn't differentiate between them. Michael had been dead for nearly two years, but Conrad hadn't had the heart to erase all traces of his son, however misguided Michael had been.

"Come on, Danny, let's get to the studio before someone calls the bomb squad."

"But s-sir, the time. I think you sh-should—"

"Should *what*, Danny?

"Get to the tr-tr-tram."

"Of course that's what I *should* do, Danny. The mayor and the governor are waiting. But once again, I'm left to clean up your mess. And this time, it's a *hell* of a mess, isn't it? The tram will have to wait."

"I'm sorry, sir, b-b-but—"

"But what? Jesus! Why couldn't you be more like your brother? Every time I give you some responsibility, you completely screw it up. At least when Michael screwed up, he was trying to make history. You screw up booking guests on a radio show, for Christ's sake."

"Bu-bu-but . . . I . . . I—"

"Enough! We've got no time. You've jeopardized Project PAT and possibly created a citywide panic. Either way, you've allowed someone to sabotage BioWorld, and now I'm going to find out if it was deliberate or accidental," Conrad stated emphatically, walking into the atrium and past a rosebush bursting with the enormous blue flower he and his mother had created for themselves so many years ago.

Daniel trailed behind him, trying to keep up.

"But D-D-Dad . . . I thought I shouldn't st-stop her because it was maybe a j-j-joke like *War of the Worlds*."

"What the hell are you talking about? What have world wars got to do with anything?"

"No, *War of the Worlds*, Dad, sir . . . 1930s ra-ra-radio show about Mar-Martians attacking Earth. They didn't say it was pretend, and people k-k-killed themselves. I thought the psy-psychic, you know, would say, 'J-Just kidding, folks.'"

"*'Just kidding, folks'*? That's your reasoning, Danny? I know you're a dropout, but are you a complete imbecile?"

"I'm sorry, sir. Let me . . . f-fix it. Please, leave for the ceremony. The mayor, the governor, they're waiting at the tr-tr-tram for you to go to the island."

Conrad checked his watch. In a few minutes he was scheduled to ride across to Roosevelt Island with the mayor and governor to open the Supercomputer Re-Creation Center. After that, he was going to stand in front of the TV cameras and make what he knew would be one of the most monumental announcements in the history of science.

"You're absolutely right, Danny, I should leave now. But first I have to find out how much damage has been done. You take the tram and make my apologies to—"

"Oh, no . . . no! Please don't make me do that! I'm too ner-ner-nervous to—"

"For God's sake, you've got to get your act together. Today the Dinnick name will be written in the history books once again. So stand behind me, keep your mouth shut, and at least *try* to act like the heir to an empire!"

Conrad and Daniel arrived at WARP as Security Chief Wilson emerged with a tall red-haired woman wearing a white silk blouse and black tailored slacks. She looked dazed.

"Mr. Dinnick, sir, this is the psychic, Katherine Haywood," Wilson said.

"Let's cut to the chase, Miss Haywood: Whom are you working for?" Conrad demanded.

"Sinatra," Katherine said dreamily.

"What did you say?" Conrad asked.

"Frank Sinatra," she repeated.

CHAPTER 10

JACK MORGAN SNAPPED THE COVER FROM HIS
MOTORCYCLE like a stage magician. And there it
was, his 1969 Harley-Davidson chopper, a replica
of the bike Peter Fonda had ridden as Captain
America in the movie *Easy Rider*.

When Jack was a teenager, the bike had
been the ultimate rebel machine. But today, the
extended front forks, "ape hanger" handlebars,
and Stars-and-Stripes gas tank looked ridiculously
old-fashioned and silly.

*But who cares what it looks like? Just get on, find
that woman, and stop her lying once and for all.*

Susan had loved the Harley, and while Jack
hadn't sold it, he also hadn't started it since she'd
died. Six or seven years ago, he'd told Mohammad
across the street that he could use his garage for
storage as long as he watched over the bike and
kept it clean and in working order.

Jack opened the garage door, eased himself
onto the seat, and with a single kick, the Harley

jumped to life. He revved the engine wildly for a minute before strapping on his Captain America helmet.

The last time Jack had been in the city, the BioWorld Tower hadn't even existed, but he had no trouble finding it. Within minutes, he was speeding across the Brooklyn Bridge and could see the ugly black colossus towering over the city like a tombstone. He automatically glanced to his left, where the Twin Towers had stood, and felt like someone had punched a hole through his chest and yanked out his heart. He thought of Liam.

Don't. Just don't. Don't even think about it.

Jack headed off the bridge onto the FDR Highway and came to a dead stop. Both north-bound and southbound lanes were jammed solid. He maneuvered onto the road's narrow shoulder that ran north along the East River and twisted the throttle, flying up the highway. He was almost in the BioWorld Tower's shadow when he saw flames on the river. A fire department water boat was hosing down a small blue and white cabin cruiser.

Looks like an NYPD Harbor Unit, Jack thought. *Hope none of our boys got hurt.*

Jack pulled off the highway to find police barriers blocking traffic from getting onto York Avenue. He navigated through a dozen or so demonstrators protesting in front of the Tower.

"Hey, Captain America, nice hog. But the street is closed—didn't you see the barriers? Or maybe you think the law don't apply to Easy Riders."

Jack looked at the uniformed officer walking toward him and pulled his badge from his back pocket.

"Captain Jack Morgan, *homicide*. Got someone I need to talk to inside the radio station," Jack said, looking at the Tower's marble staircase and wondering if his battered body would make it to the top.

"Jack Morgan? Get the hell outta here! You're kiddin' me, right? Jesus Christ, that's a good one . . . Crazy Jack Morgan," the officer said, laughing in Jack's face until he looked at the badge. "Holy shit, I didn't mean no disrespect, sir. Nothing like that at all. I mean, you're a legend at the academy. Best homicide close rate in department history until you . . . um . . . you know. I just thought you were like retired in Florida or something."

"I've been on special assignment, sort of low profile. Listen, will you watch my bike for a few minutes? I've got to get to this suspect before—"

"You looking for the psychic?"

"Why do you ask that?"

"Whaddaya think we got the street closed for? They're expecting a little protest 'cause of something she said that's got some people in the city spooked. Nobody tells us uniforms on the street nothing. All I know is a bunch of other shields were supposed to be heading down to talk to her, but I guess they got detoured when that Harbor Unit exploded."

"Yeah, I saw that. What happened?"

"Dunno. I hear maybe a gas line or something. They're still looking for two of our guys."

"That's rough."

"Got that right. Yeah, so I guess some of the guys are tied up over there. Plus, this traffic is just nuts. I've never seen it so bad—like everybody's trying to get out of town before noon or something, huh?"

"Yeah, it's bad all right. Watch the Harley, okay? If I'm not back in 20 minutes, the bike's yours," Jack said.

"Yeah, that's a good one, but sure, I'll watch it. Hey, Captain, I was real sorry to read about your son. That was a tough day for everyone, huh?"

"Yeah . . . a tough day," Jack said, turning toward the stairs.

"What did that psychic do to piss everyone off so much, anyway? Predict that the Mets would whip the Yankees?"

"That's exactly what she did."

"Well, she should be shot for that. Right, sir?"

"You can count on it," Jack said, slipping his hand into his jacket and gripping the handle of his .38.

He began climbing the marble stairs to the Tower.

CHAPTER 11

ZOE HURRIED TOWARD WARP'S FLASHING NEON SIGN. She navigated through the atrium's strange, genetically engineered foliage, hoping that by holding her tiny palmtop computer out in front of her, she looked like a busy environmental inspector.

The palmtop was a small but powerful investigative tool that had helped her bag a lot of exclusive stories. Its flip-up lid doubled as a digital video camera with a high-powered parabolic microphone capable of recording conversations from 100 feet away—just about the distance between her and the three men surrounding Katherine Haywood outside WARP's front door.

"Kaaaa-ther-innnne . . . you got some 'splainin' to do," Zoe whispered, taking cover behind what looked like a miniature palm tree. She zoomed in on the group, framing them on her little computer screen, then fished out a wireless earphone from her pocket. She popped the earphone in place, established an audio signal, and hit Record.

"Frank Sinatra?! You think this is a god-damned joke? Do you realize what you've done? The damage? The panic you've created? *Who* are you working for? Is Sinatra some kind of code name?"

Zoe didn't need to look at the screen to identify the angry voice vibrating in her ear. It belonged to Conrad Dinnick, gazillionaire genius, two-time Nobel Prize winner, presidential adviser, and at the moment, a super-pissed-off radio-station owner.

"Code name? Who do I look like, James Bond? I've told you everything I know! Please listen. This is *so important*. I think New York is going to be attacked *today!* Stop wasting time—we've got to talk to the police."

"Don't worry, lady, you'll be talking to the police. But not until I know who you're working for. So who is it? A pharmaceutical company? Al Qaeda?"

"*Al Qaeda?* What are you talking about? I'm an American citizen—and a *Democrat*. I'm not a terrorist!"

"Who then? The Syrians? Hamas? *Tell me!*"

"I'm a psychic, for God's sake. The only people I've been talking to are dead. Energies. *Spirits.*"

"So spirits told you New York was going to be attacked?" Conrad sneered at her.

"Yes, in their way, that's exactly what they did."

"And what's Frank Sinatra—chairman of the spirit board?"

"No . . . he's not related to the bombs. It's something else . . . and it's not *about* him, it's something to do with where he's *from*. . . ."

"Vegas?"

"No! Sinatra was from across the river in Hoboken. And it has to do with driving to Sinatra, or Sinatra Drive . . . I don't quite know yet. Look, we don't have much time."

"Sinatra Drive in Hoboken?" Conrad grabbed Katherine by the shoulders. "What about Sinatra Drive in Hoboken? *What are you saying?* There are bombs planted in Hoboken?"

"Stop it, you're hurting me," she tried to shake Conrad's grip. "I'm still trying to understand it myself. Julia loved Sinatra, so she used him as a reference. And maybe something about Abe Lincoln, too."

"What? Lincoln? Who's Julia? What does she know about Hoboken?" Conrad's fingers were digging into Katherine's flesh.

"Let go of me *now!*" Katherine said, pushing Conrad away. "*Just listen to me.* Julia's not in Hoboken. She's dead. She's a good friend of mine, and she's doing her best to help me, to help us all. I think she was trying to tell me that people might get sick there—*really* sick."

"Okay, this all makes sense now. A dead woman told you that people will get sick in Hoboken, right?"

"Not just with words. She *showed* me. It's one of the ways I get messages. And yes, she *said* that unless I get to Hoboken, everyone would get sick.

Now, please, *please*, I'm begging you. Someone get the police right away!"

Katherine was becoming frantic. Her voice was so piercing that Zoe had to turn down the volume on her palmtop.

"Mr. Dinnick, sir, you have to get on the tram. Let me take this lady somewhere less public, somewhere I can do a thorough interrogation," said the man standing to Conrad's right.

Zoe zoomed in on the blond man with the crew cut and sleek suit. He was in head-to-toe Armani, but she could tell from his ramrod posture and severe manner that he was military through and through.

"Give me two minutes alone with her, and I'll be able to establish if she's working with someone or just a lunatic. Please sir, leave this to me," the blond man said. "You've got to get on that tram before it leaves for the island—and you better hurry. The front desk reports that there's a small group gathering outside to protest the radio show. I'll have one of my men escort you."

"That's very thoughtful, Wilson," Conrad said sarcastically. "But if you were more concerned with security and less concerned about my social calendar, I'd already be on the tram. Isn't that right, John?"

John Wilson? Zoe wondered. *General John Wilson . . . right! Former Special Forces guy in charge of finding chemical weapons in Iraq. Founder of the New Homeland Militia. He had so much power that the Army refused to fire him even after he publicly accused the White House of being weak-kneed and the Pentagon of going soft on terror. He wanted to nuke half the Middle East to get rid of terrorists. Oh yeah . . . now I really remember this winner. They called him the "Eye-for-an-Eye GI" because of all the Old-Testament "vengeance-is-mine" type quotes he spouted on CNN during the Iraq War. He's a certifiable Dr. Strangelove. But I thought he was still in the Army. Why's he doing BioWorld security?*

"Look, sir, for your own safety, I suggest you leave for the tram now. I'll deal with our friend here," Wilson said.

"Do it, D-D-Dad . . . get on the tr-tram . . . now. Before it leaves."

Zoe adjusted the zoom again, bringing the face of the third man in the group into focus. *Well, well, if it isn't the sole heir to the BioWorld billions.* Zoe had never met Daniel Dinnick, but she'd researched him inside and out for a profile she almost wrote on the Dinnick twins.

Would have been a great story, too, if only brother Michael hadn't stuck a gun in his mouth and blown his head off, Zoe recalled, wryly remembering how her five-page feature became a half-page obituary after Michael committed suicide.

"Haven't either of you two been *listening?*" Conrad shouted at Daniel and Wilson. "This woman obviously knows about our Biosafety Level 4 lab in Hoboken. She even knows it's on Frank Sinatra Drive. And whoever she's working for also knows. So stop worrying about the stupid tram and start worrying about a nightmare scenario. I've got to get Washington on the phone. . . ."

Holy Mary . . . a Level 4 lab in Hoboken? Zoe was astounded. *If that's true, Conrad must be working with the Pentagon. How else could he be running*

one of the few high-security labs licensed to handle the
world's deadliest viruses, from Ebola to the plague?
There are only a few of those labs in the entire coun-
try—the nearest one off the coast of Long Island.
But was there really one just across the river from
Manhattan? Without anyone even knowing about it?
Unbelievable!

"Sir, again, let me do my job. This woman is
a celebrity. She's like an actress. It's unlikely that
she has any terrorist links, but I assure you, if she
does, I'll find out and call Washington personally.
This ceremony is so important for you, for everyone. Don't let her keep you from it—get on the
tram," Wilson said to Conrad, his tone sounding
almost like he was issuing an order.

"Yes, call Washington . . . call the President,"
Katherine pleaded. "I don't know anything about
your Level 4 or 5 or whatever it is. But I do know
that people are going to die unless we do something right now. I can't let this happen again, so
I'm leaving. I'll find the police myself, and then
I'm going to Hoboken. Abe Lincoln must mean to
take the Lincoln Tunnel. See ya."

Katherine turned away, but Conrad caught her
arm and spun her around. "You're not going anywhere near Hoboken. You've caused enough—"

Katherine grabbed Conrad's wrist and tried
to break his grip. "That's the second time you've
laid your hands on me, Mr. Dinnick. Who do you
think you are? If you don't—" Katherine froze in
mid-sentence. Her psychic senses were still wide-
open from the radio show, and she connected with
Conrad's energies as soon as she touched him.

"Wait," she said. "Stop. I'm getting someone here . . . I think it's for you." Katherine looked at Conrad. She was trying to focus on an image that was flashing in her mind of a woman. "It's a grandmother or mother energy. Definitely a mother. . . ."

Katherine's grip on Conrad tightened, and she began speaking rapidly. "Is her name Lily? She's showing me a flower. No, not a Lily . . . she's showing me a . . . is her name Rose? But I don't think that's her name . . . no, it's a blue rose. Did you and your mother grow blue roses?"

"Stop it! Just stop it!" Conrad yelled, trying to break the psychic's hold on his wrist. "You can learn everything about me and my family in a two-minute Internet search, so don't try your tricks on *me*. I'm a scientist, and at the very least, you're a charlatan and a cheat—and quite possibly an accessory to terrorism."

Katherine ignored him, speaking quickly and with increasing urgency.

"There's a son on the Other Side, your mother is bringing him through . . . they're together, and she says she met him when he crossed. Oh . . . it was violent . . . a very violent passing. Trauma to the head. It was sudden . . . like a gunshot . . . he was a Gemini? There's a strong twin energy . . . and a name . . . D-N with a long 'e' sound like Denny or Donny or maybe Danny. I'm seeing flashing red lights again. It's a warning . . . another name . . . Mac or Mick . . . no, it's Michael . . . and he's very ill. . . ."

Zoe heard the smack before she realized she'd seen it on the screen. The sound echoed across the atrium like a gunshot, so sudden and unexpected that it felt like she'd been slapped herself.

On the monitor, she saw a crimson imprint of five fingers surface on Katherine's right cheek. Blood dripped from her lip, staining her white silk blouse just above her heart.

Conrad's arm shot into the air, catching the back of his son's hand as it came swinging toward the psychic a second time.

"What are you doing, Daniel?! What's gotten into you?" Conrad asked in astonishment, his voice painfully loud in Zoe's ear. But she understood his bewilderment—the Daniel Dinnick she'd read about was a timid man, spooked by his own shadow—not the kind of guy who'd smack a woman across the face and then go at her again.

"She sh-sh-shouldn't talk about Mi-Mi-Michael like that!" Daniel gasped.

Conrad shook his head and turned to Katherine. "I apologize, Ms. Haywood. My son's behavior is inexcusable . . . but certainly understandable. I've never seen Danny raise his voice, let alone his hand to another person. But you use his radio station to spread fear and panic, and then you have the audacity to pretend to talk to his dead brother, whom he deeply loved—and his grandmother—it's too much. You've gone too far, way too far."

Katherine looked stunned. She pointed at Daniel.

"*This* is Danny?" she asked.

Conrad nodded to Wilson. Zoe heard a metallic clack and zoomed out to see that Wilson had stepped behind Katherine and handcuffed her wrists behind her back.

"Now you'll get what you want—a good, long visit with the police," Conrad said to Katherine. He turned to Wilson and Daniel as he began walking toward the security desk. "Gentlemen, let's take Ms. Haywood outside and hand her over to the authorities. I have a tram to catch."

CHAPTER 12

FRANK JUMPED FROM THE TRUCK and was running toward the mosque's courtyard when he collided with a man blocking the sidewalk.

"Whoa . . . slow down there, buddy. Where's the fire?" said the man, planting his hand firmly on Frank's chest and pushing him back several feet. The man looked to be in his early 40s and was of medium height with a wiry build, but Frank could tell from the pressure on his chest that the guy was solid muscle.

The man took one step back and placed both hands on his hips so that his jacket rode up, exposing the badge and gun clipped to his belt.

"Hey, Frank, how ya doin'?" he asked with a twisted grin.

"We know each other?" Frank asked, still feeling the effects of the shove to his rib cage. He glanced over at Samantha through the gate and saw her kneeling down.

"Sure, Frank . . . at least, I know *you*. I feel like we're old buds . . . but I guess we've never been formally introduced. Detective Kevin Christie," he said, extending his hand. Frank ignored the gesture.

"Yeah, well—Christie, is it? What do you want? I gotta get my daughter and get outta here."

"What's the big hurry, Frank? Can't we have a pleasant little chat for a couple minutes?"

This must be the goon who was driving the Lincoln Town Car that was tailing me all morning, Frank realized.

"Look, I don't know why, but you've been following me, right? Why? Did a guard on the island tell you that I stole lawn supplies? Well, I didn't, and I don't have time for bullshit, so please get outta my way. Like I said, I've gotta get my daughter."

"Come on, Frank, play nice."

"Nice? In case you didn't hear, there's been some kind of bomb threat . . . there might be a terrorist attack today. So maybe there's something else you should be doing while I get my kid away from here?"

"What bomb threat would that be, Frank?" the detective asked, his hand casually slipping to his gun.

"I just heard it on the radio."

"Really? You hear anything 'bout a bomb threat or terrorist attack, Big Davie?"

Spinning around, Frank saw a second man standing directly behind him.

"Nope," replied the other man. "You'd think they'd let us know about these things, seeing as we're on the anti-terrorism task force and all."

Frank rarely needed to look up to make eye contact with anyone, but this guy towered a good six inches over him. The man's skin was so dark that it looked blue against his white shirt. His stance was the same as the other cop, his massive right hand resting on his sidearm with a relaxed readiness. There was a shovel in his left hand, which he twirled between his thumb and forefinger as though it was as light as a pencil.

"Found this in the back of your pickup, Frank. Quite the lethal combination you've got in there: a couple hundred pounds of fertilizer, a big ol' can of gas, some coal fuel. All the fixings for an explosive little cocktail."

"Explosive? Yeah, if you're an idiot . . . and that's a $60 shovel in case you're planning to steal it," Frank said.

"Steal it? Just looking, Frank. I've developed a sudden interest in lawn care."

"This is my partner, Detective Paul Davie," Christie said. "Call him Big Davie, okay, Frank? We're all friends now, right? So what radio station did you hear that bomb threat on, Frank?"

"I don't know. I think that idiotic show with the guy who screams like Tarzan."

"*The Jungle Hour?* Hey, that's solid journalism . . . just a sec," Christie said, pulling a cell phone from his jacket pocket.

Frank looked through the fence again at Samantha, who was touching her forehead to the prayer mat. He wished he could get her attention. He had a sick feeling in his gut, and all he wanted to do was grab her and get the hell out of

Manhattan. First he's accused of stealing fertilizer, then he hears someone screaming about a terrorist attack, and now two cops are shaking him down. He could taste the bile rising in his throat.

"You can stop panicking, Frank. Just talked to headquarters. You were right—there *was* a bomb threat on *The Jungle Hour,* but it's nothing to worry about. They've got some crazy psychic on the radio today making some spooky predictions. Just bullshit. The DJ already apologized, said it was all a bad joke . . . real funny, huh?"

"Yeah? Maybe it's a joke to you, but I don't take chances with my kid. If you guys really are on the anti-terrorist task force, you should know better than to dismiss any bomb threat. Now if you'll excuse me. . . ." Frank tried to move past Christie, who once again pushed Frank back, away from the gate entrance.

"Oh yeah? Guess you'd be an expert on bomb threats, Frankie," Christie said.

Frank stared hard at him.

"Look, if you want, I'll come to your office tomorrow to talk, but not now. My little girl's sick. I just want to get her home. I don't know what the hell you want to talk to me about anyway. I don't know anything about any terrorists."

"Well, that's not exactly a true, is it Frankie? I mean, you do know *something* about terrorists, don't you?" Christie said.

"Not good to start a new relationship with a lie, Frank," Big Davie said from behind.

"I don't know what you're talking about." Frank sidestepped to get a better view of Samantha, and to get the big detective away from his back.

"No? Come on, Frankie, let's be honest with each other," Christie said. "You look a little nervous. And I sympathize, I really do. I mean, here we are, knowing everything about you, and you don't know me or Big Davie from Adam."

"Sammy!" Frank called to his daughter through the fence, but his mouth was dry and his voice stuck in his throat.

"Don't worry, Frank, she'll be fine. So, like I said, we know you, but you don't know us. How 'bout we play a game, huh? You show us yours, and we'll show you ours. And to prove we're good guys, we'll go first. Sound like fun, Frank?"

"I'm asking you nicely. *Please* get out of my way!"

"You've got a tone there, Frank. Didn't I already say to play nice?" Christie smirked as Big Davie laid Frank's shovel against a parking meter and stepped toward him.

"That's okay. I'll still show you ours," Christie continued. "We know you were a real big shot in Iraq. A war hero even—Purple Heart and everything. A top guy in EOD—Explosive Ordnance Detail, right?

"Explosive Ordnance *Disposal*," Frank corrected. "And that's all classified information."

"Yeah, right, whatever," Christie said, taking a notepad from his pocket and flipping it open. "Let's see," he continued. "You spent four months interrogating captured Taliban and Al Qaeda bomb makers in Afghanistan, Pakistan, and Iraq. Now, I gotta say, that qualifies you as knowing terrorists."

Christie wet his fingertips with his tongue and leafed through his notes. "Then there's a two-year tour in the Gulf pulling boom-boom pins out of hundreds of old mines that the towel-heads left lying around for our boys to step on. Oh sorry, Frank . . . the term *towel-head* offend you? Big Davie, I think I offended him."

"Maybe 'cause he married a towel-head and had a towel-head baby," Big Davie said.

"Oh, that's right, Sarah Mustaffa . . . got a picture of her right here. Not bad-looking, actually. Little Iraqi freedom fighter you hooked up with over there, eh, Frank?"

"She worked for Save the Children, she was an American citizen, and I suggest you watch your dirty mouth, you racist bastard," Frank said, taking a deep breath. For the second time that morning, he tried to use Samantha's relaxation trick, but it wasn't doing much good.

"Touchy, isn't he, Davie? Here's where we get to the sad part, and I must say, I'm real sorry to hear about what happened to the missus, Frank. An M16 can make an awful mess of someone. Terrible mistake, but I guess all towel-heads look the same over there. Must be tough . . . raising a sick kid all alone? Especially on such a tight budget."

"If you have a point to make, I suggest you make it now."

"I'm almost finished with my turn, Frank. Like I was saying, you marry little Miss Mustaffa, move to Jersey, and the Army loans you to the UN as some kind of a bomb expert-at-large. Says here you can take a nuke apart and put it back together blindfolded! That right, Frank? Some cojones on this one, eh, Big Davie? To wrap it up, your wife goes to Iraq to help the war orphans, gets shot accidentally by a U.S. soldier, and you get out of the Army and take over your dad's landscaping biz. That about sum it up, Frankie?"

"Yeah, that's real good—you've got my whole life in a file and actually know how to read. Now what the hell do you want?" Frank demanded, mentally measuring the distance between him and the two detectives.

"What we want is for you to answer some questions for us. First, why does an explosives expert who's pissed off at the U.S. Army for killing his wife go to work for Conrad Dinnick, a guy with access to weapons-grade germs? Second, why do you show up at this mosque every Friday, all buddy-buddy with a cleric who has ties to Islamic extremists? And third, why the hell have you stockpiled enough fertilizer in the past year to blow up Grand Central Station? Anything I'm missing, Davie?"

"As a matter of fact, yeah. Frankie, what were you doing at Roosevelt Island today when you weren't scheduled to be there—coincidentally a couple of hours before the mayor and governor are supposed to arrive, and just before a police boat mysteriously blows up?"

"You guys can't be serious," Frank croaked. "You think *I'm* a terrorist? I've spent five years straddling bombs for this country . . . they gave me the Medal of Honor, for Chrissakes!"

"Yeah, you're a real freakin' hero. Come on, you heard what we've got on you . . . you've got to admit it doesn't look good." Big Davie shook his head.

"Looks bad, Frank, real goddamn bad," Christie said. "But I promised you'd have a turn, and this is it. So go ahead, clear the air. If you've done nothing wrong, you've got nothing to worry about. Give us something to go with."

"I got nothing to give you, man. I don't know anything about a boat blowing up. I was on the island to make sure the job was done. The only fertilizer I have is on my lawn or in the back of my truck, and I've got nothing stockpiled. And the cleric here helps out with my daughter and—," Frank realized it didn't matter what he said. These guys were looking at him like he had TERRORIST tattooed across his forehead. They'd reached their verdict: guilty.

"If you think I'm a terrorist, why are you talking to me on the street? Why not just arrest me, label me an enemy combatant, lock me up, and throw away the key?"

"Oh jeez, Frankie, didn't I mention that?" asked Christie, his sardonic smile spreading across his face. "You *are* under arrest . . . we're just waiting for Social Services to get here and take away your kid."

Frank's heart pounded against his chest, and he could feel the oxygen squeezing out of his lungs, the way it had the first time he'd been in combat. He gulped for air.

"Social services . . . my daughter . . . please . . . she's sick, very, very sick . . . she can't be away from me . . . it will kill her . . . please . . ."

"You have the right to remain silent," Big Davie recited, reaching behind his back and producing a set of handcuffs. "Anything you say can, and will, be used against—"

As Big Davie grabbed his wrists, Frank dropped into a squatting position and then thrust upward with all his strength. The top of Frank's skull caught Big Davie under the jaw, and he heard the bones crack. Frank jabbed his left elbow into the detective's solar plexus, and the big man dropped to the cement.

Detective Christie was pulling his gun from his holster when Frank grabbed the shovel from against the meter and swung it in a sweeping arc. Its steel blade smashed against the side of Christie's head, knocking him face-first onto the sidewalk.

"Oh shit, oh shit, oh shit!" Frank cried out, dropping to his knees and collecting the guns and badges from the unconscious detectives.

"Daddy?"

Frank looked up into his daughter's pale, frightened face.

"Sammy, *get into the truck now!* Oh, honey, it's going to be okay. These are bad men . . . they were going to take you away from me."

A handful of women who had been praying were looking through the gate, pointing at Frank. He scooped up Samantha in his arms and stumbled to the truck.

"Why would they take me away? Why did you hurt them?"

Frank started the engine and pulled into traffic, trying to think straight . . . and trying to map out the fastest route to the Lincoln Tunnel.

He looked at his daughter, who was holding her prayer mat to her chest and staring at him, horrified.

"Don't look at me like that, Sammy. I'm not a monster. I'm not sure what just happened myself, but it's got something to do with me being in the Army and your mom being Iraqi . . . it's all so mixed up, I just can't explain it right now. Please believe me, I did what had to be done. And I promise, promise, promise that I'll make it right. Okay?"

Samantha began to weep.

CHAPTER 13

ZOE DUCKED BEHIND A HELIX-SHAPED FOUNTAIN as the handcuffed psychic and her three grim-faced companions crossed the atrium toward her. She snapped her palmtop shut and pulled out her earphone, dropping both into her bag. Crouching on the floor, she waited for the group to pass and plotted her next move.

She'd definitely recorded enough material for a blockbuster news item and could envision the headline: PSYCHIC TERRORIST? RADIO READING PANICS CITY!

She also had a national scoop and potential Pulitzer Prize for reporting on BioWorld's secret Level 4 research lab in Hoboken.

She smiled, but then she had a realization: *This should be a slam dunk, but what do I tell the boss? Um . . . just FYI, I committed a felony by impersonating a government official. And, oh yeah, you know all those quotes? Obtained illegally while recording a private conversation.*

Zoe knew the editor would have two choice words for her: *You're fired*. Then he'd send another reporter out to scoop her on her own story.

No way will I let that happen. . . . Right now I gotta get a quick interview with Katherine to back it all up. I need her on the record. I'll research Hoboken later. I gotta follow them outside and get to her before they cart her off to police headquarters—or the loony bin.

Zoe peered around the fountain as Katherine walked past, looking as though she was being marched to the gallows. Zoe checked her watch to give the group a two-minute head start before tailing them to the front door. As she waited, Zoe saw something she'd never seen before: a perfect blue rose, the deep color of a sapphire. There were dozens of them, each one more beautiful than the next. She waited another minute, and then began moving through the foliage, jumping across a small stream and sliding across some mossy stones before emerging from the atrium forest and nearly running headlong into Conrad Dinnick. She took a few steps back and sat down on a small bench.

Conrad and the others had stopped in the front lobby. Katherine was staring at Daniel, but the three men were looking up at an enormous monitor suspended above the security desk. They were watching a live broadcast from the Roosevelt Island tram wheelhouse. The camera panned across the platform packed with city dignitaries and local celebrities, all jostling each other to be photographed with the mayor and governor.

A fidgety young reporter, identified at the bottom of the screen as a science specialist for

New York First News, stared out mutely from the screen. Off camera, someone was loudly whispering, "You're up, you're up!" The reporter cleared his throat and launched into a nasal-voiced commentary:

"Good morning. We're coming to you live from the Roosevelt Island Tram as it launches into the future on what could ironically be a historic journey. In a minute or two, our camera crew will board the tram with the mayor, the governor, and the many distinguished guests you see behind me. We will then travel over the East River, reaching a height of 250 feet, before descending to the island to be on hand when BioWorld founder Conrad Dinnick officially opens his multibillion-dollar Supercomputer Re-Creation Center. Whoa . . . try saying that ten times fast!

"No, just joshing you, folks. What a treat it is to be here. This new Center is the most expensive single structure ever built in New York, and is home to the most advanced computer system in the world—reportedly capable of sequencing genes hundreds of times faster than any other computer now in existence. Its potential for advancing genetic research is, well, mind-boggling.

"And I can't neglect to mention that the center will create hundreds of high-tech and biotech jobs right here in the heart of Manhattan—a big boost in these troubled times.

"So don't touch your remote, because right after the ribbon-cutting ceremony, Mr. Dinnick will be making a major announcement. No one knows the details, but we're told it has something to do with a process called 'genetic regeneration.' I can promise you that it will be big news. The last time Conrad Dinnick held a

news conference, he announced that he'd isolated and 'turned off' the celleptic cancer gene . . . you'll recall he received his first Nobel Prize for that one. So stay tuned to New York First News, folks. Our exclusive coverage of this historic . . ."

A Dixieland band pushed through the crowd playing a peppy rendition of "When the Saints Go Marching In." The music drowned out the reporter, who, after trying to shout above the racket, shrugged and held his microphone toward a rail-thin banjo player who was singing:

> We are trav'ling in the footsteps
> Of those who've gone before
> But we'll all be reunited,
> On a new and sunlit shore,
>
> Oh, when the saints go marching in,
> When the saints go marching in . . .

"Well, there they go. I missed my ride," sighed Conrad, watching the mayor and governor wave from the TV screen and step onto the tram. Everyone else on the platform—the band, reporter, camera crew, and several police officers—climbed on board with them. The doors slid shut, and the tram jerked from the platform, crossing over Second Avenue. The reporter, who was inside the tram squeezing himself between the governor and mayor, went back on camera.

"Fasten your seat belts, folks. We're heading into the future, and it's going to be one heck of a ride," he said, as the tram climbed toward the top of the Queensboro Bridge.

Conrad turned away from the screen. "We'll take Ms. Haywood outside and let the police deal with her, and I'll take the company boat across to the island. Let's go," he commanded, motioning to Wilson and Daniel to follow.

"Daniel and I will monitor things here, sir, but first we'll escort you to the dock," Wilson said. "I'll have a boat pilot standing by, and you'll arrive on the island at the same time as the tram."

"Good."

As they passed the security desk, the guard who'd questioned Zoe earlier yelled after them, "Mr. Dinnick, Mr. Wilson, please use the side exit. We have—"

Conrad silenced the guard with a dismissive wave. "What we *don't* have is any more time to waste," he asserted, striding across the front lobby and out the revolving door.

On the street below, dozens of demonstrators were shoving against a line of police in riot gear. The crowd became frenzied when Katherine appeared above them, standing at the top of the Tower's marble staircase.

A wave of angry shouts rolled up the stairs as someone threw a bottle that shattered at Conrad's feet. Zoe stepped outside and was hit by a flying brick. It only grazed her cheek, but it sent a flood of adrenaline coursing through her body.

"We've got to get you out of here *now!*" Wilson shouted, releasing his hold on Katherine and grabbing Conrad by the arm. "Move back into the building. You can take the chopper across the river."

"Yes, the ch-ch-chopper . . . Dad, let's go back inside," Daniel said worriedly, taking Conrad's other arm.

"Do you see what you've done? *Do you see?!*" Conrad yelled at Katherine, as Wilson and Daniel pulled him backward toward the revolving door.

Katherine didn't hear him. She stood frozen, staring at the sky in wild-eyed panic as the bright red Roosevelt Island tram glided above them and out over the East River.

Zoe ran toward Katherine, hoping to talk to her before the protesters reached them. She reached into her bag for her recorder.

"That's it!" Katherine screamed, looking at the tram. "That's it . . . *that's it* . . . that's the ski lift I saw . . . we have to stop it . . . it's going to . . . someone stop it before it . . . it's going to—"

A man halfway down the stairs, wearing a leather jacket and a Captain America helmet, was glaring at Katherine. "Hey, psychic! I see someone already cuffed you. I guess I'm too late to make you my last collar!" he yelled. "How dare you talk about my son . . . they handed out those medals for bravery and sacrifice—not for phony psychics to exploit!" He opened his jacket and began pulling something out of his pants pocket.

But all Zoe saw was the butt of a gun sticking out of the man's leather coat, and his hand moving toward it. Instead of her recorder, Zoe pulled the latest-model stun gun from her reporter's knapsack, jerked her arm up, and squeezed the trigger. Two darts hit the man's chest, pierced his skin, and pumped enough electricity into him to completely disrupt his nervous system. His gun fell out of his jacket and clattered down the steps. He collapsed, convulsing violently until Zoe released the trigger. She looked at him, then back at Katherine, making eye contact with the psychic for the first time.

"I'm too late. . . ." Katherine said, looking up at the tram.

Zoe opened her mouth to ask her what she meant, but didn't get the chance. The blast hit her like a sledgehammer, lifting her off her feet and slamming her against the Tower wall. She dropped to the ground and rolled onto her side, with the wind knocked out of her and her stomach muscles contracting violently as she tried to breathe. She was beginning to black out when the air finally filled her lungs in a hot, acrid rush. She gagged, coughing until she thought her ribs would crack. Her eyes burned with ash and smoke, and she rubbed them hard until she could see.

Everyone who'd been near her—the police, the demonstrators, Conrad and his son, Wilson, and Katherine—had been knocked down. Zoe looked toward the river. The center tower of the Queensboro Bridge was listing to the northeast like the topmast of a sinking ship. A great, yawning groan of stretching steel filled her ears, ending with an abrupt snap. She stared in disbelief as hundreds of people leapt from their cars onto the swaying bridge and ran for their lives.

The bridge seemed to moan in pain for several minutes before its upper roadway collapsed onto the lower level, crushing hundreds of cars. The whole structure shuddered, and a long section dropped into the East River, creating huge waves. Several abandoned cars teetered on the edges of the severed bridge before slipping over and dropping into the water below. Dozens of vehicles bobbed downstream, spinning around in the current once or twice before sinking beneath the surface. Except for the terrified neighing of a few police horses, there was a moment of stunned silence.

Then the screaming began.

The bridge's wounded tower screeched as it twisted around, snagging and breaking the steel cable supporting the tram. The wire whistled as it snaked though the air, and the tram plunged toward the water more than a hundred feet below, disappearing in the thick cloud of smoke now blowing across the river.

Zoe looked over at Conrad, who'd gotten to his feet just in time to see the bridge's pillar break away from its moorings and slice his Re-Creation Center like the blade of a giant guillotine. A series of explosions ripped through the length of the building, culminating in an enormous blast that sent entire sections of steel wall sailing off both sides of the island. A fireball shot up, leaving a thick, dark cloud hanging in the air.

Conrad stared at the crumbled, fiery ruins of the Re-Creation Center. Burning ash landed on his sleeve, and he ripped off the smoldering jacket, tossing it to the ground. From the top of the BioWorld Tower steps, he had a panoramic view of the devastation. Fire was everywhere.

"Oh my God, oh my God. My Center . . . and all those people," he moaned, dropping to his knees and burying his face in his hands.

Some of Conrad's security detail rushed to his side.

"Grab that psychic!" Conrad ordered. "Find out what's going on. How did she know? Find out if this attack was directed at me."

Then he suddenly looked up, turned westward, and gasped.

"We have to stop them," said Conrad, jumping to his feet. "Whoever did this—if they get to the lab in New Jersey, they could kill us all. We have to get to Hoboken!"

CHAPTER 14

THE DODGE JERKED FORWARD, and Frank thought he'd been rear-ended until he heard the explosion—a boom so powerful that it shook the buildings along Lexington Avenue.

"Daddy?" Samantha asked, clutching his arm. "What is it? Did a plane crash?"

"Jesus."

"Daddy . . . is it a plane crash?"

"No, no honey, it's not a plane. It sounded like a bomb, a big one. But it's a long way from here, so don't worry," Frank said, flooring the gas pedal and screeching down the street.

He sped through traffic like the truck had a force field he was sure other vehicles couldn't penetrate, cutting off two taxis and a dump truck to get into the buses-only lane.

It was a risky move. Driving in the restricted lane increased his chances of being pulled over, but he had no choice. He had to get to the tunnel before the cops he'd knocked out at the mosque came to and reported him.

If they ever come to, Frank thought. *I hit them both so hard that I probably killed them . . . but don't think about that. Focus, Frank, focus.* He pounded his fist against the steering wheel when the bus he was following stopped to pick up a long line of passengers.

Frank looked over at Samantha. Her eyes were closed, and sweat dripped from her forehead. Her face was ashen and her lips were trembling. He brushed his fingers across her arm, felt the coldness of her skin, and panicked.

"Sammy? Sammy?" He shook her roughly. "Wake up honey! Please wake up!"

"I *am* awake, Franklin."

"How you feelin'?"

"About you beating up two policemen? Not good."

"Well, no, not that. I mean, how are you *feeling* feeling? You're sweating, but you're cold. Your lips were trembling."

"I feel a little sick, but I think it's because of your driving. I'll be okay when we're home."

"We'll be home soon."

"And my lips weren't trembling; I was praying."

"Jesus, honey, you just finished praying at the mosque."

"Yeah, well, that was before you hit those guys. That'll take *lots* of praying to square with You-Know-Who."

"Sammy, you know I don't believe in hurting people."

"You've got a funny way of showing it."

Frank pressed down on the truck's horn and held it for a good 30 seconds. *Move it, move it, move it.* The bus driver stuck a hand out his window and pointed his middle finger upward at Frank.

"Damn it, Sammy! Those guys were assholes. I mean *really bad* guys! They would've taken you away and stuck you in a foster home. Just because they've got badges, Sam, doesn't mean . . . look, they're exactly like the ignorant jarheads who killed your mom for being a Muslim and—"

"I heard what they said. I know what they think. I know you're scared for me. But you shouldn't have hit them."

"Sammy, you've *memorized* the friggin' Bible, right? What about 'an eye for an eye'?"

Samantha sighed. "Exodus 21:23 . . . *life for life, eye for eye, tooth for tooth* . . . that sort of thing?"

Frank nodded, "Yeah, exactly. See?"

"No one poked out your eye, Frank. And Jesus revised Exodus in Matthew 5:39: ' . . . *whosoever shall smite thee on thy right cheek, turn to him the other also.*' You didn't do much cheek turning back there, did you, Frank?"

Frank checked the rearview mirror. Traffic was bumper-to-bumper as far as he could see, but there was a flashing red light about 20 blocks back, moving slowly through the gridlock toward them.

"Okay, okay. Sammy. Let's skip the Bible lesson. I hit them, and I shouldn't have. I hope they're okay. Is that why you're praying, so they'll get better?"

"No, I was praying we get the hell out of here before you get arrested. So *please*, Frank, if we're heading for the Lincoln Tunnel, get off Lex, cut through Central Park, and then head south."

"Okay, Sam, jeeze," Frank laughed. "Better make up your mind what you're going to be when you grow up: a preacher, a shrink, or a taxi driver because you—," Frank stopped in mid-sentence and bit his tongue.

"It's okay," Samantha said quietly. "You can say, 'When you grow up.' I'm going to, you know, and I'm going to be all those things. . . . I just have to wait until my next life, that's all."

Frank turned right on to 72nd Street, reaching out to touch Samantha again. She was a little warmer. Sometimes that's how it was for her after chemo: shivering one minute, warm the next.

I've got to get her somewhere safe, get her to bed, he fretted.

They stopped for a red light at Madison Avenue, and he checked the rearview mirror again. No sign of the cops. Leaning over, he kissed his daughter's cheek.

"Listen, kid, I've screwed things up royally, and I've got to make them right. So, instead of going home, I'm taking you to your Aunt Lucy's in Connecticut for a couple days, and she'll drive you up to your Aunt Lorna's in Toronto, okay?"

"What? Go to *Canada?* Why can't we just go home?"

"Because the police know where we live, and they'll find us at Lucy's soon enough. If you stay here, they'll try to put you in a foster home, and that's not going to happen."

"But, Daddy—"

"It's going to be okay. I'll come up to visit you

next weekend. I just have to straighten things out with the police, and then we'll be together."

"Swear, Daddy, swear you're telling the truth."

"I swear it."

"Swear on Mommy's grave."

"Sam . . . I—"

They heard another explosion, much smaller than the first.

They both turned, looking through the rear window at the giant plume of smoke rising up behind them, somewhere near the East River.

"Daddy?" Samantha clutched his arm. "What's happening? Is it another bomb?!"

"No, Sammy, don't worry about bombs. Someone's probably just setting off some fireworks."

"But you said it was a bomb, Daddy!"

"Forget what I said."

Frank floored it, screeching across Madison Avenue toward Central Park.

CHAPTER 15

JACK OPENED HIS EYES. His ears buzzed, and his mouth tasted of burnt toast. He tried to move, but couldn't, so he lay still, staring into the fading sunlight.

He didn't have a clue where he was, but recognized the nasty lump of remorse churning in the pit of his stomach. It was the same sickening feeling he used to get every Monday morning after waking from a bender. No memory of the weekend, just a gnawing sense that he'd done something ugly and would pay for it later.

I haven't touched a drink in years . . . right? He tried to remember, realizing that he didn't know where or *when* he was. He closed his eyes. Fragments of memory began banging against each other: Susan's face, a carriage ride, a gunshot, his motorcycle, a bridge, a gun, that voice . . . the same voice that was calling to him now.

"It's not your time just yet—hang on, you'll be okay."

Jack opened his eyes. Someone, a woman he thought, was hovering over him, her face hidden in shadow, as a dark cloud began to swallow the sun.

"Susan?" he whispered.

"No, but Susan's here with us," she said softly.

Jack recognized the voice but couldn't place it.

"Your name's Jack, right? Yes, Jack. We don't have much time, so listen closely. Susan has a message for you that I'm trying to understand . . . something happened, something horrible. Whatever it was, she needs you to know that it wasn't your fault. She passed so you'd be here today. You have to finish something. I don't know what this is, but she's saying, 'Follow the story.' Now she's . . . I'm sure of it . . . she's showing me a baby, in the arms of St. Thomas. To me that means that she wants you to forgive yourself for something and start living again. And Jack, she also says, 'Tomorrow will be a better day.' Do you understand this? 'Tomorrow will be a better day.' Do you under—"

The woman's face vanished, and her last sentence was drowned out by a commanding male voice shouting, "On your feet, psychic, you're coming with us!"

Psychic? Jack thought, the events of the day breaking through his delirium. *Oh God, what did I do? Why didn't I just kill myself . . . I must be—*

"Crazy Jack Morgan! It is you, isn't it? I knew I recognized that helmet. What in the hell are *you* doing here?"

Another female face was looking down at him. But the sun was now completely engulfed by clouds, so he could easily make out her features. *She's beautiful,* Jack realized, staring into her eyes—the soft green color of old Coke bottles.

"Who are you? Where am I?"

"My name is Zoe Crane. You'd better relax for a minute. I zapped you with my stun gun when you went for your pistol. You should be fine in a couple minutes, but if you mess with me, I'll stun you again."

"I can hardly breathe, lady. I'm not going to be messing with anybody."

Zoe looked at him warily, then cradled his head in the crook of her arm and held a bottle of water she'd fished out from her knapsack to his lips. As Jack gulped down the water, Zoe looked at the handsome face encased in the ridiculous helmet—the same one he'd worn in the photo accompanying a story she'd read about him in *The Trumpet* archives. *Poor guy sees his wife get whacked right in front of him . . . but why the hell does he go postal a decade later? And why today of all days? There must be a scoop here somewhere.*

She took the bottle away from his lips and gently wiped the soot and ash from his eyelids.

"Feel better?" she asked.

"All pins and needles."

"Good, the shock's wearing off. Let's get you up."

She slipped her arm around his shoulders and pulled him until he was sitting up, facing the river.

The breeze off the water burned Jack's face. He rubbed his eyes, and then he rubbed them again. He stared at the dozens of people at the bottom of the steps: Some were coughing, others were calling for help, and many more were being tended to by police officers.

He looked up at the Queensboro Bridge, shrouded in smoke billowing from a huge fire in the center of Roosevelt Island. As the smoke cleared for a second, Jack saw the gaping hole in the bridge's crippled frame. Struggling to catch his breath, he gasped, "Holy Mary Mother of God, what's happened? What the hell has happened?"

"I don't know," Zoe replied. "I guess it was an explosion."

"Again. They did it again, didn't they? Another attack? Those goddamned, murderous bastards!" Jack shouted, then turned to Zoe. "How many . . . how many did they kill this time?"

"I don't know. I saw people running off the bridge and people running on the island . . . I just don't know. But what the hell do you care? You showed up here with a gun trying to kill people yourself!"

"What are you talking about? I didn't try to kill anyone."

"You were pulling a gun out of your jacket. You were going to shoot the psychic, Jack. I saw you, and I heard you. I *stopped* you, for Christ's sake!"

"I wasn't going to shoot her. I was just going to show her something that belonged to my boy and tell her to stop exploiting people's sorrow. I wasn't going to kill *her*. Not that it's any of your business, but I was going to kill *myself* today. I'd already be dead if I hadn't heard that psychic on the radio."

"That's pure bullshit. Going to kill *yourself?* Yeah, like I'm going to buy that line, especially from Crazy Jack Morgan."

"Look for yourself. There's only one round in the cylinder, and that bullet has my name on it. I just wanted to scare her. I would never shoot an unarmed woman."

"What, are you a chauvinist, too?"

Jack grabbed Zoe by the arm, pulling her toward him until their eyes were just inches apart.

"Who *are* you?" he demanded.

"I told you—Zoe Crane. I'm a reporter." She hesitated. "For *The Trumpet.*"

"*The Trumpet?* Oh, that's just perfect!" He turned his back to her and stared at the growing fire across the river. "Got yourself a nice little story, don't you?"

Zoe picked up Jack's gun and opened the cylinder. *Like he said, just one round in here.* She shook the bullet into her palm. *Jesus, he literally meant that it had his name on it.* She read the words etched on the casing of the bullet: *Jack Morgan: Guilty of uxoricide.* Zoe had read enough autopsy reports to know that *uxoricide* meant murdering your wife.

Zoe slipped the bullet back, closed the cylinder, and handed the gun back to Jack.

"It's your gun, and it's your life, so do what you want with them. You said the psychic was a liar. Maybe . . . that's pretty much what I've always thought, too. But that woman predicted that this would happen today, and she predicted there'd be more explosions. I don't know what Katherine Haywood ever did to you, or why you want to kill yourself, but take a look out there," she said, pointing to the ruined bridge and wounded people. "If anything like *that* is going to happen again today, I need to find out where and when. So I need you to tell me what she said to you," Zoe said.

"What do you mean, what she said to me?"

"When you were lying here. She was leaning over you, talking to you. What did she say?"

"That was *her?* I thought I was hallucinating."

"You weren't. Did she say where the other bombs might be?"

"What? No, she . . . she said . . ."

Suddenly Jack remembered: *She said that tomorrow would be a better day . . . the same thing Susan said to me every morning. How could she have known?* Jack wondered, incredulous.

"Well? Are you going to tell me?" Zoe insisted.

"I can't remember," Jack said, thinking he really must have been hallucinating.

"No comment, huh? Well, I'm a reporter, and right now she's the only story in the world, so I'm following her."

"What?" Jack said.

"Katherine seemed to know exactly what was about to happen. She knew about the explosions and the tram, so I'm going to follow the story. Maybe I can write something that matters for a change."

"Wait! She said that to me. She said, 'Follow the story.'"

Jack and Zoe stared at each other. There were wailing sirens coming from the street and helicopters swarming overhead.

"Tell me something. Are you still a cop?"

"Technically, yeah, until the end of the day."

"Really? You've got a shield?"

"Yeah."

"Good. I think Katherine is going to Hoboken; I overheard her saying it. But by now the tunnels will be closed to civilians because of what's happened here. Will you help me get across the river?"

Jack looked at the burning island and collapsed bridge. "Yeah, I'll help you," he said at last, "and I'll make her my last arrest. But I don't know if I can get to my bike—it's hard for me to move. "

Zoe lifted Jack's arm across her shoulder and hoisted him up. She helped him down the stairs, through the mounting frenzy on the street, to the curb where his battered Harley lay in the gutter.

"I don't have the strength to lift it," Jack told her.

"Don't worry—six years of sparring might finally pay off," Zoe replied, grabbing a long handlebar and the frame just beneath the seat, then pulling the bike upright.

Jack eased onto the seat, kick-started the bike with relatively little effort, and took off his helmet and passed it to Zoe. As she climbed on the seat behind him, he said, "Wear the helmet and tell me which way to go."

"The tunnel. Take the Lincoln Tunnel."

CHAPTER 16

CONRAD STOOD ON THE EASTERN EDGE of the BioWorld Tower roof, staring down at the fire raging on Roosevelt Island. A menacing cloud was forming over the island, and the orange and blue flames shimmered savagely in the spreading darkness.

The blades of the BioWorld helicopter were slicing the air in a high-pitched whine when Wilson approached Conrad. "The bird's ready to fly, sir. Time to board."

Conrad walked toward the helicopter. Wilson held Katherine's cuffed wrists; Daniel crouched by the cockpit door talking to the pilot; and a half-dozen guards stood around the chopper, rifles at the ready.

Katherine leaned over, pressing her mouth against Conrad's ear so he'd hear her over the spinning blades.

"Don't get in that helicopter—it's dangerous. I need to talk to you alone, *now*," she said.

Wilson immediately yanked Katherine from Conrad and dragged her to the helicopter as she screamed, "No, no, no! Dear God, don't put me in there. I'm not getting into that death trap! Let go of me! *Get your stinking paws off me!*"

She twisted around and kneed Wilson in the groin. He doubled over, and she made a run for it, straight into an armed guard standing at the roof's only door.

I'm 120 stories up—where in heaven's name am I going to go? she thought desperately, spinning to make a last-minute appeal to Conrad.

"Please . . . this helicopter . . . it's not safe!"

Wilson had recovered and was heading straight for her.

"Conrad, believe me, this man is not acting in your best interests . . . or mine. He's dangerous."

Wilson grabbed her, slapped his hand over his mouth, dragged her to the helicopter, and threw her in. A guard was already sitting in the passenger cabin, and Wilson told him: "Keep her quiet. Do you understand what your other orders are?"

"Yes, sir," the guard said, looking across the roof at Conrad.

"Wilson, that Haywood woman is in hysterics," Conrad said with concern. "Are you sure this helicopter's safe?"

"Absolutely, sir."

"Even with the solar storm?"

"No problem, sir," Wilson assured his boss, starting to climb into the passenger cabin.

Conrad caught him by the sleeve.

"Wait, Wilson. I don't want you to come with us," Conrad said.

"Excuse me, sir? The city and BioWorld may be under attack. I'm not leaving your side. Besides, Hoboken is a prime target."

"Don't you think I know that? I need you to contact Washington and the New York National Guard. We need to at least *triple* our security presence at all our facilities—especially the Level 4 lab in Hoboken!" Conrad ordered.

"Of course, sir, I'm on it already—I guarantee I'll take care of it personally. As far as security is concerned, you have nothing to worry about."

"Then I don't need you in Hoboken. I need you here to protect my son, and to protect our headquarters. Guard the building at all costs—my life's work is in here. I want you to seal the Tower tight and start up our oxygen-production units. If anything goes wrong in Hoboken, the Tower is the safest place to be."

"Sir, I don't—"

"That's an order, understood?"

"Yes, sir, if you insist."

"Fine. And please take the cuffs off Miss Haywood."

"Unadvisable, sir."

"She seems ready to talk, but might not be so forthcoming if we still have her chained up."

Wilson reluctantly gave an order to a guard inside the helicopter, and he unlocked Katherine's cuffs.

"Let me out of here! Let me out of here!" she began screaming again, banging on the window.

The guard restrained Katherine, pressing his thumb and forefinger against her throat, and in a few moments, her head dropped forward.

"What have you done?" Conrad yelled.

"Relax, sir," Wilson assured him. "Our man just performed a standard Army hold used to subdue unruly prisoners. He simply stopped her oxygen supply for a few seconds to put her to sleep. She'll be awake and screaming before you get to Hoboken."

"I'm starting to wonder about your tactics, Wilson."

"Just doing my job, sir. And don't worry, your son is safe with me," Wilson said, saluting and walking over to the pilot's window to issue some final orders.

Conrad approached Daniel and wrapped his arms around him. It was the first time he remembered hugging his son since he was a child. He hated to admit it, but he knew he'd always favored Michael. And after Michael had gotten sick, then committed suicide, he took much of his anger out on his surviving son.

"Danny, I've said some terrible things to you today, and over the last . . . well, I mean, I've never really been a good father to you. This morning's ceremony was to have been dedicated in Michael's memory . . . Project PAT . . . all his work . . . and now . . . and now—"

"Don't . . . wor-wor-worry about it," Daniel said, breaking the embrace abruptly.

"I'll make it all up to you, Danny. I have so much to make up for." Conrad began climbing into the helicopter, but turned back to face his son. "I, uh . . . I love you, Danny. If anything happens to me, BioWorld is yours. Finish Project PAT."

Conrad slid the cabin door shut and sat down beside Katherine.

"You can count on it!" Daniel yelled from the roof as the helicopter lifted off.

Wilson walked over to Daniel and put his arm around his shoulders, saying, "Don't worry . . . it's all for the best."

Conrad fastened his safety belt and leaned over to clasp the belt of the still-unconscious Katherine.

"Are you're sure she's all right?" Conrad asked the guard.

"She's fine, sir."

The helicopter lifted off the roof, swung out over the East River, U-turned toward Hoboken, and began flying over Midtown.

Katherine woke with a start, looked out the window, and saw scores of flashing red lights hundreds of feet below.

"Oh God . . . how could you have let them put us in here? I told you this was dangerous. You'll get us both killed," Katherine whispered frantically to Conrad.

"Calm down, you're fine. And we'll be perfectly safe, Ms. Haywood . . . we'll land in Hoboken in five minutes. What happened to the bridge and on the island will be nothing, *nothing,* compared to what could happen if someone attacks the other lab. Now, you said you wanted to talk to me. If you do, you'd better start now. What you said on the radio this morning about the explosions . . . I want to know how you knew about them."

Katherine looked at the guard, then back at Conrad.

"Put on your headset, would you?" Conrad asked the man. As soon as the guard's ears were covered, Katherine began talking urgently.

"First of all, we're in real danger. We should never have gotten on this helicopter, and—and—there's so much coming through to me. Wait, let me focus . . . I have an older female coming through to me . . . like a mom . . . and her son or grandson . . . wait, wait . . . they want you to trust me . . . look, I may have predicted what happened at the bridge, but I had nothing to do with it. Do you believe me?"

"Believe *what?* That spirits confided in you about a bomb plot?" Conrad was incredulous. "I don't believe in spirits or an afterlife. Maybe you've been hypnotized or have some form of extrasensory perception . . . so if you sense something about Hoboken, I'm all ears and willing to listen. But don't expect me to believe in spirits. I already told you, I'm a man of science."

Katherine put her hand on Conrad's. "How do you think I knew about your mother and the blue roses?"

Conrad sighed, "Newspapers, magazines, television—take your pick."

"Then how can I know that when you were a boy your mother told you that you could play God?"

"Radio, Internet, chat groups, private detectives . . ."

"And how," Katherine squeezed his hand tightly, her voice filled with alarm, "do I know that you murdered your mother?"

Conrad didn't have time to respond. In one swoop, the guard sitting across from them lunged at Conrad, unfastened his seat belt, and slid open the passenger cabin door.

"Sorry, sir, this is where you get out."

"Are you crazy?!" Conrad yelled at the man, kicking him with both his feet.

Katherine screamed. The helicopter suddenly rolled to one side, and the guard, reeling from Conrad's blow, stumbled backward and out the door.

Katherine held on to Conrad's arm, preventing him from falling out as well. They could both see the guard tumbling through the air until he smashed into the roof of St. Patrick's Cathedral.

"What did I tell you!" Katherine shouted, and then immediately began centering herself. She closed her eyes and concentrated on channeling positive energy, visualizing the two of them emerging safely from the helicopter.

Conrad closed the door and pounded on the glass wall separating the passenger cabin from the pilot.

"What the hell is going on?!"

"A solar storm is frying my instrument panel . . . hold on, I've got to try to put this thing down!" the pilot responded, his voice barely audible through the glass.

The BioWorld helicopter dropped suddenly, falling hundreds of feet in seconds. Conrad saw the crowded square of Rockefeller Center hurtling toward him, and he turned to Katherine and said, "I'm sorry."

Katherine began pounding her fist against Conrad's chest.

"Why didn't you listen to me? I told you, I warned you that this would happen."

"I know, I know," Conrad groaned, wrapping his arms around her tightly.

The helicopter pulled up just above the ground, passed over the center's concourse, banked hard to the left, and headed north up Fifth Avenue. They were flying so close to the ground that Conrad could see the faces of startled tourists videotaping them from the open upper level of a double-decker bus.

They shot up Fifth, passing between The Plaza Hotel and Trump Tower, and crossed into Central Park, clipping treetops along the way.

Katherine and Conrad clung to each other as the helicopter began spiraling downward. As the ground rushed up, Conrad's mind went blank except for a single memory: the day he brought his sons to Central Park on their eighth birthday, a crisp December afternoon. His gift to them was to be their first skating lesson, but as soon as they'd arrived at the rink, he was called away to the lab. A nanny taught them to skate.

The helicopter plunged into a clump of trees, and everything went dark.

CHAPTER 17

FRANK BARRELED ACROSS FIFTH AVENUE and entered Central Park at 72nd, realizing too late that the park was closed to vehicles at that hour. He smashed through a groundskeeper's wooden traffic barricade, which bounced over his hood, cracking his windshield. The road forked immediately, and he made a fast left to head southbound toward the tunnel.

"Daddy, *look out!*" Samantha shouted.

A young mother was pushing a stroller across the road directly in front of them. Frank cranked the steering wheel so hard that the truck's right wheels left the ground, nearly flipping the pickup onto its side. The tires screeched as the truck hit the pavement again, fishtailing downhill in the wrong direction.

"Damn it, I missed the turn! I'm going north!" Frank shouted, honking at a throng of pedestrians gawking at the dark cloud of smoke rising over the Upper East Side. "You okay, Sammy?" he asked his daughter.

"Please—please, please, *please,* slow down, Daddy. You're going to kill someone. You're really scaring me."

"I'm sorry, sweetie, but we've got no time. I won't hit anyone, I promise." He glanced at his daughter and forced a smile. "Hey, people are easy to miss. You should try driving through a minefield with tank gunners shooting at you. At least no one's shooting at *us,* huh?" Frank said nervously, trying to laugh.

"No, but they will if you don't *slow down.* You're not even supposed to be driving in the park. The police are probably looking for us everywhere and—"

"Don't worry *too* much about the police, Sammy. They've got lots of other things to worry about at the moment."

She sat silently for a minute, then looked sternly at her father.

"I want you to tell me something, Frank, and tell me the truth."

"Anything, Sammy."

"How'd you know it wasn't a plane crash we just heard?"

"How did I—," Frank swerved again, this time narrowly avoiding a pack of cyclists.

Jesus, don't these people even know what the hell is going on? He stuck his head out the window and yelled back at them, "The goddamned city is blowing up, for Christ's sake!"

As they passed behind the Metropolitan Museum of Art, he said, "I know I just said not to worry *too* much about cops, but we've got to worry a little. They could be coming up behind us, so I can't turn around. So hang on, kid—I'm going to detour."

He veered left, jumping the curb and ending up on the bridle path. A half-dozen horses bolted with their riders as Frank pulled a U-turn in front of them, heading up a steep embankment and onto the jogging track circling the Central Park reservoir.

"All right, okay. We're halfway home, Sammy," he said, gunning the engine and racing westward around the southern end of the track.

"Stop, Daddy, *stop!* I'm going to be sick. . . ."

Frank pulled off the path, parking in the shade of a tall maple tree.

"What is it?" he asked, unfastening her seat belt and taking her into his arms. "I'm so sorry, honey . . . but I've just got to get you out of here before it's too late."

Samantha pressed her head against his chest. She was cold and shivering. Her breathing was shallow, and she was wheezing.

"Okay, I guess we can stop for a minute. We'll take a little breather, and you'll feel better. Okay, honey? You just need some air."

Samantha rarely let Frank carry her, but for the second time today, he cradled her in his arms, and his heart broke at how thin she'd become. Samantha closed her eyes for a moment. When she opened them, she saw her mother standing on a sunny patch of grass just a few feet away. Her eyes closed again.

Frank carried her from the truck, took a bottle of water from the cooler in back, and set her down gently on a bench overlooking the reservoir. A small bronze plaque affixed to the backrest was engraved, *"In loving memory of Maria Christoff."*

"This is a pretty spot, Daddy. When you get paid for the Roosevelt Island job, will you buy me a memorial bench here?"

"Don't start, Sammy. You'll be buying *me* a memorial bench. And don't forget, you promised to dance with me at your wedding." Frank looked at his watch and softly pinched Samantha's small wrist between his fingers, hoping to discreetly gauge her pulse.

"It's very weak today, isn't it," she said faintly, and then turned and vomited on the grass. "I'm sorry, Daddy. I wish—"

"Why are *you* sorry?" Frank held her close, wiped her face, and kissed her forehead. "I'm the one who's made you sick with my crazy driving." He gave her a sip of water to rinse her mouth.

"No, the cancer made me sick. Your driving always makes me puke," Samantha laughed weakly.

"Oh, honey . . . you're so cold."

"I'm scared."

"I know you are, but we gotta get out of here now. You'll feel better at your aunt's. It's safe there."

"I'm not scared for me. I'm scared for you . . . and for everybody else in the city. Daddy?"

"Yeah, Sammy?"

"Pray with me?"

Frank stroked his daughter's neck tenderly, resting his fingers on her throat and counting her heartbeats. Her pulse *was* weak, but at least it was steady. He rubbed the back of her neck, and she began to feel warmer.

"Please pray with me."

"You know that's the only thing I can't do for you, sweetie. Please don't ask me to."

"Daddy, you have to stop blaming God for what happened to Mommy, and for what's going to happen to me."

Frank was silent for a moment. Finally, he said, "If I did believe in God, I'd have to hate Him for taking your mother from us, and that's something I can't do. So I don't believe in Him, Sammy. Not anymore. Let's drop it, okay?"

"How many times do I have to tell you, Dad," Samantha reminded him with a fragile smile, "God's a *woman*."

"Oh yeah, I forgot," Frank laughed. "Then, I don't believe in *Her*. Honey, we've really got to go now."

"Wait."

"What is it?"

"How did you know it was a bomb, Frank?"

"You know my Army job was doing bomb stuff, remember? To this day, I still recognize the sounds of those things."

Frank stood up with Samantha in his arms. She rested her head on his shoulder, and whispered, "Wait."

"Now what?"

"If you don't believe in God . . . if you don't ever pray again . . . how will you hear me talk to you when I'm gone?"

Frank walked silently to the truck, trying not to let Samantha see his face as he gently placed her on the seat and leaned over to fasten her seat belt.

That's when he heard it.

A thick stand of pine trees blocked his view, but he knew the sound. It was a chopper in distress.

What the hell? Can't be, not here. Is this some kind of flashback? Am I going nuts? Frank thought. But then suddenly, it was above them, maybe a hundred yards away—a private helicopter struggling to stay up, but quickly heading down.

The pine trees in front of him began snapping like dried wishbones as the battered fuselage of the chopper plowed through the grove. It burst from the tree line, skipped across a patch of lawn like a stone skimming across a still lake, and slammed into an old oak tree less than 20 feet from Frank's truck.

Frank jumped into the cab and reached for the ignition. "The keys! Where are the freakin' keys?"

"Go help them!"

"Sammy, the goddamn gas . . . give me the keys, I've to get you out of here. *Give them to me!*"

"Go help them, Frank!"

Frank jumped from the truck, choking on the spreading fumes, and splashed through a puddle of leaking fuel toward the downed chopper.

He saw the pilot's grotesquely twisted head sticking through the shattered windshield and knew instantly that he was dead. The cabin door was open, so Frank pulled out the first body he saw: a man with a blood-covered face. Frank plucked a shard of glass from the man's temple, wiped his eyes with his sleeve, and turned him in the direction of the Dodge.

"Can you walk?" Frank asked.

"I think so."

"Good. Then *run* to that truck."

As the man moved toward the truck, he yelled back to Frank, pointing into the chopper's cabin. But Frank couldn't hear a word the man was saying—his voice was completely drowned out by a familiar, angry thrum that sent a shiver down his spine.

Frank looked up. Hovering just above him was a U.S. Army Apache attack helicopter, its two 30mm machine-gun cannons pointed directly at him, and its 16 Hellfire missiles fastened to its underbelly, ready to launch.

My God, this is becoming a freakin' war zone! Did the Army just shoot this chopper out of the sky!? Frank wondered.

The Apache suddenly pulled up and away from him, banking low and to the east until it was out of sight.

Frank stepped into the cabin of the downed chopper. A red-haired woman was slumped over, tangled in her safety belt. He put his hand on her chest and pushed down hard, trying to slip the shoulder strap around her. She opened her eyes, looked at his hand, smacked him hard across the face, and passed out again. Frank managed to pull the woman through the straps, hoisted her long body over his shoulders in a firefighter's carry position, and sprinted back to the pickup.

The bleeding man was sitting in the back, so Frank let the woman's body slide from his shoulders onto the man's lap.

"I'll pay you $100,000 to take us to Hoboken," the man said.

"Buddy, you'll be lucky if I can get you ten feet before that thing blows," Frank said, jumping into the cab and sticking out his hand to Samantha.

"Keys!"

"I put them in the ignition."

Seconds later they were zigzagging across the park's Great Lawn. Frank looked into his rearview mirror and watched the flames of the exploding helicopter shoot into the sky. Then he looked at his daughter.

He could see her lips moving, but he could barely hear what she was saying. She was whispering so softly: "Okay, Mommy . . . I will . . . I promise . . . don't worry."

CHAPTER 18

THE LIMOUSINE IDLED 30 FEET BELOW THE STREETS OF MANHATTAN as the driver waited in darkness for the massive garage door to open.

This door of the BioWorld Tower was known in engineering circles as the strongest ever manufactured—a massively thick gate of solid tungsten that was capable of withstanding a direct hit from high-powered explosives.

A series of heavy metallic cracks echoed as the door's bolts retracted, followed by a steady hissing as the Tower's air lock was broken. The door rolled up like a two-ton Venetian blind.

As soon as there was enough clearance, the dark limo emerged from the basement, heading up the ramp toward York Avenue.

But before it reached the street, a dozen NYPD Operation Atlas officers had the car surrounded. They all wore gas masks and bulletproof vests and had their weapons trained on the long, dark car.

"Stop or we'll shoot!" shouted one of the officers. His order was muted, muffled by the thick gas mask, but his intent was clear.

The limo halted immediately, and as the tinted rear passenger window rolled down, a hand emerged and presented a BioWorld Security DNA/Photo ID, and a security pass issued by the Department of Homeland Security.

The lead officer approached with his shotgun leveled at the window, leaned forward, and inspected the credentials.

"John Wilson, BioWorld Security Chief," Wilson said, from inside the car.

"General John Wilson? Boy am I glad it's you in there, sir. I wish circumstances were different. Damn city's blowing up around us, and—"

"Do I know you?"

"Sir, yes, sir. Sergeant Peter Crighton—um, well, you knew me when I was *Captain* Crighton, sir. It was my honor to serve under you in Desert Storm," the sergeant said, slipping his gas mask up off his face so it sat on his head like a baseball cap.

"Your weapon is in my face. Please lower it."

"Sorry, sir," Crighton said, pointing his shotgun at the ground and signaling his men to do the same.

"That's better. Of course I remember you. Fightin' Crighton—the man who single-handedly took out three Iraqi tanks in ten minutes. You're out of uniform, soldier."

"No, it's just a different uniform these days, sir. I'm 12 years now with the NYPD, third in command of Operation Atlas. That's the anti-terrorism—"

"I know what Atlas is," Wilson interrupted. "I'm the one who requested your detail to secure BioWorld. That was 20 minutes ago. Nice of you to finally show up. Now, kindly get the hell out of my way—"

"Sorry, sir. No can do."

A blue armored personnel carrier with an image of a rearing cobra painted across its front rolled up to a stop at the top of the ramp.

"COBRA?" asked Wilson.

"Yessir: Chemical, Biological or Radiological Actions unit."

"I know what it stands for!" Wilson yelled from the car. "I invented the goddamn unit! What I want to know is why it's *here*."

"Because of the radiation traces, sir. Lots of 'em all over the street, the ramp, and especially the garage door you just drove out of—the entire place is a freakin' hot zone. We have to search the building for dirty bombs . . . and sorry to report, sir, we have to search your vehicle and everything inside."

At the top of the ramp, the door of the COBRA carrier flew upward, as if the jaws of the painted snake had snapped open.

A team dressed in yellow radiation suits moved quickly down the ramp, each carrying a halogen Geiger counter that emitted high-pitched warning beeps, like a truck backing up.

"Listen to that, sir. It's contaminated here, and I have to order—"

"Listen to *me*, Captain. See that smoking bridge across the river? It could have been taken out by a dirty bomb. That means fallout everywhere around here. On top of that, we're being bombarded by the biggest solar storm in 150 years. There's no way you'll get anything close to an accurate radiation reading today—especially not in this neighborhood. Now kindly get out of my way."

"I've considered all that, but with respect, General, the garage door you came through seems particularly hot, and I have to insist—"

"That *door* can only be opened by a control panel in Conrad Dinnick's private penthouse suite. Now, his close friends—the mayor, the governor, and the *President of the United States*—don't think he's hiding nukes in here, and neither do I. Do *you?*"

"Again, with all respect, sir, none of that matters. The city's Office of Emergency Management is in that building. If there's a radiation trail leading to it, I have to—"

"Listen, Crighton, I showed you my Homeland Security ID, I have security clearance higher than you can imagine, *and* I'm still a general in the U.S. Army. I'm issuing you a direct order to—"

A halogen Geiger counter by the garage door interrupted him with an ear-splitting shriek.

"Sir, that door is hotter than a thousand-dollar hooker," Crighton said. "There must be—"

Just then, the ground shook beneath a dozen fire engines as the trucks raced up York Avenue toward the Queensboro Bridge, distracting both Crighton and his men.

Wilson seized the moment to leap from the car. "I ordered you to stand down, Crighton," he hissed, pressing the long barrel of a silver-plated pistol against the sergeant's temple. "Now before we have a bloodbath, tell your men to lower their weapons while we talk."

The noise of the fire engines faded. Wilson cocked the hammer of his pistol. The officers surrounding the limo raised their weapons, and the ramp echoed with the clicking of the pump-action shotguns.

"Hold your fire, but maintain your positions!" Crighton ordered his men. "If he fires his weapon . . . kill him."

"The solar storm has knocked out communications, and without electronic communications, there's no way to know what's happening. We could be at war, Crighton," Wilson barked at him.

"Yes, sir, but it's still my duty to trace all radiation trails."

"You have no idea what's going on here, son."

"Sir, as an NYPD sergeant and unit leader—"

"You're a West Point grad, Crighton. You know the reasons we fought in Iraq—to protect our constitutional rights—the freedoms we all have under the writ of habeas corpus?"

"Of course I do . . . why are you giving me a history quiz with a gun to my head?" Crighton said through gritted teeth.

"No, Crighton, a *current-events* quiz. Tell your men about the only time habeas corpus can legally be suspended."

"Sir, I don't understand what you want me to—"

"The U.S. Constitution, Crighton! Article 1, Section 9. When does military authority supersede civilian authority?"

"Sir?"

"Answer me. Say the goddamned words."

"In cases of rebellion or invasion."

"In cases of rebellion or invasion. In case you haven't noticed, Crighton, we're at war. The infidels are at our gates—"

"Infidels?"

"The godless, suicide-bombing terrorists, Crighton. You're as blind and stupid as everyone at the Pentagon. For the last time, I am on a Code Red mission. Millions of lives are at stake, and you're in my way."

"I have my orders, sir."

"I'm giving you *new* orders. For all we know, this city could be under martial law. Under Article 1, Section 9, and the provisions of the Terrorism Prevention Act, I'm taking command of your unit. Now, order your men to fall back and clear this ramp, or so help me God, I'll put a bullet in your brain in three seconds. One, two . . ."

"Lower your weapons. Stand down. Do it!" Crighton shouted to his men. "I'm relinquishing command to General Wilson."

The officers lowered their guns and stepped aside as the COBRA vehicle backed off the ramp.

Wilson removed his pistol from Crighton's head.

"That's what it's all about, Crighton—the chain of command. Your orders are to secure the Tower's perimeter. All essential personnel have been escorted in; all non-essential personnel are gone. The building is in 24-hour lockdown until we ascertain the current threat level. No door or window can be opened—it's airtight and impenetrable. You'd need a goddamn nuke to get inside there now, son. Guard it with your life, and try to stay alive." Wilson clapped the soldier on the back, said, "Nice seeing you again, Crighton," and hopped back in the limo.

The car was off the ramp and heading south on York Avenue before Wilson had tucked his gun into its holster.

"You play a lot of games with people," Daniel ventured, as the general settled back into his seat and pulled a briefcase onto his lap.

"I don't play games, son. I give orders, and soldiers—even ex-soldiers—obey. That's what we program them to do."

Daniel looked at Wilson doubtfully. "But the chopper?"

"It should have returned for us. Whatever happened to the chopper wasn't because my orders weren't followed."

"And the bridge. Why?"

"Necessary diversionary tactic."

"Those people were innocent . . ."

"Unavoidable. Collateral damage." Wilson was stoic.

"It . . . doesn't seem—"

"Seem what? Right? Fair? Remember, my boy, all is fair in war, and this is war," Wilson said.

"But, *Dad* . . . I mean . . . I'm sorry . . ."

"It's all right, I understand that you're a little confused. It's okay to call me Dad if you want. You know you're like a son to me."

Daniel sighed heavily, then looked at his watch. "We'll never make it."

"We'll make it if there aren't any more god-damned delays. Traveling over ground makes the timing very tight, but we'll make it."

Wilson leaned toward the driver. "Slap that flashing light on the roof, and take 42nd Street across town. The police will have shut it down for emergency vehicles only. When we get to the Lincoln Tunnel, take the north tube—it's the shortest route across the river."

Turning back to Daniel, he opened the brief-case.

"Look at it. It's a beauty. I made it myself—C4 packing, random alpha-cryptic trip-wire protection and satellite phone detonator. It's guaranteed to satisfy. The only thing I didn't bank on is a solar storm messing up our satellite system. What are the chances of being hit by one of those today of all days?"

"Astronomical," Daniel said sardonically.

"But it won't be a problem; the phone has a roving trigger that's programmed to continually attempt an uplink—as soon as the first functional satellite comes online, it'll bounce the signal back here, and we'll have a connection. Then all we do is flip this," Wilson explained, pointing to a gold switch attached to the phone.

"Once that's done, the clock starts ticking down. Thirty minutes later, it will take out the primary target, and then the briefcase will self-destruct. I've put enough plastic explosives in this case to take out a city block, so we have to make sure we're in the air and on our way to

South America when the timer reaches T-minus zero. Once the switch is flipped, nothing can stop it except for a disconnection code that only I know."

"But maybe . . . it won't work. Because of the storm. Maybe it's not supposed to work."

"Not *supposed* to work?!" Wilson shouted incredulously. "Supposing has nothing to do with it. This is a military operation, and I'm a military expert, son. Just sit back, enjoy the ride, and have a little faith."

CHAPTER 19

THE PICKUP SKIDDED ACROSS THE GREAT LAWN, its rear tires spitting chunks of turf through the air.

Frank crossed the quarter-mile-long field in less than a minute—more than enough time to see that the city had changed. Manhattan was suddenly defined by the black cloud drifting westward across its skyline, and by the police helicopters buzzing over the island. The scene reminded Frank of his last tour in Iraq when he'd been clearing cluster bombs from a playground and his squad leader had stepped on a land mine. There was a look on his face during the split second between the clicking of the mine's trigger and the man's realization that he was going to be blown to bits that haunted Frank to this day. It was the same look he saw now, etched on the faces of everyone he passed in the park: the hot dog vendor, the nanny pushing the stroller, the dad piggybacking his son, the old lady feeding pigeons.

It was the look of terror.

The memories of September 11, 2001, locked tight in the minds of so many New Yorkers, burst open and flooded the city with the horror of history repeating itself almost six years later.

From the corner of his eye, Frank could see Samantha signaling to him. Her eyelids were barely open, but she was holding her left arm in front of her, insistently pointing at something through the windshield.

"The castle in the sky, Daddy," she said weakly.

Frank was focused on navigating through the human stampede sweeping across the park. There were now hundreds of people running over the lawn, desperate to reach shelter, get to their homes, and find their families. He was certain that his daughter was hallucinating.

"Sure, Sammy, I see it, floating way up there. Now close your eyes and get some rest. We'll be home soon."

"No, Franklin . . . look up at the castle in the sky! We used to come here all the time with Mommy."

She was right. There it was, towering before them: Belvedere Castle. A medieval fortress in the heart of Manhattan, perched on top of a granite cliff—the highest point in Central Park. He'd taken Sarah and Samantha there for Sunday-afternoon picnics to, as Sarah loved to say, "dine like royalty with the richest but least expensive view in the city."

Perfect spot for a sniper nest, Frank thought, surveying the walkway on top of the castle wall. He spotted them instantly: at least six camouflaged soldiers with high-powered rifles taking position in the castle's battlements.

Great! A pickup truck driven by a wanted man, fleeing a chopper crash at high speed across a crowded public park. I might as well draw a bull's-eye on the roof. Not only am I a dead-easy target, I'm a justifiable kill. And at this distance, even these weekend warriors couldn't miss.

"Daddy?"

"Sammy, *not now.*"

"But I need to tell you something."

"*What?* I'm trying to drive."

"I decided I want you to sprinkle my ashes from the top of the castle—"

"*Samantha!* If you mention dying one more time, I swear to God I'll—"

"Thought you didn't believe in God, Frank," Samantha said sarcastically.

"Mock me later," Frank told her, flooring the gas pedal and sending the truck hurtling straight toward the pond beneath the castle.

He swerved to the right at the last minute onto a pedestrian walkway leading out of the park, laying on his horn, which screamed as he sped down the crowded path. Frank glanced at his daughter and said, "If you feel like praying again, Sammy, this would be a good time. Pray I don't hit anyone, because I'm sure as hell not slowing down."

The Dodge shot on to Central Park West, which was hopelessly jammed with cars and pedestrians fighting to get home, unable to move in any direction. A female traffic cop, who'd cleared a narrow path in the gridlock for an approaching ambulance, motioned for Frank to stop. He ignored her, plow-ing across the busy intersection to West 81st Street, forcing the cop to dive out of the way to avoid being mowed down. Even so, she knocked against the side of the truck as she jumped, cursing at Frank as she hit the ground.

"Oops," Frank said, seeing the cop in his sideview mirror stand up, brush herself off, and flip him the finger. Then he spotted the banners hanging over 81st Street.

Finally, a stroke of luck! The entire street had been closed off in preparation for a sidewalk fes-tival. Frank cut through a line of pedestrians and smashed through a thicket of metal police bar-ricades.

"We've done it, sweetie! We've got an open route west clear across town. If 11th Avenue isn't blocked, we'll be in the tunnel in 12, maybe 15 minutes, tops. That was some good praying, Sammy. Way to go, girl!"

"Not *that* good, Franklin. You nearly ran over a policewoman."

"I didn't run over anyone."

"Yes, you did."

"I did not."

"Did."

"Well . . . I didn't run her *over* . . . I just clipped her. If the city doesn't get blown to hell today, she can claim whiplash and take a six-month disabil-ity vacation in Florida. See? I did her a favor."

"*Dad!*"

"Sorry, Sammy. I could have hurt her; it's nothing to joke about. I'm just nervous. But I can't believe you're busting my chops. One second you're quiet, the next you're citing me for traffic violations."

"I feel a bit better . . . but I don't know about them."

"Them who?"

"Back there," Samantha said, jerking her thumb over her left shoulder like a hitchhiker, toward the bed of the truck.

"Oh shit, shit, shit!" Frank cried, remembering his unwanted cargo.

Then he spotted the police roadblock two blocks ahead.

Damn it, he realized, *I'll never get past them with two blood-covered crash victims in the back.*

He slammed on the brakes, reached under the seat for one of the detective's guns he'd stashed, and jumped out of the truck.

Then man he'd rescued had made a mattress for his female companion using fertilizer bags, tucking a small roll of sod under her head for a pillow.

She was unconscious, but Frank saw that her breathing was regular and deep.

"Thanks for picking us up," the man said.

Frank pointed the gun at him. "Two questions, and don't even think about lying to me," he barked. "Who the hell are you, and why was the military chasing down your chopper?"

"My name is Dinnick, I'm the—"

"*Dinnick?*" Despite the mask of dried blood plastering the man's face, Frank now recognized his wealthy employer. "I know who you are, Mr. Dinnick. Why were they after you?"

"I honestly don't know *who's* after me anymore."

"Well, you better come up with something fast."

"Maybe you don't know about the attack," Conrad said, emphatically, "or at least, about the explosion at the Queensboro Bridge. Half the bridge is in the water, and the Re-Creation Center I built on Roosevelt Island is completely destroyed. So I think—"

"That was the explosion I heard? The bridge . . . the Re-Creation Center, destroyed?"

"That's right. They must be shutting down airspace over Manhattan like after 9/11, and . . . look, it's too complicated. I work with the Army, with the government. Someone in my company, or terrorists or a foreign government . . . *someone's* trying to kill me because of something I know. I don't have time to explain it all to you. I said I'd give you $100,000 to take me to Hoboken. Put the gun away, and I'll make it $200,000. You have no idea how high the stakes are—"

"Well, aren't you generous, Mr. Dinnick. You already *owe* me $200,000 for landscaping your island, and I'm still waiting for the check, pal."

"I had no idea who you—"

"Never mind," Frank said, waving the gun toward Katherine. "Who's she?"

"A psychic."

"Oh, of course, a *psychic*. Who else would you drop out of the sky with? Wait—she's that TV psychic . . . Katherine what's-her-name, the one freaking everyone out on the radio with bomb threats . . . on *your* radio station, right?"

Frank pressed the gun against Conrad's ribs. "I don't know what kind of sick game you're playing here, but pick up your girlfriend right now and haul your trillionaire ass out of my truck before I blow a hole in—"

"Daddy!"

Samantha had slid open the small rear window and was staring at them. The dirty frame accented the dark circles under her eyes and the paleness of her face.

Frank immediately hid the gun behind his back.

"Sammy, I swear I'm not going to hurt anyone else, but we've got to get to your aunt's right away. We can't take these people—"

"Mommy says to take them with us."

"*What?*"

"Mommy just talked to me. Stop looking at me like that—she did, really. She said we all have to go together."

"Okay, honey, that's good. Now shut the window and fasten your seat belt. We're leaving in a hurry."

Samantha closed the window and dropped out of sight, and Frank turned back to Conrad.

"I don't want to hurt you, but I will. It looks like the Army's after you, and I *know* the police are after me, so we don't make a good team. Now get out. You see how sick my little girl looks, she's delirious—"

"She's dying."

"What did you just say?"

"Chronic genocalimic leukemia, right?"

"How the hell did you know that?"

"Because I went to med school, and I'm a geneticist. I can't promise you, but I think I could help her—"

"You could what? You lying bastard."

"If you know who I am, then you must know what I do. There's a new gene therapy I'm developing. It's still in trials, but I think it could reverse the disease."

"I don't believe you."

"Your oncologist must have told you what I can see just by looking at her face: She's got weeks, maybe only days. Get me to Hoboken, and I'll do what I can for her, I swear. I've developed a new treatment. I'll have a team of doctors working with her day and night."

"What the hell is in Hoboken?"

"In the right hands, global protection. In the wrong hands . . . a new virus that could kill a million New Yorkers in a month. I told you, I do work for the government—I develop vaccines to protect us against biological attacks. Get me to my lab, and I'll help your daughter."

"If you're lying to me, I'll kill you."

"If that bug gets loose, I'll be *begging* you to kill me."

The two men stared at each other for a second.

"It's a deal. I don't know if they'll let us past the roadblock up ahead, but I'm going through one way or the other," Frank said, tucking the gun into the waistband of his jeans.

He stuck out his hand and shook Conrad's hand. "Frank Dell," he offered cautiously.

"Conrad Dinnick," Conrad replied.

"Looks like we're both trying to do the same thing—save lives," Frank said, pulling one of the detective's badges from his back pocket and handing it to Conrad. "Take this. When they stop us at the roadblock, show it to them and say your name is Big Davie."

"I don't need a badge," Conrad said, pulling a wallet from his pants pocket. "I have top Pentagon clearance and a Class-10 Homeland Security pass. If we needed to, we could walk into the Oval Office for tea."

"Let's just hope we can get into the Lincoln Tunnel."

Upon hearing the word *tunnel,* Katherine stirred in the back of the truck. Now semiconscious, she began softly mumbling. Neither of the men could hear her, and even if they had, they wouldn't have been unable to understand what she was saying: *Tunnel . . . limo . . . virus . . . Sarah . . . twins.*

Samantha was asleep when Frank climbed back behind the wheel. Conrad's pass got them through the police on West 81st Street with no problem. They headed south down 11th Avenue, the Hudson River on their right. Frank looked across the river at the condos going up along Hoboken's abandoned piers, and farther south toward the little patch of green he seeded once a year called Frank Sinatra Park.

Conrad's pass got them through six more police checkpoints. They made it all the way to the Lincoln Tunnel's north tube entrance in less than 15 minutes.

A National Guardsman shook his head while inspecting the truck and its disheveled occupants, but waved them past after checking out Conrad's credentials.

The white tiles on the tunnel wall had yellowed, like the teeth of a lifelong smoker. They reminded Frank of the YMCA swimming pool he'd gone to when he was Samantha's age. Swimming made him feel like he was weightless, practically flying—the way he felt now looking at his daughter and wondering if Conrad really could heal her. Samantha met his gaze, flashing him a dimmer version of her thousand-watt smile. She saw her mother again, standing at the entrance of the tunnel as they moved underground and beneath the river. Sarah was smiling as always, and the weary girl heard her say, *Soon, Sammy, very soon.*

"I'm going home, Daddy."

"I think so, baby. I think maybe you're right. There *is* a God, and She just answered our prayers."

CHAPTER 20

"I NEED TO KNOW . . . IS HE . . . IS MY FATHER DEAD?" Daniel asked haltingly.

"Turn on the all-news station," Wilson commanded the driver.

A male voice vibrated through the limo's speakers. The announcer grew increasingly emotional and incoherent as he described the events unfolding around him.

" . . . *we just don't know how many people have been hurt or killed, but the bridge has collapsed, it's collapsed! Rescue workers are trying to reach the island, but the fire . . . the fire is so big . . . oh God! . . . it's 9/11 all over again . . . it must be another terrorist attack . . . there's no other—"*

There was a sudden thud, as though the microphone had been knocked over, and then a calm female voice began reporting.

"You're listening to Action News Radio. There have been erroneous reports of a terrorist attack in the city, but this has not, I repeat, not *been confirmed. The*

facts we know so far are as follows: Approximately half
an hour ago a massive explosion on Roosevelt Island
damaged or destroyed much of the Queensboro Bridge.
As of yet, there has been no public statement from the
mayor, governor, or police commissioner.

"Fire Commissioner Erwin Douglas says that so
far the explosions seem to be related to a rupture in a
large natural gas line on the island. No group or indi-
vidual has claimed responsibility for the explosions.

"Police anti-terrorism units and the New York
National Guard are patrolling the city, but they say
that there's no sign of any type of ongoing terrorist
attack.

"So, although the situation may look chaotic in
the streets right now, the most important thing is not
to panic, folks. This appears to be an accident—not
an attack. Stay tuned to Action News Radio for up-to-
the-minute coverage of this breaking news story."

A sudden burst of static shot through the
limo, and the driver moved to turn the volume
down.

"Leave it on," Wilson ordered. He opened his
briefcase and checked the satellite phone. "No
connection yet."

The newscaster continued.*"What's even more*
frightening is the ongoing solar storm, which is mak-
ing it difficult for New Yorkers to use their phones or
the Internet to communicate. Again, this is not due
to terrorism. It is, believe it or not, a weather-related
problem, although it's quite a serious one. People are
advised not to look at the sun, as sudden bursts of light
during severe solar storms have been known to cause
blindness, burn skin, and even start forest fires. The
storm has already damaged scores of communication

satellites. More than 300 of our sister radio and television stations across the country have been knocked
off the air. If the same thing happens to us, do not
adjust your dial. We're told that the disruptions will be
intermittent, and likely temporary. Again, we urge you:
Stay tuned to Action News Radio for up-to-the-minute
coverage.

"Now, recapping the facts. What we know so
far is that approximately 35 minutes ago, a large
explosion on Roosevelt Island destroyed much of the
Queensboro Bridge. The new BioWorld Supercomputer
Re-Creation Center under the bridge, which was scheduled to open today, has been completely destroyed. A
fire at the site, at the moment believed to be from a
ruptured gas main, is burning out of control. Several
hundred people had assembled for the center's opening
ceremony, but remarkably, we've received no reports of
casualties so far, although that could change. . . . We
just don't know at the moment."

The limo was moving west across 42nd Street
when hundreds of anxious-looking people began
to pour into the street from Grand Central Station.
Police pushed the crowds back onto the sidewalk
as emergency vehicles flew down the road toward
the East Side.

"The subways are emptying—" Wilson remarked
to Daniel.

"Sir," the driver interrupted Wilson nervously,
"the road's getting so crowded that I'm having a
hard time getting around these people."

"I don't care if you drive *over* them. You've got
20 minutes to get to the Jersey side of the Lincoln
tunnel. Turn on the siren and flasher, and *move!*"

When the limo's siren began wailing, several police officers stepped out on the road and opened a clear path. The car began speeding through Midtown toward the Hudson River.

And on the radio: *"We have another breaking development: Subways in all five New York boroughs are being evacuated as a precautionary measure. Once again, there's no, I repeat, no confirmation of a terrorist attack—just a lot of confusion and, naturally, anxiety.*

"We're still waiting for a news conference with the mayor, governor, and police commissioner . . . but . . . what? We've just received a report that the mayor and governor may have been on the Roosevelt Island Tram when the bridge collapsed, but there's no word on their whereabouts or condition, although some fear that they must be seriously, or fatally, injured. I apologize for the vagueness of the report . . . the solar storm is making any form of communication with officials or our reporters in the field virtually impossible. . . . It's like we're being thrown back in time."

"It sounds like the beginning of the end," Wilson said wryly, as the limo crossed 8th Avenue.

Daniel looked up and saw the giant neon signs of Times Square that were filled with images of the day's news. First there were the pictures of the burning Queensboro Bridge, then some of the mayor and governor, followed by an image of his father. Then there they were—he and Michael, a 40-foot high photograph of the Dinnick brothers—being broadcast above the world's busiest intersection.

Daniel was startled by seeing his brother's face in front of him so suddenly, staring at him like a ghost from above. *What is that expression on his face?* Daniel wondered in disbelief, his heart beginning to race. *It's accusation . . . he's accusing me . . . he's blaming me!*

His mind drifted back to the day in BioWorld's Hoboken lab, when everything between the two brothers changed. He felt like he was watching a movie of a moment in his life being played back for him: Daniel walking in on Michael . . . catching him conducting experiments on himself, using a hypodermic air gun to inject cloned human embryo cells into his brain stem.

"What you're doing is wrong. Not only could it kill you . . . it's a crime against God," Daniel had said, threatening to go to their father to report his brother. Michael had been laughing and laughing—so smug—mocking Daniel.

"Go ahead, go to Dad and report me. But while you're at it, tell him about all the BioWorld money, the hundreds of millions of dollars that *someone* has been diverting to supply developing countries with free antiviral drugs—drugs that BioWorld should be *selling* on the open market for profit. They call that theft, embezzlement, larceny—take your pick. It's just the kind of thing Dad would love to hear about."

"I don't know how you know about that, but it's different. I'm trying to help millions of people. I'm doing God's work," Daniel had explained.

"So am I, Danny, just in a very different way. Now if you want to keep doing what you're doing, you'll let me do what *I'm* doing. So it's our little secret, agreed?"

"All right . . . for the common good."

"For the common good," Michael had repeated. Then he held up the hypodermic gun and walked toward Daniel, saying, "There's just one other condition I have. . . ."

Everything was fuzzy after that—sickness . . . a tumor . . . and Wilson, helping out, covering something up . . . what was it? *What had happened?*

He pulled back from his daydream as the image of his father's face flashed back on the screen.

"Dad?" Daniel asked, staring through the window then turning to Wilson.

"With the phones out and satellites down, there's no way to be sure *exactly* what happened to him, but I think we both know," Wilson told Daniel. "But remember that whatever happened, we agreed it was for the best," Wilson said, closing the briefcase.

"Right . . . for the best . . . but the vaccine— there isn't enough . . . not yet . . . not for everyone."

"We don't need it for everyone, and as long as we can re-create it, there's not a problem," Wilson reassured him.

As the car pulled onto the ramp for the tunnel, the female newscaster's professional delivery evaporated, developing a hysterical edge.

"Oh my God . . . we've just received a confirmed report that . . ."

The radio fizzled out completely.

A group of National Guard soldiers were lined up along the entrance of the Lincoln Tunnel as the limo descended the ramp to the north tube.

A group of soldiers approached the limo, brandishing M16 machine guns.

"Authorized personnel only," said one of the soldiers as others inspected the underside of the limo with long-handled mirrors.

Wilson produced his identification. "Here's my authorization."

The soldier saluted, saying, "Go ahead, General, sir."

As they passed into the tunnel, the speakers began crackling again.

"We're losing radio transmission. The storm's knocking everything out," Wilson said.

The reporter's voice began cutting in and out. *". . . all tunnels and bridges leading in and out of the city are being closed until—"*

The radio died completely.

Wilson leaned forward and put his mouth next to the driver's ear.

"This tunnel is just under a mile-and-a-half long, then it's a three-mile drive to Hoboken. There's a group of people waiting for us there, the kind of people you don't keep waiting. If we don't meet them in exactly 15 minutes, it's likely we'll all be dead . . . and I'll make sure you're the first to go."

CHAPTER 21

JACK TWISTED THE HARLEY'S THROTTLE BACK until the roar of the engine almost deafened them, and then popped the clutch. The chopper's front wheel jumped off the ground, the rear tire screeched against the pavement, and the bike shot forward at a gut-wrenching speed.

"Whoa!" Zoe yelled, the acceleration whipping her against the backrest, nearly spilling her onto the street.

She grabbed Jack's leather jacket, then slid her arms around his waist.

"Never been on a Harley before?" Jack yelled to her.

"Believe it or not it's—"

"What? Can't hear you."

Zoe put her lips against Jack's right ear. "I said, believe it or not, it's my first time on a motorbike."

"*A motorbike?* What are ya, British?" Jack asked in his thickest Brooklyn accent.

"*Excuse me*—I've never been on a motor*cycle* before, and for the record, I'm a Joisey girl."

"From New Jersey *and* a reporter?"

"Yeah, well, nobody's perfect."

Jack swerved to miss a pothole, and Zoe shrieked.

"Listen—don't be scared," he assured her. "We'll only get into trouble if you tense up. Try to relax, don't fight the motion, and just follow the movement of my body. When I turn right, you lean right. If I turn left, you lean left. Don't worry, you won't fall off . . . and always keep your feet on the foot pegs. I'll be moving fast, cutting through heavy traffic and taking a few shortcuts, so hang on tight. Get it?"

"Got it."

In spite of the heat, Zoe was trembling violently. She pressed herself against Jack's body and tightened her arms around his midsection. She could feel his solid stomach muscles through the thick leather and began calculating his age.

What am I doing? she wondered. It dawned on her that she hadn't been this physically close to a man since the day she quit the beauty-pageant circuit.

"Hey, you're really squeezing the breath out of me!" Jack yelled over his shoulder.

"Oh, sorry," Zoe said, embarrassed. She tried to release her grip but couldn't. Jack's left hand had wrapped around her interlaced fingers and held them in place for a second.

Jack laughed, "No, you gotta hold on tight. I just meant, you're really strong, that's all. I don't mind, I'm just surprised, 'cause, you know, you're kind of petite . . . I mean . . . you must, you know, work out a lot or something."

"Boxing."

"Say what?" Jack shouted.

Zoe put her mouth against his ear again. "I said, I box for exercise. I'm a boxer."

"A boxer? What? Like Rocky Balboa?" Jack laughed.

"Yeah, just like Rocky," Zoe replied, surprised to find herself laughing as well.

"So if you're a boxer, why'd you need a stun gun to take out a broken-down old man like me?"

"You had a gun! You were acting crazy—oh, sorry . . . but you were—"

"Fuhgettaboutit, I deserved it. I guess I am a little crazy. Besides, I haven't felt anything that intense since . . . well, in a long, long time."

Zoe paused, squeezing her arms around him a little tighter. "You're not an old man."

"Say what?"

"I said, I'm cold, really cold . . . man," Zoe answered, realizing she couldn't stop shivering.

"CIS."

"What?"

"Critical Incident Stress. Your body's trying to protect itself. Your blood pressure's dropped, so you feel cold. Basically, you're in shock. You just saw some horrible shit back there, but I can't do anything for you right now. Just hold on tight, kid, and try to keep warm against me. If you get dizzy, tell me right away."

"What? You go to medical school before becoming a cop?"

"Nah . . . my son's a . . . my son was a para-medic."

"Yeah? What's he doing now?"

"I can't talk about it. Gotta focus on the road."

Zoe sensed she'd opened a deep wound.

"I'm sorry," Zoe said, and was silent for a moment. Then, in a soft voice: "I know what it's like to lose a child."

It was the first time she'd ever said that out loud; she wasn't sure why she'd said it or even if Jack had heard her. She began shivering more violently and held Jack tighter, pressing her face against his back. Until she realized his leather jacket was wet, she hadn't even known she'd been crying.

As they began turning west, away from the East River and toward the tunnel, Zoe took a last look over her shoulder at the broken, smoldering bridge. Then she closed her eyes and kept them shut until she stopped crying.

Jack was true to his word: His riding was fast, furious, and dangerous—mounting sidewalks and terrorizing pedestrians one minute, and suddenly cutting in front of a bus the next. He headed the wrong way down one-way streets, played chicken with oncoming traffic, and ignored stop signs and traffic lights.

Within five minutes, they were in the heart of Midtown.

Zoe opened her eyes and was amazed at what she saw. They were less than a dozen blocks from the burning bridge, yet no one seemed to know what had happened to their city. As always, the streets were filled with people, some had even stopped walking and were looking up at the smoke in the eastern sky. But there was no panic, no screaming, no run-for-your-life hysteria.

Just like September 11th, she thought. *They don't know, just like I didn't know.*

Even a hardcore news junkie like Zoe had been late to catch on about the significance of 9/11. She'd been scheduled to fly to Albany to report on a mob-related Supreme Court hearing and was sitting on the stoop of her uptown apartment waiting for an airport limo, sipping coffee and reading *The Trumpet,* when the first plane hit. When the second one hit, she was still reading the paper, wondering why her car was so late.

She found out that the city was under attack when the limo dispatcher called on her cell phone explaining that her car would be delayed due to bad traffic downtown.

That had always stuck in her mind: *Delay due to bad traffic downtown.*

"Yeah, so, this is New York. Traffic's always bad," Zoe had answered.

"Yes, Miss, that's true . . . but the planes crashing into the World Trade Center have really fouled things up—"

"What?!" Zoe had yelled, only then noticing the smoke rising over Lower Manhattan.

She got on her bicycle and pedaled like crazy. She was only blocks from the World Trade Center when the South Tower came down, the dust storm blowing her off the bike and into a story she would cover for the next year. Despite the pain and loss she'd reported on, she tried to never let it get to her. She threw herself into her work, determined to beat the competition and get the most heart-rending stories possible.

The Trumpet offered free trauma-therapy sessions for reporters who'd covered the events, but Zoe didn't attend any of them. She'd dealt with what she'd seen that day in the same way she'd dealt with her so-called mother: She turned her back and left it in the past, where it could never hurt her again.

But everything she'd walked away from was beginning to seep into her heart and mind now as she sped through the streets of Manhattan after another catastrophe, entrusting her life to a crazy man she'd just met during what amounted to a shoot-out.

She now remembered that it was after 9/11 when she first heard of Katherine Haywood. Someone in her office had a friend who'd seen the psychic pass out during a group reading three days before the attack, then wake up with a splitting headache—and a premonition of an airplane crash in lower Manhattan.

At the time, Zoe dismissed the rumor as the self-promotion of an opportunistic business-woman trying to tap in to a market of bereaved New Yorkers. But years later, after she'd been assigned to the Your Lucky Stars column, Zoe had come across two others who'd been at that same reading. Both of them—one a doctor, the other a district attorney—swore that Katherine had predicted the terrorist attack.

Oh God, I've done everything I possibly could to screw this woman's reputation in my columns, and she might have been telling the truth all along? Zoe wondered.

"Jack," she suddenly yelled, "do you think maybe this psychic is for real?"

"What? Not a chance."

"But how could she have known about the explosion? And the things she said to Dinnick, things she just had no way of knowing . . . the tram, the explosions. How do explain that?"

"*I'm* supposed to be the crazy one, not you."

"No, but really, what if she's the real deal? What if it's possible that the people we love are really still around, and someone like Katherine can talk to them?"

"Listen, all I know is what I know: When you're dead, you're dead."

Zoe pressed close to Jack again, this time whispering urgently, "Hurry, Jack, please."

Jack revved the engine higher, weaving like a drunk through the busy streets.

They raced across Midtown in what had to be record time, even for a cop. But when they reached Times Square, they abruptly stopped.

News of the explosion had spread slowly at first, creeping beneath the radar, before exploding in a burst of panic that infected the center of the city with desperation. It was like New Year's Eve without the celebration.

Hundreds of people jammed the streets, trying to hail taxis that couldn't move, and flocking to subway entrances already packed with commuters evacuating the underground stations.

Police and military vehicles cordoned off the square as helicopters hovered overhead. Pictures of the burning bridge flashed everywhere—on massive digital billboards, on the television display screens of discount electronics stores, and embedded in the news crawlers snaking along the facades of building after building.

"We'll never get out of this mess," Zoe said.

"Oh, yes we will!" Jack shouted. "Don't you worry, I'm going to get you through this. I won't let anything happen to you, kid. The cops will have cleared out 42nd Street as an emergency route—that's just two blocks south of here. Hold on!"

Jack revved the bike, popped over the curb and through the gate of a construction site, crossed 43rd Street, and headed in to a parking lot that emptied out onto West 42nd.

He tore down the street, just ahead of the roadblocks that were being set up. Jack knew that the Lincoln Tunnel would likely be shut down, but that the north tube would be reserved for police and fire department use, so that's where he headed.

He rode down the ramp and stopped behind a black limo being checked out by a squad of National Guard soldiers.

Two NYPD officers carrying 9mm Glocks approached the motorcycle, and a pair of National Guardsmen aimed machine guns at Jack and Zoe from the tunnel entrance.

"Back off, back off now!" one of the officers shouted at Jack, his pistol pointed at Jack's chest.

"Don't move, don't even twitch," Jack muttered to Zoe, and then yelled out, "I'm a cop . . . can I open my jacket to show you my shield?"

"Move slow, real slow," the officer cautioned. His partner stood back, keeping his gun aimed at Zoe.

Jack opened his jacket just enough to display the badge attached to his belt. The lead cop approached him hesitantly, and then said, "Jack? Is that really you?"

"Yeah . . . hey, Bobby, how ya doing, man?"

"Not so good today," said the cop, lowering his gun. "Can't believe we're going through this hell again. Hey, I thought they bounced you for messing up that priest's face."

"Nah, just stuck me under a mountain of paper. I been working cold cases for the last 100 years."

"Well, better than still pounding a beat at 50."

"So can we go through? I've got a suspect I really need to question in Hoboken."

"Sorry, Jack, nobody's allowed through the tunnel unless they have a military pass."

"Come on, Bobby, cut me some slack. I'm following up on a lead in Jersey that could connect with this mess. I gotta follow up. I'd call the feds in, but none of the damn phones are working."

"Sorry, man, they're making no exceptions. The National Guard's calling the shots on this one. You believe this? Nearly 30 years on the force, and I'm taking orders from some Army brat with zits on his face."

"I hear ya, pal. Hey, how's your boy doing? Still with the hook and ladder?"

"Yeah, yeah. Get this: The kid's a captain now, running his own firehouse. Remember when he and Liam used to play in your backyard and . . .

uh, Jack, I'm real sorry. It's been so long since I've seen you. We were all torn up about Liam—"

"Thank you," Jack answered abruptly, looking down. "This mess kind of brings it all right back."

"Don't you know it. My stomach flipped when I heard the blast." Bobby looked Jack and Zoe over carefully, and then said, "You really got a lead on this—someone connected to this bridge thing?"

"Swear to Christ, Bobby. It's from a cold case I been working on, a bomb maker in Hoboken. I don't know if it'll pan out, but if it does, maybe it could save a couple of our boys from getting blown to hell."

"Yeah, I hear ya. But I like I said, the Guard's in charge now. I tell ya what . . . for old time's sake, I'll make it right with them. But before I stick my neck out, tell me something straight. Are you still crazy, Jack? I mean, riding around on that chopper like Peter freakin' Fonda?"

"No, man. I saw a shrink for years. I'm good. I swear to Christ, I'm on the job. The Harley's the best thing to get through traffic, that's all."

"Who's she?"

"Her? This is my girlfriend. Now, ask yourself: Could an old slob like me land a babe like her if I was crazy?"

"Good point."

"I just didn't want to leave her in the city with all that's happening."

Zoe leaned forward and kissed Jack on the cheek. "He *is* crazy—crazy in love," she said.

"Uh-huh. I think you're a little young for him, sweetheart, but what the hell, we could all be dead tomorrow, right? Wait here. And, Jack, take my advice, don't move till I come back."

Jack looked at the young soldiers nervously fingering their machine guns, and nodded his head. "You got it, Bobby."

"So, introducing me as your girlfriend already?" Zoe asked sarcastically, as Bobby walked over to the soldiers.

"Maybe I should have introduced you as a cop-bashing, lie-spinning, sleazeball tabloid reporter?"

"Ah, no—girlfriend was a good idea."

Jack saw Bobby arguing with the soldiers. "This could take some time," he said.

"Jack, I think we're just about out of time."

CHAPTER 22

FRANK SQUINTED THROUGH THE PICKUP'S CRACKED WINDSHIELD, trying to see beyond the mist rising up in front of him after he'd entered the tunnel.

It was the strangest thing he'd ever seen—as though they'd driven into a dense white cloud, visibility went from 100 percent to practically zero in seconds.

This is too weird . . . I can't see anything, Frank thought. *Nothing at all. Where in the hell are we?*

. . . there is no hell. Franklin, I love you . . .

I love you, too, Sarah, Frank thought, and then shook his head to clear the cobwebs.

What, am I hearing things now? he wondered, then looked at his daughter.

"Did you just say something to me, Sammy?"

"No, I didn't, but this fog is really cool, isn't it?"

"I wouldn't call it 'cool.' Are you sure you just didn't say something like 'There is no hell' . . . and

'I love you'?"

"No . . . I mean, yeah, I know there's no hell, and *of course* I love you . . . but I didn't say anything." Then she gave him a sudden look of excitement.

"Oh, Daddy, are you starting to hear God language, too?"

"What? 'God language'? No, Sammy. It's been a long, long day and . . . where the hell is this fog coming from?!" Frank shouted, confused by the strange mist, and angry that he was moving so slowly. He turned on his headlights, but the beams just bounced back into his eyes.

He rolled down the window and stuck his head out. The mist felt warm and soft against his face, like a caress. And the smell was so . . . sweet, like the fragrant jasmine potpourri Sarah used to leave all over the house in her hand-painted ceramic bowls.

Frank pulled his head back inside, thinking, *What* is *this stuff?*

They'd passed the halfway point of the tunnel, crossing the New York–New Jersey border, and were moving beneath the Hudson River, nearly a hundred feet underwater.

But the cloud, or fog, or whatever it was, kept closing in on them, tighter and tighter, until Frank couldn't see at all.

Thank God they've closed the tunnel, or we'd have had a head-on collision by now.

He knew that they had to be close to the New Jersey exit, but he had to slow the truck to a crawl.

"Hurry up, Daddy. They're waiting for us," Samantha said impatiently.

"Who's waiting?"

"All of them. . . ."

"Well, whoever you're talking about, Sammy, is going have to wait a little longer. This fog . . . I've never seen anything like it. I have to stop for a few minutes until it clears or I'll hit something."

Frank put on his hazard lights, pulled over to what he guessed was the side of the road, shifted to neutral, and killed the engine. He turned on the radio to see if he could get a report on where the tunnel fog was coming from, but there was only static. Then the radio died and the headlights went out. He tried to start the engine, but nothing happened.

Now the battery's dead? Frank looked at his daughter in confusion, and said, "Listen, Sammy, if you've got nothing else to pray about right at this moment, you might consider praying that no cars come up behind us because—"

But before he'd finished his sentence, they were rear-ended hard enough to push the truck down the tunnel several yards.

Frank's chest bounced off the steering wheel.

"Son of a bitch!" Frank yelled into the rear-view mirror at the limousine that had plowed into them. His anger was instantly usurped by panic when he saw that Samantha had undone her seat belt just after the impact, slid onto the floor, and was now curled up in the fetal position.

Frank reached down, lifted her into his arms, and shouted, "Sammy! Sammy! Wake up! Please talk to me. Please, honey!"

Samantha's eyes were shut tight. He couldn't understand why she'd be unconscious—the collision had been a relatively minor one, not too much worse than a bad fender bender.

Frank shook her gently, tears welling up in his eyes. "Come on, Sammy," he pleaded. "For Daddy, please. Just open your eyes."

Her eyes opened. She focused on her father's face and smiled. "I'm okay, Daddy. I just had a really, really bad feeling about what's behind us, and I guess I got scared for a second. I'm all right now."

Frank laughed in relief, and kissed her all over her face and forehead.

"When I saw you lying on the floor, I got a bad feeling too," he said, instinctively checking her neck and collarbone for fractures. She seemed fine . . . more than fine. There was color in her face, and she was warmer than she'd been all day. He checked her pulse; it was strong and steady. In fact, she looked better and seemed livelier than she'd been in months.

"Do you hurt anywhere, honey? Your head? Your tummy? Your back?"

"No, Daddy. Like I said, I just got scared . . . and that scared me even more, because you know I'm almost never afraid."

"I know, Sammy. It's this fog we're stuck in. It feels so spooky."

"Oh, no, it wasn't the fog. The fog is friendly— it loves us. It's what hit us that's scary."

"The fog loves us? Whatever you say, kid. Can you sit tight for a minute? I have to check on our passengers in the back, and then I'll see who hit us to make sure they're not too evil, okay?"

"Okay, but please be careful."

As Frank stepped out of the truck, the lights running along the length of the tunnel's ceiling blinked out one at time, like a mile-and-a-half-long line of fluorescent dominoes disappearing into the distance. He should have been standing in complete darkness, but there was a pale glow emanating from the fog itself, as though the mist was charged with some kind of internal energy source.

This is absolutely freakin' weird, Frank thought, looking back at Samantha. Aloud, he told her, "Now I mean it, Sammy. You stay right there— don't move until I check things out."

"See ya later, alligator," Samantha laughed. "But everything is okay now. I just realized that we're safe. We're here . . . we're finally here."

We're stuck *here, that's for sure,* Frank realized, moving to the rear of the truck.

He looked into the back and saw Katherine and Conrad digging their way out from beneath a pile of turf.

"Everyone alive back here?" Frank asked, sticking his hands into a thick sod roll and shoving it aside.

"I think we're fine," Conrad said. "This grass really cushioned us. What did you hit?"

"I didn't hit anything; someone hit us," Frank said, already walking toward the limo that had stopped about 15 feet down the tunnel, and which was barely visible in the hazy light.

The hair on the back of his neck stood up, and his soldier's survival instincts went on high alert when he saw BIOWLD2 stamped on the license plate.

BioWorld? Why do these guys keep smashing into my life? Do I have the cops and *the BioWorld goons chasing me?*

When Frank got to the limo, he saw blood splattered on the inside of the windshield and the driver's body slumped over the wheel.

What the hell? Did he smash his head against the glass?

He tried the door, but it was locked. Then he began rapping on the window.

"Hey, buddy, you okay?" he asked.

The man didn't move. Frank leaned in closer and noticed a hole in the side of the driver's head, and a gun on the passenger seat.

Frank jumped back.

What's going on here? Why did this guy shoot himself? This is all too much. . . .

The rest of the limo's windows were darkly tinted, and all the doors were locked. Frank banged on the roof, but there was no reply.

He walked back to the pickup and found Conrad and Katherine kneeling on the truck bed, brushing dirt off each other.

"What happened?" Conrad asked Frank.

"You tell me. It was one of your damned security limos that smashed into us."

The truck's back window slid open, and Samantha's face appeared. She surveyed the back of the truck, then looked at Katherine and asked, "Are you Kathy?"

"Yes, I am," Katherine replied, crawling over to the window. She gently touched the little girl's face and asked, "Are you hurt, sweetheart?"

"Nope, just really, really sick."

"I know," Katherine said, grimacing for several seconds as a scorching pain passed through her body. "You've been hurting for a long time, haven't you?"

"Yeah, but my mom says it won't hurt much longer, and she said you'd help me."

"Your mom . . . Sarah, right?" As Katherine spoke the words, she remembered Italy and knew instantly that this little girl was the same one she'd seen in the vision that had pulled her back to New York.

"Yeah, Sarah's my mom," Samantha said.

"She's with us."

"She's been talking to me all day in God language."

"Well, now she's showing me a picnic basket. Do you know what that means?" Katherine asked.

Frank's hand landed heavily on Katherine's shoulder, and he pulled her away from the window.

"What are you talking to my daughter about?!" Frank shouted. He looked at Conrad angrily. "Who the hell does this woman think she is?"

"She's a psychic. She's . . . *odd*. Christ, I don't know anymore. I think she might even be on the level."

"Yeah, well, she should stay away from my daughter." Turning to Katherine, he fumed, "What do *you* know about Sarah?"

"Not much. I'm just feeling her energy now. She was funny and very kind, she gave herself to others, and she loved you—both of you—very deeply. I know that much. She's showing me an old potbelly stove . . . a Franklin stove . . . is that your name?" Katherine paused and looked Frank in the eye. "Do you have any idea how open your daughter's faith has made her to the spirit world?"

Frank stared in disbelief.

"I know how you feel, Frank," Conrad sympathized. "But she kind of grows on you after a while."

"Thanks a lot," Katherine said wryly. "But that's a pretty cheap compliment coming from a trillionaire."

"You're right, you deserve better," Conrad said, reaching over and pulling a clump of sod from her long red hair. Then he turned and looked out at the glowing ring of white mist surrounding them. "Where are we? What is all this fog?"

Katherine wasn't sure what it was, but she felt its energy penetrating her very being. It was the same feeling she'd get when she conducted a highly charged group reading.

"We're nearly through the tunnel, but the truck's battery is dead. We're going to have to walk out of here and hitch a ride to Hoboken," Frank told the others.

Then they heard a car door open, and General Wilson stepped out of the back of the limo, saying, "We're the only ones going to Hoboken. None of you are going anywhere—*ever!*" He had a briefcase in one hand and his silver pistol in the other.

"Wilson? What are you—I told you to stay in the BioWorld Tower, to stay with Daniel."

"I'm afraid the Tower will be closed for a century or so, Mr. Dinnick, and I *am* with Daniel . . . *sir.*"

The young man got out of the limo behind Wilson.

"Danny, why are you here? What's going on?" Conrad asked, completely perplexed.

"I've g-got . . . bad news . . . D-Dad."

Katherine climbed down from the truck, rubbing her eyes as she stared at Daniel—but the vision was still there. Superimposed just above his head was an image of the Archangel Michael.

"Michael," she whispered.

CHAPTER 23

"YOU'RE A DIFFICULT MAN TO KILL, MR. DINNICK," Wilson said, pointing his gun at Conrad through the mist. "I should have taken care of you myself. I don't know how you survived the helicopter 'accident' I had planned for you, but I assure you, you won't escape this tunnel."

Frank moved forward, quickly placing himself between Wilson and Samantha.

"Nobody moves—including you, gardener, unless you want me to put your daughter out of her misery right now."

"Stay in the truck, sweetie," Frank ordered Samantha over his shoulder, never taking his eyes off the man with the gun. To him, Frank said, "I know you. You're General John Wilson . . . you got me hired to landscape the island."

"Affirmative, Sergeant Dell. Amazing how much the Army's simple psychological profile reveals about a person, isn't it? Yours just screamed *fall guy.* If our plans fouled up at any point, all we had to do was hang everything on you—the embittered explosives expert; an Islamic sympathizer, flat broke, with a dying daughter and extreme animosity toward the U.S. government for killing his wife. You were *perfect*."

"You set me up?" Frank was incredulous.

"Your profile also said you weren't the swiftest dog in the race. Now use your left hand to remove that gun sticking out of your pants, drop it on the road, and kick it toward me. And don't forget, I can shoot your daughter as easily as I can shoot you."

Frank dropped the gun and kicked it hard. It clattered across the pavement and was swallowed up by the wall of mist.

Wilson looked at his watch, then at Daniel. "I have no idea what this fog is, or where it's coming from—maybe a burst steam pipe. Looks like our car is out of commission. And I've dealt with that incompetent chauffeur. But if we take their pickup truck, we can still make our meeting. We'll be there in less than ten minutes, make the delivery, get the cash, and then catch our flight."

"The satellite phone?" Daniel asked.

"It's still searching for a signal. It'll let us know as soon as it's found a viable satellite and is connected. After that, it's countdown time. By then the briefcase will be in Hoboken, and we'll be on our way."

"What's he talking about, Danny? What cash? What flight?!" Conrad demanded, jumping from the back of the truck. "What have you gotten my son involved in, Wilson? Are *you* the terrorist? I entrusted you with my business, my labs, my boys' safety—my life. You're a general in the U.S. Army, for God's sake, an American soldier, a *patriot*. But I guess you're really nothing but a filthy, murderous traitor, aren't you? *My God! The bridge, the tram . . . all those people!*"

"A traitor?" Wilson laughed. "To *what?* A country with no moral values, where Presidents have sex with interns in the Oval Office, where women are promoted to be five-star generals over men like me, where gays marry each other, and where 70 percent of our citizens are too cowardly or too fat to fight for their flag?

"I've betrayed nothing—it's patriots like me who've been betrayed. But thanks to you and your money, Mr. Dinnick, I can set up my own army, establish a state where true Americans— and American values—will be embraced and defended."

"What are you talking about?!"

"Nothing you would understand, Mr. Dinnick, *sir,*" Wilson spat out bitterly. "Frankly, you've always disgusted me. That's why I singled you out years ago to bankroll my plans. You think you're a god, but all you've ever done with your money, privilege, and power is undermine the security and the values of this once-great nation."

"I've done nothing but serve this country and save lives my entire career," Conrad said, shaking his head in disbelief.

"You've done nothing but make yourself rich off the rest of us!" Wilson yelled at him. "You convinced our so-called government that your bioscience and vaccines can defend us against terrorists. The President should have nuked all the terrorist states into submission years ago—that was our only sure method of defense. But that fool wouldn't pay attention to me because he was listening to people like you. Now they're convinced we're safe from germ warfare, when really it's only a matter of time—"

"Oh, God!" Katherine cried, her ears pounding with the sickening rhythm of marching boots, her mind reeling from the sights and sounds of soldiers . . . screaming children, street battles, tanks . . . a city in flames. "He's planning some kind of coup . . . to overthrow a government . . . somewhere . . ."

"Shut up, psychic! For someone who earns her living selling foresight, you've failed to glimpse the greatest future ever envisioned," Wilson smirked.

He turned back to Conrad. "You said I was an American soldier. Well, I *am*, but *this* is no longer my America. Thanks to your money, and your son's inventiveness, I'll soon be running my own nation-state in South America—still an *American* country, but one a man can be proud to call home."

"You're a lunatic! And you're insane to think I'd ever finance whatever evil plot you're trying to hatch!" Conrad screamed.

"You don't have to, because your son already did. Do have any idea how many mercenaries I can buy with $30 billion?"

"What $30 billion? What's he talking about, Daniel?"

"Not Daniel . . . *Michael*," Katherine corrected, standing at Conrad's side.

"Katherine, *please,* I told you: Michael's dead and gone. Daniel is the only son I have left."

"No! *Daniel* is dead, but trust me, he's not *gone*—he's here with us now."

"Your time is up, lady," Wilson said to Katherine, leveling his gun at her. "I don't know how or why you ended up at the Tower this morning, but you've caused nothing but trouble. It's going to be a pleasure to send you to—what do you call it—the *Other Side?*"

The briefcase in Wilson's left hand beeped three times, and a thin, electronic voice announced: *Viable satellite detected. Estimated time to connection . . . five minutes.*

Wilson handed the briefcase to Daniel, keeping his gun trained on Katherine and the others. "It's almost time, son. In a few more minutes, we'll flick the switch and get out of here."

"Yes, sir," Daniel answered firmly, kneeling on the road and opening the case.

"Daniel, what are you doing—"

"Well, it's like Mr. Wilson has been saying to me for the past two years, Dad. Today is Judgment Day."

"I don't understand . . ."

Daniel looked at his father with contempt, and when he spoke, his voice was clear and even. "Dad, can you explain to me how someone who advises the President and has two Nobel Prizes can be so blind and stupid?" He laughed sarcastically.

"*Michael?*" Conrad gasped. He looked at Katherine, who nodded at him sympathetically, and then he turned back to his son.

"Michael, is it really you?"

Michael smiled. "In the flesh, back from the dead, and never to return."

CHAPTER 24

**CONRAD STARED AT THE YOUNG MAN IN FRONT OF
HIM** in complete confusion, desperately trying to
understand what was happening. "But . . . if you're
Michael . . . then Danny is—"

"Dead, of course," Michael said flatly.

"Did you—"

"Kill him? No, he killed himself. I won't say I
was *completely* guiltless. We had an agreement—I'd
let him steal money from you, and he'd let me—"

"Danny steal from me? That's impossible.
He wouldn't know how, and it would be totally
against his nature."

"That's so like you, Dad. You never did give
Danny any credit, did you? He was actually quite
brilliant, even daring—a regular modern-day
Robin Hood. You looked at him and saw a stuttering loser, but for years he was quietly siphon-
ing billions away from you to build factories in
developing countries so that they could make
their own affordable medicines, instead of buying

them from BioWorld. So he not only took your money, he used it to flood your biggest customer base with cheap, black-market drugs."

Conrad was stunned. What Michael was saying actually made sense. His accountants had told him only that morning that huge sums of money had "gone missing." And BioWorld's lucrative sales of antiviral drugs to the developing world had plummeted in recent years. This also explained Danny's sudden interest in working at the Hoboken lab after Michael's death—or what he'd *thought* had been Michael's death.

"You've been pretending to be Danny for two years so you could keep conducting your own experiments in Hoboken?!" Conrad asked in disbelief.

"Ah, the blind begin to see," Michael said calmly, enjoying his father's rage. "But as I was saying, I do share some of the responsibility for Danny's suicide. He knew that my experiments were illegal, and I knew about his thievery, so we agreed to turn a blind eye to each other . . . on the condition he let me use him for a few Project PAT experiments."

"My God, Michael, you didn't! PAT is years away from human trials. That's why I built the Supercomputer Re-Creation Center—to test it. Injecting Danny would have—"

"Killed him? No, I'd tested it on myself many times first, and I'm perfectly fine. But unfortunately, poor Danny developed that malignant brain tumor and couldn't face a long and painful death."

"What? No . . . if you've injected yourself with PAT, your mind must be so mixed up, your thinking so muddled. Oh, Michael, you've made yourself so sick. What have you done?" Conrad cried out.

"Don't worry about what I've done in the past. It's what I'm going to do now that will really impress you, Dad. Your Project PAT is child's play, nothing but a joke. I've gone light years beyond your research. Didn't *you* name it PAT, for *Project Aeternus Eternus*—life everlasting? But you just can't envision that, can you? All you can imagine is 'creating' transplant organs, or developing vaccines, or curing diseases. Remember when I told you that death was the sickness we had to end? That *that* should have been the goal of PAT? Well I've been working on it for years, and I'm going to do it—end cellular decay and stop the biological clock from ticking on toward death."

"Michael, son . . . only a madman would try to completely *end* the aging process. PAT was created to cure disease, to allow people to live healthier, more productive, and yes, even *longer* lives—not to conquer death. It's insane to even think it's possible—"

"No, Dad, I'm completely sane, and it *is* possible, which I'll prove in just a couple more years. All I need is my own lab, where people won't constantly question my methods. And with the help of Mr. Wilson, in a few days I'll have that lab and—"

"Wilson? How is he going to help you do anything but destroy your life? He's a paranoid, homicidal maniac."

"Maybe so, but you better remember that this 'maniac' has a gun pointed at you," Wilson broke in. He looked at Michael. "Let's cut this short, son. I can take care of them now, and we can be on our way."

"Why do you keep calling him 'son,' you psychopath?" Conrad yelled.

"Wilson's been more of a father to me than you ever were!" Michael spat out at Conrad. "And who are you to call anyone homicidal? You killed everything Danny and I ever loved. First you pushed Mother out of our lives forever, then you *murdered* Grandmother."

Conrad blanched. "What are you talking about?"

"Danny saw you kill her, saw you stick a needle in her arm and pump her full of poison until she stopped breathing. He told me everything—the image haunted him for the rest of his life, and he was never the same. Why do you think he started stuttering? He use to have such a sweet voice. Remember how he used to sing for us? But you killed that, too."

"No, no, no, Michael! No one saw that . . . you boys were in the—"

"How would you know where we were? You *never* paid attention to us!"

"I didn't murder her. She was so sick . . . in such pain. I just increased the dosage of the medication she was already on. She begged me to release her!" Conrad cried, visibly upset by the memory.

"No! You were playing God, like always," Michael said.

"No, he wasn't," Katherine countered, while placing a comforting hand on Conrad's back. She had a fleeting image of Conrad at his mother's bedside, sliding a needle out of her arm, his eyes brimming with tears as he kissed her good-bye, and his mother thanking him over and over.

"Conrad, you did what your mother needed you to do—ease her pain," Katherine said. "She thanks you for ending her suffering. I sensed that you'd caused her passing when we were in the helicopter, but I didn't see how until now. . . . She's showing me her symbol of love for you, Conrad: blue roses."

Katherine turned to Michael. "Your grandmother wants to help ease *your* pain, too, Michael. She's showing me a darkness around you . . . that you've brought a terrible sickness upon yourself . . . but I feel that the darkness isn't permanent, that you can find help . . . you must—"

"Ms. Haywood," Michael snapped in disgust, "I'm a great believer in the untapped potential of the mind. I actually believe that you possess a unique ability. You've shown consistent and extraordinary prescience throughout the day. Of course there's no afterlife, but obviously an area of your brain has developed in greater proportion to the rest of us. I'd love to have your brain removed and preserved for future study."

"I'm not quite done with it," Katherine bristled.

"You will be soon!" Wilson told her, as the computerized voice in the briefcase Michael was leaning over announced: *Satellite connection established. Trigger function operational.*

"Well, Michael, that's our cue. It's time to go. Flip the switch, I'll get the package out of the limo, and we're out of here," Wilson said.

"Just a few more minutes, Mr. Wilson?" Michael asked, suddenly looking faint and holding his head.

"What's wrong with you?" Wilson demanded.

"Nothing, I'm fine . . . I mean . . . ," Michael replied, recovering his composure. " . . . I mean, I'd like a few minutes with my dad—kind of a going-away present. He was supposed to have been killed in the helicopter, but by some incredible coincidence I've met up with him one last time in this tunnel—"

"There are no coincidences. The fact that your production assistant found me in Italy and got me to come back here is proof of that," Katherine insisted.

"Fine, fate brought us together—whatever. It's my chance to show my dad what I'm going to achieve after he's dead. How much greater a scientist I'll be than he ever was."

"Michael, you're sick," Conrad pleaded. "All those injections have damaged your mind, and Wilson has obviously brainwashed you, but I can help. We can hire specialists—"

"Help me what? Find the real *Aeternus Eternus*—find immortality? Because that's what I'm on the threshold of finding myself, Dad. That's probably part of the reason why Danny killed himself—he realized that after all those years of arguing with me, I'd been right—God really was just a myth. It must have been too much for him to bear.

"He left a suicide note. Want to know what it said, Dad? *'Of every tree of the garden thou mayest freely eat: But of the tree of the knowledge of good and evil, thou shalt not eat of it . . .'* After all those years at divinity school, you'd think he'd come up with more poignant parting words. Let's face it, Dad, Danny just didn't have our stomach for the forbidden fruit—that lust to tease the hidden secrets from the double helix."

"That's from the Bible, what he said . . . Genesis 2:16–17!" Samantha shouted, climbing down from the cab of the pickup.

Wilson swung his gun in her direction, and Frank jumped in front of her, imploring, "Please don't. She's just a child!"

"She's a precocious little towel-head brat who refuses to die. I've memorized your profile, gardener, and the cancer should have killed her long ago."

"You're right, maybe she is a brat. She's got a photographic memory and likes to quote the Bible. She's got a big, big mouth, but she's still just a little girl."

"I'm not afraid of him, Daddy. Mom says not to be afraid."

"Shut up, Sammy!" Frank pleaded.

"No, I won't. What that other man said about tasting the forbidden fruit, that's only part of the verse. It finishes: *'. . . for in the day that thou eatest thereof thou shalt surely die.'*"

Frank clapped his hand over Samantha's mouth.

"Shut that kid up or she shall surely die *right now*," Wilson said to Frank, then looked at Michael. "You have a green light, so flip the switch. We have to go soon or risk missing our connection."

"Mr. Wilson, please. I've done everything you've asked, and it's all in motion . . . just a few moments more," Michael said, looking at Samantha. "That's right, little girl," he told her. "If you know the Garden of Eden story, I'm sure you know that God didn't forbid Adam and Eve to eat the fruit because it would kill them, but because He was afraid it would give them the same knowledge He possessed. That it would make *them* Gods."

Samantha pushed her father's hand away from her mouth.

"No, mister, that's just what the devil said to trick Eve. In Genesis 3:4—"

"*Sammy, shut up now!*" Frank yelled.

"That's all right, let her speak. She reminds me of myself at her age. Ever have her IQ tested?" Michael asked, turning his attention away from briefcase.

"What?" Frank asked.

"Her IQ . . . did you ever have it tested?"

"What does—"

"For Christ's sake, answer the man!" Wilson yelled impatiently. "If you say *what* again, I'll shoot her."

"Yes, yes, yes, we tested her . . . it was over 200," Frank spat out. "They said it had to be a mistake. They wanted to test her again, but she got sick and I wouldn't let them."

"Over 200? Just like Conrad over there, and just like me. You know what they call that, gardener, having a 200-plus IQ?"

"Yes, some kind of genius," Frank answered, his arms wrapped protectively around Samantha.

"Some kind of genius? That's your brilliant summary? They call us immeasurable geniuses. I scored 212. Since the gene therapy, I've jumped to over 280."

"Impossible," Conrad murmured.

"Quite possible, Dad. And it's only the beginning. The potential for PAT is immeasurable." The briefcase speaker punctuated his sentence: *Trigger active: on standby.*

"What *is* that?" Frank asked, staring at the flashing lights and wires inside the case, already fearing the worst.

"That's something right up your alley, Mr. Dell," Wilson said. "It's a detonator for a dirty bomb in the basement of the BioWorld Tower. I wanted to leave this country making sure that Conrad Dinnick was not only dead, but also that the world wouldn't remember him as the great man of medical science he pretends to be. Instead, he'd be remembered as the man who spewed radiation into the heart of Manhattan."

"How did you get a dirty bomb into New York City? With all the new security precautions, it's impossible," Frank said.

"Not impossible for a U.S. Army general," Wilson snapped.

"Is that what you're using my money for, Michael?" Conrad asked incredulously. "To bomb New York and hurt thousands of innocent people?"

"What?" Michael sounded confused, and held his head in his hands again. He stared at the briefcase, then at Wilson, and finally at his father. "No . . . no . . . the Tower's been evacuated and sealed," he continued. "No one's going to get hurt . . . only the building will be contaminated. Isn't that right, Mr. Wilson?"

"Yes, that's right, son," Wilson said. "But don't start losing it now, Michael. Keep yourself together until we've made the pickup and delivery in Hoboken."

"A pickup in Hoboken? Michael, please tell me you haven't taken anything from the Level 4 lab," Conrad pleaded with him, sounding increasingly panicked.

"Well, Dad, I'd already given Mr. Wilson all the money left over from Danny's stealing so that he could hire soldiers and build my lab in South America, so we needed something else to give the terrorists in exchange for the bomb."

"Terrorists? Oh God in heaven! Michael, you didn't give terrorists one of our viruses? You wouldn't have."

"Not one of *our* viruses, and not one of *your* viruses. It was all *my* creation," Michael said, sounding like a proud little boy.

"God, no . . . what have you made?"

"I call it Seventh Heaven, Dad."

"Seventh Heaven?"

"It's a beautiful bug; you'd be proud. A new family recipe. The engineering was tricky, but basically it's just seven extremely deadly viruses: Ebola, smallpox, Marburg, hantavirus, SARS, Lassa virus, and a dash of Spanish influenza. You mix them all together, then reduce it to an aerosol, and there you have it: Seventh Heaven."

"No, no, no," Conrad mumbled, his shoulders sagging with the realization of what his son had done. "Please, tell me you didn't."

"Oh, but I did, and it's lovely. An airborne virus that will spread like a brush fire in a high wind and has a 95 percent mortality rate. I even have the vaccine. Not enough yet, but I will as soon as . . ." Michael's voice trailed off, as though he were drifting into a stupor.

Conrad pulled himself together and shouted, "Michael, listen to me! Where have you stored it? If something like that ever gets loose . . . please, tell me it's safely stored."

"Huh? What? Of course I stored it safely, Dad," Michael responded, alert again. "It's locked up in the Hoboken Level 4, and of course, I have full access to it. In fact, we're going there now to get the new virus and give it to our friends. And then we'll leave the briefcase in the lab to make sure all your most precious buildings are destroyed. Thirty minutes after I hit this little switch, the world will remember you as it should, just like Mr. Wilson said: not as the brilliant scientist, but as the Monster of Manhattan."

"You can't do this! Son, you need help! We'll cure you, I swear. I'll move heaven and earth to help you. I'll stand by you to the end."

"Really, Dad?"

"*This is the end!*" Wilson broke in, slapping Michael's face. "Snap out of it, boy. I *need* you to get into the lab. Remember our plan—our mission isn't completed yet."

Wilson reached down into the briefcase, but Michael pushed his hand away. "No, it's mine . . . I'm going to do it. I'm going to play God," he whined, sounding even more like a little boy.

"Then shut up and do it!" Wilson growled.

"What have you done to my son?" Conrad demanded.

"Nothing. Nothing at all. Whatever he is now, it's because *you* made him that way," Wilson snapped. Then he yelled at Michael again: "Do it now!"

At the sound of the harsh command, Michael suddenly came out of his daze. He put his finger on the gold switch.

"Wait, mister," Samantha said. "You don't want to destroy everything, do you?"

Michael paused, looking at Samantha. "I'm not destroying, kid, I'm creating. How would you like to play a little game my brother and I used to play when we were kids? We called it 'Creation.' I said everything started with the big bang. He said everything started with God. Do you know anything about creation myths?"

"Yeah, lots—and my name is Samantha, not kid," Samantha said.

"All right, *Samantha*, the Egyptians believed that—"

"Nun, the God of watery chaos created the—"

"Very good," Michael said, running his finger over the switch. "How about the Africans?"

"Which ones?"

"Oh, let's say . . . Zulu."

"The creator Unkulunkulu brought people to the earth," Samantha answered.

"Hey, gardener, your kid's a real brainiac—too bad she's dying. I'll need bright people like her when I set up my new world," Wilson told Frank. "She must have gotten her smarts from her towel-head mother, because you're clearly a moron."

"My mother says you're a bad, bad man!" the little girl announced.

"Really? You talk to her?" Wilson asked with a gleam in his eye. "Well, say hi for me. Last time I saw her was when I gave the order to have her shot so I could set up your daddy. Don't worry, though, I made sure she died quickly."

"You goddamn murdering bastard—you killed Sarah!" Frank screamed, rushing at Wilson.

Wilson cocked the hammer of his gun and pointed it at Samantha's head.

"Frank, stop! The child!" Conrad yelled.

Frank stopped dead, eyes wild with rage, his chest heaving.

"You may not be very bright, Dell, but you *are* an arms expert. Tell me . . . what am I holding in my hand?" Wilson asked.

"A .44 Magnum," Frank rasped through clenched teeth.

"Is it an effective weapon?"

"Extremely."

"Then if you don't want me to use it on your kid, I suggest you step back against the truck and don't move again. Let Samantha and Michael finish their nice little chat so I can get him out of here before he loses his wits completely."

"This isn't a nice chat," Samantha said to Wilson. "And my mom says that you're sicker than

I am . . . and that she's looking forward to seeing you real soon."

"Isn't that sweet," Wilson smirked.

The circle of fog that had been surrounding them began closing in, becoming denser and brighter.

Michael looked into Samantha's dark eyes. "You've got guts, kid, I'll give you that. Now come on, let's finish our game . . . what about Buddhism?"

Samantha crossed her arms in front of her chest. "I'm not playing anymore," she said.

"Samantha, please, *for me?* Answer him!" Frank pleaded.

"Okay . . . for you, Frank. Buddha began his journey toward enlightenment after leaving his palace as a little prince and wandering among the poor and sick and—"

"Right on the money. How about the Hindus?"

"Hindus believe that the thousand-headed God of Immortality, Purusha, wrapped his arms—"

"You've almost won the big prize," Michael praised.

"Mister, it doesn't matter what different people in different places believe about how the world began. Almost all of them believe that our spirit moves from this world to the next. That it's how we live our life, not how life began, that's important, and that—"

"Now you're sounding like my brother," Michael said wearily. He shook his head. "I just have one last question, Samantha. What about the Jews and Christians?"

She answered, "Out of the void and chaos God said, 'Let there be light.'"

"Right again," Michael answered. "Now, here's your prize. Something you've never read or heard anywhere—not a creation myth, but a creation *fact*. It goes like this: *And in the tunnel deep beneath the waves, Michael Dinnick wrapped his finger around the switch and said 'Let the New World begin.'*"

He began to push the switch but stopped. He stood up, looking around, lost and bewildered. He looked at his father, and then he looked at Wilson.

"I can't," he said. "People . . . people . . . will be *hurt* . . . Mr. Wilson . . . please don't make me."

"You sniveling wimp!" Wilson yelled, shoving him out of the way as he bent down, stuck his hand in the briefcase, and flipped the switch. Then he turned and faced the group, pointing the gun at Conrad. "You go first, Dinnick."

But before he had a chance to pull the trigger, a single beam of light pierced the mist, followed by the high whining of a fully revved, rapidly approaching engine.

Wilson shielded his eyes against the blinding brightness of the motorcycle's high beam. He pointed the gun toward the light and pulled the trigger.

The shot echoed down the tunnel.

The intense blue light of a .38-caliber muzzle flash pierced the thick mist.

Wilson's hands flew up to his chest, pawing briefly at the gaping wound that tore through his heart, before he collapsed onto the road.

The Harley burst through the wall of mist. Jack was holding his service revolver in one hand, trying to control the bike's handlebars with the other. Zoe clung to Jack as he hit the brakes, sending the motorcycle into a tire-screeching skid. The big bike dropped onto its side and came sliding toward them in a shower of red and orange sparks.

"Daddy!" Samantha shouted.

Frank grabbed his daughter and jumped into the rear of the truck.

The motorcycle's front tire hit Michael just below the knees, tossing him high in the air.

He vanished into the fog.

CHAPTER 25

"SAMMY, ARE YOU ALL RIGHT?"

"You're crushing me, Frank."

"Sorry."

Frank sat up quickly and noticed that the fog was thickening around them. He lifted his daughter and held her tightly against him—she felt cold again, and her pulse was weak. He wanted to run out of the tunnel with her, but he still couldn't see anything beyond the mist engulfing them.

Samantha began choking, gasping for breath. Noticing that her pale skin was turning blue, Frank ripped off a strip of material from his shirttail and wrapped it around her mouth.

"Breathe through this, sweetie. Maybe it will help."

He peered into the darkness. There was nothing, just the harsh sound of her labored breathing.

"Is anyone else alive?" he shouted. His voice sounded muffled, lifeless in the fog.

"I'm okay, I'm right behind you. I'm not hurt," Katherine said.

"Try to get into the back of the truck. God only knows what will happen if another vehicle comes through here," Frank said. "Conrad, are you out there? Are you okay?"

They could hear him somewhere in the distance, calling out for his son.

"Michael, where are you?"

There was no reply.

"Conrad, come back to the truck! Don't get lost in the mist—there's something very strange happening here!" Katherine called out.

Conrad's voice grew fainter. "Michael . . . where are you, son? Michael . . . come to me, come to your father."

"Conrad, get back here!" Frank yelled. "Jesus, I can't see more than a foot in front of my face. We need some light."

Samantha began to cough harder, a deep rattle echoing in her chest.

Frank heard someone crying several yards away and called, "Who's out there?"

The crying stopped. A gentle female voice was softly pleading for someone to get up. Then the gentleness faded, and the voice grew increasingly stern and demanding: "You stop this, Jack! Do you hear me? You said you'd get me through this. Now say something to me right now! Wake up! Wake up, you crazy bastard!"

They heard the sound of flesh slapping flesh.

"Ouch! Jesus Christ, I've been shot. You didn't have to hit me, too, didja?"

"Oh, Jack, thank God you're alive," Zoe squealed. "You're shot? Where? I don't feel blood."

"I've been shot enough times to know when I've taken a bullet and—ouch, ouch, ouch."

"I found where you were hit."

"I noticed—hey! Watch your hands, woman!"

"Relax. I need to get your belt off so I can use it as a tourniquet. You've been hit in the right thigh, and there's a lot of blood. But you're lucky; I think the bullet missed the femoral artery."

"Suddenly you're a doctor."

"Basic Red Cross field training, and I used to hang out at the morgue a lot."

"The morgue? I don't want to hear about it . . . but how can you tell the bullet missed my—whaddaya call it? My immoral artery?"

"*Femoral* artery. I know it's not severed because if it was, you'd have bled to death by now. But it could be nicked, so shut up while I tighten this belt." Zoe continued to work on him.

"Forget about me. How are *you?*"

"I'm fine. I did like you said and just held on to you. The only thing that hit the ground was my backpack and head. If I hadn't had your helmet . . . but what was that Wild West show you put on before we crashed? Who are you, Quick Draw McGraw? You're not getting crazy on me again, are you?"

"I dunno . . . I saw a guy with a gun, and something or someone guided my hand. Believe it or not, after all those years of being a cop, that was the only time I ever fired my service revolver."

"Well, whatever it was, you only had that one bullet—the one with your name on it. So I take it you won't be shooting *yourself* anytime soon?"

"Let's take it one bullet at a time," Jack grimaced, as Zoe tugged on the belt.

Frank had been listening to the conversation without a clear sense of where the voices were coming from. He felt like he was lost at sea, unable to gain his bearings.

"Where are you—*who* are you people?" Frank asked again.

"My name is Zoe Crane," she answered. "I'm a reporter, and I have a wounded police officer with me. His name is Jack Morgan."

"Does the headlight on your bike work? We need some light," Frank asked.

"Not a chance, pal. It's more busted up than I am," Jack said wryly. In a softer tone, he asked Zoe, "Do you have matches?"

"No, but I have a flashlight in my bag. Just a second . . . oh damn! It's smashed. Oh, wait, there's a spotlight on my palmtop!" Zoe yelled.

A faint orange dot appeared near Frank.

"That's your spotlight?" he asked incredulously.

"No, that's the Record-Active light. The camera's recording, but the spotlight is broken . . . and the damn cigarette smokers in my office must have stolen my matches and lighter."

"So we've got to find our way out of here in the dark?"

Zoe snapped her fingers. "Maybe not. I just remembered that I've got something else in my bag that might work."

There was a crack, then a small pool of red light opened up the darkness.

Emergency road flare, Frank realized, looking down at Samantha. He placed his hand on her chest, distressed by its feeble rise and fall. Pulling the cotton cloth from his daughter's face, he peered into her eyes as best he could in the dim light. Her pupils were glassy and unfocused.

"Oh, my sweet girl, hold on," he whispered.

She drew a crackly breath that made his heart pound. The whistling in her lungs was identical to the noise made by a wounded soldier he'd once carried to a field hospital. The man—only a boy, really—had two punctured lungs and labored for breath as Samantha did now. That soldier had died in Frank's arms.

"We're almost home now, right, Daddy?"

"Almost, Sammy. Just hold on a little while longer."

It was difficult for Frank to catch his own breath. He felt light-headed and struggled to assess the situation rationally. *We'll all die in here like rats. Oh, Sarah, please help me.*

"Don't be frightened," Samantha whispered. "Mommy hears you."

Her voice was so faint that Frank couldn't make out what she was saying. "Don't speak, Sammy, save your breath," he told her, then turned in the direction of the road flare that was illuminating Zoe and Jack.

"Hey, lady—I mean, Zoe, do you have any more flares with you?" Frank asked.

"No, just that one, and it's old. It might last 20 minutes, tops," Zoe answered.

"Why are you carrying a flare, anyway?"

"Because I'm a reporter, and I covered 9/11 from Ground Zero with nothing but a notebook and pen. After that, I vowed never to go anywhere in this city without my emergency bag."

"What else have you got in there?"

"What do you need? Water, bandages, disinfectant, a thermal blanket, a radiation meter, anti-radiation pills, a stun gun, superglue, a tube of Chanel lipstick, two tampons, an oxygen canister, a whistle—"

"Oxygen?"

"Yeah, one canister—30 minutes' worth."

"Please, my daughter can't breathe—"

"One second," Zoe said, tightening Jack's belt just below his hip. "You stay put," she told him, carrying her bag to the pickup and getting her first look at Samantha.

"Oh, she looks really sick—," Zoe started saying, handing Frank the small oxygen cylinder.

"I've got to get her out of here, but this fog . . . I can't move anywhere, and I can't figure out what it is or where it's coming from," he said, putting the oxygen mask over Samantha's mouth.

Frank began twisting the tiny airflow knob at the end of the cylinder. "Damn it, it's stuck! Which way does it turn?" he asked nervously. "I don't want to snap it off . . . I need more light!"

"Wait," Zoe motioned, pulling her camera from the bag. "The damn digital video recorder won't shut off, so everything is being taped, but the LCD screen should be a little brighter."

She held the palmtop's small, glowing screen over the canister, giving Frank enough light to see the arrow pointing left. He twisted the knob, and the cylinder hissed softly.

Samantha's breathing eased immediately. Her eyes focused on Frank's, and she smiled at him.

"Mom says, 'Hello,' Daddy, and . . . she heard you."

"Yeah? Tell her 'Hey' right back. But for now, I need you to lie still and breathe slow and deep," Frank told his daughter, easing her down on the tailgate. He picked up two rolls of sod, tossed them toward the flare, and turned to Katherine.

"Please watch her for just a second. I'm going to try to make her more comfortable until this steam, or whatever it is, passes."

"Of course," Katherine replied.

"I'm going to make you a little Kentucky blue-grass bed, okay, Sammy? I'll be back in a flash."

"Peachy-keen, jelly bean." Samantha smiled.

Katherine squatted down beside her and took her hand.

"Sarah's with you, isn't she, honey?" Katherine whispered.

The little girl nodded and smiled. Then she pointed at Zoe's computer.

"What's that?" Katherine asked Zoe as she glanced at her palmtop.

"A palmtop computer. They're new—it's a computer, phone, video camera—"

"No," said Katherine. "I mean, what's the picture on the screen?"

Zoe looked down. "That's the last image in the still-photo memory. I took it just before I left the office this morning. I forgot all about this! It's a picture of the mannequin the police found under the Queensboro Bridge before the explosion. Maybe that was where the bomb was planted."

"Can you enlarge it?" Katherine asked.

"I paid $18,000 for this thing; I better be able be to enlarge it," Zoe said, pressing a button. The image painted on the mannequin's torso came sharply into focus.

Katherine gasped. "The Tower card! That's the reason I'm here."

CHAPTER 26

"IT'S A TAROT CARD!" ZOE BLURTED OUT, remembering the lesson her assistant had given her on the ancient tools that some psychics used in their work.

"Not just any tarot card, but one of the most powerful of the Major Arcana," Katherine explained.

"Why do you think someone would paint it on the mannequin?"

"I have no idea, but if this was the bomb that brought down the bridge and destroyed the computer center, maybe it was a last laugh at Conrad—the man who built the world's largest tower."

The two women stared at the frightening image filling the computer screen—a bolt of lightning striking a gray, lighthouse-type tower, shattering its top and setting it on fire. A king's crown toppled toward the ground as people plummeted through the air toward the earth.

"God, it looks like what happened at the World Trade Center," murmured Zoe.

"Well, that's often what the card represents: sudden and unexpected change—which is often destructive and irreversible."

"Just like what's happening now."

"It would seem that way," Katherine agreed. "But the Tower card can also mean positive change when things seem like they're at their worst, like the arrival of a new child, or the beginning of a happier phase in one's life. It's a burst of universal energy, a force that affects a major turning point in a person's path. A friend once told me that I'd have to help interpret this card at a crossroad in my life—and I think I'm at that point right now."

"I think we all are," Zoe replied.

Katherine stared at Zoe in sudden recognition. "You're that reporter who earns her living writing nasty things about psychics—including me—aren't you?" she asked.

"Well, it hasn't been much of a living," Zoe replied.

"Maybe that's about to change . . . we'll have to wait and see," Katherine said.

Frank returned to the truck. "How's my girl?" he asked.

Zoe gave him the thumbs-up. He lifted Samantha out of the truck, making sure her oxygen mask didn't slip off.

"Let's gather 'round that flare and figure out what to do to get out of here," Frank said.

"Good idea," agreed Zoe, placing her palmtop on the hood of the pickup, its small orange Record light flashing like a tiny beacon in the mist.

They all moved toward the red glow of the road flare, where Jack was sitting propped up against the wreckage of his Harley. Frank laid Samantha down carefully on the mattress of soft grass he'd prepared for her. Zoe squatted beside Jack to check his leg—even though no main arteries or veins had been severed, it was a nasty wound and still bleeding heavily. She dug into her bag for her first-aid kit and brought out some thick cotton bandages and a roll of gauze.

"Jeez Louise, it looks like a shark chomped on you," she muttered, placing the dressings over the wound and winding the gauze around it a dozen times. "Jack, put your hand on the bandage and keep pressure on it, okay? Now, you're still losing a lot of blood, so I'm going to tighten the belt around the wound, and it's going to hurt like hell."

Zoe looked him in the eye, and Jack smiled at her. She pulled the belt as tight as she could, and he kept smiling.

"You have an incredibly high threshold for pain."

"You have no idea," he said, reaching out and brushing Zoe's hair from her eyes. "Are all the nurses in this tunnel as pretty as you?"

"Jack Morgan, you *are* crazy. Earlier this morning you were planning to blow your head off, and now you're flirting with a complete stranger."

"I'm not flirting, and once you've been on the back of my Harley, you're no stranger."

In the dim light, she could barely make out his face. She touched his hand and whispered, "Jack, I'm really scared."

"Don't worry. I told you I wouldn't let anything happen to you. See how well I'm protecting you? You're trapped 100 feet underwater with a crippled old cop, breathing in a vapor made of only God-knows-what—"

"Stop it! I told you: You're not *old*."

She sat beside him. The group had formed a little circle around the flare like kids sitting around a campfire.

They sat in silence, shrouded in the persistent fog and at a complete loss as to what to do or say about the surreal situation in which they were trapped. For those few moments, the only sound in the tunnel was the steady hiss of Samantha's small oxygen tank. Then they heard Conrad, emerging from the mist, calling out for help. His son was slung over his right shoulder, and Wilson's briefcase was in his right hand.

"He's badly hurt. Please help me lay him down," Conrad pleaded, moving into the small circle of light. Frank jumped up and helped get Michael to the ground.

"Is he alive?"

"Yes, but it doesn't look good. He was barely conscious when I found him . . . and Wilson's dead," Conrad paused, then collected himself and pointed to the briefcase. "And that is a very, *very* serious problem," Conrad noted, laying the case on the road and opening it up.

An electronic voice startled them: *T-minus 25 minutes.*

"If what Michael said is true, then in less than half an hour this thing is going to set off a radioactive bomb in my Tower—*in the middle of Manhattan!"* Conrad's voice rose. He sounded increasingly panicked.

Frank knelt down and studied the briefcase. Twenty-six wires, each marked with a different letter of the alphabet, ran from the satellite phone into a block of plastic explosives as thick as a phone book and twice as wide. The neon numbers on the digital clock attached to the top of the plastic flashed rhythmically, counting down to zero.

"It's an ETD," Frank said.

"What's that mean?" asked Conrad, his voice now thin and weak.

"An explosive triggering device. When the timer runs down, the phone signals a receiver to detonate whatever it's wired to, and then this transmitter will self-destruct. That means this briefcase will blow up. And there's enough explosive in here to knock a hole the size of a house through this tunnel and let the entire Hudson River come pouring in on us."

"Can you turn it off?" Conrad asked, kneeling beside Frank.

"No."

"Please . . . you have to . . ." He grabbed Frank's arm tightly.

"I wish I could, but I can't. I'm taking my daughter to New Jersey, to a hospital. And far away from you and Manhattan and this mess you've made possible—"

"No, Frank, please! I'm being told you have to disable it now!" Katherine said firmly, putting her hand on his shoulder. "There's powerful energy all around me. I feel the presence of a female figure, a wife . . . it's a love bond. And she has an 'S' name . . . like Susan, yes, Susan. But your wife's name is Sarah—I'm confused. There are two 'S' names, two wife energies coming through together. . . ."

Frank brushed her hand away. "And exactly who's telling you all this?"

"*They* are—the spirits."

"Listen, Katherine," Frank spat out angrily, "there are 26 wires here! If I cut the wrong one, this thing will detonate, and then we'll all be dead. So if your supposed spirits can tell me which wires to cut, how many to cut, and in what sequence to cut them, I'll do it. Otherwise, Sammy and I are outta here."

The briefcase squawked: *T-minus 21 minutes.*

"No! You have to listen. They insist! *You can do this.* You can defuse this before it's too late. Sarah says—"

"Don't say my wife's name to me again! She's dead. I don't believe in what you do, and I don't have any time to waste. That oxygen tank is all that's keeping my little girl alive, and the air is running out!" Frank yelled, hot tears flooding his eyes as he looked at Samantha lying on the patch of bluegrass.

"Do you know what will happen if you leave without at least *trying* to stop this thing?" Katherine pleaded.

"Yes, I do, and I also know what will happen if I stay," Frank answered, watching Samantha cough into her mask, small pink bubbles forming at the corners of her mouth.

For the second time since they'd entered the tunnel, he closed his eyes and silently asked for help he didn't believe existed.

Please, Sarah, show me what to do!

CHAPTER 27

THE ROAD FLARE SPUTTERED AND DIED, leaving them in complete darkness except for the eerie, unnatural glow of the mist swirling around them. The hiss of Samantha's oxygen tank stopped abruptly.

Then the tunnel was suddenly alive with voices. The fog thickened, and a dazzling burst of blinding light flooded the group. Rays of a thousand different colors shimmered about them as if they were in the center of a crystal prism.

A heavy layer of mist rolled over them, so impenetrable that Frank lost sight of everyone, even Samantha, who'd been lying right beside him.

Then he heard her voice, at least a dozen feet away. He jumped up and ran toward the sound as the fog moved around him like a river, filled with shifting pools and eddies. For a moment, the air cleared, and he saw Samantha skipping in circles near the edge of the deepest bank of fog.

"Daddy, Daddy . . . we're inside a rainbow," she giggled, before she was once again shrouded in mist. He heard her voice clearly but could only catch glimpses of her as she moved through the cloud.

"Sammy, stay put for a minute. Let me look at you," he laughed. "You look so . . . so . . . healthy! Are you feeling better?" he asked in wonderment, stretching his arms out to her for a hug.

"You're silly. Of course I feel better," she continued skipping. "I told you: We're *here*."

"I know we're here, honey; we're still stuck in the tunnel. But I can hear voices and see lights, so there must be a rescue party nearby. Now come over here and give me that hug."

"Frank?" Katherine said carefully.

"Not now," Frank replied with some impatience, delighting in the sight of his daughter skipping happily.

"Daddy, you won't forget, will you?"

"Forget what, sweetie?"

"About my bench in Central Park."

"I promise, Sammy, but you won't need that bench, not for a long, long time. Come here, now."

"Frank . . . ," Katherine persisted.

Samantha performed a little pirouette and a curtsy.

"Thank you, kind sir," she said, giggling again.

"Frank, *please!*" Katherine pressed a third time.

"Listen to Katherine, Daddy. She's talking to Mommy. I'm not going anywhere yet."

"She's 'talking to Mommy'?" Frank asked. He looked at Katherine, who was gazing at Samantha in amazement. The psychic's face was glowing, a serene smile lighting her face as tears rolled down her cheeks.

"What's wrong? Why are you crying?" Frank asked, confused.

"It's so beautiful, more beautiful than I ever imagined," she whispered. "I can hear them all so clearly . . . it's like the most wonderful music. . . ."

"Who can you hear?"

"It's who you thought, Frank. It's a rescue team, but it's not going to be the kind of rescue you were expecting," Katherine explained softly.

"What do you mean? Sammy, where are you? Where'd you go?"

Frank was suddenly alone with Katherine, but vaguely aware of the others still there, standing in the luminous pool of light.

"Listen, Frank—*all of you,* listen to me," Katherine said gently. "There's a veil between this world and the next, a very thin veil. Few people realize that energies on the Other Side are continually trying to communicate with us. We either block them out because we're too afraid to listen, or because we just refuse to believe they exist. But right now, here in this tunnel, something unbelievably special is happening that I've never experienced before—*something wonderful.* The veil is being lifted."

She turned to Frank, taking both of his hands in hers. "Frank, your daughter has a wonderful gift she's been trying to share with you for a very long time, but you've never allowed yourself to open your mind—to open your heart—and accept her offer. She's been a patient teacher, but you've been a poor student. You've allowed your pain and grief to build a wall between you and the love you never really lost, the love of your family . . . Sarah's love."

"What are you telling me?"

"I'm telling you that your eyes have been open, but you've failed to see what Sarah's been trying to show you: that she's there for Sammy, ready to help her cross over to the Other Side and begin her new journey. The same way Sarah's mother, Fatima, was there to greet her when she passed over."

Frank looked at Katherine, beginning to panic.

There was no way she could have known that Sarah's mother's name was Fatima . . . unless she really could talk to the dead. He was terrified—not only of the enormity of what he was hearing, but by all the years he'd refused to believe Samantha when she insisted Sarah was still with them.

"You're ready, Frank. Turn around," Katherine said softly.

Frank turned, but he couldn't understand what he was seeing. "No," he whispered, and closed his eyes. *It's not real, it's not real, it's just a dream*. He opened his eyes, and then he did something he hadn't done for years. He crossed himself.

Standing before him was his wife, her beautiful face framed by soft, dark curls . . . her eyes looking at him with such love.

"Sarah," he moaned. "Oh, I'm sorry, I'm so sorry . . . so sorry," Frank said, falling to his knees.

"Sarah, my sweet love, where have you been? Why did you leave? Please come back . . . come home to me. I miss you, I *miss* you . . . I've tried to be a good father to Sammy, to raise her the way you would've wanted, but it's been so hard without you . . . she's been so sick since you left, and she needs her mother back . . . oh, please, Sarah." Frank's throat was swollen with the words and feelings he'd buried so deep, that had burned unspoken in him for so long.

Sarah smiled at him but said nothing.

"She hears you, Frank, and I hear her . . . more clearly than I've ever heard anyone from the Other Side. She says you've been a wonderful father, and she knows how much you love her. She carried your love with her when she passed and feels it still. She says your love fills her . . . but she also says you threw something away because of her, and it pains her. She says you must embrace it again, Frank. You must find what's been lost."

"I don't understand." Frank shook his head in confusion.

Sarah's image began to shimmer, slowly retreating into the mist.

"Wait . . . oh God, not again, don't leave me again!"

"She has to go, Frank. What do you want to tell her?"

"That I'm sorry. I'm sorry that I was angry at you when you left . . . oh, Sarah, please forgive me for not kissing you good-bye. . . ."

Sarah's translucent face was suddenly only a breath away from Frank's. He looked into her eyes and felt the fire of her lips brush softly across his, then she was gone . . . and Frank slipped to the ground, his hands covering his face as he laughed and cried and cried and laughed.

"Daddy?"

Frank looked up. Through his tears, he watched Samantha blow him a kiss.

Oh, Sammy, I was going to dance at your wedding, he thought.

Samantha winked at him and said, "Don't worry, Daddy, me and Mommy will dance at *your* wedding."

Then Sarah took Samantha's hand in hers— and together his daughter and his wife smiled at him . . . and walked away into the mist.

THE OTHERS HAD BEEN WATCHING in stunned silence.

Katherine spun around and looked at Jack. "Do you hear that, Captain?"

Jack heard the clanging bell of a fire truck sounding deep within the tunnel. Not a real fire truck, but a toy, like the one he'd given Liam on Christmas morning many years ago. He could see nothing in the white fog until Katherine stepped in front of him.

"There are two strong energies coming through for you. One's the female companion figure who came through earlier today." Katherine smiled. "Now I understand why two female 'S' energies were coming through to me: first Sarah for Frank, and now *Susan* for you.

"She's laughing at you . . . she says your back wouldn't hurt so much if you'd stop sleeping on the sofa bed in the guest room."

"Susan . . . Susan . . ." Jack repeated softly, watching in disbelief as she slowly materialized before him. She was wearing her wedding dress and holding out her left hand, pointing at the tiny diamond he'd placed on her ring finger when they took their vows.

"She says, 'The smallest diamond shines the brightest.' She's laughing again—what a kind, funny energy she has, Jack. And tender . . . so tender. She's worried about you, though. She says your life is yours to live—not to throw away."

"I see her, I see so clearly," said Jack. "But I can't hear her voice."

"She hears you, Jack, and she's repeating what she said this morning: 'Forgive yourself . . . stop dying and start living' . . . now she's laughing again."

Then, for the first time since they'd climbed into that carriage in Central Park the night she was killed, Jack heard the music of Susan's soothing, loving voice.

"I can hear her . . . I can hear her lovely, sweet laughter . . . I can hear my beautiful wife!"

"She wants to know who you've been fooling around with on the Harley. . . . She says she's cute," Katherine laughed. "Susan says to help the pretty girl find what's been taken from her, and you'll find what *you* need. Her energy is pulling back."

Jack reached up to stroke Susan's face as she began to fade into the air. He touched her, and his entire body flooded with warmth. For the first time in years, he felt no physical pain at all.

"Don't go!" he begged, reaching out into the fog to touch Susan one last time. Instead, he found Zoe's hand waiting there for him, so he took it in his and squeezed tightly.

Then Susan was there again, holding a little boy by the hand. She vanished, leaving the boy with Jack.

"Liam! It's my son! I see him, but . . . he's just a boy. Liam!" Jack stared at the little fellow, who was wearing his favorite pair of cowboy pajamas and holding the new toy fire engine in front of a Christmas tree.

"You're seeing him the way you love remembering him most," explained Katherine. "But I'm also seeing a uniform, flames . . . a plane crash. He passed violently, but very, very quickly. It was an honorable passing. He was, oh, dear Lord, when he died, he was in—"

"The World Trade Center. He was one of the first firefighters in the building. We never found him," Jack wept, his chest heaving as he squeezed Zoe's hand.

The image of small Liam morphed into a handsome young man in a firefighter's uniform.

"He's showing me that day. He carried a lot of people out of the tower. He kept going back in . . . he was a hero, Jack. He wants you to know he felt no pain—and no regret. He passed doing what he wanted to do, saving lives. But he says he feels *your* pain—he says it's all around him. He wants me to tell you that suicide is never the answer. That you only end up hurting others and yourself."

"But I feel like I *did* hurt him. The last time we spoke, I was angry at him. I never even said good-bye."

"Are you carrying something of his? He's showing me a badge, or some kind of medal."

Jack reached in his pocket and pulled out the medal he'd received after Liam's death. He wanted to show it to Liam, but when he looked up, his son was gone.

"He sees it, Jack. And he says to tell you to remember what that badge means, to honor his memory and his sacrifice, not to let the pain of his passing destroy you. He's repeating Susan's words: *Forgive, live, love.*"

Jack couldn't see Liam, but he heard his son's voice as clearly as though the boy were standing beside him.

"I know how much you loved me, Dad, and how proud you are . . . but you've been locking yourself inside your house, and outside of your heart. That changes today. This is my ultimate rescue. Let me rescue *you*, Dad."

Liam reappeared for a moment, smiled at Jack, then looked at Zoe and said, "You'll be a great mom."

Liam's image began to fade. "Remember . . . it all changes today, Dad."

"ZOE, THERE'S A FEMALE ENERGY here for you," Katherine told her. "It's a mother energy, but not a birth mother. You were adopted," Katherine said with realization.

"Me? . . . Yes, I was," Zoe said, feeling intensely uncomfortable.

"This energy, it's so heavy . . . I can barely stand under the weight of her remorse . . . her name is Abby . . . or—"

Zoe saw a shadow hovering behind Katherine. "Her name is Abigail, and she can go to hell, if she isn't there already!" she screamed.

"She understands your anger, Zoe. She's showing me a crown, like a tiara. That usually means victory and achievement to me . . . but this tiara is black . . . pain and suffering and loss . . . it's attached to so much loss. Do you understand any of this?"

"You bet I do," Zoe said bitterly.

"She wasn't a very nice person . . . not a good mother to you," Katherine continued.

"She was evil."

"She wants your forgiveness, Zoe. She knows how badly she hurt you, that she wounded your heart and made it so difficult for you to trust . . . to love."

"It's typical of her—she wants my forgiveness, but she won't even show her face to ask for it herself."

"She wants to show herself to you, Zoe, but even here, in this tunnel of light, your emotions are so dark that they're blocking her out," Katherine said.

"Tell her to leave me alone! I'm not interested in what she has to say!" Zoe sobbed, squeezing Jack's hand, which had never left hers.

"She's showing me a hospital . . . a maternity ward. . . . Did she force you to give up a child?"

"Please stop, Katherine! I don't want to remember."

"She doesn't expect you to forgive her, Zoe, even though she wants it very much. She accepts responsibility for what she did, but she wants to help you. She says a pony came to you recently . . . or something by pony express. Does that make sense to you?"

"A pony? Yes, a picture of a pony on a letter. It came in the mail today, and I pinned it up over my desk at the office . . . but why would she—"

"Do you have a daughter?"

"No, I don't . . . I mean, I don't know, I'm not sure . . . they wouldn't let me see—," Zoe began weeping. "I had a baby! I had a baby, and they took it away from me. I don't know if I had a boy or a girl. All I know is I had a baby, and I've never held it in my arms."

"She says to find the girl who sent the letter, the pony girl, and you'll find your daughter . . . that's Abigail's way of showing you her love, Zoe."

The dark shadow behind Katherine flared briefly to a vibrant pink before it withdrew into the mist.

A dog barked in the distance. "Rewrite? That's Rewrite! That's my puppy," Zoe said in amazement.

"That's one more way Abigail is trying to reach you with love. She wants you to know that Rewrite is okay . . . and waiting for you."

KATHERINE LOOKED AT FRANK, JACK, AND ZOE. She felt a sense of peace among them, but could sense a wave of pain behind her. She was being pulled toward Conrad and Michael—she knew she was needed.

Conrad was staring into the wavering haze and strange vapor that had isolated him from the rest of the group. Katherine's voice was coming at him from all directions, and high above him, he heard a child's playful laughter.

Conrad held Michael's head in his lap, caressing the bruised and battered face of a man, but remembering him as a boy, especially the trusting eyes with which his son had always looked upon him.

I pressured you too hard to succeed. I pushed you too far, right over the edge of sanity, Conrad thought. *And Danny, poor Danny, I drove him away—all I cared about was my work, and all I achieved was killing everything I ever loved.*

He looked up. Katherine was beside him, smiling. "Your *sons* are here; both of them are with you now. One on this side, one on the Other Side. And there's the mother energy that's been around you all day . . . that's always around you. . . ."

"No, this can't be. There must be a gas leak . . . I must be hallucinating. This can't be happening," Conrad murmured. But then he looked up, and his heart began to melt.

"Mother?"

He saw her through the fog, sitting at her workbench in the greenhouse back in Iowa. Her hair was pinned up, the way it always was when she worked; and she glowed with the vibrant, lush beauty of youth and health.

The scene was cloudy, like the kind you'd see in the swirling liquid of a just-shaken snow globe. But as the vision became clearer, he recognized the exact moment in time: It was his 8th birthday . . . she was just 30, and so lovely . . . then he was beside her. She was showing him a flower . . . he could hear her words echoing back to him from the past. . . .

It's your turn to try, Connie. If a farmer's wife can play God, I don't see why a farmer's son can't, do you?

His heart was pounding . . . it was her birthday present to him, his first glimpse into the wonders of DNA, into the secrets of life itself. The vision clouded, diminishing . . .

"She has great regret, Conrad. She says she was wrong to tell you to play God," Katherine said. "She wishes she'd told you to *embrace* God, in whatever way, in whatever form you could . . . that all you ever needed to know exists within that embrace."

Michael stirred in Conrad's lap and sat up, looking at Katherine in bewilderment.

"She's pulling back . . . she's sending love to you, showing me blue roses . . . again, she's thanking you for easing her pain, for helping her pass. She's gone, but she's bringing through a male energy . . . a very old soul. His energy has also been with us all day."

"Where? I can't see anything," Conrad said.

"He says he's sorry for leaving the way he did, for the pain he caused by taking his life. He says not to remember the way he passed . . . but remember the song."

"Is it Danny? What song? What song does he—"

Suddenly, Conrad was sitting in a school auditorium more than 30 years ago, with a young

Michael by his side. It was a special night, a rare occasion where he'd taken time from work to attend one of his boys' school events. Danny stood in the center of the stage, his face beaming with pride as spoke to the crowd.

I dedicate this song to Conrad Dinnick, my dad, and to my best friend in the whole world—my brother, Mike, Daniel said clearly, with no a trace of a stutter.

"Michael, look, it's Danny . . . look there . . . Danny's back!" Conrad exclaimed.

Michael's eyes widened. He whispered: "It's Danny's song."

Danny began to sing in a sweet, lyrical voice that seized Conrad's heart.

> *Oh Danny boy, the pipes, the pipes are*
> *   calling*
> *From glen to glen, and down the moun*
> *   tain side*
> *The summer's gone, and all the flowers*
> *   are dying*
> *'tis you, 'tis you must go and I must bide.*
> *But come ye back when summer's in the*
> *   meadow . . .*

"Danny, please forgive me," Michael muttered, getting to his knees. Conrad sobbed, as the light on the stage brightened so intensely that Danny appeared translucent.

> *And if you come, when all the flowers*
> *   are dying*
> *And I am dead, as dead I well may be*

> *You'll come and find the place where I*
> *am lying*
> *And kneel and say an "Ave" there for me.*
> *And I shall hear, tho' soft you tread*
> *above me*
> *And all my dreams will warm and*
> *sweeter be*
> *If you'll not fail to tell me that you love me*
> *I simply sleep in peace until you come*
> *to me.*

The stage light waned. Danny, now a grown man, stood before his father and brother, his arms across his chest, hands clasped above his heart.

"He says he's at peace, but asks your forgiveness—and he wants both of you to forgive yourselves, and each other," Katherine said.

"Danny!" Conrad and Michael cried out in unison.

"He's showing me *he's* healed, but he needs you to know that you can heal each other—it's not too late. You *can* find the cure in the embrace. He's pulling away . . . he's gone. . . ." Katherine's voice trailed off.

KATHERINE DROPPED TO THE TUNNEL'S FLOOR, alone in the mist, utterly drained.

Never in her life had she felt the energy of spirits surge through her with such force and power. It was as though she'd stepped across to the Other Side and, for a few brief, glorious moments, had walked among them, talking to them effortlessly, hearing them with complete clarity. She actually felt their thoughts and emotions as they had them.

She realized that the Other Side had needed her here to be a conduit to the people she'd been thrown together with today. Her presence had been necessary, but this had drawn on every ounce of her psychic ability. She knew it was an honor—but it was an honor she never wanted to have again.

Since the energies had retreated, she was left with only silence . . . and a sense of overwhelming loneliness. She was more exhausted than she'd been in Italy, more tired than she'd ever been in her life.

She barely had enough energy to keep her eyes open.

I'm crossing over, she thought. *I'm spent . . . I'm finished.*

CHAPTER 28

"HI, KATHY. THERE'S SOMEONE HERE WHO WANTS TO TALK TO YOU."

Katherine opened her eyes and saw Samantha's smiling face looking down at her. There was an intense but lovely expression in the child's eyes. Her skin glowed with a rosy hue in the shifting light.

"Sammy, am I—," Katherine began to ask.

"Of course not. Don't be silly," Samantha scoffed.

"Are you—"

"So many questions from someone with a visitor waiting to see her," she giggled.

"What visitor?"

"Her," Samantha said, pointing behind Katherine, but the exhausted woman continued to stare at the girl's gleaming smile. Then she felt a presence behind her emanating such intense love that she was afraid to turn around. She closed her eyes as the familiar strains of Sinatra filled her mind.

> *. . . painted kites, those days and nights*
> *went flying by . . .*
> *. . . then softer than a piper man, one*
> *day it called to you . . .*
> *. . . and I lost you—to the summer wind . . .*

"Don't be afraid, Kathy," Samantha said gently.

Katherine opened her eyes and saw the friend she'd loved more than any other, the person who'd believed in her and opened her mind to a world of books and music and wonderment. The person who'd guided her to her life's work, and whose absence had left a gnawing emptiness.

"Julia," she whispered, "where have you been? Why have you never come through to me? Why did you leave me all alone?"

"She says you should know why," Samantha said. "You knew each other so well that you'd never believe it was her if she *did* come to you. You'd think you were tricking yourself into believing."

Samantha's laugh echoed in the mist. "She says you must be losing your touch—she's been sending you messages since Italy to get here. . . ."

"The tower images?"

"You got it!" Samantha exclaimed.

"Julia, I need you. I'm so, so weary . . . I can't go on with the work. I have nothing left to give anyone."

"She's asking me who you are," Samantha relayed.

"She can't see me? She doesn't know?" Katherine cried in confusion, tears streaming down her cheeks.

"Oh, she sees you, all right. But she says the Katherine Haywood she knew wasn't a quitter—she's strong, a warrior."

"I have no fight left . . . I can't help anyone anymore."

"She says to stop it. You've helped *everyone*. You've turned the Tower card around, you've drawn the light from the darkness, turned negative force into positive energy . . . and now she says to reach out."

"Reach out where?"

"To *her*, silly. She says to put out your hand."

Katherine offered her hand to her old friend and felt an electrical current run up her arm and around her skull. A flash of white light exploded in her mind, and she could feel Julia's presence in every cell of her body as strength and energy pulsed through her.

For a moment she saw her father and grandmother standing beside Julia.

"I told you that you were special, sweetheart," her father said, beaming. "You just had to grow into your specialness."

"Remember to look both ways before crossing the road, little Kathy," her grandmother chuckled sweetly.

"Oh, Dad, Grams . . . I love you," Katherine whispered, as her family faded from view. She stretched her arms wide and breathed deeply, feeling renewed and regenerated.

"My God, I've never felt so . . . alive," she said in wonderment.

"Her gift to you," Samantha explained, smiling, "but she still has something to say to everyone here."

Julia's image became brighter than any they had seen so far, and suddenly they could all hear her voice: "You've been given a gift, each of you. You've looked into a world few ever see without first being touched by death. You were brought together to heal yourselves, to know you can move forward, and to understand that you must use the time allotted to you on this physical plane to grow, to learn, and to love. These lessons you must share with others beyond the walls of this tunnel—especially the lessons of love and forgiveness—because that's what endures and binds all our energies together."

"But—," Zoe began to say, unsure of how to address this vision.

"Your question is about *him*," Julia said, looking through the clearing mist at Wilson's lifeless body, barely visible a few yards away.

"Yes," Zoe said. "How can we love or forgive someone like him . . . is he in hell? Or does evil energy exist where you are?"

"His hell is to realize, relive, and personally experience the same pain he's inflicted on others. He must atone for his actions . . . and has much to atone for . . . but he will."

Katherine looked up at Julia as the image began to waver and fade.

"Julia! Will I hear from you again?!" Katherine cried out.

"We're always together, Katherine, and we'll be together again, but not yet. Your work is far from over. Remember what I told you the first day we met. Even the darkest tunnel can open up onto the brightest of lights, and right now there are many dark tunnels in the world. New York is just the beginning; your mission is destined to take you to many places. You have a light, Kathy, and you must let it shine," Julia said, and she was gone.

A fog enveloped the group, leaving everyone but Katherine in a semiconscious state.

Katherine looked to Samantha to thank her for bringing Julia through. The girl was gone, but she could hear her voice.

"Please, Kathy, help my daddy."

Somewhere in the tunnel, an electronic voice announced: *T-minus five minutes.*

"WAKE UP, WAKE UP! Wake up now, Frank!" Katherine shouted, shaking him violently by the shoulders.

"What's the matter, Sarah?" Frank asked sleepily. "It's Saturday morning, my turn to sleep in—*your* turn to take Sammy to temple. . . ."

"It's not Sarah, Frank; it's Katherine. Get up—the bomb is about to go off!"

"What . . . what's happening?" Frank said in confusion, sitting up and looking around groggily. "Sammy . . . where's Sammy?"

"She's safe, Frank . . . but the rest of us aren't."

"What?!" he exclaimed, now fully alert.

"Frank . . . the bomb!" Katherine screamed.

T-minus two minutes.

"Oh my God! Two minutes? Jesus, it's too late

for any of us to get out!" Frank realized, crawling over to the briefcase and peering inside at the many wires and flashing lights. "I can't . . . I can't—"

"Yes, you can, Frank. Sarah is telling me you must find what you threw away when she died."

"I don't know what you mean! I have no idea! The bomb . . . its trigger is too complicated. I gotta think . . . I gotta think."

"You think too much, Frank. Listen to your heart," Katherine told him. "Find what you lost when Sarah died."

Frank thought of Sarah's funeral. He remembered standing by the coffin, dropping his crucifix inside before he closed the lid, the crucifix his mother had given him before his first communion, engraved with the words: *Franco, Non perda mai la vostra fede.* Frank, never lose your faith.

He reached into his jeans, pulled out his pocket knife, and held it over the mass of wires.

T-minus 1 minute.

Frank opened the blade and put it under the wire with the letter *F* stamped on it. He hesitated. Then he thought he heard Samantha's voice behind him.

"It's in your heart, Daddy."

T-minus 30 seconds.

He took a deep breath and sliced through the *F* wire. Nothing happened.

He moved the knife expertly, like a surgeon, and cut through the *A* wire, then the *I,* the *T,* and the *H.*

There was a hard metallic click, and the speaker in the briefcase announced: *Countdown aborted at T-minus 9 seconds.*

The fog began to lift.

"I don't understand what's happening," Frank said, looking behind him through the thinning mist to the small patch of grass where he'd left Samantha. There, he saw her lifeless body, with the plastic oxygen mask still strapped across her face.

The howl formed in the center of his being, churning in his gut until the pain forced it into his throat like a fist, breaking through his mouth and screaming down the length of the tunnel like a wounded animal.

"Noooooooooooooooooooo!"

"Shhhhhhh, Frank, it's all right." Katherine tried to comfort him as she knelt beside him.

"Oh God, Sammy, don't leave, don't leave me here alone . . . don't go—"

"She's already gone, Frank, but you know she hasn't left you," Katherine told him with conviction, placing her hand over his heart. "She says she'll always be right here . . . just never lose faith."

Frank collapsed onto the asphalt.

EPILOGUE

THE STATIC FROM THE RADIO IN THE PICKUP TRUCK WOKE HIM UP.

Frank rolled onto his side and saw that the truck had returned to life, its headlights cutting a double path of light leading to the end of the tunnel and illuminating the bodies scattered on the road. The radio emitted a low, crackling buzz.

As he walked toward the patch of green, he could hear everyone breathing and saw that they were all beginning to move—all but Samantha.

Frank kneeled beside her and carefully removed her oxygen mask, wiping the traces of blood from her lips and chin.

"Sammy," was all he could say, leaning down to kiss her forehead and cross her arms over her chest.

Her right hand was balled into a fist. He gently opened her fingers and saw it glitter in her palm: the cross he'd dropped into Sarah's coffin.

It can't be . . . it just can't be . . . but here it is!

With tears in his eyes, Frank took the crucifix from her hand and kissed it. Then he slipped the gold chain around his neck, and tucked the cross into his shirt.

He felt Katherine's hand on his back. "The world is full of miracles, Frank—big and small. We just have to look for them. She's all right, you know. She's happy, she's safe, and she's with Sarah."

"I know she is," he admitted tearfully, getting to his feet and looking at the psychic.

"But . . . are *you* okay, Frank?"

Tears streamed down his face. "No, I'm not . . . but I know I will be. She taught me how to live, and how to believe. But it's so hard. It's so difficult to know *what* to believe."

Katherine put her arms around him, hugging him tightly while he sobbed on her shoulder.

"It takes time, but it will come to you," Katherine said compassionately.

Behind them Zoe was leaning over to help Jack get up, but he bounced to his feet before she had the chance.

"Hey, be careful, Jack, your leg! You'll hurt yourself getting up so quickly. Are you okay?" she asked.

"I've never felt better in my life," he told her. He glanced at his leg—his wound was healed. Then he looked into Zoe's soft green eyes, took her hands in his, and kissed both.

"Wow," she said, with a surprised smile.

"Thank you," he told her as he gazed at her appreciatively.

"For what?"

"For everything you've done for me, starting with the stun gun—when you shocked me back into the world of the living."

"Well, you're welcome, and thank *you!*"

"For what?"

"For everything you're *going* to do for me. . . . because I know you're going to help me find my baby . . . my daughter."

Conrad had lifted Michael to his feet and was walking with him toward the others. Michael seemed dazed.

"What happened, Dad? Where are we?"

"You got sick, Michael . . . and you've had an accident. But we're going to get you better, I promise. I know just what to do. You're going to be fine—we're both going to be fine."

Conrad and Michael stood beside Frank and Katherine.

Conrad looked down at Samantha. "Oh, no! Frank, I'm so sorry. Oh, God . . . I know how painful it is to lose a child . . . and to almost lose another. I—I don't know what to say." Conrad hugged him.

Zoe ran over to Frank and threw her arms around him. "She was a beautiful, beautiful girl!" she exclaimed.

"She *is* a beautiful girl. She *is,*" Frank said.

"I've been where you are, and I know there isn't much I can say to ease your pain, except that she's part of all of us now, and always will be," Jack told him.

Frank acknowledged Jack with a nod, and then they all stood in silence, looking down at

Samantha, each saying farewell in their own way.

Then they looked at each other, no one quite sure what to say or where to start.

"Do we all know what we've just been through?" Katherine asked.

Everyone nodded.

"But no one outside this tunnel is ever going to believe it," Jack said.

They were all silent again.

"Then let's not tell anyone else. What happened in the tunnel stays right here," Frank suggested.

"Except that I've got this," said Zoe, picking up her palmtop from the hood of the truck. "I've been writing about this stuff for so long, but I never believed a word of what I wrote . . . and now that I finally have proof, I don't need it."

She popped the disk out of her small computer. "It was recording the entire time. Everything that happened is probably documented on this—it's the story of a lifetime."

They all looked at her, waiting, expectant.

Zoe took a deep breath and sighed. "Oh, well. My horoscope this morning said to perform a selfless act, and that it was time for a career change." She laughed, handing the disk to Katherine. "It's yours to do with what you want."

Katherine smiled, putting the disk into her pocket. "Welcome to your crossroads," she said to Zoe.

"Look, everyone, this is far from over!" Conrad said. "Just for starters, there's a new virus in my Hoboken lab I have to take care of—and no one outside this tunnel should ever know about it. Agreed?"

"Agreed," they all said.

"There's also a dirty bomb in my Tower in Manhattan that we have to try to defuse quietly so we don't panic an entire city."

"I should be able to handle that," Frank volunteered, "but something that serious is going to be hard to keep quiet."

"I have friends in high places who can help keep a lid on it. It's not something they're going to want to advertise," Conrad said, looking over at Wilson's body on the road. "As far as my son is concerned, he'll have to answer for whatever part he played in what happened at the bridge and for any other crime he's committed. And finally, there's a group of terrorists in Hoboken waiting for Wilson to show up with a package."

Conrad turned to Jack and said, "I never had a chance to thank you for saving my life. So thank you. Are you really a cop?"

Jack checked his watch. "I'm on the payroll until five o'clock. But I'll get the information about the terrorists and Wilson to the right people: the police, the FBI—whoever it takes."

"Okay, but before we do anything, we have to get out of this tunnel," Frank said. "Neither of these vehicles are going anywhere, so it looks like we're walking."

Conrad went first, his arms around Michael to support him as they left.

Zoe turned to Jack. "Do you need a hand to walk?"

"Do I look like an old man to you? I'll race you to Joisey."

"No, just walk beside me, Jack," Zoe told him, taking his hand.

Frank bent down and lifted Samantha into his arms.

"Do you want some company, or should I leave you alone?" Katherine asked.

"No, please walk with us," Frank said, as he began the final journey with his daughter to the end of the tunnel. "She really liked you, Katherine—you understood her so well. I wish I could have done that sooner."

"Oh, no, Frank, don't regret anything. All I could see was how close she was to the Other Side. You had her love, and you knew her heart."

"It's going to be hard without her . . . not hearing her voice."

"You know, Frank, you *will* be hearing from Sammy again."

"I know I will," Frank said, then smiled. "Sammy would laugh if she heard me quoting the Bible, but there's something she used to say to me all the time that just popped into my head: *There are three things that last forever: faith, hope, and love. But the greatest of them all is love.*"

THE HIGH BEAMS ON THE TRUCK cast them all in silhouette against the growing light at the end of the tunnel.

The static on the radio was slowly replaced by the sharp, clear voice of a female reporter:

". . . is improving as the solar storm moves away from Earth's atmosphere and into deep space. The

electrical grid is slowly getting up and running again, and telecommunication systems around the world seem to be coming back online.

"Here at Action News, our field reporters are starting to call in with some amazing stories. As I've said already, this has been a phenomenal day in New York City. The main explosion on Roosevelt Island that severely damaged the Queensboro Bridge has been extinguished, and city engineers say initial estimates are that the bridge could be completely repaired within six to eight months.

"The mayor and governor and many City Council members are being treated for abrasions and broken bones after the Roosevelt Island Tram they were riding in dropped safely onto a sand barge passing beneath the bridge moments before it collapsed.

"Once again, as remarkable as it sounds, everyone who was on the bridge at the time of the explosion seems to have escaped with minor injuries, and while the numbers are not yet final, at this moment we have no confirmed reports of any fatalities—no fatalities at all.

"It's seldom you'll hear a news anchor say this, but folks, if I was told I had to sum up today's events in one word, that word would have to be: miraculous!*"*

ACKNOWLEDGMENTS

SANDRA—YOUR UNCONDITIONAL LOVE AND SUPPORT allows me to do everything that I do.

Justin—you're the reason I can't wait to come home . . . always remember that Daddy loves you.

Carol—if I could get you to stop stealing pens from hotels and my desk . . . some might consider you perfect. . . .

Isabel, Lucille, John, Ruth, Phil, and Kelly—a special thank you and all my appreciation for always going above and beyond in all that you do.

Joanne—you will always be King of the Forest to me.

Jolie and Roxie—you're still my girls.

Jon—wooooooooooooooooooooooooooooooooo ooooooooosh!

Stacy—thank you for your continued support and friendship and . . . you know!

Reid Tracy—thank you . . . again and again and again.

Jill Kramer, for all that you do.

Gina Rugolo—your enthusiasm and energy are such a help in my achieving my professional goals.

Marc Chamlin—thank you for your sage advice and counsel and for always being there.

Corinda Carford—you are my sage.

Jill Fritzo—for your hard work, support, and friendship.

Natasha Stoynoff—a few years ago you were brought into my life to write a story about the subject matter of life after death. That turned into a great friendship that took us across the world, where you helped me write Part III of my journey in this work. Now . . . I think we've found a great place where both our creative minds have come together to tell a story that will be entertaining, and enlightening as well. I look forward to what's next. . . .

Steve Erwin—(no, not the crocodile guy!), thanks for all your invaluable help you gave to your wife, Natasha, on her spiritual adventure.

There are so many other people that I could mention here, but that would be another book all unto itself. I know you all know who you are. . . .

— **John**

───────────

Thank you to my beautiful colleagues at *People* magazine, who hid me when I slipped in late and wrecked after all-night writing sessions.

Many thanks to Lou Stanek, for her much-needed guidance.

Many thanks to Jill Kramer, who didn't complain when I begged for deadline extensions and then worked miracles.

Much gratitude to sweet Miss Mellie, aka Norris Mailer, for her constant encouragement and inspiration. Put Paris and our Southern epic on the to-do list. . . .

Thank you to the loved ones on the Other Side whom Steve and I miss terribly, and who helped write this book. You know who you are. Come and visit more often.

Thank you to John Edward, a fellow number "9," who had the movie version of this book cast even before we'd written the first word! Thanks for your invaluable friendship, patience, trust, and Other Side insight. You have enriched my life.

And most of all, thank you to my dear husband, Steve, whose endless talent, ideas, research, energy, faith, passion, and too many years of watching bad-brother movies all added up to help make the finest moments in this story.

— **Natasha**

If you enjoyed *FINAL BEGINNINGS* and want
to continue with this spiritual adventure to see
what happens next,
look for *INFINITE ENDINGS* . . .
coming soon . . .

ABOUT THE AUTHORS

John Edward is an internationally acclaimed psychic medium, and author of the *New York Times* bestsellers *One Last Time, Crossing Over, After Life,* and *What If God Were the Sun?.* In addition to hosting his own syndicated television show, *Crossing Over with John Edward,* John has been a frequent guest on *Larry King Live* and many other talk shows, and was featured in the HBO documentary *Life After Life.* He publishes his own newsletter and also conducts workshops and seminars around the country. John lives in New York with his family.

For more information, see John's Website at:
www.johnedward.net

Natasha Stoynoff is a staff correspondent for *People* magazine, and this is her fourth book collaboration, following *Life's Little Emergencies* with supermodel Emme; *Never Say Never* with former CBS sportscaster Phyllis George; and *After Life* with John Edward. She has worked as a news reporter/photographer for *The Toronto Star* and as a columnist for *The Toronto Sun.* Her work has also appeared in cover stories for *Time* magazine.

Natasha lives in Manhattan with her husband, writer/journalist Stephen Erwin, and is currently working on her first screenplay.

THE JOHN EDWARD NEWSLETTER
"BRIDGES"

The John Edward newsletter, "Bridges," is a quarterly magazine-style publication that includes:

- Inspirational stories
- A Q & A "Ask John" section
- Spiritually related areas
- Reader validations and experiences
- Special subscriber offers
- Guest contributors
- Other related material

To order your subscription of the **"Bridges"** newsletter, just fill out the order form. In addition, as a special gift from John for purchasing both this book and a **"Bridges"** newsletter subscription, you will receive three (3) free John Edward Appreciation Pins (a $20.70 value).

Due to overwhelming demand, you must send the original form below, not a copy.

Please make check payable (in U.S. dollars only) to **Get Psych'd, Inc.**, and mail your order to:

Get Psych'd, Inc.
P.O. Box 383
Huntington, NY 11743

Allow 4–6 weeks for delivery.

Visit our official Website at: **www.johnedward.net**

$\mathcal{P}$

SERPENTINE

A remote Florida island is the perfect wedding destination for the upcoming nuptials of Anita's fellow U.S. Marshal and best friend, Edward. For Anita, the vacation is a welcome break, as it's the first trip she gets to take with wereleopards Micah and Nathaniel. But it's not all fun and games and bachelor parties. . . .

In this tropical paradise, Micah discovers a horrific new form of lycanthropy, one that has afflicted a single family for generations. Believed to be the result of an ancient Greek curse, it turns human bodies into a mass of snakes.

When long-simmering resentment leads to a big blowup within the wedding party, the last thing Anita needs is more drama. But it finds her anyway when women start disappearing from the hotel, and worse, her own friends and lovers are considered the prime suspects. There's a strange power afoot that Anita has never confronted before, a force that's rendering those around her helpless. Unable to face it on her own, Anita is willing to accept help from even the deadliest places. Help that she will most certainly regret—if she survives at all, that is. . . .

PRAISE FOR *LAURELL K. HAMILTON* AND *THE ANITA BLAKE NOVELS*

"If you've never read this series, I highly recommend/strongly suggest having the Anita Blake experience. Vampires, zombies, and shifters, oh my! And trust me, these are not your daughter's vampires." —*Literati Book Reviews*

"A sex-positive, kick-ass female protagonist." —*Starburst*

"Number one *New York Times* bestseller Hamilton is still thrilling fans . . . with her amazing multifaceted characters and intricate multilayered world, a mix of erotic romance, crime drama, and paranormal/fantasy fiction. Her descriptive prose is gritty and raw, with a mosaic of humor and horror to tell this complex, well-detailed story. But it's her enigmatic stable of stars that continues to shine, managing their improbable interpersonal relationship dynamics." —*Library Journal*

"A first-class storyteller." —*St. Louis Post-Dispatch*

To Jonathon, my husband, who let me take time out of our romantic getaway to finish this book and stayed at my side while I did it. Real love is about consistency over time, battles won, battles lost, the pain, the pleasure, the sharing.

To Genevieve, my first girlfriend
and the only woman in my life. Yes, dear.

To Spike, poly partner, helpmate, romantic battle buddy.
Strength shared is strength multiplied.

ACKNOWLEDGMENTS

Shawn, what a long, strange journey it has been, my friend—here's to happiness and new adventures. Will, who made me feel safe and reminded me that I am my own surety. Jess, who has performed miracles of organization in helping Sherry and Theresa battle on against the tide of artistic clutter. To all my fans and readers, who have fallen in love with my world and characters. To Zannah, Keiko, and Mordor, the office pack. To Eomer and Grizzy, office cats, at last.

1

I WAS STANDING in the air-conditioned hush of Forever Bridal in Albuquerque, New Mexico, but since all I could see was a rack of plastic-wrapped wedding dresses taller than my head, I could have been in any bridal shop in any part of the country. The dresses were ones that had needed tailoring to fit their brides. I stared at the different shades of white, from dazzling white like fresh snow in sunlight to a cream so dark it was almost a pale brown, or maybe taupe. I was always confused by taupe. Who wouldn't be confused by a color that couldn't decide if it was gray or tan? The dress they'd finally let me try on was black, because the pale teal that matched the maid of honor's dress had looked so bad on me that even Donna Parnell, the bride-to-be, had conceded that we could try the dress in black for me. Since I was the best man, or best person, on the groom's side of the aisle and the men were in black tuxes with teal ties and cummerbunds, putting me in black would make the wedding party look more balanced, or that's what the store manager had finally said.

I stood clutching the overly long black skirt in one hand, so I didn't trip, as I talked to Micah Callahan on my new smart-phone, which was actually so smart I felt uncomfortable using it, as if the technology were silently judging my lack of tech savvy.

"So, your clients have finally given you permission to share more info with your police girlfriend?" I said.

I could feel/hear the smile in his voice as he said, "They're not clients, Anita. I don't take money for helping people who are desperate." Micah was the head of the Coalition for Better Understanding Between Human and Lycanthrope Communities, colloquially known as the Furry Coalition. They traveled the country, some internationally, to help keep the lycanthropes and the humans safe from each other. Sometimes it was just to give lectures to the local police to help them deal better with this very special minority in their cities; sometimes it was to settle disputes between different wereanimal groups before they became violent. The Coalition never went into another city without an invitation from someone among either the local lycanthropes, the police, or even medical professionals. One of the most frequent things the Coalition did was help victims of wereanimal attacks recover and come to terms with turning into their attackers come the next full moon. Micah had been a survivor of an attack, just like the people he tried to help. He'd been hunting with his uncle and cousin the year between college and high school when they were attacked by a wereleopard. He had been the only survivor, so he had serious street cred when he spoke to victims.

"You take donations," I said.

"If they can afford it, yes, and if it's a city government, we'll take a fee, but for individuals in need we waive fees, so they are not clients."

"Sorry, I didn't mean to step on an issue here."

"It's okay, Anita. I'm sorry—this . . . case is getting to me. When you see the pictures, you'll understand."

"Okay, if they aren't clients, what word do you want me to use in conversation?"

"Shapeshifters," he said.

I glanced around the store to see if there was anyone within earshot, but all I could see were wedding dresses on one side and another rack of dresses on the other, this time in a myriad of colors for other hapless bridesmaids. Turning just that much made my breasts slide out of the halter top of the dress, which had been designed for someone with a very different figure. I transferred my hand to clutch the top instead of the hem of the dress. As long as I didn't try to walk, the yards of extra fabric wouldn't trip me. My dignity was in more danger from the dress than my body was. Solution: I would stand still and do my best not to flash anyone. "I came out of the changing room because I could hear everything in the next stall. I've got as much privacy as I can find here, but there are certain words that make civilians perk up their ears and listen harder." I lowered my voice even more and said, "*Shapeshifter* would be one of those words."

"That's fair," he said, and sighed, not like he was happy. "You can use the word *client* for now, but I see myself more as their advocate. But that's beside the point. Use whatever vocabulary you think will keep this between us, Anita. They're finally letting me send you pictures, and those absolutely must be for your eyes only."

"I'm a U.S. Marshal, Micah. I know how to keep details to myself." I realized that it sounded a little crankier than I'd meant it to.

"Are you okay?" he asked, taking my crankiness for my feeling bad, and not taking it personally. There were so many reasons we were engaged to each other.

"Yeah. I mean, I can't believe that Donna decided at, like, the eleventh hour that I couldn't wear a tux like the rest of the men, but I'll live, once they figure out a way for the halter top not to make the wedding an accidental PG-thirteen."

He laughed, then said, "Ask Nathaniel to take pictures of the dress before they fix it."

"You can see my breasts without a dress next time we're in the same state," I said, but I was smiling, which is probably why he'd said it the way he had. Micah knew when I needed cheering up, or coaxing out of a cranky mood.

"We haven't been in the same state much lately," he said, and sounded sad again.

"You and I both travel for our jobs."

"I know, but I miss you."

I stood there in the ill-fitting dress with our shared boyfriend only yards away from me and was suddenly so lonely for the touch of Micah's arms around me that it was almost a physical pain. I could remember the last time we'd slept in the same bed, but I couldn't remember the last time we'd made love. It had been weeks. Had we gone a month, it was a first in the five years we'd been together. "I miss you, too. I want to do more than just sleep in the same bed in between business trips for our jobs."

"Nathaniel is staying in town with you, so I know you're getting sex."

I'd never heard Micah sound even a little bit jealous of Nathaniel before. "He's our shared boyfriend, shared fiancé, and you're planning to marry him legally, like I'm marrying Jean-Claude," I said.

"I know, and if we could marry more than one person at a time, the four of us would marry one another, though I admit the idea of me marrying any man but Nathaniel, even Jean-Claude, would be weird."

"And do you have another woman in mind that you'd like to add to the group?" I asked, making sure my tone of voice was teasing.

He laughed. "No. The other women in our poly group are lovely, but it's not about the sex; it's about the emotion and being a couple together. I'm a couple with you and Nathaniel, but not really with anyone else, not the way the two of you are with some of the others." His voice had already lost that edge of laughter and was back to sounding tired.

"What's wrong, Micah? Besides this case, I mean."

"I told you what's wrong, Anita. I'm feeling crowded. It's not marrying Nathaniel; I love him. I understand that if you marry anyone legally, it's got to be Jean-Claude. He's the king of all the vampires, and he's close to being the king of all the supernatural citizens in this country. He has to be the one that marries the princess."

"I'm not the princess in this story," I said.

"You're not the damsel in distress, but as far as everyone in the media is concerned, you are the princess to be married off to the prince, or king."

"Nathaniel is enjoying the idea of all the weddings more than I am."

"He's enjoying it more than I am, too, but I think what's throwing me is the two-groom wedding. I always pictured a white-dressed bride coming down the aisle toward me."

"Nathaniel would probably wear a white dress if you really wanted him to," I said.

Micah laughed. "I know he would, but I think I'd prefer him in a white tux with tails."

"He's so happy you accepted his proposal."

"I'm sorry I hesitated even for a little bit. I just had to work through my issues."

"Nathaniel is your first-ever boyfriend. I know you never thought you'd be marrying another man."

"I hope he doesn't think I've been ignoring him since I said yes. There have just been so many out-of-town issues that needed attention."

"You spend time with us when you can, just like I do. Nathaniel got to travel out of town with you to Florida the time before last."

"And you couldn't go because you had bad guys to catch," he said.

"When we all go down for Ted and Donna's wedding we'll have some time to enjoy ourselves, because I won't be crime-busting and you won't be saving other shapeshifters."

"Did Nathaniel tell you that the shapeshifters down here wouldn't let me bring him to the meetings, so he had to go sight-seeing by himself with only a bodyguard for company?"

"He mentioned it, but we'll have time to sight-see before and after the wedding. Besides, if Nathaniel hadn't got to sight-see, he would never have found the hotel where Donna and Ted are getting married. She's getting her beach destination wedding and he's getting to be somewhere we can all stay armed and our badges are still legal."

"I know it worked out," Micah said, "but I feel like I'm not getting any time with either of you lately."

"It does seem like either you're out of town or I am the last few months."

"It does, and it's moments like this when I think that I need to start cutting back on all of it."

"Why don't you? I mean, that would be great if you could, but you know I would never ask you to compromise your job."

"Because you would never compromise yours," he said, but not like he was exactly happy about it. It wasn't like Micah to be this unhappy about things, about us and our complicated personal lives, or our complicated professional lives. My chest felt tight, my stomach started to knot, and those negative voices in my head tried to be louder, saying, *See, see? This is the moment that Micah stops being perfect and drops the other shoe right on our heads.*

"I don't know what to say to that. I'm a marshal. It's who I am, not just what I am."

"I know that. I knew the kind of person you were when we met. I don't want you to change, Anita."

"Good. You had me scared for a minute there."

"I'm sending you the first picture; let me know when it comes through."

The change of topic back to the business he'd called about was so abrupt it caught me off guard, but I didn't protest. I was happy for a change of topic. My phone dinged to let me know the picture had arrived, but I had to take the phone away from my ear to look.

"Do you want me to put you on speaker while I look at the picture?"

"No, just look at it. I'll wait."

I did what he asked, going to his texts and seeing the image of a man I'd never met. He was bare to the waist, lean upper body, but not like he worked out—more like he was just young and naturally thin. He looked ordinary, except there was something wrong with his right arm. I thought at first it was a tattoo, then a tentacle, which would have been weird enough. I used my fingertips to expand the picture and found that the "tentacle" had a head where the hand should have been. It looked like the man's arm turned into a snake, complete with a triangular venomous head. I widened the image further. It was blurry now, but I could see the yellow eyes on the snake head, with slits for pupils, like it was some kind of viper.

I got back on the phone and said, "It's a camera trick, Micah. No one changes shape like this. You have weresnakes, you have beings like lamias and *nagas* that are part snake and part human, but the head wouldn't be at the end of an arm."

"It's not a trick."

"You saw it, in person?" I asked.

"Yes."

"I've never seen anything like that, ever."

"I'm trying to get their permission for you to show it to Edward. If anyone else might have seen something like this before, it would be him."

"Agreed. I could show him—"

"No, it would be a betrayal of their trust, Anita. Don't act like a cop on this one, okay?"

"I am a cop, but okay. There's no crime involved, right?"

"Right. I've sent you a second picture."

The phone dinged, and he said he'd hold again while I looked at it. It wasn't the same man; this one looked older, heavier, not in bad shape, just not with the slenderness of the first. It was his left arm this time, and it wasn't just one snake head. It looked like his arm had sprouted a bouquet of snakes, all the way up into his shoulder. It was very Medusa, but in movies there was something vaguely erotic as well as horrific about the Gorgon; here there was only the horror.

I took a deep breath or two before I got back on the phone with him. "Did you see this one in person, too?"

"Yes," he said, voice soft, and I realized his unhappiness wasn't just travel and being away from me.

"Is their form change tied to the full moon like most shape-shifters?"

"At first."

"What do you mean at first?"

"This is a large extended family, Anita. Most of them all seem perfectly human at first, but some of them start to manifest this . . . change in early adulthood. The youngest male started to change at fifteen; the oldest was almost forty. If they make it to forty without this happening, they seem to be safe from it, but they can still pass it on to their children."

I said, "The only lycanthropy that I've ever seen run in families is the weretiger clans, but that's like regular lycan-thropy, when they start to change in adolescence. It's a whole-body change, not piecemeal like this."

"It usually starts like the first picture, with a hand or arm or some small piece changing, but then it grows worse over time, like the second photo."

"You hinted that it's tied to the moon at first. I take it that later on it happens more often."

"Yes, just like regular lycanthropy: Stress, anger, any strong emotion, can bring it on, and sometimes the changes become permanent."

"Does it get any worse than the second picture you showed me?"

"I sent you one last picture. It's worse."

The phone dinged and I didn't want to look at it. I saw my share of awful crime scene photos—hell, I had waded through my share of serial-killer crime scenes—but I still didn't want to see worse this time. Micah had seen it in person. If he could see it live, then I could look at a picture.

The upper-right side of the man's body was a mass of writhing snakes. The right side of his face was covered in livid green scales. I expected his eye on that side to be like the snake's eyes, but it was still a human eye, brown and ordinary. Coming out of the side of his neck and trailing up the edge of his face were more snakes. It was as if his human body was turning into a mass of serpents.

I got back on the phone; my voice was as empty as I could make it. The picture was too awful for me to add more emotion to the situation. "Do they eventually change into a whole bunch of snakes? Does the human body lose integrity and just become individual serpents?"

"And that's one of the reasons I wanted to talk to you about it. That's a question I never thought to ask. If the answer is yes, does it change anything?" he asked.

"Maybe. I mean, do they just become a mass of snakes and never re-form into a person, or do they stay attached to one another like a really creepy version of Medusa?"

"I'll ask."

"Does their snake, or snakes, become a beast like yours and mine? I mean, my inner beasts have thoughts, emotions, and if my body would let the change happen, if I could really turn into the physical form of my beasts like you can, the beast is sort of independent. It's its own being, animal, personage. Is one snake arm like that?"

"No, it's more like that rare medical condition, alien hand syndrome, where one hand begins to act independently of the person. They'll get flashes from the snakes, but it's mostly about biting, attacking, violent impulses."

"Are the snakes afraid of the human body? I mean, does the snake want to get away like a real snake would want to hide from humans?"

"I don't know, and I'm not sure they know either. They see it as a curse, Anita, a true curse, so they don't spend a lot of time trying to communicate with the monster parts of themselves."

"Surely you've told them that if you cooperate with your

inner beast, you can control it better. The more you fight the change, the more violent it is, and the less control you have as a beast."

"I've explained that to them, but they don't want to make peace with it. They want it gone."

"A lot of new lycanthropes feel that way."

"But this isn't like regular lycanthropy, Anita. They aren't becoming their animals; they're losing pieces of themselves in a way I've never seen. Their minds never stop being human and being horrified at what's happening to them. There's no moment when they can embrace their beast and enjoy the release of simpler, more linear thinking. Giving over to my leopard is peaceful sometimes, almost meditative."

"Do you think there's any chance of them finding peace with their beast parts?"

"You've seen the images. I get the feeling that there's worse to come, but they either don't want even me to see it, or they suicide before it gets much worse than the last picture I showed you. By the way, that's one son, one father, and one uncle."

"Is it only men in their family?"

"No, but it manifests differently in the female line, and it's less prevalent."

"How differently?"

"You mentioned Medusa. It usually starts there, like one snaky curl, or one picture is a snake curled between a woman's breasts, but the snake just happens to be growing out of the woman's ribs. It's usually calmer and it seems to be a different species of snake. It can also appear years earlier, even in early childhood."

"Can you send me a picture of it, the snake at least?"

"Hold on a second; there's someone at the door." He put me on hold.

I was left staring at the bridal dresses again in their plastic cocoons, waiting for the big day when they would come out and turn into beautiful brides and friends in rainbow colors. I wondered if anyone in the family Micah was helping saw marriage the same way. Did they tell their would-be spouses that any children might suffer the family curse? At what point in dating do you tell someone that particular truth?

"Anita, are you still there?"

"For you, always," I said.

"Thank you," he said.

"For what?"

"For reminding me that you're there for me. I don't know why this is bothering me so much."

"It's pretty terrible, Micah, and you can't figure out how to save them from their fate. Your inner white knight is really unhappy with that."

"You know me too well."

"No such thing, between us," I said.

"True," he said, and his voice sounded lighter. "Sorry, the witch has a few questions for me before we fly home to St. Louis. She's willing to see what her magic can tell her about the curse. More information is what I'm hoping for, but of course the family wants a cure."

"Is it the witch my friend recommended to the Coalition?"

"Yes, but I really don't think any modern witchcraft can cure this. If it's a curse, then whatever power was behind it is not like anything we can do today."

"Yeah, witches can't turn you into toads or any of that kind of stuff."

"I'm trying to talk them into a multiprong attack—magic, medical science, and gathering information from anyone old enough to have seen this kind of thing before—but if they won't share information, or allow me to share information, then there's not much we can do. Honestly, I'm not sure there's much we can do if they do come completely out of the closet. I've just never seen anything like this."

"What did they expect you and the Coalition to do for them, Micah? I mean, why did they call you in?"

"They want a cure."

"No type of shapeshifting is curable," I said.

"They want help, Anita. They've been very careful about who they let me see, but they are a big family, and the curse, or whatever genetic disorder this is, is getting worse."

"Have you seen any of them where the change is permanent?"

"No."

"How do they function with part of their body like that? I

mean, how do they go out and about if it doesn't go away? It's not like they can hide it."

"If it's just an arm, they put it in a cast or a sling. If it spreads to the point of the last picture I sent you, and it's permanent, the family hides them away, or they suicide. Though I'm not certain about that last part; they won't say *suicide* out loud, but it's implied loudly enough. Too many stories about family members who become less and less coherent when they change form, and when I ask how bad did it get, they get vague. They say grandparents can't live forever, or they have accidents, lots and lots of sudden, fatal accidents."

"Maybe they're not saying *suicide* because it's closer to assisted suicide, or even murder."

The silence on the other end of the phone was heavy. He sighed. "I guess I didn't want to think about that, but of course, you're right; that's probably what's happening. I'm not certain on that last part, because they won't confirm it as a solution, not out loud, but it's implied."

"Have they tried cutting off the arm when it's just one snake?"

"If you chop it off with a blade, it either goes away for a month until next full moon, or it splits and becomes multiple snakes faster, and the multiples become the form from the full moon onward."

"It sounds like the Lernaean Hydra from the Labors of Hercules. Every time you cut off a head, two grew back in its place."

"The family has Greek ancestry. They believe that their curse goes back to ancient Greece."

"What did their ancestor do to piss off the gods?"

"A seduction gone wrong and maybe turned into a rape, depending on which side of the story you're on."

"You know this can't really be a curse by the gods, right? It's some kind of genetic lycanthropy that we've never heard of, but it's not a curse."

"Some people still see turning into a wereanimal once a month as a curse, Anita."

I wanted to argue that with all the new laws nobody still thought that way, but I knew he was right. Prejudice against the lunarly challenged, or the terminally furry, to coin just two polite euphemisms, still ran strong in some places. I went back to trying to fix the problem, or at least trying to understand it better.

"Have they tried not chopping it off, but surgical amputation?" I asked.

"They have. Surgery works better; at least they don't split into multiples right away. They've got one cousin that's missing his arm from the elbow down because they've amputated it multiple times. He's willing to give up an arm to keep it from spreading through his body."

"Wait—how can a surgeon be treating him if it's still a secret?"

"They've got one doctor in the family who agreed to help."

"Okay. Has the patient made it through a full moon yet?"

"Three full moons. They've amputated his arm each time as it started to grow back as a snake."

"The Lernean Hydra was defeated by cutting off a head and burning the neck stub, according to legend. Fire still works on regular lycanthropy. If you cut off a shapeshifter's arm or leg and burn the end, it doesn't grow back. Fire cleanses or kills everything."

"That's been tried in the past," he said.

"Jesus, Micah, the Coalition is good, but what can you guys do for them?"

"I told you what they want, Anita: They want a cure."

"I didn't ask what they wanted; I asked what can you and the Coalition reasonably do to help them?"

He let out a shaking breath and whispered, "I don't know."

"If there's nothing you can do for them, Micah, come home."

"I am planning to come home tonight, but I hate to leave them without any hope, Anita."

"Being a police officer has taught me that you can't save everyone, Micah. I hate that we can't, but we can't."

"It just seems so terrible to leave them with nothing."

"I know, and I'm sorry for that. Have they tried modern genetic counseling? I mean, it might not help the adults that have it already, but they might be able to fix their babies in the womb if they could figure out what part of their genetics is causing it."

I couldn't really argue that. We were all polyamorous, which meant to love more, a flavor of consensual nonmonogamy, but Nathaniel was probably the least monogamous person in our committed relationship. Hell, he was one of the most poly polyamorous people I'd ever met.

"Anita, you still there?"

"I'm here, just trying to decide if I've ever heard Nathaniel ask for fewer people in the bedroom."

"The answer is no," he said.

"Probably," I said.

"Not probably," he said, "but if he were less of a group animal, I might not be in your life. You met Nathaniel first."

"That's true," I said.

"So, can I bitch about his love of more people, when I benefited from it?"

"Sure you can," I said. "I do shit like that all the time."

"But I try not to," he said.

"I know. You are the better person between us, Micah. I never doubt that."

"I do. I've got to go, Anita."

"I know, you have to introduce a witch to her potential clients before you fly home," I said, trying to keep my voice light.

"She has some of her magic group with her, so she won't be on her own."

"If she'd been on her own, you would have stayed," I said.

"We did ask her to consult on an impossible case, so probably."

"Go and play ambassador between the shapeshifters and the coven, and then come home to me."

"They prefer the phrase *magical working group*, and you're not at home."

"I guess *coven*, like the word *witch*, does come with a lot of baggage. The mystical community seems divided on whether to try to take back certain terms or discard them altogether."

"There's one out in California that calls itself a white-light study group."

"Really?"

I could hear the smile in his voice as he said, "Really."

"Our flight leaves tonight for St. Louis, so we'll be home soon."

"Sorry I had Jean-Claude's private jet on this trip, or you could have used it."

"A plane is a plane, Micah. I'm phobic of them all, but having to go through Minneapolis for a layover does make me miss the jet."

"Let me go play ambassador, so I can come home sooner."

"Yes, please," I said.

"I love you, Anita."

"I love you more, Micah."

"I love you mostest," he said and hung up.

It was usually our third who finished the last part of our three-part *I love you*. One of us would say "I love you," and then we'd say our parts. "I love you mostest": Until today I'd believed that Micah, Nathaniel, and I meant that to one another. Now I was left wondering if our so-very-understanding Micah might be coming to the end of his patience with the added lovers. I knew there were days and nights when I didn't know what to do with them all. Usually it was Micah soothing me about it. I wasn't sure I was going to be as good at soothing him.

2

"ANITA, ARE YOU all right?"

I jumped, tripping over the hem of the dress and jerking the top of the dress hard enough that one breast popped out. I did manage not to drop my phone, though.

Donna, the bride-to-be, laughed and then looked away quickly as I fumbled to try to cover the breast that had escaped. There were enough laugh lines in her face to let me know she did it often. As her face relaxed, she looked younger—dare I say glowing? She just looked happy, and nothing makes someone as beautiful as happiness and being in love. No makeup or youth serum can come close to that beauty secret. "I've never seen you startle like that," she said with an edge of laughter still in her voice. "You and Ted are usually so hyperaware of your surroundings that I didn't think it was possible for me to sneak up on either of you."

"I'm fine, just a little jumpy apparently," I said, but I was mentally cursing myself because she was right. I was in a public place and I'd had to hand over my gun and knives to our bodyguard, Nicky, because there was no way to have any weapons while we tailored the dress. If I'd been thinking, I would have brought a thigh holster and my Sig Sauer .380. Thigh holster was one of my least favorite ways to carry, but at least I could have kept one weapon on me. A belt holster on a formal dress had nowhere to hang, so I'd handed my weapons to Nicky. We had two more bodyguards outside the doors to the bridal shop, so I was safe, but I still didn't like that Donna had been able to sneak up on me. Micah had talked to Nathaniel before he'd asked for privacy and just me. Whatever he'd said to Nathaniel had left our shared boyfriend smiling, so Micah's doubts had only come to me—lucky me. I think I meant it on the lucky part; one of the three of us should be enjoying themselves today.

"Whatever you were thinking about just now isn't fine," Donna said, raising a hand as if to smooth her hair back behind her ear. But the new hairdo was all soft, short curls that didn't encroach on the smooth curves of her ears, which bore two delicate stud earrings. Her hair had been brown, but now it was almost blond, with just hints of her underlying brown, as if the sun had bleached it golden, but I'd been told she'd gone to a great hair stylist.

"You said it yourself, Donna. I let you sneak up on me in a public place. I could have been flashing a stranger."

She chuckled. "The halter dress looks great on Denny, but you . . ." She waved vaguely at me and shook her head, still smiling. "I'm sorry, I didn't think about how different you and Denny are built when I asked for you to match her dress."

"Denny's inseam must be seven inches longer than mine, Donna. Plus, she's a serious runner and does triathlons, so she's built long and lean. I'll never be either of those things."

Donna hugged me, which was a little more awkward than normal, because I could only use one arm to hug her back unless I was willing to do a lot more than flash one breast. The thought of pressing my bare breasts against Donna in a close hug made me wildly uncomfortable. If I hadn't been dating women, would it have bothered me as much? I think so. It wasn't the girl-on-girl thing; it was the Donna thing.

"I forgot how much shorter you were than Denny; you always seem to fill up more space than that, just like Ted does." She drew back and I was happy the hugging was over, so I could try to rearrange the halter top as best I could.

"I forget that he's only five-eight sometimes, too," I said.

"He seems like he must be at least six feet tall, doesn't he?" she said.

I smiled and agreed because she was right. Nathaniel was actually an inch taller than Edward, but I always forgot that until they were standing next to each other for comparison. Part of the reason was that Nathaniel had only been five foot six when we met, so sometimes I remembered him as shorter than his full height.

"Thank you again, Anita, for flying to New Mexico this close to the wedding. I know how you hate to fly, and now you'll have to fly home and then fly to Florida, so three flights instead of just one."

"Only your tailor here in New Mexico was going to be willing to make time in their schedule this close to the wedding, so I had to come to you."

"You didn't have to come; you could have told me to go to hell and you were wearing a tux like we planned."

I smiled. "I could have, but I'd rather not have a fight with you and Ted this close to your wedding. I'm his best man; I have to act like the better man, or better person, or whatever."

Donna's eyes narrowed, small frown lines appearing between her eyes. She reached out toward me and for a second I thought it was the beginning of another hug, but her hand sort of hovered near my left shoulder. "I've never seen that one before. I guess your usual shirts cover it."

It took me another second to realize she meant the scar on my collarbone.

"How did it happen?" she asked, voice soft.

"A vampire did it," I said.

"It doesn't look like a vampire bite."

"He wasn't trying to drink my blood. He bit me so he could tear me up; he bit through my collarbone and just kept worrying at me like a dog with a bone."

Her face started to show horror, but she got control of herself until when she asked the next question she looked neutral. I knew she didn't feel that way, but I gave her points for the control.

"What about the bend of your arm?"

I looked down at my left arm with its mound of scar tissue. "Same vampire."

"God, he just wanted to hurt you, didn't he?"

"Yes."

I made a fist, flexing my arm. There was a lot more muscle on the arm than there had been when I got the injury. A doctor had told me I'd lose partial use of my arm if I didn't do my physical therapy and start lifting weights. It had been the first thing that got me into the gym seriously. Keeping the use of my arm was a much better motivator than fitting into a smaller size of jeans. Both scars were white and slick now, but the scars in the bend of my arm would always be raised and feel like there was something under the skin, because so much scar tissue had formed at the wound as it healed. The vampire hadn't even broken my arm, but the scar was worse all the same. The scar between my shoulder and neck was flat to my skin except for the one area over my collarbone that would always be raised. It wasn't rougher, exactly, but it was as if I could still feel the broken edges of the bone sticking up underneath my skin, though it was just scar tissue, not bone. Both injuries had healed years ago, but when it got damp or cold, or if I ever laid off the weight lifting for the arm for too long, they would ache. I realized with a shock that they didn't ache like that anymore, or very rarely. I had too much magic in my veins now, too much power. It made me more, or less, than pure human, depending on whom you asked. Micah wasn't the only one who got casual death threats from hate groups.

Donna misunderstood the look on my face, because her eyes got shiny and her voice had a catch in it when she said, "Anita, I am so sorry that I tried to make you wear a dress that shows all your . . . job-related injuries. I know how many Ted has, and I should have known that you'd have them, too. If you had said something, I would have understood."

I looked at myself in a way that I didn't normally. The scars were just a part of me. The cross-shaped burn mark on my left forearm I'd gotten from the same attack as the other two injuries. It had been the first time Edward and I worked together on a case. It sort of set the tone for our working relationship. The burn had been from the vampire's servants branding me so I'd look like a vampire who had had a holy object burn her. It had amused them while we waited for darkness to fall and their master to rise. It had amused them right up to the moment when Edward burned the house down around them and nearly around both of us. I'd never liked him using the flamethrower after that. Hell, I didn't like flamethrowers in general after that, but he was the only vampire executioner I'd ever known who would actually use it in the field.

Donna's hand hesitated above my arm, as if she was going to touch the claw marks just below the burn. The scars from the shapeshifted witch made the cross a little crooked. Edward hadn't been there for that wound. I'd been working with the police on my own that time, before I had a badge and was officially on the job myself, back when I'd just been a vampire executioner, consulting with the police. Edward had just been Edward, cold-blooded assassin who specialized in killing monsters, both human and otherwise. I hadn't even known he had a legal identity as Ted Forrester, bounty hunter. Now we were both U.S. Marshals with the Preternatural Branch. We did the same job legally and, for Edward, for far less money.

She pointed vaguely at the small slick scar on the side of my arm, and then the thin, almost dainty scar on my right arm that was barely noticeable. "I know that's a bullet graze and that's a knife wound, because Ted has similar ones." She looked at me, her brown eyes going large in her tanned face. She looked suddenly younger, or more innocent, as if I got a glimpse of what she might have looked like at fifteen. "I stopped asking about where the other scars came from, because Ted told me the truth and they were almost all stories like the werewolf attack that killed my first husband, except that Ted goes out hunting the monsters. The monster that killed Frank broke into our house. It was a once-in-a-lifetime tragedy, but Ted and you go out looking for it."

"We hunt rogue vampires and lycanthropes that have murdered people. We keep people safe by killing the things that kill them."

She nodded, biting her lower lip, the frown lines deep between her eyes. There was real fear in them. Maybe she was remembering the death of her first husband, and that was probably in the mix of terror, but I thought it was more anticipating future tragedy than dwelling on the past. I looked into Donna's eyes and saw the fear that every time the man she loved left for work, he might not come back. I could tell her that he was more likely to die in a car crash, or from a dozen innocent household accidents, than be eaten by monsters, but it wouldn't help the emotions I saw in her eyes.

"I know you and Ted save lives. I know you keep other families safe from the monsters. I know that."

I reached out and touched her arm. "You know that Ted is the best, the absolute best at this job."

She nodded again, a little too fast and a little too often. "He says the same about you." She grabbed my hand where it touched her arm and held on. "I always feel better when you're with him, because he says you're the best, next to him."

"He helped train me, so he's still complimenting himself." I smiled when I said it and got a weak smile in return.

"I don't know what I'd do if anything happened to him," she said. She started tearing up. I hugged her because I didn't know what else to do, but apparently it was the wrong thing, because she started crying harder, clinging to me like she was really going to start sobbing. Fuck, what did I do now? How could I make her feel better about one of the truths of our job?

She went very still in my arms, and the crying slowed. She pushed away with her face still wet with tears and asked, "What's on your back?"

"Nothing," I said.

"I felt it."

I half turned and she touched the edge of the place where a vampire servant had tried to drive one of my own wooden stakes into my back. It was low on my back, and they'd just tried to shove the stake in without using a mallet. It doesn't work that way in real life, not if you're only human-strong, anyway. Lucky for me it had just been a human in league with the vampire I'd been hunting, and not a vampire.

"That's one of your own stakes driven into you, isn't it?" she asked. She wasn't crying anymore, so it was better, right?

"Yeah," I said.

"Ted has one like it; that's why I know what it is. You know, it's right there." She touched the side of my hip where bathing suits and underwear covered.

"I've never seen that one."

"Oh," she said, and looked confused.

"I've never seen Ted nude, so I missed that one."

There was a derisive snort, half laugh and half just rude noise, from the other side of the dress rack. Dixie, one of Donna's oldest friends and a bridesmaid, came into view. "That's such bullshit," she said, and her voice was as bitter as the look on her face. Dixie might actually have been an attractive woman, but she so seldom smiled or did anything pleasant that she came off as unattractive. Who wanted to be around a constant stream of negativity? No one, that's who. I had no idea what Donna saw in her as a friend except for the fact that they'd been friends since high school and they were now in their forties; well, duration counted, I guess.

"Don't start again, Dixie," Donna said.

"It's bullshit that Anita has never seen Ted nude."

"Why, because we work together?" I asked.

"No, not just because of your jobs, though that does give you the perfect cover story."

"I don't know how it works at your job, Dixie, but at mine we don't see our coworkers nude all that often."

"Is there a reason you came to find us, Dixie?" Donna asked, stepping closer to the other woman and blocking our view of each other, as if she were stepping between two kids on the playground about to fight.

"The tailor has another client in an hour that needs major alterations, so she needs Anita and the dress right now." Dixie put her hands on her hips, scowling at both of us.

I gathered up more of the voluminous skirt and said, "Let's get this over with, then."

"No, you don't have to wear the dress," Donna said, voice soft.

"You're finally kicking her out of the wedding; fabulous," Dixie said. She sounded happy, pleased with the world. She was even smiling, though her eyes stayed mean, almost predatory, like she smelled blood in the water.

"No, of course not. I'm just not going to make her wear a dress that's identical to Denny's. There's no reason the maids of honor have to match exactly; they just need to wear something that sets them apart from the rest of the wedding party."

"Thanks, Donna, I appreciate that, a lot."

She looked at me, touching my arm. "The tailor said that there was no way to fit your curves in this dress anyway." She laughed a little. "But I wouldn't make you appear in such a public venue with all your scars on display like this. I wouldn't do that to anyone."

"Why are you being nice to her?" Dixie demanded.

"She's my friend, Dixie."

"The fact that you're both sleeping with the same man doesn't make you friends, Donna. It makes her a whore and you stupid."

"Donna," I said, because I'd just about had enough of Dixie, and I wasn't sure how to ask permission to punch her friend in the face.

"Ted and Anita are not sleeping together. They are just partners and best friends; that's all," Donna said.

"You're the one that told me they were having an affair!" Dixie said, raising her voice a little. I was pretty sure it was on purpose. If she was going to embarrass us, she wanted an audience.

"I was wrong. I just didn't understand Ted being so close with another woman. Our therapist has helped us work through all that."

"Your therapist believed they were screwing each other, Donna!"

"Because I told her they were, and she only had my version."

"Ted admitted it!"

"Only because I told him that I wouldn't marry him unless he admitted they were having an affair."

"He lied to you!"

"Only because I wouldn't believe the truth."

Dixie pointed at me. "She admitted it to you, too."

"Ted asked her to lie, if I asked her directly."

"That's ridiculous! Who the hell would lie about something like that if it wasn't true?" Dixie said.

"It was ridiculous," I said.

Dixie looked at me in triumph. "See, she admits it!"

"No, Ted and I are not now, and never have been, lovers, but the fact that he asked me to back up his lie about it was ridiculous. I still can't believe that he asked me to compromise us both like that. I didn't think Ted would ever let anyone emotionally blackmail him into anything so stupid, and then ask me to back him in it."

"He was buying time so he could explain the truth in therapy to me and our therapist," Donna said, and she was smiling now, her face filled with that radiant glow that only true love can give you.

"That is the most insane thing I've ever heard. You wouldn't marry him until he told you the truth, so he told you the truth, but then he manipulated you and your therapist into believing that he's innocent and Anita isn't his slut on the side."

"Are you trying to pick a fight with me, Dixie?"

"No, just calling a spade a spade."

"Glad to hear you're not trying to pick a fight, but if you call me a whore or a slut again, it will be a fight, just to be clear."

"Anita is going to be Ted's best man in our wedding, Dixie, and that's that. You need to find a way to deal with that."

"I am dealing with it."

"With more grace than this, Dixie. I mean it."

"Grace, grace . . ." She looked astonished, shocked. "How can you ask me to be okay with this, Donna? Once a cheater, always a cheater. Don't start your marriage with his mistress in the wedding party."

Mistress was a step up from *slut* and *whore*, damn it. I was almost disappointed that I couldn't at least scare Dixie into leaving me the fuck alone. "I am no one's mistress, but least of all Ted's."

"I know you're not his mistress, but you got mad at me calling you what you are." She gave me that mean look again. I just knew Dixie had been one of those mean girls in school who made other girls' lives hell. Some people never grow up; they just grow older.

I took a step forward.

"Anita, no, please, she doesn't understand that you won't fight like a girl," Donna said.

"I can take care of myself, Donna," Dixie said.

Donna put a hand on her arm. "No, Dixie, you can't, not with Anita."

"Why do you keep defending her? She's fucking your husband-to-be!" She started toward me, pushing against Donna's hand.

Donna put a hand on each of her arms and pushed back, not letting her get closer to me. I noticed for the first time that there were muscles under Donna's tanned skin. I knew she had been working out for the wedding but hadn't realized how much until that moment. Good for her. Dixie didn't have muscle to push back, but she tried. I realized in that moment that she was one of those people who wanted to take her bad mood out on someone, anyone. I understood anger issues, but she'd picked the wrong woman to start a fight with.

"I'm not protecting Anita. I'm protecting you."

"Protecting me from what?" Dixie yelled, trying to push past Donna.

"From her."

"What?" Dixie stopped pushing and looked at Donna like she was crazy. "She's five inches shorter than I am. She's tiny."

"Size isn't everything," I said, voice quiet, because I realized I would enjoy an excuse to hurt Dixie. I wouldn't hurt her much, because I wouldn't need to, but she was getting on my nerves and we hadn't even flown to the destination for the destination wedding yet. It did not bode well for Dixie and me.

She tried to push past Donna again, and this time Donna let her, moving just enough to one side so that Dixie's pushing carried her forward, stumbling. Dixie had made the rookie mistake of getting stuck on pushing against someone: Just stop holding them up and they'll usually fall. Donna used small, fast hand movements to help Dixie to the floor, using one arm as a lever, or maybe a leash; it depended on what you wanted to do next. Dislocate her elbow, face-plant her on the ground, so many options.

Dixie cried out in surprise. She looked and sounded as surprised as I was that Donna had done it. When I met Donna she'd been useless in a crisis and she would never have done anything this physical, this soon. Yay, Donna!

"If I can do this to you, Dixie, Anita would destroy you." She let go of her friend and stepped back out of reach, just in case. You never know how someone is going to take an object lesson that includes physical force. Major brownie points to her for treating her best friend like anyone else you've forced to the ground.

Dixie knelt on the ground cradling her arm like it hurt. I knew it didn't hurt. Donna hadn't done anything to hurt her, yet. It had been very controlled. Violence and control had been two things Donna didn't have when Edward first introduced us. I hadn't known until this moment that he'd been teaching her how to fight. Since I was insisting that everyone close to me learn at least the basics of self-defense, I approved.

Dixie started to cry, softly, as she knelt on the floor, still cradling her arm. "You heartless bitch, you deserve to be cheated on." Maybe Dixie just called everyone insulting pet names. If I'd known that, I might have let the *whore* and *slut* comments go.

Donna was clear-eyed, calm, and determined as she said, "Anita, go find Nathaniel and help him pick out a new dress for you. Dixie and I are going to stay here and talk things over."

"You could have broken my arm, you bitch!"

"Go on, Anita. I've got this," Donna said in a voice so sure of itself that I could almost hear the echo of Edward in it. Or maybe I was doing her a disservice; maybe this surety had always been inside her and Edward had just helped her find it. Either way, I honored that strength in her and did what she asked without questioning if she could handle the situation. She'd proved she could handle herself and Dixie. So I left her to handle things and went to find Nathaniel and get out of that dress.

3

NATHANIEL FOUND ME before I could start wandering the store in search of him, which was just as well since I'd tripped again. The only thing that saved me from flashing again was that I had so much of the skirt in my hands that it hid my chest, which begged the question of what I had tripped on: I thought I had all the damn skirt in my arms.

"You are adorable," Nathaniel said. His arms were full of black and teal cloth, presumably more dresses.

I glared at him as I tried to get my one high heel free of the single edge of hem I'd managed not to pick up. "It is not adorable that this dress is trying to kill me."

His face was shining with suppressed laughter. His eyes had darkened from lilac to lavender with the effort not to laugh at me. His driver's license said his eyes were blue, but they weren't; they were shades of purple like flower petals. Strangers asked if they were colored contacts, but they weren't. The eyes sat in the middle of a face that was more beautiful than handsome, but I preferred my men on the pretty side of masculine, so it worked for us. He'd pulled his thick auburn hair back into a ponytail, but it wasn't quite long enough, so strands of it escaped and trailed around his face. Once his hair had been down to his ankles, and it had been midcalf length when some very bad vampires chained him up and cut it off. They'd done it with me tied up and forced to watch. They'd planned to torture and mutilate him to get to me, and it would have worked, except that we escaped and killed them first. His hair was growing back, but it was a constant visual reminder of what we had almost lost.

There were reasons for the two bodyguards, Millington and

Custer, who were hanging near the front of the store, one outside and one inside near the door. Millie's white-blond hair was
still cut high and tight, as if he'd never stopped being a Navy
SEAL, but Custer, nickname Pud, had let his brown hair grow
out enough that it almost touched the tops of his ears. Millie
was starting to tease him about being a hippie. I trusted them
to make sure that no one who was a threat to us entered the
shop. But it was Nicky Murdock, who came down the aisle
behind Nathaniel like a blond mountain, whom I trusted the
most. I would never risk Nathaniel like that again, not if I could
avoid it, and I knew that Nicky understood that. He was our
main bodyguard for that and a lot of other reasons. His shoulders barely fit between the clothes racks on either side of the
aisle. He was a fraction of an inch shorter than six feet. Millie
was taller at six feet plus, but though the ex–Navy SEAL was
in great shape, he looked almost fragile when he stood beside
Nicky. Pud was a little bit shorter than either of them, and
slightly broader through the shoulders than Millie, but nothing
close to Nicky. We had plenty of bodyguards who were taller
than Nicky, but almost none of them were as broad through the
shoulders. He'd been a big guy to begin with, but a devotion to
weights and the natural genetics to bulk had made him huge.
He was like a smiling blond colossus trailing behind Nathaniel,
and I knew that he was even more dangerous than he looked.

Nicky was good-looking, but in a much more masculine way
than Nathaniel. He had squarer features, and just to set off the
rugged look, he was missing his right eye. Where it would have
been were slick white scars, in a harsh contrast to the blue eye on
the other side. His yellow hair was long on top so that it fell
forward toward his face, but the sides were almost shaved. The
longer spill of hair almost seemed to be pointing at the missing
eye so you wouldn't miss it; before he cut the hair, the yellow
point had cascaded down over the scars, hiding them. It had been
a sort of anime version of an eye patch. I wasn't sure if the haircut was a show of solidarity with Nathaniel, or if Nicky had
simply been ready to face the world head-on with no hiding. He
still got uncomfortable now and then, when people stared, but he
stared back and they usually dropped their gaze and tried to
pretend they hadn't been looking. He was one of only two lovers
in my life who had more spectacular scars than I did.

He smiled as he said, "I thought for a second I'd have to save you from putting Dixie in the hospital."

I finally got my heel untangled from the hem. "I didn't think we were being that loud, and I wouldn't have hurt her that badly," I said.

"We're lycanthropes. We'd hear almost everything in a store this size," Nicky said.

"And Dixie is usually loud," Nathaniel said, and he looked unhappy.

"I take it you've about had it with her, too," I said.

He nodded. "I think even Donna is getting fed up."

"Donna just did my job for me and put her friend on the floor," Nicky said, smiling. "I don't think she's getting fed up; I think she's there."

"I didn't know Donna had it in her," I said.

"Me either," Nathaniel said.

"Edward's been teaching her some of his moves," Nicky said.

"Ted has been teaching her moves," I corrected.

"I know better than to make slips like that. Sorry."

"It's not my forgiveness you'll need if you do it in front of the wrong people, Nicky."

"I don't want to go one-on-one with . . . Ted."

"Even though he's straight human and nothing supernatural?" I asked, studying his face.

"Ted isn't like anyone else; you know that." Nicky's face was very serious as he said it.

I nodded. "True. I just wasn't sure you'd think so. You outweigh him by at least eighty pounds of pure muscle, have longer reach, and preternatural strength and speed to his human-normal. I guess I just thought you wouldn't see any straight human as that big a problem."

"Like I said, Ted is different. He may not be a supernatural citizen, but I think calling him 'straight human' may be stretching things," Nicky said.

"There's something scary about . . . Ted," Nathaniel said, voice soft and eyes sort of distant, as if he was remembering something grim. Was he remembering Ireland, where he'd lost his hair and almost his life? Edward had been there with us. He'd brought us in to help him hunt the vampires that had been threatening

Dublin. One of our people had died there. Domino had died there. I made myself say the name, at least in my own head. My therapist said I felt guilty about his death. Damn straight I did.

Nathaniel touched my face, made me look at him and see the gentle smile on his face. "If you think happy thoughts, so will I."

I smiled at him because he made me want to smile. "So we can fly?"

His smile brightened. "No flying off to never-never land until after this wedding. I've still got a to-do list to go over with the bride. No one goes anywhere until we get them down the aisle."

"Isn't the maid of honor supposed to do that kind of stuff?" Nicky asked.

"Yes, but Denny isn't good at wedding stuff, and she's been training for triathlons through most of the wedding prep."

"So how did it become your job? You're like the third bridesmaid," Nicky said.

"Dixie had started doing it," Nathaniel said, looking back at the taller man.

"And how was that going?" I asked.

Nathaniel looked back to me. "Dixie is competent enough to do it all, but she's been pissed that Donna made Denny maid of honor over her. She was doing the duties of a maid of honor without the title, and she made sure we all knew that every time she talked to us. A few phone calls from her and I was so over it."

"I thought you volunteered to be Donna's bridal helpmate because you love weddings," I said.

He grinned. "That, too, but mostly to save Donna, Denny, and Dixie from having a fight that would have ended twenty years of friendship."

"Why didn't she just make Dixie the matron of honor in the first place? After knowing her that long, Donna had to know what a bitch Dixie would be about it if she didn't," Nicky said.

"I know this one," I said. "Dixie was her maid of honor for her first wedding and Donna was her matron of honor, but they both promised that if they married a second time that Denny would be their maid of honor. I think they were both sort of joking, because neither of them planned to marry again."

Nathaniel nodded. "And the irony is that I don't think

Denny cared about being maid of honor; she just wanted to be in her best friends' weddings."

"Agreed. Denny is almost as uninterested in wedding stuff as I am."

Nathaniel raised the dresses in his arms like he was gesturing with them. "Now let's find you another dress, so you never have to wear that one again."

"Yes, please," I said, and started moving toward the dressing rooms. I tripped over some piece of the dress that had fallen out of my arms. I caught myself on a clothes rack or I'd have hit the floor.

"I could carry you," Nicky said, voice deadpan, but with an edge of teasing he wasn't really trying to hide.

"No."

"I am your bodyguard and I think that dress is a danger to you." His voice was even flatter and more serious.

I glanced back at him. His face matched the voice except for the twinkle in his eye that let me know there was laughter struggling to get out.

"I think I can walk a few yards to the dressing rooms without injuring myself."

"If you say so," he said.

Nathaniel said, "I'd pay to see the looks on the other bridesmaids' faces if we show up with Nicky carrying you. I could undo my hair, shake it out, and make my clothes look messy like we'd been fooling around."

"I know you're teasing me, because you value their good opinion as much as, or more than, I do."

"True, but I'd still do it, just to see Dixie's face."

"How do you know she's back with the other bridesmaids and not still having a heart-to-heart with Donna?"

"We heard them walking back," Nicky said.

I looked from one to the other of them and knew he meant it. I hadn't heard anything except us and the air-conditioning struggling against the New Mexico heat. I said, "Let's just go back and get this over with."

We were within sight of the rest of the bridal party and the tailor when I tripped again and flashed them all. Maybe I should have let Nicky carry me.

4

LESS THAN AN hour later I was standing on a small raised dais surrounded by mirrors. Donna and Dixie had given their thumbs-up and -down on the many dresses I'd tried on, until we all found, if not the One, then at least the It'll Do. I'd have thought Dixie might have stayed angry, but she was better behaved and even seemed calmer. Maybe having her BFF put her on the ground had put things in perspective for Dixie, or maybe she was one of those people who responded better to bad treatment than good. If I'd known getting physical with her would have fixed the problem, I'd have done it sooner, or asked Donna to do it.

The seamstress was putting the last pin in the skirt so she could hem it later. Other than being too long, which every-thing was, the dress didn't need any other tailoring. It was a vast improvement on the first dress. This one was black with a much more modest *V* neckline. My chest still filled the avail-able space nicely, but I wasn't in danger of flashing anyone. I didn't even mind the teal sash that tied into a neat bow in the back. I normally hated bows, but the teal matched the brides-maids' dresses perfectly and was a nice splash of color in all the black.

"It's getting late, Anita," Nicky said.

I started to look toward the windows to judge the amount of daylight left. "Don't move!" the seamstress said.

"Sorry," I said to her, then glanced at Nicky. "It doesn't feel that close to sunset yet."

"What do you mean it doesn't 'feel' close to sunset?" Dixie asked.

Donna chimed in with a voice that was a little too cheerful. "They've got a plane to catch back to St. Louis tonight."

"We either need to make this flight or be in Santa Fe, but either way, we have to be out of Albuquerque before sunset," Nicky said.

Nathaniel said, "My phone says we still have two hours."

"Making your flight I get, but what's wrong with being in Albuquerque after dark?" Dixie asked.

Nicky, Nathaniel, Donna, and I all exchanged glances with one another. It was Donna who said, "Obsidian Butterfly, Albuquerque's Master of the City, has some . . . issues with Anita."

"What, did Anita try to kill Albuquerque's Master of the City, like she does to most of the vampires she meets?" Dixie's voice had that cruel undertone that was almost her usual tone. Apparently, whatever nice she'd gotten from the "talk" with Donna had been used up and she was now back to her usual bitchy self.

I hadn't tried to kill Obsidian Butterfly. She thought she was an Aztec deity, and since she had been worshipped as one once, who could blame her for the delusion? She was powerful enough that the old vampire council had declared Albuquerque off-limits for other vampires. Their Master of the City was powerful enough to frighten the other monsters, which meant that she was powerful enough that both Edward and I tried to leave her the fuck alone. My first case in New Mexico, we had needed the goddess's help. That was also the case where I'd first met Bernardo Spotted-Horse and Otto Jeffries, fellow U.S. Marshals now. We were nicknamed the Four Horsemen of the Apocalypse, because individually and together, we had the most kills of any of the other marshals. Bernardo was going to be at the altar as one of Edward's groomsmen. Otto hadn't been invited to the wedding.

I didn't owe Dixie that much history. "There are a lot of vampires in my life who would disagree with that statement, including Jean-Claude," I said. I didn't even feel defensive about it. She was too wrong for it to be offensive.

"Your fiancé, Jean-Claude, is like a male version of Snow White. Did you take one look at him asleep in his coffin and just couldn't put a stake through his heart?"

Ted Forrester's good ol' boy drawl came from behind us. "Jean-Claude sure is pretty; that's for sure." He pronounced *pretty* like "purdy." When Edward was in full Ted mode he sounded like you think southern cowboys talk, if there was such a thing as a southern cowboy.

I started to look over my shoulder but remembered not to move just in time and just used the mirrors to watch him. The big smile on his face that made his blue eyes sparkle was all Ted, as were the white cowboy hat, the white short-sleeved dress shirt, and the cowboy boots. But the undershirt that showed at the neck was black, tucked into the black jeans, and the cowboy boots were black, too. It was as if he could pull off the white dress shirt and be in all black in an instant like Clark Kent changing into Superman.

He took off the hat, and his short blond hair was tight to his head because he'd worn Ted's beloved Stetson all day. Edward didn't wear hats, and if he had it wouldn't have been a white cowboy hat.

"I didn't know you thought he was pretty, Ted," Dixie said, and just her tone let you know that the next thing out of her mouth was going to be something unpleasant.

"Everyone thinks he's pretty, Dixie. I'm just secure enough in my manliness to admit it." The accent helped make it a teasing statement. He stepped around the seamstress and me so he could kiss Donna.

She wrapped her arms around him and turned the kiss into a little bit more than just a normal hello. It made me smile and I caught Nathaniel's glance, so we smiled together. We were like most happy couples; we enjoyed seeing other people happy, too. Nicky's face was impassive in the mirror.

"God, Donna, stop acting like a teenager in public. It's embarrassing at our age."

Donna pulled back from the kiss, but Edward wouldn't let her step out of the embrace. "What does it matter what anyone thinks but us?" There was less Ted and more of Edward's middle-of-nowhere, middle-of-America nothing accent in the question. For him to lose his accent in public like that meant he was upset.

Donna smiled up at him as if he were her whole world and then leaned in so they could kiss again. Good for them.

The tailor stood up, hesitating a little as if her knees were an issue. Nathaniel offered her a hand and she took it, smiling at him. "Thank you, young man."

He flashed her a watered-down version of the smile he used at Guilty Pleasures when he was dancing. She blushed. Nice to know Nathaniel had that effect on women of all ages. He offered me a hand down from the dais, though he knew I didn't need it. Once upon a time, not that long ago, I wouldn't have taken it, because I didn't need the help, but just as Edward could admit that Jean-Claude was pretty without it compromising his masculinity, I could let my fiancé help me down a step without losing my independent-woman card.

He flashed me the smile that no one at his job got, the one that said *love. I love you* with just his eyes. I smiled back at him and knew that my eyes and the rest of my face showed just how much I loved him, too. We leaned toward each other for a kiss, because that's what you do when you love someone. His lips were soft, warm, gentle, because it was that kind of kiss.

"So just you and me, left out in the cold," Dixie said.

The bitterness of the comment made us both draw back from our kiss to look first at Dixie and then at Nicky, when we realized that was whom she was referring to. He looked back at her, face utterly calm. "I'm not out in the cold, Dixie. That's just you."

"Well, I don't see anyone kissing on you either."

"I'm working," he said.

"What does that mean?" she asked.

Edward answered in Ted's accent, but they were his words. "It means that Nicky is a professional bodyguard."

"So what?"

"So he's guarding Anita and Nathaniel right now. Kissing her would be a distraction and unprofessional."

"What he said," Nicky said.

"I don't believe it," she said. "You're all just teasing me."

"What part don't you believe, that I'm one of their bodyguards or that I'm one of Anita's lovers?" Nicky asked.

"Bodyguard I believe." She looked at Nathaniel. "Are you just going to let him claim your girl like that?"

Nathaniel smiled. "Anita's not my girl, she's my fiancée,

and I like sharing with Nicky." He offered a fist and Nicky bumped it gently.

"The news says she's marrying Jean-Claude, so she can't be your fiancée."

"Actually, we found out that there's no law against how many fiancés you can have; you just can't legally marry more than one of them," I said.

"Not yet," Nathaniel said.

I kissed him lightly and said, "You are being awfully optimistic about the government of our country. It was hard enough to get the United States to allow same-sex marriage. I don't see multiple partners being legal anytime soon."

"Are you saying you'd actually marry Nathaniel and Jean-Claude if it was legal?" Dixie asked.

"And Micah," Nathaniel and I said together. It made us grin at each other in that stupid-happy way.

"What about you?" she said, motioning at Nicky.

"What about me?"

"Doesn't it bother you that Anita just said she'd marry three men, but you're not on the list?"

"No," he said.

"Of course it bothers you. It would bother anyone to be left out like that," Dixie said.

"I don't feel left out."

"Don't lie. Just tell them they hurt your feelings and it was rude."

"My feelings aren't hurt and they aren't the ones being rude."

Edward said, "Go change out of the dress so you guys can make your plane." He kept the accent, but somehow the tone was colder than good ol' Ted usually sounded.

I didn't argue, because he was right. Nicky handed me a small pack that he'd had slung over one shoulder. I took it and went into the dressing room. The pack contained the two guns, extra ammunition, and knife that I'd get to carry onto the plane. I'd taken the training as a sky marshal, years before 9/11, and so far, it let me carry on a plane, though there was talk of that changing. But for today I was the only one of us who wouldn't have to put their weapons in luggage.

I could hear Dixie still trying to start some sort of jealousy issue between Nathaniel and Nicky. It wouldn't work. Nathaniel was the least jealous person I knew, and Nicky just didn't think like that.

Edward's voice cut in. "You almost dressed in there, Anita?"

"Almost." I was in my own black jeans, black boots, and red T-shirt, with a black suit jacket over it all to help hide the weapons. Just because I could carry legally didn't mean I wanted to flash my weapons at everyone. One, it made people nervous, and two, if it did turn into a fight, I didn't want the bad guys to know what I was carrying or where on me I was carrying it.

"Dixie, stop picking at Nathaniel and Nicky. I don't know what's wrong with you lately. You're supposed to be one of my best friends, Dixie. Why aren't you happy for me?"

"I've already told you why I'm not happy for you, Donna."

"If I believe Ted and Anita aren't having an affair, why can't you?"

I fussed to get my inner pants holster a little more comfortable, but really I was dressed. I just didn't want to walk out into the middle of this conversation. If I hid, would it be cowardice? Yes, damn it. I opened the door and said as cheerily as I could, "I'm dressed. Let's head for the airport."

Dixie kept talking as if I hadn't said anything. She was looking at Donna with an intensity that made the rest of us irrelevant. "I don't believe him because no man would admit to an affair he wasn't having. It's hard enough to get them to admit to ones they are having."

I sighed and said what I was thinking. "It was pretty stupid." Everyone looked at me.

"Having an affair is pretty stupid," Dixie said.

I shook my head. "There is no affair, never was, never will be, but Dixie's right on one thing—it was stupid of Ted to confess to something he wasn't doing. It was stupid of me to let him talk me into going along with the lie. It was convoluted thinking beyond anything I've ever thought for him to use a false confession to have time to talk to Donna and their couples therapist while the wedding plans went ahead."

"You went along with it," Ted said, but not in his friendliest tone.

"I didn't say I was the brightest bulb in the box when it came to relationships either."

That got smiles and laughs from everyone but Dixie. "I can't take this anymore. I'm done."

"What do you mean 'done'?" Donna asked. "You don't mean the wedding . . ."

Dixie moved her gaze from Donna to Ted. She stared at him like she personally hated him. I'd only seen genuine bad guys stare at him like that. It was strangely more unnerving coming from a supposed friend.

"If you are going to marry him, I'll be there, and when she finds out you are a cheating son of a bitch, I'll be there to hold her hand, just like I did after Frank died." And with that, she left.

5

SOME SILENCES ARE louder than noise. This was one of those silences. None of us knew what to say to fill that awkward moment, or rather, I knew what I wanted to say, which was some variation of "Kick Dixie out of the wedding," but it wasn't my place to say it. It was Edward's.

"Donna, we need to talk about Dixie and the wedding," Edward said.

"She's one of my oldest and dearest friends, Ted. She was my maid of honor the first time, and I was her matron of honor."

"I know that, honeybunch," he said, sliding back into Ted's accent, "and I know you were close when her sons and Peter were younger, but now that all the boys are college age, it's changed."

Donna nodded. "The last time Dixie and I had a shopping trip, just us girls, we took Becca with us. Dixie said she wished they'd had a little girl. Someone close to Becca's age so we'd all be doing dance classes and theater together, the way we used to do sports with the boys."

"Peter was in martial arts with their youngest son, but we didn't do what they did. They spent every weekend and most evenings at one sporting event or another with their two boys."

"Peter did all the sports that the other boys did," she said.

He smiled at her with a look that was all warm and happy, and a little something that I couldn't define. "Peter didn't like team sports. We didn't force him to stay in everything the way that they did with Benji."

"It was just that their oldest was like Ray and Dixie; he loved all the team sports and was good at them."

"Benji was good at a lot of them; he just hated playing," Edward said.

"We're going to have to leave soon for the airport," Nicky said. "If you need to discuss the wedding and Dixie with Nathaniel or Anita, you need to do it soon."

Donna started to try to get a little offended, but Edward said, "Nicky is doing his job, honeybunch. Do you want Nathaniel to help us decide about Dixie?" I didn't mind that he dropped me off the list of people to consult. He knew what my vote would be.

She looked up at Edward. "Are you actually asking me to kick Dixie out of the wedding?"

"Dixie said it, that since she doesn't have a daughter Becca's age we don't do as much with them as we used to, so she hasn't had a chance to call me a cheating bastard in front of Becca, but once we get to Florida we are on a small island. We are going to be in each other's pockets, honeybunch. Do you really think she can control herself in front of the kids and our other friends?"

"She wouldn't say things like that in front of Becca. She helped me shop for Becca's flower girl dress and the three of us had a wonderful time. Dixie said it was like the old days when the boys were little."

"Donna," Nathaniel said.

She turned and looked at him.

He was very serious as he asked, "Do you really want my opinion on this?"

She smiled at him. "I know you stepped in because Dixie wasn't helping me the way she should have, and I will always be grateful for that."

He smiled back at her. "But I'm not one of your oldest friends, and you don't want my opinion on this."

She moved away from Edward so she could grip Nathaniel's arm. "No, that's not what I meant. I've come to value your opinion on so many things, Nathaniel. I admit that I invited you to be part of the wedding party with the idea that with you around Ted wouldn't be so tempted with Anita, but you turned into the best bridesmaid I've ever had."

He grinned at her. "Thank you. I've really enjoyed most of it."

Her own smile faded around the edges. "I'm sorry that Dixie kept trying to get you to complain about Anita."

That was news to me. I looked at Nathaniel, and he shrugged. "When it was just us girls"—he made quote marks around the last word—"Dixie tried to make it a bitching session about our significant others, like she tried to get Nicky to admit he felt left out of the kissing earlier."

"You never mentioned that to me."

"You've met Dixie before this. Are you really surprised?"

I thought about it for a second and then shook my head. "I guess not."

Nicky said, "Ten minutes, and then we have to leave."

"Dixie compares her husband, Ray, to any man she's around. 'Why can't you be in shape like Nathaniel? I bet he can lift more than you in the gym.' That kind of thing," Nathaniel said.

"You're almost the age of her oldest son. Ray can't compete with a younger version of himself," Donna said.

"She told him that Peter can lift more in the gym than he can now."

"I told her that was totally unfair, that it would be like comparing us to nineteen-year-old girls," Donna said.

Nathaniel smiled. "That did shut her up for a while."

"You'd kick her out of the wedding," Edward said.

The smile left Nathaniel's face as he answered, "Part of Dixie's bitchiness is because she's not the matron of honor. If you kick her out of the wedding completely, then the friendship is over. I wish I had any family or friends that had been in my life for twenty years. I won't be the deciding vote that ends a relationship that's lasted that long."

Donna hugged him and said, "And that is why you are the best bridesmaid ever."

Edward was looking at Nathaniel as if he wanted to say something to him.

"Time's up, or we're going to miss the flight," Nicky said.

And we had to leave it there, because Nathaniel was right: It had to be Donna's decision because Dixie was her friend, but she didn't have much time to decide. The wedding was in a week.

6

THE HOUR LAYOVER in Minneapolis turned into three because our first plane never got off the ground due to mechanical trouble. Hey, at least the issue happened while we were still on the ground and not in the air. I'd had mechanical issues happen in midflight before; it was one of the things that had contributed to my fear of flying. Five hours later we were almost home but got stuck in traffic out in front of the Circus of the Damned. Even though it was late, people were still lined up on the sidewalk to get into the remodeled warehouse that housed the Circus, and other people were driving by trying to find a parking place now that the customer lot was full. We were stuck in the traffic, inching along in front of the building. The huge fanged clowns still rotated endlessly on the roof, and large, lurid posters still covered the front of the building, though some of the acts had changed over the years. One poster showed a wolfman with blue eyes: *Hear Professor Wolf Read from His Latest Book of Poetry*. Zeke, like Micah, had been punished by the same sadistic ex-leader, forced into beast form until they couldn't come back completely. Micah had gotten lucky just losing his human eyes. Zeke had started the poetry as therapy to deal with all that he had lost, and then his wife suggested he put a video up of him reading his own poetry. He'd become an Internet sensation, and then there'd been that late-night show appearance, and suddenly Professor Wolf was one of our star attractions. Another poster showed a truly nightmarish image that looked as if it had been skinned alive: *Come See the Nuckelavee, Fairy's Most Frightening Monster*. I knew some other creatures of fairy that might argue the "most frightening" title, but nothing in our country could top him. We were almost at the end of the front of the warehouse when a poster proclaimed, *The Lamia, Half Snake, Half Woman*. The poster didn't really do Melanie justice: As a woman she was more beautiful, and her serpent half more sinuous. She'd tried to kill me when she first got to town years ago, but when I killed the ancient vampire who was controlling her, she stopped being on his side. Jean-Claude had offered her a job, and she'd been a big hit with the customers.

"Sorry that we hit traffic. If I'd been thinking it was Saturday night I would have avoided the front of the Circus," Millington said from the driver's seat.

"It's okay, Millie," Nicky said. "I didn't think about it being the weekend either."

"Thank you, sir," he said.

"Millie, I'm not a sir."

"Thanks, Nicky."

"Not a problem."

The SUV finally made the corner and started to leave the bright lights of the front behind us as I had an idea. Melanie only became a snake from the waist down, and she'd been born that way; as a lamia she was a partial shapeshifter, and it was inherited just like that of the snake shapeshifters in Florida Micah was trying to help. Why hadn't I thought of Melanie when Micah showed me the photos? Hell, why hadn't Micah thought of her? Though I wasn't sure that he'd ever met her in person, and the posters were purposely done in a rougher style, like an old-fashioned traveling carnival, so they looked half fake.

"What's wrong, Anita?" Nathaniel asked from beside me.

"Nothing's wrong; she's happy," Nicky said from the other side of him. The other bodyguards were in the front seats acting as chauffeur and riding shotgun.

"Her heart rate and breathing are up; that could mean something is wrong."

"I can feel that she's happy, not scared. If the two of you would drop more of your psychic shielding you'd be able to feel that, too."

"We like to keep a little more mystery in our romance," I said.

"I'm your Bride, Anita. You can't lie to me. I know that's not why you all still shield from each other."

"Let it go, Nicky."

"We do fine with a closer psychic connection. I don't know why the idea bothers you with Nathaniel and the others."

"I don't have a choice with a Bride. I have a choice with the others."

"I know, but what I don't know is why you choose to keep one another at the limits of your psychic connection."

"Drop it, Nicky, and by drop it, I mean stop talking about this."

"Whatever you say."

"Besides, I can lie to you. You'll just be able to tell I'm lying," I said.

"Not always. Sometimes it just feels like you're unhappy or cranky when you're lying."

"When has Anita lied to you?" Nathaniel asked.

"She hasn't, but she lies to other people when I'm with her sometimes."

"Stop talking about me like I'm not here."

"Sorry," they said together.

"Thanks."

The back of the Circus was dark and quiet, with only a few streetlights illuminating the employee parking lot here and there. There were a couple of our guards on either side of the entrance. They waved us through, but if they hadn't recognized the car they would have stopped it and made sure it was an employee and not just a customer trying to find parking. Business was good, but we still weren't willing to give up part of the rear parking for customers. We were looking at buying a secondary lot and shuttling the crowds from there to here, but until we got that set up, the customers were parking anywhere they could. We parked in a spot near the door beside my Jeep.

If we hadn't had extra guards with us, I'd have just opened my own door, but they get testy if their protectees open their own doors, especially outside in open areas like parking lots. We were all equally well armed now, so why did I let Custer stand in front of my door on alert for me? Because it was his job and there were people who wanted me dead, and if that happened on his watch, I was pretty sure Jean-Claude would kill him. So, since my life and theirs might be on the line, I let Custer and Millie look around the darkened parking lot and decide it was safe before Custer opened my door for me and Millie stood on the other side of the door blocking me from the rest of the angles they could control. You can't control every angle in the open, you just can't, but good bodyguards can control most of them. Nathaniel got out on the other side when Nicky opened the door for him. We'd already discussed that he was in charge of Nathaniel's safety until we were inside. I wasn't completely comfortable with me having two guards on my side of the car and Nathaniel having only one, but three wasn't an even number of guards, so there had to be some unevenness on the coverage.

"What made you excited and happy, just then?" Nathaniel asked as he and Nicky joined me. Millie stayed beside me and Custer fell in behind us like a walking body shield. I was pretty confident at our safety in the parking lot because I knew there was a hidden observation post near the roofline of the Circus, complete with a trained sniper, most of the time. Even we didn't have enough snipers for 24-7 coverage. Tonight, the guards in the crow's nest, which was our current guard-speak for it, were probably watching us through the scopes of their long guns.

"I may have thought of something that could help Micah out with the latest shapeshifter issue."

Nathaniel reached out for my hand, but it was my right hand and he knew in public I liked that free for weapons. "I think you're safe to hold hands for a few yards," Nicky said.

"That has to be Anita's call," Nathaniel said.

If he'd just taken my hand because someone else told him it was okay, I'd have probably protested, but he'd said just the right thing. "I think we can chance it," I said, smiling at him and holding out my hand.

The smile that Nathaniel gave me made it all worthwhile, made me wish that I was less pedantic about keeping my gun hand free more often. We made it safely to the back door of the Circus hand in hand, grinning at each other like there was no one else in the world in that moment.

"Kitten has a Robin to deliver," Nicky said, apparently to

the air, but I knew it was actually into the earpiece he'd slipped on when we got closer to home.

"I hate that call sign," I said.

The lock made a thick *thunk* sound, and then the back door to the Circus started to swing open.

"You wouldn't pick a code name," Nicky said.

"Everyone picked one but you, Anita," Nathaniel said, smiling. He'd chosen Robin after Batman's boy-wonder side-kick. I guess anything was better than the code names based on chess pieces. I'd been the black queen, Jean-Claude the black king, and so on . . . It had all seemed too obvious who was who, so we'd decided to let all the protectees choose a code name. Everyone had had fun doing it except me. I couldn't decide. They all seemed silly, or not right, but almost anything would have been better than *Kitten*.

The door opened and I couldn't see anyone through it, which meant it wasn't one of the newer guards, or one of the ones from "civilian" backgrounds. If the police and the military kept their policy of kicking people out if they tested positive for lycanthropy, we were going to have enough of their exes to field our own small army.

"All you have to do is pick a different one, and we'll use it," Nicky said as Millie moved up so that he'd go through the door first.

"Oh hell, Nicky, if it was that easy, I'd have done it already."

We finally stepped into the small area between the door that led into the Circus and the door that led to the underground where Jean-Claude lived and where I spent more than half my time. One direction was bright lights, carnival games, food booths, rides, and the sideshow where Melanie the Lamia would be entertaining her fans. I must have started toward the door toward the midway instead of the one that led to the underground apartments, because Nicky said, "Jean-Claude and Micah are waiting for us."

That stopped me from doing anything stupid. If Micah didn't want me to share the pictures with Edward, he certainly wouldn't want me to share them with Melanie. "I didn't realize Micah was already here."

"Jean-Claude's jet doesn't have mechanical issues," Nicky said.

"Right," I said, but I was already thinking that I could run the idea of talking to Melanie by him. Surely the shapeshifters in Florida would give the okay. Hell, Melanie was from ancient Greece originally, or maybe even older than that, but lamias were part of Greek legend, so she might have answers that no one else would.

Nathaniel tugged on my hand. I looked at him and then at the door Nicky was holding open. I couldn't do anything until I talked to Micah, so I let him lead me to the other door. Besides, we had about a mile of stairs to walk down before we reached the last door into the underground. I wasn't joking about the mile, and the steps were carved from the bedrock, so they weren't perfectly square, or perfectly even, and they were oddly spaced, as if whatever they were originally designed for hadn't moved on two legs like a person. If you couldn't do the cardio, you'd be exhausted before you ever got to the big door at the bottom. I wondered if anyone had ever broken in and just given up before they finished the stairs.

As if he'd read my thoughts, Millie said, "My wife says I'm in the best shape she's ever seen me, and the only difference to my exercise regime is these stairs."

"These damned stairs, you mean," Custer said.

"I thought SEALs never complained," I said.

Custer laughed. "Oh hell, no, who told you that?"

Nathaniel and I laughed with him. Nicky remained happily stoic beside me. "Fair enough. I thought SEALs didn't complain about physical hardships," I said.

"We don't," Millie said.

"You just did," Nathaniel said, smiling and glancing from one to the other of the men.

"This isn't hardship," said Custer.

Nathaniel and I digested that thought for a second or two. "Some SEALs bitch, some don't," Nicky said.

"How do you know that?" I asked.

"I used to work with a lot of contract workers; that runs high to special teams, even Navy SEALs."

"Contract workers, contractors," Custer said, "sounds like temporary office help. What happened to soldier of fortune, mercenary, and all the other cool names I remember from old movies?"

"Try putting soldier of fortune down on your tax return and see how well that works," Millie said, smiling back at us all.

"Have you tried?"

"No, and I'm not going to. I've got a wife and kids. I don't need to play fuck-fuck games with the IRS."

Both of the SEALs had relaxed once we got on the stairs, which said, clearly, they thought we were safe here. They were probably right, but it was still interesting seeing them start to loosen up on the job. When they first came to us from the military, they'd barely speak when they were working. I preferred chattier to silent. Millie and Custer had both adapted to that preference. It was one of the reasons they were doing more guarding for me.

Once we got our cardio on the stairs, there was a locked door that looked like it led to a dungeon or a smallish castle. If it was locked, even Nicky, with all his strength, enhanced by being a werelion and the weight lifting, wouldn't get through the door easily. He'd have to pound or tear his way through it, which would give more guards on the other side a chance to get ready for whatever was strong enough to get through the door. There was another pair of guards on the inside of the door to the underground and another pair on the other side of the living room / receiving area. There was another pair of bodyguards guarding the long hallway that had been carved out of bedrock and the natural caves that had been down here eons ago. Then there was another set of bodyguards outside one of the doors before we finally got to the pair outside of Jean-Claude's bedroom door. They let us in, saying, "Renard and Wolverine said to let you in without announcing you first."

Renard was Jean-Claude, and Wolverine was Micah. I did not like the new call signs, which was probably part of the reason I was having such trouble choosing one for myself. The guards opened the door to Jean-Claude's bedroom, and Milligan and Custer were dismissed, not officially in a military way, but they'd delivered Nathaniel and me to our "base."

The door closed behind us, and I for one let out a long breath and the tension between my shoulder blades that had been building up somewhere between all the guard checks. I'd agreed to Claudia trying out a new guard rotation, but I hadn't quite realized what it might mean for just everyday life inside the Circus. If Micah had been feeling overwhelmed by the number of people in our lives before, this wasn't going to help. I'd expected to find Micah and Jean-Claude in the custom-made orgy-size bed that dominated the bedroom, but the glow from a single bedside lamp showed the bed empty. It was even still neatly made up: Today's comforter was royal blue, with pillows in matching colors interspersed with deep red ones at the head of the four-poster bed, which probably meant the silk sheets underneath it all would be red to match the accent pillows. The lamp left most of the room in shadows, but it gave enough light to see by. The faux fireplace against one wall, a fur rug and grouping of chairs in front of it, was empty, too. Usually I was disappointed not to find Jean-Claude waiting for me first thing, but today an empty room seemed good. It was as if seeing more people right that moment would have been too much, no matter who it was.

"They're in the bathroom," Nicky said.

"You can hear them?" I asked.

"And smell the bubble bath."

Nathaniel sniffed the air. "Lavender," he said.

I couldn't smell a damn thing from that far away, but then, when it came to scent tracking, I was only human.

"Before we go into the bathroom, can we talk about all the guards that we just went through?" Nathaniel asked.

"Sure," I said.

"Do we need that many guards?" he asked.

"No," Nicky said.

"Claudia talked to me about trying out a new heightened security guard rotation," I said.

"Is there a new threat I don't know about?" Nathaniel asked.

"No, and that's the point. She wanted to try out the new heightened security before we needed it, so we could work out the bugs," I said.

"It's not just the Circus," Nicky said.

"I know, we're testing the new security across all the businesses," I said.

"You could have mentioned it to us, or did you tell everyone but me?" Nathaniel said.

I squeezed his hand, which was still in mine. I was happy he hadn't pulled away. "I didn't think to mention it to anyone in our poly group, Nathaniel. I'm sorry—you're right. I should have given all of you a heads-up, but between trying to do three weddings, work at Animators Inc., and be a marshal, plus the poly group, I think I'm just losing track of it all."

Nathaniel squeezed my hand, which made me look at him. "Wow, you! Admitting that you can't keep track of things before they blow up in your face. Yay, therapy!" He smiled at the end, but I didn't smile back.

I felt that spurt of anger inside me that was always there like a pilot light just waiting for the right spark, but I breathed through it. I counted and breathed and remembered that I was in love with Nathaniel and he was right.

His smile faded around the edges and he looked at me with those big, beautiful eyes of his, waiting for me to fall back into old patterns and start a fight that didn't need to happen, or do my famous pull away, or even runaway, from him, from the relationships, from everything. I forced myself to relax all the way down to the hand that was holding his and said, "Yeah, yay, therapy."

He gave me a smile that made me happy that I'd been smart instead of stupid, and that I was working through my issues rather than letting them blow my life up. He came to me then, leaning his forehead down so that he touched the top of my head. "I love you so much right now."

I grinned and moved so I was looking up at him. "Why, because I'm working on my issues?"

"Yes," he whispered and kissed me.

"They know we're out here," Nicky said.

I drew back from the kiss. "I figured they did."

Nathaniel started leading me across the carpet and toward the closed bathroom door. Nicky said, "You were really bothered by the extra guards. I thought you liked crowds."

"I like group sex, not crowds," Nathaniel said.

"So, are you feeling overwhelmed by this many people, too?" I asked.

"I don't mind people I'm sleeping or playing with, but most of the guards are just guards. I like an audience, but they aren't good for that."

"We're supposed to be protecting you, not watching the show," Nicky said.

Nathaniel paused with his hand on the door to the bathroom. "Can't you do both?"

"Not really and not well."

"The other guards stopped at the door. Are you still guarding us?" Nathaniel asked.

Nicky smiled. "No, I'm just going to say hi and do this." He drew me into his arms, all that muscle wrapping around me as Nathaniel let go of my hand. Everyone I dated was strong, but Nicky had a way of making me aware of it that was exciting and just the tiniest bit scary. I knew physical potential, and if it ever came down to a real fight, I couldn't win against the strength that pulled me in against his body. Lucky for me, I wanted to be in his arms. He kissed me and put a lot of body English into it, so that he finally picked me up, and my feet left the ground. I tried to wrap my legs around him, but the gun at his waist got in the way. He put one hand underneath my ass, so he held me in place and turned the awkward attempt to wrap my legs around him into something sexy. It was like a good dance partner turning your stumble into part of the dance.

He drew back from the kiss with me still held in his arms. "I've been wanting to do that all day." He set me back down with my legs so shaky that he and Nathaniel had to catch me. That made them both laugh that masculine chuckle that either is at your expense or is a compliment. I took it as the second, because they both knew better than to laugh at me, and we loved one another. Laughter edged with love is always good.

7

NICKY OPENED THE door and Nathaniel helped me through while my knees recovered from the kiss. We were all half laughing as we stepped onto the black carpet of the black-on-black bathroom with its black marble, double sinks, and silver fixtures, but what was waiting in the big bathtub at the end of the room stole the laughter and made my knees threaten to go weak again.

The bathtub was big enough for four large adults, so Jean-Claude and Micah didn't have to be next to each other, but they were. Micah's hair was so wet it was black, and slicked back so that the bones of his face were bare in a way that they weren't when all the deep brown of his curls framed him. His tanned skin looked even darker against the utter whiteness of Jean-Claude's chest. The vampire's hair was up in a loose man-bun that looked careless, but I'd been dating him and Nathaniel too long to believe the illusion. It was one of those hairdos that looked messy at first, but the longer you looked at it, the more artful it was, with curls trailing around the edge of his face, tracing the curve of his cheek, the line of his chin, so that his lips seemed framed by white skin and raven black hair. His curls were dry except for a few small ones low on his neck. He had an arm across Micah's shoulders, so the contrast between their skin colors was framed against the black marble of the tub edge and the mounded bubbles, which were only a little less white than the vampire's skin.

Micah blinked green-gold leopard eyes at us, trapped forever in his human face from too much time in animal form, so that he couldn't come completely back now. He wasn't wearing his new glasses, which helped his cat eyes see far away, and I wondered how well he could see us in the doorway.

Jean-Claude gestured with one pale long-fingered hand and my eyes followed the movement so that I was left staring at his face. It wasn't a face that had launched a thousand ships, but it might have launched a thousand seductions in old Europe. Even though Micah's face was finer boned, and he was just more delicately made overall, it was Jean-Claude's face that was the more femininely beautiful, more ambisexual. If I hadn't had their faces so close together, I would have thought it was Micah who would be closer to feminine, but some line or curve just made his face more male.

"I'm going to leave the two of you to stare at your shared boys," Nicky said.

It startled me, as if I'd forgotten he was standing with us for a moment. I felt instantly guilty. I started to try to protest, but he waved it away. "It's okay. This show was for you and Nathaniel, not me. I'm not anyone's lover but yours, and Jean-Claude doesn't need blood from me when he has the three of you."

"You do not have to go on my account, Nicky," Jean-Claude said, "for I will have to be getting dressed for work."

I must have pouted, because Jean-Claude laughed, that wonderful touchable laugh that could caress places in my body that no hand could ever reach. It made me shiver and clutch at Nathaniel, who clutched me back. That sensual laugh didn't just work on me.

"It's okay, Jean-Claude. I'll hit the weight room while I can."

"You would leave such bounty for the gym?"

Nicky grinned and shook his head. "If I were more into men, then the gym could go fuck itself, but I'm not, so I'll go and let the four of you have some alone time."

It seemed funny to say "alone time" with four people in a room, but Nicky left, closing the door softly behind him. Nathaniel and I were left standing at the door like we didn't know what to do next.

Nathaniel stripped off his shirt in one smooth motion and threw it to the floor. He started toward the tub, stripping off clothes as he went. Okay, maybe *I* didn't know what to do next.

8

NATHANIEL HAD KICKED off his shoes and was finishing wiggling out of his jeans by the time I started taking off my jacket and the guns hiding underneath it. There was so much less sexy spontaneity when you were carrying multiple weapons.

"Come join us, *ma petite*, *mon chaton*, before I have to leave to attend to much less pleasant duties," Jean-Claude said, reaching out toward me with one pale, muscled arm. He would never bulk the way Nicky did, or even as much as Nathaniel, because he was built like a long-distance runner, tall, lean, graceful lines that moved with strength, but nothing would make him be bulky.

Looking at Jean-Claude had made me miss some of Nathaniel's undressing, so that he was just suddenly nude moving up the three steps of the bathtub. I got completely distracted watching the back of his body from shoulders to legs as he climbed into the sudsy water.

"I can never decide if you look better coming or going," I said.

"I think, *ma petite*, the phrase you are searching for is *dat ass*."

Hearing him say the slang in his usually elegant voice made us all laugh. "Yes, that was what I was trying not to say out loud."

Nathaniel looked back over one shoulder at me, flexing his glutes so that his ass flexed like you would to make a biceps harder. It made me laugh again, an edge of almost nervousness to it. I wasn't sure there would ever come a point when I didn't have my moments of, *Golly gee whiz, I can't believe I get to play with all these wonderful toys.* Sex was a type of play and recreation for me. I'd worked through most of my issues about that, or maybe I'd just accepted that it was supposed to be this way, full of joy, playfulness, and shared humor.

Micah stood up, the water and bubbles clinging to his body, some of the suds beginning to slide down his skin as he reached for Nathaniel. I wanted to help the suds caress his skin, wanted to help them hurry down his thigh, cup my hand over that strangely thick pile of bubbles on the front of his body. The first time we'd ever made love together there had been suds and water involved.

I laid the guns and knives on a corner of the black marble where most people would have put candles, and put the holsters on the edge of the sink, farther away from the potential splash zone of the bathtub. Free of the holsters and all the weapons, I could finally start to pull my shirt over my head, but Jean-Claude said, "*Ma petite*, come here, let me undress you."

He'd come to the side of the tub while I'd been watching Nathaniel and Micah. How had I missed him just feet away moving through the water? He was on his knees, hands resting on the edge of the tub so that he lifted himself half out of the water toward me. I was suddenly staring into the midnight blue of his eyes, the darkest blue I'd ever seen, so that it was almost black, almost, and then he'd turn and the light would catch it, and the deep blue of his eyes would gleam to life. The night sky is never truly black, it just looks like that when there's no light to see by, but I could always see the light in Jean-Claude's eyes, no matter how dark.

I went to him and he raised himself even higher from the water. I had a moment of thinking of mermaids lifting themselves up on rocks at the edge of the sea to kiss their sailors, or princes. Of course, the raven-haired beauty offering me a kiss was a king. Did that make me the mermaid? Nah.

I met his lips with mine so that we kissed with me still dressed at the edge of the marble tub. I felt his fingers on the bottom of my T-shirt. "Sit on the edge of the tub, *ma petite*, so I can use both hands."

I did what he asked, because who wouldn't? He leaned

back into the water enough to make room for me, face lifted toward mine, so that it was the most natural thing in the world to meet his lips with mine. He slid his hands underneath my shirt, lifting it upward as we kissed. I raised my arms so he could pull it over them, but he stopped with it up to my shoulders, and kept kissing me. I pressed into the kiss as I felt his fingers at the back of my bra. The snap gave and his hands glided under the line of my bra, spilling over my breasts, and the kiss grew. I pressed my mouth against his, my tongue sliding between his lips and oh so carefully between the dainty hardness of his fangs. His hands touched my breasts with the water still clinging to them, so that he made my breasts as wet as other parts of me were starting to become.

He finally drew my shirt over my head and the kiss had to stop. I glanced over to find Micah and Nathaniel in their own kiss, though since they were both naked and one of them was wet and covered in suds it distracted me a little more than it should have in Jean-Claude's arms. I turned to him to kiss him again, to apologize for ogling other men while I was almost in the middle of a kiss with him, but he was looking at the other men. I wrapped my arms across his shoulders, pressing my breasts against the wet slickness of his skin, and put my face against his while we watched our two shared men share a very passionate kiss.

Jean-Claude put his arm around my waist and sighed. "We are lucky, you and I, *ma petite*."

"We are, but I'm wearing too many clothes." I whispered it against his face.

"You are," he whispered back.

Micah and Nathaniel came up for air, half laughing. "I think we're distracting them," Nathaniel said.

"I think you're right," Micah said, and he aimed a smile around the edge of Nathaniel's body. It was a smile that would have been more at home on Nathaniel's face, or Jean-Claude's, but there it was on his face, a look that said he knew his worth and he knew just how hot he was, all wet and wrapped around our shared boy.

Nathaniel kissed his cheek and said, "We better stop distracting them, so Anita can get naked." He pulled Micah with him through the water to settle against the far side of the bath.

He threw an arm across Micah's shoulders and drew him in against his body, because it was always easier for the taller half of the couple to throw an arm across. Micah cuddled in against him, tracing one hand over the other man's chest. Nathaniel raised Micah's hand and kissed his palm.

Micah closed his eyes as Nathaniel kissed across his hand and licked delicately across his wrist. "Stop that or we'll just keep distracting them."

Nathaniel rose from Micah's wrist, smiling. "I'll behave myself until Anita is out of her clothes, then no promises."

"Off with the clothes," I said.

"Yes, please," Nathaniel said, grinning at us.

"We'll watch you and Jean-Claude now," Micah said.

"We must make it worth your while, then, *mon chat.*" Jean-Claude turned to me and said, "Give me your foot, *ma petite.*"

"I'm wearing combat boots, not high heels."

"It does not matter what you wear. I would still want to help you out of them."

That made me smile, and I lifted my leg up so he could reach my boot. He unlaced it slowly, making what would have been awkward for anyone else graceful, sensual. He pulled the boot off, and there was the thick boot sock, about as unromantic as it gets, but he just tossed the boot to the floor and then reached up under my jeans with those long, slender fingers, rolling my sock down slowly. He did the same on the other side, and once I was barefoot, he helped me stand up on the top step leading to the tub so that he could unsnap my jeans. I reached to help him unzip them, but he moved my hands away, shaking his head at me. I let my hands fall to my sides and he began to pull my jeans down my hips. He pulled the lacy thong down with them, so that as he pulled the jeans he revealed me nude. He got the jeans to midthigh and then leaned in and laid the gentlest of kisses against that line where thigh and hip meet. It brought my breath in a sigh, my head falling back, my eyes closing as he kissed the other side where my hip met more intimate things.

He eased the jeans downward, placing kisses on my legs as he did it, until he licked behind my knee, which was a ticklish spot, and I squirmed for him. "No fair, no fair."

"I think it is very fair," he said and licked behind my other knee.

I laughed, squirmed, and tried to cover the backs of my knees, but my ankles were still trapped in my jeans, so it was like being in soft ankle-cuffs, which meant that squirming around on a marble step wasn't my best move. I fell trying to "get away" from the tickling.

Jean-Claude caught me, but I was trying to catch myself at the same time and we both fell into the water. I remembered to hold my breath as we went through the suds and underwater. I started to try to swim my way to the surface, but Jean-Claude stood up with me in his arms, water and suds streaming off both of us. I was coughing and sputtering. He didn't have to breathe, so at least he wasn't dealing with that. My jeans were soaking wet and trailed down from my ankles, trapping them even more than when they'd been dry. Jean-Claude's careful hairdo was a wet mass, and whatever had been holding it in place was still trying to hold on with the heavy wet curls, so that it was just tangled around his face and neck but wasn't free of the bobby pins, or combs, or whatever.

I wiped suds from my face, and he was trying to blink them out of his eyes because he was using both hands to hold me. Nathaniel and Micah were both laughing. I reached out and wiped the bubbles out of Jean-Claude's eyes and started to laugh.

"The first time we made love I fell into the bath with all my clothes on," Jean-Claude said.

"Well, at least it's just my jeans getting wet this time."

"I have been a ladies' man for centuries. I am truly suave and debonair, except with you, *ma petite*, except with you."

"I think I told you, it was a hint, that first time."

"You did," he said, and smiled.

Nathaniel asked, "Are your lower legs as tangled as they look?"

"Wet jeans cling like crazy," Micah said.

"We could use the jeans for bondage," Nathaniel said.

I shook my head, laughing. "No, not tonight. I just want to get the jeans off so that I can get in the nice hot bath with the rest of you."

"You do not want me to simply stand here and hold you, *ma petite*?" Jean-Claude's smile widened as he said it.

"No," I said, laughing.

Nathaniel reached up to take one leg of the jeans and Micah took the other. There were suds in their hair and I realized we'd splashed them when we fell in. We'd also splashed my guns, but lucky for me, the days of having to keep your powder dry so that a gun would fire were long past. Most modern guns could be dragged through water, or even mud, and still shoot.

They got me out of the jeans and Nathaniel tossed them over the edge of the tub to the floor. The fall into the water had broken some of the momentum to rush into sex and gave me time to remember the idea I'd had about the lamia and helping Micah's clients in Florida.

I was still in Jean-Claude's arms when I said, "Have you thought about talking to Melanie about your clients in Florida?"

Jean-Claude put me down into the hot, sudsy bathwater and there was that moment when my body just relaxed into it. It wasn't about sex or anything but my body letting go of more of the stress that I seemed to carry around.

"What did you say about Melanie?" Micah asked.

"She's a lamia," I said.

He blinked at me and then said, "I can't believe I didn't think of talking to her. I've been agonizing about this for weeks and it never occurred to me to talk to her."

"You are talking about the sad shapeshifters that Micah and the Coalition have been trying to help," Jean-Claude said.

I looked up at him from the water, nodding. "I don't know how much he told you, but the lamia is the closest to their type of shapeshifting that I've seen."

"He told me some, but I was more intent on the two of us spending time together, to ease each other's . . . stress, than talking about work." There was something in his voice that made me look up at him again. All the warmth and laughter of a few seconds ago was gone. His face was still lovely to look at, but the cold expression made it more like a statue, a work of art that you could look at but weren't allowed to touch.

I reached out to touch his arm and he actually moved back from me. I knew something was wrong, but it took Nathaniel moving back to join Jean-Claude on their side of the tub before I realized what.

"We're all naked in the bathtub and I'm talking business," I said.

Nathaniel nodded. Jean-Claude just looked at me. It was one of the downsides to being polyamorous: You could get the same looks from more than one person at the same time when you fucked up.

"I'm sorry, Jean-Claude, Nathaniel, but Anita knows how much this has been bothering me," Micah said, coming up to hug me. I think he needed the same reassurance I did, that not everyone in the tub was angry with him.

"And we don't know how much it's been bothering you?" Nathaniel asked, arms crossing over his chest so that I noticed the swell in his biceps, but the attitude that went with it made it less sexy and more *You don't get to play with this*.

"Of course you both know. You went with me to Florida and they were so protective of their secret that I had to keep sending you off by yourself with just a bodyguard," he said, and then looked at Jean-Claude. "And you've just spent time helping me climb out of the darkness in my head from this case."

"And yet, it is Anita that knows how much it is bothering you?" Jean-Claude said, and it was that girlfriend/boyfriend accusatory voice.

Micah hugged me a little closer and I hugged him back. I didn't want this to turn into a fight, but I wasn't always good at avoiding them. I finally decided to be very honest. "I don't want this to turn into a full-fledged fight. I'm sorry that I just blurted out the idea of talking to Melanie about the other shapeshifters, but I was just excited that I might have a clue that would help Micah."

"More excited than being with us?" Nathaniel said.

"Have we become less exciting than your cases, *ma petite*?"

Oh shit. "No, of course not."

Micah tried to help me dig myself out of the hole that our evening was rapidly disappearing into. "Please, Jean-Claude, Nathaniel, we were both thoughtless and careless of your feelings, but no one is as important to us as the two of you."

"Please," I said, "it's the first time the four of us have been together in weeks. Don't let this ruin the evening."

"And that is exactly why it hurts so much, *ma petite*."

I looked at Micah. "You try. I can't seem to keep my foot out of my mouth."

"I am sorry that we started talking business in that moment, but Anita is the only one who has seen the pictures of what is happening to the family down in Florida. It's awful enough that it's haunting us both."

"They wouldn't let me see them in animal form," Nathaniel said.

"And perhaps if you had shown me the same pictures you showed to Anita, I would have thought of sending you to Melanie, as well."

"You're right, you're both right, but I know that Anita sees worse on her job than I do on mine, so I knew she would see it as part of the job. I didn't want to burden the two of you with things that give me nightmares."

I hugged him tighter.

Nathaniel's face softened and Jean-Claude stopped looking so still and statue-like, as if he'd finally allowed himself to start breathing again. "We are not children to be protected against the harshness of your job, Micah," Jean-Claude said.

"I didn't mean it that way . . ."

Jean-Claude waved him to silence. "It is a noble sentiment, Micah, but it is not necessary for me. I have seen more blood spilled and lives lost than you have. I would say that all four of us have seen horrors that haunt us. We are none of us sheep that need to be tended and watched over; we are wolves to hunt together. I do not know when you decided that you and Anita were wolves to our sheep, but it is not true. We must be equals, or at least the power must not be so uneven as this."

Micah opened his mouth, closed it, and didn't seem to know what to say. I hugged him, rubbing one hand along the smoothness of his back. I finally said, "What can we do to fix the mood?"

"I did not realize that the three of you would be home and unoccupied tonight, or I would have not agreed to the regular business meeting being moved to tonight, so my time here is limited. I will have to start over with my hair, and that will take more time."

"So, we've ruined the mood and spoiled the evening," Micah said.

I shook my head. "Wait, I know I fucked up the way I said it, but if Melanie does have information that could help the other shapeshifters, then that's important. It's not more important than the two of you, or the four of us, but moments like this are what make Micah and me not talk about work with the two of you. You're complaining that Micah shares more information with me than with you, but in the same breath you're saying you don't want us to talk about work."

"No, *ma petite*, we are complaining that you thought to speak of work in the middle of foreplay."

I didn't have a comeback for that, because there really wasn't one. Not a good one, anyway.

"That's fair," Micah said, "and I apologize for my part in it. I am obsessed with this case."

"As we discussed, *mon chat*, you must find someone trustworthy enough to send out on some Coalition business without you, for there is too much for you to oversee everything personally."

"It was a great idea, Jean-Claude. I am thinking about people I could send."

"Is this business, or can I offer a suggestion?" I asked.

"It is," Jean-Claude said, "but make your suggestion, *ma petite*."

"Socrates was really good with the marshal that got lycanthropy on the job with me. He talked to her family and everything."

"I remember you telling me about that," Micah said. "He might be able to take some of the survivor interventions."

"I would trust him to handle survivors," I said.

"So would I," Nathaniel said.

"Now that we have settled some of our worries, I must wash my hair and begin to get ready for the business meeting."

Nathaniel hugged him, putting his face on his shoulder. "No, I just got here."

I half walked, half swam through the water to him and took

Jean-Claude's arm. "We haven't been here that long; do you really have to go now?"

Jean-Claude looked down at the two of us and smiled. "Such faces, you really do not want me to go."

"Of course not," we said together.

"I can feel your sorrow at the thought of me leaving, *ma petite*." He kissed the top of Nathaniel's head. "And you, but not so loudly, our pussycat."

"Can you read my feelings?" Micah asked.

"Only as one person knows another; you are not tied to *ma petite* in a way that allows me access to your inner thoughts and feelings."

"Sometimes I'm happy about that and sometimes it makes me feel left out."

"I'm sorry for the latter, *mon chat*."

"This wouldn't have been enough time for the four of us to have sex, even without the misunderstanding. You don't really have to leave for your meeting yet, do you?" Micah asked.

Nathaniel and I went still beside Jean-Claude. "It will take longer to get ready now that my hair is wet. I had put it up for a reason."

"That doesn't answer Micah's question," I said, studying his face.

"No, it does not. I wanted to see if you truly would be sorry that I had to leave before I had joined you for sex, or if you did not care."

I looked at him, and even with his wet hair clumped around his face, in probably the worst hairdo that I'd ever seen on him, he was still so beautiful that I felt like, what was he doing with me, but then who could equal him? When you're a twenty-one on a ten scale of beauty, you have to date someone. When he first started trying to date me, I was so insecure about it. It took me a long time to realize that no matter how beautiful or handsome or graceful or smart you are, you still have insecurities. We all have them—even kings, even Jean-Claude.

"It was childish to need the reassurance, *ma petite*."

I touched his face, moving closer so I could kiss him. "I love you all the more for needing the reassurance, but I'm sorry that I caused the need."

"When you mentioned Melanie to Micah, you were concentrated solely on the business at hand, as if I was not holding you in my arms. Your single-mindedness can be a bit intimidating, *ma petite*."

I wasn't sure what I thought about that, but Micah saved me from having to answer. "We can talk to Melanie on one of her breaks between shows tonight, but not before we give you and Nathaniel the attention you deserve."

"How much time do you really have with us before you have to get ready for the meeting?" I asked, wrapping myself around him and finding Nathaniel's arms on the other side, so we entwined him, pressing our naked chests against his.

"I do have to fix my hair."

"Sorry I got you wet."

"It's you we need to get wet," Nathaniel said.

"How much time, Jean-Claude?" Micah asked.

He looked at the other man, and it was almost not friendly. I looked from one to the other of them and felt that weight between them, of two strong, dominant men who would never have chosen each other, yet here they were, domestic partners. This was not the mix of people Jean-Claude had planned to be in his bathtub and headed down the aisle with, but these were the men who had been willing to work their issues and help us work ours. Sometimes you fall in love all at once, and sometimes you fall in love gradually, and sometimes you look up and are surprised as hell at whom you're in love with.

"Forty-five minutes, and then I must ready myself for the meeting."

"A quickie, then," I said.

Jean-Claude smiled. "With all three of us, *ma petite*, you insult us."

"Fine, a quickie for you," I said, smiling back.

"Maybe enough time for Anita and me to apologize for talking business," Micah said.

"Nathaniel and I eagerly await your apologies."

"Eagerly," Nathaniel said, smiling like the cat that ate the cream, or was hoping to eat it.

9

JEAN-CLAUDE DID a quick wash of his hair, though we offered to help him. He said that it would be faster if he did it himself, and he was right, but just his turning down extra pampering from us let me know that we weren't the only ones who were eager for each other's company. Micah surprised us by keeping himself and Nathaniel in the bathroom and sending Jean-Claude and me out to the bed. Jean-Claude protested, but Micah said, "You and I talked about more than just my work, Jean-Claude." He'd pushed aside the thick strands of his own wet hair to show two dainty fang marks.

"I'm sorry I missed watching the two of you together," I said.

"It's always so hot when you take blood from Micah," Nathaniel said.

"Thanks, but we did it that way on purpose."

"I don't understand."

"I'm not the only one getting tired of the group activities, no matter how much we love everyone involved," Micah said.

I started to try to pick at the comment, but he held up a hand and said, "We have less than an hour before Jean-Claude has to dress for the meeting. If we divide and conquer, we have enough time to apologize to both Jean-Claude and Nathaniel."

I looked from one man to another, and everyone seemed happy with the arrangement, so I stopped arguing after that. I can be taught.

We spread a body-size towel over the crimson silk sheets, so Jean-Claude could lay all that long black hair out to dry without ruining the silk. The towel was even a red to match the sheets, so he lay back against a perfect background of rich, perfect red, or maybe the perfect part was how his pale skin looked against the color. It brought out the blue undertones in his skin, so that the whiteness of him seemed to have more color, as if he were blooming with health, but I knew that wasn't it; he was blooming with Micah's blood. Vampires usually fed on ordinary humans because there were more of them, but supernatural blood had more kick to it, like a higher-octane fuel. Jean-Claude lay back on the bed damn near shining with the power of feeding on Micah.

"*Ma petite*, as much as I enjoy you admiring me, we do not have much time."

"The day I don't stop and admire the view before we have sex, either I've lost my mind or I'm dead."

He smiled and held out his hand to me. "Come to me, *ma petite*."

I climbed up on the bed, taking a good grip of the sheets, because I'd learned that silk is slippery. At least I wasn't wearing hose—that was a combo with these sheets that had sent me sliding off more than once. Once I was safely on the bed, I was kneeling at his feet, with those long legs stretching up and up, toward where he lay nestled against the front of his body. He was already a little happy to see me, but then I was as nude as he was, so apparently he was admiring the view, too.

I loved going down on him before he was completely erect, so I could feel the change in his body as he grew harder. If I took my time and kissed my way up his legs, I'd miss all the softness. I compromised and didn't start at his ankles, but moved up to his lower thigh first. I didn't so much kiss his thigh as brush my lips just above the skin, so that the tiny, pale hairs on them tickled along my lips, and I used my breath to help me caress his skin. It was the lightest of touches, too light for some people to enjoy, but Jean-Claude shivered for me as I worked my way up his thigh toward one of my goals.

By the time I got to the top of his thigh, there wasn't much soft left for me to go down on. He was already long and hard against the front of his body. I licked along the line where his thigh met his hip and had to work hard not to touch anything else.

"You are teasing me now," he said, voice a little breathless.

I drew back enough to look up at his face and saw a need there that I hadn't expected. We were both having sex with each other as part of our poly group, and I knew that we were both having sex with other people when we weren't together, so why the raw need in his face?

I kept eye contact with him as I lowered myself back toward his body and flicked my tongue along the most tender part of him. His eyes closed and a look almost of pain crossed his face. "If I was so slow with you, you would be angry."

He was right, so I licked down the front of him from top to bottom and then slid over the tip of him and down, so that he filled my mouth and then my throat. I came up for air and then moved so that I was up on my knees to get a quick, deep angle so that I could go down as far as we both wanted, but not stay so long that my body fought to breathe too much. I spread his legs so that I could kneel between them and get a better angle to slide my mouth over just the smooth head of him to roll against the roof of my mouth, over and over, and just the sensation of it made me shiver and cry out around him.

He made a wordless, wonderful sound, his upper body coming off the bed as he cried out, *"Ma petite!"*

I slid my mouth farther down him, so I could feel the slight change of texture where his foreskin covered the shaft; it was just a slight change in texture over the hard eagerness of him. I pushed myself down that length until Jean-Claude cried out again. He sat up and pulled me into his arms. He kissed me so fiercely that I had to open my mouth to his eagerness or one of us would have cut our lips on his fangs. He pressed me back against the bed and I expected him to be on top of me, but he leaned off to one side and it was his fingers that he put between my legs. He slid one finger inside me and said, "So wet just from holding me in your mouth."

"I started to get wet just seeing you lying there on the bed."

He smiled down at me as his fingers found that sweet spot between my legs. I shook my head. "We don't have time; this takes the longest for me." But my voice was already breathy.

"To finish you, no, but to bring you to the edge, yes."

"What?" I asked, and was having trouble focusing on his face.

"One good tease deserves another," he said as he leaned in and kissed me. His fingers kept playing between my legs and there was the beginning of that heavy warmth between my legs, but it was a slow build. I was always a slow build by hand.

He knelt between my legs, spreading my thighs as I'd spread his earlier, one hand playing over that outer sweet spot, and the fingers of the other hand sliding inside me to find another sweet spot. His long fingers knew just how to curve inside me and find that spot just inside the opening, so that he was working both at the same time, but the inner spot always distracted me from the outer, so that doing both didn't really work for me, and he knew that.

My voice was strained and breathy as I said, "I won't tease you again, if you just stop doing that."

He drew his fingers out and just caressed over that one spot on the outside of my body, and some combination of everything we'd done brought me suddenly. My body bucked under his touch, the orgasm filling my body with heat and pleasure, so that I cried out. He kept playing over that one spot until I was making softer noises, and I tapped on the bed, letting him know I was done and I couldn't talk yet.

He was suddenly above me, while my eyes were still only half focused. I felt him begin to slide himself inside me while I stared up into his eyes. They'd bled to solid blue, gleaming with his own inner fire, as if the night sky could burn with a cold, cobalt blue flame. He held his upper body above me, so that it was halfway between a push-up and a cobra yoga position. He found a rhythm that was just right, not too deep, not too shallow, not too fast or slow, but so that his body rolled over and over the spot that his fingers had already teased to near orgasm. I felt the weight of it begin to build again from his body caressing over and over and over, while I watched his eyes like blue flame above me.

"Let me in, *ma petite*."

I found enough voice to whisper, "You're in, so in."

"Drop your shields, *ma petite*. Let me in."

I had a moment of hesitation, and then the next stroke of his body brought me screaming up off the bed, my hands scrambling in the sheets as if the world were flying apart and I needed something to hold on to, and my shields came down with the orgasm. It happens sometimes, but he had asked, and he almost never asked.

The orgasm that had been fading roared back to life, and I was suddenly screaming underneath him and the blue fire in his eyes filled my vision. It was like falling into a soft blue ocean of light, with wave after wave of pleasure spilling over and through me and through him. I could feel Jean-Claude's body inside mine, and then I could feel his body on top of mine, so that I could curve my arms around his shoulders and my fingers found his back, to set my nails into his flesh as I clung to him in the blue light that seemed made of pleasure. I dug my fingers into his back and my legs around his hips to hold myself steady in the ocean of power that was Jean-Claude's eyes.

He cried out, his face buried in my hair, his body convulsing inside mine as he finally lost his rhythm while I was still lost in his eyes, even though my hands and body told me that I was no longer looking into them. His hair was across my face, my body was wrapped around his, but all I could see was soft, warm, blue light, as if happiness had a color and we were swimming in it. I cried out as he thrust himself inside me one more time, and his body convulsed so hard that it fought to escape my arms and legs, as if I were trapping him instead of the other way around.

We lay there relearning how to breathe together. I felt the small sharp pains where her nails had cut my back. I felt his heart fluttering frantically against my body. I felt my body buried deep inside the warm, wet tightness of her. It had been centuries since I'd had a body that could be inside a woman, and then I knew it wasn't my thought, or my body, and for a second I didn't know whose body I was supposed to be in; was I him or her? What the fuck was happening? And that sounded like me, not him.

The floating blue light started to darken, as if night were falling on it, but it wasn't blackness that spilled across the blue; it was brown, as if someone were holding up cognac diamonds to the sun. It dazzled our eyes and splashed dark rainbows through the blue light, and whereas the blue had been only pleasure, there was pain in the whiskey-colored light, pain and pleasure intermingled, and I began to climb back into my body. I knew who I was and that I was not him.

He raised himself enough so we could gaze into each other's eyes again. His were still drowning blue light, and in that light I saw a reflection of a darker light. I had one more dizzying moment of seeing what he saw as he stared down at me. My eyes had bled to solid brown, but with a light sparkling behind them so that it was dark amber fire.

I felt the flash of fear in him, afraid that I'd panic at the power and push him away. I did my best to not be afraid of what I was, what I'd been for a while. I was a living vampire, but it was still a kind of vampire. I just fed on sex and rage instead of blood. I knew what I was, and it wasn't bad. I wasn't evil, and neither was the man in my arms. He felt my fear subside, felt my acceptance, felt the closest thing I had to peace inside me.

"Je t'aime, ma petite," he whispered.

"I love you, too, Jean-Claude."

10

FABULOUS SEX AND metaphysics faded along with the fire in our eyes, and then Jean-Claude had to rush to dress for his big meeting. It was with the managers of all his clubs, plus some salespeople who were regulars for the clubs. They'd be using the new conference room in the upper part of the Circus in the expanded offices over the Circus big top. Before we expanded the offices there, the only conference rooms were here in the underground, and from a security standpoint you don't want anyone but your most trusted people inside your inner sanctum. You certainly don't want to invite the guy who supplies you with fresh linens to walk past the bedroom of the king. Not to mention that a lot of our suppliers were human and there were a lot of not-human in the underground. It wasn't just our safety that we'd been concerned about.

Micah and Nathaniel came out of the bathroom in time to watch him rush around. They climbed under the sheets and coverlet with me so we wouldn't be in the way. It was like watching Jean-Claude get ready for work. We'd dated for seven years, but I'd never been this wide-awake in his bed while he got ready for business. I think I'd slept through it, but I wasn't even sure of that. I worked a lot of nights, too, so I cuddled, with Nathaniel in the middle between Micah and me, while Jean-Claude slid into a pair of black jeans so tight that I'd have given up. He made it look easy, not to mention that watching his ass while he got into the jeans was a very happy thought. His ass in the jeans was pretty darn good, too.

He added one of his signature white lacy shirts, tucking it in and adding a belt that I knew was custom made, or at least the belt buckle was, because it looked like silver but was actually white gold, because too many of our sweeties were "allergic" to silver. There was also a single black diamond set in the buckle, very understated unless it caught the light. He put on a black velvet choker with an antique cameo on the front of it. I knew it was a genuine antique because I'd bought it for him. He left the high lace collar open so it framed the cameo. It made me smile, more than the engagement ring he took out of the safe, because the engagement ring he wore most of the time had been his choice for his hand, not mine. The only reason he had an engagement ring was that I told him if he didn't get an engagement ring, then I wouldn't accept one either. I'd hoped it would get me out of having one, but I should have known better. Jean-Claude liked jewelry a lot more than I did; besides, he was a king, and kings did not get to skimp on jewelry. The people making our rings were also making tiaras—read *crowns*—for both of us. Mine was to hold a veil in place; his was because I refused to wear one unless he did. I was so going to have to stop using that as my ultimatum.

We'd finally gotten an engagement ring for everyday wear that worked. Jean-Claude had a matching one, but it wasn't his favorite. It was a platinum band with two channel-set sapphires on either side of a brilliant white diamond, also set flat. The flashy ring that he'd first given me was all white diamonds and a princess cut of epic proportions. It had been impossible to wear to do anything ordinary like put my hand in a pocket. He had a diamond-and-platinum ring that was as ridiculous as mine, but he also had a platinum band set with two large white diamonds with a larger blue sapphire in the center. He got out the flashy one, of course. It looked like a medium-size star set in platinum, winking and catching the light as if small planets should find his hand and start orbiting it, or maybe that was just my discomfort with that level of consumerism. I just couldn't get used to wearing a ring that cost more than most people's houses.

We'd finally come up with a design for a wedding set that made us both happy, but the jewelers were still creating them, so until then we had the everyday rings and the original ones.

He opened the wardrobe that was against the far wall and got a pair of over-the-knee boots out of it. Sitting on the bench seat that sat to one side of the wardrobe now, he unzipped the backs of the boots so he could fit his feet inside.

"Do the boots zip all the way up?" I asked.

"Not all the way up," he said, as he rolled down the soft leather tops of the boots to midthigh and drew garters out that went around the tops of the boots, holding them in place.

"Are those real diamonds in the garters?" I asked.

He raised his head enough to smile at me. "Of course."

"Of course," I said, smiling. "I love you in boots."

He kept smiling, but he was concentrating more on the boots as he said, "I am aware of that, *ma petite.*"

"I like you in boots, too," Nathaniel said, his voice lazy with good sex and an edge of sleep. He was already snuggled down into the covers so that only his face showed. His head resting on Micah's sheet-covered thigh was the only way he was able to see Jean-Claude at all.

"I am aware of that, too, *mon chaton.*" He took the time to raise each long leg up toward the ceiling while he zipped them from ankle to midthigh. I was already thinking about how fun it would be to unzip them later.

"I don't know what I like you in yet," Micah said.

"You did not expect to be romantically tied to another man, let alone two of us. It is all right to be unsure of your preferences in a sex you were never attracted to before you met us."

"Thank you for understanding," Micah said.

"I understand better than you think. I played the game if I was forced, but I was never a man for other men until I met Asher."

"You had to be in your late twenties by then," Micah said.

He laughed. "I wasn't twenty; I was already dead by the time I met him." With that he went into the bathroom and did a few minutes of blow-drying with a diffuser, so it wouldn't damage his curls. He was already wearing five keep-in hair care products to tame the nearly waist-length curls. Without all the product, his hair would almost do the white man's 'fro like mine and Micah's.

Micah turned to me while we listened to the blow-dryer. "Did you know that Asher was his first man?"

"Yes."

"Yes," Nathaniel mumbled sleepily, sliding off Micah's thigh so he could bury himself deeper into the covers, between us.

Jean-Claude came back out with his hair mostly dry and his curls laid in careful disarray. He got a short velvet jacket out of the wardrobe and pulled the white lace of his sleeves through, so it spilled out of the end of the jacket sleeves in a graceful fall around his slender, strong hands. He stopped in front of the full-length mirror in the corner, settling the open lace of the collar out over the black velvet of the jacket so that it lay just so and the cameo had pride of place at his neck. I knew he liked the necklace, but he was wearing it tonight for me, so I could see it on his neck. It was one of the moments when I began to understand why he wanted me to wear his ring.

He stalked toward the bed in the new boots and the rest looking like someone's wet dream, or maybe it was just my wet dream. Either way it made me smile as he came to the edge of the bed and kissed Micah first, and then had to climb up on the bed to lean past him to kiss Nathaniel, who drew a bare arm out of the covers to wrap around Jean-Claude and draw him down to the bed across Micah's lap.

"Non, *mon chaton*, I must go to work."

"Stay," Nathaniel said in a sleepy, happy voice that had made me late for work more than once.

Jean-Claude laughed, and Micah helped him get free by putting himself in the way of the entwining arms of our shared boy. Jean-Claude got to knees and hands and leaned across the men to kiss me. We'd just started pressing into the kiss, my hand on the edge of his face to help steady myself, when arms came up around us both and tried to drag us down to the bed. We opened our eyes to find Nathaniel doing his sleepy, teasing best to pull us down to the bed. I let him pull me close, but Jean-Claude pulled away laughing and slipped gracefully off the bed.

"I will come back and allow you to pull me into your warm nest after my meeting, but it will not be a short meeting, so sleep and I will wake you when I return."

Nathaniel made sleepy, happy noises and curled back under the covers. Micah called out to Jean-Claude as he went for the door. "We may try to talk to Melanie tonight in between shows."

Jean-Claude looked back with his hand on the door. "Remember that Melanie is thousands of years old and has never been human. It makes her arrogant, among other things."

"We'll take security with us," Micah said.

"You have little choice in that, with the new security regimen." Jean-Claude said it like he wasn't entirely happy with it either. "But I was not thinking of that. You wish information from Melanie, if she has it to share. I was merely reminding you that she might not respond to your questions in the way you expect. If you wish to learn what she knows, you must keep her uniqueness in mind."

"I've dealt with her before. She didn't seem that different for questioning," I said.

"She was still trapped as the animal to call of a vampire and was not the master of herself as she is now."

I thought about that for a second or two. "Point taken."

"I would ask you to wait until I can help you question her, since I have more experience dealing with her day to day, but I know you are both too impatient to wait, so I will not ask it of you."

"Sorry, but you're right," I said.

"I did not doubt I was right, *ma petite*, and now I truly must go. This has been a wonderful respite, and I go forth to this tedious but necessary meeting with renewed vigor and enthusiasm." He blew us kisses and left.

I looked at Micah across the bed. "Do you feel full of renewed vigor and enthusiasm?" I asked.

He thought about it for a moment and then smiled. "I do, actually."

That made me smile. "Good, me, too."

He grinned.

Nathaniel reached up and tried to pull us both down into his nest of covers. "Stop sitting up and lie down with me."

"We're going to go talk to Melanie and see if she knows anything to help the shapeshifters in Florida," I said.

That made him blink awake. "I thought I dreamed that part."

"No," Micah said.

"I'll come with you." He sat up, wiping his hand across his eyes.

"You enjoy your postcoital nap; we'll come back and join you after we talk to her," I said.

He shook his head. "When's the last time you talked to Melanie?"

"Years, like right after we killed her master and Jean-Claude gave her the job."

"I've talked to her a lot more than that. I'll come help you talk to her."

"Why are you and Jean-Claude both so worried about us talking to her?"

"Not worried, just the two of you are too blunt sometimes; you have to sweet-talk Melanie."

"Are you friends with her?" I asked.

"No, but we used to be fuck buddies."

That made both Micah and me stare at him.

"What? Why the looks from both of you?" Nathaniel asked.

"I don't know," I said. "I just remember her as unpleasant. I mean, she did try to kill me."

"Weren't you trying to kill her, too?"

"Not technically, but since she was his animal to call, me killing her master could have killed her."

Nathaniel shook his head and started crawling out of the covers. "You'll treat her like a suspect and that will get you nowhere."

"How long ago were you and she fuck buddies?" Micah asked.

"Four or five years ago." He crawled off the bed and went to the wardrobe for some of the clothes that we all left there.

"So, before you started dating Anita."

"Before I was even Anita's *pomme de sang.* I was a good little apple of blood and treated it like the relationship I was hoping it would turn into." He pulled out a pair of black jeans and a matching T-shirt.

We were both still in the bed watching him. I wasn't sure why, but knowing that he'd slept with Melanie bothered me. I knew he'd slept with a lot of people, but this one bugged me.

He stopped with the jeans on, the shirt still in his hands,

and looked at us. "What is wrong? Melanie is a beautiful woman and I didn't belong to anyone back then, so I could fuck who I wanted, and I did."

"I know," I said, "but Melanie, I mean . . ."

"Is it because she's a lamia?" he asked.

I thought about that for a moment. Was that my issue? I hoped not, because that would be shitty and racially horrible. Would it make me a racist or a species-ist? "I don't think that's what's bothering me. I think I just find her creepy, and she tried to kill me and damn near succeeded, and she can turn human men into these half-snake creepy things, so the thought of willingly having sex with her sort of creeps me."

"Fair enough," he said, as he slid the T-shirt over his head.

"I think it's the first time you've said you were lovers with someone that tried to kill one of us. I think that's what's bothering me."

"Jean-Claude gave her a job at the Circus. I figured if he trusted her enough to get her a green card, then she was trustworthy enough to date. I'm saying *date*, because both of you seem to tense up every time I say we were fuck buddies."

"Sorry, but the level of casual really bothers me," I said.

"It doesn't bother you, Anita; it confuses you," he said.

"True."

"Now, are the two of you going to get dressed so we can question Melanie, or can I get undressed and climb back into bed, because I would way rather cuddle up for a post-sex nap."

"It sounds better to me, too," I said.

"And me, but I want to know if Melanie knows anything that can help us," Micah said.

"Then get dressed, but I'll warn you that once we've talked to her I may be so wide-awake that I'll need more sex before I can nap again."

"Oh darn," I said.

"I think we can manage that," Micah said, smiling.

"So, get up and get dressed, so we can come back and get undressed and fuck like bunnies."

Micah and I both laughed out loud at the phrasing and the look on Nathaniel's face that went with it. We'd question the lamia and then we'd come back and fuck like bunnies.

11

I TEXTED NICKY and Micah texted Bram to let them know we were going to be on the move soon. We also let them know that Nathaniel was going to be with us, so they could bodyguard appropriately.

Nicky was showered, changed, and ready at the door for us. He'd brought Rodina and Ru along, looking like smaller, freckled shadows of each other. They looked delicate standing next to Nicky, and since they were both inches taller than me, I must have looked tiny beside him. Rodina and Ru looked like they were in their late teens—twenty would be stretching it—but they were centuries older than Jean-Claude and had once been personal guards to the Mother of All Darkness, the Evil Queen of the old vampire council, though R and R were the only two of the Harlequin I'd ever heard call her that as if it were her title. They thought I was their new evil queen since I'd killed their old one. I wasn't sure about the evil part, but I'd stopped arguing that I was the heir to the power of Mommy Darkest. To the victor go the spoils and all that shit.

"Bram is en route," Nicky said, and he was every bit the bodyguard in charge of my safety; the man who had kissed me so passionately in the bedroom was gone until he wasn't on the job again.

Rodina quirked a smile at me; her curly blond hair had grown out enough to touch the lower part of her face. She'd put a streak of pink in the almost white-blond curls. It was wash-out dye, so that if she needed to blend in again she could get rid of it. It was the third color she'd tried a streak of in the last few months; once she realized that we didn't have any restrictions on what our guards did with their hair or body, she'd started experimenting. She and Ru were both pale blonds with light enough skin that they had a dusting of golden freckles across their cheeks and noses. You expected blue eyes with all that, but their eyes were black, as in a brown so dark that you couldn't tell where their pupils stopped and their irises started. Rodina used black eyeliner to emphasize the improbable eye color and had even persuaded her twin brother Ru to use guy-liner; that, coupled with the all-black clothing they wore, made them look very Goth. The first time I'd remarked on that, Ru had said, "No, we're from Wales." I gave up trying to explain that I hadn't meant Visigoths, because he kept trying to talk real history instead of modern cultural references.

"You aren't happy to see us," Rodina said. "Would you prefer someone else in our places?"

She was right, and she felt what I was feeling just like Nicky did, and for the same reason. All three of them were my Brides—Brides of Anita instead of Brides of Dracula—and all for similar reasons, because I'd been desperately trying to save myself or save the people I loved, or both. When I met R and R in Ireland, they'd been R, R, and R, triplets, but their brother, Rodrigo, had given his life to save ours. It was good that he'd sacrificed himself, because it had saved me from killing him for killing Domino. Being able to turn him into a Bride had changed him from would-be assassin and kidnapper to rescuer. If I hadn't been able to work that bit of magic, then Nathaniel would have lost a lot more than just his hair. So why wasn't I happy to see them as our bodyguards? Because it was like Nathaniel's short hair; every time I saw what was left of the trip-lets, I was reminded about what had happened in Ireland, or what had almost happened, and I didn't love the twins the way I did Nicky. I'd figured out how the Bride thing worked by then, and I hadn't accidently bound myself to them emotionally the way I had with Nicky. I was free to remember that they would have happily tortured Nathaniel and me to death if I hadn't been powerful enough to mind-fuck them. It made it hard for me to like them. The fact that Ru looked exactly like his dead brother, who had done horrible things to me, didn't help either.

"I'm working my issues about how we met in Ireland, but I'm not there yet," I said.

Nathaniel walked up and put an arm across each one's shoulders. His black T-shirt, black jeans, and black boots matched their outfits, except their boots were less club and more SWAT. The three of them were within an inch of the same height. Rodina and Ru put an arm around Nathaniel's waist as if it was the most natural thing in the world. Rodina even managed a smile, suddenly looking as young as her body did; even her posture changed.

"I've started requesting them for my guard detail," he said, smiling at me, his face leaning down so that he and Rodina posed for a minute like a high school couple. Even Ru being a slightly less comfortable third wheel was very high school, or maybe college.

"I didn't know that," I said.

"Neither did I," Micah said.

"You've both been traveling a lot," Nicky said.

"Why?" I asked.

"Why have you been traveling so much?" Rodina asked, voice friendly and unfriendly all at the same time.

"I do not think that is what she means, Sister," Ru said, his voice far more uncertain than his sister's usually was.

"Nathaniel, why request them?" I said.

"Because we won in Ireland, Anita. I know bad things happened, awful things, but we won, and you keep acting like we lost."

"We are like trophies to Nathaniel," Rodina said, "trophies of victory like slaves brought back after a war." If she resented being brought back as a "slave," her voice and face didn't show it. Her body language stayed friendly and open as she stood there holding Nathaniel.

I resisted an urge to tell her to stop touching him. Ru stepped away so he wasn't touching Nathaniel, but she didn't. Nicky was compelled to keep me happy, and Ru seemed to be as well. It should have worked the same with Rodina, but she liked pushing limits, and she didn't seem as invested in keeping me happy. Nicky said it actually caused him pain to have me near him and unhappy. Maybe Rodina was a masochist.

Nathaniel looked at her. "Do you really think I treat you like a slave, or are you just trying to get a reaction?"

She looked at him, really looked at him as if it mattered to her. The hard-edged teasing fell away for a few minutes. "No, but you do see us as living trophies of your victory."

He drew away from her, or tried to, but she held on a little and I realized that he mattered to her more than I'd thought. What else had I missed while I was at work?

Ru said, "She doesn't mean that as a bad thing, Nathaniel. She just means that you look at us and see that fought and won."

"Ru and I like being your victory march," she said. She turned those dark eyes to me and said, "It's better than being Anita's funeral dirge."

"What the fuck is that supposed to mean?"

"You never look at us without remembering the death of your weretiger, and you never look at Nathaniel's shortened hair without remembering what might have happened. You are haunted in your mind and heart by it. Warriors do not let fear steal their victory after they have won, Anita, and that is what you are doing."

"I don't need a lecture from you."

"You need it from someone," she said.

"That's not your call."

"I'm sorry you lost your lover in Ireland, but has it occurred to you that Ru and I lost our brother there?"

I had a moment of not knowing what to show on my face, because I didn't usually think of it that way. "I'm sorry if you're mourning him."

"If? After a thousand years you mourn enemies, Anita. He was our brother, our triplet; we shared a womb together; you can't imagine the bond that forged between us."

"One close enough that when I mind-fucked Rodrigo it fucked all three of you. So, yeah, I have some idea how close the bond was." I still sounded unsympathetic.

"Rodrigo stepped between you and a shotgun blast. He died to save you and Nathaniel." She finally sounded angry.

"Yeah, and I'm grateful for that, I really am, but Rodrigo killed Domino in front of me and made me drink his blood. I don't know how to forgive that, Rodina."

"It was stupid and cruel. Rodrigo could be like that sometimes," she said.

"He gave his life to redeem his mistake," Ru said.

"No, he gave his life because once I made you my Brides he had to do everything he could to keep me happy and alive. You all did; you all still do."

"We are well aware that we are tied to you in a way that should not be possible. We are part of the Harlequin. Even you should not have been able to make us into your Brides. Our ties to our vampire master should have kept us safe from that particular insult."

"Your master didn't have enough juice to keep me out of your heads."

"No, he didn't, and that is why we know you are the true heir to our dead queen." She didn't sound happy about the fact.

And just like that I didn't know what to say to her. I never seemed to know what to say to either of them. If Rodrigo had not forced Domino's blood down my throat, then I wouldn't have been powerful enough to roll his mind. He had accidently fulfilled the prophecy of me "marrying" one of the clan tigers, because the prophecy didn't mean marrying for life; it meant taking in their life, their essence. One cruel act had given me the fuel I needed to save us. If Domino had not died, if Rodrigo hadn't tried to terrorize me with the blood of my dead lover, then Nathaniel and I would have died in Ireland. Not just died, but died by torture, like serial-killer-worthy torture. Rodina was right: I couldn't let it go, couldn't get past how narrow the escape had been. I was stuck with the thought that Domino's death and Rodrigo's cruelty had saved the day; that two events that I would have given almost anything to change had saved Nathaniel's life and mine. I hated that, hated it so much. It made me want to hate Rodina and Ru, as if I could blame them for it all and that would make it better.

Micah touched my arm, and I fought the urge to pull away from him. I was so angry, and I so wanted to be angry at someone. I wanted a target, so badly, but I knew better than to take it out on Micah. He hadn't even been in Ireland. None of this was his fault. No, I'd been the one who'd endangered Nathaniel, not him.

"What have I missed?" Bram asked.

I looked up to find the six-foot-tall guard coming down the hallway behind Nathaniel and the twins. He looked slender until you noticed the muscle definition that the short-sleeved

T-shirt didn't hide. He was wearing one of the black body-armor vests that we'd started giving the guards an option to wear. Most of the ones who were wearing one put a man's sleeveless undershirt under the vest, then a larger-than-normal shirt over the vest, and then a suit jacket over the top of that so they were layered and it wasn't obvious that they were wearing body armor. Bram's vest was on the outside of a form-fitting black T-shirt. The big Glock .45 in its hip holster, complete with a strap around his thigh to hold the gun in place so he always knew where it was in relation to his body, wasn't going to be hidden by a suit jacket. He and several of the other ex-military guards had started dressing in a civilian version of full battle rattle, at least inside the Circus. Bram's recently cut hair was back to military short. He'd tried to let it grow out, but it was curlier than mine or Micah's. He could grow an Afro for real and he wasn't prepared to deal with it.

He came up behind Rodina and she moved so that she didn't give him her back. It wasn't that she thought he'd hurt her; it was just automatic. It meant there'd be no more hugging with Nathaniel unless he moved closer to her, and if he did, we'd be having a talk later. Our poly wasn't closed poly, which would have meant that we were "monogamous" within our poly group and no one else could be added; because we weren't closed poly, new lovers could be added if everyone agreed to it. We had veto power over new people coming in, but it was a possibility. Until a few minutes ago I'd have said that there were no new candidates on the horizon.

"I'll ask again: What did I miss?" Bram said.

"Nothing," I said.

"Do I state the obvious?" he asked.

"Drop it and I'll fill you in later," Nicky said.

"There's nothing to fill in," I said.

Micah took my hand in his and tried to hug me, but I put a hand on his chest and shook my head. Hugging was too much touching for the level of anger I was experiencing. Too much touching when I was this pissed just made it worse.

"Is this 'nothing' going to impact our ability to guard you?" Bram asked.

"We're ready and willing to give our lives in defense of our queen and her princes," Rodina said.

The anger flared hotter at her wording. I glared at her because I knew it had been a deliberate reminder of her brother's sacrifice, which I did not need. My inner beasts began to stir, rising to the bait of my rage. I knew the anger was disproportionate to what had just happened. I knew it was because of other emotions—fear, sorrow, love, hate, lust, confusion—and all those emotions were translating into anger, because being angry felt better than being afraid or sad. Anger was what I put in front of love, if loving someone confused me too much, like Nathaniel's attention to Rodina was confusing me now. Anger had been my coping mechanism for most of my life. Therapy was helping me find other ways of coping, but it hadn't gotten rid of my anger issues. It was just helping me not let my inner rage tear my life apart anymore.

I went to stand against the cool stone wall of the hallway. I leaned back, closed my eyes, and started counting while I took deep, even breaths. I had to get a handle on this, damn it. I sank in against the cool stone, placing my palms flat against it so I could feel the grain of the stone, the chill of it. I pressed my feet into my boots so that I could feel that I was standing here in my human body. This was me. I grounded myself in the feeling of myself leaning against the wall, and then I let myself notice the beasts inside me. One of the things that you have to do to stay sane when you catch lycanthropy is to find a visualization, a way to "see" your inner beasts, because otherwise they just try to claw their way out of you. It's as if giving your human mind something to concentrate on that makes sense to it gives you more control over the animal parts. I saw the place where they lived inside me as darkness, the darkness at the center of me, like a well, but the moment I "looked" at it, the darkness became hints of jungle and trees, and there was ground for the beasts to stand on, for me to stand on. I'd worked hard so that I could draw them out one at a time rather than as a snarling mass. Thanks to Jean-Claude's vampire marks, I couldn't actually change shape to any of my beasts, so having that mob of claws and teeth trying to work its way out of me had hurt like hell, with no possible relief. My frustrated beasts and I had been forced to find a compromise.

I looked into that dark, shadowy place deep inside me and called, or thought, and the first image to gleam to life was a lion, but it wasn't my usual gold lioness; it was a big male with a thick reddish black mane. My pulse sped, heart rate faster, and that let him step farther out of the shadows and growl at me. He put one big clawed foot onto the ground and snarled up at me with amber eyes so dark they looked orange.

"You're new," I said, and it must have been out loud, because Micah was there, asking, "What's new?"

I spoke carefully, softly, as if the lion were down the hallway and I didn't want to spook it. "Male lion."

"Where's your lioness?" he asked.

I thought about it, and she was there, beside him, as if the darkness turned gold and grew fur and golden-amber eyes. She panted up at me, and there was something in her . . . face. It was a demand, a question, except that's not how lions think, not real ones, anyway; but then, she'd been trapped inside me for a few years now. It made us both a little confused.

I stared into her deep golden eyes and heard/felt/knew she wanted what was beside her in the dark. The big male looked up at me with his orange eyes and I realized he wasn't as real as she was, not yet.

I heard noise outside myself, like someone sniffing the air, felt the displacement of space as someone larger than me or Micah got too close. My lioness snarled at that, and the sound trickled across my human lips. Fuck, that wasn't good.

"It's me," Nicky said. "You smell like lion." He put his arm near my face so that I could smell the faint scent of lion on his skin, drawn to the surface by the nearness of mine. My lioness growled and hissed at the scent. That wasn't right either; it should have calmed her down. The big male beside her gave a coughing roar—not the big one that we all think is the only roar, like the Hollywood lion, but the more typical cough.

"Whatever just happened, my lion doesn't like it at all," Nicky said.

"Male coughed, roared," I said.

"You can't have a male lion inside you, Anita," he said.

"Lioness wants him."

"I'm right here," Nicky said.

I felt my head shake as I stared into the lioness's amber eyes. "You're my Bride; you can't be my lion to call; you can't be both."

"I know that."

I stared into her amber eyes until it was like falling into them, almost like falling into a vampire's gaze; so many impossibilities. I let myself fall, let myself lean my forehead against hers the way a housecat will bump its head against you. I felt the fur of her face under my hand; for a second it was more real than the wall I knew I was touching. She and I leaned against each other for a moment, and I knew what she was trying to tell me.

She vanished into the darkness like smoke, and I knew the big male would be gone with her, because he wasn't as real as she was; he wasn't as real as the other movements in the dark: Leopard, wolf, rat, hyena, and a rainbow of tigers moved like thick shadows in the dark. The lioness was the most real of them for some reason. I didn't know if they had agreed to that among themselves, or if she was just that strong, but then I knew as if I'd always known. It was her need that was stronger than theirs. She had been inside me longer than rat or hyena, and they were the only ones that didn't have a mate on the outside of me. The lioness wanted a lion to call.

I opened my eyes, utterly calm, and told Micah and Nicky and everyone else in the hallway what had happened. "Can she do that? The lioness, I mean? Can she create a male . . . counterpart inside Anita?" Nathaniel asked.

"No," Nicky said.

"Did you smell a second lion on her skin?" Micah asked.

"No, just her lioness."

"That's all I smelled as well, so the male lion wasn't real."

"Her lioness is more powerful than normal because Anita is more powerful than normal," Rodina said.

"It's never done anything like this before," I said.

"I've never heard of anyone's beast being able to do this," Micah said.

"Our old queen could call all the cat lycanthropes," Rodina said.

"Moroven had seals as her animal to call," I said.

"She was M'lady, not our dark queen."

"My sister means the Mother of All Darkness," Ru said.

"What does that have to do with anything?" I asked.

It was Bram who said it. "I think she's saying that your cat forms may have gotten a boost of power from you killing the dark mother."

"I killed her a couple of years ago; nothing like this has happened before."

"But you only killed Moroven a few months ago, less than a year," Rodina said.

"I didn't think I gained any power from that; I mean, it wasn't even me that actually killed her."

"Moroven believed that when you slew the Mother of All Darkness, her power scattered, seeking out vampires that were suitable for each power. She thought she had gained all the power except what went to the old council member, the Lover of Death, and you. You killed him, and his power went to you, so she was going to kill you and get it all."

"I remember her doing her villain speech and explaining all this while I was chained up," I said, scowling at her.

"What if the crazy bitch was right? What if when she died you really did gain more of the power from our dark and evil queen?"

I shook my head. "I didn't feel any different, and I did feel different when the mother and the Lover of Death died."

"You'd just used necromancy to control thousands of ghosts. Would you have felt the rush of more power in all that?" she asked.

It was a good question, a smart question. It was the kind of thinking that had made us keep the two of them around. I looked at Micah and Nicky, who were still standing the closest to me in the hallway. "What do you think?"

"I think it's something we should talk over with Jean-Claude," Micah said.

"Yeah," Nicky said.

"Are you saying that Anita's lioness created a real male lion inside her?" Nathaniel asked.

"No," Rodina said, "I think the lioness created a thought, or a message for Anita."

I nodded. "She wants a mate. She wants me to find a male lion to be my animal to call. She's tired of waiting, or she feels the need of backup, or something."

"I felt it when the male roared inside Anita. I felt it like a punch almost," Nicky said.

"Is that typical when another male roars at you?" Micah asked.

"No, I'm the Rex of our pride; no one has that kind of power here."

"Anita does," Rodina said.

"Not as a lion, she doesn't," Nicky said.

"But she's not just a werelion," Ru said. "She's our evil queen reborn, or reimagined."

Rodina nodded. "Our evil queen had enough power to back down any of the cats, large or small."

"I really wish you would stop saying *evil queen* every time, and just say *queen*."

Rodina gave me a smile that was part joy and part evil, the kind of smile that her brother had on his face when he fed me Domino's blood. I fought not to shiver but failed. She knew that she creeped me out sometimes. She enjoyed it.

"But, Anita," she said in a sweet voice, "we don't want a fair and just queen to follow. We of the Harlequin want our motherfucking evil queen back."

"I am not your girl, then."

"Oh, Anita, don't be modest. I've seen you drain the life out of one of the Selkies until he was just a dried, screaming husk. That's not white magic, my queen."

"I was out of options to save our lives," I said.

"And you were ruthless enough to use black magic."

"It's not black magic," I said.

"Well, it sure as hell isn't white."

"It's a psychic ability, not magic."

"Pronounce it tomato or tomahto; it's still a red, squishy vegetable."

"Actually, it's a fruit," Bram said.

We all looked at him.

He looked as close to being embarrassed as I'd ever seen him. "Well, it is a fruit."

"Okay," I said.

Rodina laughed. "Fruit or vegetable, it's still dark magic, and you are the first full-fledged necromancer in thousands of years, Anita. There are videos of you on YouTube raising an army of zombies in Colorado."

"The Lover of Death had raised an army of undead. I had to do something to stop them from killing more people."

"Your motives were good," Rodina said.

"You saved hundreds of lives, Anita," Micah said.

"I don't doubt that," Rodina said.

"Then what is your problem?" I asked.

She smiled that happily evil smile again. "I don't have a problem with the fact that you're the evil queen in this story; you have a problem with it."

"Anita is not evil," Micah said.

Rodina shrugged. "Necromancer, succubus, can feed off anger and suck the life force right out of someone. What on this list makes her not our evil queen?"

"She doesn't lash out with her power just to hurt us," Ru said, voice soft.

Rodina glanced back at her brother.

He looked uncomfortable, as if something in her face wasn't happy with him, but he spoke up in the face of his sister's disapproval. "It is not power that makes someone evil; it is what they do with that power."

"A pretty thought, Brother, but you know what they say about power corrupting."

"I do, but I was not as happy with our old queen as you and Rodrigo were. She was petty, ill-tempered, mad, and had enough power to destroy the world. We were all afraid of her, even you."

"Evil queens are meant to be feared."

"And that is my point, Sister. Anita works very hard to be fair and just, and not frightening."

"So you're saying that she's the good queen—the white queen and not the black?"

"Yes."

It was interesting watching them talk about me almost as if I wasn't there, but Ru seemed to be winning the argument, and I wanted him to win, so I just listened. We were all listening to them, and the siblings talked as if none of us mattered in that moment but the two of them. I wondered if they missed Rodrigo in these brother-sister moments.

"If you're evil, you can't just decide to be good," she said.

"If you're evil, no, of course not."

"Well then?"

"If you decide day after day to make good, positive, moral choices, then you are not evil. In fact, you would be the definition of a good person."

"You're saying that she's not evil because she has decided to be good?"

"That is the only way any of us are ever good. We choose to do what is right instead of what is wrong," Ru said.

"That would be so boring," she said, rolling her eyes.

"Good isn't boring," I said.

She gave me a disdainful look.

"I'm in love with three of the men in this hallway, and that's a very good thing."

"But morally it makes you a whore," she said.

Micah stiffened and made a movement toward her, but I touched his arm. It made him look at me, and I let him know with a glance that I had this. He let me speak for myself, which was one of the things I loved about him.

"You think being good means that very narrow fundamentalist Christian or Muslim or Jewish definition, but it always comes down to fundamentalism of some kind. Is that what you think good is, Rodina?"

"That's what everyone thinks good is," she said, rolling her eyes again.

"No, that's not what everyone thinks good is; it's what the world tells us is the definition of good."

"I thought you were Christian; you even go to church, so by your own beliefs you are not a good person."

"My path of faith is between me and God, and He's okay with it."

"You can't know that your god is okay with what you do."

"I know that when I pray, demons can't touch me. I know that my cross still shines with holy fire when I'm faced with a vampire. If I was damned like the Catholic Church said when it excommunicated all the people who could raise zombies, then my cross wouldn't work, my prayers wouldn't work, but they do."

Rodina stared at me. "You're joking."

I shook my head. "I would never joke about that."

"You cannot be good."

"Why not?"

"Your faith cannot be that pure."

"Why not?"

"Because you feed on sex and rage and raise armies of the dead."

"I was a little worried about all that, but apparently God is cool with it, and if He doesn't have a problem with it, then neither do I."

"No," she said, and she sounded angry, flustered even.

"Let it go, Sister."

"No."

"Why not let it go?" Bram asked her.

She looked at him and then back at me, hands in fists at her sides. "Because if she's not evil, then she won't let us do the things I want to do."

"What do you want to do?" I asked.

"You met my brother."

"I did."

She just looked at me until I finally said, "Oh, sorry, but I'm not evil enough to let you do the kind of shit Rodrigo enjoyed."

She closed her eyes, took a deep breath, let it out in a rush, and then settled like a bird shaking its feathers into place. She gave me calm eyes. She was still and silent and contained. It was scarier than the temper tantrum had been.

"I serve you because I must, but I hope you fall from grace just far enough to let me enjoy the rest of my eternity."

"I'll do my best to be just evil enough so that you won't be bored."

She bowed then, very formally, and I remembered Moroven complaining about that and forcing her to curtsy even though she was wearing pants. Moroven had left her in that low curtsy until her legs ached, because once you bow or curtsy in front of your queen you aren't supposed to rise again until they notice you.

"Nice bow; now let's go talk to the lamia between shows."

Rodina looked up at me, face still unreadable, but she stood up straight, military straight rather than her usual. She suddenly had the bearing of a soldier. "Thank you, my queen, for noticing."

Nathaniel came to hug me and said, "Let me talk to Melanie first."

"Why?"

"Because I'll sweet-talk her, and you and Micah will just interrogate her."

"If it will get us the most information with the least amount of fuss, sure," I said.

"You know her better than we do," Micah said. "We'll follow your lead."

"You'll have to let me see the pictures from Florida, so I know what I'm talking about."

Micah nodded. "I know, and I'll have to break confidence to show Melanie as well."

"Aren't you going to have to check with your clients to do all that?" I asked.

"I'm making an executive decision that they're being insane about this level of secrecy. I need information to be able to help them, and I can't get that without telling people the truth."

"Great. That means we can show Edward when we see him."

"No, I promised I wouldn't show the pictures to anyone who might hunt them down for execution without their permission."

"Damn it, Micah."

"That is a reasonable fear, Anita. Even you don't share everything with Edward, because you don't want to endanger some of us."

"Fine, but I do share most things now."

"Good to know," he said.

Nicky said, "If you want to catch Melanie the Lamia between shows, we need to hustle."

"Are we going to have to run the stairs again?" Ru asked, sounding sad.

Nicky grinned. "Not if we hurry."

Suddenly, we were all willing to hurry. Nice to know even the immortal hated extra cardio.

12

MELANIE DID HER show in one of the tent-fronted areas to the side of the midway. It was designed to look like the food stand and game area of a traveling carnival that would go through the middle of the country in the summer. We even had rides: Tilt-a-Whirl, Ferris wheel, mirror maze, and the fun house, though the rides weren't really why people came to the Circus of the Damned. You could get more spectacular rides elsewhere. You could get cotton candy and a corn dog, play ring toss, and win prizes like a big, flappy rubber bat or a stuffed toy wolf that howled when you squeezed it. You could do everything you did at traveling fairs without the heat and dust, but that wasn't why we had lines out the door and around the block. The permanent big top, with its striped tent entrance, was just to the left of the main doors. Its one-ring show was definitely one of the reasons for the crowds. The sideshow was more than halfway into the huge warehouse space, because if the line for the big top converged with the one for the sideshow, it became an impassable mass. So now the tented fronts of the sideshow attractions didn't start until you'd walked through the games, food stalls, and rides. It also meant people did more impulse buying, which was nice for the bottom line, but the main reason to move the two main attractions farther away from each other was crowd control. The security people had requested it, along with the fire marshal.

Melanie's area was the last in the line, closest to the back door that led to the underground, which made our bodyguards' jobs easier since there was less crowd to wade through. Nicky led the way, Bram brought up the rear, and Rodina and Ru took left and right, so the three of us moved in a bubble of their arms suddenly moving outward to stop people from getting too close. We didn't really expect a problem that the three of us couldn't have handled on our own. The four of them were mainly helpful getting through the crowd and discouraging anyone who might know us through the media. Micah was on the news a lot representing the lycanthrope community, and I'd become a social media darling since the proposal and wedding announcement to Jean-Claude. Nathaniel under his stage name, Brandon, had gotten stopped by fans for years. He'd actually had less of that since his hair was cut, which was one of the few pluses to it for me. There were more of our guards scattered throughout the midway. You could pick them out by the bright orange shirts with *Security* in large white letters on the back; smaller letters on the front read, *Circus of the Damned Security*. They were keeping the crowds in line outside the sideshow from blocking the food and gaming booths across from them. It was also part of the deal with the fire marshal to keep the aisles free. It was one of the places where we actually needed more security.

Nicky started us wading through the line. Some people complained, but he glared at them and they thought better of it. One of the security guards came toward us, saying, "No line cutting." He was tall and athletic-looking like most of them, built closer to Bram's body type than Nicky's. I couldn't put a name to the strong, lithe-looking man. The fact that he didn't recognize any of us on sight might mean that I had never known it.

It was Rodina who called out, "We're working."

He looked at her and then at Ru, and then at the rest of us. His eyes widened when he got to me and Micah. I think he recognized us from TV and social media, if nothing else, or maybe Claudia had started showing our pictures to the new hires.

"Sorry, Roe, Ru, I didn't see you behind the big guy here."

The new guy tried to get introductions, but Nicky and I both shook our heads. We were in a crowd of strangers. They didn't need to know our names. If you had enough threats to your safety to need bodyguards, any time you could be anonymous was good, and bodyguards don't like people to know their names, because then strangers can yell out their names and distract them at the wrong moment.

The new guy's name was Jamie and he looked like a hundred other college-age guys across the Midwest. He wasn't unattractive, but he was attractive in a way that was so generic that it left no impression. He'd have been a great spy because he could have blended in so many places. He'd have been killer at undercover on a college campus, but instead he was working security for us, which meant he was a wereanimal, because he wasn't a vampire and we only hired supernaturals for security. Jamie hid his energy well; I got only the smallest flare of power from his anxiety about dealing with three of the primary people security was supposed to guard. Nicky and Bram made him a little nervous, too, but I think that was just him doing the big, athletic guy math of, if there was a problem, he wasn't sure he would win a fight against them. The fact that neither Rodina nor Ru nor the three of us made him do the math made me take more points away from him. Bigger didn't always mean tougher in a fight. It sure as hell didn't mean it when some of the smaller people were armed.

Jamie did escort us through the line and hold the tent flap so we could go through into the lamia's lair, which is what the poster above her tent called it. There was a small entryway/waiting room with another tent flap in front of us.

"Let me go see where she's at with the people ahead of you," Jamie said. He didn't wait for us to say yes or no; he just disappeared through the next tent flap and left us standing there. There were a handful of chairs against one soft cloth wall, a rug on the floor that looked Persian, and a small table in one corner with what looked like little catalogs and pamphlets. There was a price list attached to the tent wall. I moved close enough to see that it was a price list for pictures and signatures from the lamia. It was extra to get your picture taken with her above and beyond the price of both the unsigned picture of your choice and the signature itself. I knew that you had to pay for a ticket to watch Melanie just stand in front of you and change from human shape to half snake, but I hadn't known that there were so many other ways Melanie made money for herself and us. The last time I'd paid attention to the lamia, she'd just stood on a raised stage so everyone had a good view and then changed shape. She hadn't talked to the crowd or answered questions or much of anything. Apparently, she was much more interactive now.

Jamie opened the tent flap and leaned in, whispering, "She's almost done; just keep your voices down."

He held the flap open for us and we were suddenly inside *The Arabian Nights*, or what Hollywood thought the interior of *The Arabian Nights* would have looked like. It was all Persian rugs on the floor and wall hangings and cushions in brilliant colors and a wide variety of cloths and textures. There was a small knot of people near the middle of the room. Two security staff stood to either side of the people, so I was pretty sure that Melanie was the center of all the small group's attention, but I couldn't see her at first. Then movement near the floor caught my attention and I realized it was her tail trailing through a pile of multicolored cushions; the pattern of her scales had been strangely camouflaged until she twitched the tip of her tail. The rest of her was still hidden behind the small group of fans. They had to be fans if they were willing to pay not just to see her transform but extra for an intimate meet-and-greet, as the price sheet had said. I realized that the crowd had to move through this "intimate" room to get to the main stage. I'd have thought it would be the other way around, but then I saw the lounging couch on the far side of the room. It was made up like a bed in a harem costume drama, and I think that was the point. They'd take the crowd through and let them build up their own fantasy about what *intimate* might mean, if they were willing to pay to find out.

There was a small table to the left of the door where a woman wearing an orange shirt with a cartoon version of the fanged clowns on the roof done large across the front of it was ready to sell us things. The Halloween shade of orange marked her as staff, but the image was one of the ones we sold as souvenir T-shirts in other colors. I knew the staff were issued two shirts in that shade of orange, but with designs that we sold. We had two different fanged-clown shirt designs.

The woman at the table wasn't selling shirts, though; she was selling pictures and pens, all with Melanie's image on them.

There was another price sheet pinned to the wall behind her.
The woman started to smile at us and offer us a chance to buy,
but Jamie explained we weren't here for that.

Micah whispered to me, "Lamias are Greek; Mediterra-
nean, not Mideastern."

"I know that and you know that," I whispered back.

Nathaniel leaned in and said, "They tried Greek at first, but
white togas and a faux Greek temple made people think she
was supposed to be Medusa. It confused people."

"So they didn't believe her real origins?"

"The only half snake that most people know about is Medusa."

Micah cursed softly and got his phone out. "You need to
see the pictures before we talk to her."

Nathaniel moved closer so he could look over Micah's
shoulder as he found the pictures he'd texted me. Jamie tried
to look, too, but Nicky moved to block his view. It meant that
Nicky would be able to see, but Micah didn't tell him to move,
so apparently he really was going to share information as he
saw fit, instead of asking for permission constantly. Rodina
tried to peek, but Micah told her no. Ru took the hint and just
stayed staring around the room looking for dangers. Bram did
the same, but then he'd been one of the only people allowed
into the meetings with Micah, so he didn't need to look at the
pictures; he'd seen the real thing.

I realized that we hadn't really prepared Nathaniel for seeing them, because we hadn't been planning on bringing him
to see Melanie until he suggested it. I had a moment of regret
that Nathaniel was going to get dragged into the bad side of
our jobs again. I wanted to protect him, but it seemed like no
matter what I did lately, he ended up involved in the bad stuff.

His face was somber as he looked at the pictures. Nicky's
face showed nothing, but then he truly was a sociopath, so he
didn't have the depths of feeling that Nathaniel did. I was
Nicky's conscience, his Jiminy Cricket, he'd called me once.
Nathaniel didn't need me to help him feel empathy.

The people were being ushered out by one of the security
guards near Melanie. We were next and there wasn't time to
see how the pictures had affected Nathaniel. We'd talk later.

Right now, we could see the lamia, because that's what I thought of first: not Melanie, but lamia. Her skin was darker than I remembered it, as if she was getting a summer tan. I guess when you belong to an ancient vampire you don't get out in the sunlight much, but now she belonged to herself and she could tan if she wanted to. Her hair was still long and thick and black. Her upper body was covered by a short silk robe that looked more Oriental than Arabian, but since she was already a Greek myth, we weren't really going for authenticity. The robe hid where her human body met serpent, so that it was like watching an attractive woman standing there, except where her legs should have been were the coils of a giant snake flexing and moving against the bright carpet and scattering of pillows. She turned with a wide, professional smile; then she saw me, and the smile vanished. Her golden eyes with their slit pupils looked even more exotic with tasteful but dramatic makeup around them, though it was hard to get more dramatic than snake eyes in a human face. She gave me a look that seemed to hold actual hatred in it. I didn't like her because she was dangerous and had tried to kill me, but I didn't hate her, so what had I done to make her hate me?

Nathaniel let go of my hand and flashed her one of the smiles that made customers at Guilty Pleasures rain money on the stage. Her glare at me shifted to something softer. He walked toward her with his hand out toward her. Rodina and Ru started forward to flank him like good bodyguards, but he told them to stay back.

They stopped moving, but they looked at me for confirmation. I just nodded. I don't know if Nathaniel noticed the exchange, but Melanie did. She smiled even more warmly at him and reached out toward his offered hand. Nathaniel said, "How do you get to be more beautiful every time I see you?" his voice holding that edge of teasing that had never worked on me, no matter who used the tone.

She smiled at him, taking his hand in hers and drawing him in for a hug. "Maybe you prefer your women darker-skinned," she said, looking at me. I was pasty white compared to her tan or Micah's or even Nathaniel's own skin tone. Nothing I could do would ever make me tan; burn, but not tan.

"You look amazing with or without the tan," Nathaniel said, trying to draw back from the hug. Melanie held on, pressing her breasts against his chest, making way more of the innocent hug than was polite. She looked directly at me while she did it. Something personal was going on that I had no clue about, and then I got a clue as I watched her hands explore Nathaniel's body. He had to move her hands off his ass, laughing and kissing her cheek as he did it, so that she didn't take offense at it. Was she jealous of Nathaniel? Did she see him as having left her for me? Just because he thought of them as fuck buddies didn't mean that's how she'd seen it. Great, just what we needed: a jealous lamia.

Nathaniel turned with her hand in his, smiling, as if he hadn't just had to move her hands off his ass. I was used to shit like that at his job, but outside of it, it pissed me off. That probably showed on my face, because Micah drew me in against him, which made me look at him instead of them, or maybe it bothered him, too.

I looked at him, and he gave the smallest shake of his head, which could have meant a lot of things. I'd ask later. Melanie couldn't make me jealous because there was no reason to be jealous of her and Nathaniel. There just wasn't. He was here to help Micah get information out of Melanie, and that was all.

Micah said, "Melanie, I'm sorry to barge in here like this. I know you only have a short break before your next group of fans."

"Nathaniel texted that you needed my expertise about some Coalition matter, though I cannot imagine what expertise I might possess that would aid you." She was calmer than I'd expected, or remembered. Of course, when I'd first met her, she'd spent centuries enslaved and controlled by an ancient vampire; maybe that would make anyone cranky.

"You should drink something while we talk to you. You still have quite a crowd waiting to see you," Nathaniel said.

She looked at him, smiling, and again her face softened more than I thought it should have. I was pretty certain that Melanie thought of him as an ex, not just a fuck buddy she stopped fucking. I wondered if the concept of fuck buddies had existed in ancient Greece.

Nathaniel led her over to the couch, and I was fascinated

by watching the muscles in her tail move. She moved just like a snake, strong and muscular, except the top part of her was held aloft more like a snaky centaur, or maybe it was just Nathaniel holding her hand so that the human part of her seemed more human. When I'd seen her in this form years before, she'd moved forward much more like a serpent that just happened to have human parts. Tonight, she moved like a person with a snake's tail. I wasn't sure I could have explained the difference out loud, but it was there.

One of the security guards pushed back a wall hanging to reveal a small refrigerator. He pulled out a bottle of sparkling water and had it opened and ready for Melanie by the time Nathaniel got her settled on the couch. He tried to let go of her hand and join us, but she pulled him down beside her on the couch. He sat beside her as if that was dandy with him.

"Ask your questions, Callahan; as Nathaniel said, I have a lot of fans still to see."

Micah came forward with his phone, and Bram trailed him like a shadow. Micah didn't tell him to stay back—I'm not sure it occurred to him to tell his tall, dark, right-hand man to stay behind. Bram went with him almost everywhere, even if it was just a few yards across a room.

Micah did make the security guard who had handed her the water and was now standing beside the couch back up. He didn't even try to explain why, just called the pictures up on his phone screen and tried to show them to her, but she ignored the phone to look at his hand. She set the water bottle on the floor and touched Micah's hand to turn it, and I realized she was looking at his engagement ring. Nathaniel had proposed to Micah, but he hadn't done it with a ring in hand. He'd waited until Micah accepted the proposal and then he'd surprised him with a thin gold band channel set with yellow and green sapphires all the way around. It was originally designed as a women's anniversary band, something a couple added to the woman's original wedding set at ten years, or twenty, depending. The wedding bands were being custom made in *mokume-gane*, which was a Japanese metal technique originally designed for swords. Their rings would look like wood grain with no wood involved.

Melanie looked at the ring the way that women who wanted

one on their own finger looked at them on other people's hands: part admiration, but mostly jealousy. "So it's true; Nathaniel proposed to you."

"Yes," Micah said.

"We found a ring in purple sapphires for me, but my hand is bigger, so we either have to have it sized up, which isn't easy with a ring that has stones all the way around, or we find me a different engagement band and just match the wedding bands."

Micah had to put his phone in his other hand because she wanted to see that the sapphires went all the way around. "Very pretty," she said at last, but not like her heart was in it. Again, I had the impression that she'd cared for Nathaniel a lot more than he'd cared for her, which surprised the hell out of me. Not because Nathaniel wasn't wonderful, because I thought he was, but because Melanie had seemed crazy and to care for no one but herself when I first met her.

Micah tried to show her the phone pictures again, but she looked past the phone to me, and she wasn't hostile this time. "You aren't wearing the ring that's in all the videos," she said.

"It's for formal occasions," I said.

"What do you wear for everyday?" she asked.

She was a lamia, her dead vampire master had said she was the last one in the world, but she still wanted to see the ring. Melanie might be more girly girl than I would ever be, even with the snake tail.

"I'll show you the ring if you'll please look at the pictures and answer our questions."

"I was going to answer Callahan's questions."

"Then it's a win-win," I said and went to show her the ring and see if we could get past the weird interpersonal shit and actually learn something. Nicky came with me, and I didn't tell him to stay back. I knew that between those red lips were retractable fangs with the type of venom that had almost killed me once. Did I think she'd try to bite me tonight? No, but with Nicky at my side, I knew if she did try, she'd die failing.

13

"WHY WOULD I know anything of this abomination?" she asked after she'd looked at the pictures.

Micah answered, "They think their family curse originated in ancient Greece, and you were alive then, and in the same area of the world."

"So you thought because my beauty reminds you of these monstrosities that I would know how they came to exist?" Her voice was rising.

"I had hoped you would know something that might help them."

"Help them? Help them how?" She stood up, if that was the right word. She was taller than both Micah and me. Given how much tail she had left lying on the floor, she could have been taller than Nicky if she'd wanted to be.

"They want a cure," Micah said.

"If it is a curse, there is no cure, only another spell."

"Do you think it's a curse?" Micah asked.

"No, curses in my time were aimed at one person, a tribe, or a city perhaps, but not a family line. If the gods wished to destroy a family, they would destroy the bloodline. There would be no descendants left."

I had to ask. "Did the gods actually curse people back then?"

"Of course they did."

"Did you ever see a god or goddess curse someone for real? I mean not just a story you heard, but with your own eyes."

She looked disdainfully at me, rising a little higher on the muscular reach of her tail so she could look even farther down her nose at me. "I was worshipped as a goddess once, Anita. I know the gods cursed mortals."

What are you supposed to say to that?

"We meant no insult," Micah said.

She raised herself higher yet, stretching up on that long, multicolored tail so that it gave the illusion she was literally growing above us like some stage giant. She hissed and I saw the fangs between those ruby red lips. Her forked tongue flicked out between them.

I felt Nicky tense at my back and said, "Silver bullets don't work on her."

"How about lead?" he asked.

"Nope."

"Would you kill me, Anita Blake? Would you finish what you tried to do years ago?"

"You threatened me first," I said.

"Anita killed your old master and freed you, Melanie," Nathaniel said, voice mild and soothing. He was trying to talk her down and maybe remind me that I didn't need to add fuel to her fire.

"She did not do it to free me. She did it to save herself and Jean-Claude."

"True, but she still freed you from someone you hated."

She lowered herself a few inches. "It is good not to be enslaved."

Micah said, "I didn't think that the snake lycanthropes in these photos were lamia, or anything close to you."

"Then why bring them to me?"

"Because there aren't that many snake shapeshifters of any kind, and I hoped you might know more than I did about them."

"Do you know every type of feline supernatural being or shapeshifter in the world?" she asked. She was calmer now. Her temper used to be a lot worse than this. Maybe she'd gone to therapy, too, or maybe just being enslaved to the Earthmover had made her crazier.

Micah smiled and shook his head. "No, no, I don't."

"Then why should I know all the snake ones?"

"Fair point, but you are from ancient Greece and the family traces itself back to there."

"Just because they are of Greek descent doesn't mean I

would know the family. Callahan is an Irish last name; do you
know all the people of Irish descent?"

He sighed, still smiling. "Of course not."

"Does it amuse you to waste my time?"

"No, no, I'm laughing at myself for wasting both our times
and grasping at straws."

"Grasping at straws—what does that mean?"

"It means I'm desperate to help this family, and I'm willing
to do almost anything to find a way to do that."

"Why do you care so much about them?" she asked.

"If you'd met them, seen the despair, then you wouldn't
have to ask."

She was down to her usual height. She looked at him with
her gold, slit-pupiled eyes, and I couldn't read the expression
in them. They were different enough from any of the eyes that
I knew how to read that she was blank to me.

"I do not think I would be as moved as you were by their
plight."

"It's not like any shapeshifting I've ever seen. The snakes
are separate from them. It's not them turning into the snake,
but as if their body parts are being changed into individual
serpents. But the human part of them continues to be separate
from it. The snake part doesn't communicate with the rest of
them as a normal lycanthrope's beast does."

"My tail does not talk to me either. It is part of me, not
some animal trapped inside me as yours is."

"What is happening to this family is neither true lycanthropy nor the ancient magic of the lamia."

"Then they are damned like Sisyphus in Tartarus with no
possibility of rescue."

Jamie said, "Sorry, Melanie, but the crowd is getting rest-
less."

"I'll be ready in a moment, Jamie. Callahan and Anita were
just leaving." She leaned down to get her bottle of sparkling
water and sip from it again. She kissed Nathaniel on the cheek,
but the rest of us didn't even get offered a handshake. We were
dismissed.

14

THE NEXT GROUP of fans was already being ushered through the door as we went out the exit. The noise of the midway seemed louder for some reason. Maybe I was just tired. Yeah, I was suddenly exhausted. Nathaniel squeezed my hand and got me to look at him. "Are you okay, Anita?" He had to almost yell over the music from the nearest gaming booth, or maybe it was the Ferris wheel, which towered over everything.

"Tired. I think the time-zone change and all the issues with the flights are finally catching up with me," I said, leaning in toward him so I didn't have to yell.

"I know I'm tired," Micah added from the other side of Nathaniel.

Nicky added, "The interview with the lamia was hard on Anita."

We all looked back at him, because he'd let Bram take lead on the return trip. "Why?" Nathaniel asked, looking at me.

"I associate Melanie with a lot of stressful events, Nathaniel."

"Anita almost died twice thanks to the lamia's old master," Rodina added from beside me.

"So Melanie is sort of a trigger for you," he said, studying my face.

I nodded and looked away, because I didn't want him to accidently read my thoughts in that moment, because they weren't fair to him.

"Did you know how close Anita came to dying before you dated the lamia?" Rodina asked.

He shook his head. "The last one, because that was in public so everyone in the preternatural community here in St. Louis knew, but I didn't know about the other attack until I'd been in Anita's life for a while."

"He didn't betray you with her, Anita," Rodina said.

I frowned at her. "I never said he did."

"You feel it, though, and I am forced to feel it with you."

Nathaniel stopped walking so suddenly that Nicky almost ran into us.

"You don't normally share out loud the emotions Anita is feeling, in front of the people she's feeling them about," Nicky said.

"Oh, sorry," Rodina said, and she closed her eyes, looking almost pained. "Well, if that burst of emotions is any indication, I have fucked up royally."

"Yeah," I said, "thanks."

"Do you actually think I betrayed you with Melanie?" Nathaniel asked.

"Let's get out of the crowd before we do this," Bram said from in front of us.

I looked at the person running the pellet-gun booth. I'd thought he was human, but a moment of concentration and he was a shapeshifter of some kind. A lot of our employees weren't human anymore, which meant they could hear above the crowd noise. Great, just great.

"Thanks, Bram, yeah, get us some privacy."

The three of us kept holding hands, but we were quiet. Bram opened the door in the back wall but went through first rather than hold it for us, because bodyguards always go through the doors first if there are enough of them for it. Ru caught the door and held it for the three of us and Nicky, so that he and his sister brought up the rear. The guards in the little entry room had changed shift, and I knew these two.

Peppy—Pepita—was a little taller than me, darkly Hispanic, with her straight black hair cut even shorter than when she'd come to us, so that it was shaved on the sides and only a little longer on top. She was built like a square, with a pair of shoulders that would be the envy of any man. In the black on black of the behind-the-scenes bodyguards, she looked very masculine. The body-armor vest hid her chest and made it look more like nice chest muscles than breasts. She was partnered with Roger Parks, who was bigger than anyone in the room but Nicky, and taller than anyone but Bram. Roger was a nice guy who looked like he'd take your head off and shit down the hole. He played to the menacing looks, but in a fight Peppy was the more dangerous of the two, partly because she couldn't count on people backing down from just her appearance. I had to work harder, too.

She grinned at me. *"Hola, gatita negra."* She used the nickname that the wererats had given me; I was their black kitten. I didn't like being called just Kitten, but somehow being their black kitten wasn't the same.

"Hola, Peppy," I said, and I turned to the other guard. "Hey, Roger, Roger Parks."

Roger smiled and shook his head. "Hey, Anita. Are you always going to greet me like that, with both my names?"

"It's how you introduced yourself to me the first time," I said, smiling.

He rolled his eyes. "I remember."

"It makes me remember you."

The far door opened, and Claudia came through it with Pride at her back. "If we keep hiring new people, even I won't remember everyone's names."

Peppy and Roger did the civilian equivalent of coming to attention. I'd seen some of our ex-military types salute Claudia before they could catch themselves. She was head of security at the Circus, which meant she was in charge of the main security for Jean-Claude and the rest of us principal clients. Though I wasn't sure *client* was the right word when we were their bosses and paid their salaries.

Claudia was also six feet, six inches tall and built so that she could have walked into most fit-model or Ms. Olympia contests and won by sheer intimidation. Her straight black hair was back in a tight ponytail like usual. It left her face clean and very unadorned. She had strong features, very Hispanic, and since she never wore makeup, her face and the rest of her were so damned intimidating it took a while to realize that she was actually beautiful. She was *guapa*, which is a Spanish word for a woman who is handsome rather than pretty, like the difference between Nathaniel and Nicky in attractiveness.

Pride was a few inches over six feet tall, but beside Claudia he looked shorter. Only his shoulder spread was wider than hers; he didn't hit the weights as hard as she did, but then few of the guard did except Nicky. Except for him and Roger, even the other men in the room looked delicate beside her. Though as Claudia walked farther into the room, I realized that Peppy's shoulder spread was wider. It wasn't that the girl was lifting heavier than Claudia; it was just natural body shape. Peppy had fabulous shoulders and arms if you were wanting to lift or box.

Pride followed Claudia like a blond, golden-skinned shadow. His short hair curled too much to avoid it unless he wanted to shave it down, so it spilled artfully or messily around his handsome face. He was model handsome, like most of the golden-clan weretigers, with blue-on-blue tiger eyes adding to the exoticness of his skin tone. He wasn't a blond who had tanned to a light gold; his natural skin color was golden, like most of his clan.

"Are you saying that you're having trouble keeping the new security hires straight, too?" I asked Claudia.

"I remember their faces, but names are starting to be a problem."

"Then we need to put a hiring freeze on," I said, "if you agree?"

"I agree, but it's not up to me. I'm only in charge of the security at the Circus and the main security around Jean-Claude and the rest of you. Hiring for other clubs and the overall hiring isn't up to me."

"Fredo would agree with you," I said.

"Fredo is still out of town on that special assignment," she said. Fredo, like a lot of the wererats, did contract work overseas, though I'd thought he was past the age for it. Wereanimals age slower than humans do, but he looked well over fifty, and that's old for contract—read *mercenary*—work. Fredo had two specialties, knives and driving, so wherever he was, either he was driving someone who needed protection, or he was doing something with knives that I probably didn't want to know about.

"I thought you were in charge until Fredo got back from his assignment," I said.

"So did I."

"Okay, who's hiring all these people, then?"

"Each animal group gets to bring in people of their choice," she said.

"Yeah," I said.

"After the last few years they're trying to recruit people that can help them fight, if it's needed."

"Logical," I said.

"People who are good in a fight aren't always good at working in anything else, Anita."

I looked at her, trying to think my way through it. "Are you saying that the animal groups in town are bringing in fighters and then expecting us to find places for them to work in our security without asking first?"

Micah said, "Claudia, you should have said something to us."

"You're busy helping other cities with bigger issues than this," she said.

"Then you should have brought it to me," I said.

She gave me a look, one hand on her hip, and I realized that though her nails were trimmed as short as possible for fighting and weapons practice, they were painted red. I'd never seen her use polish before.

"You're traveling out of town for the Marshals Service and to raise the dead almost as much as Micah is lately. Besides, Anita, this is my job."

"And you're great at it," I said.

"But it's not your job to talk to animal groups outside of the wererats about their new people," Micah said.

"No, it's not. Our king tried to speak with some of the other leaders, but they accused him of trying to serve the interests of the wererats over the rest of the groups in town."

"It shouldn't have fallen to Rafael to try to fix this," Micah said.

"Then just stop saying yes to employing them as part of our security force," I said.

She closed her arms over her chest and scowled. Her arms tensed and all that muscle stood to attention. It was sort of eye-catching, but I made myself raise my eyes to look at her face in case she thought I was staring at her chest instead of her arms. I think she was grinding her teeth.

"Wow, you're pissed. What happened, or what else happened?"

"They were recruited to the various animal groups and invited to move to St. Louis with the understanding that they would be guaranteed employment."

"It's not our job to guarantee them employment," Micah said. "That needs to come from you or Anita."

"Why hasn't Jean-Claude stepped in and stopped it?" I asked.

She shook her head. "He told me to talk to his accountant. He sees it as a money issue, and there's money to pay them. What there isn't, is work for them, and too many idle fighters are bad news."

"Agreed," I said.

"I'll talk to Sylvie about the payroll and then to Jean-Claude about what I learn," Micah said.

"You leave again on Friday," Claudia said.

"I'll talk to them before we leave for the wedding on Friday. I promise."

"And I'll explain to Jean-Claude that it's more a security issue than a money issue," I said.

"We can always use really good people," Claudia said.

"I'm confused," I said.

"I don't want to pass up people like the SEAL team, Anita, but we don't need more people whose only experience has been as college bouncers, or college athletes that didn't quite make the cut to professional."

"May I add one?" Pride asked.

Claudia nodded, once down, once up.

"We don't need more martial artists that have never had a fight outside of a tournament."

"Sorry, Claudia," Roger said, "but I was a bouncer at a college bar and I was in martial arts and wrestling all the way through college myself."

"Yeah, but you don't suck like most of them do."

Roger grinned at her. "Thanks, boss."

Peppy added, "A lot of the new wereanimals aren't very good with violence."

"They're wereanimals," I said. "They hunt animals; that's violence."

"Hunting for food isn't the same thing when the food has fangs, claws, and fists of its own," Claudia said.

"Fair enough," I said, "but we don't need people that can't fight for real on our payroll."

"I couldn't agree more," she said.

"And you say you brought this to Jean-Claude's attention?" Micah said.

"I did, but as I said, he saw it as a payroll issue, not of the new hires being below the standards that the wererats had set for your bodyguards."

"Yes."

"You didn't push the topic until he understood what you were worried about, did you?" Nathaniel asked.

"I talked to him," she said, scowling at him.

Nathaniel faced her angry face and smiled. "But you didn't push."

She glowered at him. He just looked at her and smiled, and gradually the anger left her, so that she looked chagrined, a look that I'd never seen on her face before. "Maybe not as hard as I should have."

"Why not?" I asked.

Her eyes flicked to me and then to Nathaniel, who seemed to already know the answer. Pride touched her arm, lightly, and said, "You need to tell Micah and Anita."

"Tell us what?" I asked.

"I assume you're headed back downstairs to sleep," she said.

"Yeah, trying to get there."

"Let's talk on the stairs, then," she said.

We didn't argue, just moved for the door that she and Pride had just come through. If they didn't like the idea of going back down the stairs after just getting to the top of them, neither of them showed it. The rest of us just followed them back down the steps until Claudia thought we were far enough down to not be overheard from above.

She turned, leaning against the wall while the rest of us fanned out along the steps. "I didn't push the topic because Jean-Claude makes me nervous," she said, looking at the floor and then up at me as if daring me to make more of it than there was to make.

I met her angry, defiant look and didn't know what to say. I finally looked at Nathaniel. "And you knew this how?"

"I've been in the room for a lot of her reports to Jean-Claude," he said.

"God, I hate that it was that obvious," she said.

"It wasn't that obvious—I swear."

She looked at him as if she didn't believe him, but then some tension left her. She was like most powerful shapeshifters and could smell when someone was lying. Apparently, Nathaniel was telling the truth.

I started to ask, *Why does Jean-Claude make you nervous?* but Nicky touched one arm and Nathaniel touched the other. I looked from one to the other of them. What was I missing?

Micah asked, "Has Jean-Claude done anything to make you nervous around him?"

I frowned at the two men touching me, as if to say, *See, it wasn't just me.*

"No, he's always the perfect gentleman."

"It's not just you that's nervous around him," Pride said.

I looked at him. "What am I missing here?"

"It's not just Anita who has gained power as our evil queen," Rodina said.

"Will you please stop calling me that?" I said.

"As you wish, but you are heir to our dead queen's power, and through you it flows to all of those metaphysically tied to you."

"We all share power, so what?"

She looked at me as if I were being silly, or deliberately stupid.

Nathaniel answered, "Jean-Claude's sexual attractiveness has gone up."

I frowned at him. "That's not possible."

"It's possible," Pride said. "I'm completely heterosexual, but I'm noticing Jean-Claude in a way that I didn't before Ireland."

"Pride is right. It all started after Ireland," Claudia said.

"Are you saying that Jean-Claude's natural charisma has gotten that much better?" I asked.

They both nodded.

"And when was someone going to tell us that?" I said.

"They just told you," Nicky said.

"Are you both having trouble being alone with Jean-Claude?" Micah asked.

They exchanged looks with each other. Claudia shook her head and said, "I make sure I'm never alone with him."

"Are you saying you don't trust him alone with you?"

"Anita, don't make me say it."

"I'll say it for both of us," Pride said.

"One of you say it," I said.

"It's not Jean-Claude that we don't trust; it's us," Pride said.

"Are you saying that you're afraid that you'll . . . what? Throw yourself at him?" I asked.

"Not exactly," he said.

"Then what?" I asked.

"If he asked us to donate blood to him, I don't think we'd refuse," Claudia said.

"You don't donate blood to anyone," I said.

"I know."

"We're saying that if Jean-Claude wanted to take advantage of the leveling up that you've all done, he could," Pride said.

"Are you having issues around any of the rest of us?" I asked.

"Not like we are with Jean-Claude," she said.

"I like women and I'm still not having as much trouble with you as I am with him," Pride said.

"Good to know," I said.

"Are you truly happy knowing that they are more attracted to Jean-Claude than to you?" Rodina asked.

I nodded.

She laughed.

"What?" I asked.

"Most women would be bothered by that," she said.

"I'm relieved," I said.

"Why?" This was from Ru.

"I don't want people attracted to me by magic; that's just creepy."

"There are men and women through the ages that have paid fortunes to seek out the very spells that you do not want," Ru said.

"Love potions and charms and all that kind of stuff are illegal for a reason," I said.

"They're illegal because people will use love spells, if they can find ones that work," Rodina said.

"I didn't think there was such a thing as a real love spell," Micah said.

"Not true love," Rodina said, "but lust; there's plenty of those."

"Lust is easier than love, always has been," Ru said.

Rodina nodded, face solemn.

I looked at the siblings and felt like there was a story there. I debated on whether it was any of my business. Ru looked at me. "I feel your curiosity. I would ask what I have no right to: Please do not ask this story of us."

I looked into his black eyes with the guy-liner done heavy around them and thought that if he was going to do the eyeliner, he needed to do something less conservative with his hair. Out loud I said, "You can keep your story, Ru."

"Thank you, my queen." He did a bow that went with the title.

"No need to bow," I said.

"You are being generous in your treatment of us. I wish you to know that I appreciate it."

"Okay, and you're welcome," I said.

"Do you want us to talk to Jean-Claude about this?" Micah asked Claudia.

She looked shocked. "About the payroll and the guards, yes, but about the other, absolutely not."

"Pride?" he asked the man.

"No, not unless it gets worse."

"Promise to tell one of us if it does grow worse," Micah said.

They both promised and went back up the stairs. We continued down them toward our bed. I was suddenly tired.

"I'm sorry that seeing Melanie bothered you," Nathaniel said as we walked down the endless steps.

"I'm sorry that seeing her interact with you made me feel sort of jealous."

"I was never with her while we were dating."

"I believe you," I said.

"It bothered me, too," Micah said.

"Why? You've seen me with ex-lovers before."

"I'm not sure I have," Micah said.

"He didn't come to town until after you were with me," I said.

He hugged Micah. "I'm sorry, I forgot."

Micah hugged him back, smiling. "It's okay. I didn't think it would bother me this much."

"I think what bothered me was that you called Melanie a fuck buddy, but she seemed to be a lot more serious toward you than that," I said.

"I noticed that, too," Micah said.

"I can't help what she thought or even felt. I can only tell you that I was sleeping with a lot of people at the same time."

"Did she know that?" Micah asked.

"Yes," he said. "I was still working as a paid escort, for one thing."

"Were you sleeping with other people off the clock?" I asked.

"Yes, and I made no secret of it. I was slutty, but I made sure everyone that was interested knew it before I slept with them. I'd stopped taking drugs and was in a program to stay off of them, but I was using sex as my drug; I just didn't realize it."

I wasn't sure what to say to that and finally settled for, "Yay, therapy."

He nodded. "I was afraid to sleep alone, and the only reason that people sleep with someone is sex, so I made sure I was having enough of it that I was never alone. It was all pretty desperate."

"I'm glad you don't have to be desperate anymore," I said.

"Me, too," he said, smiling.

"Me, three," Micah said, and came in to take us both into a hug. We held on to one another on the stairs. It felt so good, I just wanted to go back to the bedroom and curl up between them and sleep.

"Would it be really weird to say I'm tired and I just want to curl up between the two of you and sleep?"

"That would work for me," Micah said.

"I'd be lying if I said that I wasn't disappointed," Nathaniel said, "but we did have great sex earlier, so you might persuade me to just sleep if you promise to wake me up with great sex."

"I think we can manage that," I said, half laughing.

"I'll do my best to make sure the sex is great when we wake up," Micah said.

"Then let's go to bed," Nathaniel said, grinning at both of us.

And for once, the three of us stripped off our clothes, crawled into the big bed in Jean-Claude's room, and just slept. We were waiting for him when he finished his meeting, just before dawn. He stripped off his clothes and crawled into bed next to Micah with a murmured, "So warm." He had time to fall asleep with us in a tangle of arms and legs and spooning bodies before the sun rose aboveground and he died for the day.

15

MICAH AND I talked to Jean-Claude about the security hiring issues before we had to fly out on Friday for Edward and Donna's wedding. A phone call for another treaty-dispute issue between animal groups out west came up as we were packing. Normally, Micah would have blown off the wedding to take care of it, but he sent Jake and Kaazim in the private jet. They'd both been with him on the last trip to deal with the same two groups, so they knew the situation as well as he did. That meant that we suddenly had to find tickets on commercial airlines to Key West. Having to do last-minute ticket shopping helped us make the decision to limit the number of bodyguards we were bringing with us. On one hand we were all feeling a little suffocated about having so many bodyguards around; on the other hand, we'd had a ton of bodyguards in Ireland and still almost come to grief. Choices, choices.

Nicky and Bram were givens, but after that it got trickier. Jake and Kaazim would have been our next top picks, but they were handling Coalition business so Micah could enjoy the trip. Jean-Claude insisted if we were taking so few guards that two of them be Harlequin. I couldn't argue, but then Micah insisted that none of the extra guards be ones we were sleeping with since this was supposed to be a couple trip for the three of us. That was fair, but one or more of us was sleeping with the rest of the Harlequin we trusted. Yeah, yeah, we've got to stop sleeping with our employees or we're going to need an HR person. Because I couldn't come up with a better idea, Rodina and Ru were in coach behind us.

They'd shown up in oversize black T-shirts with young-

angry-person slogans, baggy khaki shorts, and combat boots.
The 5.11 boots were the only thing that was part of their normal clothes—well, and the black eyeliner. It didn't look very
bodyguard professional, but honestly what bothered me most
was that I was wearing almost the same outfit, except I was
wearing a plain black tank top over blue jean shorts with a
black boyfriend-style shirt over the tank. I was even wearing
my own 5.11 boots, the pair with side zippers, perfect for going through the airport. If I'd seen their clothes first, I might
have changed, or made them change. I was supposed to be the
boss, after all.

I hadn't chosen my clothes just for comfort; I'd chosen
them because I knew they'd help hide the gun at my waist. I
had the sky-marshal training, so I was allowed to carry on the
plane, but a lot of people get nervous around guns, and the last
thing I needed was some Good Samaritan thinking I was going to hijack the plane while Nicky and Bram were only a few
seats away. The poor Samaritan wouldn't know what hit him.
So, in the interest of everyone's safety, I chose clothes that
would keep the gun our little secret.

Bram was the only one of us in jeans with a white tank top
tucked into them, and a black shirt unbuttoned like a jacket
over the first shirt. He was wearing black 5.11 boots just like
the three of us. Nicky had a black tank top with a large Hawai-
ian shirt in a bright pattern unbuttoned over it. The bold pattern would hide his gun, as would Bram's black shirt—once
we landed and they could get their weapons out of the checked
luggage. Nicky's thighs wouldn't fit in most shorts, so he was
wearing jean cutoffs that he'd sort of made himself. He'd gone
for black slip-on Vans instead of combat boots.

I'd known the wedding was in Florida. I'd known that the
closest airport was in Key West. What I hadn't realized was
that the airport isn't big enough for really large airplanes, so
it was two seats on one side, a single seat on the other side of
the aisle, and a round metal tube that was far too small for my
claustrophobia. I wasn't the only one I knew with a fear of
flying, aviophobia, but I was the only one I knew with the
combination of phobias. I'd thought I was getting better at flying because of how well I'd taken the flights to New Mexico
and back, but this trip was teaching me that though my fear of

flying might be easing through a sort of immersion therapy from all the business flights, the claustrophobia hadn't really improved much. I'd loved small spaces until I'd had a diving accident that involved a cave underwater, in the dark. That had been the start of it, but I'd also woken up in a couple of coffins when vampires captured me and decided to save me as a snack for later. Waking up in the pitch black with a dead body beside you that you know in a few hours will come to "life" and feed on you . . . I'd earned my claustrophobia.

I sat in the small airplane thinking this was so much better than being trapped in a dark coffin with a vampire. It was, it really was, and this plane was fully functional, not like the one that had nearly crashed with me on it a decade earlier that had given me my fear of flying. I'd been in a helicopter that crash-landed more recently, but it hadn't made the phobia worse. It just hadn't made it any better.

I sat beside the window because that helped ease the claustrophobia. If only looking out and seeing clouds and the ocean so far below didn't make the aviophobia worse. I closed my eyes and tightened my death grip on the arm of my seat. I tried not to grip Micah's thigh quite as tight as the chair arm. I'd been holding his hand, but he'd lost feeling in his fingers, so he'd moved my hand to his jeans and the thigh underneath. On one flight I'd actually bled him through a pair of jeans, so I was really trying to monitor my grip. He shouldn't have to bleed because I was a great big baby on planes.

The plane shook and then hit some bumpy air, like a car hitting a rough spot in the road. With my eyes closed, my stomach rolled from the movement, so I had to open my eyes. I'd never thrown up on an airplane and I didn't want to break that streak.

"Anita, honey, it's okay," Micah said.

I turned and looked at him. Sunlight from behind me spilled across his face, making the pupils of his eyes spiral down to a pinpoint so that the green and gold of his irises filled his eyes. They were framed by his new glasses. We'd finally persuaded him to get colored frames. They were a mix of brown and green tortoiseshell that made the green in his leopard eyes more prominent than the yellow, but maybe that was partly the forest green T-shirt he was wearing and the tan.

As a human he'd had perfect eyesight, but cats, even leopards, are nearsighted, and now so was Micah. I was actually feeling better, just gazing at him, when the plane shuddered again. It sort of slid sideways as if there were ice on some invisible celestial highway. I suddenly didn't feel well again.

"It's okay, Anita. It's just a little bit of turbulence."

"Easy for you to say." It sounded grumpy even to me, and I didn't want to be grumpy at him. A few nights sleeping home in St. Louis with us had helped chase away the dark mood he'd been in about the Florida case. Some really great sex as a threesome had helped, too. I didn't want to rain on his brighter outlook because I was being cranky.

His smile widened, as if I hadn't just grumped at him. "You know how I feel about your fear of flying."

I frowned at him because I couldn't help it. "You sort of like that I'm afraid of it."

"I don't like that you're afraid, but that I can be brave for you is kind of nice."

"We could talk about work; that usually distracts me."

Nathaniel leaned across the aisle from the one seat on that side and said, "I like that you're both big and brave for me, but no work talk. You promised." He smiled and offered a hand to Micah, who took it, and between them they had enough reach to be able to hold hands across the aisle. I'd have had to squeeze Nathaniel's hand and let it go.

Since Nathaniel was the only one of us who didn't have a concealed-carry permit, he didn't have to stick with dark colors or patterns that would conceal things later, so he was wearing a pale lavender tank top, black khaki shorts, and purple jogging shoes. The tank top showed off the muscles in his shoulders and arms and the shorts managed to be tight across his ass but loose elsewhere. I wasn't sure how the shorts managed that, but it meant that he looked great coming and going.

"No work talk at the wedding unless something new happens with my . . . clients," Micah said. His face was already losing some of its happiness, the tension singing down his body where I was touching him.

"Thank you," Nathaniel said, and lifted Micah's hand up so he could plant a light kiss across his knuckles. Micah smiled and some of the tension eased away. I kissed him on the cheek and he turned and looked at me, smiling again.

The announcement for landing came on, and my pulse instantly tried to climb out of my throat. It was so ridiculous that my phobia was still this bad. I clung to Micah's thigh through his jeans, took a few deep breaths, and concentrated on controlling my breathing. He put his hand over mine, which made me look into his eyes. He smiled and there was such confidence, such surety that we were going to be fine. In the face of his calm it was hard to be afraid. He'd been my steadying force from almost the moment we met. He fit a role in my life that I hadn't even known I needed filled, as if he'd shown up for a job I hadn't been advertising but that I really needed someone to do.

He leaned in to kiss me, and we were still kissing when the plane's wheels bumped onto the tarmac. I startled away from the kiss, staring into his face from inches away, but we were on the ground and my phobia was over until the next time. The plane jerked hard, as if the pilot was shoving his foot as hard as he could on the brakes. We were thrown forward, and the brakes were still being stamped on; the plane slid a little to one side, as if we were leaving the runway.

"It's okay, Anita," Micah said, "it's a short runway. The pilot has to use the brakes."

My mouth was dry as I said, "Short runway; are you saying we're going to run out of runway?"

"No," Micah said, gripping my hand, "we'll be fine."

The plane finally shuddered to a stop.

Bram said, "I'm betting the pilot is fresh out of the navy."

"Why?" Nicky asked.

"He lands like he's trying to put a fighter onto a carrier deck. Now, that's a short runway."

I had to swallow hard to get past the dryness in my throat and to say, "Remind me to never try to land on an aircraft carrier."

"We'd first have to get you into a fighter jet," Bram said and shook his head.

"You're right—you'd have to drug me like Mr. T from the old A-Team to get me on a fighter jet, let alone a landing more exciting than this."

The seat-belt sign went off and the clicks of seat belts being unbuckled filled the plane as people got to their feet and crammed themselves into the aisle. Nicky and Bram got to their feet and blocked everyone else on either side of us so that Nathaniel and Micah could get to their feet and get the carry-ons from the overhead. I got my brief bag out from under the seat and stood up, still trapped near the window. I had to bend over or I'd have bumped my head. There was more than one reason that Nicky and Bram had aisle seats, or Nathaniel for that matter.

Nicky's broad shoulders acted like a wall to the people filling the plane behind him. People ahead of Bram waited as near the outer door as the flight attendants would allow, while we all waited for the door to open.

Bram got his oversize backpack settled into place and then glanced at me. "If you thought it was essential for you to get on a fighter and land on a carrier, you'd do it. No Mr. T bullshit needed."

"Define 'essential,'" I said.

"Saving lives."

"Oh, that essential," I said. "Well, yeah, if you put it that way and there was absolutely no other way for me to get to where I needed to go."

"I hope you never have to do a carrier landing, because you would hate it, but I know you could do it if you had to."

"How do you know?" I asked.

"Because you can't let anything beat you."

"I was going to say because you're just that brave, but what Bram said works," Nathaniel said.

I wasn't sure what to say to all the compliments. I wanted to squirm with some vague embarrassment and wasn't sure why. "My grandmother would have said it was because I was just that stubborn."

"That, too," Micah said, and moved so I could wedge myself in beside him as the door opened and people finally got to deplane. He gave me a quick kiss before we started shuffling in line behind Bram. Nathaniel slid in behind us and Nicky brought up the rear like a movable wall. We were sandwiched between the bodyguards, safe as houses, but I was worried about Nathaniel. Micah and I could take care of ourselves, but our shared boy didn't train as hard as we did. He didn't need to for his job, so as we shuffled down the aisle with Bram and Nicky bookending us I felt safe enough, but for the first time my claustrophobia took a backseat to my worries about Nathaniel. The plane was a controlled environment, two guards were plenty for that, but once we were through the door into the wide world it would be anything but controlled. I was suddenly wishing we'd been able to put Rodina and Ru in the front of the plane near us, but that was silly, because we could only exit the plane one at a time. We'd wait on the tarmac for them to catch up with us, but it hit me again that I was unreasonably worried about Nathaniel's safety. I knew it wasn't logical, but some things aren't about logic; they're about feelings, and feelings are some of the most illogical things in the world.

Bram was in the doorway, the sun so bright it made a halo around his body. I realized belatedly that sunglasses would have been a good idea. I glanced back and found that the other three men had changed to dark glasses. It was just me fumbling at the top of the stairs trying to find my glasses in the big purse/briefcase combo that a friend had talked me into buying. It was supposed to be the perfect travel bag, but as always when it came to women's purses, it was a lie. Every purse comes with its own movable black hole that eats things and spits them back out later. Screw it. I could squint until we got inside the terminal.

16

WE WAITED ON the tarmac for Ru and Rodina to work their way free of the plane. It gave me time to fish my sunglasses out of my new purse/briefcase. R and R finally came down the stairs, laughing and looking relaxed, as if they'd enjoyed the flight. Glad someone had. They moved out to either side of us like they had at the Circus. Bram kept the front and Nicky brought up the rear. I felt like we suddenly had a sign above us that read *Bodyguards!* but it was probably less obvious than it felt. If it bothered Nathaniel or Micah, I couldn't tell.

The three of us walked hand in hand across the tarmac toward a long, low building that had large writing that read *Welcome to the Conch Republic*, as if we were entering a new country. As we got closer I could see there was much smaller writing saying *Welcome to Key West* underneath what looked to be statues above the doors leading into the airport. The statues, or whatever they were supposed to be, had what looked like parents with two kids on one side with the wife reaching out toward three people on the other side. The three were probably meant to be a family, too, but there was no mother figure, just an older man, a younger man, and a boy. The two older men were reaching out toward the woman. It was like they were trying to reach around a big thing in the middle that read *90 miles to Cuba, southernmost point*. I guess everyone needs a selling point.

"What the heck is the Conch Republic?"

"Key West tried to secede from the Union once and even declared war on the rest of the country," Micah said.

"You're kidding," I said.

He smiled at me, his eyes hidden behind the prescription sunglasses. "You can even get a passport from the Conch Republic. It's not a real passport, but they still offer it."

"Did you learn all this on your business trips?" I asked.

"We went on the tram tour," Nathaniel said.

"Was it interesting enough to do it twice?"

"Totally," he said, and he swung my hand in his as Micah agreed.

"Anything the three of us can do together will be wonderful," he said. We were all smiles and happy, but I had a thought for the big man who was bringing up our rear guard. Nicky was my lover—we loved each other, not the same way I loved the two men holding my hands, but it still felt odd to leave him out of so much. We'd all discussed this ahead of time. Nicky would be working along with Bram, which meant while he was on the job he wasn't my lover, or Nathaniel's bro, or anything but a bodyguard. It had to be that way, or we would have needed more guards. But I still had a moment of feeling unfair to Nicky.

Rodina moved up so that she was behind Bram, and Ru dropped back to be with Nicky as we walked through the doors and into the airport. I glanced back at Nicky, but he was looking around the airport for danger. He was on the job; any longing looks I wanted to share needed to be aimed at Micah or Nathaniel until we were safe somewhere inside, and even then, it would depend on where we were and what was happening. He was a bodyguard first this trip, and everything else second. It had to be that way, but I still felt weird about it.

The four bodyguards were all searching the crowd for trouble, but since most of the crowd had just gotten off the plane with us from St. Louis, they'd already looked at each of them as they boarded the plane. Bram, Nicky, Ru, and Rodina stood around us like boulders of various sizes in the middle of a river, so that the crowd flowed around us, because there were suddenly more people than our medium-small plane could have held.

"Did another plane land ahead of us?" I asked.

"No," Nicky said.

"I told you, it's a small airport," Micah said.

I looked around and realized that the car-rental agencies, all three of them, were against the far wall. There was a small loop of conveyor belt that stuck out from the wall to the right, and a juice and drink bar in the middle of the room. The wall behind us, where we'd entered, was covered in advertisements and flyers for local attractions. I wondered what the Dry Tortugas were and why I would want to visit them.

"Where's the baggage-claim office?" I asked.

"Far left as we come in the door, past the other luggage belt," Bram said.

"The luggage isn't off-loaded yet," Micah said. "We have time."

"How do you know that? Maybe they're quick today," I said.

He smiled at me and shook his head. "I've flown in here three times in the last month and a half. It's a small airport with a small staff. They get it all done, but you might as well start adjusting to island time."

"What's island time?" I asked, instantly suspicious.

He smiled. Nathaniel laughed and said, "I loved the laid-back attitude here, but it irritated Micah after a while and you will probably hate it."

"How laid-back is it?" I asked.

"It's island time," Micah said.

"What does that mean?"

"That you better hope whoever you need didn't blow off their job to go diving or sailing or fishing," Bram said, and he sounded disgusted.

"That's not everybody," Micah said.

"It feels like it," Bram said.

"But we're on vacation," Nathaniel said, "so it doesn't matter as much."

"If we can come up with a way to help the people that live on Kirke, I am going to do some work, Nathaniel."

Nathaniel's face sobered. "I've seen the pictures now. If we could really help them, it would be worth sacrificing part of our first-ever vacation."

Micah pulled him in closer so he could give him a quick kiss. It was rare for Micah to be the one who elicited a public kiss from the other man. It brought the smile back to Nathaniel's face like sunshine after rain, as if there should have been rainbows in his eyes from the happiness.

"Thank you for understanding," Micah said.

"We'd understand better if we'd seen the pictures, too," Rodina said.

"It's a need-to-know basis," Micah said.

"And we don't need to know," she said.

"No."

"Nicky and Bram have seen them, Sis," Ru said.

"And we just have to trust them to share information with us if it's needed?" she said.

"Yes," he said, and he seemed at peace with the division of labor.

She sighed but let it go.

"Be happy you didn't have to see the pictures," Nathaniel said.

Micah and I both hugged him at the same time, and only long practice at group hugs kept us from getting in one another's way. "I'm sorry that I had to bring more horrors into your life," Micah said.

"It's for a good cause," Nathaniel said, and then leaned back enough so he could see Micah's face. "But that doesn't change the fact that I don't want you to get dragged into work if it won't help or it won't change anything." He looked serious now; not sad, but determined.

"I will do my best."

Nathaniel looked suspicious.

"I need this vacation, too," Micah said.

"All right, but I'm serious, Micah, and you, too," he said, looking at me.

"What did I do?" I asked.

"Nothing yet, but you're as bad as he is about work." Nathaniel gave me a look that I guess every spouse sees eventually. It's the I-know-you-too-well-so-don't-even-try-to-tell-me-I'm-wrong look. We weren't married yet, but we'd been living together for five years. Some things don't need a wedding ring, just time.

"I won't apologize for my work," I said.

"I don't want you to, but I do want this trip to be about the wedding and just enjoying ourselves."

"Micah's work will be harder to avoid, but I'll do my best unless bodies start dropping."

"Is this where someone says, 'It's quiet, too quiet'?" Nicky asked. I looked at him, but he was still scanning the crowd, as if he hadn't spoken.

"Or 'I have a bad feeling about this'?" Bram said, and he was still looking at the milling crowd, too.

"Don't you start, too," I said.

"Who's supposed to pick us up?" Micah asked.

"I'm not sure."

"Donna said that whoever was free would be here. It wouldn't be her or Ted," Nathaniel said.

"God, I hope it's not Dixie," I said.

"Would I do that to you?" a man's voice said, and then I could finally see Bernardo Spotted-Horse through the crowd.

17

HE WAS TALL, dark, and handsome, with those perfect cheekbones that only certain ethnicities would give you. His was Native American. A red tank top looked great against the perfect brown of his skin. The shirt was loose over a pair of blue jean shorts. The body that showed around the tank top and the shorts was muscular and spoke to a lot of gym work. He'd have looked even better if he had tucked the shirt into his shorts, but then the gun in the waistband of his shorts would show. How did I know he had a gun in his waistband? Because the tank top showed too much skin for a shoulder holster and the shorts showed clearly that he wasn't wearing an ankle holster. How did I know he had a gun on him? Because it was the only explanation for the shirt being loose instead of skintight, and it was Bernardo. Also, the only way Jean-Claude had agreed to us traveling with so few bodyguards was the fact that Bernardo, Edward, and other law enforcement officers were going to be nearby for the visit. Almost all the groomsmen were either cops or military, so if anything happened, we had backup, or something like that.

The moment I realized I wasn't the only one in our group with a gun, a tension I hadn't known I was carrying eased. Nicky and Bram were both great hand to hand, but one silver bullet from a distance and none of that mattered. I was really glad to see Bernardo and know that we had at least two guns.

I may have wasted more smile on him than normal because of it.

Nathaniel got to him first, shaking hands and then hugging at the same time, in that one-sided guy hug that seemed to scream *We are not gay!* as if any physical contact between friends was potentially questionable. I wasn't a guy, so I could have given him a normal hug, but that wasn't really the kind of friendship Bernardo and I had. We were more work friends, so I offered my hand. He shook it, wrapping his much larger hand around mine, and then he drew me into the same one-armed, awkward guy hug that he'd given Nathaniel. Except that I was five inches shorter, so my face was buried against the firmness of his chest, so it was even more awkward, but he moved me to the side like a dance move, so that awkward turned into graceful.

I drew back and said, "We're not on the clock; you could have just had a hug."

"Now you tell me," he said, and laughed. I noticed some of our fellow passengers eyeing him covertly, or not so covertly. He was Hunger to Edward's Death and my War. Why Hunger? Because he was so handsome that he made people hungry for him, but he couldn't satisfy them all, so he left them wanting. I thought it was stretching the metaphor for him to be Hunger, but he had the fourth-highest kill count among the preternatural marshals, so he got to be one of the horsemen. Bernardo acted like he didn't notice the people looking at him, but I knew he saw it; he always saw it, but he never got obnoxious about it. He was a good-looking man, he knew it, and there was nothing wrong with owning that and enjoying it. My own issues about beauty would never allow me to be that relaxed, but, hey, that was me.

Nicky and he just shook hands and then he introduced Bram to Bernardo. I'd forgotten that they'd never met. Sometimes I forget that all the people in my various friend groups don't know one another.

"Bernardo, this is Micah," I said, smiling, because again it seemed like they should have met by now.

Bernardo shook his hand, saying, "I see you in my news feed so often, it feels like we've already met." He smiled as he said it.

Micah smiled back. "And I've heard so many stories about you, it feels like we should know each other."

Bernardo looked at Rodina and Ru, who were still watching the crowd. "But these two are new."

"Bernardo, this is Rosemary and Rue Erwin." Those were the names on the passports they'd used at the airport. All the Harlequin had legal identities, though after a few hundred years, *legal* and *real* weren't the same thing. It wasn't like they could produce birth certificates from when they were born. Nobody was doing birth certificates before the fall of Rome.

Rodina smiled and rolled her eyes as she held out a hand to him. "I know, terrible names, aren't they, but Mom was seriously into gardening." Her accent was perfect midwestern American. Her word choices were suddenly late teen, early twenty-something. She was going to play the younger side of her apparent age. I don't know why that bugged me, but it did.

"Hey, at least she didn't stick you with a boy's name the way she stuck me with a girl's," Rue said. The quiet, almost shy boy-man was gone, and he was a much more forceful teenage boy. I wondered if they'd pop in and out of character the way Edward did with Ted.

Bernardo looked at me. "Babysitting, or did you bring friends for Peter?"

I didn't know what to say, because I sucked at subterfuge. They hadn't done anything but use the other names until that moment, so it had caught me off guard.

"We've made you unhappy again," Rue said.

"What do you want us to be?" Rodina asked.

"Older," I said.

Nathaniel said, "You need to be old enough to get into a bar or a club."

"Fine," she said and put all the teenage angst into that one word. She turned and smiled at Bernardo, and she was just suddenly older. It was subtle, but it was like a different person inhabiting her skin. It was a little disturbing.

"Morgan Erwin, Dr. Erwin, but I say it second, so people won't think I'm a medical doctor."

Bernardo shook her hand, looking a little bemused, but he'd been friends with Edward long enough to go with it. "What are you a doctor of, if not medicine?"

"History."

"Do you teach?"

"No, I was a curator of antiquities at one point."

"At a museum?" he asked.

"Something like that." She smiled sweetly as she said it but kept a certain world-weariness in her expression that helped her look older than twenty.

Bernardo turned to Ru, held out his hand, and said, "I can't wait to hear who you are."

Ru gave a wider smile than I'd ever seen on him. "Dr. Wyatt Erwin, but I'm not a medical doctor either."

"History?" Bernardo asked.

"No, literature."

"Which means he's spent his postcollege years asking people if they want fries with that," Rodina said.

Bernardo looked from one to the other of them, and then at the rest of us. "I can't wait to hear all about what's new in your life, Anita."

"I can't wait to tell you."

"The luggage is starting to come through," Nicky said.

"Great," I said, and I meant it. Luggage I understood. The last few minutes with our newest bodyguards, not so much.

18

WE HAD ALL the other suitcases in tow before we went to the room with the sign above it that read *Luggage Claim*. We showed our IDs and claimed our locked bags from the man in the room. Micah only had one gun in a lockbox with extra ammo, but the rest of us had at least one large equipment bag that was almost as long as I was tall. It took less time to get our weapons than to get our regular luggage.

I let Nicky take one of my equipment bags so I could sling the other across one shoulder and still keep my hand free for my gun. Until we had a chance for everyone else to rearm in the parking lot or the car, Bernardo and I were still the only ones armed. As we stepped out into the blaze of sunshine outside the airport doors, it bothered me more than normal that we weren't all armed like a platoon. At least I'd remembered to put my sunglasses on this time.

It was just a short crosswalk to the parking lot. Apparently, Bernardo had rented an SUV just before we landed so he could chauffeur us around. "Who dropped you off?" Micah asked.

"The hotel has a car and a driver that you can use if no one else has reserved it. They had an opening to drop me at the airport, but then they were booked for the return trip," he said as he led the way through the open parking area and underneath a large covered area. He went directly to a white SUV without having to double-check the numbers on the parking slots. He'd scouted it before we landed.

"Do you want to just load up the luggage and I'll drive you to the boat?" he asked as he opened the back of the SUV.

"Boat?" I said.

"Didn't anyone tell you Kirke Key is an island off the coast?"

"Crap, they did. I just didn't put it together."

He flashed a white smile in that dark face of his. "It's not like you to miss something that obvious, Anita."

"It's been a hard year." I tried to make it light, but it didn't come out that way.

"I'm sorry about Domino."

I realized that he had met Domino on at least one case. "Thanks," I said. I didn't know what else to say, so I got very interested in loading the suitcase with my clothes into the open back of the SUV. He took the hint and let it go. Guy rules meant that unless I opened up, he wouldn't push. Sometimes guy rules were exactly what I wanted.

Nicky put his equipment bag up next to my suitcase and started unlocking it. Bram moved so the view was blocked. Rodina and Ru got the hint and helped hide the fact that Nicky was getting his handgun and belt holster out. The three of them kept looking out at the empty parking structure while Nicky armed himself. Micah moved behind the wall of bodies and let them hide him while he opened his own lockbox and got his gun out. He had an inner pants holster, because his shirt wasn't as loose as Bernardo's or as patterned as Nicky's. Legally we could have armed ourselves in plain sight of the entire airport, but just because it's legal doesn't mean that people don't freak out about it, so it was just polite to be circumspect about it.

Everyone but Nathaniel put on at least one gun. Everyone but Micah and Bram added knives. Yeah, that counted me. Guns could run out of ammo, but a sharp blade was always ready.

When we were armed, we locked the cases back up, stowed everything in the back, and could have gotten in and driven away, except I was finally ready to talk to the newest members of our merry band.

"What's with the pretending to be someone or something you're not?"

Rodina and Ru looked first at each other and then at me. "We spent most of the last thousand years as spies. It's automatic to have a part to play," Rodina said.

"That won't work this trip. You are bodyguards, period. Don't overcomplicate it."

"How do we explain that we look like teenagers but you trust us enough to guard your back?"

"We could tell the truth," Nicky said.

"No," Rodina said.

"No," Ru said.

"Why not?" I asked.

"If you wish to tell people that we are older than we look, that's fine, but we have lived in subterfuge for lifetimes, Anita. We are not ready to be completely open with strangers." She was as serious as I'd seen her since she arrived in America.

"What do you think, Ru?" I asked.

"Use the names on our passports and we will be your bodyguards." He was as serious as his sister.

"Is it that uncomfortable for the two of you to be out as bodyguards?" Micah asked.

"If you let us be part of your group but not obviously guarding you, then if we are attacked they will see we are delicate, young, and assume inexperienced. It would give us a few minutes' advantage while they underestimate Ru and me."

"So the whole *let's pretend to be doctors* wasn't just to be irritating and difficult?" I said.

"We weren't pretending on the doctor part," she said.

"What do you mean?"

"We were in one city for a very long time," Rodina said.

"We both have several academic degrees," Ru added.

"Really?"

They both nodded.

"Is it really history and literature?" I asked.

They nodded again.

"Were you really a curator of antiquities?" I asked.

"Yes."

"At what museum?" Micah asked.

"The vampire council's collection."

We stared at her then. "I didn't know they had a museum," I said.

"It wasn't a formal one, but vampires collect things. We keep souvenirs to remind us of the life we had, or might have had, or even souvenirs in the way that modern serial killers do."

"You said *we*, but you're not a vampire," Bernardo said.

She gave him the full weight of those black eyes. "Not in the way you mean, no, but then neither is Anita."

"She's human and you're not that either."

"You are the marshal the other officers have named Famine or Hunger." It wasn't exactly a question, but he answered it with a nod.

"Do you really believe that Anita, who the marshals named War, is human?"

"Yes," he said.

"Completely human?" Rodina made it a question with the uplift of her voice.

"I'm not sure what that means anymore," Bernardo said.

She smiled, and her face finally held that teasing, almost cruel edge that was her usual expression. "That is either a diplomatic answer or an honest one."

"It smells like the truth," Ru said.

The two of them looked at me in unison, which was an unnerving habit I'd almost broken them of, because it unnerved me and it bothered them that I didn't like it. But sometimes they couldn't help it—the habit was too ingrained.

"We are sorry to make you uncomfortable," Rodina said.

"But we must find our place among you," Ru said, finishing his sister's thought.

I looked at the two of them. "I guess it has been a big change for you coming to us in America."

"If you make us behave as Nicky and Bram do, then when we are attacked they will try to take the four of us out first," Rodina said.

"But if you let us hide," Ru said, "then they may leave us unharmed long enough for us to kill them and save the three of you."

"You're twins, aren't you?" Bernardo said.

They turned their heads to look at him as if there was one brain moving both of them. "No, we aren't twins," Ru said.

"We were triplets until Ireland," Rodina said.

"We had a brother," Ru said.

"What happened to your brother?" Bernardo asked.

"He died," she said.

"He sacrificed himself to save Anita," Ru said.

"He took a shotgun blast to the chest," I said.

"Rodrigo saved Anita and me," Nathaniel said.

Bernardo looked at him, at me, and then at what remained of the triplets. "So, you lost your brother, your triplet."

They nodded.

"That's hard."

"Yes," Rodina said.

"We miss him," Ru said, and then he looked at me. "I'm sorry that makes you feel bad, Anita, but the grief over Rowan's death deadens my ability to feel your pain."

I almost asked who Rowan was, but Rodina said, "Rosemary, Rowan, and Rue Erwin were our names."

She didn't want me to use Rodrigo's name any more than her real one. He was dead and she still wanted to help him hide his identity. It was a level of hiding in plain sight that I would never understand, but I didn't have to understand it, not really.

"We'll need a cover story that makes more sense than either of the ones you told Bernardo in the airport," I said.

Rodina smiled at me and then Ru echoed it. "Thank you, our queen."

"First of all, you can't call me that on this trip. It'll give everything away."

"As our queen wishes," Ru said. For a second I thought he might be joking, but he wasn't.

19

THE SUV LOOKED big until we tried to stuff all of us in it. Nicky rode shotgun because his shoulders squeezed us in the backseat, though since we had to unfold two extra seats just in front of the luggage, weren't they the backseat, and Micah and I were in the middle seat? Rodina and Nathaniel squeezed in the backest seats. Micah was pressed between me and Ru. Bram managed to get his six-foot-plus body folded between me and the door. There was a bodyguard for each of us so that if someone tried to hijack the car, everyone could be covered.

Bernardo drove out of the parking area and we'd barely turned onto the next small road when the ocean was suddenly visible, shining and spreading out toward the horizon. I'd seen the ocean on the West Coast, up and down the East Coast, and in Ireland, but I'd never seen ocean that was this blue. It was aquamarine, turquoise, pale sapphire, as if God had ground up jewels and turned them into water.

"Wow," I said, "I've never seen water that color before."

"It gets even prettier as we drive up toward the Middle Keys," Bernardo said. He turned left, and I watched the shining water dotted with sailboats and motorboats, though some of them looked big enough to be called something else. How big does a boat have to be before you call it a ship?

I settled back in the curve of Micah's arm and the back of the seat and looked out at my first Caribbean blue ocean. I suddenly felt like we really were on a vacation. We weren't on the road long before we turned left again onto the Overseas Highway, U.S. Route 1. "It's the only highway in the Keys," Bernardo said.

"Must make it hard to get lost," I said. Small trees had closed around the highway, but even without the ocean visible you wouldn't have mistaken it for the Midwest or either coast. I wasn't sure what kind of trees were hugging the road, but they were unique enough that it felt foreign, as if it weren't America anymore, but someplace new. The short trees vanished, and now there was ocean on either side of the road, though one side was an overall pale turquoise green, and on the other side of the road it was as if the water was striped, pale turquoise, and then so many shades of blue, from sky blue to royal blue, cobalt, and finally a navy blue that was almost black. The darkest blue reminded me of Jean-Claude's eyes, and I was sad that he wasn't here.

"The darkest blue looks like Jean-Claude's eyes," Nathaniel said from behind us.

I turned so I could see him as I said, "I was thinking the same thing."

"Even if he was with us, he could never see the ocean looking like this," Micah said.

I turned back to look at him, pressed so close to him that I had to move my head back to focus on his face. "What do you mean?"

"Sunlight," he said. "It doesn't look like this at night."

"Oh," I said, "I knew that. I mean, I know, but . . ."

"But you forgot anyway," he said, hugging me with the one arm around my shoulders and kissing me gently on the cheek.

Bernardo said, "Did you forget that Jean-Claude was a vampire?"

"Not exactly," I said. It seemed terribly sad that Jean-Claude could never see the ocean spread out to either side of the highway in shades of blue and green, shining in the sunlight.

"He could see it on a video," Nathaniel said.

I turned to give him a smile. "We could take a video and send it to him."

"And pictures," Micah said, smiling.

I nodded and cuddled my face against his.

"You're really going to miss him," Bernardo said.

I looked up from Micah to see Bernardo looking at us in the rearview mirror. "Why do you sound surprised?" I asked.

He glanced back at the road and then back at us. "I see how you are with Micah and Nathaniel and I just don't know how there's more room for anyone else."

"I figured of all people you'd understand being attracted to multiple people at once," I said.

I caught his grin in the mirror before he turned back to watching the road. "I can be attracted to a lot of women at the same time. It's one of the reasons I've never been married. Monogamy just didn't seem reasonable when the world is full of so many beautiful, funny, smart women."

"Thanks for adding the funny and smart part," I said.

He laughed. "I don't just go for looks all the time."

"Just most of the time," I said.

"You really don't have room to throw stones at my glass house, Anita." He was still laughing as he said it, but I think he meant it.

"What's that supposed to mean?" I asked.

Micah hugged me a little tighter. "Honey, you don't date unattractive people."

"You date people because you find them attractive," I said.

"Belle Morte would be happy with the men and most of the women in your life, Anita," Rodina said.

"And she collects only the fairest of them all," Ru said.

"They can't all be the fairest of them all," I said, glancing at him where he sat on the other side of Micah. I don't know if my irritation showed on my face or if he could feel it.

"I'm sorry if that offended you, my queen."

"It didn't offend me, Ru. It just didn't make me happy."

"All I know is that you are unhappy with me and I would do anything to make you happy once more."

"Don't say anything," I said.

"But it is the truth."

Nicky spoke from the front seat. "Anita tries not to think about what it means that we are her Brides."

"Wait," Bernardo said, "I knew Nicky was your Bride, but are you saying that Ru is, too?"

"And me," Rodina said from behind us.

"So you're both part of the poly group?" Bernardo asked.

"No," Rodina said.

"Not yet," Ru said.

I leaned around Micah and glared at Ru. "What is that supposed to mean?"

"We are your Brides. That means that we serve you in any way necessary or desired by you."

"I get that; so what?"

"It's okay, Anita," Micah said, stroking his hand down my bare arm the way you'd soothe a horse or a dog.

"Do you want them to be part of our polycule?" I asked, glaring at him, because my confusion was turning into anger and any target would do.

"No, I really don't, no insult to either of them, but there are so many people in our poly group now that it's hard to know how to take care of all of them."

"Then why are you trying to soothe me, after what Ru said?"

"He's your Bride. Doesn't that mean that he's supposed to be willing to do anything for you?"

"Yeah, but I didn't ask him to feed the *ardeur* with me. He's just here as security." I sounded angry, even to me.

"If that is all you need from me, then I am happy to be of service," Ru said, leaning around Micah so he could see my face more clearly.

"I just need you to protect Nathaniel, Micah, and me; that's it."

"Of course," Ru said.

"We have guarded queens before you and we will guard queens after you," Rodina said.

Nicky said, "Is that a threat?"

"No, just the truth. Before our first evil queen died, I thought we would guard her all our days. It has left me with doubts about the permanence of anything, or anyone."

"The queen is dead, long live the queen," Ru said.

"And that's not a threat?" I asked.

He looked surprised, but then his face went back to unreadable blankness, which seemed to be his most common expression. "We would never threaten our dark queen."

"I'm not even sure we're capable of threatening Anita," Rodina said.

I glanced behind me at her. "What does that mean, Rodina?"

"We must take care of you. We are compelled by your emotions more than our own. If you are unhappy, it is almost a physical pain until you are happy once more."

"You are a pain in my ass a lot of the time, and that makes me unhappy."

"I told you, Anita, I like being a pain in the ass. I even like the pain when you're unhappy with me sometimes."

"Why?" Micah asked, glancing at her.

"I think it helps me mourn our brother. I want to hurt, maybe even need to hurt, while I mourn."

"I do not enjoy pain," Ru said.

"I'd have totally pegged you for the submissive and Rodina as the dominant," I said.

"You should know not to judge people like that, Anita. So many of us don't wear our kinks on our sleeves the way that Nathaniel and Nicky do. You don't."

"We are not talking about our kinky preferences in the car like this," I said.

"Does Mr. Spotted-Horse not know your preferences by now?" Ru asked.

"What's that supposed to mean?" I asked.

"Both of you like beautiful lovers, you are polyamorous, and he stated that he wasn't monogamous. Why have you not explored the possibilities of each other? Since you work together, being lovers would be practical; it would help you feed the *ardeur* while you are being a marshal."

I studied his face, because he was so serious. "I can't argue with your reasoning, but I'm just not that practical."

"I would say you are one of the most ruthlessly practical people I have ever met," Ru said.

"Do I say *thank you* or *I'm sorry*?"

"Neither. I am your Bride; you owe me no explanations."

"You say that, but you don't seem to mean it," Micah said.

"I do not know what you mean, my king."

"You say that Anita owes you nothing, but you want things from her and you want her to give them to you."

"What do I want from our new queen?"

"To belong," Micah said, looking into Ru's face from inches away.

"We belong to the Harlequin," Rodina said.

"But the Harlequin belong to Jean-Claude and Anita."

"Yes, which means so do we," Ru said.

"No," Rodina said, "we belong to each other, Little Brother."

She was angry; it spilled around the edges of her words and began to trickle energy through the car.

"If you lose control and bring Anita's beasts, I will be pissed at you," Nicky said.

"I do not want to raise her beasts."

"Then control yourself."

"What's wrong, Rod . . . Morgan?" Nathaniel asked.

"Our Nimir-Raj is right; we wish to belong, truly belong. We are lost without our brother. He was my right hand, as Ru is my left. I feel amputated from the person I was, the life I thought we were living. I would give almost anything to have Rowan here in this car helping protect you all. I miss his smile, that look of evil mischief in his eyes."

"You are mourning someone I would have killed for what he did to Domino."

"We think that's partially why he sacrificed himself at the fight in Wicklow," Ru said.

"What do you mean?" I asked.

"He was your Bride. We can feel what you are feeling most of the time. We all knew you meant to kill him when you had the chance. We all felt your hatred and loathing of what he had done to your tiger."

"He knew you would never let him leave Ireland alive. We all knew it," Rodina said.

"I won't apologize for wanting to avenge Domino."

"We are not asking that of you; we would never ask that of you," she said.

"Then what are you asking?" Micah said in a calm voice.

"Let us mourn our brother, and stop hating us for it."

"I don't hate you for mourning your brother," I said. "I hate you a little because you remind me of him, and, no, I can't forgive what he did to Domino and me."

"He's dead, Anita. He gave his life to save yours. As revenge goes it's quite complete," she said.

I turned in Micah's arms, so I could see her sitting there beside Nathaniel. "No, that's not revenge. Revenge would have been plunging a sword into his lungs and heart the way he did to Domino. Revenge would have been killing him myself!" I felt the first stirrings inside me of my beasts. It forced me to start doing my breathing exercises. I had to be more in control than this—I had to be—or the beasts inside me would rise to the bait of my rage and try to tear me apart.

Nathaniel reached out to me and I moved in Micah's arms so I could take his hand. If Rodrigo hadn't sacrificed himself, Nathaniel could have died in Ireland. I hated that the same person had done something so evil and something so good. It messed with my head and my heart. The moment Nathaniel touched me I felt calmer; the anger was still there, but it was muted. I was glad to be touching my two men, glad to be driving with them on our first-ever vacation together with the ocean spilling out on either side of the road like some impossibly beautiful postcard. I was happy for all that, so very happy, but I still regretted not having killed Rodrigo myself. Was that crazy, sociopathic, psychotic? Maybe? But it was still how I felt, and one thing I'd learned in therapy was that you had to own your feelings, all of them. You didn't have to act on them, but you had to acknowledge them. Buried feelings always found a way to uncover themselves. You could do it voluntarily and have some control over it, or you could stuff them down into the darkest part of your psyche and give your inner demons new ammunition to use against you. I was really trying not to do that anymore.

I said the truth out loud in a voice that was so strained and careful it almost didn't sound like me. "I hate that I owe Nathaniel's life to the same person who killed Domino. I hate that all I can see when I look at the two of you is him. I hate that I'm still so freaked-out about almost losing Nathaniel in Ireland. I hate that I can't seem to let go of it all and just move forward. It makes me feel weak and stupid."

"You are not weak, or stupid," Micah said, kissing my cheek while I glared at Rodina.

"I will honor your candor with my own, because Ru and I have not had so much truth aimed at us in centuries. It is most refreshing," she said, but the word *refreshing* had some bite to it, like an angry echo, as if I wasn't the only one holding my inner demons back.

"Sister," Ru began, but she waved him silent and he allowed it.

"I want to hate you for what you did to the three of us. I blame you for my brother's death and I want to hate you for that, too. I want to hate you, Anita Blake, but I cannot. Your magic prevents it. Instead of being able to hate you, I am forced to care about your feelings. It causes me physical pain when you are unhappy, especially if that unhappiness is with Ru and me. You have bound us to you for eternity, or until we die saving you, or you kill us as a whim."

"I'm not very whimsical."

She made a sound that was part laughter and part exasperation. "Well, that is the naked truth. Seldom have I met anyone less full of whimsy than you, our would-be queen."

"So you're both safe," Nathaniel said, and he hugged Rodina, just a quick, friendly hug, but I felt my eyes narrow.

Micah hugged me and turned me to kiss him; maybe he noticed my reaction to their hug. "You and I are the two least whimsical people I have ever met."

"I have to be whimsical enough for all three of us," Nathaniel said, smiling.

We reached out over the back of the seat and he had to stop hugging Rodina so that he could hold both our hands. The three of us rode like that, awkwardly holding hands over the seat, as the ocean stretched out on either side of the highway, and I wished that we were heading to our wedding instead of Edward's. If we could have gotten Jean-Claude down here to stand in the sunlight with us, a wedding by the ocean sounded perfect.

20

THE HIGHWAY DROPPED low enough that the trees blocked the view and the water actually lapped the edges of the road, in the roots of the mangroves and other trees that I didn't know the names of. It bothered me that I didn't know what all the plants and trees were called. I'd have to get a plant identification book, just so I'd know what I was looking at. Yes, we had eventually stopped gazing into one another's eyes and started looking at the scenery again.

"You guys didn't tell me how beautiful it was here," I said as the highway started to rise again over one of the many bridges that spanned from one island to another. I'd known theoretically that the Keys were a series of islands, but I hadn't expected that they would *seem* like islands. I think I'd thought each one would be bigger, or maybe I'd just never been anywhere that the ocean was so present.

"We figured it would be more fun to just bring you, since we knew the wedding was coming up," Micah said. He raised my hand to kiss the back of it.

"You already feel more relaxed, and we just got here," Nathaniel said.

I turned around so I could see the smile I heard in his voice. It was worth turning around for. With the dark glasses hiding his eyes, it helped me see just how great a smile it was, though his hair had escaped the ponytail again and was falling around his face. The bright sunlight brought out more of the red in his auburn hair. I fought to just enjoy how great he looked in that moment, and not think about why his hair was short. Why couldn't I let that go?

He touched his hair, putting it behind his ear; he'd felt some of what I was feeling in that moment, what I was thinking. We all worked to stay behind our metaphysical shields with one another, but some of it leaked over. He was my *moitié bête*, my leopard to call, which meant we were closer than just lovers. I felt that he was sad, not because his hair was short, but because it made me sad.

"I'm sorry that it bothers me this much," I said.

He reached out to touch my face. "I love that I know what you're feeling, Anita; never apologize for that."

"And the rest of us don't have any idea what you were thinking, only that you were sad about it," Rodina said, her tone somewhere between disdainful and fighting not to be angry.

I looked into her dark eyes and said, "And I can't feel what you're feeling at all."

"No, because we are only your Brides; we feel your emotions, your desires, your needs, but you know nothing of our internal landscape."

"You're right, we just have to muddle through like every other person on the planet and actually talk to each other about what we're thinking and feeling."

The car slowed down. I looked back to the road because I thought we were stopping. When we kept creeping forward I looked for a car accident or something else to take us from sixty to about thirty miles per hour.

Bernardo answered before any of us could ask. "It's the Key deer sanctuary. You have to drive very slowly through here or the cops will give you a ticket."

"What's so special about deer in the Keys?" I asked.

"They're a different species, or subspecies," Bernardo said.

"They're really tiny," Nathaniel said.

I turned to look at him. "How tiny?"

"Look to the right," Micah said.

I looked where he pointed and there were two deer beside the road. Nathaniel was right; they were tiny compared to any deer I'd ever seen. They couldn't have been any bigger than a German shepherd, maybe half the size of a white-tailed deer. I turned as the car crept past them. They were watching the traffic with big, dark eyes, their ears twitching back and forth.

"They're so pretty," I said.

"Too small for much meat," Rodina said.

"Are you just trying to spoil the moment?" Nathaniel asked her.

"It's just the truth," she said.

"If you can't be positive, then just stop talking," he said to her.

She looked surprised that he'd spoken to her like that. Maybe she'd thought that his flirting with her had meant more than it had. Hell, I'd wondered about it myself, but his body posture, his whole attitude toward her, let me know that it was just his usual flirting. He'd probably started out as a flirt, but years of working at Guilty Pleasures had made flirting almost an automatic reflex. Rodina was learning that it hadn't meant anything to Nathaniel except a little fun.

"This is the first time the three of us have ever gone on a trip together. I know you're in mourning for your brother, and I really am sorry for that—I know what it means to lose a brother—but if you're going to rain all over Anita's happy moments, then we need to send you home and fly in someone else that can do their job without letting their feelings get in the way," Nathaniel said.

She stared at him for a second, openmouthed. Rodina had made the mistake that a lot of people did with Nathaniel: She'd just seen the flirtatious pretty boy, the stripper who managed to sleep his way to the top of the local food chain.

She closed her mouth and sank back into that blank face that all the really old ones could manage. "I can do my job."

"Great," he said, and that was that. He flashed me a smile and said, "We drove through the sanctuary on the way back to the airport and saw more of the deer. They came right up to the car, begging for treats."

"There are signs all over warning you not to feed the deer," Micah said.

"The deer came right up to the car windows, totally expecting that we'd give them something," Nathaniel said. His face was shining with the memory of it.

"I'd love to see more of the deer," I said.

"We'll come back, but no guarantees on seeing deer," Micah said.

"I understand, but, hey, at least I got to see two of them."

A sign let us know that we were leaving the Key deer area

and we could go from forty-five miles per hour to whatever the actual speed limit was. I'd been so busy watching the scenery and gazing into my sweeties' faces that I hadn't kept track of it. I looked at the back of Nicky's head. He was working, and he was not my sweetie when he was on the job, but it was a little weird to be so up close and personal with Micah and Nathaniel and not touch Nicky at all.

I reached up to touch the back of his neck where his hair met the bare skin of his newly shortened haircut. He responded by turning and smiling at me but said, "It's okay, Anita, I don't feel left out."

"Okay, just checking."

He smiled a little wider. "And that is one of the reasons I'm okay with it."

If he had been closer I'd have kissed him, but since he was on the job he might not have allowed it, and nothing is quite as disheartening as offering someone a kiss and having it refused.

"We still need a cover story for R and R," Nicky said.

"Whatever story you want to use, think of it fast because we're about ten minutes away from the marina and the boat to the island," Bernardo said.

I voted for the truth, but I was outvoted. Jean-Claude and I were accused of wanting to be dictators. That wasn't our goal, but every once in a while a little dictatorship didn't sound so bad.

21

THE MARINA DIDN'T look that different from ones I'd seen with my family as a kid when we visited relatives on the Great Lakes, but the Great Lakes didn't have palm trees or the ocean spreading out to the horizon like a Caribbean island wet dream. The boat that would take us to the island was at the end of the row closest to the open ocean. We shouldered the bags like we had in the airport and headed down the wooden walkway with Bernardo leading the way. The walkway was wide enough for two of us to walk abreast, but no more, so Rodina and Ru had to walk in front and behind, one trailing Bram and the other following Nicky. The three of us were still in the middle of our bodyguard sandwich. A man's voice called out, "Hey, Bernardo, let me help with the bags."

I had so many taller people in front of me that I couldn't see the man who was being helpful until Bernardo and Rodina were on the boat, with Bram standing at the end of the wharf so he could keep an eye on us. The man who was helping stow the bags was under thirty with brown curls turned gold from the sun and a tan everywhere that I could see around his white T-shirt and khaki shorts. The T-shirt had a small logo over the pocket that matched the design on his white slip-on boat shoes. When he turned around there was a slogan on the back: *Marry Me on Kirke Key, Florida.*

Micah's phone rang as I was handing my first equipment bag to Bernardo on the boat. He let Nathaniel move ahead of him in the queue as he said, "Christy, what's wrong?"

I had no idea who Christy was, so I let Nicky hand over my other equipment bag and then took Bernardo's hand to step from wharf to boat. The uniformed man was named Roberto, though he looked more like a Chad, or maybe a Ken for Malibu Barbie, but Hispanic came in a lot more colors than most people realized.

"We're about to get on the boat for Kirke," Micah answered to the mystery woman on the phone. "Damn," he said.

The tone of voice made Nathaniel say, "No work—you promised."

"Hold on a minute, Christy." He hit the button that put her on hold and turned to Nathaniel.

I let Nicky help me out of the boat and back to stand beside them. "What's up, Micah?" I asked.

"Christy's husband is one of the pictures I showed you. He's drunk at a bar, too drunk to drive home safely, and he's fighting not to change."

"Stupid; drinking lowers your inhibitions," Nathaniel said.

"Christy says she's called everyone else that could go to him. She remembered that we were arriving today, so she called."

"No, Micah," Nathaniel said.

"He'll be outed if he shifts, Nathaniel."

"He shouldn't have gotten piss-faced drunk in a public place."

"I'm going to have to agree with Nathaniel on this one," I said.

"Christy is pregnant on full bed rest. It's why she can't go get him herself."

"You're afraid that she'll go get him, if we don't," I said.

"I've met her husband. Andy was drinking to self-medicate. It actually can help them not change form if you can keep the drunk to a certain level."

"It doesn't help our form of lycanthropy at all," Nathaniel said.

"It does seem to help them, but Andy has gone from being a functional alcoholic to being . . ."

"A drunk," Nathaniel finished for him.

"Yes," Micah said.

"No, Micah, just no. It's not your problem. It's not our problem."

"The snakes that his body changes into are venomous, and non-native to this country."

"Jesus," I said, "there won't be antivenom for it if they bite one of the people in the bar."

"People could die," Micah said.

"So, if I say, no, don't go, and his snakes bite someone and they die, somehow it's my fault for wanting to protect our time together."

"I didn't say that," Micah said.

"But you can save the day, and everyone will be safe," Nathaniel said.

"That's the hope."

"Damn it," Nathaniel said, "go save them."

Micah moved to kiss him, and Nathaniel actually turned away from him. Micah's face fell, and my stomach tightened into a hard knot. I did not want this fight, not now, not at the beginning of our trip together. Nathaniel's anger trickled along my skin and through my head, cracking our careful metaphysical distance. He was furious. I wasn't sure I'd ever felt him so angry at us.

He took a deep breath, let it out slow, and then hugged Micah. "I love you, damn it."

"I love you, too," Micah said, his face concerned as he pressed himself into the hug.

Nathaniel kissed him and then turned to me. "I love you both."

"We love you lots," I said, and for the first time I wasn't sure about moving in for a hug or a kiss.

He shook his head and then grabbed me, pulling me into an embrace. I let myself relax against his body, the strength of his arms, the solidity of his chest against mine. I buried my face against the side of his neck, breathing in the vanilla scent of him. A piece of his hair tickled along my cheek, and I felt that poignant sense of loss for his longer hair, and for just . . . for surety, for a surety that I could never have. You can say all the vows you want, but they mean that death does us part, and anger, misunderstandings, much smaller things than death, can part you from people. I leaned into his body, his strength, him, even though I could still feel the tension of his anger behind the shields that he'd put back in place hard and tight so we could touch and I wouldn't know how angry he still was at me.

We kissed and I said, "I'm sorry."

"But not so sorry you won't go save the day," he said.

I didn't know what to say to that, so I just looked at him as he drew back from the kiss.

"I'm sorry you're mad."

He nodded. "I know. Now, go and help Micah."

I wanted to say more, to apologize, or to make things all right between us before we left, but I didn't have any words to make it okay. I'd learned that sometimes when words can't make it better, just stop talking and do something, so I did.

"Hand up my equipment bags," I said.

"I'll just take Bram with me."

"No, you'll take Anita with you. She's got a badge and you don't. If the worst happens and you're there with him, you'll get dragged in for questioning at the least," Nathaniel said.

"He's right," Nicky said. "They're small towns. They don't get a lot of lycanthrope-related crime."

Bernardo handed a bag up to Nicky. "Where are you going with all your gear?"

"No time to explain, just got to grab and go," I said.

Bernardo stepped from the boat back to the wharf. "Okay, let's go."

"No, Bernardo," Micah said.

"I heard Nathaniel say that Anita is coming because she has a badge; well, two badges are better than one." He lifted the hem of his oversize tank top to flash the badge tucked into his belt.

"There isn't time to argue. Let's go," Micah said, heading back down the wharf. Bram fell into step behind him. Bernardo went with them. I turned back to Nathaniel. He kissed me and then turned me around. "Go with him. I'll be fine with R and R."

Micah yelled, "Anita, are you coming?"

"Coming!" Nicky and I got our equipment bags and started moving with purpose toward the SUV. The others were already getting into the vehicle. We heard the engine start. Nicky started running toward them; if my big equipment bag bothered him, it didn't show. Within a few steps, I was cursing the bag I was carrying, but it was the purse on my other shoulder that really made me curse. If I could have remembered everything in it, I'd have left it with Nathaniel. The purse slipped down my arm until it was damn near tangling in my legs. I shifted it so I was carrying the strap balled up in my free hand, because it wouldn't stay on my shoulder with the other bag already taking up most of my back. I'd packed for airport travel, not for running to the rescue. Silly me.

22

THE BAR HAD a cheerful sign that read *Herbie's Chowder House*, complete with a cartoon fish that seemed to be fishing for itself. Herbie's looked cheerful, but the location looked as if it was in the middle of nowhere on the side of the road, maybe because of the overgrown vacant lot beside it. It wasn't over-grown with just weeds either, but with tropical-looking trees and underbrush, as if it had been vacant a long time. The bar sat right beside Highway 1, the main road through the Keys, so it wasn't as middle of nowhere as it seemed. I guess in the Keys there wasn't a lot of choice about where to put things, but the building managed to seem convenient for drive-by customers and isolated all at the same time. The gravel parking lot out front was so full we had trouble finding a place to park.

"It's just past noon; isn't that too early for a full bar?" I said.

"Some people use their vacations as an excuse to drink," Bernardo said.

"Some people travel to paradise to fall into a bottle," Bram said.

"That, too," Bernardo agreed.

We'd all talked ourselves out of putting on body armor, but I had put on a loose T-shirt over my tank top so that I could put on the custom-made knife sheath that went down along my spine and then attached with straps to my belt. The original had been part of a shoulder rig for guns, but I'd finally had a second made so I could carry my largest knife more regularly, and my regular carry for guns had become a waist holster or inner pants holster, depending on how concealed I wanted to carry.

"I'm still amazed you can carry a blade longer than your forearm and no one ever sees it," Bernardo said.

"As long as my hair is down it hides the hilt."

We all made small adjustments to our weapons, or at least touched some of them, before we got out of the car. It becomes automatic to flex your body or lightly touch to make sure that none of your weapons has shifted out of place. The trick is never to do it where people can see you, because nothing gives away the fact that you're carrying a gun like touching it to adjust it. We got out of the car with everything settled in place and threaded our way through the cars.

"Remember that thanks to Jean-Claude's vampire marks, I'm poison-proof, so if anyone has to wade into the snakes, it has to be me."

"Lycanthropes are poison-proof, too," Nicky said.

"Since this may be some ancient type of snake, let's not test how proof you and Micah are, okay?"

"I'm your bodyguard, remember."

"I remember, and I'm in love with you. I'd really rather not lose you over some macho bit of grandstanding, okay?"

Nicky gave a small smile and said, "You're the boss."

Micah said, "Bernardo stays completely away from the snakes."

Bernardo raised his hands in a sort of push-away gesture. "As the token human, I'll let you guys wrestle the deadly snakes."

Bram opened the door first like a good bodyguard, so that if the noon drunks got out of hand, they'd attack him first. I figured since no one was screaming or saying *what the fuck* that Andy hadn't changed into snakes yet. It was good to be in time to prevent tragedy, rather than just cleaning up after it.

The bar surprised me by being brightly lit and painted white, with the bar against the left-side wall and small, high tables against the right. Small family groups were having lunch at the tables. Either the licensing laws were different in Florida than in St. Louis, or everyone was ignoring them. I guessed if the kiddies weren't drinking the liquor from Dad's and Mom's glasses, we were good.

"Cheerful," I said.

"Food smells good, too," Bernardo said.

He was right. If I hadn't eaten on the plane, I'd have been more interested. Micah said, "There he is." We followed him and Bram farther into the room, starting toward the bar proper. I couldn't tell which of the hunched figures was our guy yet. One person drinking looks a lot like another.

A woman wearing the bar's logo on her T-shirt came toward us smiling. "We have bigger tables in the other dining room, or did you want to sit at the bar? I think we can just fit you all in."

"Sorry, we're here to give a friend a ride home, but we'll definitely keep your place in mind for later," Micah said, smiling.

She did an eye slide toward the bar. "Are you here for Andy?"

"I take it he's a regular," Micah said.

"Getting to be," she said. She looked back at the bar with her hostess smile fading around the edges. This wasn't a *bar* bar; it was a restaurant that had a bar in it, which meant that they would be even less happy with serious drinkers than a normal bar. I wondered if Andy had gotten thrown out of his usual bar, since he was only "getting to be" a regular here.

"He's the dark-haired one on the end," Micah said.

Bram moved ahead of Micah. There really wasn't a lot of room between the middle tables and the bar, so I went between the two rows of tables to come into the bar area from the other side, with Nicky trailing behind me. Bernardo stayed at the door. We were getting glances from some of the restaurant patrons because we weren't acting like normal tourists; we were acting like potential trouble.

Micah was talking softly to the man by the time Nicky and I were on his other side. Two of the men at the bar got up with their drinks in hand, looking more at Nicky than at anybody else. People who didn't know how to fight and were just impressed with size always looked at him first. He was like camouflage for the rest of us, unless people were trained enough to know what they were looking at.

The man we were trying to save just sat there as if nothing had changed. He was darkly tanned, with short black hair that looked coarse even from a distance. He huddled over his drink like it was the most important thing in the world, and maybe it was to him. His wife was on bed rest with their unborn baby in her body, and he was here drinking. Addicts only love their addiction. If you believe anything else, you're lying to yourself.

I was on the other side of Andy now. I could see the bloodshot eyes, the unshaven face that could pretend it was a beard, but he'd just stopped shaving. At least he didn't smell as unkempt as he looked; since we were going to be in a car with him, I appreciated that.

I could hear Micah's voice now. "Do you really want Christy to get out of bed and lose your baby?"

"No," the man said in a voice that sounded like he had gravel in his throat. I didn't know if he wasn't used to talking or if he'd screamed himself hoarse. He looked up at me as if he'd just noticed I was there. "Who's this?"

"My fiancée," Micah said.

"Congratulations," he said, and that seemed to get him up on his feet, as if just the social niceties made him think to be nicer. Hey, if social conditioning works in our favor, I'm all for it.

Andy swayed enough that Micah and I each caught an arm. Micah kept Andy's arm on the way to the door, so he didn't bump into things like the ball in a drunken pinball game. Bram came next and Nicky and I brought up the rear. Bernardo held the door and out we went.

Bernardo drove, and after some discussion Micah took the passenger seat, because if the two bodyguards were going to have to risk one of their primaries, they didn't want to risk both of us. Since I was doubly protected from venom with lycanthropy and vampire marks, I got to sit beside Andy. The fact that Micah let me win the argument was one of the reasons I loved him. It was logical that I sit beside the potential danger, but a lot of men would have rather risked their lives than concede it. Bram and Nicky had their own moment of who would sit on the other side of Andy. Bram finally won by saying, "My shoulder span is smaller; we just fit better with you against the door."

Andy let Bram buckle him in for safety, but then he slumped forward, and I thought he'd passed out, which was fine with me. I didn't think he was going to be a great conversationalist. Most drunks aren't. They think they are, but they aren't.

We were almost back to the turnoff to the wharf when Andy startled awake. He looked at Bram and at me and he didn't know where he was, or remember how he'd gotten here. "Who are you? Why am I here? No! No! Let me out!"

He reached past me for the door handle; I pushed his hand away from it. He seemed to think we'd kidnapped him. He lashed out with big fists, but we were trained, he wasn't, and he was drunk; no one is good drunk. Bram pinned his arm and I got the other arm in an elbow lock, putting just enough pressure to make him tap out and stop fighting. I felt the skin change texture and had time to let go of his arm, and then it was a nest of snakes that just happened to come out of his shirtsleeve. The pictures hadn't done it justice. I was sitting next to a bouquet of green-scaled, hissing, fang-baring snakes. I went from zero to terrified. Even if you like snakes, you don't want surprise snakes that close to you. I screamed. Micah yelled, "Anita!"

"I will kill you!" Andy screamed. "I will kill you all!"

Some of the heads were hissing in different directions like they were covering us all. Two of them reared back to strike at me, and I punched Andy in the face from inches away with as much force as I'd used against anyone in a long time.

He slumped forward, unconscious, and the snakes vanished into just his arm again. "Fuck," Bram said softly. I don't think I'd ever heard him use that word before.

"Did anyone get bit?" Micah asked.

"No. I mean, not me," I said.

"I'm good," Bram said.

"Is Andy alive?" Micah asked.

I looked at the unconscious man and was suddenly afraid for a different reason. I started searching for the big pulse in his neck. Nicky said, "I can hear his heart; he's still alive."

"Is his neck broken?" Micah asked.

I stopped fishing for a pulse and said, "I didn't hit him that hard."

"You hit him pretty hard."

"It was a good punch," Bram said.

"He startled me," I said.

"He startled us all," Bernardo said. He glanced in the rearview mirror. The rest of us looked at the unconscious man.

"Did I really hit him hard enough to worry about spinal injuries?"

"If he was human, you'd have snapped his neck," Nicky said.

"I didn't mean to do that."

"We need to find more humans for you to work out with, so you can modify your strength better," Bram said.

I stared at the slumped man between us. "Is their kind of lycanthrope harder to hurt, just like us?"

"Not just like us, but, yes, they're tougher than human-normal," Micah said.

"Good to know," I said.

Andy groaned and moved enough to let us know everything still worked. I was so relieved that I was almost nauseous. I hadn't meant to hurt him, just to protect us. Andy didn't wake up or come to, though, which was probably just as well. Bram and Nicky carried him on board the boat after we'd stowed all our gear. Roberto—the boat driver, captain, or whatever—said, "Thanks for getting Andy, Mr. Callahan."

"He changed in the car. If he'd done that at the bar, people could have gotten hurt."

"There were kids in the restaurant," I said.

Roberto looked at the unconscious man. "Andy's burned his bridges with all of us, except for Christy. She still thinks he's going to sober up and be a great dad."

"Loving an addict won't fix them," Bernardo said.

"I know that and you know that," Roberto said, "but she's his wife and about to have his kid. I guess she's got to have hope."

"Hope is a lying bitch sometimes," I said.

"Isn't that the truth," Roberto said and started easing us away from the dock. I'd have enjoyed being out on the blue, green, turquoise sea more before I had been scared shitless by a face full of snakes and nearly broken a man's neck with one punch. Micah pulled me into his lap where he sat in one of the three chairs.

"Look"—Bram pointed—"dolphins!"

I looked where he pointed, and there they were, my first-ever wild dolphins. They rolled out of the water in a line like the humps of a sea serpent. I smiled because . . . dolphins!

They leapt from the water and my heart leapt with them, because—wild dolphins!

I glanced back at the small cabin where we'd put the still unconscious Andy, and then I went back to watching the dolphins, because there was nothing more I could do for Andy, but maybe if I looked out at the ocean, felt the spray on my skin and Micah's arms around me, and watched dolphins ride the waves, just maybe I could do something for me.

23

THERE WERE TWO burly guys that looked a lot like Andy on the dock when we got to Kirke. They turned out to be his cousins. Christy had guilted them into just meeting us at the dock and bringing her husband home to her. They thanked us for bringing him back, but not like they were happy to see him. Who could blame them?

I texted Nathaniel that we were on the island. His reply text was, "At the pool enjoying our vacation. Have room keys. I love you both." It was a very dry message for him. I glanced at Micah. "I think our shared boy is still pissed at us."

"Upset. If he was still pissed he wouldn't have added the *I love you both*," Micah said.

"Trouble in paradise?" Bernardo asked.

"Nathaniel is still upset, but he has the room keys at the pool."

"Where his text says he's enjoying our vacation," Micah said dryly.

"That sounds like a girlfriend text," Bernardo said.

"How would you know what boyfriend texts sound like?" I asked, smiling up at him.

He bowed his head. "Good point—I've only dated women. Are you telling me that it's not that different dating men or women?"

"Everyone is broken," Nicky said.

Bernardo looked at him. "Are you saying you've dated both?"

"I had a misspent youth," Nicky said with an utterly flat delivery.

"Am I the only one here that's never dated same sex?"

"I didn't date, I hooked up, but yeah."

Bernardo looked at all of us and then said, "When I met Anita she was like the untouchable virgin and I was the man whore. When did I become the more conservative one?"

I laughed at the dismay on his face, and the men joined me. "Trust me, Bernardo, I never planned on being wilder than you."

"So, you're all telling me, honestly, that it doesn't matter that much whether you're dating men or women? Really?"

"Bitches be crazy, and men are stupid; it's all hard," I said.

"What she said," Nicky said.

Micah just nodded.

Bernardo laughed. "I keep hearing about the women in your life, Anita, but I'm not going to believe it until I see for myself."

"You are never going to see me making out with our girl-friends, Bernardo. Fantasize on your own time."

He blushed, which I hadn't thought possible. "I didn't mean it that way."

"Aww, you really didn't." I punched him lightly in the arm. "We really are friends now."

He laughed again. "Do not put me in the friend box."

I grinned at him. "Would it be a first for you?"

He nodded, the laughter fading to a really nice grin, not the one he must practice in the mirror every morning, not the one that melted strange women into puddles of desire, but just a grin with no agenda attached. I felt privileged to see Bernardo when he wasn't posing.

Nicky offered to stay in the lobby with the bags while we got the keys, but I said, "If Nathaniel is really upset, it could take a while."

"I'm good. Go do what you need to do," he said. I knew that part of what made Nicky so easygoing in the relationship was that he was my Bride. My happiness, my peace of mind, were truly more important than his own, but it was nice to have at least one person in my life who was low maintenance, instead of high. I wanted to kiss him good-bye to show how much I appreciated it, but he shook his head. "I'm working."

I nodded and walked hand in hand with Micah off toward the pool. Bram went ahead of us, opening the side door that led back outside through a wall that was mostly glass. "If we were looking for Nathaniel last trip, he was usually at the pool," he said.

"Because you were both working," I said.

"Yes," Bram said, leading us down a sidewalk with huge tropical plantings on either side.

"It was a business trip; Nathaniel knew that. It was even his idea to come with me on it." Micah sounded irritated.

"But this isn't a business trip and he's back at the pool by himself," I said.

Micah sort of marched through all the pretty landscaping like he wasn't seeing any of it. It made me jiggle his hand in mine to make him glance at me. "If you go out there angry, this will be a fight. Is that what you want?"

He stopped walking so abruptly that Bernardo almost ran into us. "Do you need some privacy?" he asked.

Bram just stopped on the path like a good bodyguard. The really good ones could make you forget they were there.

Micah shook his head and looked at me. His jaw was set in that determined line that could be anger or just stubbornness. Sometimes it helped get things done; sometimes it didn't. His stubbornness was like mine, part asset and part deficit, depending on the situation and what side of it you were standing on.

I watched the tension ease in his face, felt it ease in his hand. "No, I don't want to fight with Nathaniel."

"Good, me either."

"I couldn't have just left Andy at the bar to lose everything. It's my job to help people like him."

"It's not your job to be a taxi service for drunk strangers who are being self-destructive," I said.

"So you agree with Nathaniel that I should have just left Andy to his issues?"

"No, because if his secret comes out, then it endangers everyone else on the island, so I'm okay with helping him out this once."

"Didn't his wife say that she'd called other people and they refused to go get him this time?" Bernardo asked.

Micah looked up at him, and even through the sunglasses it wasn't entirely friendly.

"Sorry if it's not my business."

"Since you came to help us ride to the rescue, I'm okay with it," I said.

Micah let out a sharp breath of air. "What's your point, Bernardo?"

"The wife, Christy, called friends and family first, right?"

"I suppose," Micah said.

"People who would lose the most from the whole snake thing coming out, right?"

Micah nodded.

"But they were willing to let him hang in the wind. Ask yourself, how many times have they gone and gotten his ass? How many times have they cleaned him up and brought him home?"

"A lot, probably," Micah said.

"Not probably, Micah. They were willing to let the family secret out, to risk all of them, rather than go get Andy one more time. You only get to that point after years of this shit."

"Are you speaking from experience?" I asked.

"Not me, but my mom. It's why I ended up in foster care and why I stayed there until I was eighteen and could join the military."

"I'm sorry, I didn't know," Micah said.

"No one knows. I don't talk about it, but Nathaniel is up front about being an addict when he was on the streets. On one of his trips out to New Mexico for the wedding we talked. He has no sympathy for addicts that won't get help, especially ones that have a family and people depending on them."

Micah sighed and hugged me. "Was I wrong to help Andy?"

"I didn't say you were wrong," Bernardo said.

I pulled back enough from the hug so I could see Micah's face. "It's not about right and wrong sometimes; it's about seeing everyone's point of view."

"I'll add one thing for both of you," Bernardo said.

We looked up at him, and there was a seriousness to his face that I'd never seen before, or not about this kind of stuff. "Sure," I said.

"You are both serious white knights and serious sheep-dogs, but you need to learn that there will always be people that need saving."

"I know that," I said.

"Then do you know that if you find a little happiness, people to love, that you should put them ahead of saving strangers? Not all the time—you both have your jobs—but from Nathaniel's point of view, this isn't a work trip, and this wasn't a work emergency. No one's life was in danger. There was no murder. This was an addict doing self-destructive shit, and last I checked that's not in either of your job descriptions."

We stared at Bernardo and then at each other and then back at him. "Have you been saving this up?" I asked.

"Like I said, Nathaniel and I talked."

Micah looked at Bram, who was standing just down the path like he heard nothing. "Do you want to weigh in on this?"

"Absolutely not."

"I think that's Bram-speak for *don't drag me into this*," I said.

Bram nodded. "Yes, ma'am."

"Let's go to the pool and talk to our shared boy."

Micah nodded. "Let's."

Bram led the way down the sidewalk, having to push some of the plantings away with his hand or get hit in the face. Micah and I were short enough to go under all of it, but I heard Bernardo moving the big leaves overhead as he came behind us. Being short wasn't always bad.

24

THE POOL WAS crowded enough that I couldn't see any of our people at first. I finally spotted Rodina sitting at a table under an umbrella. She was still dressed in street clothes, probably because it's nearly impossible to hide weapons in a women's bathing suit. There were far too many drinks at the table for just her, but where was everyone else?

It was Bernardo who said, "There's Ted."

I didn't recognize Edward at first glance, first because his short blond hair looked different wet, and second because he was wearing swimming trunks. I don't think I'd ever seen him with so much skin showing. I'd seen him shirtless years ago, but I didn't remember him being in this good a shape. He had a six-pack, which takes a hell of a lot of work and nutrition. He was forty, but watching him walk to the edge of the pool, I'd have put him in his early thirties, tops. I knew he'd started worrying a little about his age, because fighting monsters was all about being physically fit whether you were running away from them or chasing them down. Apparently, he'd taken that worry and hit the gym and nutrition even harder than in the past.

Micah leaned in and whispered, "Most of the exotic dancers at Guilty Pleasures don't have abs that nice."

"Yeah, who knew?"

"You didn't know Edward looked that good out of his clothes?"

I shrugged. "I've never seen him out of his clothes."

A second man, whom I didn't recognize, came to stand beside Edward at the edge of the pool. The man had dark hair

shaved close to his head, but not like military close, more like
he was going bald, so he'd decided to shave it down rather than
have that monkish fringe of hair. He wasn't fat by any means—
he wasn't even exactly heavy—but he had enough body fat
that he looked soft beside Edward's fierce leanness.

Someone else I didn't know called out, "Go!"

Edward leapt smoothly into the water. The dark-haired
man followed a second later, not nearly as smoothly. Edward
surfaced and started making for the opposite end of the pool
in a strong Australian crawl, breathing easily with his strokes.
I'd never truly mastered the stroke because I could never quite
get my breathing in rhythm with my arms, so I ended up pretty
much drowning myself when I tried it. I know, I know, it's
supposed to be the easy stroke that everyone can do. The dark-
haired man surfaced, gulping for air before he started doing a
breaststroke that was surprisingly fast, closing in on Edward's
lead rapidly. A dark-haired woman in a pink bikini was jumping up and down yelling, "Go, Paul, go!" Other women and
some men who were already wet from the pool were yelling
for Paul, too. Call it a hunch, but I was betting that the man
racing Edward was named Paul.

We had people yelling for Edward—well, Ted—too. Bernardo joined in the yelling of "Go, Ted!" I felt silly but added
my voice to theirs.

Paul didn't pass Edward, but he got within a body length
before Edward reached the wall and a blond woman who
looked like she was in her teens but was wearing a T-shirt over
her bikini that had *Bride* on it declared Edward the winner. It
hadn't actually been that close. I mean, we could see from
where we were standing at the halfway point that he'd won,
but it was still gracious of her to declare him over Paul, who
turned out to be her groom.

"What's going on?" I asked.

"You left the men unsupervised too long, Anita," Rodina
said from the umbrella-covered table. I realized there were
umbrellas in some of the drinks on the table, too.

"What does that mean, I left them alone too long?"

"You and Donna and the rest of the wives/girlfriends. You
weren't here to be a civilizing influence and now they've challenged all the young studs to a swim meet."

I raised my eyebrows at that. "A swim meet—really?"

Edward came up to us, drying off his hair and upper body as he moved. Up close I could see a scar on his upper chest. I didn't normally notice it, but maybe the scar talk in New Mexico with Donna had made me notice it. I didn't know about any other scars, but I'd been with him when he took a wooden stake through the chest from a booby trap while we were trying to get a much younger Peter and Becca to safety. It had been the trip where I met them and Donna for the very first time.

Edward/Ted said, "We figured that all you wimminfolk would be upset if we challenged them to an impromptu fight club. Besides, swimming is the only thing that almost negates a lycanthrope's supernatural strength and speed." He started with a thick accent, or he wouldn't have used the word *wimminfolk*, but by the time he finished he had no trace of any accent, just that perfect middle-of-nowhere-America voice that was either natural or training. He didn't usually forget his Ted accent in public like this. I'd noticed he was slipping more in New Mexico, too.

"Does it really?" Micah asked.

Edward gave him a long look out of his pale blue eyes. "Your tone says you know different, pardner." Just like that, Ted's thick, vaguely Texas, or somewhere southwestern, accent was back. Why did he keep slipping in and out of character? It wasn't like him.

"Extra speed and strength seem to be across the board for most of us," Micah said.

"You also have to know how to swim better than the man racing you," Edward said, and again he sounded like himself, not Ted. Then the accent returned with a vengeance as he said, "And none of your fellow shapeshifters have ever been much for swimming, or so they said." It wasn't like him to keep losing the accent in public. I might have tried to get Edward off to one side for a whispered question or two, but Micah said, "Look." I looked where he gestured and suddenly forgot all about Edward's Batman dilemma.

A bevy of bikini-clad women parted like a curtain and Nathaniel and a blond man I didn't know were suddenly revealed, laughing and flirting with the women. Nathaniel flirted almost unconsciously, but he didn't usually turn it up this high unless he was onstage. The two men stalked to the far end of the pool, having to peel a brunette, a blond, and a redhead off of them like towels. I finally recognized the blond man; it was Ru. Out of his clothes he seemed taller, almost as tall as Nathaniel's five feet nine. In clothes he'd looked thin, delicate even; out of them he looked lean and muscular. He didn't bulk as nicely as Nathaniel did, but within the limits of his body type he was muscled everywhere that I could see. He was narrower through the hips than Nathaniel, but then Nathaniel was built like the male version of an old-fashioned pinup. Ru was built like a long-distance runner who hit the weight room. The leaner body type with its naturally lower body fat gave him one advantage; he had not a six-pack, but an eight-pack. No amount of exercise or diet will give you more than a six, but if you have the genetics for it, you can get an eight-pack. I'm told a ten-pack is possible, but I've never seen one in person. Nathaniel lost too much of his ass when he leaned down even for a six. He looked fabulous as he was. I didn't need to be able to trace my finger between the connective tissue of his abs to appreciate that he was beautiful. The gaggle of flirting women behind them was admiring both views pretty damn hard. I had time to be happy that Nathaniel was mine, and admit that Ru looked awesome, both of them in their body-hugging Speedos, purple and blue, respectively, and then they dived into the water and began to swim under the surface. I went to the edge of the pool with Micah's hand still in mine, so I had a better view. The flirting women did the same thing, but I couldn't really blame them. Who wouldn't want a better view?

They were suspended in the water side by side, Nathaniel's hair flared out around his head like an auburn halo. Ru's short hair was thick enough, or long enough on top, to move slightly in the shining blue pool. They both came up out of the water at the same time, breaking the pool's surface in bright flashes of light where the sun hit the water. I heard their breaths gasp in, and then they were swimming side by side, and I realized they were racing. Nathaniel wasn't that competitive, and Ru hadn't seemed that competitive. Of course, Ru hadn't seemed flirtatious or even that social until now.

The women trailed along the pool edge, some calling out

Ru's alias, Wyatt, and others calling for Nathaniel. Micah gave a small frown and looked at me. I knew the look. If you left Nathaniel alone long enough, he usually picked up an admirer, and he didn't always discourage it, but this seemed more than usual. I wondered if it was the addition of Ru; maybe he was more of a flirt than we'd realized.

A tall, lean man with skin the color of black coffee, wearing a slightly larger swimming suit, was standing at the end of the pool watching the two of them intently. His skin was so dark it was harder to see the muscle development, but it was there. He wasn't mine. Lieutenant Colonel Muhamad (Frankie) Franklin was one of Edward's oldest friends, though he knew him only as Ted Forrester, which was Edward's legal name and the one he'd entered the military with. You don't start out as Batman. So, oldest friend, but not that close; the close ones knew the secret.

It was hard to tell from where we were standing who touched the wall first, but when they came out of the water breathing heavy and laughing, it was Nathaniel whom Frankie pointed at as the winner.

"If you weren't taller than me, we'd have tied," Ru said.

Nathaniel just nodded, grinning. He swept his hands through his hair to smooth it back from his face. I watched his handsome face laughing in the pool, that body that he worked so hard to maintain come dripping out of the water, and I knew that I'd come close to losing some or all of that beauty, because that's what the vampire had threatened: not just death but disfigurement, torture. The helplessness of that moment haunted me, and I hated that it did, but I couldn't seem to let it go. I couldn't even stuff it to the back of my head, where I'd been shoving other bad memories for years. The memories from Ireland lived right in the front of my head, so that everything filtered through them.

Ru smoothed his hands through his own shorter hair, which seemed even brighter yellow wet. He was smiling and patting Nathaniel on the back, as if they were best buddies.

Micah whispered, "What is going on?"

I just shook my head and shrugged, because I had no idea.

I lost sight of them then as the bevy of bikinis closed around them. A few men came in and got their women out of the group, some with grace and smiles, others obviously upset that the women were flirting a little too much. None of the men who pulled them away were in the same ballpark of handsome as either Nathaniel or Ru. I was prejudiced about Nathaniel, maybe, but it wasn't sentimentality that made me think it of the other man.

Rodina came to stand next to us and spoke low. "Ru is very good at mirroring whomever he is with; it makes him a near perfect undercover spy. I told him to stay close to Nathaniel, and he has, but he's also imitated him a little too well. If one of you could claim Ru as well as Nathaniel as your lover, that would be most helpful. He's good at getting into these situations, but not at getting out of them."

"I'm not claiming Ru," Micah said.

She leaned toward me. "Before you refuse as well, Anita, let me add that if you don't play girlfriend for my brother, I'll be forced to do it."

I turned and stared at her.

"The look on your face, your feelings in my head: You find the thought of me playing his girlfriend almost as disturbing as I do; so happy neither of us finds incest fantasies enticing."

"What do you want from me, Rodina?"

"It's Morgan, and just help my brother, Wyatt, extract himself from his too-successful flirting. Morgan and Wyatt Erwin, because you wanted us old enough to teach undergrad, not be one, remember."

They came padding barefoot toward us, smiling and talking excitedly to each other, as if they really were best friends. The redhead was on Nathaniel's arm, one brunette on Ru's, but another brunette had put herself between the two men, an arm through each of their arms. Nathaniel's lavender eyes had darkened with the exertion or the excitement of the competition so that they were the color of violets. It usually took sex to make his eyes that dark. Ru's eyes couldn't get any darker, but they were shiny with laughter and a joie de vivre that I didn't think he had in him.

"Hi, pussycat. Hi, Wyatt," I said as they came up to us with the other women still in tow. I looked at Nathaniel's eyes a little closer and realized that they weren't darker from exercise; it was anger. He'd upped his flirting game with these strangers because he was pissed at us for abandoning him. I wasn't sure what to do to soothe the anger, extract him from the women, and make up for the fight that was threatening to happen, but Micah knew exactly what to do. He stepped forward and cupped his hands around the bottom of Nathaniel's face and kissed him like he meant it. Nathaniel extracted himself from the redhead like she didn't exist, putting his arm around Micah. He tried to extract himself from the brunette, but she seemed sort of frozen on his arm, as if she couldn't process the two men kissing. I always enjoyed seeing the men in my life kissing each other; the only thing better was when they were on either side of me in bed and kissed over me. The second brunette was staring openmouthed at them, too. She clung even harder to Ru's other arm. I wasn't sure if it was a possessive gesture or to steady her world. She'd thought she had a shot at one or both, and now half of the handsome duo was kissing another man. She didn't seem to have a fallback plan for this turn of events.

Ru laughed, enjoying the women's reaction. He'd been the quiet, shy one of the triplets. In Ireland when we needed to pretend to be a tourist couple, it had been Rodrigo who had smiled and flirted on my arm. Ru just didn't seem interested, and suddenly he was suave and debonair. "Hi, Anita. Your fiancés seem to have missed each other." Even his tone of voice was deeper, richer. If I'd had my eyes closed, I wouldn't have known it was him.

"Did you say they're both her fiancés?" the redhead asked.

"I did."

"They are," I said, but I was looking at Ru, trying to figure out how to do this next part. I was terrible at undercover work.

Rodina seemed to have figured out that I needed a push, because she came up to us and said, "Kiss her, brother dear, before her fiancés are done with each other and a line starts to form."

The Ru I thought I knew would have hesitated or been embarrassed, but this new person gave me a look from his dark eyes that was all male. "The invitation needs to be from the lady in question," he said in that deeper voice.

"Sure, but you better be fast before they come up for air," I said.

He managed to extract himself from the brunette who had

finally let go of Nathaniel's arm. She looked lost and about four years younger than I'd have put her when she was all confident on their arms. I'd thought she was older because she was the tallest, at least five-eight, but the look on her face and the sudden awkwardness of her body language in the bright bikini made me wonder if she was even legal.

The brunette on the other arm wasn't so easy to get rid of; she snuggled tighter to his side, putting both hands and some of her body into holding on. It was a definite possessive gesture. He'd only been flirting with her for less than two hours; how was that long enough for possessiveness? The brunette was short enough that she came in under his shoulder, which made her my height, or maybe an inch shorter. Her dark hair was somewhere between curly and wavy, which probably meant it was natural. Permanents always seem to pick one. She was tanned enough that the white bikini she was wearing made a nice contrast. Her eyes were hidden behind large round sunglasses. The glasses hid a lot of her face. What I could see was pretty, but her face was sort of round and unfinished, which made me deduct a few years off her age no matter how grown-up the body looked. She was college age, somewhere between eighteen and twenty-five, though I was betting much closer to the younger age. I think she was glaring at me through the sunglasses. I managed not to feel intimidated by the glare.

When Ru realized he'd have to actually struggle to extract his arm from her, he stopped trying to get away and gave a small shrug. "Anita, this is Bettina. She and her friends are here for their best friend's wedding."

"The blonde in the *Bride* shirt?"

"How did you guess?" He grinned, but his eyes were watching me, trying to see what I'd do. If he'd been my real boyfriend instead of a pretend one, I'd have been more aggressive, but . . . "So how did Bettina and friends get the idea that you'd be more than just flirty?"

He glanced down at the woman on his arm. "I'm not really sure."

The redhead said, "You lying bastard, you've been flirting your asses off with us." She had hands on slender hips, small breasts pointed sort of aggressively. She had the beginnings of a sunburn on her pale, freckled face and shoulders.

Micah and Nathaniel came up for air. "You're just too adorable for your own good, Wyatt," Nathaniel said with both arms around Micah, who usually didn't do that much public display of affection with Nathaniel. He loved us both, but he was still a little uncomfortable in public with his first-ever boyfriend, now fiancé. It was fun to see him feel he had to mark territory like that, and it was probably the perfect way for him to say sorry to Nathaniel.

"And now you're going to have to wait your turn, Wyatt, because here's my line," I said, motioning toward Micah and Nathaniel. They came toward me still holding hands.

"Hey, Nathaniel, are we going to race or are you going to keep kissing on your boyfriend?" a strange man was yelling from the other end of the pool. He was tall, slender, but muscled enough to have his own six-pack. I was betting he was a college athlete of some kind.

"Give me a minute to kiss on my girlfriend and then I'll be right there," Nathaniel called.

"I don't care who you kiss—just let's do this, unless you want to admit that we're going to win and just concede."

Nathaniel glanced at the redhead and the other brunette, and then back at the tall dude by the pool. "You don't care who I kiss, really?"

The tall brunette held her hands up and shook her head as she backed up. "I'm sorry, but this all got too weird for me."

The redhead looked defiant. "I'm still game if you mean it. The idiot yelling at us is my boyfriend, Randy, and I'd like to see if he really doesn't care."

The redhead came over to Nathaniel and Micah. She was almost as tall as Nathaniel but still seemed delicate beside him. She truly was one of those people who had small bones and a small body frame, and even though not a rib showed on her, she had almost no breasts or ass; she was naturally thin—because of genetics, not a starvation diet. She also looked soft, as if there wasn't much muscle tone to her, so she thought she was in shape because she was thin, but it's not the same thing as being strong. Her big hazel eyes were her best feature to me, but I wasn't the one who had been flirting with her.

Nathaniel smiled at her and said, "Just a minute, let me ask my girlfriend how she feels about it." He came to me then, still

wet here and there from the pool, but his front was now surprisingly dry thanks to Micah. I glanced down and found that
a lot of the front of Micah's clothes were now wet, as if he'd
spilled something all over the front of him. They hadn't tried
to keep any space between their bodies. Micah had made a lot
of progress to be able to kiss him like that in public; maybe it
was his version of makeup kissing.

I turned to Nathaniel and we shared a smile, both of us
proud of our shared man for being brave and owning his feelings. His smile was a real one now, without that edge of anger
in it. We came together, wrapping our arms around each other
effortlessly. We knew where our hands, arms, and finally our
bodies went as we slid as close together as we could get with
clothes still on, though the itty-bitty bathing suit he was wearing almost didn't count. He was already a little happier to be
there from kissing Micah. If he and I kissed too much, the
Speedo might not hold him comfortably. I told him so.

"I'll risk it," he said and bent those few inches downward
as I raised my face upward. And just like the rest of us, our lips
knew exactly where to go. We kissed with lips, tongue, and
finally, lightly, teeth. If he wasn't going to have to swim immediately afterward, I'd have used more teeth, but the Speedo
had to hold.

We ended the kiss slowly, reluctantly. For a moment we'd
forgotten where we were and why we were putting on the
show. We'd just got lost in each other. We stood there for a
moment sort of trying to recover from it and get back to the
reality around us.

"Wow," one of the women said.

"Randy has never kissed me like that," the redhead said.
She was almost right beside us, as if it really was a line at a
kissing booth.

"I've never been kissed like that," Bettina said.

The redhead actually touched Nathaniel's shoulder as if to
turn him from me to her. She wanted a kiss. I don't think Nathaniel would have done it, but Edward stepped between them
just in case. "No, we are not going to goad them into a fight.
We are going to finish the race, win their money, and then
we're done."

"Hey," said the redhead, "it's not your call who he kisses

unless you're his dad or something, and dads don't have abs like that." She'd managed to compliment and insult him in one sentence. It took me a moment to realize that Edward might actually be old enough to be Nathaniel's father. I never thought of him as that old, or Nathaniel as that young, but the math worked. Fuck, that sort of bothered me, though I wasn't sure why.

"How do you know that you're going to win?" Bettina asked, still holding on to Ru.

Edward gave her a look that was way more him than Ted. It made her move a little back behind Ru, though she didn't let go of his arm. It made me think better of Bettina that she recognized the look as dangerous.

"Wait, you guys have bet money on this? That doesn't sound like any of you," I said.

"Some of the other men were talking trash, so Ted suggested a friendly wager," Ru said as he tried to get Bettina to let go of his arm without hurting her.

"They implied that they were young stud muffins and some of us were more stud doughnuts now," said Sheriff Rufous Martinez as he walked back to the table with something tall and fruity-looking in a glass. He was a big guy, about six-three, and had played football in college, so I'd learned, but hadn't been fast enough for the pros, so he must have been in good shape once. Now . . . he patted the hard roundness of the belly that covered way too much of the front of his body if you were worried about heart attacks. "It was my fault. I'm the only one who likes doughnuts a little too much."

"Sweets aren't your problem, Rufous," Edward said in his Ted accent. "Fatty meat and starches are."

"You're starting to sound like my wife, there, Ted," he said, easing his bulk into a chair that almost didn't hold him. Apparently, he'd gained weight sort of all over; the belly just distracted you from the rest.

"But why are Wyatt and Nathaniel swimming against each other if it's an us-versus-them thing?" I asked.

"We both won our first matches," Nathaniel said.

"Are we racing or not?" Randy called from the edge of the pool.

Nathaniel smiled and said, "I'll be right back."

"Does that mean he thinks he's going to win?" I asked.

"Win or lose, it's quick," Rufous said.

Micah leaned in to whisper, "I'll cheer on Nathaniel; you help Wyatt get rid of Bettina." He started to walk toward the rest of the group that was moving up to watch the race. I was left facing Wyatt, um, Ru, and the pretty girl on his arm. She was pretty, or would have been if she'd stopped frowning and clinging to Ru as if only violence would remove her.

Rodina leaned in and whispered, "Please, Anita."

I looked at Ru, at this new more confident exterior and the body that had been totally hidden under the baggy clothes he preferred. His eyes started to be a little less certain as I stared at him, and somehow, I didn't want to ruin his mood. He seemed happier than I'd ever seen him. Maybe it was an act, or maybe just pretending to be happy can help.

I held my hand out to Ru, and he smiled. He gave me the hand she wasn't clinging to with both hands and some of her body weight. She pretty much had him pinned. I wondered if she was always this clingy or if it was something about Ru that made her so determined. I tried to draw him to me, but she held on as if it was going to be a tug-of-war with him in the middle. That was too ridiculous, so I moved to Ru's other side and touched his face. He slid his arm around my waist for the first time, and he felt as strong as he looked. He tightened his arm around my waist and drew me in against the side of his body. It was so much bolder than I'd thought he had in him, and for a second it reminded me of Rodrigo, who had been bold and dominant and domineering. I started to recoil from him. He felt it and the light started to fade from his eyes; that quiet, nearly beaten look was creeping back into his eyes, and I didn't want to see it back. I didn't want to be the cause of it. Rodina was right; they were in mourning, too. We'd all lost in Ireland. I stared up into his black eyes and for the first time I saw Ru, not Rodrigo, but the man standing in front of me instead of the ghosts behind me.

I smiled up into his face, let my fingers play along the water drops on his skin. That light touch filled his eyes back up with something happier. I tried to put my arm around his waist but ran into Bettina's body.

"Hey, I'm not into girls, okay?" she said.

I hesitated for a minute with my arm pushed against her

body as I tried to hug him; then I smiled up at him and did my best to let him see/feel/think what I was about to do. If it had been Nathaniel, I would have been able to just lower my shields and be sure he understood, but with Ru the connection only went one way: him sensing me. I went up on tiptoes, leaning against the line of his body and putting my lips against his; it wasn't even a kiss, just a touch. I felt his lips curl into a smile and I smiled back. I turned my arm to go around her waist, so I was hugging both of them. She made an unhappy "Hey!" I pulled harder and broke from Ru's lips to lean toward Bettina, as if I meant to kiss her. She gave an unhappy squeal and let him go, only my arm keeping her in place. If I'd been a little more perverse, I'd have gotten a kiss before I let her go, but I didn't like Bettina enough to even go that far. I moved my arm and she stumbled back as if she'd been fighting harder against my arm than I'd felt.

She was calling me names now, *lesbian* being the nicest of them. I ignored her and was finally able to look up into Ru's ebony eyes without any distractions. He smiled, I smiled, and then I leaned in toward him as he leaned in toward me. We kissed, a light brush of lips, and then his hands tightened on the back of my body, pressing us together so that there was more body English to the kiss. I felt his body through the front of his small bathing suit. It made me push away from the kiss and turn my face in against his neck. His skin was slightly cool from the pool, but it must have been a saltwater pool, because there was no hint of chlorine. His skin smelled clean and good. I wrapped myself around him, burying my face in the bend of his neck where the pulse beat underneath his skin. He was suddenly so warm, and underneath the sweet scent of his skin was heat, a heat that I could warm myself with, if only I could reach it.

I kissed his neck, pressing my lips over that warm, pulsing smoothness. I licked lightly over it and found his skin salty, and not from sweat, but from the salt water of the pool. I licked across his pulse, harder this time, licking as if I could touch that beating thing with my tongue if only I licked hard enough.

Ru shivered in my arms. He said, "Anita," in a voice that was a little breathy.

I opened my mouth enough to set teeth against his skin on either side of that pulsing, dancing point. I could feel it against my tongue like something alive and separate from him, like a tiny bird fluttering under his skin waiting for me to free it so it could fly high in a spill of crimson feathers and screams.

A hand grabbed my hair hard enough that it hurt. Under other circumstances I might have enjoyed it, but not now. I set my teeth in the flesh. If they tore me away now, they'd take his neck with me. I heard a low growl and realized it was me.

Micah's voice against my ear: "Anita, don't do this, not here in front of Edward and the wedding guests."

He could have said a lot of things, but that was a good one to bring me back to myself and wonder what the hell I was doing. I relaxed in Ru's grip and stopped biting him, drawing first my teeth and then my mouth back from his skin.

Ru's eyes were slightly unfocused, as if he'd gotten more from the partial bite than he should have. Rodina spoke low near my ear: "My queen, when is the last time you fed?"

"I had food on the plane," I said.

Micah kept his grip on my hair. He knew that the danger wasn't over yet. I almost told him, *I'm okay, I'm safe,* but I didn't know what had made me lose control, so I just let Micah draw me back from Ru. Bram stood a little ahead of Micah, closer to me than to his leopard king. If I lost control, he was going to defend his king. I was glad to know that Bram was there, because I wasn't sure what had just happened, or why. Stupid metaphysics.

Nathaniel put an arm over Ru's shoulders and drew him away from me as Micah moved me. Ru said in a voice that was still lower than normal, "I am yours in whatever way you need me to be, my queen."

I blinked and looked at Nathaniel's worried face as he stared at me. "Did you win?" I asked.

"What?" he asked.

"Did you win the race, the heat, the swimming thing?"

He smiled then, and Micah said, "That's our girl."

"I lost," Nathaniel said.

I must have looked surprised, because he added, "The guy is going through college on a swim scholarship and he's nearly five inches taller than me. He touched the wall first."

"So, did we lose the money?" I asked, as if I really cared. I didn't, but sometimes you support your people even when they do things you don't understand like bet money on winning a swim race with strangers, or try to tear the throat out of one of your friends. See, we all try to understand one another's little foibles.

"Not yet," Edward said. He was standing near us with a towel in his hands. I was pretty sure there was a weapon of some kind in the towel. I was okay with that. He was only human, after all, and the rest of us standing there weren't. He was the most dangerous human being I'd ever met and one of the most dangerous people, human or superhuman, but still, a weapon was good to have when you were dealing with supernaturals, because sometimes the only difference between a preternatural human being and a monster was a little unsatisfied bloodlust.

Bernardo was standing a little behind Edward. It wasn't that he wasn't going to help if he was needed, but he didn't have Edward's cold-blooded determination, meaning that he might hesitate if it came to killing me. I was their friend, after all. If Edward ever made the decision that I was too dangerous, he'd pull the trigger, because he trusted his judgment that completely, and so did I. Bernardo wasn't as self-contained as Edward, but then few people were.

"We're going to take Anita to the room for a few minutes," Micah said, and he looked at Edward when he said it.

Edward gave a minute nod. "Good idea," he said; his voice was tight, cold. I expected his eyes to be the pale of winter skies, which was the color that his eyes became when he was about to kill. I looked into a richer, friendlier blue than I'd expected and saw something in his eyes that I'd never expected to see: hesitation. He'd do it, but I'd crossed a line for Edward, just as he had for me. We'd pull the trigger on each other if we felt we had no choice and other people's safety was on the line, but it would cost us. Damn it.

I looked past him and saw Rufous. He'd finally stood up, too, though he looked out of shape enough that it made me worry for him, and then I saw his face. His eyes had narrowed, and for lack of a better word he had that cop look, and it was aimed at me. I'd done something interesting and not in a good way. He didn't know what was going on, but he was a cop, and if the flags go up, cops run toward the action, never away from it. Physical fitness and age had nothing to do with it. Rufous was a police officer, period. That made me wonder, so I glanced behind me toward Frankie. He wasn't a cop and never had been, but he was a man who had spent a lot of his career settling violent problems with violent solutions. He was behind us, and I finally realized that both Nathaniel and Ru had given some of their attention to the tall, dark, and potentially dangerous man. I'd totally forgotten about him, which was worse than careless; it was stupid. Just as Edward wasn't my only dangerous friend, so I wasn't his either. If you had to pick a wedding to crash, this would not be the one to choose.

Edward just kept looking at me, not even really at any of the three men around me, as if our eye contact was all that mattered. I finally gave as good as I got on the eye to eye. We were staring at each other as if that long moment was everything, and for us, it was.

"Donna and all the other women are having a spa day, so you've got some time to rest in your room before dinner tonight."

"A nap sounds great," I said.

"Don't nap too hard," he said, glancing at Ru's neck, where a light imprint of my teeth was showing on his skin.

25

WE WENT BACK to the lobby and got Nicky and the bags, and then Nathaniel led us to our rooms. Bram and Nicky's room was beside ours, Ru and Rodina's across the hall from us. We'd filled Nicky in on the adventure by the pool. He hadn't seemed surprised. "All the master vampires with Brides fuck them, Anita. All the bloodlines, not just Belle Morte's line."

I turned in the hallway just short of our rooms and said, "How do you know that?"

"I started asking around when you brought these two back from Ireland."

"Asking who?"

"I asked the Harlequin; they served the old vampire council for thousands of years."

"You didn't ask us," Rodina said.

"How could I ask you about your own fate?"

"We knew once she owned us that we were her meat if she wished it, in any way she wished it," Rodina said.

"I don't want you as my meat, either of you."

"You didn't plan on wanting me either," Nicky said, and gave me a look.

"I hear someone coming; let's finish this talk in one of the rooms," Micah said.

We were actually opening the door to our room when Donna came down the hallway. I still wasn't used to her newly lightened hair. It had so many highlights in it that it was nearly blond, but it looked natural, as if she'd just been out in the sun a lot. The hair was new enough that I was distracted by it until she got close enough that even the large round sunglasses couldn't hide the fact that she was crying. I exchanged a look with Nathaniel. He'd held her hand through the wedding process more than I had, but one look and I knew that he didn't know what was wrong either.

"Anita, I need . . . We need to talk." Her voice held tears, but it also held anger, and the dreaded phrase *we need to talk* never ended well.

My pulse actually sped up as I said, "I thought you were with the other ladies getting your nails done."

"I don't give a damn about my nails, not now."

Oh shit.

Nathaniel tried to put his arm around her in a comforting way, but she shook him off. "No, no, I don't want another man to comfort me right now. I'm sorry, Nathaniel, it's not you, or about you. I'm just feeling like all men are fucking liars right now." I didn't think I'd ever heard her say *fuck* before.

On the plus side, she wasn't mad at me, because she was pissed at men and I wasn't one, so yay for me! On the downside, the comment didn't bode well for Edward—sorry, Ted. Had she found out more about the Batman side of his life this close to the actual wedding? That would suck, a lot.

"What's wrong, Donna?" I asked, because I felt I had to ask.

She grabbed my arm and started pulling me down the hallway. Apparently, we were going to have a girl talk. I looked back at the men. "We'll handle things here," Micah said.

Nathaniel gave me a very serious and sad look. He mouthed, *Sorry.* He knew I hated handling this kind of emotional upheaval, but a lot of people assumed that, being the woman, I'd be better at it than the men. Boy, did they have the wrong girl, um, person.

I'd do my best with Donna for Edward's sake, but she and I had never been friends, really, let alone the kind of girlfriends who could grab each other and drag each other down a hallway for an emotional heart-to-heart. I had no idea what had upset her this much and made her turn to me. She had two best friends here, plus her co-owner in her metaphysical shop, so why was I the one with the sobbing bride on my arm?

Nicky tried to follow like a good bodyguard, but Donna just pointed a finger at him wordlessly. Rodina tried next, but Donna said, "I'm sorry, but I don't know you. This is private."

"I'll be okay; everyone chill," I said.

"No," Nicky said, "you can't go anywhere without at least one of your bodyguards."

"No," Donna said, "I want to talk to Anita without an audience."

"Anita goes nowhere without a bodyguard."

Donna started to try to protest, but Rodina said, "We could use the little café area at the end of the hallway. The doors are glass and we can keep an eye on Anita without eavesdropping." She smiled as she said it, exuding helpfulness. I knew that unless people were shouting around us, any wereanimal would be able to hear at least some of the conversation, but I didn't tell Donna. We all need our illusions and I was pretty sure Nicky meant his ultimatum. He was my Bride: I could have just ordered him to let me go; same for Ru and Rodina, but Bram had free will, and I was pretty certain he'd use it to support his fellow guards.

Ru and Bram stayed with Nathaniel and Micah, herding them into our room. Nicky and Rodina went with us, him in front and her behind. I think if Donna hadn't been crying so much, she'd have put up more of an argument, but she was too distressed about something to marshal her forces, so in the end she let Nicky and Rodina go outside first, and when they gave their all clear, Donna pulled me through the double doors and into the brilliant Kirke Key sunshine. It was good that they'd already declared it a safe zone, because I nearly ran into the small chairs and tiny, nearly useless tables that had been crowded onto the balcony. I should have gotten my sunglasses out before we went through the door. I couldn't even remember when I'd taken my sunglasses off. Was it my imagination or was sunlight by the ocean just brighter than normal? I squinted, shielding my eyes with my other hand, because she had a death grip on my right arm. If bad guys had jumped us, I was blind in the sunshine and couldn't have gone for my gun. Perfect. Lucky for us I wasn't on the job today, so no bad guys, just hysterics.

I used her own grip on my arm to turn her around to face me. "Donna, what's wrong?"

"Did you know Ted had been married before?"

I stared at her for a moment, and my face must have showed

my surprise, because she suddenly collapsed into one of the
little chairs as if saying it out loud had taken everything she
had. Her hands had slid down my arm so that she was holding
my hand loosely in hers, while her shoulders shook with her
weeping. Jesus, what did I do now?

I patted her hand awkwardly and waited for the crying to
pass, and then I realized she was trying to talk through the
tears. It was hard to understand her, but I caught a word here
and there. "You didn't . . . know either . . . Stupid . . . How
could I . . . Deceive us . . . You know him better . . ."

I was finally getting a clue as to why she'd come to me with
the news and not her other friends. They were her friends, but
I was Ted's best friend, so by her reasoning I should feel betrayed, too. Best friends tell each other everything, right? Not
exactly, at least not if your best friend was Edward. He loved
keeping information to himself. Though I had to admit that
this was a stupid thing not to have told Donna.

She'd taken us to one of the little seating areas that the
hotel had scattered around where there were views to be had.
I managed to hook one of the little chairs with my foot and
pull it over so I could sit down while I tried to commiserate.
"He's free to marry you, right?" If there was a mysterious first
marriage, its being legally over seemed the most important
fact to establish.

She nodded, which helped the tight feeling in my gut to
loosen. I hadn't even known I was that tense until some of it
eased away. "So he's divorced?"

She nodded again, her head almost touching her knees as
she wept. I totally didn't understand why she was this upset,
but maybe I had different criteria for keeping secrets. "How
did you find out about it?"

She mumbled something mostly into her own lap. I hated
to say it, but: "Sorry, Donna, but I didn't understand that last
part."

She raised her head enough to say, "Carol, Frankie's wife,
said she was so happy that Ted's taste in women had gotten so
much better than when he was eighteen."

"He was married at eighteen?" I asked. I couldn't picture
Edward that young, let alone the kind of young guy who would
marry just as he'd gotten into the military.

"Carol gave the ex-wife some insulting name. I really thought better of Carol than to make fun of someone's weight."

I worked with a lot of ex-military, and I was beginning to get a clue. "Did she call the woman a dependapotamus?"

Donna took a shaky breath and nodded. "That sounds right."

I smiled before I could stop myself.

She jerked her hand back from me. "It's not funny!"

"No, it's not, but dependapotamus is a nickname for a certain type of woman that hangs around the fringes of military bases and sort of preys on young military guys."

"What do you mean, preys on?"

"They are pretty and charming, but once they get the soldier to marry them, then the charm goes away and a lot of them seem to do nothing but stay home and spend the man's, or woman's, military benefits."

"Woman . . . You mean there are men that do the same to female soldiers?"

"It's less typical, but it happens."

"So you're saying that these women and men try to marry young soldiers so they can have their benefits?"

"Apparently," I said.

"But that's awful."

I nodded. "It can be. I've heard stories of men who have been deployed and their wives empty their bank accounts and file for divorce while the soldiers are still fighting for their country."

Donna looked suitably appalled. "Sending someone divorce papers while they're fighting for their lives . . ." She seemed to be having trouble finding a word to describe it.

"Some ex-military guys I know think the women do it on purpose sometimes, because if the soldier dies on active duty while they're still married, she'd get more money." Everything I was saying was true, but I was trying to give the details that would bother Donna right in her liberal, freedom-loving heart.

"That's monstrous!"

"It's hard to picture Ted that young and that naïve, but even he had to start somewhere," I said.

"I've seen pictures of him when he was first in the military. He looks so young and unfinished, as if he's not Ted yet," she said. Her voice was clear, and somewhere in all the talking the tears had stopped. We were making progress.

"Think how embarrassed Ted would be to admit that he'd been tricked into marrying someone like that."

"He'd be mortified," she said.

"Young Ted would be, but Ted now, your Ted, would have put it on the list of things that just aren't important anymore."

"What do you mean list of things? Are you saying he has more things he's hiding from us?"

Oh shit, I had to be careful here or I'd open a can of worms that Edward might never forgive me for. "What I mean is that men like Ted compartmentalize; it's part of what helps them be good at their jobs. Something like a dependapotamus that got her hooks into Private Ted Forrester twenty years ago would be put in a compartment of things that didn't affect him or his life now. It just wouldn't be important except as a lesson learned."

She took the big sunglasses off and blinked at me. Her mascara and eyeliner had run in black tears down her cheeks. It made her look fragile, like someone to protect. "Is that how you do the job, Anita? You put things in separate compartments so that the emotional things don't interfere with the job?"

And it was moments like this that made me glimpse why Edward was marrying Donna. She got it; at some level she would make the logical leap about Edward, about me, about all of us who put on a gun and went out to hunt the monsters. It also meant she was more insightful than was comfortable sometimes, but it still made me think better of her for thinking of the questions, and then for having the courage to ask them. She'd already gotten brownie points for handling Dixie in New Mexico; now she got more.

"Yes," I said, "that's part of what I do for the job."

"You're not angry about Ted being married before, not even a little bit, are you?"

"No."

"You were surprised by it, I saw that, but you weren't upset even before you figured out what Carol had meant by that horrible hippopotamus comment."

"No," I said.

She studied my face. "Why not?"

I licked my lips and tried to be very careful. "Ted and I are best friends, but we've only known each other for nine years. We don't tell each other everything that happened before that."

"But a marriage is important. I'd tell my best friends something like that."

"But your best friends are women. It's different when your best friend is a man. You talk about different things."

"You're not just his best friend; you're his work wife, his monster-hunting partner."

"Yes, but you're his real wife; even without the ceremony, you guys have been dating for close to seven years. You've made him happier than I'd ever thought possible. I didn't even know Ted wanted a family, or could see his life with one, until I got off that airplane five years ago and met you and the kids."

She smiled, but it didn't stay. Her face got all serious again. Damn it, I'd been winning. What was wrong now? "If you'd thought that Ted wanted a family and a more normal life, would you have pursued him harder?"

"Pursued him how?" I asked.

"I believe that you weren't having an affair before, Anita, I do, but there is something between you. It feels like it could have been more than just friendship. If you had thought he wanted a family and marriage, would you have tried to date him?"

"You mean would I have wanted to do the white picket fence with Ted?"

"Yes, that's exactly what I mean."

"Donna, if you haven't noticed, I'm not a white-picket-fence kind of girl."

"Every woman wants that."

"Maybe I did in college—I was even engaged for a little while back then—but I'm never going to have what you think of as a normal life."

"Would you want one if it was possible for you?"

"What would normal mean for me? I'm here with both Micah and Nathaniel. If normal means giving either of them up, count me out."

She smiled then and rubbed at her eyes as if she'd just

thought about her eye makeup, but it was too late. The black tearstains had started to dry against her skin; she'd need a makeup remover just to get it all off now.

"And you have Nicky with you again, too."

"He's my personal bodyguard," I said.

"Anita, he's more than that to you."

"Yes, he is."

"When you marry Jean-Claude, is he really not going to make you give any of them up?"

"He would marry Micah and Nathaniel along with me if it was legal."

"And Nicky?"

"He's okay with Nicky, too."

"I'll never understand how you manage so many relationships."

"Not all of them are primary relationships."

"How can anyone be okay with not being someone's primary relationship?" she asked.

"Some people don't want the pressure of being someone's one and only."

"I wanted to be Ted's one and only, but even if his first marriage wasn't important, he still has you."

"We went through this, Donna. He and I are not a romantic item."

"I believe that, but Ted still needs you in his life. I'll never be enough for him alone. He'll never be just mine."

"But we're not having an affair."

"Not a physical one, but emotionally you really are his work wife. You meet emotional needs for him that I never can. I'd almost prefer an affair, because I could make him give that up, but what you and he have is something that he won't give up."

"I don't know what to say to that, Donna, except that he is in love with you, madly, deeply in love with you. I've never seen him like this about anyone else in all the time I've known him."

"Carol said the same thing."

"And she saw him with the first wife, so he didn't love her the way he loves you."

"Then why did he marry her?"

"Because he was eighteen and maybe away from home for the very first time, and lonely as hell. It's a recipe for being vulnerable."

"I suppose you're right," she said.

I caught movement from the corner of my eye and realized it was Nicky and Rodina opening the door for Edward. He came through the door still in his swim trunks. He'd just added sandals and sunglasses. I thought he'd hurried to find Donna after someone clued him in, until I saw her face when she saw him. She looked like someone had hit her between the eyes with the oh-my-God-he's-so-sexy hammer. The British would say she was gob-smacked. Edward had come wearing nothing but his bathing suit the same way some women will wear a low-necked blouse if they want to stop a fight and turn it to other things.

I had to admit that Edward looked very nice coming through the door with the sunlight dancing over all that muscled leanness. I'd known Edward was handsome, but I'd never really appreciated that he was sexy. He was my best friend; you just shouldn't speculate about sex and your true bestie. Nope, just nope.

"Oh, Ted, I'm so sorry I was stupid about you being married once before," she said, standing up and going to him.

He hugged her to his mostly naked body as he said, "I was eighteen, it lasted less than six months, and she took me for everything I had. I'm so sorry you had to find out through Carol mentioning it."

"When Carol called your ex-wife a dependapotamus, I thought she was being mean about her weight, but Anita explained what it meant," Donna said.

He flashed me a look over Donna's head, relief and a thank-you all there in his face. To her, he said, "It's exactly what she was, but don't call her my ex-wife; she wasn't important enough to even be that."

"Anita and I couldn't imagine you that young and naïve, but I guess we all get to be young and stupid."

"Oh, I was that, honeybunch. I was that in spades." His accent had thickened. I already knew that *honeybunch* was his special nickname for her. I called Nathaniel *pussycat*, so I really couldn't bitch.

She held him tight and then raised her head so he could kiss her. The kiss got a little busy, and I suddenly wanted a graceful exit either for me or for them, but I should have known that Edward was ahead of me.

"Let's go to our room, honeybunch."

"I need to go back to the spa. I left Becca getting her nails painted to match her flower-girl dress."

"Becca will be fine with the other bridesmaids with her."

"But I ran out on Carol; she must be frantic."

"She called Frankie, and he told me, and that's how I knew to find you. Carol will explain to everyone that we needed some private time."

"I'll let the two of you kiss and make up, and I'll go back to my guys."

Donna grabbed my hand in another spontaneous gesture of how close she seemed to think we were; sometimes I thought she wanted me close so she could keep an eye on me with Edward, but then, like now, I thought she just liked me as a friend. It was all too convoluted and therapy-rich for me.

"You are the best best woman ever," she said.

"I'll second that," Edward said in his Ted voice. The smile on his face was all Ted as well. If they ever gave out Oscars for playing your secret identity, I'd vote for Edward.

They left to go to their room and I was looking forward to going to mine. I wondered if Wyatt and Bram were still with Nathaniel and Micah or if everyone had gone to separate rooms by now. I mean, we did need to talk about vampire Brides and why I'd almost taken a bite out of Wyatt's neck, but I was really hoping for separate rooms and some alone time with Micah and Nathaniel. This was supposed to be a romantic trip for us, damn it. I hadn't even seen the inside of our room yet. But, hey, I'd managed to calm Donna down, and the wedding was still on. As long as I didn't try to take another bite out of anyone, I'd put today in the win column. I started for the door where Nicky and Rodina were waiting to escort me safely back to my room. I was pretty sure the walk back wasn't going to be that danger-ous, but I wasn't a bodyguard; I was the body being guarded. The body being guarded has to learn when to shut up and let people do their jobs; I was still learning.

26

NICKY WAS STARTING to open the door for me when I was suddenly facing most of the other bridesmaids coming down the hallway. Denny, short for Denise, the five-foot-nine, golden-tanned, natural blond maid of honor, was almost in tears. Dixie was yelling at her. They were almost the same height, and thanks to good hairdressing their hair was even nearly the same shade of blond. You could see the shadow of their being athletes in high school together, though Denny was still a serious runner and even did some triathlons, which meant she was lean and muscled and had that tall athlete's body that only a lifetime of athletics and good genetics will give you. Dixie had stayed thin, but she was no athlete. It made her look ten years older than Denny.

Nicky looked at me, and I shook my head, mouthing, *I'll be fine.*

Rodina peeked around the door and said, "If you need us, just yell."

"Will do," I said, and followed my fellow bridesmaids back out into the Florida sunshine. At this rate I was going to wish I'd put on sunscreen.

"Dixie, stop being such a bitch." This from Lucy, Donna's partner in her metaphysical shop. Lucy was not a small woman, but she didn't worry about the fact that she wasn't thin, just like she didn't worry that her hair was mostly gray and white with streaks of the original blond she'd started with in among the other colors. Letting her hair go natural and refusing to use makeup made her look older than she was, but Lucy didn't seem to care about age, so it worked for her. I'd have said she looked like someone's grandmother, but she didn't; she just looked like her. She'd explained that her silver-frame glasses were invisible trifocals, which I hadn't known was possible. She was one of the most comfortable people with age I'd ever met. She was also a practicing witch, as in Wiccan, but since Donna couldn't do anything psychic, one of them needed to be talented.

"How dare you call me that?" Dixie yelled, turning to face her with her hands in fists at her sides. I really hoped she didn't take a swing at either of them; she might take manhandling from Donna, but me . . . she'd never forgive me.

"You are being awful, Dixie," Denny said, with a little hiccup that let me know she was either about to start crying or had just stopped.

"What's happened now?" I asked.

"Did you know about Ted's first marriage?" Lucy asked.

"No," I said.

Dixie made a very unattractive snort. "That's rich. Of course you knew. Men always confide everything in their mistresses."

"Would you please stop saying that awful lie?" Denny said.

"It's not a lie," Dixie said.

"How many times do we have to tell you that there is no affair?" I said.

"It doesn't matter what you say, Anita. I see the way Ted looks at you."

"He admires Anita, respects her," Denny said.

"No man respects and admires a woman unless he's fucking her."

"Were you looking for me to pick a fight?"

"No, she wants to tell Peter and Becca that you and Ted are cheating together," Denny said, tearing up again.

"Peter knows about all of it. You leave Becca alone."

"When Carol told us about the first marriage and Donna didn't know about that either, I knew it was all lies," Dixie said.

"What is your problem? Are you jealous that Donna has a second chance at happiness?"

"I'm not jealous that Donna is about to marry a two-timing liar. I want to save her from making the mistake of her life."

"She is going to marry Ted," Lucy said, "and nothing you say will change that."

"She won't forgive him for lying about the first marriage. The wedding is already off."

"Actually, they made up," I said.

"I don't believe you."

"I would say go ask Donna, but they went back to their room to have makeup sex. It'd be rude to interrupt."

"Liar!"

I looked at her and let her see how pleased I was that the news upset her. "Why should I lie when the truth pisses you off so much more?"

"I won't let her make a mistake like this, and if you were her friend, Denny, you'd be with me on this."

"Ted is perfect for her," Denny said.

"He's a lying son of a bitch."

"Donna doesn't agree, and she is going to marry him, Dixie," Lucy said.

"I'm going to tell the kids, both of them. Peter won't want his mother marrying a cheating bastard."

"We keep telling you that Peter knows the truth," I said.

"But Becca doesn't. If I tell her what Ted and you have done, there won't be a wedding."

"You leave the child alone," Lucy said, and there was a steeliness to her tone that turned her gray-blue eyes mostly gray.

"Do you not want to be in this wedding, Dixie?" Denny asked.

"Donna didn't trust Anita and Ted at her own wedding unless Anita had someone else to fuck besides Ted. She was ecstatic when you brought Micah and Nathaniel. She thought with two men at your disposal you'd leave Ted alone for this week, at least."

Denny started crying again. "You are being so horrible."

"No, what's horrible is that Donna's own son is okay with her being cheated on."

"He's Ted's son, too," Lucy said.

"No! No! I was there for Donna's wedding to Frank. That was true love! If he hadn't died, then Ted would never have gotten his . . . hands on Donna or their children. I have half a mind to tell Peter how disappointed his real father would be that he's not defending Donna's honor."

"Just leave Peter out of this," I said.

"The woman who is cuckolding my best friend doesn't get to tell me what to do!"

I almost said that I wasn't sure a woman could cuckold someone, but I figured that correcting her vocabulary would not help things.

Lucy touched Dixie's arm and said, "Let Donna handle Peter the way she sees fit, Dixie."

Dixie jerked away from her and glared at us both. "I will tell Becca and see how the wedding goes with the flower girl accusing her father-to-be of fucking one of the maids of honor."

"You will not talk to Becca without Donna's permission," Lucy said, before I could say anything.

"I was there when Becca was born. I'm Aunt Dixie. I'll talk to my niece as I see fit."

"If you really love that little girl, you will leave her alone," Lucy said.

"She deserves to know the truth."

"There is no truth to tell her," I said.

"Lying bitch," she said.

"I thought we had the talk about pet names in New Mexico."

"Donna protected you then."

"No, she protected you and she told you so, because I heard her say it."

"You are a vile woman," Dixie said, and her eyes were shiny now, too, as if the anger was turning into tears.

"Ted is the only father Becca remembers. Do you really want to take that away from her because you don't like him?"

"I am not the bad guy here," Dixie said.

"If you tell Becca those lies, then you will be," I said. Dixie went for the door, slamming it behind her so hard that for a second I thought the glass was going to break.

Denny called out, "Dixie!" and ran after her.

Lucy patted my arm. "I better go after them and make sure she doesn't do anything we'll all regret, like talk to the kids. I'm sorry this is going to be so unpleasant for you, Anita."

I actually patted her hand back and said, "Thanks, Lucy. Good luck talking sense into Dixie."

"Can you tell Bernardo what's going on? Carol told her husband and Marisol told Rufous, but Bernardo doesn't have anyone to fill him in."

"You think he needs to know right now?"

She looked at the door. "I have to go make sure Denny and Dixie are all right, but, yes, my intuition says it's important that you talk to Bernardo." She looked at me and there was weight to it; her power, her magic, whatever word, breathed along my skin. "Talk to him, Anita, and then you can go have fun with your men."

I didn't ask her how she knew I was eager to get to my men—she was psychic, after all, or maybe it was just a good bet that if I had a couple of hours before dinner I was going to be with them. Either way, I wouldn't argue with the power that goose-bumped along my arms.

I was left alone in sunshine and heat, the sound of waves on the shore below. It should have been idyllic. Peter knew the truth, the real truth, both what his mother had believed and what Ted and I had admitted to, and why we'd admitted to a lie. Peter didn't understand why she'd needed the affair to be real either, but he loved his mother and wanted her to marry Edward. We'd all agreed—Ted, Donna, Peter, and I—that Becca didn't need to know either way. She was eleven; her parents' sex lives weren't her problem. If Dixie told Becca about the affair without Donna's permission, I wouldn't have to take care of Dixie; if Donna didn't do it, Edward would. I didn't think he'd kill her for it, but Dixie didn't understand how much danger she might be in if she messed with his happy family. She saw handsome Bruce Wayne or bumbling Clark Kent, not the Dark Knight or Superman. If she pushed hard enough, she'd find out that even Superman has a temper.

27

I TEXTED BERNARDO to find out where he was, and wasn't surprised to find that the answer was "Pool." Nathaniel couldn't follow through on the flirting, but Bernardo was footloose and fancy-free. What better place to pick out his gazelle than the watering hole, where he could observe them in their natural, bikini-clad habitat? Rodina took the lead this time, so I could see around her; following Nicky was like driving behind a semitruck on the highway—it blocked all the exit signs. I remembered to put my sunglasses on before walking outside this time; that was an improvement. I could see the sunlight dazzling and dancing on the blue water of the pool, but it didn't blind me this time. There was a family group with two small toddlers at one end of the pool and a dozen young ladies in various states of undress on the other end of the pool. Two of the women were actually wearing one-piece bathing suits, so I'd have to revise my earlier sarcasm about bikini-clad gazelles.

Some of the women were sitting with their feet dangling in the water, some going in and out of the pool, more showing off their bathing suits than actually swimming. I looked around at all the tables with umbrellas and empty chairs and then realized there was one table I couldn't see because the majority of women were blocking my view. Call it a hunch, but I walked toward the table I couldn't see.

"We'll wait here," Nicky said as he took up a post at the edge of the gazelle herd.

"Good luck in there," Rodina said with a smile.

I had to weave my way through the women until I found

him sitting at the table under the umbrella, with a tall drink at hand and a pair of swim trunks the only thing covering all that tall, dark, and handsome. The only thing that surprised me was that the trunks were loose fit. I'd have bet Bernardo was a form-fitting-trunks kind of guy, but, hey, it's nice to leave something to the imagination sometimes. Besides, I'd accidently found out just how well-endowed he was, and maybe looser trunks were better. He wouldn't scare any of his gazelles prematurely.

It was hot enough that he should have had his long, thick black hair in its usual ponytail or braid, but it was loose around his broad shoulders. It was Bettina, the short brunette who had flirted so hard with Ru earlier, who came up behind him and ran her hands through his hair. Apparently, when she lost out with Ru and Nathaniel, she'd gone looking for other flirtatious men. I looked around and didn't see the redhead but did see the taller brunette in the bright bikini moving in from one side with a fresh drink in her hand. I didn't recognize any of the other women; maybe it was a fresh batch. I'd thought Bernardo would use the swimming pool the way a lion uses a watering hole, but I'd been wrong. He was using himself for bait—not to attract gazelles, but to find a lioness.

"Hey, Bernardo," I said, and I didn't try to hide the smile and headshake.

"Hey, Anita."

"Not you again," the tall brunette said.

"Are you sleeping with all the beautiful men in the hotel?" Bettina asked.

Bernardo reached up and caught her hand in his, bringing it around so he could lay a gentle kiss on her wrist. Her eyes damn near fluttered closed. That seemed like a lot of reaction for something so small, but, hey, it wasn't my wrist being kissed.

"Don't worry, baby—we're just work friends, no benefits."

"Absolutely no benefits. He's all yours, girls," I said.

Bettina wrapped her other arm around Bernardo's neck and leaned her breasts against his hair. It was such an obvious marking of territory that it made me smile. Then Bettina put both arms around his neck, which made her breasts spill around either side of his throat like bikini-clad pillows. Bernardo patted her arm but kept looking up at me as if she wasn't trying to hug him with her breasts. This wasn't the reaction she was hoping for. She didn't understand it, but she wasn't frowning at him; she was frowning at me. Why is it that women never blame the guy for ignoring them for another woman, but only blame the other woman?

"I need to ask you to give the groom a message before you retire to your room."

"I'm a little busy; why can't you tell him yourself?" he asked, and his voice sounded gruff, almost unfriendly. He moved Bettina's hand so that he could lay a kiss on her other wrist. That made her smile happily and wriggle her breasts even closer to him, though frankly she had to be driving her collarbone into the back of his head at this point, or maybe that was just me being picky.

"He and the bride went back to their room for makeup sex. I don't want to disturb them, but this is important."

"Makeup sex? What are they fighting about?"

"Ted's first marriage that Donna didn't know about."

"What? I didn't know Ted had been married before." He'd stopped touching Bettina and was sitting there with her wrapped around his shoulders like a PG-13-rated towel.

"Neither did I," I said.

He let the surprise show on his face. "I can see why Donna got pissed."

Bettina rubbed her face against his hair, which made him reach up and rub his hands down her arms, idly, like you'd pet a dog that had shifted in your lap. The other women were beginning to see the writing on the wall, and it was either going to be Bettina's name or mine, but not theirs. They were looking uncomfortable and frowning at both Bettina and me.

"I talked her down, but she confided something in Dixie, and now Dixie has shared it with the other bridesmaids and she's threatening to tell Becca, and that would go really badly."

He was serious now, watching my face, still touching the girl's arms, but even she had figured out he wasn't concentrating on her. She tried to put her leg around the edge of his chair and into his lap, I think, but moves like that look better in the movies. Her leg ended up over the chair arm but couldn't reach more than the edge of his thigh, and it looked awkward, but she kept it there because she couldn't seem to figure out how to take it back. Ah, to be a few years younger and both that bold and that bad at it.

Bernardo touched her calf, letting her know that he appreciated the effort, but most of his attention was on our conversation. "What is it? What is the crazy bitch threatening to tell the best niece in the world?"

I tried to think of a clever way to hint, but I suck at hinting. I'm really more of a just-say-it kind of person. Bettina was pouting because he wasn't paying enough attention and the other women were trying to decide if they could outflirt her. The awkward leg thing had given some of them hope. "I'm sorry, ladies. Can you excuse us for just a few minutes? I'll make it quick, promise."

"Ladies? I'm not a lady," Bettina said, standing up but keeping her hands on his bare shoulders.

"Well, you said it, I didn't."

"I meant that you know my name," she said, and I half expected her to stamp her foot at me.

"Fine. Excuse me, Bettina, but I need to speak with Bernardo for a few minutes."

She gave a little upset sniff but said, "That's better, thank you." I'd really expected her to be more insulted by all the talk of ladies, but apparently she was harder to insult than I'd thought. She flounced off to join her tall friend, who began to shake her head almost as soon as they started to talk. Bettina might still be game to try to bag Bernardo, but her friend was fed up with me interrupting their fun, or maybe she just didn't like her odds. It was quite a crowd around Bernardo.

I had to shoo a couple of them out of hearing range, because Bettina moving away had given them even more hope. Bernardo had to be charming at a couple of more, and they hovered nearby like vultures waiting for the handsome gazelle to stop struggling. Some of the women found other chairs beside the pool and tried to drape themselves artfully, or blatantly, waiting for Bernardo to finish talking to me. He ignored them all; that would have been enough to make me walk away. I don't deal with being ignored.

He pulled a chair over so I could sit and leaned in toward me. "What is Dixie threatening to tell Becca?"

I told him.

His face showed the shock. "Fuck," he said with deep feeling.

"Yeah," I said.

"But I thought that Donna and Edward cleared all that up. Donna doesn't believe you guys were an item, right?"

"Not anymore," I said.

"Then what is Dixie's problem?"

"I'm not sure."

"What can we do to minimize the damage?"

"You tell Edward when he and Donna come back out of their room," I said.

"Why can't you tell him?"

"Because this is supposed to be a romantic trip for the three of us, and Micah and I have already disappointed Nathaniel once today. They're waiting in our room for me now."

He motioned toward the waiting women. "And I don't have people waiting for me?"

"You haven't bagged and tagged yours yet; I have."

He sat back in his chair. "You think I couldn't have a woman in my bed within the next few minutes?"

I laughed. "I know you could, but would it be the one you wanted?"

"I want them all," he said, smiling and obviously pleased with himself.

I shook my head. "I know that's not true."

He looked a little less pleased. "How do you know that?"

"You're pickier than that just on the beauty scale alone."

He studied me through his dark glasses, now firmly back hiding his eyes. "So are you."

"Don't compare my dating preferences to yours. I'm a lot pickier than you are."

"That's fair," he said, and then he smiled, adding, "You know, if you wanted to join me and one of the beauties here by the pool, you could."

I laughed. "I've got my own threesome waiting for me in my room, but thanks for thinking of me."

He laughed, too. "I thought you liked girls now, or are you just dating them to make your guys happy?"

I shook my head. "I told you, Bernardo—fantasize about me with other women on your own time, and when you meet the other women in my life you will fantasize."

He gave me a smile that was almost a leer. "Can't wait to meet them."

"So, will you tell Edward?" I asked.

"I'll tell him before I pick my afternoon delight."

"You did not just say *afternoon delight*." I lowered my sunglasses enough so he could see me roll my eyes.

He laughed, lowering his own glasses so he could wiggle his eyebrows at me.

"Good luck," I said, and started to walk away. Nicky and Rodina settled on either side of me. I glanced back, and Bettina was already at his side, but then so were a few of the other women. Rodina said, "I'm beginning to see why you never slept with your work friend."

"Yeah, I don't like being part of a herd," I said.

She glanced back and said, "Moo."

I glanced back, too. Bettina had climbed into Bernardo's lap, but the other women hadn't given up yet. One was starting to give him a back rub. I followed Nicky, with Rodina bringing up the rear. I watched the back of Nicky's body, the spread of his shoulders and his ass as he walked away from me. It made me happy to know that he was mine. Micah and Nathaniel were waiting for me back at the room, and I was looking forward to joining them. I liked that I had people in my life and that we were sure of one another. We were poly, but we were secure in our group. I liked that, a lot. My own love life always interested me more than anyone else's.

28

WE WERE ALMOST to our room when I saw a tall, dark-haired man coming toward us. He had to be over six feet tall or I couldn't have seen him over Nicky's body. It took me a second to realize it was Peter Parnell, Donna and Edward's son. When had he gotten that tall and how had I not recognized him? Part of it was me still wearing the sunglasses in the dimmer hallway, but a lot of it was that at nineteen he was finally filling out into the man he'd be for the rest of his life. If I hadn't known that both Nathaniel and I grew several inches after age nineteen, I'd have said he was done.

Nicky moved slightly to the side so that Peter and I could see each other better, I think. I guess I was completely hidden behind him. Genetics and working out had broadened Peter's shoulders and just helped fill out his arms and legs and everything in between so he looked more finished than he had even a year ago. His hair had gone from deep brown to a nearly black brown. It was short except on top, where he'd left it long so that his bangs, if that was the right word, fell across the edge of one eyebrow, because he swept his hair to the side and did something to it so that it stayed that way. He had a habit of running his fingers through just that part of his hair now. I wasn't sure if it was to make sure it stayed where he wanted it, or if he'd started styling it that way because of the habitual gesture.

I studied his face as we walked toward each other, trying to see the shadow of the young boy I'd first met, but all I could see was this big, athletic stranger walking toward me. Well, not quite a stranger, because he looked so much like the picture of his dead father that Donna kept in the living room that it was a little disturbing. She was the only person I knew who kept a picture of her first husband when she was with someone else, but maybe that was because she'd been widowed. No, that couldn't be it, because my father didn't keep any pictures of my mother out, and my stepmother, Judith, didn't keep any of her first husband out either, and they were a widow and a widower. Maybe it was a Donna thing, or maybe she wanted her kids to remember him. Whatever her motive, I wondered how Peter felt seeing his dead father's face in the mirror every morning.

"Do I have something on my face?" Peter asked as we all came together in the middle of the hallway.

I shook my head. "No, well, wait, is that a five-o'clock shadow?"

He grinned and there was a glimpse of the kid I'd met all those years ago. It made me smile to see it. "Maybe I'll see if I can grow a beard."

"If you stop shaving before the wedding, your mom will kill you."

He laughed. It was a deep chuckle, and there was nothing little boy about it. I was happy for him growing up, but sometimes I missed Peter from a few years ago. I wondered if this was a tiny bit of how parents feel when they watch their kids grow up: happy and sad all at once.

Peter noticed both Rodina and Nicky, but he looked longer at the man. Peter had only been introduced to Nicky as my or Nathaniel's bodyguard on trips to New Mexico, at first. He had been fine with Nicky; he hadn't even had the issue that most men did with Nicky being physically intimidating, until he found out that Nicky was my lover. He'd liked Nicky less after that. I'd known that Peter had had a crush on me for a while, but I hadn't thought that it might bother him if I added new men to our poly group.

Nicky said, "Peter."

"Nicky."

Rodina smiled at them both and then looked down to hide it. She was the ultimate spy and centuries-old assassin; she could control her facial expressions, which meant she wanted

Peter to notice, because Nicky wouldn't care. Peter glanced at her, noticing. Why did she want him to see it? I'd ask her later, but I didn't try to hide my irritation with her. Brides were supposed to want to keep me happy, right?

I said, "Why aren't you out by the pool? I know Edward made sure you know how to swim."

He rolled his eyes, and again, that was something he'd done when I first met him. Peter was still in there, just bigger. "While Uncle Bernardo is holding tryouts for his bimbo of the night, no, thanks."

It was my turn to laugh. "Fair enough."

"I would think you could give Bernardo a run for his money with his bimbos," Rodina said.

I looked at her, but she was looking at Peter like a girl looks at an attractive guy. Was she flirting with him? Why would she be flirting with him?

I looked at Peter; I mean, really looked at him. I tried to look at him not as Edward and Donna's son, but as a person. He was a little too traditionally masculine for my preferences. I preferred pretty or beautiful to handsome, and his face was longer than I liked, but it was a good face, a strong face. The hair spilling around his eyes gave him that careless bad-boy look. His eyes were a nice solid brown, deep and dark and full of a force of personality that I liked, though not everyone likes that amount of internal fire. But I did. His lower lip was fuller than his upper one, but I could see running my thumb along that pouting lower lip. I realized with almost a shock that Peter was a good-looking guy, and there was a reason that he'd been able to pass for twenty-one before he was eighteen. He didn't look like a kid anymore and probably hadn't for a while. I just hadn't noticed.

Peter looked at Rodina. "I don't think I'm in the same league as Uncle B."

"He's a little too pretty for my taste. I like my men to be more handsome than pretty," she said. She gave him a look out from under her eyelashes. There's only one reason any woman gives that look to anyone. She was flirting. In my head I wanted to say, *But why are you flirting with him?* But her reaction to him had made me see Peter not as a kid, but as a grown-up, and if you liked your men closer to the rugged, handsome side of the scale, then he was worth flirting with, weird as that seemed to me.

"We're working," Nicky said.

"But once Anita is safely in her room with Micah and Nathaniel, then we won't be working anymore," she said.

I looked at her and had to bite my tongue, because what I wanted to say was *No*. I wanted to tell her she couldn't sleep with Peter. He was Edward's son; my bodyguards weren't allowed to sleep with his kid. But was that fair? Was it fair to Peter? Was I being overly protective? When Peter was fourteen, some very bad people had kidnapped him and Becca. It hadn't been Edward's fault. They'd been bad guys Donna's preservation society had actually gotten on the wrong side of, but it had been Edward, Bernardo, Otto, and me who had gone in and saved the kids. We'd saved them, but not in time for Peter. His first sexual experience had been abuse, and I could never make that not have happened. I could never truly save Peter, and that fact haunted me and colored how I felt about him. I knew that, but knowing it didn't make it go away. Fuck.

My phone beeped. It was a text from Micah. "What's taking so long, sweetheart?"

Nathaniel texted a second later. "Where are you?"

"What?" Peter asked.

"Texts from Micah and Nathaniel."

"Nathaniel's really been looking forward to this trip with the two of you," Peter said.

"I know," I said.

"We should get you tucked into your room so you can start enjoying your trip," Rodina said. Her face was completely blank and businesslike as she said it, but there should have been a smile with it.

"Go have fun," Peter said and turned to go.

"Don't go too far," Rodina said.

He frowned at her, as if trying to figure out if she was kidding.

Again, I had another moment of wanting to play parent or big sister or auntie, or something, and tell Rodina to back off and Peter not to sleep with her. He was nineteen, legally an adult, and I wasn't his mom, his sister, or even his real aunt. I was his father's best friend. What rights did that give me in his life? Deeply conflicted did not begin to cover it.

"We can change and go down to the pool," Rodina said.

Peter shook his head. "I don't think so."

"If you look as good out of your clothes as you do in them, I'm betting I'm not the only girl around the pool that prefers my men a little more rugged than your uncle."

"Rugged, huh." He looked at me. It wasn't a friendly look. "You told her about the scars."

"No," I said.

Rodina looked from one to the other of us. "I meant masculine when I said rugged. Anita doesn't confide in me."

"I don't believe you," he said, and he was just suddenly angry. I remembered another thing that Peter and I had in common—rage. He grabbed the hem of his T-shirt and yanked it up, showing that Edward wasn't the only one who had been working on his abs and that Peter had his own scars. The weretiger's claws had cut across his upper stomach and the right side of his upper chest, and I knew that higher up on the shoulder and his arm were scarred, too, because I'd been there when he'd almost died saving my life. It was the one and only time that Edward had brought Peter as backup for one of our "adventures." I'd made him swear that Peter wouldn't go into the family business again until he hit twenty-one. I'd have liked to get Edward's promise that Peter wouldn't go into the family business at all, but I knew better than to ask that.

Rodina raised eyebrows and smiled. "Nice."

"It's not nice," Peter said.

"You're right, it's not nice; it's awesome. Scars like that are a badge of honor, Peter. It means something monstrous tried to kill you, but you killed it instead."

"How do you know I killed it?"

Rodina smiled. "Well, I did hear the story, but not from Anita. You saved her life, getting those scars."

"Did they tell you that one of the other guards died helping me save her life?"

Rodina's face went blank and unreadable. She stopped trying to flirt. "I heard."

"His name was Cisco and he died to help me save Anita."

The anger had turned to something cold and distant, and that was more Edward's flavor of anger than mine. Peter pulled his shirt down and just walked past us all and kept walking. I don't know what Rodina had been trying to accomplish with him, but I don't think this was it.

She waited until Peter was out of earshot and then said, "I tried, Anita."

"What were you trying to do?" I asked, and I couldn't keep the anger out of my own voice.

"Help Peter feel better."

"Why do you care how Peter feels?" I asked.

"Because you care, my queen, and if Peter was happier, you'd be happier."

I frowned at her. "I don't think my emotional health is tied that closely to Peter's happiness."

"We are your Brides; we can feel when you're unhappy, and that is how you feel whenever you talk to him, or even talk about him."

I looked at Nicky. "Is that true?"

"Do you want me to answer that?" he asked.

I sighed. "You just did." I don't know what I would have said next, because Micah texted me again: "Nathaniel isn't happy. Hurry, or we're going to have another fight on our hands." Well, shit.

"Maybe you're right; maybe I am fucked up about Peter and Edward and his whole little family, but there's nothing I can do about it. But there's something I can do with Micah and Nathaniel to avoid another fight."

"Go make Nathaniel happy," Nicky said. He even moved across the hallway and motioned at the door.

"I will leave Peter alone, my queen. I'd hoped to make you and him happier, but the situation is more complicated than I understood."

I looked at Rodina's blank and unreadable face. "Thanks, I guess." I got out my key card and went for the door to our room.

29

I CLOSED THE door behind me and leaned against it, letting out a breath of tension I hadn't even known I was holding. Rodina made me so tired, because how I felt about her and her brother was so damned complicated. Being tied to her metaphysically until she died, or I died, just seemed like a terrible idea. It worked with Nicky, because he made things easier. Rodina and Ru didn't seem to make anything easier. If they were all my Brides, then why were they so different? Why did they make me feel so different? The answer of course was that they weren't Nicky. I'd made the rookie mistake of assuming because my first relationship with a Bride was this way that they would all be the same. I knew it didn't work that way with real romantic relationships; why had I assumed that the rules would be different for Brides? Wishful thinking? Stupidity?

I looked up to find there was a living room with a desk with a flat-screen above it on one side and a couch on the other side. There were closet doors to my immediate right and a half bath to my left and a long stretch of empty living room. I knew that Micah had booked us a honeymoon suite, but I hadn't expected it to be bigger, just more honeymoon-y. Right now, the room could have been simply a nice business suite.

I called out, "Hello, honeys, I'm home."

"Bedroom." Micah's voice, but slightly distant. There was one more closed door in the living room area. Chances were that was the bedroom, and since there were no other doors that made sense to open, I pushed away from the door and forced myself to stand upright, shoulders back. I centered myself and then tried to push all the other issues away. I tried to focus on just Micah and Nathaniel and the fact that they were waiting for me behind this door. We were on a romantic trip together, damn it. I was not going to be the one who dropped the ball and ruined this moment for us.

I opened the door in time to see Nathaniel jerk away from Micah's hand on his shoulder. They were wearing matching robes with the hotel logo on them. Nathaniel turned to me, and as soon as I saw his eyes I could feel the anger like heat along my skin. My own anger tried to flare up to meet his, as if his was just the spark I needed to burn us all up in one spectacular fight. I just stood there, breathing hard and trying to count slowly. I would not be the one that drew first blood. It would not be my fault if this afternoon went up in smoke. It would not be my issues that ruined today, damn it. My hands were already trying to curl into fists, my shoulders rolling forward. My beasts tried to ride the anger, but I thought at them, or myself, or both, *Don't even try it!* For once all my inner beasts just faded back, like a dog that had been chastised.

"Bettina and I are Facebook friends." Nathaniel spit it at me like an accusation.

I had to swallow hard and fight to control my voice as I said, "Why are you mad at me for something she posted to Facebook?"

"She's complaining that you tried to steal another man from her, but she won this time. She seems to think that it was the fact that she was in a bikini and you were wearing too many clothes at the pool."

The ridiculousness of this woman that we'd just met posting things about me on social media, and that causing a fight between Nathaniel and me, helped my anger start to fade. It was just too stupid a reason for us to fight. "I didn't try to steal Bernardo from her."

"But you did go down to the pool and talk to him, while you knew we were up here waiting to have a romantic afternoon with you."

I finally had a clue as to why he was so angry—to him it was just another case of me ignoring him for other people. "I didn't want to go and hold Donna's hand in the first place, remember."

"So how did it help Donna for you to go down and lounge by the pool with Bernardo?"

"Are you jealous of Bernardo?" My anger faded even more, because Nathaniel was one of the least jealous people I knew. I glanced at Micah, trying to get some clue as to what was going on. He shrugged and spread his hands, showing either that he didn't know or he didn't want to get dragged into it.

"Maybe I'm jealous of anything that seems more important to you and Micah than I do."

"I know we went to rescue the local guy, Andy, and I'm sorry that interfered with our time together. I'll give you that one, but talking to Bernardo was wedding related."

"And it was so important that it couldn't wait until after we'd had sex?" His voice was rising again, the softness around his mouth vanishing into his anger. I had to fight to keep my hands from turning into fists again, the tension in my shoulders returning.

My voice came out too soft, too controlled, closer to the way I talked when I was angry on the job and didn't want to lose my shit at a suspect. "If I hadn't given Lucy's message to Bernardo, I'd still be waiting to give the message directly to Edward. I hunted down Bernardo so that I could be up here with you now instead of in an hour."

"You know Edward's room number. You could have just told him yourself." Nathaniel's tone was sneering. I'd never heard him like this. Because it was so unlike him, it helped me to be less angry.

"He'd just taken Donna back to the room for makeup sex, and since he'd forgotten to tell her that he was married once before, and she just found out today, the makeup sex is going to have to be fucking spectacular."

"What did you say?" Micah asked.

"Edward was married before and didn't tell Donna?" Nathaniel asked.

"Yeah," I said.

Nathaniel looked shocked. "Jesus, is the wedding canceled?"

"It was, until I talked Donna down."

"Start from the beginning, Anita," Micah said.

"From where Donna dragged you off for the girl talk," Nathaniel said. He wasn't angry now; he looked shaken. Nothing like a real crisis to short-circuit a fight.

I told them everything that had happened, including Dixie's being more convinced than ever that she needed to stop the wedding, and her determination to tell Becca. "Lucy told me to find Bernardo and have him warn Edward, so I could be here with the two of you sooner."

Nathaniel sat down on the edge of the bed and put his hands in his lap, head down and staring at the floor. "I'm sorry I was so terrible when you walked into the room."

I sat on the bed beside him, leaning my head on his shoulder, taking one of his hands in mine. "I forgive you, if you can tell me what it was all about, so I won't step on that particular emotional landmine again."

"I'm not sure, not really."

Micah came to sit down on the other side of him and reached for Nathaniel's other hand, so the three of us sat in a row holding hands. "Before Anita got here, you were talking about our being workaholics, and that you needed more time with us than you were getting."

I sat up straighter, using my free hand to sweep his hair back so I could see the side of his face. "I'm sorry that we're both working so much."

"It's not just that."

"What is it, then?" I asked.

He glanced at me, and then at Micah. He took a deep breath, let it out, and then took another one as if he were getting his breathing under control for something physical. "Even when you're in town we don't always have sex anymore."

"We had great sex just yesterday," I said, and almost laughed.

He gave me an unfriendly look. "We used to have sex twice a day. Now we're lucky if it's once a day." The hurt in his eyes chased the last of the laughter away.

"Oh, Nathaniel," I said, and leaned in to kiss his cheek, "baby, I'm sorry. If I need to say it out loud, I want you. I always want you."

"Then why aren't we having as much sex as we were before?" He looked at me with such sadness in his eyes that it made me kiss him again, but he didn't respond with his usual passion. He looked at me, wanting explanations more than affection at that moment.

Micah said, "I can't speak for Anita, but sometimes I'm exhausted when I come in from a trip. My being tired doesn't mean I don't love you." He kissed Nathaniel's other cheek.

"I know you love me, Micah, but do you want me?"

"Of course I do. How can you ask that?"

"You almost never initiate sex when it's just the two of us. When we were together in Jean-Claude's bathtub was the first time you'd suggested just you and me in months."

Micah looked surprised, started to say something, and then seemed to think better of it. He sat there for a few seconds, hugging Nathaniel with one arm, while he thought about it. "I hadn't realized it had been that long, but I think you're right." He laid his head on Nathaniel's shoulder and hugged him more tightly. "I am so sorry."

"If it's any comfort, it's not just you," I said. "Micah and I aren't doing much better with just the two of us."

Micah raised his head. "It hasn't been months for us."

"No, but we're both tired, and holding each other sometimes seems like the best thing in the world."

Micah reached across to take my hand while he kept his arm around Nathaniel's shoulders, which meant we both had to let go of Nathaniel's hands to hug him and hold each other. "Falling asleep in each other's arms is the best thing ever," Micah said.

"It is great. I love it, too, but I love it most when we fall asleep after having sex," Nathaniel said.

"Well, me, too," I said.

"Am I the only who is having problems getting into the spirit of things?" Micah said.

"After seeing the pictures and knowing what you've been dealing with, I think the case is getting to you," I said.

"There have been some really hard ones the last six months." His face looked sad. His eyes were almost haunted as he stared at the wall, and he wasn't seeing the honeymoon suite. I knew that look. I had my own version of it. Sometimes the nightmares just pile up so high inside your head that you can't stop thinking about them.

"I know some of it," Nathaniel said, "and that's why I haven't been pushing this, but the fact that we've been in Florida for hours and still haven't had sex is just depressing. There was a time when we couldn't get into the bedroom fast enough to get our clothes off and fuck like bunnies."

"We fucked like bunnies this week," Micah said, smiling.

"Every other day, and that was after months of not having sex with you at all, Micah." Nathaniel looked at him.

Micah looked uncomfortable and drew a little away from both of us. "I'm allowed to be tired and stressed from work, Nathaniel."

"You are, but I'm allowed to miss you, miss us together, and to be sad that you find more time to have sex with Anita than with me."

"We discussed this before I said yes. I'm still not completely comfortable with . . . sex with men. I feel bad that there are things that I still don't do for you that you do for me."

Nathaniel took his hand and said, "I know I'm your first-ever boyfriend, and that you never expected to be in love with another man. I know that you're heteroflexible at best, not bisexual like I am. I love that you love me enough to push your boundaries as much as you do, and I told you that because you let me sleep with other men in our polycule, so that I get those needs met elsewhere, that I can live with you not doing certain things with me."

"I am sorry that I'm still not there completely with you."

"If we were monogamous, it wouldn't work, but we're not, so I can get my guy-on-guy needs met. But that you don't reach for me as much as you reach for Anita . . . that hurts."

"I didn't realize it had gotten that bad," Micah said.

"I think it's because you and Anita are out of town and in town opposite each other a lot lately. When she's with us you think of sex more, because there's a woman in the bed, not just another man."

"I can't even deny it. I just hadn't realized it."

"I wasn't going to bring it up on our trip. I thought we'd catch up on all the sex and nefariousness together, but when that didn't happen I just couldn't take it anymore."

"You needed to tell us," I said.

He looked at me. "I know you've worked hard to control

the *ardeur* better, Anita. The fact that you can go more than twenty-four hours without having to feed is great for traveling with the marshals, or going out of town to raise the dead, but I miss you reaching out to me like you did before. Feeding the *ardeur* is such a high."

"I can't feed on the same people every time without risking draining them to death. I don't want to risk either of you."

"And I love that you want to keep us safe, but now that you can go longer between feedings, that means that the *ardeur* isn't pushing us to have as much sex as it was before, and I'm beginning to think the *ardeur* was the reason we had as much sex as we did."

"Probably," I said.

"Passion doesn't stay at the same level all the time," Micah said.

"It does for me," he said.

"I don't think I can do sex twice a day, every day, forever," Micah said.

"I can," Nathaniel said.

Micah smiled gently and touched Nathaniel's face. "I'm sorry, but I'm not as multiorgasmic as you are."

"I'm a girl, so I can have sex twice a day, every day, if the scheduling works."

Nathaniel smiled and kissed me.

"I'll try to do better, but Anita's right—this case has just drained me. I can't seem to get it out of my head, and that is a serious mood killer."

"If Anita releases the *ardeur*, you'll be in the mood."

"I fed on Jean-Claude before we left, so I don't have to feed, but I can feed again if we all agree to it."

"Do you ever get full from the *ardeur*, like having too much chocolate cake?" Micah asked.

I smiled. "There's always room for chocolate cake."

Micah smiled back, his eyes filling with heat that had nothing to do with being a wereanimal and everything to do with being lovers. "Yay, cake," he said, his voice low.

Nathaniel stood up and untied the sash of his robe, proving that he was as naked under the robe as I'd thought. "Eat me."

"Before or after I release the *ardeur*?"

"Yes," he said.

30

MICAH TOOK OFF his robe, too, and the two of them lay down on the bed side by side. They were both strong and fit. Nathaniel lifted more weights, so he had more definition, but Micah was lean enough that what muscle he had showed. He might not lift that much, but he did fight practice more than Nathaniel did. It was like looking at two different male ideals—the fit model and the martial artist. Micah would have argued that he wasn't able to practice as much as some of the guards did, but then, he wasn't a bodyguard. He practiced as much as he did because all wereanimal leaders could be challenged to defend their positions. Sometimes one could choose a champion to fight in his place, but most lycanthrope cultures didn't allow that. I worked out to stay in shape for my job, too, and I was just as likely as Micah was to end up with my physicality being the difference between coming home safe and not coming home at all. We didn't talk about it much because there was no point; it was our reality.

I stood there admiring the view of my two men, and by the time I crawled onto the bed between them their bodies had already started to prove that they were admiring their view of my body, too—or maybe I was being too egocentric, and it was the view of each other's bodies. I didn't care—I loved and desired them both.

"Release the *ardeur*, Anita," Micah said as he helped Nathaniel pull me down between them.

"Before we've done any foreplay?"

He went up on one elbow, so he was looking down at both of us as we lay looking up at him. "If we get to a certain point and then you release the *ardeur*, we'll finish like we always do, and that's fabulous, but I'm willing—no, I want—to try something different."

Nathaniel went up on his elbow on the other side of me so he could look across eye to eye with Micah. "We usually release the *ardeur* when everyone's dick is where they want it for orgasm."

"Which means I'll be in someone's mouth or inside Anita," Micah said.

"I'm okay wherever I end up, and whoever ends up in me," Nathaniel said.

I was left looking from one to the other as they talked over me. I was okay with that; this was more their issue than mine.

"That's not true," Micah said. "I'm too wide even for you to want me to do anal on you."

"But you don't enjoy anal in any way, so unless it's my idea to put you back there, even with the *ardeur* it won't occur to you."

"I'm sorry that neither of us likes anal," I said.

Nathaniel smiled down at me. "I have other people in my life who do, but it does disappoint me."

"I love you, Nathaniel. I love both of you, and I want to be with you both, really be with you both."

"I love you even more for trying, but if we release all our inhibitions this early, I know what I'm going to want to do, and if we don't use lube, then even the *ardeur* can't make that part of the body make its own lubrication, which means it may feel good while we're doing it, but once we sober up from the metaphysics it's going to hurt. I do not want the first time we do anal to be painful."

"All right, then let's put lube in first, just in case."

Nathaniel raised his eyebrows at that. "And how do we do that in a way that you'll enjoy?"

"Get the gloves and the lube and I'll explain."

"I should say *What a wonderful gesture* and talk you out of it," Nathaniel said.

"Why?" Micah asked.

"Because you don't really want to do this, and you're using the *ardeur* as sort of getting drunk to relax into it."

"I love you. We're getting married. I want to try."

Nathaniel looked down at me. "What do you think?"

"I think we either try it or we do something more normal for us, and think on it some more."

He looked back at Micah. "I really appreciate the offer, Micah. I really do. I love you even more for it, but I want the first time to be special, not a drunken orgy."

"I might not ever be able to do it without the *ardeur* helping me lower my inhibitions."

"I know that, but let's work on exploring anal with smaller, gentler things before we go for it, even with the *ardeur*. I love you too much to hurt you. The same goes for you, Anita."

"How did I get into this discussion?"

"You know what they say—everyone has an asshole."

I laughed, because I couldn't think what else to do. "I already have an opening that works just fine for both of you."

"We'll discuss it later," he said, smiling.

"We will, will we?"

He nodded, grinning.

"Well, I don't know about that, but I do know that I want one of you to go down on me, and I want to have both of you in my mouth at least once, and I want you inside me."

"We can do that," Micah said.

31

MICAH PUT ME across his face, so I could look down my body and see his eyes looking up at me as he licked and sucked between my legs. We'd put his hair back in a ponytail to help keep it out of the way. My hands held on to the headboard, because I couldn't reach anyone else to hold on to. Nathaniel was behind me going down on Micah. I prided myself on having control of my gag reflex for deep throating, but Nathaniel didn't have a gag reflex at all. The only challenge for him with Micah was the width, and even there his mouth was bigger than mine. I looked over my shoulder to try to watch a little of it, but Micah did something with his tongue that made me gasp and turn back to staring down into his chartreuse eyes.

I felt his body shudder and I knew that something that Nathaniel was doing behind me was bringing him close. It almost distracted me from Micah's mouth between my legs, but he was too good at it for me to be distracted for long. He sucked on that sweet spot and I felt that warm weight between my legs growing heavier, and from one movement of his mouth to the next he drew me over the edge and brought me to screaming. I clawed at the headboard and yelled wordlessly, head thrown back. His tongue and mouth kept going until I was trying to find my words to tell him *Enough*, but I felt his body shudder again, and this time it made his mouth hesitate, lose its rhythm, and I looked down to see his eyes flutter closed, and watched them lose focus, felt his body go from straining to limp, and I knew that Nathaniel had brought him to orgasm, as Micah had brought me.

Nathaniel was suddenly kneeling behind me, his voice growling in my ear. "You didn't release the *ardeur.*"

I managed to shake my head. I was still trying to recover from the afterglow of the orgasm.

He put his lips near my face, so his breath was hot against my skin. "I want you to release it when I'm fucking you."

I nodded, still having trouble talking.

Nathaniel lifted me off Micah and half carried, half dragged me down the bed and put me on all fours so that my knees were between Micah's legs, my arms on either side of his hips. I was suddenly staring down at his groin; his body wasn't completely hard anymore, but he still wasn't small.

I felt Nathaniel pushing himself against my opening. "God, you are so wet. I'm going to fuck you while you lick Micah."

Micah managed to say, "Too sensitive."

"I know," Nathaniel said. "That's why I want her to do it. You were willing to let me fuck you in the ass. I think you'll enjoy this more."

I might have protested, but he grabbed my hair, just tight enough to click that internal switch over so that I wanted to do what he wanted. He pushed himself inside me, and just having him inside me when I was so wet and so sensitive from the oral made me cry out. Nathaniel found a rhythm, pushing himself in and out, sliding over that one spot inside as if he could feel exactly where it was. He used my hair to push my head down toward Micah as he slid himself in and out of me. I licked Micah and found that he was harder than he had been just seconds before. He was enjoying watching us together.

Nathaniel started moving faster in and out of me. I felt the thick, heavy weight of pleasure start to build inside me. "I'm going to fuck you hard, Anita, and I want you to suck Micah's dick until I tell you to stop and then release the *ardeur* and feed on me. Do you understand me?"

I managed to say, "Yes."

"Then put your hand around Micah's cock and suck it, while I fuck you."

I did what he asked, because in that moment it all seemed like such a good idea. Micah filled my mouth and more, but I didn't have to deep throat him; he was too sensitive for that now, anyway. I could stay higher up on all that thick hardness and make small noises around him, as Nathaniel fucked me hard and fast, so that I screamed around Micah's body, which made him cry out, "God!"

Nathaniel brought me screaming, with Micah's body like a living gag to soften the noises. "Stop sucking him." I did what he wanted, letting go of Micah as Nathaniel used my hair to raise my body back up to all fours as he fucked me as hard and fast as he could, and brought me again to orgasm, screaming without Micah's body to muffle the noises.

"The *ardeur*, Anita—now, now!" His voice was strained as he fought his body to hold on one more minute, while I unleashed that part of me that could feed on what he was about to do. The power washed over both of us and it, or Nathaniel, or both, brought me another climax, as Nathaniel thrust inside me one more time. I felt his body convulse, felt him pulsing inside me, and I fed on the feel of him pushed as deep inside me as he could, fed on the strength of his hand in my hair, his other hand on my shoulder, fingers digging in as he spilled himself inside me and I drank him down everywhere his body touched me.

He called out my name and then he half collapsed across my back and let go of my hair. "God, I love you," he whispered.

"I love you, too," I said in a voice gone hoarse with screaming.

"I love you both so much," Micah said from the bed just underneath us.

My knees gave out and I collapsed on top of him, with Nathaniel on top of me. Micah laughed, and petted our hair while we waited to be able to move again. We'd clean up and then we'd be able to sleep in a sexy cuddle pile just the way Nathaniel had wanted.

32

WE WOKE STILL spooned together in a warm nest of sheets and bodies. It felt so good that I just lay there listening to them breathe, feeling the rise and fall of their bodies against mine. Nathaniel was still deeply asleep, but Micah moved restlessly. If I wasn't careful I'd wake him on one of the few mornings that we could all sleep in together. I slowed my breathing down, deepened it, and did my best to pretend to sleep while my eyes were still open, so I could see the line of sunlight from the crack in the drapes. We'd have to remember to close them better tonight, but this morning I liked watching the light play in Micah's curls and along his naked back. If I could have figured out a way to turn over and see the light on Nathaniel, I would have, but I knew that would wake Micah.

I lay sandwiched between them, listening to their breathing, feeling the beat and pulse of their sleeping bodies. I memorized the feel of it all, so that later it could be one of my happy thoughts. I was kissing the back of Micah's neck and waking us all up with more cuddling and maybe more sex, when there was a knock at the door so loud and authoritative that I knew it was a cop, or someone who had been a cop of some kind. They all had that loud, resounding knock that made your heart beat faster and your pulse jump to your throat for a second, even if you were innocent. The sound alone was sort of scary.

"What is that?" Nathaniel said, raising his head but hugging us tighter to him.

"I don't know—maybe someone complained about the noise," I said as I tried to get up.

"You are a screamer," he said, but he was still holding me tight, his heart thudding against my back.

"The complaint should have come in last night, not this morning," Micah said, lying very still in the bed, as if he were listening harder than I could. He was a wereanimal, so his hearing was better than mine.

I had to tell Nathaniel to let me go so I could check the door. I put on one of the robes that we'd used last night after we cleaned up. I tossed the other one to Micah in the bed. We were both more modest than Nathaniel. I belted the robe tight and put my Sig Sauer .380 in the right-hand pocket, got my badge in its little wallet cover out of the drawer beside the bed, and went for the door. I was pretty sure it was the police, and if I was answering the door armed, I wanted my badge with me.

I glanced back to find Micah standing by the bed with his robe tightened in place. Nathaniel was still in the bed with the sheets covering him.

The knock sounded again. I called out, "I'm coming. I'm coming." I let myself sound as cranky as I felt about the interruption. A man's voice said, "Kirke Key Police. Open the door!"

I couldn't think what we'd done to earn an early morning wake-up call from the local police. I checked the peephole just in case, but it was a uniformed officer at my door. Edward had even sent me a text of the local uniforms in the area before I got on the plane. I'm not sure I would have thought of it, but it was Edward: He pretty much thought of everything when it came to the job. It was the right uniform.

I opened the door enough to see and be seen, but not like I was inviting him in to visit. Just because we were both cops didn't automatically make us buddies. Besides, I didn't really want him to see the men tucked into the room behind me if I could avoid it.

"Can we come in for a minute and look around?" the tall officer asked.

"What's this about, Officer"—I read his name tag—"Dunley?" I asked.

"Are you alone in the room?"

"No, I've got friends with me."

"We need to speak with your friends," he said.

I flashed my badge. "Marshal Anita Blake."

His eyes widened. He hadn't expected to find another cop of any flavor in the room. He got control of his expression and said, "Still need to speak with your friends and anyone else in the room, Marshal."

"Why? What's the problem, Officer?" I said.

"Reports of a woman screaming last night," he said.

"Sorry about that. I guess we got louder than I thought."

"Were you fighting with your friends?"

"No, we were having sex." I could have lied, but why? Once he got inside the room and saw the men, especially Nathaniel in the bed, what else could it be?

But the truth threw Dunley for a second. He looked at me, frowned, almost smiled, got control of his face, and said, "Well then, you won't mind me seeing your friends and getting their side of things."

"And if I do mind?"

"The more you don't want me in the room, the more I want inside. If you're on the job, then you know what I mean." *If* I was on the job, he'd said. I looked at him a little harder. He was taller than me, no big surprise; he had more weight around his middle than was probably good for him, like the beginnings of the gut that Rufous had on him. The weight drew the eye down to his duty belt, where it strained at his waist, so you might underestimate his height and the rest of him, but I had to look a long way up to meet his brown eyes, which put him over six feet. He had to be at least six-three, and the biceps that bulged at the short sleeve of his uniform shirt showed that underneath the recent weight gain there was still plenty of muscle. His brown eyes weren't unfriendly, but they did that narrow cop thing, and then a dark eyebrow arched. Apparently, I wasn't meeting his idea of cop perfection either.

"I really need to see your friends and anyone else in the room, Marshal."

"It's two friends and me, but sure. Why not?" I opened the door and ushered him into the room. He stopped at the bedroom door. I glanced toward the bed and found Nathaniel sitting up with the sheets in his lap, smiling at the officer as if he were about to be introduced to him on the street, somewhere nice and not embarrassing. Micah stood beside the bed, trying to look relaxed and failing. He'd have been happier with clothes on. Me, too.

"And your names are?"

"Micah Callahan."

"Nathaniel Graison." Nathaniel smiled, trying to be pleasant.

"Did you participate in a swim race at the pool here yesterday?"

I hadn't expected that question. It wasn't just a noise complaint question. Nathaniel's smile faded a little around the edges. "I did."

Dunley looked at me then, and I realized that he'd kept the door open behind him. There were hotel employees hovering in the hallway. "Marshal Black, was it?"

"Blake," I said. So much for me being well-known in police circles.

"Well, Marshal Blake, did you have an argument with another woman down by the pool?"

I shook my head.

"You didn't fight with another woman about her paying too much attention to Mr. Graison here and another gentleman?"

"It wasn't an argument, but I did have to explain to a couple of women that Nathaniel wasn't free to follow up on any perceived flirting."

"Did you also feel that you had to explain that one Bernardo Spotted-Horse, also a marshal as it turns out, was also unable to carry through on his flirting?"

I smiled. "No, I just needed to discuss some wedding details with him that I didn't want half the beautiful women in the hotel to overhear, so I asked for some privacy."

"And it's just a coincidence that the same woman was involved in both altercations?"

"It wasn't an altercation or a fight or anything like that. I gave my message to Bernardo and left him to carry on with his flirting, or whatever."

"How did it make you feel knowing that Mr. Spotted-Horse was going to have sex with a woman you'd already fought with over Graison here, earlier today?"

I frowned at him, feeling like I was missing something important. "Bernardo is just a work friend and fellow wedding member; that's it. He and I have never been an item. He can sleep with anyone he wants."

"If you've never been an item with Mr. Spotted-Horse, then why did you get angry at him interacting with other women?"

"I told you before, I wasn't angry about anything. I just needed to tell him something about the wedding."

"And what did you want to tell him that was so private?"

"Something private," I said, because I was so not going to tell the local cops about the supposed affair. No way.

"Funny, that's what Spotted-Horse said, too. I'd really like to know what wedding detail could be so top secret that you couldn't say it in front of other people."

I shrugged, because nothing I could say would help, and if he kept me talking I might give him a hint. I did not want to do that. Besides, if he thought I was arguing with other women about Nathaniel and Bernardo, his thinking I was having an affair with the groom would just confirm that I was pathological about men.

"Why are you asking us all this?" Micah asked, still standing by the bed.

"Did you sleep with Ms. Bettina Gonzales, Mr. Graison?"

"No, I've been with friends since I left the pool yesterday."

"We'll need the names of those friends." He actually got a small notebook out of his pocket and started riffling through the pages. I didn't know that anyone still used notebooks like that.

"Micah was with me the whole time."

"And what is your relationship to him?"

"He's my fiancé."

Dunley raised eyebrows and looked at Micah. "Is that right, Mr. Callahan? Are you and Mr. Graison engaged?"

Micah nodded. "Yes."

Dunley turned to me with his notebook and pen in hand. "Someone told me that Mr. Graison was your fiancé, Marshal Blake."

"He is."

Dunley looked at me and then back at Nathaniel and Micah and then back at me. "How does that work, Blake? Bigamy is still illegal."

"Marrying more than one person is illegal, but there's no

rule against being engaged to more than one person, as long
as everyone knows about everyone."

Dunley frowned, staring down at his notebook as if he
wasn't sure that what he'd written made sense. "So you're all
engaged together?"

"Yes."

"All the news says that you're engaged to the master vampire of St. Louis, this Jean-Claude."

His asking that meant he'd known exactly who I was before
he ever knocked on the door. "I am," I said.

"So are any of you actually going to be marrying each
other?"

"I'm not sure what that has to do with anything, but I'm
going to be marrying Jean-Claude, because as you said, we
can only legally marry one person at a time."

"And you, Mr. Graison, who are you marrying?"

"Micah and I are planning a wedding," Nathaniel said. He
was watching the police officer's face now. He was still trying
to look pleasant, but I knew his eyes and they showed that he
was thinking hard, trying to figure things out. What the hell
was going on?

"So, Blake, you're planning to marry someone that isn't
here this weekend, but you're engaged to the two gentlemen
here, and you're sleeping with Mr. Spotted-Horse and Mr. Wyatt Erwin." Knowing Ru's name meant he had probably talked
to the others first.

"I told you I'm not sleeping with Bernardo, and since you
brought it up, I'm not sleeping with Wyatt either."

"You're not sleeping with either Spotted-Horse or Erwin."

"No," I said.

"And yet you got into a fight with another woman over both
the men you're not sleeping with, plus a fight over Graison
here."

"I told you, I didn't fight with anyone, over anyone."

He looked back to the two men at the bed. "But you are
sleeping with these two gentlemen?"

"Yes," I said.

"And all the men are okay with you sleeping with all the
other men?"

"We share really well," Nathaniel said, drawing his knees

up to his bare chest and trying for winsome, but mostly hitting lascivious, or maybe that was just how he made me feel. Was he trying to distract Dunley, or just tired of the questions?

"Mr. Graison, are you sleeping with Mr. Callahan?" Dunley asked.

"I am." Nathaniel smiled as he said it.

"What about Mr. Spotted-Horse?"

"No."

"Mr. Erwin?"

"Nope."

"And you, Mr. Callahan, who else are you sleeping with?"

"Why the twenty questions, Officer Dunley?" I said.

"Just trying to get a sense of what happened, Marshal Blake."

"What has happened, Officer Dunley?"

"What do you think has happened?"

"Oh, for the love of God, Dunley, just tell us what's happened."

"So you're lovers with Callahan, Graison, Spotted-Horse, and Erwin?"

"I'm just work friends with Spotted-Horse, as I keep telling you. Erwin is just a friend and employee."

"According to witnesses, you were in a passionate embrace with him at the pool yesterday."

"I really can't explain what happened with Wyatt by the pool, or if I can, I don't owe the explanation to you."

"Well, I'll make a note that you don't want to be helpful in this investigation."

"What investigation?" I asked. Something bad had happened, and whatever it was had probably happened to Bettina, last name Gonzales. I wondered if Bernardo had even known her last name before they had sex. I doubted it, but maybe last names weren't that important for a one-night stand.

"Are you sleeping with anyone else in the wedding party, Marshal Blake?"

"No."

Dunley nodded and made another note. "How many other men here in town are you sleeping with that aren't in the wedding, Marshal?"

I debated whether I should answer at all, or if it mattered

that the police knew about Nicky and me. "And if I was sleeping with anyone else in town, why would that matter?"

Dunley had to look back through his notes and made enough of a big deal out of it that I wasn't sure if he really needed to check his notes, if it was something he did to give himself time to think, or if it was supposed to mess with our nerves. If it was the latter, he could have saved the act.

"So the three of you are all lovers, all engaged to each other; is that it, Ms. Blake?"

"It's Marshal Blake, and yes."

"You don't seem to care if I call Marshal Spotted-Horse mister."

"He's not here to feel insulted. I am."

"You're standing here in a robe in a hotel room with a naked man in your bed, and a second man in a matching robe, and I'm insulting you by calling you Ms. Blake as opposed to Marshal Blake; really?"

"Are you implying that a woman who has multiple lovers is such a slut that she can't be insulted, Officer Dunley?"

He looked at me and thought it through; then he glanced back at the still-open door. Another officer had shooed away the civilians sometime during it all, but still Dunley didn't want to get accused of some kind of sexual insensitivity, not unless he could prove it was all part of his clever questioning technique.

"I would never use that word, Marshal Blake."

"Good to know, but it is what you think of a woman who would sleep with multiple men, isn't it, Officer Dunley?"

"Absolutely not, Marshal Blake."

"Really. I could have sworn that you implied that rather strongly just now, Officer Dunley."

"I most certainly did not."

"Then what are you implying, Officer Dunley, and why do you have this intense curiosity about our personal lives?"

"Just trying to get an understanding of what might have happened between you and Bettina Gonzales."

"Nothing happened between us, Officer Dunley."

"That's not what her friends say."

"I can't help what other people say, Officer Dunley."

"Don't you want to know what her friends said happened between the two of you?"

"You've already told me what they said."

"No, Marshal, I did not."

"Yes, you did," Micah said from the bed.

Dunley frowned for a second and then recovered with a smile that I think was supposed to be disarming but wasn't in the least. He was questioning us like we were suspects or at least persons of interest. Something bad had happened to Bettina. She wasn't my favorite person, but she didn't deserve whatever would make the police question people like this.

"What's happened to Bettina—Ms. Gonzales?" I asked.

"You tell me."

"I would if I could, but I left her by the pool with the rest of Bernardo's harem of possibilities."

"So it doesn't bother you that Spotted-Horse fucked Ms. Gonzales?"

He'd used the word on purpose, hoping to shock me. "I think it's probably bad judgment on his part, but other than that, no."

"Why is it bad judgment on his part?"

"Bettina seemed a little high-strung and definitely possessive after a very short amount of time."

"What do you mean a little high-strung?"

"She took insult really easily, even where none was intended."

"Her friends say that you fought with her."

"They're wrong."

"They say things got heated between the two of you after you tried to kiss her, and she rebuffed your advances."

I laughed before I could stop myself. "*Rebuffed your advances.* I haven't heard that one in a long time, but trust me, I did not try to kiss Bettina."

"Several witnesses say differently."

"I may have implied that I'd kiss her to make her leave Wyatt alone."

"Why would that make her leave him alone?"

"She was homophobic, and letting her think that Wyatt and I were angling for a three-way made her retire from the field."

"*Retire from the field.* Now who's using old-fashioned terms?"

"Sorry, you're right. Let me just say that using her homophobia against her was a way to avoid a fight, though it was totally Wyatt's fault for flirting that hard when he didn't mean it."

"I'm sorry, Anita, honestly; it was just so much fun to flirt with all of them. We got carried away," Nathaniel said.

"How carried away did you and Bettina get, Mr. Graison?"

"I meant Wyatt and myself. We were both flirting with the bridesmaids from other weddings and we may have gotten carried away."

"How far did you get carried? What plans did you or Mr. Erwin make with Bettina Gonzales?"

"None."

"I find that hard to believe, Mr. Graison. Were you jealous when she slept with Mr. Spotted-Horse?"

"I didn't know she slept with him until you told us a few minutes ago, but no, it doesn't make me jealous. I had no intention of actually sleeping with any of the women by the pool."

"Then why flirt with them?"

"It was fun."

"Was it fun when you arranged to meet with Ms. Gonzales later?"

"No. I mean, I didn't arrange anything with her."

"How angry were you when she chose Spotted-Horse over you?"

"If you want to look at it that way, I chose Anita over Bettina, so it's Bettina that should have been pissed, not any of us."

"How far would you have gone to make sure Mr. Graison there chose you over Bettina?"

"I don't have to go far. He's my fiancé; he's already chosen me."

Dunley had to look at his notes again, but this time I was pretty certain he was giving himself time to think. "But you have no idea where Mr. Erwin was last night."

"I'm sure his sister can vouch for them since they were sharing a room," I said.

Micah said, "What has happened to Bettina Gonzales?"

"I didn't say anything had happened to her."

"Stop the game playing, Dunley," I said. "Obviously something has happened to her, or you wouldn't be here asking twenty bajillion leading questions about the day's events."

He smiled before he could stop himself as he said, "I don't think I've hit a bajillion yet."

"It feels like it," Nathaniel said.

"Oh, this is nothing, Mr. Graison. You should see a real interrogation. Now, that may be a bajillion questions by the time everything's said and done."

"This isn't an interrogation, Dunley, and you and I both know it."

"Do you want it to be an interrogation, Blake?"

"No. Do you have enough to bring any of us in for one?"

Dunley gave me the hard cop-eye stare, but it wasn't his serious best, so I didn't flinch. "Not yet."

"You're fishing, talking to anyone who saw her."

"What's happened to her?" Micah asked again, voice more impatient.

"When's the last time you saw Bettina Gonzales?"

"We told you, by the pool before we came upstairs," Nathaniel said.

"I told you, by the pool with Bernardo and his bevy of beauties," I said.

"Spotted-Horse is lucky that her friends came and picked her up at his hotel room door. If we didn't have witnesses that said she'd left his room happy and healthy, we'd have him in a room answering questions right now."

"Why?" I asked.

"Bettina Gonzales is missing." He'd telegraphed it so hard, it wasn't a surprise to any of us.

"I thought you had to be missing twenty-four hours before the police would look for you," Micah said.

"Normally, or even forty-eight hours," I said.

"Neither of you seems surprised she's missing," Dunley said.

"You telegraphed it pretty hard," I said.

"Sorry, but if that was you being subtle, it didn't work," Nathaniel said.

"Why are you looking for her so soon?" I asked. "Please tell me you didn't find anything like blood, or . . . things."

"Like what things?"

"I work with the preternatural branch of the Marshals Service, Officer Dunley. That means I see some really horrible things as part of my job. I can think of a whole bunch of stuff that I hope you haven't found in connection to Bettina Gonzales."

"Why would you care that much about a woman you fought with twice and had to chase away from your man—sorry, men."

"Look, we didn't fight, and I don't chase anyone away from my men. If they're my men, as in my lovers, then I don't have to defend my territory, because they're happy to be with me. Bettina didn't strike me as someone I wanted to become bosom buddies with, but there didn't seem to be any harm in her. I hate the thought of her family and friends here to celebrate a marriage and now they're searching for one of their loved ones. I've seen enough awful things in this world. I really just wanted to enjoy Ted and Donna finally tying the knot and enjoy being in the Florida Keys for the first time ever."

Dunley studied my face as if trying to read more in my eyes than there was to read. He looked at Nathaniel and asked, "Do you have any idea what might have happened to Ms. Gonzales?"

"No, but if I did, I would tell you."

"Did she talk to any other men, flirt with any others?"

"Not that I saw."

"Me either," I said.

"Mr. Callahan, do you have any idea what might have happened to Ms. Gonzales?"

"No."

"Can you think of anything else that might help us locate her?"

We all shook our heads. "We'd help if we could, Dunley."

"I want to believe you, Blake."

"I want you to believe me, because it's the truth."

"Come on, Blake. You're on the job. You know the rule."

"Everyone lies," I said.

He nodded. "Even U.S. Marshals," he said.

"We're Feds. You local guys think we have horns and tails hidden under our clothes."

He looked at me, and this time he let his eyes go up and down. I realized that the front of the robe had gaped a little so that he'd gotten to see more of my breasts than I'd wanted to share. Damn it. I glared at him, as defiant as I could make it, because bold, self-righteous anger was the only defense I had against the embarrassment that was trying to make me blush. I finally lost the battle and closed the robe a little bit more, holding it in place this time.

"How can someone with this many lovers blush?" Dunley asked.

"Anita is a delicate fucking flower," Nathaniel said.

I glared at him as I tried not to blush even harder.

He smiled at me. "I love that you still blush."

"I'm amazed you still blush," Dunley said.

"Get out of our room," I said.

"That doesn't sound like you want to help us find the woman."

"We'll help all we can, but right now we've given you all the information we have."

He held out a business card to me and gave me two extra ones so that he didn't have to walk to the bed and give them to the men directly. Maybe he was more bothered by the almost naked men in the room than he'd let on.

"If you think of anything that will help us in our investigation, call."

"We'll do that."

"Enjoy the rest of your day, Marshal Blake."

"We'll do that, Officer Dunley."

He left. I shut and locked the door behind him and said, "Well, fuck."

So much for a leisurely room service breakfast and more sex. I was pretty sure the mood was ruined for all of us.

33

"HOW COULD YOU get involved in a case on our wedding trip?" Donna asked all of us later, as if we'd planned the whole thing. And by *us*, I mean everyone who got questioned by the police and knew both the lie and the truth about the supposed affair.

We were in a conference room in the hotel. We were supposed to be double-checking if we liked the room for the rehearsal dinner; instead we were on the verge of another argument.

"Now, honeybunch," Edward started in his best Ted voice.

"Don't you honeybunch me, Theodore Magnus Forrester! You promised no crime-fighting on this trip. You gave me your word!"

"Magnus?" I said, smiling.

That stopped Donna's rant long enough for her to turn to me, frowning. "You didn't know his middle name?"

"Nope."

"How can you share information about you and your life so differently between us?" she said, turning back to Edward.

"According to you and your therapist, the fact that I share different parts of my life with both of you is the entire point of me living with you and working with Anita." His voice had dropped down into that low, middle-of-nowhere accent that was Edward. He didn't even fight to keep Ted's smiling eyes and pleasant expression going; he just looked at her. I knew he loved her to pieces, but in that moment I realized it was possible for her to wear him down enough that down the road it might not be her who called the relationship quits. He'd marry her and it would work for years to come, but that one look said he was already tired of some of her shit, and she was certainly telling everyone around us that she was tired of his.

Donna nodded and said, "That's true, but . . . I'll never understand it."

"And I'll never understand why you had to tell Dixie about Anita and me in the first place. If you hadn't shared the lie with her, then she wouldn't be trying to tell Becca."

"I thought it was the truth, and we are not changing topics yet." She actually walked up to him with her finger pointing at his face like he was five and she was scolding him. "You promised me no police stuff on this trip."

"Ted didn't plan on one of the other hotel guests going missing," Micah said.

She turned on him as if trying to find a reason to scold him, too. He just stood there, smiling softly, his hair still loose around his face. He'd left it down because he knew how much Nathaniel and I both loved it. Maybe he was also seeing if he could distract Donna for a minute. I hadn't tagged her as a long-hair fan, but a pretty man is a pretty man. Or maybe she just couldn't find anything to yell at him about, and that was probably exactly why he'd spoken up.

She turned to Bernardo, as if Micah hadn't said anything. She wanted a fight and she was going to have it. "And you—if you could keep it in your pants, the police wouldn't be questioning all of us."

Bernardo actually took a step back from her shaking finger. "Hey, I'm in the clear. Her friends can testify to the fact she left my room happy and healthy."

Donna gave him a look of such scorn that he started looking guilty. I hadn't been sure he could feel that where women were concerned. "You wouldn't need an alibi for the girl's disappearance if you hadn't fucked her."

I think Donna had cussed more on this trip than I'd ever heard her. The shock was beginning to wear off.

"I'm not the one getting married to you, so who I fuck is none of your business."

"How dare you talk to me like that?" She turned to Edward. "Are you going to let him talk to me like that?"

"You yelled at him first," Edward said in a voice that was

cold and even, and very not the Ted she thought she was marrying.

"So you're taking his side against me?"

He gave her as cold a look as I'd ever seen him give her and said, "No, Donna, I'm taking mine."

"What does that mean?" she said, and she was still angry, but there was an uncertainty to her voice now. Maybe he'd never aimed this much of the real Edward at her before.

"It means that this isn't one of our cases. We did not seek this out or bring this to our door. You, on the other hand, told Dixie our secret. The secret that you made me swear not to tell to any of my groomsmen. You said that it would be humiliating and that they wouldn't understand the arrangement we all had. I kept my word, but you told one of your bridesmaids. Why? Why did you do it, when you'd expressly forbidden me from doing the exact same thing?"

She actually started to blush, but her words were still angry and strong. "How can you compare the disappearance of a young woman to me telling what I thought was the truth to one of my oldest and closest friends?"

Edward stared up at her from the chair that he was sitting in, and I watched his anger slide through his eyes. I'd never seen him this kind of angry with her. "Why, Donna? Why tell anyone?"

"I . . . I needed to tell someone. I needed a friend to talk to about it."

"Why?"

She turned to me, because she was one of those women who didn't like being the only woman in a group, but it just seemed weird that she kept turning to me since I was the other woman. "I just needed to be able to talk about it with another woman that isn't my therapist. You understand that, right, Anita?"

I looked at her, trying to figure out what to say that wouldn't make things worse.

Nathaniel tried to help, stepping in and taking my hand in his, which made her look at him. "Anita's not like that, Donna. She doesn't feel that compulsion to talk about everything with her girlfriends."

"Well, I do," she said, and she reached out toward Edward

in his chair. "I didn't know that it would affect how Dixie felt about you and Anita. I swore her to secrecy. She promised she wouldn't tell anyone. I even told her that I just needed one friend to know the whole truth, so I could vent from time to time."

"So she broke her word of honor to you," Edward said.

"Yes, and I never thought she'd obsess about it like this."

"She's still threatening to tell Becca," he said in a voice so cold and so full of icy anger that I didn't blame Donna for flinching. It was a shame the make-up sex had been wasted on the news about Dixie and her threat.

"I talked to her about that, Ted. She says she won't tell Becca."

"Did she give you her word of honor that she won't tell Becca?" Edward asked, still in that cold, angry tone.

"Yes, she swore to me, promised me."

"The same way she promised she wouldn't talk to anyone else about your secret?" he asked. His eyes were that pale, winter blue now; it was almost a gray. It was the color his eyes went when he was being Edward the assassin. Edward the cold-blooded sociopathic killer had eyes the color of winter skies.

Donna went pale. "Don't look at me like that, Ted, please." That meant that she'd seen the look on his face before, but never aimed at her. It also meant she had some idea what that look in his eyes meant. I almost felt sorry for her, but she had brought it on herself.

"If Dixie tells our daughter, it could change how she sees me forever, Donna. I won't be Daddy anymore; I'll be the lying bastard that's cheating on her mommy."

Donna started to tremble, and then her eyes filled up, and I knew it was only a matter of time before the tears started. I did not want to stand here and watch her cry. I did not want to be part of this fight. Apparently, I wasn't the only one, because Micah said, "We'll give the two of you some privacy to talk this out." He touched both Nathaniel and me on the shoulder and started ushering us toward the door. Nicky, Bram, Ru, and Rodina were by the door, trying to be bodyguards and not get dragged into anything. Bernardo followed us toward the door. We were all wanting out of the fight, but sometimes no matter how hard you try, you can't get out of it.

"And Anita won't be Aunt Anita anymore. She'll be the lying bitch that's betraying her mommy by sleeping with her daddy. Is that what you want Becca to think about both of us?"

The huddled group of us froze. Nicky had his hand on the doorknob. Damn it! "Please, Ted, don't drag me further into this than I already am."

"Do you want to lose Becca as your niece?" he asked, still in that cold voice.

"No, of course I don't." I stayed looking at the door, though. I wasn't turning around and losing the few steps of freedom I'd gained if I could hold on to them.

"I didn't mean . . ." Donna's voice shook, and I didn't have to turn around to know she was crying. "I didn't want to damage anyone's relationship with Becca. She's recovered so well from what happened, and she loves you so much."

"You have to think things through, Donna, especially where the kids are concerned."

"I always think about the kids first." That was less tearful and angrier again.

"Do you, or do you think about your feelings first? Because that's the only reason you told Dixie—so you would feel better."

"I thought we all worked through the mess with Dixie," Nathaniel said.

I wanted to grab him and say, *Don't*, but I guess he was invested in the wedding further than the rest of us.

Edward answered, "We've been having to hide Becca from Dixie. I don't see how she can be in the wedding."

"And now you're involved—you're all involved—in a police investigation on our wedding trip," Donna said.

I don't know what would have happened next, but we heard Peter yelling and a woman's voice raised. Nathaniel opened the door and led the way out. In that second, I think all of us preferred whatever fight was in front of us to the one in back of us.

34

PETER WAS CARRYING a screaming and struggling Dixie across his shoulders in a fireman's carry. She was wearing a one-piece bathing suit and looked to be still wet from the pool. He was wearing baggy swim trunks and a soaking-wet over-size blue T-shirt. He had her arms and one leg pinned, but her other leg was kicking out wildly. She was also yelling, "Put me down, you son of a bitch! How dare you! I used to babysit your ass!"

I knew Peter was better at hand-to-hand fighting than Donna was. If all he'd wanted to do was to take Dixie to the ground like Donna had done in New Mexico, he'd have been efficient and quick. But unless he wanted to hurt Dixie, or had zip ties or restraints of some kind, it was hard as hell to make someone go with you if they really didn't want to. He'd also been socialized not to hit a girl, but the girl had no problem hitting him.

Lucy was behind them in a flowing swimsuit cover-up. Her gray hair was still dry, so apparently she hadn't even had time to get in the pool before whatever the current crisis was had struck.

"What the hell is going on?" I asked.

Peter said something, but Dixie was yelling so much that I couldn't understand it.

I realized that part of the problem was that Donna was yelling at Edward in the room behind us, so that we were getting a double dose of yelling women. Edward's voice was a low, angry rumble; he was holding on to his control and his temper. Donna seemed to feel that all bets were off, because she was cursing like a sailor.

It was Wyatt who leaned in and told me, "Peter said he doesn't know how to put her down without hurting one of them again."

I wasn't really sure what Peter meant about getting hurt again, but I looked at Peter and the woman across his shoulders and did some quick physical math. "We're too short to make a smooth transfer," I said.

"I'm not," Nicky said, "but I'm working."

"We'll cover for you," Rodina said.

Nicky looked at Bram. "Let's help the kid."

Bram shook his head. "I'm working. Nothing takes precedence over that."

Bernardo came over to us. "I'm not on the job."

"Let's do it," Nicky said.

They moved toward the struggling pair. Peter's lips moved again, but I still couldn't hear him. Nathaniel leaned in and said, "Peter said be careful, she bites and scratches."

"Look at Peter's right hand," Micah said.

I looked and there were bloody nail marks in Peter's hand, where he was still fighting to keep the leg from kicking along with the other leg that he hadn't managed to pin. I saw the bloody marks on his thigh about the time that Nathaniel said, "Jesus, look at his thigh."

"I didn't know Dixie had that kind of fight in her."

The men shook their heads in agreement.

Bernardo grabbed the one leg that Peter hadn't managed to pin. Dixie started to scream louder, which I hadn't thought possible. "Let go of me! Help me! Someone help me!" But no matter what words she was using, she didn't sound scared; she sounded pissed.

Nicky wrapped his hands over the one hand that Peter was using to pin her wrists. Bernardo got both her ankles in his hands. They said something to Peter, or to each other, but all I could hear was Dixie calling them sons of bitches and to let her go. I'd underestimated Dixie; she was hell on wheels when she finally got going. It was going to take all three men to get her off of Peter's shoulders and to the floor without hurting her or letting her hurt any of them. If they'd been willing to hurt her, it would have been easier, a lot easier. She certainly hadn't minded hurting Peter. I wondered where she'd bitten him.

Bernardo and Nicky held and lifted as Peter did a sort of overhead press with the main part of Dixie's body. All that weight lifting paid off, because her body weight didn't seem to be hard for him. What was hard was that the "weight" was wiggling and struggling as hard as it could. He didn't exactly drop her, but he wasn't able to hold on to her past a certain point, and Bernardo and Nicky suddenly had all of Dixie's body weight just at the ankles and wrists. They didn't drop her, but she probably thought they were going to, because she stopped struggling as hard but gave a nice blood-curdling scream. If hotel security hadn't been alerted before, someone was sure as hell going to call now. Great.

They laid Dixie's body on the floor but didn't let go of her. Bernardo pinned her legs between his arms and body, which cut down on a lot of the squirming. Nicky was having more issues with her arms, because when he tried to change his grip, he got closer to her face and she snapped at him like a dog. Fuck.

The noise brought Edward and Donna out of the far room, so they were with us when Rodina joined Nicky and took one wrist and arm. Dixie went wild as they pinned her more securely to the floor. She kept trying to bite something or drive her nails into someone. It was like she didn't know where she was, or didn't care.

Peter went to his mother and said, "She's your friend, Mom. Tell her we'll let her go if she stops trying to hurt us."

Donna went forward reluctantly, as if she were a little afraid of the struggling woman, too. I didn't blame her. I was pretty sure that Dixie would hurt any flesh she could reach. She seemed like she'd gone a little crazy. I wasn't sure Donna would be able to calm her down. It looked like a kind of violent hysteria.

Donna bent over so that she could be sure that the other woman could see her, but Dixie didn't stop struggling or screaming. Donna yelled her name until the struggling slowed down, and then she told the other woman, "If you stop struggling, they'll let you go. Do you understand that, Dixie? If you stop trying to hurt them, they'll just let you go."

The woman on the floor stopped moving and just lay staring up at Donna.

"I think you can let her go," Donna said.

Edward said, "Don't let go of her until she says something coherent to Donna."

Donna started to protest that, but Peter stepped into her line of sight again and pulled his T-shirt down at the neck to show a bloody bite impression of Dixie's teeth in the top of his shoulder and back. She'd damn near taken a piece out of him.

"Talk to her, Mom."

Donna looked a little pale after seeing the bite and him holding up his bleeding hand. She didn't argue with him anymore, just went back to talk to Dixie. She kept talking until Dixie started talking in full sentences and seemed to be making sense. Even then, when Bernardo, Nicky, and Rodina let go of her, they counted to three, let go at the same time, and moved back fast from her. She actually lay there for a second or two, as if she didn't realize they'd let her go. Donna offered her hand and Lucy came to take her other hand, and together they got her on her bare feet. Dixie stood there in her yellow one-piece bathing suit holding her friends' hands. She seemed very quiet, too quiet, as if she'd gone somewhere deep inside herself. It was almost as unnerving as the screaming and fighting had been. What the hell was going on?

Peter stood to one side, close to Donna, but not too close to Dixie. I think he'd had all of her he wanted for the day, or forever. "She's your friend, Mom, and this is your fault."

"What are you talking about, Peter?"

Lucy chimed in, "Dixie was determined to tell Becca at the pool. The little girls were playing together, being so happy."

Dixie looked angry again at that. She jerked her hands away from the other women and backed up into the corner where there was a chair, but she didn't sit down in it. She stood beside it with the wall at her back, one hand on the chair as if to steady herself.

Donna had gone pale. "Did she tell Becca?"

"No," Peter yelled, "because I stopped her."

"He tried being polite first," Lucy said, "but Dixie wouldn't shut up. She said that Becca deserved the truth, that she should know what kind of father she was getting."

"You did not," Donna said, staring at Dixie.

Dixie gripped the back of the chair hard enough for her

hand to mottle with the pressure. "She does deserve the truth, just like you deserve a husband that won't cheat on you."

"I told you that it's not true, Dixie. Ted isn't cheating on me with anyone. If you tell Becca the lie, then I don't . . . I don't think I can forgive you for it."

"You'd throw twenty years of friendship away over me telling the truth?"

"Becca doesn't need to know everything about our grown-up problems. Her therapist explained that some things are not supposed to be shared with children until you have run out of options, and it's not true, so there are lots of options."

"Why did you tell Dixie at all? Even when you believed it was true, why tell her?" Peter asked.

"I have a right to talk to my friends."

"Not when it impacts Becca and me to this degree. You're the mom, the grown-up. That means that you suck it up and deal instead of messing up our lives because you can't deal."

"How dare you talk to me like that."

"If you don't want me to talk to you like that, then act better, do better." He was waving his arms wide as he talked, big, upset gestures. Donna looked small beside him, but she didn't flinch and she didn't give ground.

"I'm sorry that Dixie didn't keep my confidence, but it was bothering me more than I thought it would, Peter. I thought I could do it. It was knowing that I've never had Ted's undivided attention. Them getting involved in a case on our wedding trip proves that even if they're not having an affair, it's still true."

"What's true, Mom?"

"That there are parts of him that he never shares with me, but only with Anita. It hurts me. Don't you understand that?"

"You aren't a marshal, Mom. He can't share work with you."

"But he shares with her in ways he doesn't share with Bernardo."

"What made you think they were more than just best friends?" Peter asked.

She gave him a scathing look, one hand on her hip. "You see how they are together."

"Yes, I do, which is why I'm asking the question that I should have asked months ago. What made you think they were more than friends?"

"He talks to her more than he talks to me. He confides in her the way a man does to his wife."

"Maybe some men, but Ted's not like that, Mom."

"I've been married before, Peter. I know how marriage works and what husbands do."

"You know how your first marriage worked. You know how Dad was with you, but from what I remember, he was nothing like Ted. They are such different men, Mom. Didn't it ever occur to you, or your therapist, that they might be very different husbands? If they're very different men, then they would be just as different in a relationship with you."

"I think I know more about marriage and relationships than you do, Peter."

"You've seen Anita with Micah and Nathaniel—hell, with Nicky now. She treats them completely different from how she treats Ted."

"I've always valued how respectful Anita and Ted are when they're around us. I know they're not having a physical affair, but I appreciate that they modify their emotional behavior when they're around me," Donna said.

"I have seen Ted with Anita when you're not around, Mom. They don't act like a couple, and they sure as hell don't interact the way she does with Micah and Nathaniel."

"They're engaged to each other; of course she acts differently with them."

Peter shook his head. "No, Mom, it's not that. She's not engaged to Nicky, but she treats him more like a boyfriend than she's ever treated Ted."

Dixie had caught on. "No, just no. You are not magically going to say there is no affair, so you can marry her now? That's just bullshit and more lies."

"If Anita had been a male friend from the Marshals Service, would you have suspected that Ted was having an affair with him?" Micah asked in a soothing voice, the kind of tone that you use to talk children back to sleep, or jumpers away from windows.

"You mean suspect Ted of being gay?" she asked.

"Yes."

She laughed as if it was too absurd to even think about. "Of course not."

"Are you saying that Anita's being a woman is the only reason you thought it was more than friendship?" Micah asked.

"No, of course not."

"Then what made you suspect?" he asked.

"He confides in Anita. He's always coming back from seeing her with every other sentence 'Anita this' and 'Anita that.' There's this look in his eyes when he talks about going out on a case with her that he doesn't get when he's home." Her voice grew soft at the end, as if she didn't like admitting that last part.

I knew that look in Edward's eyes wasn't about sexy time with me. It was about the fact that working with me usually meant it was going to be a tough job. Something that would challenge his skills, push his limits, allow him to use that part of him that enjoyed the action, the danger, and the violence. Sometimes that last part wasn't fun, but if we didn't enjoy it at some level, we'd have different jobs, or we wouldn't be good at the one we had. That was the real truth that Edward hadn't been able to explain to Donna.

"I told you that it wasn't Anita as a woman that made me act like that," Edward said.

"You told me it was the job, the action, the thrill of the chase, or some bullshit like that." The scorn in her voice was thick enough to walk on.

"Why didn't you believe him?" Micah asked quietly.

"Because it's too ridiculous. You put on a badge and a gun to protect people and put away the bad people, but the violence is a necessary evil, not the reason for it all."

I looked at Edward with renewed respect. "You really did try to tell her the truth."

He nodded. "I would never have asked you to tell such a complicated lie if I hadn't tried to tell Donna the truth first." His voice was still empty of accent, but now he sounded tired.

"He really did try, Anita," Peter said.

Donna and Dixie were looking at all of us. "What the hell is going on?" Dixie asked.

Edward ignored them both and talked to me. "Thank you for going along with the lie, Anita. I know it bothered you, and I know you thought it was ridiculous to confess to an affair we weren't having just so Donna would marry me."

"'Ridiculous' about covers it."

He smiled, but it left his eyes tired and unhappy.

"No," Dixie said. "You are not going to get out of the affair that easily."

"We can't get out of something we were never in to begin with," I said.

"But you are still involved with Anita in your work, Ted."

"I can't change my work, Donna."

"But on our wedding, Ted, to get involved in a case on our wedding."

"We're not involved yet; we're just being questioned like almost everyone in the hotel."

"But if they ask you to help with the case, you will. I know you will."

"I love you, Donna. I love that you wear your heart on your sleeve, but I hate that you let your feelings overwhelm you to this degree. I accept that it's two sides of the same coin, that maybe you can't be as open and caring unless your emotions rule you, but I've let you manipulate me into a no-win scenario. I win, Donna, I always win, except with you. I let you win a lot. I should have just stuck to the truth and kept on living together, but I had this stupid idea that I wanted to marry you. I wanted to be the legal father for Peter and Becca. I wanted the white picket fence with you, enough to lie, enough to pretend that I was something I wasn't. I would never have an affair, never cheat you and our family like that. But now it's about emotional cheating. I don't even know what to say to that, Donna. I gave in on the stupid affair thing, and now you think I'll give in if you just push hard enough. Well, I won't. I can't."

"Ted," Peter said, "don't, please don't." Peter looked on the verge of tears.

Edward gripped his arm. "I'm sorry, Peter, sorrier than I've ever been about anything."

"No," Donna said, and started to cry. "No, don't . . . I love you. I love our family. I love the life we have together."

Edward looked at her, his face still empty, as if he'd shoved all his emotions away so that no one could see them. If you control your outside demeanor, sometimes you can almost pretend that you control your inside feelings; almost.

"Oh, Ted, don't look at me like that," she said, and started to cry harder.

Edward started to let go of Peter's arm, but Peter put his bigger hand over Edward's and kept them touching. The first tear slid down his cheek, his face struggling to stay in control the way Edward was controlling his. Peter didn't want to be like his sobbing mother; he wanted to be like Edward, and that had been true almost from the first time I'd seen them all together.

"How do you want me to look at you?" Edward asked in a voice that was empty. I'd heard him hurt people with that emptiness in his voice. Donna flinched as if she'd never heard it before, and she probably hadn't. If she only knew that it wasn't an affair with me Ted was hiding, but something much more violent and dangerous.

"Like you still love me," she said in a voice that was choked with tears, "like we're still a family."

Edward's eyes flinched then, because that was really it. He, Donna, Peter, and Becca were a family, and he wanted them to keep on being together. He'd wanted it so badly that he'd compromised who he was, and who we were, so that Donna would marry him. My chest was tight watching the three of them. I swallowed hard, because I would not cry here. This was their moment to cry, or not cry. I didn't want to take away from that by drawing attention to me.

"I want to be a family with you, all of you. I wanted it so much that I was willing to confess to an affair I wasn't having, because you wouldn't believe the truth. I love you and Peter and Becca, and those stupid fluffy dogs back home, so much that I convinced my best friend to confess to an affair she wasn't having either. But now you want us not to cheat emotionally. We're best friends. We have an emotional connection, Donna. That's what *best friends* means."

"Oh, Ted," she sobbed, and then wrapped her arms around him. He didn't hold her back, just let her hold him. Silent tears were running down Peter's face as he stood there watching them.

Nathaniel grabbed my hand. I glanced at him and watched a tear trail down his face. He'd spent more time with Donna and both kids than I had. He was Uncle Nathaniel to Becca. This would be a loss of more than just the wedding for a lot of us.

I squeezed his hand and then had to look away, because if

I'd kept watching him tear up, I couldn't have stopped myself from joining him. I would not cry until it was done, for better or worse.

"I'm sorry that I'm insecure about Anita. I will do better, I swear, and if the police need you to help find that girl, of course you can help, of course."

Donna pressed her face harder into Edward's shoulder, the tears coming in huge, wracking sobs that seemed to be breaking her shoulders and back, she was shaking so hard from them. Slowly he raised one arm and wrapped it around her. It made her cry even harder, which I hadn't thought was possible, and she wrapped her arms tighter around his waist, as if holding on so that she didn't fall. Peter stepped into them and wrapped his arms around them both. Edward hugged him back and the three of them held one another. The only dry eyes were his, but he was holding them. I just wasn't sure if it was a good-bye hug or a sign of reconciliation from him.

"You can't just ignore that he's having an affair because you love him, Donna." It was Dixie who had stepped closer to them, her hands in fists, her eyes shining with rage. She really was beautiful when she was angry. It gave her color so there was more contrast between her pale skin and dark blond hair; even her eyes were a richer blue when she was angry. The question was, why was she this angry about Donna's love life?

Donna ignored her, or maybe she was crying so hard she hadn't heard. Peter was bent over so that his head was buried on the other side of Edward's head so he couldn't see Dixie. After the damage she'd already done to him, that seemed unwise, or maybe he knew that Edward could see her, or maybe he trusted all of us. He'd literally brought the problem, Dixie, to us; maybe he did trust that we would fix it now. Looking into her fever-bright eyes, I wasn't sure that was going to work. You can't fix crazy.

Ru put a hand on Nathaniel's back and my shoulder, leaning close, and whispered, "What's wrong with her?"

I shook my head. "I don't know."

Nathaniel whispered back, "Is she going to hurt them when she gets close enough?"

Micah came in close to my side, finding my hand to hold. We all seemed to need a reassuring touch, because there was just something in her face as she crept toward them. I was really glad she didn't have a gun in that moment, because as illogical as it seemed, I wouldn't have trusted her with it. I wasn't sure she was even seeing Edward, Donna, and Peter, because her reaction didn't match the tearful forgiveness and love in front of her. Dixie looked like she saw something terrible, frightening, or even disgusting.

Bernardo moved toward them, slowly. It took me a second to realize he was trying to get between Dixie and the family. He was right; there was something wrong with the look on her face. She'd already tried to be inappropriate by telling a child personal grown-up things, and the damage she'd caused to Peter should have been reserved for someone who was hurting her.

She kept creeping closer to the family as they hugged. Bernardo kept creeping closer to her, just in case. The tension that had dissipated when they all started to hug was back, but it was a different kind of tension. Dixie wasn't done yet.

It was Lucy who stepped in, putting a hand on Bernardo's arm so he'd move and let her closer to the other woman. "Dixie," she said in a low, soothing voice. There was no reaction, as if she hadn't heard. "Dixie," Lucy repeated in a louder tone, "Dixie, look at me." Still no reaction. All Dixie's attention was aimed at the hugging family.

"You can't take him back, Donna. Don't do it. Once they cheat on you, you can never trust them again." Dixie said it as if Lucy wasn't trying to talk to her, as if there was no one in the room but her and Edward's family.

"Dixie!" Lucy said it sharp now.

Dixie blinked once, and some of the fever intensity on her face softened as she turned to look at Lucy, who was close enough to touch now. Dixie blinked again, and more of the emotional turmoil vanished from her face. She straightened her shoulders so that she wasn't hunched, but her hands stayed in fists at her sides.

"Dixie, can you hear me?" Lucy asked, voice softer again.

Dixie nodded wordlessly, but now her face looked too smooth, too empty. Her blue eyes were back to their paler shade of normal, but they were too big in her face, like people look when they're in shock. It was as if she'd expended too much emotion in the last few minutes, so she had to teeter-totter to no emotion. Whatever the rest of us thought about Donna and Edward and the kids, or how Peter had solved the problem of getting Dixie away from Becca, it wasn't how Dixie saw any of it. Something about either the coming nuptials, the supposed cheating, or the kids, or something we couldn't even guess at, touched her at levels that no one was going to understand but her.

"Dixie, honey," Lucy said, "I need you to say something, anything."

Dixie shook her head.

Lucy reached out slowly to touch her shoulder. Dixie was fine right up until her hand touched her bare arm, and then she flinched. Touch wasn't good for her right now, so Lucy drew her hand back. "Honey, Dixie, are you all right?"

She nodded, and then in a voice that was empty of all emotion but very clear, she said, "Yes."

The answer was so obviously a lie that I'd have been tempted to say, *No, you're not*, but Lucy was smarter than me. She said, "All right, honey, let's go back to your room. You need to shower off from the pool and get dressed."

Dixie nodded again, but her eyes were still too big, and her hands were still in fists at her sides. Something was still deeply wrong, but I had no idea what it was or how to deal with it. Lucy started trying to herd Dixie down the hallway without touching her, which is harder than it sounds, but it worked. Dixie moved ahead of her. Bernardo stepped out of the way. Dixie's eyes flickered up to him, and there was a flash of rage in her eyes. Just a blazing glimpse, and then her eyes were empty again, and she let Lucy ease her down the hallway.

Edward, Donna, and Peter, with tears still drying on two of their faces, were watching now. Edward's face showed no emotion, but Donna's showed enough for both of them. Peter just looked confused, like he was trying to figure it out. So was I, but as long as Dixie went elsewhere to calm down, I was good. I'd learned a long time ago that you can't fix everyone, but Peter was nineteen; he didn't know that yet.

"Did I do that to her?" he asked in a low voice.

"No," Edward said.

"I'm not sure," Donna said, which wasn't helpful to her son.

Peter looked at her, his face stricken. "I didn't know what else to do to keep her from telling Becca."

"I know," she said, hugging him closer. "You did the best you could."

"You were trying to remove her from the situation without hurting her," Edward said.

"Yeah," Peter said.

"But she didn't feel the same way about you," Edward said and motioned down so that they all looked at Peter's leg. There was blood actually running down his thigh from underneath the baggy swim trunks. That was some scratch.

Donna gave a little scream of panic. Not helpful. She tried to pull up the leg of his trunks, and Peter pulled away. "I can do it, Mom."

He pulled the leg of his shorts up, and it wasn't a scratch. It was a stab wound. "That wasn't done with fingernails," Rodina said.

"No," Edward said and knelt so he could see the wound better.

Donna started to cry again, as if the tears were still too close, or maybe she just didn't know what else to do. She had her moments, but unless she worked at it, she wasn't always great in an emergency.

"What did she stab you with?" Bernardo asked.

"A fountain pen," Peter said. "She grabbed it off a table as we passed it. I didn't even know she'd grabbed it until she stuck it in my leg. If it had been a real knife, she'd have really hurt me."

There was a lot more blood than I would have expected from just a fountain pen. Then the blood blurped out of the small hole. That was bad.

Edward was leaning close to the wound. He raised the hem of his white T-shirt to gently wipe away the blood. "I think a piece of the pen is still in the wound."

"I didn't think it was bleeding this much," Peter said.

"It probably wasn't," Edward said, "but the piece that broke off kept working in deeper as you walked."

"Why is the blood coming out like that?" Donna asked.

"I think the piece in his leg nicked an artery."

She made a small sound and went pale.

"Don't you dare faint," I said.

She flashed me a look that wasn't entirely friendly. "I'm allowed to be upset."

"Yeah, but if anyone gets to faint, it's Peter. It's his leg."

She frowned at me, but her color was better. Her anger with me was fine if it meant she held her shit together and didn't make the current emergency more about her.

"I'm not going to faint," Peter said.

"Bring that chair here," Edward said.

Bernardo went to get the chair that Dixie had been leaning on earlier.

"I can walk to the chair, Ted," Peter said.

"Walking is what worked the shrapnel into your artery. No more walking until a doctor okays it."

"Doctor? I'm not that hurt."

Bernardo had the chair behind Peter, who started to sit down, but Bernardo grabbed his arm and Edward got up and took the other. "Keep the leg straight, no bending at all."

I started forward, but Nathaniel beat me to it, kneeling to help steady Peter's leg at either side of the knee so the leg stayed straight.

"You guys are scaring me."

"Good," Edward said. "We need clean towels or something to hold on the wound, but we can't press hard like normal to get the blood flow stopped."

"Will napkins do?" Rodina asked.

"Depending on what they're made of, yes," Edward said.

She went back down the hallway in search of napkins.

He called after her, "If you see a staff member, ask if they have a doctor on call for the hotel and if he's in residence. If the doctor is on-site, then send him to us. If an ambulance would be quicker than a doctor, then have the staff call one."

"I'll go with her," Micah said. He kissed me on the cheek and then followed Rodina down the hallway. Bram followed them without consulting anyone. He was Micah's shadow, period.

"An ambulance?" Peter said. "She put a fountain pen in my leg, not a blade. If I need stitches, can't you just drive me?"

Edward slipped his white T-shirt off completely, flashing

that unexpectedly great upper body again. He knelt and put the white cloth carefully over the wound. We needed to get the bleeding stopped, but we didn't want to press on the piece of shrapnel and force it to tear the artery more. The white shirt started turning scarlet. Peter's foot twitched and the shirt was suddenly heavy with blood, as if a lot of it had come out in an instant.

"Did it hurt when I touched the wound?" Edward asked.

"Not much, but I'm having trouble keeping my foot still."

I knelt behind Nathaniel and supported Peter's foot on my knee. He looked embarrassed. "You don't have to do all this. I've been hurt a lot worse than this before."

He was right. I'd seen him in the hospital after a weretiger had cut him up. He'd been sixteen and done it to save me after the same tiger had nearly gutted me. Why was it that almost every time I saw Peter something bad happened to him?

"You've had bigger wounds, Peter, but just because a wound is small doesn't mean it's not serious," Edward said. It made me look at the shirt he was holding against the wound. It was almost completely soaked with blood. That had happened quick; fuck.

Micah was back with an armful of nice linen napkins and Bram. "Rodina is double-checking on the ambulance. I thought you'd need the napkins sooner." He looked at the now-dripping shirt and just held out the napkins to Edward.

"I can hold them on my wound," Peter said.

"Just sit still, Peter. The more you move, the faster you bleed," Edward said.

Donna was just standing there staring at everything. Her uselessness was beginning to piss me off. She whispered something and then said it louder. "This is my fault. If I hadn't told Dixie, this wouldn't be happening."

I agreed with her, so I lowered my face and looked at Peter's leg in my hands, which was weird, so I looked up at Nathaniel's broad back kneeling just ahead of me, and then to Peter's face. He was pale; his brown eyes looked darker even than I knew they were, because his skin was a bad color. He was naturally darker than either Edward or me, but in that moment we both had more color. I prayed, *Let it just be shock and fear; don't let him be pale from blood loss.*

"I'm sorry, Peter, Ted."

"I can't believe you told Dixie, of all people, Mom. She would never help you feel better about anything. She's one of those people that turns everything into some kind of drama. How did you think confiding in her would be a good thing?"

"I thought she'd understand, because her husband cheated on her, too."

I looked up at her then. We all did.

"Ray is a cheating son of a bitch," Peter said. "He doesn't have a girlfriend; he has hookups."

Donna stared down at him, looking shocked. "How do you know that? How do you know any of that?"

"Because their son Benji has been in martial arts with me for years. Everyone thinks the kids don't know about stuff, but it's kind of hard to miss when Benji's dad would pick us up for carpool smelling of perfume and it wasn't the kind that Benji's mom wore."

"Dixie told me that Ray cheated on her a couple of times but swore he'd stopped."

"We drive ourselves to class now, so maybe he has sworn off other women, but all of the kids in carpool knew that he was fucking around."

She corrected him automatically. "Don't say *fucking*, Peter."

"Is that really more important than what I'm telling you?"

"No, of course not, but I didn't know it was that bad."

"Because when you saw Ray at parties he was all cleaned up and presentable and stayed by Dixie's side. Anyone can pretend for an afternoon or an evening dinner party, Mom. Outside of that she was hostile to him, she knew, and he knew she knew, but he didn't stop and she didn't divorce him. Benji chose a college out of state so he didn't have to deal with it."

Donna looked horror-struck. "Why didn't you tell us?"

"Tell you what? That Benji's dad would drop us off smelling of his aftershave and pick us up smelling like perfume? You wouldn't have believed me when I was little, and by the time I got big enough to explain it so you might have believed me, I'd given up trying to tell you a lot of things. Besides, it would have embarrassed Benji if you had tried to talk to his parents about it, and you would have taken me out of their carpool. You'd have told the other parents because you'd have felt it was immoral or a bad example for the kids. You'd have tried to make it better and it would have just been worse. Like today."

"Peter," Edward said, that one word a sort of warning for him to mind how he spoke to his mother.

Peter glared at him. "Tell me I'm wrong. Tell me she wouldn't have done exactly that."

Edward met the weight of his son's gaze but said nothing. He kept holding more napkins against Peter's leg, and they started to turn red. Where the fuck was the ambulance?

"So this is all my fault," Donna said. "The fact that you and Anita are having an affair, or maybe you really aren't, but you let me believe it, because I wouldn't believe the truth. Which sounds ridiculous."

"Benji's mom hates his dad, and she shows it when there are no grown-ups around. Was it her who started convincing you that you couldn't live with a man that cheated on you?" There was sweat beading on Peter's forehead now as he glared up at his mother. His big hands were gripping the bottom of the chair as if he needed to hold on to stay in it. When had he started the death grip on the chair?

Bernardo moved behind Peter, putting a hand on either shoulder. He was careful not to move him more, but he was there in case the kid's death grip on the chair failed. The napkins were filling up with blood. Was it my imagination or was Peter's leg heavier than it had been a second ago?

Edward said, "Peter, look at me."

Peter did what he asked, and lowering his head was better; some of the color came back to his face. He was still sweating, though.

"You're right, Peter," Donna said. "Dixie was trying to convince me that I couldn't marry Ted unless he gave up Anita."

Peter looked back at her, but his head leaning back wasn't good. Bernardo pushed his head forward and a little down. "You don't have to look up to talk," he said.

Peter swallowed hard, as if his mouth was dry. "Would water help?" Micah asked.

"Ice chips," Edward said.

"I'll see what I can find." Micah started down the hallway at a slow jog, with Bram at his heels.

Peter said, "Why didn't you ask Ted to give up Anita, if you really believed they were lovers?"

"I did."

Peter tried to look up, but Bernardo held his head and shoulders downward. "Easy, kid."

I must have looked surprised, because Donna said, "Ted didn't tell you that, did he?"

I went back to staring at Nathaniel's back. I so wanted out of this conversation, out of this moment. Where the fuck was the ambulance?

Edward said, "I told Donna that Anita was my partner. She was the person I trusted most at my back in an emergency. The one I trusted to bring me home safe to you, Becca, and her. I asked her if she really wanted me to give that up."

"I couldn't ask him to give her up then, because all I could think was that if something happened to Ted on the job and Anita wasn't there to save him, it would be my fault. I couldn't stand that, so I thought I could live with the affair, and now I know there was never a real affair."

"Donna," Nathaniel said, "you're being so sexist."

"What? How have I been sexist?"

"You admitted that if Anita had been a man, you would never have accused them of an affair. If she'd been another man, you would have just thought they were partners."

"Yes, I did say that, but it's not just that she's a woman."

"When I look eager about going out with Anita, it's about the job, not some imaginary affair, Donna."

"No, it's not just that."

"What then, Mom? What is it? What made you believe it?" Peter asked.

She was quiet for so long I thought she wasn't going to answer, but then, finally, in a voice that was low and embarrassed, she did. "It's because she's a beautiful woman."

That made me look up at her. She was blushing, so she was embarrassed. Good, she should have been.

"There's just something about you, Anita. It's like you give off this sexiness like you enjoy it and you'd be good at it." She blushed harder, because now I was looking at her and letting her see what I thought of her reasoning.

"Don't look at me like that, Anita."

"How do you want me to look at you?"

"Like I'm not crazy, like I didn't let my insecurities wreck my wedding and injure my son."

I didn't know what to say to that, so I did the best I could. I looked away from her.

"The ambulance is coming," Nathaniel said.

"How do you know?" Bernardo asked.

"I can hear it."

"I can't."

"Me either, but if Nathaniel says he hears it, he does," I said.

"It'll be here soon, Peter," Nathaniel said.

"Good," Peter said, his voice a little thick.

His leg got very heavy all of a sudden. Nathaniel said, "It's okay, Peter, we got you."

"Hold on, son," Edward said, "just hold on."

I could hear the ambulance now. Ru knelt beside Bernardo so he could put steadying hands on Peter's chest. Nathaniel and I held his injured leg still and straight as he passed out. Edward kept both his hands on the wound and the blood-soaked napkins. We all held Peter and waited for the ambulance.

Donna wiped her eyes and got a handle on herself. She stopped crying and started helping us do first aid on her son. It was like she'd fallen back into the old Donna, the pre-Edward Donna, and suddenly, when she realized the shit was hitting the fan for real, she found that strength I'd seen in the bridal shop when she put Dixie on the ground. I liked the new, strong Donna, but I couldn't have dealt with the weak version. Good thing I wasn't the one marrying her. Though looking at Edward's face at that second, I wasn't sure he was going to be marrying her either.

35

EDWARD RODE IN the ambulance with Peter. He'd grabbed my arm as he moved beside the gurney and made me run with him. "Take care of Becca; keep Dixie away from her."

"I will."

They loaded a still-unconscious Peter into the ambulance, and Edward squeezed in with the EMT in the back, still shirt-less. His bloody shirt had been discarded on the floor some-where. Doors closed, and they were off, sirens screaming, lights swirling. Donna was left staring after the ambulance, as if looking at it hard enough would make it travel faster, or some other magical thinking. Edward had told Bernardo to keep an eye on Donna, so he was standing near her, waiting for her to react. I thought that Donna should have been looking after Becca, rather than needing anyone to look after her, but that was just me.

Becca was with Nathaniel. She was tall for her age, but she'd still wrapped herself around him like she was half her height and years younger than almost twelve. She'd buried her face against the side of his neck, his hair just long enough to spill across her face.

Micah and Bram were standing by Nathaniel and Becca. Micah was trying to help comfort her. Bram was watching the crowd that had gathered to watch the show. If he was uncom-fortable, it didn't show. Carol had insisted on her husband coming with her to take their daughter, Ellie, the other flower girl, away from the sight of blood and the potential trauma of watching someone she knew being loaded into an ambulance. Lieutenant Colonel Franklin hadn't wanted to go, but he gave in to his wife. The rest of the wedding party had found us, attracted by the lights and sirens. Becca had tried to go with Peter, but when she realized she couldn't go but Edward was going, she'd let Uncle Nathaniel pick her up and carry her out of the way.

Ru and Rodina were standing a little apart, between where Nathaniel and Micah were standing with Bram and where I was standing with Nicky. Nicky showed nothing about the drama. He was his usual calm self.

Lucy and Dixie were talking to the two uniformed policemen who had shown up just after the ambulance. I realized that one of them was Officer Dunley from earlier. He caught my eye and motioned me over toward them. I glanced back at Becca and the men. They seemed to have things as under control as they were going to be for a while, so I went to join the uniforms and the hysterical woman, because Dixie was hysterical. She seemed to be upset that Peter was so badly hurt and was hiccuping between sobs, "I didn't mean to hurt him." Lucy was patting her shoulder and trying to help explain what had happened to the stoic policemen. Nice that there was one other woman involved who wasn't having a hissy fit.

Officer Dunley raised an eyebrow at me and let me see an expression that matched it for a second before he went back to blank face. He was a good cop; he'd do his best to add no emotion to the situation.

He couldn't quite keep the irony out of his voice as he said, "Marshal Blake, I take it you're involved in all this."

"If you mean I know everyone involved, then yes."

His mouth quirked just a bit at the corner, as if he found my wording amusing but was fighting not to show it. He took me off to one side and left the other uniform to continue to try to talk to Dixie, with Lucy helping as best she could.

There was a slight settling of his broad shoulders when he got us to a quieter part of the parking area near the ever-present palm trees. "Did you witness the assault?"

"No, just helped give first aid until the ambulance arrived."

"Witnesses say the man involved abducted the woman from the pool area."

I realized in that moment that this could go entirely badly for Peter. He had taken Dixie against her will and carried her fighting and screaming through the hotel. Witnesses would be able to testify to that. I didn't know how Florida law was written. Did his just carrying her away like that constitute assault?

"I wasn't there."

"You said that you didn't witness the assault."

"When you said assault, I thought you meant her attacking Peter."

"Ms. Carlitos says that she didn't mean to hurt him as badly as she did, but she was afraid for her safety."

I narrowed my eyes at him. "I'm betting that's not what she said."

"Then you tell me in your own words."

"Look, Peter is only nineteen."

"And over six feet tall, big guy, a lot of women would be scared if he picked them up and manhandled them like that," Dunley said.

"Maybe, but that's not my point."

"And just what is your point, Marshal?"

I resisted the urge to call him Officer. "He's nineteen and he's never had to try to deal with a woman that he didn't want to hurt, but who didn't give a damn if she hurt him."

"You make it sound like Ms. Carlitos started the fight."

"I'd call it a disagreement, not a fight."

"Disagreement, huh? Parnell just got rushed off to the hospital with a stab wound. That's one hell of a disagreement. In fact, I'd call it a fight when a woman is so afraid of a man that she stabs him."

I didn't like the wording again, but I couldn't really argue with it at face value, so I ignored it. "Dixie did start things off."

"In what way?"

And here we were back to the fucking lie again. I cursed Edward for dragging me into it, and cursed myself harder for letting myself get dragged into it. I was debating how much to tell him when a man in a polo shirt and slacks walked up to us. I thought at first it was someone from the hotel, but Dunley stood a little straighter and sighed. It made me look at the new guy, and the moment I really looked at him I knew we were in trouble, or Peter was, because it was a detective. How did I know? Maybe it was the gold shield. I hadn't known that the Kirke Police Department was big enough to have detectives, but there it was, slipped into the pocket of his polo shirt. The way that Dunley gave ground to him, not only was he a detective, but either his rank was high enough or he was respected or scary enough that Dunley wasn't going to fight for it.

The detective was maybe five foot nine at best, built slender, so that he looked almost fragile beside Dunley. His hair was a rich chestnut brown, a little long for most cops—I mean, you couldn't even see his ears—and just long enough that it was beginning to wave, or maybe settle into loose natural curls. It didn't seem to be a fashion statement, more like he hadn't seen a barber in a while. I wondered what could have made a police detective ignore the boys' club haircut for that long. He was also tanned, as if he spent a lot of his off days doing something outdoorsy. Then I looked into his eyes and all pleasant speculation stopped. It wasn't the color of them, which was a brown so dark they looked black. I'd seen more exotic and more ominous eye color. No, it was the cold, nearly unfriendly calculation in them. His intelligence and intensity were all there trapped in his eyes, while he tried to play to the fact that he wasn't physically imposing, that he didn't look like a cop. Maybe the hair was on purpose. It certainly helped him look a little disheveled, and it distracted from the neatness of his clothes and the precision of the mind staring back at me.

"Detective Terry Rankin, this is Marshal Anita Blake," Officer Dunley said.

"Dunley tells me you're in town for a wedding."

I nodded. "That's right."

"So you're a bridesmaid."

"No, I'm the best man," I said, staring into his dark eyes. If he thought I'd flinch because of really good eye contact, he was wrong. I loved eye contact.

He blinked then, and it was nice to know that I could make him blink. "Best man. So you're standing up with the groom, not the bride?"

It was my turn to blink. I'd hoped for at least a few comments about whether I was the best man for the job or something, anything to break the tension that seemed to roll off of the detective.

"Yes," I said.

"What's your relationship to Peter Parnell?"

I fought to keep my face blank and pleasant as I said, "He's the biological son of the bride and the stepson of the groom, and he's also a groomsman in the wedding."

"Stepfather—are the bride and groom already legally married and this is just a renewal of vows?"

"No, but the family has been living together for years. Call the wedding a legal formality."

"So you just know him as their son?"

"I've known Peter since he was a kid."

Rankin nodded as if that was somehow significant. "So you're close to him and his family?"

"Close enough that I'd like to see about getting more of us to the hospital to check on Peter." I was really wanting away from the detective, because something was up, something more than just the mess between Peter and Dixie. You didn't get a detective on something that could be put down to high jinks gone wrong.

"How well did Parnell know Bettina Gonzales?" Rankin asked.

It took me a second, because I wasn't used to thinking of Peter by his last name. The confusion over the name probably saved me from looking shocked, because I was. I totally hadn't seen that coming and I should have. They had a woman vanish from their hotel earlier today, and then another woman being carried off against her will, so scared about it that she stabbed the man doing it. Any cop would try to put the two events together.

I shook my head. "Not well."

"Really. A nineteen-year-old boy and a twenty-one-year-old girl hanging out by the pool, but you're sure they didn't talk to each other."

"I answered the question you asked, Rankin. If you have another question, ask it."

"When you say they didn't know each other well, what does that mean?"

I shrugged. "It means what I said."

"You really don't know if he talked to Bettina Gonzales, do you?"

"I don't know what Peter is doing every minute of the day, if that's what you mean."

"So you wouldn't know if he and Bettina hooked up, would you?"

I opened my mouth, closed it, and tried to think. "I didn't see Ms. Gonzales paying any special attention to Peter. She seemed pretty focused on Bernardo Spotted-Horse last time I saw her."

"Dunley told me what you had to say about Spotted-Horse and our missing woman." Again he hadn't given me much to talk to, or about. He was trying to get me talking. I knew that Peter wasn't involved in whatever had happened to Bettina, but I also knew that anything I said could be used against Peter. It was amazing how innocent comments could sound guilty once the police finished with them. I was a cop. I knew how this game worked.

"Then you know everything I know."

"I doubt that, Blake. I really doubt that." He made it sound sort of ominous, as if he knew I was hiding things and he would dig out my deepest, darkest secrets. I wasn't hiding anything about any of this, so my secrets wouldn't help him find the missing girl. I don't know why, but I kept thinking of Bettina as a girl. Twenty-one was legal, but she'd seemed so unfinished and insecure. It was hard to think of her as all grown-up.

Rankin gave me the serious eyes again, trying to make me fess up if he'd just stop staring at me. I stared back and managed a friendly smile. I wasn't sure it reached my eyes, but it was the best I had under the circumstances.

"I need to check on Peter's little sister. She's pretty upset, watching him get carted off in an ambulance." I actually turned away, but Rankin wasn't done with me.

"I notice you're not defending Parnell's innocence."

I turned back and didn't try to keep my eyes friendly now. "Innocence for what, Rankin? Peter is the one that got stabbed so deep in his thigh that his artery got nicked."

"He's also the one that dragged a screaming woman out of the hotel pool and carried her against her will through most of the downstairs area of the hotel. We have a dozen witnesses that say Ms. Carlitos was begging him to let her go and calling for help from passersby."

"If they really thought she was in danger, why didn't they help her?"

"Parnell is over six feet tall and in good shape. They were afraid of him, Blake."

I tried to see Peter that way. Tried to see him as a big, athletic guy people would be afraid to mess with, but I couldn't. "I'm sorry, Detective Rankin, but I know Peter too well to see him like that."

"You wouldn't be afraid of a six-foot-plus man who was carrying a screaming and obviously frightened woman through a hotel?"

"No."

He let me see that he didn't believe me.

"I'm with the preternatural branch of the Marshals Service, Rankin. I spend my time hunting vampires and lycanthropes. A tall guy with a struggling woman doesn't even step foot in the ballpark of what I'm afraid of."

"I know who you are, Blake."

"Then you know that I'd do the same thing you'd do if you really thought a woman was being abducted right in front of you. We'd both double-check what was actually happening, and if it was an abduction, we'd stop it."

"Most men wouldn't see you as much of a threat," he said.

"Most men are stupid."

His mouth quirked as if he almost smiled, but if I'd amused him, he managed to fight it off. He went right back to that serious intensity of earlier. "You've known Parnell since he was a kid, but you still haven't defended his honor. Most people tell me how their friend couldn't have done it, that they're too nice a guy, they'd never hurt anyone. I find the fact that you aren't protesting like that interesting, Blake. It's like you know something we don't about Parnell and the missing woman."

"Do you want me on the record saying the usual shit that everyone says? He didn't do it. Well, of course he didn't. I don't have to defend Peter, but right now I do have to check on Becca and her mother and get us organized to head to the hospital and check on Peter."

I walked away then, and, yes, Rankin called after me, but I wasn't under arrest. I didn't have to keep talking to him, or

any of them. I knew the rules and how far they could be bent.
I would gain nothing by talking to Rankin and Dunley, but
things I said could hurt Peter later. He was innocent of Bettina's disappearance, but if things went wrong, he might end up
charged for what he'd done with Dixie. Assault maybe, or even
holding someone against their will. Who knew? If the local
cops wanted to make a big deal out of this, they could. Peter
might have more problems than just a stab wound. Of course,
he had to live through the last to worry about the first. Did I
really think Peter would die from what Dixie had done? No,
but there was a tightness in my chest that was less sure.

36

EDWARD LET US know that Peter was in surgery. Donna was already there with Uncle Bernardo. Sheriff Rufous and his wife, Marisol, were still out sight-seeing and no one had been able to get ahold of them yet. Lieutenant Colonel Franklin came to offer to take Becca to their room to hide out with their little girl, but I had to say no. Until Edward relieved me of duty, Becca was with us.

The police were still interviewing people, and that included Micah, Nathaniel, Ru, Rodina, Bram, and Nicky. I wasn't sure why they wanted to question Nicky—he hadn't even been at the pool—but the police were very insistent on it. Once Detective Rankin showed up, the police were suddenly way too interested in everyone I was traveling with, or maybe it was just them being thorough and me being paranoid. But for whatever reason, I was suddenly out of bodyguards, and even lovers. Rather than feel nervous about it, I was almost relieved, as if maybe I needed a little more alone time. I felt almost guilty taking Becca back to her room to change, just her and me, as if I needed permission from Nicky or someone to be out by myself. The hotel was swarming with police. I figured I'd be safe enough.

The top of Becca's head came to my shoulder, but she still took my hand in hers and swung it between us as we walked. She'd liked to swing hands like that since I'd met her, but what was adorable at six was a little odd at eleven, or maybe it was just the realization that she was going to be taller than me. If she came up to my shoulder now, by the time she was fourteen she'd be as tall as I was, just like Peter had been. She might not reach his full height, but I was remembering one of those articles I'd read when I was waiting somewhere. It had said if you take a man's height and subtract five inches, then that's how tall he'd have been as a woman. If you added five inches to a woman, that would have been her height as a man. I wasn't sure it was true, but I'd liked the idea that I'd have been five-eight as a man. If I took Peter's height for Becca, she might end up five-ten at least.

"Aunt Anita," she said in a voice that was way more serious than her usual cheerful tone. I waited for her to continue, but she didn't. I glanced at her as we walked down the hallway to their room, and still she didn't say anything. She looked down at the floor as we walked, swinging our hands back and forth as if she didn't realize she was doing it. Maybe it was a comfort thing for her.

"What's up, Becca?" I asked.

"Aunt Dixie was yelling things at the pool before Peter took her away."

My stomach clenched tight and I damn near stumbled. I did not want to have this conversation with Becca. I sure as hell didn't want to have it with just the two of us. Nathaniel was better with kids than I was, and Micah was calmer with nearly everyone and everything. One of the things I'd learned was that calling someone your other half, or other halves, doesn't mean you're not whole without them, but you do divide up your life according to each other's strengths. Talking to an eleven-year-old about the supposed affair I wasn't having with her dad . . . Hell, maybe there was no good way to have this conversation. I was just being cowardly wanting to have the men with me, but right that minute I would rather have faced a bad guy than have this particular talk.

I took a deep breath, let it out slowly, and said, "What kind of things?"

"That you and Daddy were . . . like, boyfriend and girl-friend, like, dating each other. That's not true, is it?" I was almost a hundred percent certain those hadn't been the words Dixie used, but I could work with them.

"No, Ted and I aren't dating."

"That's good, because he can only date Mom, right?" She stopped and turned to me in the hallway, still holding my hand, so that I had to stop, too. She stared up at me with those sincere brown eyes of hers, so direct, so convinced I'd tell her the truth. She hadn't changed all that much since she was six. "I mean, I know that you date Uncle Nathaniel and Uncle Micah and they date each other, but that's not what Mom and Dad do, right? They don't date other people, right?"

"That's right, they're monogamous."

"And you're poly-whatsit," she said.

I couldn't help but smile. "Polyamorous, yes."

"But Dad and Mom aren't polyamorous; they're the first one, they're monogamous."

"Yes."

"Then why did Mom's friend say that?"

"I'm not sure why Dixie did it."

"Is she crazy?"

I thought about the look on Dixie's face earlier. "Actually, I think she might be."

"I've never seen anyone that's crazy before. It was scary." She shivered a little.

I hugged her, pressing my cheek against the top of her hair. "Let's get you out of the bathing suit and into some street clothes," I said.

"Can I wear my pink dress?"

"Are you telling me you only brought one pink dress?" I said.

She pulled away from the hug enough to smile up at me. "One pink dress, but I have pink shorts, pink jeans, pink sandals, and my pink cowboy boots, plus pink shirts!"

I laughed. "Do you think that's enough pink for one trip?"

She smiled even broader, and shook her head hard enough that her hair fluttered around her face.

I laughed louder, and she joined me. We got to the door to their room, still shiny with laughter. I fished in my pocket for the key card. "Why don't you ever wear pink, Aunt Anita?"

"Not really my color," I said as I slid the key card into the lock and got a green light. I opened the door, and a deep voice called around the corner of the hallway nearest to us. "I would like to see you in pink, Anita."

I pushed Becca into the room, told her to change, and turned to face the corner as the owner of that voice came into view. At seven feet, his bald head nearly touching the ceiling, he'd kept the black Vandyke beard and mustache. It gave form and helped highlight his face, so that it wasn't just the black arch of his eyebrows that gave his face color. I could see that he might be considered handsome by some women, but I knew too much about the inside of his head and heart to ever see him that way. His eyes weren't just a dark brown that looked black like Detective Rankin's; they were black like Rodina's and Wyatt's. I wondered if there was Welsh ancestry in him somewhere. But his eyes were more disturbing, because they were set so deeply in his face that they were like twin caves.

"Olaf," I said, and the only thing that kept me from drawing my gun was that Becca was trying to come back out of the room.

"Anita," he said, watching me with a look that was almost hungry, like he was a lion and I was the gazelle. He was a werelion now, but I was no gazelle.

"Uncle Otto!" Becca cried out and managed to slip under my arm and run toward the big man.

"Uncle Otto?" I said, and it was all I could do not to say, *When the hell did you become Uncle Otto?* Becca flung herself into his arms as if he wasn't a sociopath or a serial killer. But as U.S. Marshal Otto Jeffries, he wasn't either of those things. I watched him swing the little girl up in the air, and the smile on his face seemed real enough. What the fuck was going on?

37

HE TRANSFERRED BECCA to his left arm, so his right was free. He'd seen me almost go for my gun. I still wasn't sure that it wasn't my best move, but if I didn't want to explain an affair with her father to Becca, I sure as hell didn't want to deal with her watching me shoot Uncle Otto to death in front of her when he hadn't done anything in front of her to warrant it. The things we do for children.

"What the . . . What are you doing here, Ol . . . Otto?"

"I was invited to the wedding," he said, smiling at Becca as she put her arms confidently around the smooth-muscled strength of his neck. I'd never seen him look so normal or so happy, but then I'd never seen him interact with Becca like this either. I was pretty sure it was cause and effect.

I was so taken by his act as he moved down the hallway that it took me a second to realize what he'd said. "Ted didn't tell me you were coming."

He stopped feet short of the door and set Becca down on the carpet. "Go change like Aunt Anita told you to, *kleines Mädchen*." Thanks to my German grandmother, I knew he'd just called her *little girl*. His voice matched the smiling face, but the little girl couldn't see him now, so his eyes were all for me. There was nothing friendly, or uncle-ish, in that black gaze.

I was in front of the door, but Olaf stayed those awkward few feet farther from the door than social norm would have dictated. Whatever we were doing on this trip, he didn't want to spook me—yet.

Becca looked from one to the other of us. Olaf was still

smiling and she couldn't see his eyes well enough from where she was standing, but either my face gave it away or she was sensing the tension between us. "Is everything all right?" she asked in an uncertain voice.

"Yeah," I said.

"Of course," he said smoothly and filled his eyes up with the smile that was still curling his lips so that he looked like a friendly giant.

"Go change, Becca, while Uncle Otto and I have a little talk."

"Are you going to fight?" she asked.

That seemed to startle both of us. "Of course not," I said, but not like I meant it.

Olaf said, "I will try not to make Aunt Anita angry with me."

Becca narrowed her eyes at us. "Promise you won't fight while I change?"

"I will promise if Anita promises."

I looked at him, but he was smiling down at the child and ignoring me. "I don't want to fight with Otto, so if he behaves himself, so will I."

"Aunt Anita," Becca said, stamping her bare foot, "that's not promising."

I sighed a little loudly and smiled through gritted teeth as I said, "I will do my best not to fight with Otto while you change clothes."

She gave me a look that reminded me of her mother when she was fed up with all the guy stuff. "All right, Aunt Anita, but you promised, no arguing."

"Do you ask your mom and dad not to argue like this?" I asked.

"Sometimes," she said, and with a last disapproving glance at both of us, she went into the room and closed the door behind her. The hallway seemed very quiet suddenly.

"Edward doesn't know you're here, does he?"

"My invitation came with a note from the bride."

"What kind of note?"

"That she wasn't sure why Ted and I had fallen out, but that she hoped we'd mend our friendship at the wedding."

Fuck, and this is what comes from having a secret identity. If you can't come out as Batman to your fiancée, then it's hard to explain that Uncle Otto is really the Joker, so maybe don't invite him to the wedding. I don't know what showed on my face, but it made him chuckle—a deep, rumbly, pleased sound that under other circumstances and coming from a totally different person might have been a sexy laugh. Honestly, I hadn't thought Olaf had that kind of laugh in him anywhere.

"Donna didn't know any better, but you did. You know that you and Edward aren't going to kiss and make up, so why did you come?"

"He's not the one I want to kiss."

"The last note I had from you said you were staying as far away from me as possible; you didn't want me to tame you the way I had Nicky."

"The note said I was staying away from you until I found my way as a werelion, so that your vampire wiles could not turn me into another pet cat for your harem."

"I don't remember the note saying *vampire wiles* or *harem*," I said.

He smiled and it almost reached his eyes. "Perhaps not, but both were implied."

I took a deep breath, let it out slowly, and tried to be reasonable. Olaf was actually behaving himself admirably. He was doing his best not to scare me, or even be creepy, which was a big deal for him. I would behave if he would. Besides, if it came to a real fight, I wanted Edward and Bernardo with me, and they were both at the hospital.

I thought of something. "How long have you been in town?" I asked.

"Not long."

"Did you get here in time to see all the police?"

"I watched Edward drive off in the ambulance and Bernardo follow with Donna in the rental car. Why are the police so interested in all of your people?" He was looking at me very steadily as he said it.

My pulse started speeding up, so I breathed in slowly and evenly through my nose. If Olaf had still been purely human he might not have noticed, but as a werelion he'd know I was fighting to keep my heart rate down. He'd just admitted that he'd waited until all my backup was either gone or tied up with the police before he showed himself. He smiled, and this one wasn't safe for children. It was the kind of smile that says not only is a man undressing you, but he's thinking of what he'd do to you once you were naked.

"So, you watched Peter get hurt and didn't do anything to help?"

The smile faded. "I did not see the attack happen, or I would have helped him."

I had a moment to think what kind of help he would have been, and part of me was sorry he'd missed it, but the sane part of me was glad. Peter might be charged with assaulting Dixie, but if Olaf had helped him out, I was pretty sure assault would be the least of our worries. Though honestly I'd never seen him injure a woman who wasn't a villain. Edward had seen Olaf's handiwork once, and what he'd done to the woman had haunted Edward. But it had been done in another country by Olaf, not by Otto Jeffries, who was Olaf's Clark Kent. Otto Jeffries was a marshal in good standing. Hell, Jeffries wasn't even on Interpol's radar. It was a clean identity and I probably didn't want to know how the military, or a government or two, had given Olaf a clean identity after some of the shit he'd done. Of course, there might be people on the planet who thought the same thing about Edward and Ted Forrester, but Edward was my best friend and Olaf wanted me to be his serial-killer girlfriend, or that had been his couple goal last time we talked.

"But you did wait for everyone to go to the hospital?"

"I thought we should talk alone first," he said, and his face was serious, no leering. I wasn't sure if that was reassuring or not.

"So you found out which room I was going to and came up the other side so that I wouldn't hear you following us."

"Yes," he said, face still serious.

"You work fast."

He bowed his head, acknowledging the compliment, though honestly it wasn't exactly meant as one. If I hadn't been working hard at not teasing him and making things worse, I'd have told him what fine stalker skills he had, but I knew better. I would behave myself if he would, until the point came when one of us did something to piss off the other one. Because there would come a moment when it all went to hell. I just didn't want to be alone with him when it happened, or maybe I did. I guess it depended on if I was going to kill him or if he was trying to kill me at the time. For the first I didn't want witnesses; for the second I'd want help.

"You are still the only woman I have ever known that is comfortable with silence."

I realized that he thought I was waiting in companionable silence with him while Becca changed clothes. I just never knew what to say to Olaf that wouldn't piss him off. "I try not to talk unless I have something to say."

"It is an admirable quality in both men and women."

Once he would have just said *women*. "Agreed," I said, and then thought to ask, "Do you know how Peter got hurt, or do I need to fill you in on the details?"

"The desk clerk said that he attacked a woman and she stabbed in defense of her virtue." He said it with no affect, empty face, empty voice, nothing, as if he wasn't in there somehow. I realized that his energy was the same now as it had been before he caught lycanthropy. I should have been able to feel his inner beast or some extra energy, but there was nothing. He was shielding hard and tight and perfect. Most lycanthropes never mastered shielding to that degree. He hadn't been a shapeshifter that long, only two years, give or take. It was impressive, but I wasn't sure if remarking on it would upset him, so I talked about something that upset me.

"He didn't attack anyone. He removed her from an area and did his best not to hurt her. She didn't feel the same way about not hurting him."

"Why did he remove the woman by force?"

I really didn't want to go into details, but Olaf was the only other person besides Donna whom Edward and I had lied to about our relationship. To Donna it had been because she wouldn't believe the truth; to Olaf it was because having me as Edward's girlfriend meant he'd respect Edward's threat more than just mine. Edward had marked me as his, as territory, and put up *No Trespassing* signs for Olaf by a look here, a hand hold there, a hug, a snuggle. Some of it had been done in front of other police officers, which hadn't helped either of our reputations, but Edward had thought it was worth it to keep Olaf at arm's length. I'd agreed and now I got to tell the truth, sort of.

He looked angry by the time I'd finished, and the barest

hint of warm energy breathed through the hallway. God, his control of his energy was amazing. If I hadn't known what he was now, he could have passed for human even to me. Of course, he was shielding and I wasn't trying to call his inner beast, but it was still impressive.

"Why would this other woman want to tell the child?"

"Her own husband cheats a lot and frequently, apparently. She stayed with him out of duty, but she doesn't want Donna to make the same mistake. "

"You are Edward's only weakness. He will not fall again."

"I can sort of see why Dixie, the woman in question, wouldn't believe that, though."

"Her husband is without honor."

"Apparently."

"Is she trained with a blade?" he asked.

"Not to my knowledge."

"Then how did she stab him with a pen and hit an artery? That takes more skill than most trained soldiers have."

"I think she got lucky, or Peter got unlucky."

"No one is that lucky."

"She was grabbing for things to defend herself with and apparently someone had left a fountain pen lying around."

"A fountain pen is rare."

"Like I said, lucky and unlucky. Then a piece broke off in Peter's leg and you know the rest."

"If Peter does not survive, neither will the woman."

"You know, normally I'd see that as a creepy comment, but I sort of agree with you."

"You would help me do this?"

"No, I know Dixie as a person. I couldn't help you do the sort of things you enjoy to her."

"Why does knowing her make a difference?" he asked, and it was a good sign that he asked the question rather than just be puzzled. I appreciated that he trusted me to ask it and that he would trust my answer.

"Doesn't knowing someone make it harder for you to hurt them?"

"Not really."

We looked at each other. "Do you have any ability to feel real empathy?"

"I don't believe so, but since I know only what I feel, I cannot be certain that what I feel is not empathy. Now answer my question. Why does it bother you more if you know someone?"

I tried to think how to explain it to him. "Dixie is a pain, and she may be crazy, as in pathological, about the whole cheating thing, but I know she has kids. I know her husband's been a bastard to her. I know that he did carpool for their son and Peter to martial arts class for years. I don't like Dixie, but she's real to me, a real person with thoughts and feelings and a life of her own. I would have more trouble hurting her or taking away her life because I know she has a life. Does that make any sense to you?"

"I understood everything you said, but I see knowing someone's details very differently than you do."

"How so?" I asked, because he'd never been willing to talk this much about himself before and I was sort of interested in spite of myself. Though if Becca didn't come out soon, I was going to be going in after her. I mean, she wasn't even a teenager yet. What the heck was she doing in there that was taking this much time?

"The more I know about someone, the more I can torture their mind as well as their body. It is often the personal details that give me what I need to break someone for gaining information."

"You mean like for an interrogation?"

"That is one use, yes."

I debated whether I wanted to ask any more. So far the discussion had been mostly academic. It was interesting without being disturbing, which was a nice change for Olaf and me.

"Sometimes strangers are more satisfying, if all I want is the blood and the pain, but sometimes a long hunt is even better. I know their facial expressions and how their body moves, so I can see their pain and fear even more than on a stranger's face."

"And there you go," I said.

"What?" he asked, and he looked genuinely puzzled.

"We were having a nice discussion, sharing insights, and then you have to go all Hannibal Lecter on me and overshare."

"You know what I am, Anita. You've known from the beginning. I never pretended with you, never hid what I was. I think that was the difference."

"You never hid because Edward told me what you were before we met."

"I'm not sure I would have pretended even if he hadn't told you. I was so angry that he brought a woman to work with us on that case. What could a woman do that he, Bernardo, and I could not?"

"I remember," I said.

He smiled then and shook his head, as if remembering, too. It was weird seeing him so . . . human. And I wasn't talking about the werelion part. Olaf had been inhuman through his hatred of women and what that rage led him to enjoy doing to them. Standing here in the hallway was the closest to a normal conversation we'd ever had.

"I wanted you from the moment I saw you," he said.

I didn't try to keep the surprise off my face. "You certainly had me fooled. I thought you were just the biggest misogynist I'd ever met, and hated my guts because I dared try to be one of the men."

"All that was true, but I hated you more because I wanted you and I knew that Edward would kill me for it."

We stood there looking at each other. I debated letting the silence stretch, asking what I wanted to ask, or checking on Becca. Most people would interrupt before I had time to decide, but Olaf would let me be quiet as long as I wanted to. I could think and he could enjoy a woman who didn't talk much. It was a win-win.

"I can ask what I actually want to ask, or I can check on Becca."

"Ask," he said.

"So only Edward's threat kept you from trying to kill me the first time we met?"

"Yes."

"And now?"

"I read Sherlock Holmes."

The change of topic startled me, so that I couldn't think why it was important, and then I did remember. An offhand comment that I'd made and he'd taken way more seriously than I'd meant it.

"What did you think of the stories?" I asked.

"I enjoyed them, and I liked Holmes's attitude toward women."

"I thought you would like that part but wasn't sure how you'd feel about the stories themselves."

"You are *the* woman for me, Anita. No other has made me want to modify my urges so that I did not hurt them."

"I'm flattered," I said, and I meant it. Anything that kept Olaf from trying to kidnap, rape, and torture me to death was a good thing. My understanding from Edward was that before me, that had been his endgame with any woman he "dated."

"Once you would have been angry or horrified," he said.

"I've grown as a person," I said, trying to make it a joke, but he didn't take it that way.

"So have I."

"I appreciate that," I said, "but I better check on Becca. She should have been changed and out by now."

"You are my Irene Adler," he said, and he seemed serious.

"So, what, I call you Sherlock?"

"I would like that. Couples usually have private names for each other."

I kept my face turned away from his gaze by getting the key card out of my pocket. By the time I looked up I had my face under control, or hoped I did. I tried to make a joke of it. "Would you prefer Sherlock, or Holmes?"

"Either. Would you prefer Irene or Adler?"

I used the key on the door and pushed it open as I said, "I'm not sure; can I think about it?"

"Of course. I will wait here in case the child is still dressing."

"Thanks," I said, and made sure that I didn't turn my back on him or lose sight of him as I went through the door and shut it behind me. I set the safety bar on just like they tell people to do, but I knew it wouldn't hold if Olaf wanted inside. He wanted us to have pet names for each other. Sweet Jesus on a stick, what was I supposed to do with a semi-tame serial killer? I had no idea. Okay, where was Becca? I'd start with that. Surely an eleven-year-old girl would be easier to manage. Yeah, yeah, everyone out there who's a parent, laugh it up.

38

BECCA HAD TAKEN a shower, carefully braided her hair in a complicated style that I could never have managed, and then gotten into her mother's makeup. It wasn't that the makeup looked bad on her. It was more that she looked like a sexy twenty-five-year-old from the chin up and a gangly eleven-year-old from there down. The pink dress with its white appliqué daisies was definitely a little girl's dress. I think she'd even had a similar one in yellow when she was six.

The makeup let me see the preview of what she might look like in a few years. She would be gorgeous. Watching her make the duck-lip pout at the bathroom mirror, I was suddenly a little worried about how grown-up she would be when the rest of her matched the makeup job. She saw me in the mirror then and her brown eyes went wide inside the thick eyeliner. She suddenly looked years younger, even with the makeup.

I found makeup remover in the expensive debris scattered across the sink area and we started trying to get all of it off. She didn't argue with me about taking it off, but she did ask me to take a picture of her with the makeup on. We compromised. I took the picture with my phone, not hers, and I'd keep it until Donna and Edward said it was okay for her to have it.

"What do you want the picture for?" I'd asked as I started to scrub her face.

"To put up online, of course." She said it with a tone that implied, heavily, *What a stupid question.*

That led into me having to lecture her on how a picture like that would attract boys much older than she was, and pedophiles as well. She gave me rolled eyes as if she'd heard this lecture before. I was so going to be talking to Edward about Becca's web access at home and on her phone. What surprised me the most, I think, was that she wasn't like other little girls her age. She had been kidnapped at six and tortured. They'd broken some of her fingers. They'd healed and her hand seemed fine, but she knew "the great bad thing" was real. Becca knew that there were bad people out there who would hurt children. They hadn't touched her sexually, but I'd been tied up by bad guys and hurt. It had left a lasting impression on me. I looked into Becca's eyes and didn't see the caution that I expected. Was that why she was fine and Peter wasn't? Was she that untouched by it? Did she even remember?

She stared up at me with half her face smeared clean and the other still showing that disturbing adultness. "What's wrong?" she asked me, and she looked older again, more serious. It was like another shadow of things to come, except this one was intelligent and perceptive. I suddenly wondered if she'd been as oblivious about what was happening out in the hallway as I'd thought.

"Nothing," I said automatically.

She gave me a scathing look. "Why does everyone lie to kids?"

"Because we think it's something the kid doesn't need to know." I gave her my own look back.

She crossed her slender arms over her chest and I realized there was muscle under the tanned skin. She'd been in dance since she was tiny, and I suddenly thought of Nathaniel's body and some of the professional dancers, including ballet dancers, I knew. Becca wasn't just going to be beautiful; she was going to be fiercely in shape. I was suddenly conflicted about that.

"Do you still want to be a ballerina when you grow up?"

"Yes." But she said it like she didn't mean it, or she didn't want to answer the question.

"You don't sound very convincing about it," I said as I went back to cleaning her face.

"It's just that when I say I want to be a ballerina, people think I'm like all the other little girls who say it. I'm working so hard, and every time I tell an adult, they pat me on the head and say, 'Isn't that nice,' or smile like I'm still six. I've started saying I want to be a professional dancer because I'm tired of people treating me like I'm playing dress-up and spinning around the living room to classical records."

"I can understand that," I said.

"But now they ask if I want to be on *Dancing with the Stars*, or *America's Got Talent*, and that's not what I'm giving up nearly every single afternoon and weekend for. I want to be a dancer, a real one. I want to do pointe when I'm old enough. My teacher says I have the lines for it and that I'm going to be tall enough."

"That's great, Becca. I took just enough ballet as a kid to know that I didn't want to do pointe, and I was too short to be a prima ballerina anyway."

She grinned up at me. "It would be hard to find you a partner the same size as you, and you need to match for the ballet."

"I have a guy friend who's my size and he's a professional dancer."

Now I had her attention. "What kind of dancer is he?"

"Ballet," I said.

"Where does he dance?"

I told her what company he was with, and from that point on she asked questions I couldn't answer, but I promised to ask my friend some of her questions next time I spoke with him. She was excited and chattering about ballet and dance and performance and a lot of details that were frankly over my head. I'd been younger than Becca when I stopped taking ballet.

It did give me an opening to call the men. I started with Micah, but I ended up in voice mail. I left a cheerful message that Becca and I were up in the room and Otto Jeffries had arrived for the wedding, with his invitation coming directly from the bride. I called Nathaniel next and left a similar message, adding that Otto was waiting for us in the hallway. I called Nicky and left a message about Otto being a surprise. I didn't want the message to be that a serial killer was up here scaring me when I couldn't prove anything. I started to call Ru and Rodina but realized they didn't know who Olaf was, so I couldn't think of a good generic message for their phones. No one got back to me. Why were the cops questioning all of them this long? Then I realized I'd been slow, or stupid.

Bettina Gonzales was a short, dark-haired woman, which

made her exactly fit Olaf's preferred victim profile. I had only his word that he'd just arrived. Maybe he'd been here for days watching all of us, waiting for a chance to see me alone. Did that sound paranoid? Maybe, but the difference between paranoia and caution is one simple thing: Are they really out to get you? Olaf had already made it clear that he wanted to be more than friends. Edward was afraid that if I totally turned him down, he'd move me from potential girlfriend to potential victim. I was worried about that, too. Was I going to have to have cocktails with Olaf, a coffee date? I already knew I didn't want to date him; the preliminaries weren't really necessary. What do you do with a serial killer who's offering to behave himself if only you'll date him? Hell if I knew.

39

I MADE ONE more phone call before we went back out to visit with Uncle Otto. I called Bernardo. I would have called Edward, but I didn't want to make him feel like he had to choose between being at Peter's side and being at mine. I was a big girl; I could take care of myself. I was a U.S. Marshal, too. Hell, I'd been a vampire executioner longer than Bernardo—long before we got grandfathered into the Marshals Service. So why did I feel the need to call for backup when Olaf hadn't done anything to threaten me yet? Because he scared me—there, that was the irritating truth. I hated that he made me want a man by my side, even if that man was Edward. I could take care of myself, damn it! I believed that, I really did, but . . . I called Bernardo just in case. Just in case what, I tried hard not to think about.

I went to his voice mail just like everyone else's, but while I was in the middle of leaving my message he picked up. "Anita, the text of your voice mail mentioned a fellow marshal." He was trying to play it cool, which meant Edward or Donna had to be close by. I heard voices and knew the rhythm of Edward's voice enough to know it was him. I couldn't understand anything he was saying, but I knew it was him talking.

Bernardo lowered his voice and said, "Is Olaf, Otto, really there?"

"Why would I make that up? Of course he's here."

"Sorry, I . . . Jesus."

"Yeah," I said, "how is Peter doing?"

"Still in surgery, but once they got the bleeding stopped the surgeon came out to ask some questions."

"What kind of questions?"

"If Peter had the anti-lycanthropy shot when he was at-tacked by the weretiger."

"Why would that matter enough for the surgeon to pause in the middle of things?" I asked.

Becca grabbed my arm. "Is Peter okay? Is he hurt worse? What's happening?"

I looked down at her, having to struggle to keep the phone to my ear. "They've got the bleeding stopped," I told her.

"So why did they stop in the middle of the surgery?" she asked.

"They're asking questions about when Peter was attacked by the weretiger," I told her.

"Why?" she asked.

"Is Becca right there with you?" Bernardo asked.

"Yeah."

"Put me on speaker for a minute." I did what he asked, and his voice changed to cheerful. "Hey, tiny dancer."

"Hey, Uncle Bernardo, is Peter okay?"

"Peter is going to be fine. In fact, the surgeon came out to talk to your mom and dad because he's doing better than they'd hoped. He wanted to come out and reassure everyone that it's good news."

"You promise that's the truth?" she said, face as suspicious as the words sounded, and again there was that echo of the older Becca she was going to become.

"I promise, honest Injun."

She rolled her eyes and said, "Uncle Bernardo, you know that's, like, racist or something. I used the word at school after hearing you use it and I got in trouble."

"I'm sorry, kiddo, I didn't mean to get you in trouble, but tell your teacher that your uncle is a real-live American In-dian, so he can say *Injun* if he wants to."

"I did, but she didn't believe me."

"I can come visit your school, if you want."

"Will you promise to say *honest Injun* in front of my teacher?"

He laughed. "Promise."

She smiled. "And Peter really is going to be okay?"

"That's what the doctors are all saying."

"When can I come see him?"

"He'll be in surgery for a little bit longer, and then you'll have to wait for him to sleep off the medicine they gave him, so two to four hours."

That seemed to satisfy her. Bernardo said, "Take me off speaker, Anita."

"Are you guys going to talk grown-up stuff?" she asked.

"Probably," I said, and suddenly had Bernardo's voice in my ear again. I asked him, "What's up, Bernardo?"

"Peter is healing faster than human-normal. Medical team saw the scars from the weretiger attack; that's what got them asking about the vaccine."

"Okay," I said, "why?"

"Apparently, people who got the live vaccine after an attack have been exhibiting enhanced healing ability. There's been a paper written up in a medical journal about it."

"Interesting," I said.

Becca was watching me suspiciously, trying to figure out what we were talking about that we didn't want her to hear.

"Blood work still comes back human, but they have enhanced healing, and some of them seem to be exhibiting better-than-normal reflexes."

"But Peter wasn't vaccinated," I said.

"That's what's keeping the doctor asking questions, I think."

Then I had a thought. "The vaccine is just a different kind of lycanthropy, right? The idea is that they'll cancel each other out."

"Yeah, and it seems to be working. They've got, like, an eighty percent success rate with the vaccine preventing attack victims from catching it, if they cross-match it so it's not the same kind of lycanthropy."

"Wow, eighty percent. That is good odds," I said.

"But Peter didn't get the shot," Bernardo said.

"No, but . . ." I looked at Becca. "Can you go in the bathroom and shut the door for a minute, please?"

"No, but I'll go out and wait with Uncle Otto and tell him you're talking grown-up stuff you don't want me to hear."

I debated whether I was comfortable with Olaf being a babysitter even for a few minutes and finally decided I was: If he wouldn't hurt me for fear of Edward, then his harming Becca was right out. "Okay, I'll be out in just a few minutes."

She gave me that eye roll again and then opened the door and went out, speaking to Olaf as she closed the door behind her. Her voice was full of disdain as she said, "She's talking to Bernardo, but Peter is going to be fine, or that's what they're telling me."

I waited for the door to close and then said, "I'm alone."

"What did you want to say that you couldn't say in front of Becca?" he asked.

"When Peter got hurt, one of our wererat bodyguards got injured with him. Cisco was hurt so badly that he died from his wounds, and he bled all over Peter."

"Are you saying that the wererat blood acted like its own vaccine?"

"Yeah, tell the doctor that when Peter was attacked, another wereanimal tried to protect him but ended up bleeding out on top of Peter."

"If the doctor asks where the other wereanimal came from, what do you want me to say?"

"Make him an innocent bystander, or just don't answer the question, or let Edward answer it. He was there, too."

"So was Otto," Bernardo said.

"I know. By the way, Otto Jeffries got an invitation to the wedding with a personal note from Donna in it."

"What?" I was glad to hear his voice as outraged as I'd felt. "What did the note say?"

"Something about her hoping that Ted and Otto would work out their differences and mend their friendship at the wedding."

"She did not," Bernardo said.

"Oh, yes, she did. Doesn't it sound like something she'd do?"

"Yeah, I guess it does."

"But if Ted had told her the truth, that he was afraid of Otto, thought he was dangerous, then this wouldn't have happened. Lies catch up with us, damn it."

"Donna couldn't keep the supposed affair between the two of you secret. Do you really think she'd be able to keep her mouth shut about something as big as that?"

"No," I said, rubbing my eyes as if I was tired. I shouldn't be tired. I was on vacation.

"I'll tell Ted and Donna that Otto is at the hotel. I'll make sure Ted knows that he doesn't have to rush off and rescue you from the big bad, but if I tell him about the note from Donna, there may be another fight."

"I can't help that. Do what you think best."

"I know he loves her, and the kids are great, but . . ."

"I know, I don't get it either."

"But, hey, I'm never going to marry and settle down, so what the hell do I know?"

"And I'm trying to marry more people than the law will allow, so I'll keep my opinions to myself."

"That's not what Ted told me."

"What do you mean?" I asked.

"He told me you didn't like her."

"I never said that."

"But it's true," Bernardo said.

"And do you like her?" I asked.

He was quiet for a second. "Not really, but he really loves her, like madly, truly, deeply shit."

"She makes him happy most of the time," I said.

"That's more than I've ever had with anyone," Bernardo said.

"I'm sorry to hear that," I said.

"I'm not looking for Ms. Right, and I'm having a hell of a good time looking for Ms. Right Now."

That made me laugh. "I noticed that out by the pool."

"I see the doctor—I'll go tell him about your wererat friend."

"We'll see you at the hospital later," I said.

"Yeah," he said, and I heard him talking to the doctor before the phone cut off.

I put the phone in my back pocket, stood up a little straighter, squared my shoulders, and went out to face Olaf and Becca. I opened the door to hear my chosen niece say, "I don't know if Aunt Anita is dating Uncle Bernardo. Neither one of them is monogamous, so they could be."

Olaf looked at me, and there was a lot of rage in those dark, cavernous eyes. So much rage that his power trickled through the hallway like a breath of wind off the scalding fields of hell.

Fuck. I should have known that with the level of control he had this quickly he'd be a powerful motherfucker. Like he hadn't been dangerous enough before he became a werelion. And I so did not need a jealousy issue between him and Bernardo.

"I am not dating Bernardo. The doctor had some questions about Peter's injuries. The ones he got when Otto and Peter were helping me in St. Louis." I gave Olaf a look and tried to convey with my eyes that I needed him to think, not get all pissy.

He looked confused for a minute.

"Why couldn't I hear about that?" Becca asked. "I've seen his scars. It's why he wears a T-shirt in the pool all the time now."

I remembered that he'd had a wet T-shirt on when he carried Dixie to us, but I hadn't thought about it. I'd work on his comfort level with his scars later. "Bernardo needed to ask some questions from someone who was there when Peter got hurt."

"But why?" she asked.

"Yes, why?" Olaf asked.

I just looked at him and said, "Later."

He glanced down at Becca, who was watching me far too closely for comfort.

"We will talk later."

"Yes," I said, relieved he was letting it drop.

"About many things," he said.

So much for my being relieved.

40

THERE WERE SECURITY cameras in the elevator and there usually weren't on the stairs, so the three of us were waiting for the elevator. Becca had my left hand in her right, and Olaf's right hand in her left, and was swinging our hands back and forth as she twisted on the balls of her feet to make the skirt of the pink dress swish back and forth. I realized there was some sort of slip or something underneath the skirt part that was making it billow out and make a sound like a different type of cloth was underneath, something that made that *swish, swish* sound as she twisted back and forth. She'd done the same kind of thing at six. She was suddenly back to being a little girl again. It was comforting, and at the same time I knew it wouldn't last. She was a little girl, but the teenager was in there peeking out more and more.

I glanced at Olaf. His face showed nothing. It didn't bother him that we were standing there holding on to Becca while she twirled, but it didn't seem to make him happy either. I turned back to look at the shiny doors of the elevator and realized that my expression was about the same as his. I guessed I should stop throwing stones at Olaf unless I was willing to have them thrown back at me. We waited stoically for the elevator doors to open while Becca half danced between us.

The elevator doors opened and Rufous was standing there. His face was grim and almost angry, and then he was smiling. He looked so pleased to see us that I'd almost have thought I'd been wrong about the grim expression before, but I knew what I'd seen.

"There you are, Jeffries. I was just saying earlier today that we were missing one of the Four Horsemen, and here you are," Rufous said, and ushered us onto the elevator.

I started to get on, leading Becca. Olaf hung back a second, and since he still had Becca's other hand in his, I couldn't get on the elevator without letting go of her. Olaf said, "Weren't you getting off at this floor, Martinez?"

"Actually, I was sent to check on Anita and Becca. Marisol was wondering what took so long for the little one here to change into a pretty dress," he said, smiling at the little girl.

She let go of our hands, put her arms up gracefully above her head, and did a complete pirouette so that the skirt flew out around her and I got a glimpse of the crinkly chiffon underneath. She came down to first position, her feet in their white sandals at that odd and artificial angle that is the beginning of all ballet.

"A very pretty dress, indeed," Rufous said, beaming at her. She beamed right back at him.

The elevator started to make a high-pitched buzzing sound. Rufous must have hit the button to make the doors stay open, and now the elevator was protesting. I put a hand on Becca's shoulder and got us both in the elevator beside Rufous. He'd seemed really tall earlier by the pool. Now I didn't feel nearly as short beside him. Something about standing next to someone who really is seven feet tall makes everyone else seem smaller.

Olaf followed us into the elevator and it suddenly seemed more claustrophobic, as if there wasn't room for Olaf and Rufous in the same small space. They were both really big men; it was just that some of Rufous's size was wide, not tall. Looking at them standing there in front of me, I could suddenly see that Rufous was at least twice as wide through the shoulders as Olaf. That wasn't middle-aged spread; that was just being a really big guy. I realized that Rufous had moved slightly in front of me and Becca. It was subtle, but he'd never done a thing to make me think he felt protective of me before. He thought Olaf was Marshal Otto Jeffries, officer in good standing, so why the change in behavior?

Olaf noticed it, of course, and he looked down at Rufous in that way that really tall men can do when they want to emphasize to another man that they're bigger. Most women miss it, but I worked with too many men not to notice.

Rufous smiled up at him with that good ol' boy smile that he usually wore, but I realized that he had his sidearm on and I was pretty sure he had his ASP, a collapsible baton, in one pocket of his shorts. I knew he had something in that pocket. A lot of police never go completely unarmed if they can help it, but Rufous wasn't usually this obvious about it. What the hell was going on?

Olaf frowned slightly, turning his head as if he was trying to see Rufous better. It wasn't aggressive, but puzzled. Olaf didn't know why Rufous had come to find us armed and ready for trouble either. Usually I like not being the only one who doesn't know what's going on, but there are only a small number of things that will make a man behave like this, and none of them were true for Rufous and me. Maybe he was protecting Becca from Uncle Otto? What had changed?

I thought of it about the same time that Olaf did. He smiled, but it was a superior smile, condescending. "I did not think my having lycanthropy would bother you this much, Martinez. I had hoped better of you."

"I don't think that's it," I said. "Rufous is cool around Micah and Nathaniel."

"If the Marshals Service sees fit to keep you on, Jeffries, then that's good enough for me. I got no problem with you failing your blood test. I was sorry to hear that you caught it on the job."

Olaf frowned harder, looking almost angry. He and I did share anger as our go-to emotion unless we worked at it. "Then why are you here?"

"I'm staying in the hotel for the wedding," Rufous said, smiling.

"As am I."

"Are you mad at each other?" Becca asked, and that meant she was picking up way more of the social context than I would have at her age.

Rufous started to look behind him at her but stopped himself and kept his attention on the other man. Even if Olaf hadn't been a werelion with more than human speed, the elevator was too small for drawing guns or batons or even blades. What most people don't realize is how fast an unarmed person can close with you. In an elevator there wouldn't be time to draw weapons, and Rufous might have been a big guy and a football player once, but he was no match for Olaf, even fully human, but now . . . A lycanthrope in an elevator is going to win unless you have your gun out and aimed and are willing to shoot them before they get a chance to move. Hell, a human with good reflexes is going to close with you, and then you get to wrestle for your gun. Not good odds. I knew logically that Olaf wouldn't want to be caught on security video behaving badly, but the little moving box was feeling awfully claustrophobic about now.

"No, honey, we're not mad, are we, Jeffries?"

"I am not," he said in that careful voice of his. I realized that it was his version of Edward's voice going empty. I hadn't realized that I knew Olaf's voice that well.

The elevator doors opened at last. Rufous pushed the door-open button and said, "Ladies first."

I gave Becca a little push toward the door. She reached back for my hand. "You come with me." She had that stubborn set to her face that reminded me of Peter. I gave her my left hand and let her lead me toward the doors, but I wasn't leaving without Rufous and Olaf. I wasn't sure what was going on, but I wasn't letting the doors close behind me with them still inside—mainly because I didn't know why Rufous had ridden to the rescue. It wasn't like him, at least not around me.

I stopped in the doorway, putting a hand on one side of the doors just in case. "Everyone out," I said, smiling.

Olaf got out first, and then Rufous followed, but neither one of them looked away from the other completely. Rufous had started it, but Olaf was too aware of violent possibilities not to add his paranoia to the other man's. I'd have done the same thing.

One of the hotel employees came from behind the desk to ask us to please stop holding up the elevator. Rufous smiled and said, "Sorry about that."

The four of us stood in a little group. Becca still had my hand and was looking from one man to the other as people walked past us in the lobby. There was a uniformed officer at the main desk talking to the manager. There was absolutely nothing wrong, and yet Rufous was still tense. He could smile all the down-home smiles, but his body language still showed the subtle signs of a big man who was ready for trouble.

I felt a warm trickle of energy from behind us. It made me turn, with Becca's hand still in mine, so that I could glance behind me and keep an eye on Olaf.

It was Nicky moving toward us, not hurrying exactly, but moving like he had a purpose. Something tight and tense loosened in my chest. I had backup I trusted now, backup that really could go up against Olaf and have a chance.

Rufous was a cop, but he was only human, and an out-of-shape human at that.

I wanted to touch Nicky so badly when he came to stand beside me, but I acted as professional as he did.

He said in a low, tight voice, "Otto."

"Nicky," Olaf said.

Becca moved a little closer to me, as if she was picking up on the tension.

"Where is everyone else?" I asked

Nicky said, "The police are still questioning them."

"Why would they let you go and keep the others?" Olaf asked.

"Murdock is the only one who never met the missing girl," Rufous said.

"They would have let Bram go, too, but he was arguing with the cops that he was going to wait for Micah."

"He's Micah's bodyguard," I said.

"There are more useful things than arguing with cops." He looked at Olaf, who smiled.

"No arguments," I said.

"I could hear Morgan and Wyatt. It seemed like they were both winding down."

"How did you hear them?" Rufous asked.

"Through the walls. They aren't that thick."

"I keep forgetting that preternatural hearing," Rufous said. "What about Micah and Nathaniel?"

"The police are still questioning Nathaniel, and Micah insisted on being with him or the interview had to end. I'm still not sure why the cop listened to Micah and not to Bram."

"Why are they still interviewing Nathaniel about what happened between Peter and Dixie?"

Nicky's smile slipped around the edges. There was suddenly a cynicism to his face that made me grab his arm and say, "What's wrong, Nicky?"

"They ran everyone's name through the database and Nathaniel's popped with his juvie convictions."

I frowned at him. "What does that have to do with what happened earlier today? Nathaniel didn't do anything but help with first aid."

Nicky looked at me as if I were naïve.

"What am I missing here, Nicky? Just tell me."

Rufous made a throat-clearing sound that no one ever used for clearing their throat but was only to get attention. We gave it to him.

"Do you know something about this, Rufous?"

He looked embarrassed, which I hadn't seen on him before. It made me even more nervous. "Let's find my wife. Ted asked her to come in from sight-seeing when Peter went to the hospital just for you, button," he said, smiling down at Becca.

"Ted call you?" I asked.

Rufous nodded.

"I'm not a baby, Mr. Martinez. Is something wrong with Uncle Nathaniel?"

"No, button."

"And stop calling me button. I'm not an article of clothing; I'm a person. I'm just little, but I'm still a person."

I had to turn my face away and swallow hard to stop from laughing or giving her a high five. Both seemed good.

"How much time did you say you were spending with Button here?" Rufous said.

Becca glared at him. I fought not to laugh at her—one, because she was right, and two, because her dignity was on the line. People treat children as if they don't have dignity, but they do, or they can.

"How do you know this is my influence?" I asked him.

"Well, it didn't come from her mother," he said, and there was a note of unhappiness in his voice. I hated that I agreed with Olaf on this, but I did.

"Actually, my mom won't let just anyone call her names like honey or sweetheart or button," she said, arms crossed over her thin chest. That stubborn look that reminded me so much of Peter when he was younger was back.

"She lets Ted call her honeybunch," I said.

She rolled her eyes at me as if I was being stupid. "That's Dad. Of course he calls her that. She calls him teddy bear."

Nicky and Olaf were alerted to someone walking in our direction. I had to move slightly to see around Nicky. Rodina and Ru were walking toward us.

"Teddy bear, huh?" Rodina said.

"No, Morgan, don't even think about it," I said.

"I do not encourage it," said Nicky, "but if you are going to call Ted teddy bear, then I want to watch."

"As do I," Olaf said.

Rufous said, "Me, too."

"If I do it, I'll try to make sure I have an audience," Rodina said.

"If they wanted to keep Nathaniel longer, why are you free this soon, Wyatt? You flirted with her as much as Nathaniel did."

"I'm not sure," he said, but looked uncomfortable.

"I see the little woman," Rufous said, raising his arm to attract the attention of a woman who was almost as tall as he was, but without the middle-aged spread. Her hair was salt-and-pepper in careless curls cut just above her shoulders. There was a heat and happiness in Rufous's face as he looked at the tall woman all the way across the lobby that made me happy to see. As I got closer to my own wedding I liked seeing couples with a decade and counting of happily ever after. She turned and her face broke into a huge smile that made her eyes sparkle far enough away that I wasn't sure what color they were, and it was all for Rufous.

"I thought college football players were supposed to go for short cheerleaders," I said.

"Nope, I like 'em tall, and you can keep your cheerleaders. Marisol was a track star. She nearly made the Olympics," Rufous said, grinning and moving to meet his wife, so after they'd kissed each other thoroughly their conversation was private. Maybe he didn't want us to hear their terms of endearment for each other.

I fought off the urge to ask about Nathaniel again, because we had managed to distract Becca from it. I could have opened the link between Nathaniel and me and seen, or at least felt, everything he was experiencing, but opening a link that wide can alert others with psychic ability. Some police departments were starting to hire psychics or witches to monitor stuff like that. I didn't want to get Nathaniel in more trouble or explain how deep our connection went. Besides, if I kept my mouth shut and was patient, Rufous's wife, Marisol, would take the little girl somewhere else. I almost had to count under my breath to stop myself from asking what I wanted to ask. Luckily, they didn't keep us waiting long.

They came up hand in hand, both grinning like a couple of schoolkids. It made me feel better to see them all shiny after decades of marriage. I think they'd celebrated twenty-five years together, or maybe that was Frankie and Carol. Edward and Donna had a lot of friends who had hit the twenty-plus mark, and I'd been introduced to most of them in the last forty-eight hours, so they were beginning to glom together.

I wanted to know about Nathaniel, but I wasn't sure about letting Becca out of my sight until Edward relieved me. As if he knew, I got a text from him that told me Marisol was on Becca duty now. *Focus on Otto!*

Becca didn't want to go with Marisol. She wanted to stay and find out what was happening with Nathaniel. I'd finally had enough. "Becca, this isn't negotiable. You go with Marisol now. We need to talk about things and I'm not sure if you need to hear them or not, and until I am sure, you need to be elsewhere."

"What if I don't go?" she said, crossing her arms and getting that stubborn look again.

"Do you really want to help Nathaniel?" Nicky asked.

She looked suspicious but said, "Yes."

"Then do what Anita says, because the sooner we can talk to her about Nathaniel, the sooner we can help him."

She opened her mouth to argue.

My stomach had tightened into a harsh knot at the phrasing. Nathaniel needed help, damn it. "Becca, this is one of the loves of my life and you're delaying my ability to help him by being a brat." Was that harsh? I didn't know, but we'd wasted enough time being nice about this.

"I'm sorry," she said, but still sounded angry about it.

"Don't be sorry; do better. Now go, so I can find out what's happening."

Marisol held out her hand and said, "There's supposed to be a great cupcake place nearby."

"I don't want a cupcake," Becca said as they walked out of hearing range across the lobby. What kind of eleven-year-old doesn't like cupcakes?

I turned back to Nicky and Rufous. "One of you talk, now."

Ru looked like he was afraid he was in trouble, too, but Rodina seemed eager, as if she was glad someone was in trouble.

"You know Nathaniel has a record for soliciting and a few other things. He pled out and never saw jail time, but he has a record," Nicky said.

I nodded. "I know. What has that got to do with anything that happened today?"

"You knew?" Rufous asked.

"The first time I ever saw Nathaniel, he was in a hospital bed recovering from an attack by one of his customers."

"And you dated him knowing that he had been a whore?" Olaf asked.

I turned on him and gave him the look the word deserved. "First, never use that word in connection with Nathaniel again. Second, yes, I knew he was a high-end and very specialized escort when I met him."

"He was more than that, Blake," Rufous said.

I looked at him. "You ran Nathaniel's name through the system, didn't you?"

"When he came to New Mexico to help with the wedding the first time, he was spending a lot of private time with Peter, and Becca was all over him calling him uncle, so, yeah, I ran him. He may have been a high-end escort when you met him, but his record is for streetwalking and drugs. One of the conditions of the plea was that he go to rehab."

"He went," I said, "and he's been clean ever since."

"He's still got a very colorful past, Blake. I talked to Ted about what I found and was reassured that he knew all about it, and that Graison was one of the rarities, someone who truly turned their life around. I was happy to hear it."

"What does Nathaniel's past have to do with the police questioning him about Peter and Dixie's . . . altercation?"

"They're not questioning him about that," Rufous said.

"Then what are they questioning him about?"

"The missing girl, Bettina Gonzalez."

"What?" I asked, and it was loud enough that a few people looked our way. I lowered my voice and said, "What are you talking about, Rufous?"

Rufous answered, "You have a badge, but you've never been a regular cop. You don't understand how we see certain things."

"Then enlighten me," I said, and I'd stepped closer to him, my hands already starting to make fists.

He didn't tell me to calm down; he just did what I asked. "A young woman flirts with a few young men; then she goes missing after having sex with one of them. The lover is in the clear through witnesses, but one of the other men has a record for prostitution and drugs, and Graison got pulled in by a cop the first time when he was, like, ten, so that's child prostitution."

"He was the victim," I said.

"Yeah, but it's still going to be a hell of a background for someone to overcome. You know that abusers usually start out as victims, Blake."

"I know that's the prevailing theory."

"I've seen it happen, and if Rankin has been on the job long enough to make detective, he's seen it, too."

"So because Nathaniel was everyone's damn victim, the police are going to victimize him again?"

"The missing girl was hanging all over him and Erwin here." He pointed at Ru. "Then she goes and sleeps with someone else. The cops are going to wonder if Graison is the jealous type."

I laughed. I couldn't help it. "He's one of the least jealous people I've ever met."

"Nathaniel likes to share," Nicky said.

"But the police here don't know Nathaniel like the two of you do. To them he's a man who was flirting with the missing woman, then lost out to another man, and then his record pops with all kinds of bad shit. They are going to look at him hard for this. They'd look at anyone connected to the girl whose name popped in the database."

It was so unfair. I had to count slowly to ten, and forced myself to unfold my hands one stiff finger at a time. "Fine, fine, but they have no reason to hold him."

"Blake, he's a shapeshifter."

"How is that relevant?"

"How would they know what he was?" Olaf asked.

"You Google his name and he comes up under his stage name at Guilty Pleasures. There are pictures of him in his leopard form on the website," Rufous said.

"But I'll say again: How is that relevant?"

"Blake, come on. Shapeshifters may have legal rights and Florida is a more forward-thinking state than some of the Western ones, but people are still afraid."

"It's the big, bad wolf syndrome," Rodina said, "or in this case big, bad leopard."

"Come on, Blake. You hunt rogue lycanthropes. You know what they're capable of," Rufous said.

I tried to be reasonable. I tried to think like a cop and not Nathaniel's fiancée, but I was having serious trouble separating the two in that moment. "I know you're right, Rufous. I know I sound like every other girlfriend in the world who says, *But my boyfriend would never hurt anyone.*"

"I've had women and men say it to me with their faces covered in bruises from the boyfriend who would never harm anyone," Rufous said.

"I know, I really do, but it doesn't matter, because it's Nathaniel."

"And he's your boo."

I smiled. "Yeah, he is."

"One of them," Olaf said.

I looked at him, fighting not to frown. "Yeah, he's one of my boos."

"You do have more serious boyfriends than anyone I've ever met," Rufous said.

"I'm poly; it kind of goes with the sexual orientation."

"I thought it was a lifestyle choice," Rufous said.

I shook my head. "Not for me."

Rufous shook his head. "Marisol is enough for me. Normally, I'd say if you find the right one, all the rest just sort of fade into the woodwork, but I've seen you with your fellas, Blake, and it seems to be the real deal."

"Thanks, Rufous, I appreciate that."

"Now, go help your boo."

Olaf tried to go with us, but I didn't have to interfere, because Rufous did it for me. "I need to talk to Jeffries for a minute. You go on."

I wanted and needed to go to Nathaniel, but I didn't want Rufous alone with Olaf until I understood why he was being protective of me. "Rufous, can I talk to you for a minute?"

"Jeffries and I will be fine."

"I don't doubt that Otto will be dandy, but I need to ask you something before we all go our separate ways."

He didn't like it, but he came off to one side of the lobby with Nicky and me. Rodina and Ru stayed with Olaf. I heard Rodina say, "So you're Plague."

"Yes," Olaf said, and then we were out of my hearing range.

"Why are you suddenly treating me like a girl, Rufous?"

"You are a girl, Blake," he said with a smile.

"But you've always treated me like one of the guys until just a few minutes ago. Why do you suddenly feel protective toward me?"

"I'd feel protective of most of the men I know if they were going up against Jeffries."

"How did you know he was even here?" I asked, and then I realized. "Ted called you."

"He couldn't leave the hospital, but he told me that Jeffries has damn near been stalking you and he didn't want you to be alone with him. Don't worry, he swore me to secrecy. I know you don't want the other marshals to see you as needing to be rescued, but, Jesus, Blake, most men would need rescuing if Jeffries put a target on them. There's no shame in saying you're outmatched with someone like that. He's a freaking giant."

Like all great lies, it was almost the truth. I nodded. "I've worked too long and hard to be one of the guys to want to be shoved back in the girl box, Rufous."

"I understand that."

"What talk do you want to have with Otto?"

"I'll just tell him to back off."

"It's not your job to have that talk with him," Nicky said.

"Ted told me that he's let people think he's a couple with Anita to keep Jeffries off of her at work."

"I'm her bodyguard. I'll talk to Otto," Nicky said.

"Nicky . . ." I started to say.

"No, Anita, it's better coming from me than from Rufous."

I couldn't argue that, but I really didn't want either of them alone with Olaf. He scared me in a way that very few people did.

Nicky, letting the bodyguard stoicism slip, smiled. "I've got this. You go help Nathaniel."

"You can't scare Otto off," I said. "He doesn't scare."

"I'll remind him of how I got my job as your bodyguard," Nicky said.

Nicky was saying that he would threaten Olaf with me making him a Bride, which would mean I would own him, control him, the way I did Nicky. It was Nicky's fate as my lion Bride that had made Olaf stay away from me in the first place. He'd even written a note to me saying he didn't want to end up like Nicky.

I glanced back to find Rodina invading Olaf's personal space, but her body language wasn't threatening; it was seductive. Did she think he was handsome, or was she throwing herself on the landmine? I hoped she wasn't. I might not like Rodina, but she didn't deserve to be served up to Olaf.

"I'll be with him, Blake. Jeffries won't try anything against both of us, and one of us with a badge."

I didn't argue with him, but I knew that if Olaf thought he needed to kill both of them, he would, or he'd die trying. Nicky might have a chance of killing him first, but Rufous would just die. I didn't want to widow Marisol.

"Let's do this, Murdock," Rufous said. He sounded a little eager, as if he was hoping for a fight, or at least a little excitement. Had he been wanting to try his luck with Olaf, or was it just the typical cop love of action?

"I haven't agreed to either of you handling this for me," I said. Nicky frowned at something, which made me look. Ru was smiling and walking toward us as if he didn't have a care in the world. He looked slender and almost fragile compared to Rufous, Nicky, and Olaf, and he played to it, doing his best to radiate harmlessness and what I supposed was meant to be sex appeal. What the hell was he doing?

I glanced across the lobby to Olaf, who was watching us all as if he'd memorize us down to the buttons on our jeans. Maybe his being a stalker wasn't so far from the truth after all. Ru put his arm around my shoulders in an overly familiar way. I tensed up as he leaned in and whispered, "You flirted with me at the pool, in front of witnesses. Do you want to explain to the police why we're not flirting now?"

And, see, that was the problem with lies and pretending. Once you started, it was hard to stop. I put a smile on my face and slid my left arm around his waist, being careful that my hand slid high enough to avoid the gun at his waist. Cuddling was always harder with weapons, but with Olaf showing up unexpectedly and the police trying to pin a woman's disappearance on us, we'd work around the weapons.

Olaf started walking toward us, with Rodina trailing behind, a smile on her lips. She looked entirely too pleased with herself.

"What have the two of you been telling Otto?"

Ru kissed my cheek, touching the side of his face to mine.

Olaf said, "Are those your teeth marks in his neck?"

I gaped at him, because of all the questions he could have asked, this wasn't one I'd expected. If Rufous hadn't been there, I might have lied just because I didn't like the emotion coming off Olaf, but Rufous had seen me do it.

"Yeah."

"You bit him in a passionate embrace?"

"Yes."

Heat rolled off him, his beast breaking over us.

"You've taken another lover?"

"That's none of your business, Jeffries," Rufous said.

Olaf turned on Rufous, but Nicky stepped in and said, "Did the girl try to seduce you first?"

It distracted Olaf, made him turn to Nicky. "Yes. Has she tried with you as well?"

"No, but she tried with someone else, because she thought it would make Anita happier."

"I don't understand," Olaf said.

"When you turned her down, Wyatt showed you his neck, right?"

"Yes."

"Rufous here is protecting Anita because that's just the kind of guy he is, but you knew me before I met Anita. I wasn't a self-sacrificing kind of guy. Neither were Morgan and Wyatt before they met Anita."

Olaf looked at Nicky, and then at Ru, and finally at Rodina as she joined us.

"You're trying to distract me from Anita, at any cost."

"Which is why we all need a little talk without Marshal Blake being present," Rufous said.

Olaf didn't even protest. He'd gotten Nicky's message that Ru and Rodina were my Brides. Maybe it would make him rethink wanting to play Sherlock to my Irene Adler. I sent Rodina off with them, just in case. Ru stayed with me, on the condition he be more bodyguard and less flirt. He agreed. He was my Bride—he had to agree to almost anything.

I needed to see Micah and Nathaniel and figure out how I could convince Detective Rankin that my boo wasn't his guy.

41

THE HOTEL EMPLOYEES were impressed by my flashing my badge; the local police were not. "You aren't part of this investigation, Marshal," the uniformed officer standing at the head of the hallway, blocking my way, said. Down the hallway were the conference rooms they were using to question people.

"I just want to talk to my people; that's all."

"Unless you're part of the investigation, you don't get past me. Those are my orders." He was completely unapologetic about it, which meant I probably couldn't bully my way past him. He looked young enough to be new on the job, but there was something about the way he held himself and the buzzed haircut that said he'd been military first. The kind of military who join the police are usually combat veterans. They don't bully easily, and I certainly wasn't going to scare them. He stood at relaxed attention, perfectly content to stand there for hours. No one was shooting at him; it was a good day. When no one trying to kill you is your definition of a good day, it's damn hard to impress you.

I continued to stand there in front of the officer whose name tag read *Evans*, but I got my cell phone out and texted Micah. "I'm outside the room. Uniform won't let me in. Are you or Nathaniel officially being held?"

"I'm not," Micah texted back.

My stomach did its hard-knot thing again. "Is Nathaniel?"

"Tried to get up & leave. Rankin is trying for material witness."

"He has no grounds," I texted back.

"But he's local, we're not, could he get a warrant?" Micah texted.

I looked at the screen and thought about it. Could Rankin get a material witness warrant against Nathaniel if he got the right judge? Probably. We'd have Nathaniel out before you could say *lawsuit*, but with the right judge and enough people prejudiced against him for his past and being a wereleopard, it was possible. But one thing I knew for sure was the longer you talked in an interrogation, the more information you gave them to use against you. Hell, if you talked in an ordinary interview for enough hours, you'd end up saying things you didn't mean or wished you could take back. Hours of questions and answers were designed to break you down, to exhaust you, and to make you say things that would incriminate you. Innocent people would confess to things if they were questioned long enough and hard enough.

"Not sure, but either stop talking & say lawyer, or get up and walk out."

"Rankin will imply that we aren't free to go again."

"If he doesn't produce a warrant, he's full of shit."

"OK" was the only reply. I put my phone away.

"What's going on?" Ru asked.

"They're coming out," I said. I believed that; the hard knot in my stomach wasn't quite sure.

I heard my text go off again. When I checked, it was Micah. "We keep trying to leave, but not leaving."

"Why?" I asked.

"Unsure."

That wasn't like either of them. Micah worked with the police for the Coalition and Nathaniel had had enough experience with the police early on that he knew not to talk without a lawyer, or he should have known. So why were they still talking? I'd been so busy being scared for Nathaniel that I hadn't been logical, and logic stated that they should have walked out of there a while ago. No bluff should have kept Micah there, and he'd have insisted Nathaniel go with him. And it was a bluff, because no way did Rankin have a warrant yet.

Officer Evans could keep me out of the room physically, but I had other options and I was willing to use them now. I lowered my shields and reached out toward both of my guys, but I forgot that I was already standing beside someone I was metaphysically connected to. The side of my body closest to Ru ran with goose bumps, all the hairs on my arm standing up. I turned to look at him and found him rubbing the arm closest to me, as if I wasn't the only one who'd felt it. His eyes were a little wide, his breathing quicker.

"What is that?" Ru said.

I stared at him from inches away, and just like I had at the pool, I had a sudden urge to touch him. I shut the link down, putting my shields back in place, so that we were left staring at each other.

I stepped back from the officer and the hallway, and Wyatt followed my lead like a good dance partner. We found a quiet piece of wall and I said, out loud, "I don't know what's wrong with our connection, but it's not like this with Nicky or Rod . . . Morgan."

"You and Nicky have a solid connection. You know what you are to each other. Morgan hates you; it helps her keep you out of her head."

"And you and me?" I asked.

"I mirror the energy around me, the behaviors of the people around me, which makes me nearly perfect at undercover work, but it also means that I'm vulnerable to getting lost in my cover."

"You mean you start believing your cover story?"

He nodded.

"So why does that make my energy weird around you?"

"Nicky said it last night: Brides are food or cannon fodder. We aren't meant to be kept around this long, Anita. I'm trying to become whatever you need me to be, and for your powers, that's food—either through blood, meat, or sex."

"Are you saying you don't care which I choose?"

"I'd rather not die, so I'd prefer not to be your meat." He leaned his face close to mine, his arm going around my waist and automatically sliding high enough to not compromise the gun at my waist, just like I had with him earlier. "If you were a true vampire I would happily donate blood."

I spoke with my lips almost touching his cheek. "I'm not that kind of vampire."

"No, through Jean-Claude's powers you're a succubus like

Belle Morte." He nuzzled his face against mine like a cat scent-marking its favorite people.

"I have enough lovers; nothing personal."

"I am not asking to join your poly group, my queen, only to be your food."

I drew back enough to look into his eyes. "You know that I can feed on energy without sex."

"Yes, but of all the ways you feed, sex seems to be the most pleasant. I would like to take the pleasant option, if you would allow it."

I felt my energy rise like someone had added hot water to a cooling bath. Ru shuddered beside me, as if the energy had traveled from me to him. It was as if a part of my power had been cut off, or dampened, and it was suddenly bright again. I knew who it was before I saw them. Micah came out of the hallway behind us with his hand on Nathaniel's arm as if he were leading him. Officer Evans was looking behind them as if for orders—did he stop them or let them go?

Detective Rankin stepped into sight behind them. Evans asked him something and Rankin shook his head. Wyatt and I started walking toward Micah and Nathaniel. They saw us and moved in our direction. Nathaniel did a long blink and then took Micah's hand, rather than having to be dragged along. I was already holding my hand out to them as if that would help close the distance between us. Micah took my hand, and that helped, but it wasn't enough. I kept his hand in mine and threw my other arm around Nathaniel's neck. He wrapped his free arm around my waist and we held on. I buried my face against the side of his neck and the scent of his skin, like warm vanilla. Micah wrapped his arms around us both, and I turned so that I could bury my face against both of them together. Micah smelled spicier than Nathaniel, like the difference between cinnamon and vanilla, both sweet, but in different ways.

It was Nathaniel who reached out and drew Ru in at my back. It was totally unexpected, because Ru wasn't part of our poly group. Power thrilled over my skin and the comfort of holding the other men changed to something more urgent: less romance and more lust. It was like that was the last ingredient we were missing. We were all about the completion of the act;

it was our legacy through Jean-Claude's bloodline. There might be teasing in there, but it was only as foreplay. We delivered on what was promised. The four of us looked up as one, across the lobby at Rankin.

He looked more attractive than I'd remembered him, and I knew nothing had changed. Well, one thing had changed: He'd used magic to keep Nathaniel and Micah in the room with him. He'd used a spell or a natural ability, or something, to make them want to stay with him, to make them want to answer his questions when they both knew better. The edges of that power were still clinging to him, so that I noticed the lean muscles under his clothes and saw the black depths of his eyes shine for a second. I wasn't sure if the last part was real or part of the illusion, because that's what he was: He wasn't the reality of Jean-Claude and the rest of us. He was the tease, the lure, the promise of things, but he had no intention of coming across. He could make you want to talk to him, want to be with him, want to stay with him, when logic told you to run away. Rankin had figured out how to make what could have been just a great way to pick up people at a bar into something that compelled suspects to keep talking. It was impressive and completely illegal.

He stared across the lobby at us. We stared back. He knew we knew. He also knew we couldn't prove it. I couldn't go to his superiors and say I felt him working a spell, because it wasn't a spell. I was almost sure of that. Was it magic? Psychic ability? Both? I didn't know, and if I didn't know I couldn't explain it enough to get him in the trouble he deserved. We all stared at one another until Officer Evans asked Rankin if anything was wrong. He shook his head.

What are you? I thought, as if I expected him to answer me. He shook his head again and walked down the hallway with Evans following him. I didn't know what Rankin was, but I knew what he wasn't: human.

42

WE DECIDED TO go back to our hotel room to regroup. Ru stayed with us and Bram found us. He'd complained his way up the food chain that he needed to see his boss, and had been told the same thing: "Your boss is free to go, but his fiancé is being questioned." We'd gotten as far as the hallway outside the door when my phone rang. It was Edward's ringtone. Nathaniel said, "What is it about this hallway and all the interruptions?" as I answered the phone.

I opened my mouth to tell Edward about Rankin, but he said, "Peter's doctor didn't seem certain about much except that he's healing faster than he should be."

"Can we see him? Or does he need to rest?" He sounded distracted and uncertain. It was so unlike him, but then this wasn't the job; this was his kid.

So I stuck to kid topics. "Becca is with Rufous's wife. Do you want us to bring her with us?"

"I don't really want her here, but if Dixie tells her, then Peter got hurt for nothing." He sounded just a little bit angry. I couldn't blame him.

I took a deep breath, let it out slowly, and that was enough for him to say, "What happened? Did you let the bitch get to our daughter?" Definitely angry and looking for a target.

"No, Becca heard enough at the pool before Peter carried Dixie away."

"So it was all for nothing," he said.

"No, Becca doesn't believe that you would cheat on her mother. She just flat doesn't believe it. I told her the truth, and she thinks that Dixie is crazy."

I heard his breath go out on the other end of the line. I think it was a relieved sound. "Good, one less thing to worry about." He tried to crawl his voice back up into his normal empty range, but he couldn't do it. I'd never heard so much uncontrolled emotion in his voice. I don't think I'd realized how well he controlled even the tone of his voice until that moment. Edward was all about control.

I heard voices on the other end of the phone. "Doctor's here again. Gotta go."

The phone call was over. I didn't question it, but as we headed for the parking lot, I realized I needed to talk to Marisol or Rufous about keeping Becca with them, and I needed to tell Becca that she was with them until we got back from the hospital. I shared all that with the men.

"I have the numbers for everyone in the wedding," Nathaniel said, "so I have Rufous's number, but not Marisol's."

"Better than I have," I said. "Can you let him know we're headed to the hospital? I'll call Becca."

Nathaniel stopped in the middle of calling Rufous. "I can stay here with Becca."

I shook my head at the same time Micah said, "No."

"I agree with Micah. The three of us are staying together, and away from Rankin." No one argued with me except Becca.

"Why can't I go to the hospital with you?"

"Because Ted needs to take care of Peter and your mom and know you're safely out of it."

"But why does he need you and the others? Is Nathaniel all right?"

"He's with me. I'm taking him with me to the hospital."

"To keep him away from the police?" she asked, and again her insight was a little too good for her age, but she'd been Ted's daughter since before she was six. I guess it was hard not to pick up a few things about the business.

"Something like that," I said.

"Maybe I can find Ellie and hang out with her?"

"You do that," I said. I got off the phone, rolling my eyes and feeling stressed.

"What's wrong?" Micah asked.

"I wasn't sold on this whole kid thing before, but dealing with Becca makes me think I'll never be ready for it."

Micah and Nathaniel hugged me at the same time, timing it so that their arms went around me just right so that it was cuddly and not awkward. There had been a learning curve on group hugs, but we'd aced the curve a while ago. "They don't pop out as almost twelve-year-olds, Anita," Micah said.

"I don't think anyone is ever ready for kids," Nathaniel said.

I pulled away from the group hug enough to look at him. "Other people seem sure."

"Nathaniel's right," Micah said. "I'm not rushing us, but I don't think there's ever a perfect time to have children."

I closed my eyes, sighed, and said, "Fine, I won't hold any of this against us."

Nathaniel kissed me, which made me open my eyes and look into his happy face. He was the one who wanted the baby the most. Micah had had a vasectomy years before I met him, so it wasn't going to be him who was the bio-dad. If it was just the two of us—well, three counting Jean-Claude—we'd have gone on to our happily ever after childless and content, but we were a foursome, or a three and one, or two couples, or . . . You do the poly math. And the part of our poly group smiling at me with his big lavender eyes wanted a child, badly. He wasn't twenty-five yet, but I was over thirty. The combination was pushing us to rush, in my opinion. I'd already voiced all my doubts to everyone out loud when we first started talking about babies. Today I'd keep my opinions to myself, because I wasn't up to another discussion about when we should take me off birth control and start trying, especially not today. With anyone but people in the core of our poly group I added condoms to the birth control, just to be extra safe.

But baby issues could wait; we had more pressing issues: hospital and talking to Peter's doctor. And I hoped to have an opportunity to tell Edward and Bernardo about Detective Rankin's secret. How did I know it was a secret? Because there were no non-human police in America, not officially. That was one of the reasons that letting officers who contracted lycanthropy on the job keep their badges was such a big deal. If it worked, then maybe someday having lycanthropy first wouldn't keep you out of becoming a cop, or maybe even some of the vampires who had been forced off the force after becoming the undead could rejoin. I knew my friend Dead Dave, who owned and ran a bar of the same name, would have still loved to go back on the job. Witches and other practitioners of the mystical arts, like me, had only been allowed on the job in the last few years, and even that was on a person-by-person basis. No, whatever Rankin was, the majority of the officers he worked with didn't know he was anything but straight-up vanilla human. If he kept fucking with us, I'd find a way to prove otherwise. If he left us alone from this point on, I'd think about doing the same.

43

WE FOUND NICKY and Rodina before we went to the hospital, because no way was I leaving them and Rufous off talking to Olaf without knowing how the "talk" had gone. Nicky told me it had gone as well as could be expected. Rufous said, "That arrogant son of a bitch."

"I take it Otto wasn't impressed with the talk," I said.

"He isn't afraid of me; that's for damn sure. He respects Murdock more, even Morgan more, than he does me."

"I'm a shapeshifter—that's all that impressed him," Rodina said.

"Maybe, but Ted's threat is something Jeffries believes, and the rest of us . . . It's like he was laughing at us, as if he thinks he's untouchable." I sent Rufous back to his wife and Becca. He wanted to come with us, but Edward had called and asked Rufous to help take care of Becca, and that gave Rufous a way to save face. The rest of us headed for the hospital. It turned out that there wasn't going to be a beach wedding, at least not one with Peter standing at Edward's side. His mix of lycanthropy, like my own, seemed to be giving him superhuman healing abilities, but if the artery tore open again, he might bleed out before he could be gotten to an ER, so either the wedding was canceled, or Peter couldn't be there. None of us were looking forward to telling the bride, but Donna surprised me again. Her face might have been red and puffy from crying, and the makeup she'd been wearing wiped away hours ago, but a determined look came over her face. It reminded me of Peter and Becca's stubborn look. "Of course we can't go ahead with the wedding tomorrow as planned," she said in a very matter-of-fact tone.

They went into Peter's room together to tell him they'd just have a civil ceremony back home in New Mexico when he was well enough. The rest of us were leaving to get coffee and tea when the yelling started. Peter's voice: "I got stabbed so you could get married tomorrow! Don't you dare cancel it."

We heard a murmur of Donna's voice but couldn't make out what she said. "No, you aren't bringing everyone to my room. You are going to have a wedding on the beach like you planned, damn it!" Then his voice went lower, and then the rhythm of Edward's voice came through the door.

"If he finds us eavesdropping, will he be mad?" Ru asked.

We all looked at one another, and that included Bernardo. All of us looked guilty, like kids caught outside a teacher's door, or maybe kids overhearing their parents fight. Micah said, "Let's give them some time and space." He started walking toward the elevator.

"No," Nathaniel said, "I've spent too much time and energy on this wedding. If we're going to change things by tomorrow, I need to know as soon as possible. Donna isn't in any shape to make all the phone calls and face down the wedding coordinator, and neither is Dixie, if she's still in the wedding after what happened between her and Peter." Nathaniel's voice was rising as he talked. He wasn't yelling, but he was angry. He started pacing the hallway, waving his hands around as if he'd grab something from the air. It wasn't like him to display this kind of temper in public, or at all, really. The rest of us just watched. I, at least, wasn't sure what to do, except watch and let him get it out of his system. I realized for the first time that the wedding—this wedding and all he'd done to help pull it together—mattered to him far more than I'd realized, and a hell of a lot more than it did to me.

I wondered if it had been our child bleeding out, would we all have been our normal calm selves, or would we have struggled to hold our shit together, too? Did the fact that your child was the one injured make that much difference? I didn't know, and I didn't like not knowing, and I didn't want to find out the answer; I really didn't.

"How about Denny?" I asked.

"I haven't even seen her since yesterday," Nathaniel said.

"She wasn't in the hotel when Peter was taken off in the ambulance, was she?" I asked.

"I don't remember seeing her," Bernardo said.

"Nor I," Bram said.

R and R both said that they hadn't seen her either.

"Anita's right. She wasn't in the lobby with everyone else when the ambulance came," Micah said.

"Wait, are you saying that none of us have seen her since yesterday?" I asked.

We all looked at one another, and then slowly we all shook our heads. "Shit," I said.

"She's not as close to any of us. She could have just been hanging with the other bridesmaids, Anita," Micah said.

"Nathaniel, call her. She knows you better than any of the rest of us."

He didn't argue, just got out his phone and started pushing buttons. "It's ringing," he said, eyes distant with listening.

We waited. We waited until her voice-mail box kicked in and said it was full. Nathaniel lowered his phone and looked at me. "Denny should have come down when the ambulance came. No matter what her issues with Edward or you or even Dixie, she's known Peter since he was a baby."

"Shit," I said with real feeling.

"One of you call Detective Rankin," Bernardo said.

"Why one of us?" I asked.

"Didn't you all talk to him more than I did? I mean, I got lucky and Bettina's friends were able to alibi me."

"He still should have talked to you more than just a hi and a bye," I said.

"He found my conviction when he ran my name, and my being a shapeshifter on top of it . . . He's sure I've done something." Nathaniel's voice was bitter.

"Prejudiced bastard," I said.

"It's not just that, Anita. The cops in St. Louis know me. Some of them helped me when I was a kid. To a strange cop who doesn't know me, I will always be my record. I will always be a strung-out street whore, and it doesn't help that I'm a stripper. Most people think that's just one step above prostitution, and if they've seen the porn I did, then they don't believe I'm a reformed anything."

"None of us can call Rankin," Micah said.

"You have to do it, Bernardo," I said.

"One of us can do it?" Rodina asked.

"No," Nicky said. "None of Anita's bodyguards can attract more attention to her, or to Nathaniel and Micah."

"I'm sorry about how he treated Nathaniel, but that doesn't mean the rest of you can't call him and tell him about Denny. What aren't you telling me?" He gave me suspicious eyes out of that handsome face of his.

I told him the *Reader's Digest* version.

"Are you saying he used magic to keep you in the room for questioning?"

"He used something," Micah said. "It was only after Anita tried to reach out to me that I sort of woke up and realized we could just walk out."

"I know not to talk to the police," Nathaniel said, "but somehow every time I tried to leave, Rankin would make it seem reasonable to stay."

"That's so illegal," Bernardo said.

"And so hard to prove," I said.

"Do you think whatever he does works on straight-up humans like me?"

I shrugged. "I don't know what he is, so I can't answer that."

"You don't know what he is? You're, like, the queen of supernatural knowledge. Edward goes to you when he doesn't know."

I shrugged again. "Sorry, but this time I'm stumped. He hit my radar as normal, vanilla human, but the power he was wielding was sophisticated and takes practice."

"Couldn't he just be psychic, or a witch?"

"Maybe, but if he is, it's a type of psychic power I've never seen, and a flavor of witchcraft that's never come near me before."

"You only got it from a distance, Anita," Micah said.

"So?"

"If he did it to you in person, you might learn more."

"No, just no," I said.

"None of that matters right now," Nathaniel said. "Someone call about Denny not answering her phone or showing up for the ambulance."

"Wait—call Lucy or Rufous or Frankie and have them check at Denny's room," I said.

Nathaniel nodded. "Yeah, of course, why did we just assume something terrible had happened to her?" He started to dial his phone again.

"Because it's us," Micah said.

"I was thinking it, too," Nicky said.

Micah smiled at him. "You're part of us."

Nicky smiled back at him.

"Am I part of 'us,' too?" Bernardo asked.

"No," Micah said.

"Why not?"

Nathaniel was talking on the phone, so we all stopped to listen. "Lucy, it's Nathaniel. Have you seen Denny since you tried on the bridesmaid dresses?" Silence. "You haven't either. Could you go check her room? Yeah, I tried to call her, and it went to a full voice-mail box. Thanks, Lucy. Text me if she's there and phone if she's not." He hung up and we all waited. I was praying for a text.

"Come on, Callahan—why am I not 'us'?" Bernardo asked.

"You still think being tall, dark, and a ladies' man should get you ahead of the rest of us, for one thing," Micah said.

"Hey, until Anita, it was working pretty good for me."

"I'm not the only woman that's ever told you no."

He gave a little eye roll and the barest raise of his shoulders.

"Oh, come on."

"Well, since I hit my growth spurt in my teens."

"And that's exactly what I mean," Micah said.

"What? Because I've been suave and debonair for most of my life, I can't be part of the inner circle?"

"That can't be why, or Jean-Claude would be excluded," Rodina said.

"See?" Bernardo said.

Nathaniel checked his phone as if the text sound wouldn't have clued him. How long would it take Lucy to get to the room? Nathaniel spoke without taking his eyes from the phone screen. "Do you really want to be part of our poly group?"

"Maybe?"

"Then you'll have to come across," Nathaniel said.

"I've been trying to get Anita to do that since we met," he said, aiming that smile he had that had made more women drop their panties than Elvis in his heyday.

"Not Anita, Bernardo," Nathaniel said, and he did look up then, meeting the taller man's gaze square on with his own big lavender eyes.

"Sorry, bro, but I don't swing at boys."

"And that's why you can't be in our poly group."

"I thought Nicky didn't like men either."

"I like men better than you do," Nicky said, which made Bernardo stare at the other man.

"And just how well do you like men?"

"I don't like them as well as Nathaniel does."

"Only I like men as well as Nathaniel does," I said.

"Actually, Anita, you like them more than I do, and I don't get to say that about many women." Nathaniel grinned as he said it, just in case I took it wrong.

I didn't, and I had a smart-ass comeback all ready, but Ru said, "Would I have to sleep with Nathaniel to be part of your poly group?"

"No," I said.

Nathaniel said, "I don't force myself on anyone."

Nathaniel's phone rang. Denny wasn't in her room. Her bed was still made. Her clothes and suitcases were still there. Her room key was on the bedside table; her purse was beside it. Her bathing suit was laid out on the bed as if she'd started to change to meet everyone at the pool before Peter and Dixie had their incident. That had been nearly five hours ago. If she was truly missing and not just off having a triggered gestalt moment on the beach somewhere, then either the same bad guy had taken them both—Bettina and Denny—at almost the same time, or we had two bad guys abducting women from the same hotel on the same day, at almost the same time. Vegas wouldn't have taken the odds on either, but I knew real cases where both scenarios had happened.

I went to tell Edward. Bernardo headed back to the hotel.

The other three stayed with me, because whatever Rankin was, we were stronger together. He'd been hot and heavy after Nathaniel before; this wouldn't make him change his mind. There was more connection between Nathaniel and Denny. Hell, all of us had more of a connection to Denny, except maybe Bernardo. To my knowledge he hadn't slept with Denny. I hesitated as I started to knock on the door of Peter's room. Bernardo visited Edward more than I did because they lived closer to each other. I really didn't know how well he knew Denny. I pushed the thought away and knocked. One complication at a time.

44

DONNA STAYED WITH Peter, but the rest of us headed to the hotel. I'd have left Nathaniel, Micah, and Bram there to help calm them, but they wouldn't stay. "This isn't a case, Anita. You don't get to leave us behind that easily," Micah said.

"I know Denny a lot better than you do. I want to help search for her," Nathaniel said.

Ru had shrugged and said, "I don't know her at all, but I know that in animal form all of us could track her through the hotel."

"I've done that for you when you were on a case," Nathaniel said.

"Those were special circumstances," I said.

"Less special than this?" Micah asked.

"We're rolling out," Edward said. "Debate in the car on the way to the hotel." We all piled into our rental cars and continued to debate.

"I don't really like Nathaniel being near Rankin again," I said.

"Then you should have said that instead of trying to get me to stay with Donna and Peter," Nathaniel said.

"All right, I'd rather you wait at the hospital with Donna and Peter so we can keep you farther away from Rankin."

"Who's Rankin?" Edward asked, and I realized that he'd been at the hospital since the detective showed up.

It was easy to explain that Detective Terry Rankin was the lead on Bettina's disappearance. What wasn't easy to explain was the fact that we were all sure he wasn't human, or at least not straight-up vanilla- or chocolate-flavored human. He was definitely something exotic, like rocky road or Chunky Monkey.

"Explain to me how you know Detective Rankin isn't human."

"I love the fact that you just accepted that if we said he wasn't human, he wasn't," Nathaniel said.

"Nothing personal, Nathaniel. You're Uncle Nathaniel to the kids, but I accepted it because Anita said he wasn't human."

"I know that, but I enjoy the fact that you just rolled with it. No questions asked."

"She's earned that level of no questions asked from me."

"Thanks, Edward," I said, smiling.

Edward scowled at all of us. The look was enough. I knew the next thing out of his mouth would be on point. He'd had enough emotional bonding for one day. "So, explain to me about the detective. What did he do that made you peg him as not human?"

I did my best to explain, but like a lot of mystical stuff, it didn't translate well. "If I said you had to be there, would you understand?"

"If I had been there, would I have sensed anything?" he asked.

I had to think about that one, and look at the other men in the car. They basically all shrugged and turned it back to me.

"You spend the most time with him. Would he have sensed anything?" Micah asked, finally.

"Even I've never sensed anything quite like this," I said.

"The question isn't would Edward know what Rankin was doing, or even what he was, but would he have sensed any of the hocus-pocus?"

"I don't know. Edward isn't head-blind to psychic stuff, but he's not psychic either."

"Everyone in the car needs to start calling me Ted again, because we're almost to the hotel."

"Good point, Ted," I said.

"I've spent more time calling you Ted than Edward lately. I think I'll remember, Ted," Nathaniel said.

Edward actually smiled his real smile for that. "If I haven't said it before, Nathaniel, I really appreciate all the help you've been with Donna and the wedding."

"I enjoyed most of it. I wish we could have a beach wedding."

"We could have one, if that's what you really want," Micah said.

"Let me survive walking on the beach in bedazzled flip-flops and a formal-length dress first, then ask me again," I said. That earned me some laughter; then we pulled up in front of the hotel. Police were everywhere, as if someone had emptied out a bag of them in front of the building like toys, but there was never anything playful about having this many police at a scene.

Rankin was standing outside under the covered parking area. He seemed to be searching the crowd, as if he was waiting for someone and they were late. We pointed him out to Edward. "He looks like one of your men here."

"What do you mean?" I asked.

"Not too tall, slender but fit, good-looking but sort of androgynous. He's not as pretty as most of your men, but if you dropped him into the crowd, he wouldn't stand out."

I looked at Rankin as if I hadn't really seen him before. "I can see some of that, but he doesn't really float my boat."

"He floats mine," Nathaniel said.

Micah and I looked at him. "I don't think you've ever remarked on another man in front of me," Micah said.

"He looks like you," Nathaniel said.

I looked from Micah back to Rankin where he was still scanning the crowd, as we waited for the traffic to clear out enough for us to park. I tried to see what Nathaniel was talking about. The hair was too short, the color too dark, not nearly as curly. He was slender built like Micah, but he had a longer torso, and something about that made them look less alike to me. I wasn't even going to try with the facial features, because Rankin just lost out there, at least to me.

"I'm having trouble seeing it."

"There's some superficial resemblance, I suppose," Micah said.

"Am I the only one who thinks he looks like Micah?" Nathaniel asked.

"*Yes,*" Ru and Rodina said in unison.

"It's like Edward said: Rankin looks like he could be part of the team, but I don't think he looks like Micah," Nicky said.

Nathaniel was looking at the detective—no, not just looking, staring almost . . . longingly. He was mooning over him; that's what my grandmother would have called it. I touched his shoulder and he didn't react. I gripped his shoulder and gave him a little shake. He blinked and looked at me.

"Are you all right?" I asked.

He frowned. "I think so."

I touched his face and looked into his eyes from inches away. They were still big and lavender, like spring lilacs. He smiled at me and leaned in for a kiss. I gave it to him, but he pulled back first, which was unusual for him. He was the touchiest and feeliest of all of us. His gaze slid past me to something farther away. I turned to see what he was looking at, but there was nothing to see, not really, not yet. There were people and movement and too many police, and I finally realized there were too many police for just a missing person's case, even with two women missing.

"That's a lot of police," Rodina said.

"Too many, and there's an FDLE car here," Edward said.

"FDLE?" Ru asked.

"Florida Department of Law Enforcement. They have a local field station, but if more of them show up it's because the locals needed more resources."

"Have they found something?" Micah asked.

"If they have, it's nothing good," I said.

Nathaniel shook his head and then shook himself on the car seat, almost like a dog shaking off water, but there was nothing for him to be shaking free of that I could see. He took a couple of deep breaths and blew them out slow and steady.

"Are you okay?" Ru asked.

"No," Nathaniel said. "It's only thinking about what Anita said, that the police are here because they found something bad, that maybe Denny or the other girl is dead. Only concentrating on Denny and how much I like her as a person and that all that could be gone, dead; only that is helping me clear my thoughts."

"Clear your thoughts of what?" Edward asked.

"Rankin."

"What do you mean, Rankin?"

"The moment I saw him I wanted to get closer to him. I can

remember what he said to me, that I should tell him what I did with the woman, and I want to tell him."

Edward asked, "Did you do something to Bettina Gonzales?" I was glad he asked, because I wasn't sure I could have.

"No," Nathaniel said, and his body language said just how absurd that was, but then he frowned and tried to look through the crowd back to Rankin. "No, I swear I didn't touch her, but he thinks I did—no, no, that's not it. He wants me to say I did. He wants someone to say they did and he makes you feel like you want to confess to things that you didn't do."

"Do you feel a need to confess, too?" Bram asked Micah from the far backseat.

Micah said, "I didn't feel compelled to confess, but I did have trouble leaving. I'd be at the door, and then suddenly Rankin would say something. I don't even remember what, but then I wouldn't open the door; I wouldn't quite finish leaving. It happened more than once, but I can't remember what he said to keep me in the room."

"He just kept asking me different variations on what had I done to Bettina? Where was she? I remember what he said to me," Nathaniel said, "but that isn't why I didn't leave. I'd think, *I should stop talking and get out of here,* but then he'd brush his hand against my arm, or his body would rub against my back, and I wouldn't want to stop."

"Wait, he touched you? He, like, caressed you during an interrogation?" I asked.

"No, nothing that obvious. He literally would brush against me as he paced behind me. He patted my hand or clapped my back a couple of times, but most of the touches were really small ones."

"I didn't see him do more than touch Nathaniel's arm like he was trying to be his buddy. It didn't look sexual or inappropriate at all," Micah said.

"The effect was," Nathaniel said, almost a whisper.

"Then we need to keep you away from him," I said.

"Why didn't you say all this before?" Edward asked.

"I didn't remember until I saw him, and then you said that there are too many cops here and I thought about Denny. I mean, I don't want anything bad to have happened to Bettina, but I didn't know her. Denny is my friend. The thought of something really bad happening to her is helping me keep my head clear of whatever Rankin did to me."

"Are you having any issues, Callahan?" Edward asked.

"No. I knew he was doing something to me in the interrogation. I knew he was messing with both of us. Anita connecting with me gave me enough willpower to walk out on him and bring Nathaniel with me."

"You had to grab me by the arm and drag me out, didn't you?"

Micah put his hand on the back of Nathaniel's neck underneath the fall of his hair, the way he'd done when there was so much more of it, and leaned their faces close together. "I thought you were just nervous being questioned."

Nathaniel leaned in, resting his forehead against Micah's. "I was nervous, but that wasn't why I didn't want to leave. You touching me helped; all of you touching me helped more. It's like whatever is wrong with Rankin, whatever he's done to me, is the promise of touching, so real touching trumps it. Does that make any sense?"

"It does," I said.

"Yes," Micah said.

"Is it just Micah and Anita touching you that helps, or will any real touch help?" Edward asked.

Nathaniel closed his eyes and leaned in against Micah. "I'm not sure."

Nicky put his hand on Nathaniel so that he was touching him, too. "Any better?"

"I'm not sure; I don't feel like myself."

"Are you saying that if someone isn't touching you, Rankin could lure you into his interrogation and force you to confess to things you didn't do?" Edward asked.

Nathaniel opened his eyes and drew back enough from Micah to look at Edward. "I'm not sure."

"But it's possible?" Edward asked.

Nathaniel nodded.

"You're a wereanimal; you guys are harder to bespell than a plain human."

"Which makes me wonder how many humans have confessed to crimes they didn't do because Rankin told them to do it," I said.

"I'll bet his closure rate is a hundred percent," Edward said.

"No one's closure rate is that high," I said.

"What's closure rate?" Ru asked.

"How many cases you close, as in find the person you think did it," I said.

"So how many people you get convicted?" he asked.

Edward and I both shook our heads. "Convictions are for the lawyers; closure for us means we turn over the whodunit to them. What happens after that doesn't affect a cop's closure rate," Edward said.

"Are you telling me that if you give the lawyers a terrible case with someone who confessed but couldn't have done it, you still get the points for closing the case, even though it doesn't work at trial, at all?" Ru asked.

"Pretty much," I said.

"Yes," Edward said.

I added, "If you get a reputation for sending bad cases up the line, ones that fall apart consistently, then that will eventually hurt you, but short of that, you're good."

"If Micah hadn't come in the room and helped me, I might have said anything the detective wanted me to say," Nathaniel said.

"I'm betting Rankin uses his mind-fuck powers all the time," Edward said.

"You really think he'd force his closure rate to a hundred percent?" I asked.

He nodded.

"If it is that high, then we might be able to use that against him if we need to," I said.

"How could you use it against him?" Ru asked.

"It would be like getting a hundred percent on all your college finals year after year. No one is that perfect, so you have to be cheating," I said.

Rodina nodded. "I get it, but cheating on tests is easier to prove than whatever this is."

"It would be undue magical influence, or even magical malfeasance, especially if someone he coerced died. They have the death penalty in Florida," I said.

"Isn't magical malfeasance an automatic death penalty in every state?" Ru asked.

We all said yes, in unison.

"But if he'd done it in a state without the death penalty, then he might not be risking getting charged with magical malfeasance to the full legal definition, and that's what will get you executed," I said.

"It's unlike any other death penalty sentence," Micah said. "You don't sit for years on death row. The trial is almost unconstitutionally quick, and then the order of execution is issued and usually carried out in less than a week."

"I hadn't thought about it before, but sometimes you work on the other side of the issue from Anita and Ted," Ru said.

"I've tried to get a few lycanthropes out of the system alive, but once they get charged, it's almost impossible to save them."

"Which means that Nathaniel stays as far away from Rankin as possible," I said.

We all agreed.

A uniformed officer finally came to the window of our car. He had to lean down a ways to talk to us. Edward and I flashed our badges. The officer's comment: "I didn't think the preternatural branch got called in until we were sure it wasn't human."

"What made anyone think it wasn't human to begin with?" I asked.

"You'd need more than fingernails and teeth to do that to a body." His face got that distant look, as if he could still see whatever had put that haunted look in his eyes.

"Bad?" Edward asked.

"Worst thing I've seen, and I thought I'd seen bad."

"Which of the missing women is it? Do you know yet?" I asked. I prayed silently that it wasn't going to be Denny. I liked her, and the thought of her dying in a way that made a police officer look haunted . . . I didn't want it to be her.

"Dark hair, so we think it's the first missing girl, but you know how it is: We won't be sure until fingerprints or dental come back."

A tightness in my gut eased, and then instantly I thought, *How dare I be relieved that it was Bettina Gonzales?* I was happy it probably wasn't Denny, but I couldn't be happy it was Bettina. I hadn't liked her much, but she had seemed harmless enough. Pettiness and a tendency toward jealousy about men

weren't crime enough for her to deserve ending up like this. I
hadn't even seen the body yet, but just the little information we
had was enough to make me know it had been a bad way to go.
No one deserved that.

Micah whispered, "Rankin's coming."

"We'll park and then do what we can to help find the second missing woman," Edward said.

The officer nodded and stepped back, pointing us through
the mess. We tried to get moving, but Rankin literally slapped
both his hands on the hood of our rental car. Unless we wanted
to run him over, we had to stay put. He was so angry, he was
damn near vibrating with it as he stalked up to the uniformed
officer.

"Why are you talking to them? What did you tell them?"
Rankin yelled, getting as up in the officer's face as a six-inch
height difference could manage. It should have looked ridiculous, but it didn't, and the bigger man backed up. Maybe he
was backing up from the anger of a superior officer, or maybe
it was a case of the size of the fight in the dog, not the size of
the dog in the fight.

"They're marshals with the preternatural branch," the officer said.

"Only two of them are marshals; the rest are suspects in the
murder of one woman and the disappearance of another!"
Rankin was still yelling, and damn near climbing up the front
of the bigger man while he did it.

Micah said, softly, to me, "He's attracting attention."

Edward opened the door of the car, which made Rankin
have to move and turn away from the other officer toward the
door, the car, and people he knew weren't his friends. We'd
have been his friends as fellow lawmen—law people—but
he'd made that impossible. He turned toward the opening door
with his body language letting us know he was ready for a
fight. No, more than that, he seemed to be wanting a fight.
What the hell was wrong with him? You didn't make detective
by being a hysteric.

Rankin started shouting at Edward and tried the same
backup technique that had worked with the other officer. Edward stayed where he was and let the detective have his hissy
fit. I'd never seen another cop lose it like this in front of the

whole world, at least not this early in an investigation. Sometimes the pressure got to everyone, but he hadn't been digging at this case long enough for this kind of angry hysterics.

Bram leaned over the seat toward me and said, "There's press here."

"And smartphones," Nathaniel said.

"And they're hearing the lead detective accuse all of us of being suspects in the murder and disappearances," Micah said.

Edward figured it out, too, because he moved minutely forward, smiling and being calm, trying to talk the crazy person down in his down-home voice. He made sure some of his words carried, too, though.

"Calm down there, pardner. No need to get hysterical and start throwing false accusations around."

"I am not hysterical." Rankin started lowering his voice.

"Then step back off of me, pardner," Edward said, lowering his voice, too.

Rankin actually stepped closer, crowding him more, but his body language didn't promise violence from where I was sitting, though it probably looked it from the crowd. Rankin stuck his head in the open door, forcing himself past a surprised Edward. How had he even gotten past him? I mean, it was Edward; short of deadly force, you didn't just push past him. Rankin's voice was low and soothing suddenly. "Nathaniel, you want to confess. You want to tell everyone here that you hurt that girl, don't you?"

"What the hell, Rankin?" I said, unbuckling my seat belt and starting to move toward him.

"Yes," Nathaniel said in a voice that didn't sound like him at all, "yes, I want to tell them I hurt her." He was staring at Rankin as if there was no one else in the car, no one else to look at, no other eyes to meet.

Micah touched Nathaniel, but he never reacted to it. Nicky moved in the backseat so that his shoulders blocked the line of sight between Nathaniel and the detective. I couldn't see if it changed anything because my view was blocked, too; besides, I was moving forward on the front seat toward Rankin.

Edward spoke low next to the detective's face. "Move, or I will move you."

"Come with me, Nathaniel. Tell them you hurt her. Tell

them you turned into a leopard and killed her." He was speaking very low now. No one outside the car would hear him. Not even the uniformed officer who had been friendly earlier would be able to hear him.

Nathaniel said, "I hurt her . . ."

"Breaking eye contact isn't helping," Nicky said.

I crawled across the seat and put my hand against Rankin's shoulder to push him out of the car. He grabbed my hand, pressed it tighter against him, and looked at me. The world seemed to slow down, or narrow down to just his eyes, like black pools spreading across my vision, or maybe a night sky that stretched untouched except for a million stars, and just like that he mind-fucked me with just his gaze and his hand on mine.

45

I HAD A MOMENT of panic, of wanting to struggle uselessly, helplessly, but I'd seen darker nights and vampires' eyes filled with stars and everlasting night before. It helped me to calm the fear and to stop the panic before it grew too large, and helped me to be patient. It was like a physical fight in some ways; you protected as much of yourself as you could and tried to find a weak spot, or a chance to twist in their grip, break their hold on you, and then hit them back harder, or run away. I'd fought this kind of fight before, with vampires mostly, but one kind of fight is very like another.

I raised the shields higher inside my head, inside my heart, the walls that protected my soul from all the things that tried to grab hold of it. It should have helped, but instead the darkness in front of my eyes ate an edge of light that I hadn't even realized was still there. Shielding harder had made it worse, not better—fuck! The first spike of fear stabbed through me, and it was like stumbling in the dark. I didn't hear words, but I felt something. It was like he couldn't put words in my head, but he could put feelings in it, or longings in it. He tried to offer me desire, but I had enough of that in my life. He tried to fill me with loneliness, but I was nearly suffocating with all the people in my life. He tried to find things connected to passion, sex, seduction, that I was missing in my life, but I wasn't missing anything. In fact, I'd been pushed so far outside my comfort zones for so long that a little less adventure in the bedroom and dungeon might be nice for a change. The only things I was missing were space and time to myself, but that didn't help him gain a hold on me. Then the sound of the sea grew louder in my head, and I felt this almost irresistible long-ing for it. I wanted to step into the water, feel its coolness over my body, but fear washed over me and drowned the sound of the water and the longing for it. The last time I'd been in the ocean I'd had a diving accident that almost killed me. I hadn't been in the ocean since it happened more than ten years ago.

A voice whispered through my head: Ma petite, *what are you doing?*

I thought, *Jean-Claude.*

Oui, ma petite, *what is in your head, in our head?*

Help me fight him.

Let me inside, ma petite, *as you did when we made love.*

I wanted to argue with him that I didn't dare lower my shields with Rankin right there, but I either trusted Jean-Claude or I didn't, and I did. I whispered, "I do," and I let him inside my shields, my mind, my heart, all of me. It was like another kind of drowning, except that this water was midnight blue and glowed with power. I had a moment when I felt like I was suffocating again, and then I was being torn between black ocean and the blue night sky, but the sky burned with its own fire and the whispering depths of the ocean turned to smoke, as if the entire ocean could evaporate all at once.

I felt a kiss, and for a moment I thought it was Jean-Claude somehow magically there in the car with me, but then I realized it wasn't his lips, and for a panicked moment I thought it was Rankin, but Jean-Claude's power breathed over me, and I knew it wasn't Rankin's kiss, but Jean-Claude's. I opened my eyes to find Wyatt, Ru, kissing me, but as he drew back enough for me to see his face, his eyes were full of dark blue fire. I didn't know how Jean-Claude had managed it, but he'd pos-sessed Ru. His hands touched my face and I felt the echo of Jean-Claude's hands, as if his power were wearing Ru like a glove. I felt an almost audible click as my shields rearranged themselves to let all my people inside and keep only the bad guys out. I'd shielded too hard against Rankin and cut off my support network. It was chilling to know that alone I couldn't fight completely free of him.

I felt Rankin let go of my hand and move out of the car, and I could hear raised voices outside the car. I was still kneeling on the car seat, as if nothing strange had happened, but now

Ru was stretched over the back of the seats, his face filling my view as he leaned back from kissing me. The dark blue light in his eyes faded back to the perfect blackness of his natural eye color.

He blinked hard, as if clearing his mind, or settling himself more solidly into himself. His hand was still resting on my cheek, but it was just his hand now. "Your metaphysical shields are amazing, my queen, to be able to lock out all your allies with but a thought."

My voice was a little shaky as I said, "I didn't mean to cut myself off from all of you."

"You left us vulnerable to Rankin," Nathaniel said. He was sitting hunched, arms hugging himself, while Micah tried to hold him, but he didn't relax into the hug like he normally did. There was a stiffness, almost an anger in him, that seemed to be directed toward Micah, or at least he wouldn't let the other man comfort him out of it. I'd never seen Nathaniel react to Micah like that before. Me, yes, but never Micah.

There were people moving around the car on the side nearest to me. Someone was snapping a picture with a real camera, but more were using their smartphones. The police were pushing them back, but they'd gotten pictures of Ru kissing me, and Rankin in the car. God knew what the press, or even the Internet, would make of it. Normally it would have bothered me more, but after what Rankin had just done with some eye contact and a hand on mine, I had bigger things to worry about than my reputation in the press.

"Jean-Claude was able to use my ties to you to fill me with his power. Only the Mother of All Darkness was able to do that," Ru said, as he slid gracefully into the driver's seat, which Edward had vacated.

"Sorry," I whispered.

"I told you I would serve you in any way you desired. There is no need of sorry between us." He was smiling; he seemed happy. Nice one of us was enjoying himself.

I could hear raised voices again, as if the sound from outside was only coming back to me in pieces. I realized that one of the voices was Edward's, still playing to his Ted persona, but he was genuinely angry. I started to reach for my door handle so I could go see what all the shouting was about.

"What did Rankin offer you, Anita?" Nathaniel asked.

I glanced back at him. He still looked hunched and as if something hurt. Micah was still there trying to soothe him, so I let it go for the moment and answered his question. "Nothing."

"Nothing. You just don't remember."

"He tried, but he didn't have anything I wanted."

"I don't mean to interrupt, but you should probably get out there and help Ted with the local police," Rodina said.

"He seems outnumbered," Ru said.

I looked past Ru, through the still-open driver's-side door, and saw Edward arguing with a woman and a cluster of maybe ten other locals. "That's not even close to outnumbered for him," I said, but I got out of the car anyway. One, I needed to back my partner up, and two, I needed to help him spin a story for the locals as to what the hell had just happened in the car. I realized as I got out, making sure my badge was in clear view, that I honestly wasn't sure what had just happened between me and Rankin. It was going to make explaining it to the other cops a little tricky.

46

IT TURNED OUT that the woman arguing with Edward was not only a local cop, but also the only official psychic they had in the area. I'd always suspected that more cops were psychic than we knew, and when the powers that be had tested most of the police in the country, searching for psychics already on the job, I'd been proven right. A solid thirty percent tested high enough on the Cayce Scale to be classed as actively psychic, which was higher than most of the other professions that they tested. So the police refusing to take on psychics or witches, or whatever word you wanted to use, became moot, because they were already on the job. Officer Angela Dalton was one of the new breed of gifted police who had been recruited nationally, then assigned locally.

Officer Dalton had felt some major psychic phenomena going on in the car, and since she seemed to be under the delusion, or illusion, that Rankin wasn't psychic, it had to be all my fault. Dalton was a few inches taller than me, with shoulder-length brown hair that fell in soft waves. She was slender, with enough curves to keep her from looking boyish in her slacks and polo shirt. Her gun was holstered at her side with her badge in front of it hooked on her belt like I wore mine most of the time at work. I'm sure under other circumstances she was very professional, but right that moment she was up in my face because I'd tried to bespell one of their officers. She actually used the word *bespell*. I decided to teach her a new phrase.

"Mind-fuck," I said. I might have yelled it a little.

She frowned. "What? What did you say?"

"Mind-fuck, not bespell, mind-fuck."

That stopped her yelling at me, while she thought it through.

"If I had tried to do what you're accusing me of, Officer Dalton, it would have been a mind-fuck. *Bespell* is far too gentle a word for it."

She blinked pale brown eyes at me, one of the few cops in the group who wasn't wearing sunglasses. "What I felt in that car was awful, so you're right, except I'd say rape, mind-rape."

It was my turn to mull the word around. I nodded. "Yeah, it's closer to rape than just fucking, so, yeah, mind-rape."

"How can you be so calm after what you just tried to do to Rankin?"

"I didn't try to do anything to him—"

Rankin interrupted. "That's right, you didn't just try, you got inside my head." He almost snarled it in my face.

"Well, if that isn't the pot calling the kettle black," I said.

Dalton said, "What are you talking about, Blake?"

"He mind-fucked me, not the other way around."

"That's not true," Rankin said.

"You've felt this energy before, haven't you, Dalton?" I asked.

She nodded, frowning slightly. "Yes."

"I just got into town, so it couldn't have been me."

She blinked those pale brown eyes at me, and it reminded me of the look in Nathaniel's eyes when he fought free from Rankin's power. "No, no, you weren't there." I could see her beginning to connect the dots, and then Rankin brushed her arm with his hand. It was such a small movement. If you weren't standing right there, you'd have missed it. Her eyes went back to angry. I watched it from inches away, watched his power fill her mind back up with his lies. Fuck him.

If he'd been a vampire I could have freed Dalton; if it had been his gaze that was trapping her like it had been for me in the car, I could have broken the eye contact; but he didn't need her to look him in the eyes now. Whatever he'd done to her had become more ingrained, so he could control her without the gaze, but he did have to keep touching her sometimes. Interesting. Maybe I could work with that.

I stepped between them, forced Rankin back from her. It

forced me to turn my back on Dalton, but I kept talking to her, hoping she could hear me. "The power in the car, you said you've felt it before?"

Edward spoke behind me. "Did you say you'd felt the energy in the car before, Officer Dalton?"

"Yes, yes, I have."

I said, "Long before we got to town, right?"

"Yes," she said, and sounded uncertain, and then her second *yes* was more sure.

Rankin tried to move past me, but I moved a small step into his way. He looked at me, and I felt a brush of power, almost like a cool wind, though that wasn't quite right. I looked from his dark eyes to the lowest collar button of his shirt. I wouldn't let him capture me with his eyes again. Years of being able to look ancient vampires in the eyes had made me arrogant, but I'd spent years dealing with vampires before Jean-Claude shared his power with me and let me stare them in the eyes. Rankin wasn't a vampire, so my necromancy and Jean-Claude's marks didn't help me with him. I looked at Rankin's upper chest, as if we were in a physical fight, because if you want to know how a person is going to attack you, you don't watch their eyes or face or hands; you watch their center body mass, because all the dangerous moves start there. They can't hit you, kick you, or even reach you without moving the center of their body first. That's where their arms are attached; think about it.

He tried to move around me, but I saw his body tense for it, so I was in his way again, before he'd really moved at all. He tried the other side, and again I was in his way. Dalton was talking more and more clearly to Edward behind me. She agreed that if she'd felt the power before we arrived in town, it couldn't be us.

"It has to be someone who's local if you're feeling it a lot," Edward said in his friendly Ted voice.

"I guess so," she said, but even I could tell that she wasn't happy to say it.

Rankin called out to her, "Dalton, Angela, look at me."

Edward said, "Officer Dalton, can you come over here and see what you think of the energy of my friends in the car? That way you can be sure that it wasn't them."

I didn't glance back to see that Edward was herding Detective Dalton away from us, and most important, away from Rankin's gaze or touch. Of course, I'd forgotten about his voice. "Angela," he called out, and my skin ran in goose bumps just standing close to him when he did it.

He noticed it and dipped his head lower to whisper, "Anita," so that it slid along my skin and tried to crawl into my mind, but he didn't have eye or skin contact this time, so I was able to keep him out of my head. I whispered, "Fuck you."

He brushed his finger against my arm, and it sent a shiver of goose bumps down that side of my body. It made me shiver, which made him smile. I so wanted to punch that smug look off his face, but that wouldn't earn me any points with the other cops, and it certainly wouldn't help Nathaniel or Dalton, or find Denny.

He called out, "Angela," again, so his power slithered down my skin. Fuck, he was powerful.

I pitched my voice so the other police still in the area and any interested civilians could hear me. "This power dance between us won't help find our friend, Detective Rankin. If we work together, maybe we can find her before it's too late."

"Angela!" This time he sort of yelled it, and it held an edge of panic rather than power.

I glanced back to find Nathaniel standing very near Dalton, with Edward standing between her line of sight and Rankin. Was Nathaniel touching her the way Rankin had been touching me? The thought was enough that I could feel his/my/our finger brushing against her bare arm. The sensation of being in two places at once made me want to clang my shields tight again, but I took a deep breath, let it out slowly, and kept my shields heavier in the "front" toward the outside world, and let the ties that bound me to my people remain. I needed them, they needed me, and we all loved one another, damn it. Nathaniel hadn't tried to make me feel him touching Dalton; that had been my doing, my thought, my lack of control.

I raised my voice a little and said, "Detective Rankin, what can we do to help you find our friend before it's too late?"

He called after Dalton again, as if I hadn't said anything.

"Dalton is fine, Detective Rankin. Let us help you find Denny before it's too late and she's just another crime scene."

He tried to push past me to go to Dalton, and without thinking I grabbed his arm to keep him with me, and the power he was trying to aim at the other woman leapt from him to me. I had a moment of hearing that *shush*ing sound—was it flowing water or was it the sound of wings? But this time I got angry and let myself flex my own power, not the necromancy but the warmth of my beasts spilling like heat from my hand to his arm. It was just a swat of power; no way was I trotting out anything major with their psychic standing just feet from us.

Rankin jerked his arm free and started to rub it like it hurt, but then stopped himself in midmotion, the way you do on the practice mat when someone one-ups you but you don't want them to know it.

His voice was low as he said, "It's already too late for your friend."

My gut tightened, and I realized I'd only had one cop's word for the body being dark-haired. Sometimes blond hair can look dark with blood, or water, or just how the light falls. "Unless the body you found is Denny, we still have time to find her alive."

He shook his head. "The body wasn't your friend, but that's all I can tell you about an ongoing investigation."

"My badge is federal," I said.

"And the men in your life are suspects."

A deep voice said, "Rankin, what the fuck is going on?" The deep voice belonged to a big man, dressed in tank top, loose shorts, and flip-flops, but there was a badge on a lanyard around his neck.

"Captain Tyburn, Blake is obstructing our investigation," Rankin said.

The big man came to loom over both of us. He was well over six feet. "Rankin, my wife just sent me video off the Internet of you yelling at Marshal Blake and her friends about them being suspects. If I didn't know better, I'd say you were playing to the damn camera phones in the crowd, so don't give me shit about two United States Marshals obstructing this investigation, unless you have proof."

"You have one woman dead, and our friend is missing, Captain. We want to help find her."

"Women just keep disappearing around you and the men in your life," Rankin said.

"Am I being overly sensitive, Captain Tyburn, or is your detective trying to hint that I and the men in my life are guilty of something?"

"No, you're not being overly sensitive, Marshal Blake."

Rankin tried to say something and Tyburn cut him off. "Find us a room where we can talk in private, Detective—now."

47

RANKIN TRIED TO call Dalton into the meeting, but Tyburn overrode him, and we got to leave Dalton talking to Nathaniel, Micah, Ru, and Rodina. Bram and Nicky were there, too, but they'd gone to bodyguard mode and were leaving the metaphysical intervention to the others. I wasn't crazy about being alone with Rankin without any of my metaphysical posse, but I wasn't alone—Rankin's boss was with us. He wouldn't want to be too hocus-pocus in front of his captain. I had to believe that, because if Tyburn didn't want Dalton to come into the meeting, he wasn't going to let me bring in my boyfriends. Rankin looked back as Tyburn herded us all into the hotel in search of some privacy. Dalton looked up as if she felt him looking. Their eyes met, and even from yards away I could see her face begin to go slack, as if Rankin could capture her with a look from a distance. I stumbled on purpose and fell against Rankin. It broke his concentration, made him glance down. Edward had caught my arm, which moved him up to block Rankin's view of the parking area. Tyburn was at the door and said, "Move like you have a purpose, people."

We moved and Rankin had no choice but to move with us and catch up with his boss. Once we were through the doors and into the lobby, Dalton was safe from his mind games, at least for now. I'd do my best to find out what he was doing to her and stop it permanently, but today I'd take the smaller victory and concentrate on finding Denny and figuring out what the hell had happened to Bettina Gonzales.

Olaf was waiting for us in the lobby, or maybe he'd just been wandering through. Whatever; there he was. We tried to hurry past him, but he sort of insisted on going with us, and Tyburn had had enough of everyone apparently, because he said, "Isn't he one of your own men?"

"He is," Edward said.

He looked at all three of us as if trying to figure out where the tension was between us, but finally told Marshal Otto Jeffries to come along. So we were weirdly stuck working with Olaf again. Every time I swore that I'd never work with him again, shit like this happened, and here we were again. All we needed was Bernardo and we'd have the old band back together. The Four Horsemen of the Apocalypse ride again— fuck. How the hell did this keep happening?

Rankin took us to the room he'd used to question Nathaniel and Micah. It was big enough for all of us, but barely. Tyburn seemed even taller and wider than he had outside, as if he took up more than his share of room. He was over six feet and an eye-catcher, but that wasn't all of it. He was pissed, and his anger made him seem even bigger, like an extra invisible layer of size that filled the room and made me fight not to back up. I was glad it wasn't aimed at me, and happier that it was aimed at Rankin.

One of the things that helped me not to back up in the face of Tyburn's anger, other than just my own attitude, was that Olaf was behind me. Edward was beside me, but the tallest guy in the room was right behind me like some kind of huge sentient tree. I could feel him warm and all too real at my back. It made me glance up, and he was looking down at me with those cave eyes of his. I fought the involuntary shiver, but finally lost as I turned around and took a step forward toward Tyburn's anger. Anger I understood. Whatever the hell was going on inside Olaf's head, I didn't want to understand.

Tyburn didn't yell. In fact his voice got lower, more careful, as if he squeezed the words out past his rage. "Explain to me why you made a worse-than-rookie mistake by yelling unfounded suspicions where the press and civilians could hear and record you, Detective!"

"They are connected to both missing women, and a shapeshifter would have the ability to kill someone the way that Bettina Gonzales was killed," Rankin said.

"They are not the only two shapeshifters in town, Detective!" Tyburn said, looming over him like a white-blond mountain. If I hadn't had Olaf to compare him to, it would have been even more impressive. Tyburn had him on bulk, which was why he made me think mountain, but the mountain was nearly a foot shorter than the towering redwood of a man behind me. I suddenly felt physically small, which wasn't like me.

Rankin said, "Graison's background is what put him on my radar for the first woman's disappearance. Pandering, prostitution, assault, attempted murder, drugs, child abuse, and that's just the highlights."

Tyburn's anger began to leak away, just a little. He turned a pair of the palest gray eyes I'd ever seen on us. They matched the nearly perfect white of his military-short haircut. The only color was his boater's tan, which was damn near brown; maybe that's what made his hair and eyes look so pale.

"That's quite a list there, Marshals. It seems more than enough to warrant questioning Mr. Graison, regardless of who he's dating, Marshal Blake."

Edward put his hand on my arm and pressed, as if he'd noticed a breath I took without my realizing I was about to say anything. He spoke in his best down-home-Ted voice. "That would be plenty to make any cop interested in Nathaniel, if he was the one who had committed the crimes that Rankin just listed, instead of being the victim of all of them."

"I'm sure that Graison's version of things would make him seem like the victim, Marshals, but with charges like that on his record I don't see how you can date him, Blake, or let him near your family, Forrester," Tyburn said. His steely gaze had softened, as if he felt sorry for Nathaniel having pulled the wool over our eyes.

Edward drawled, "It's not Nathaniel's version, Captain, it's the official files. Rankin's right on the charges listed, but Nathaniel was never the perpetrator. He was referred to a social worker before age ten as a suspected child abuse victim; by ten he was being pimped out to other pedophiles."

I fought to keep my face blank, because I hadn't realized that Edward had researched Nathaniel that thoroughly. I knew most of it because Nathaniel had shared it.

"Of course Graison is going to make himself out the victim," Rankin said. "He bats those big eyes of his and sells a sob story to some social worker. He was probably as pretty then as he is now. Who wouldn't believe him?"

We all looked at him then, even his boss. "Wow," I said, "did you just slut-shame a pedophile victim because he was a pretty little boy?"

"No," Rankin said.

"It sure as hell sounded like you did. What is it about this case that's turned one of my best men into a potential lawsuit every time he opens his damn mouth?" Tyburn said, and his anger started to boil back up.

"Do you have a connection to Nathaniel Graison that none of us are aware of, Rankin? Because this is beginning to feel personal," Edward said. His accent was still thick, but it was managing to sound suspicious anyway.

"I don't have to answer your questions, Forrester. You're supposed to answer mine," Rankin said, trying to dig his way out of the shit he'd just landed himself in, but some things you can't really take back. Even if they were said out loud by accident, the officers who heard what you said are going to believe you meant them, somewhere in your heart of hearts.

"Do you have a personal connection to Graison?" Tyburn asked.

The silence in the room was suddenly thick. Rankin couldn't give his captain the same answer he'd given Edward. "How would I have a personal connection to a man I just met?"

I wondered if Tyburn would let him get away with the half answer. If he did, then Tyburn didn't want to know the truth. "That's not an answer. Do you have a personal connection with Nathaniel Graison?" I liked Tyburn better in that moment.

"I never met him before today." Rankin had gone very still, as if he were drawing himself inward and trying to hide in plain sight.

"Detective Rankin, have you had any personal interaction with Nathaniel Graison in person, or not in person?" Tyburn asked.

"No." He said it flat, final.

I didn't believe him. "It's bad enough when a fellow cop slut-shames an adult woman who's been the victim of rape, but to do the same to a child rape victim . . . What the fuck is wrong with you, Rankin?"

He gave me the full weight of his dark eyes. I moved my gaze to his mouth, so I watched him enunciate his words as if I were lip-reading. I wasn't going to get caught again. "That is not what I meant and you know it, Blake. You're just trying to get your boyfriend out of trouble."

I was about to correct him that it was *fiancé*, not *boyfriend*, when Olaf spoke for the first time. "Many men who say such things would rape women if they thought they would not be caught. It makes me wonder about you, Rankin. What would you do if you knew you would never be caught?"

"Are you accusing me of being a pedophile?" Rankin asked.

"No, I am accusing you of thinking about being one. If you already were one, you'd be more careful how you spoke in front of us."

I thought Olaf was teasing Rankin, trying to get a rise out of him, but something in his face, the calmness of him, made me think maybe he was just speaking from experience. He was a rapist who just hadn't been caught and convicted under the name Otto Jeffries. Sometimes it takes one to know one, if you know what I mean.

Rankin pushed past me, brushing my bare arm, but he wasn't trying to bespell me now; he was going for Olaf. Rankin came up to midchest on him as he pushed the bigger man with the flat of his hands against his chest. Olaf didn't even try to avoid the blow, just let Rankin have the moment, because he didn't think the smaller man could hurt him; neither did I. I mean, he was huge, and a werelion now, and, well . . . he was Olaf.

Rankin pushed him, and Olaf staggered back from it, fighting to stay on his feet. If he hadn't been able to catch himself on the wall, he'd have gone down. There was a second of stunned silence, as if we all held our breaths, and then Olaf pushed himself off the wall and went for Rankin.

48

OLAF MOVED IN a blur of speed, and within seconds it was clear Rankin couldn't match it. He blocked a feint from Olaf's right arm but couldn't move in time to block the left, which had been the real danger. The open-hand blow staggered the detective into a chair and sent it crashing along the floor. He kept his feet and managed to be facing Olaf when he came, using his knees for kicks since there wasn't room for anything else.

The room was too small for all of us and the fight. It was Tyburn who opened the door and let us escape into the hallway and gave the two men the room to spread out in. I lost sight of the fight for a moment, and then Rankin came out the door airborne, slammed into the wall on the opposite side of the hallway, and started to slide toward the floor. Olaf came out of the door and was on Rankin before he had time to hit the floor. He punched him in the throat with the points of three fingers; a human's throat would have collapsed. Rankin coughed but still managed to get an arm up to stop the left hand from hitting his face, which meant he wasn't able to block the right elbow when it hit him in the side of the head.

Rankin fell to the floor stunned, maybe knocked out; just because his eyes were still open and blinking didn't mean he was conscious. Sometimes it takes a few seconds for the brain to catch up with the damage and be peaceful about it.

Tyburn yelled, "Enough! You're done!"

Olaf tensed as if he was going to kick the fallen man.

Edward yelled, "Otto, no!"

There were a lot of uniformed men with Tyburn at the end

of the hallway. We were badly outnumbered if this spread, and the only way for me to help lower the numbers was to risk hurting people badly. I was too small and too female not to fight to put people down as quickly and violently as possible. Sometimes you could scare people with what you were willing to do, and the fight would end just because the price wasn't worth it to them. Police didn't scare that easily.

Olaf spoke into the strange, tense silence of the hallway as he stared down at Rankin. "Yes, it is over." His big hands were almost loose at his sides, not in fists, but somehow held ready to be fists, or to grab, or to be whatever he needed them to be. I'd always thought of Olaf as a two-fisted-brawler kind of fighter because of his size, but he fought with speed and finesse, not just brute strength. It was rare to find a really big man who didn't try to win through size and raw strength. It made me think better of him, and worse of him. Edward had told me to just shoot him if he ever came for me; now I knew why. I was good in a fight, but Olaf was better. Now that he was a werelion, any speed or strength bonuses I'd had with my own supernatural extras were gone.

Edward went forward to help move Olaf away from the now completely unconscious detective. He was right to move Olaf back. I don't think any of the men waiting at the head of the hallway would have willingly come close to him without wanting to use at least a Taser. Like I said, police don't scare easy, but some of them looked a little pale around the edges. Glad I wasn't the only one thinking, *I never, ever want to fight Olaf for real.* It made me feel less chickenshit.

49

I EXPECTED THE FIGHT to get us pushed as far from the case as possible, but it didn't work that way. Once Rankin regained consciousness, Tyburn still insisted he go with the paramedics to get checked out at the hospital. In fact, when Rankin was safely out of earshot, Tyburn turned to us and treated us as assets. If I hadn't known better, I'd have thought he had sent Rankin off to the hospital not for his health, but to get him out of the way. And Tyburn wasn't the only one who seemed glad that they were down a detective.

Detective Dalton came into the lobby with Micah and Nathaniel on either side of her; Ru and Rodina trailed behind them, and Bram and Nicky behind them. Dalton was pale but looked resolute, as she walked very purposefully toward Tyburn. "Sir, may I have a word in private?"

"Are you all right, Detective?" he asked.

"I am now, but I'm not sure how long it will last, so I'd like to talk to you now, just in case."

He should have told her that they had a murder investigation and couldn't it wait, but he didn't. In fact, he called another plainclothes officer over and said, "Lin, find Marshal Spotted-Horse and escort the four marshals to the crime scene."

Lin had straight black hair and just enough hints around his brown eyes and cheekbones to make me think that Lin might be his last name instead of his first. He looked at the three of us, then back to his captain. "What crime scene would that be, sir?" His tone said clearly, *You can't possibly mean for me to take strangers who just had a fistfight with one of our other detectives to see our murder scene, sir.*

"*The* crime scene, Lin. We don't have any other crime scenes today."

"With all due respect, sir—" Lin started to say.

Tyburn cut him off. "Take them to the body, Lin."

"Captain—"

"Now, Detective!" It was a growled shout.

Lin didn't jump or salute, though I saw his arm flex like he was going to do the latter. He just looked from Tyburn to Dalton and then said, "Do any of you know how to get ahold of Marshal Horse?"

I laughed—I couldn't help it—and turned it into a cough.

"It's Marshal Spotted-Horse," Edward corrected.

Olaf narrowed his eyes at me. "Why was that humorous?"

I shook my head, not trusting myself to talk, because though I'd never had sex with Bernardo, I had seen him nude once, and he was very well-endowed. How I had never shortened his name even in my own head to the appropriate nickname, I had no idea, but I hadn't. Now that Detective Lin had put it in my head, I was going to have to struggle not to think Marshal Horse or Marshal Hung-Like-a-Horse or a half dozen other inappropriate noms de plume.

Edward called Bernardo on his cell phone, as Micah and Nathaniel came up to us with the rest of our parade fanning out around them. The looks on their faces were serious enough to help me regain control of myself. "How bad was it?"

"She thought she was in love with Rankin," Micah said, voice low.

"He brainwashed her somehow," Nathaniel said, "and almost me."

I took his hand in mine. Micah was already holding the other one.

"Dalton seems free of him now," I said.

"For now," Ru said, "but I don't know if it will last if we aren't there to touch her and share some of our resistance to his powers with her."

"We can't hold hands with her forever," Rodina said.

"No, we can't," Nathaniel said.

"Hold hands with who forever?" Olaf asked. It startled me. I hadn't heard or felt him coming up on us. That was careless—not fatal yet, but I couldn't afford to let the meta-physics blind me to the real world that badly.

Olaf leaned over me and I felt a flare of his beast's energy as he whispered, "What are you talking about so secretively?"

I took a step back from him and closer to all my people. It helped chase the warmth of his energy back, though I caught a flash of amber eyes deep inside me as my lioness awoke enough to stare upward and wonder about that warmth.

"Ted will fill you in," I said.

Edward took him to one side to tell him what he'd missed.

Bernardo came striding into the lobby, and I had a moment to watch the crowd react to him. Any women who were there and some of the men followed his progress like they'd never seen anyone who was tall, dark, and handsome. Some of the other police looked at him in that *if the shit hits the fan, is he a danger to me?* way. Bernardo was tall and obviously in shape; he moved in a graceful long-legged stride halfway between the male version of a female model on the catwalk and the way most big, athletic men move. He was like a sexy predator. I thought that, even though I was standing with three men who were literally predators in one form or another.

Nathaniel leaned in and whispered, "Tell me again why you never slept with him."

Ru leaned in from behind me, resting his chin on my shoulder, and said, "I was thinking the same thing."

Rodina said, "You didn't see him by the pool with all the other women. You'd understand if you had."

We'd forgotten about Olaf having better-than-human hearing now, because he spoke low, but not quite a whisper, as he said, "Anita is not moved by the same things that move most women."

I didn't know what to say to that, because in a way he was right; if I had been, then Bernardo and I would have crossed the sexual divide the first time we met. Now I had no plans to cross it. We were work friends, maybe battle buddies, but we would never be lovers. Watching him come closer, I could admit to a tiny bit of regretful curiosity about whether he was as good as he looked, but mostly I was relieved that we'd dodged the bullet of each other. He was a womanizer of epic proportions, and when we'd met I'd still been trying for a monogamous, white-picket-fence kind of life. It would have been a disaster, and possibly ruined our working relationship. Work friends was better.

Lin put his sunglasses on and started walking toward the doors.

Then I had a thought: Rankin was going to the same hospital as Peter and Donna.

I told Ru and Rodina to make sure they were okay. Nicky and Bram stayed with Nathaniel and Micah.

I usually made it a point not to kiss my boyfriends in front of the other cops, but if I hadn't had them to rely on, Rankin would have rolled me. It didn't feel right to leave them in the lobby with just a hug. I wrapped my arms around Micah and Nathaniel and then kissed them one after the other. I turned to Nicky, but he gave a slight shake of his head. I looked at Ru. He smiled and looked hopeful. I started to kiss his cheek, but he moved so that our lips met, and I got a taste of Jean-Claude, as if he were a wine that lingered on Ru's lips, or a perfume ghosting through a room after the wearer has gone. Whatever it was, I kissed that echo of Jean-Claude, because I was suddenly missing him so much.

Edward barked, "Anita, we're moving." It startled me and helped me pull away from Ru, who looked pleased and a little dazed. I had to trot a little to catch up with everyone's longer legs, but once I got to them I could keep up. I'd been walking with taller people most of my life.

"Where are we going?" Bernardo asked.

"Crime scene," Edward said.

"How did you swing that?" he asked.

"Rankin picked a fight with Otto," Edward said.

"Who cleaned his clock," I said.

Bernardo looked from one to the other of us as if waiting for us to say we were joking. When we didn't, he said, "And that got us an invitation to their crime scene?"

Edward and Olaf said, "Yes."

I said, "Apparently."

"Glad I'm not the only one wondering what the hell is going on," Lin said, "but my captain tells me to take you to our crime scene, so I'll take you, but I don't have to like it."

"No, you don't," I said.

"I don't have to like any of you," he said.

"No, you don't," Edward said.

He looked from one to the other of us, as if wondering if we were kidding him by repeating each other. We gave him blank, innocent eyes, or I did. Edward said, "We've been partners for a while."

"You work long enough together, it's like a married couple—you start finishing each other's sentences," Lin said.

"They say married couples start looking alike," Bernardo said.

Edward and I exchanged a look. "I always wondered what I'd look like as a blond," I said.

He smiled. "Maybe you'll get taller."

I smiled back, and then Lin led us through the doors into the blinding flashes of the smartphones. Lucky we all had sunglasses.

50

I FOUND OUT THERE was a linking bridge from Kirke Key to the rest of the Keys, but the boat was considered romantic for the wedding guests. We weren't guests anymore, so we got to drive from Kirke Key to Little Coppit Key. It was my first crime scene at the edge of the ocean. The waves spilled across the small stretch of sand, rocks and shells like hungry hands trying to pull the body back out to sea. They hadn't been able to leave the body where they found it, because the ocean wanted it back, as if it were a shell washed up on the shore for someone to find, but only until the next wave came to snatch it back. So the body was laid out on a black tarp in the parking lot above the beach, though that last word conjured images of miles of pale sand stretching out and out, but it was more like a pale sand thread between the ocean and the smooth lumps of rocks, and there weren't a lot of rocks. It was as if the ocean was closer here in the Keys, a lot closer than in California, where the beach seems to give the land space to be separate from the water. Here in the Florida Keys the ocean was even more intimate, as if it wasn't sure it was finished with the land and might take it back at any minute.

It would have been easier if I had not seen the "body" when it was alive. One of the ways I stay sane is by creating a verbal distance: it's a body, not a person, not a woman; just an it, not a her. It helps me look down at what people do to other people without wanting to run screaming or throw up. I tried to stay detached so I could see and catalog anything that might help us figure out what happened. I was looking for clues, and I couldn't do that if I was emotionally involved, but all I could think as I stared down at the body on the black tarp was what Bettina had looked like by the pool. She'd been shallow and unpleasant and jealous for very little reason. I hadn't even liked her. She'd seemed so unfinished, so . . . young. We all get older, we learn our lessons, we grow, we change, hopefully we get wiser or better in some way, but Bettina Gonzales would never get older, never learn the lesson that might have kept her safe from her killer, never have a chance to grow out of the unpleasant competitiveness with other women over a man. Though, honestly, she'd struck me as one of those women who never outgrew that kind of damaging thinking that made a boyfriend, a lover, more important than friendship with another woman. When I last saw her alive I wouldn't have given her the benefit of the doubt. Staring down at her dead body, I was willing to cut her more slack, not that she cared—not that she'd ever care about anything ever again.

Her brown eyes were wide-open and staring at nothing. Her long black hair was in a tangled mass at the back of her head, as if the hair had been snagged on something, or maybe her killer had balled it up in his fist while it was getting wet. She hadn't been in the water, or even dead long enough, for much color change in her skin. From about the waist up she looked like the person I'd seen by the pool, except she was missing the top to her bikini so that her breasts were exposed, falling full and useless toward her arms. What might have been erotic if she'd been alive was just part of the horror show now, because just inches below the breasts, just below her waist, she'd been gutted. Not the way a butcher would do it, or even a hunter with a deer, but as if she were a piece of melon that the killer had hollowed out all the pulp and good stuff from, leaving only the rind behind. Enough skin was gone or peeled back that I was pretty sure I could see part of her spine. The sunlight showed everything so that there were no shadows, nothing to hide the awfulness of it, and that was with my sunglasses on. Damn, I hoped she'd been dead before he started on that part. I prayed that she'd been dead before that happened to her.

Did the same killer have Denny now? Was he doing this to that tall, athletic body right this minute? Was she screaming her life away while we stared down at the dead girl? I prayed,

Please let her be safe. I closed my eyes and prayed about as hard and fervent a prayer as I'd done in a while. *Please let us find her in time, before she's hurt. Please, God, don't let this happen to anyone else.* I got that small warm feeling that I sometimes got when I prayed. I always thought of it as God's way of saying, *It will be all right.* I took comfort from it, but I also knew that sometimes God's definition of *all right* wasn't the same as mine.

Bernardo's voice came low, next to my face: "You can't stand to look at her either?"

I opened my eyes and had to be careful how I turned or I'd have touched his face with mine, he was leaning so close. I fought not to move back, because he obviously was trying to whisper so that Edward and Olaf, standing on the other side of the tarp, the other side of the body, couldn't hear us.

"I'm praying," I said.

"It's too late to pray for her," he said, and his dark brown eyes were full of something between terror and sorrow. I wanted to move back from the intensity of the emotion, but if he could feel it, I could stand next to it.

"Not for Denny it isn't," I said.

He stared at me from inches away, face stricken; that was the only word I had for it. "I wish I had your faith," he said, and then turned and walked away from the body of his one-afternoon stand. He walked until he found a fence post to lean a hand on, as if he needed the support.

Lin, who had stayed near us, as if he didn't trust us not to touch, take, or otherwise contaminate his crime scene, said, "Captain Tyburn is en route, but he asked me to ask you what you see." Lin pulled out an iPad mini to take notes.

"You don't want us to wait for Tyburn?" I asked.

"He says get you started. I'll make sure he knows what you said." He lifted the notebook up a little, pen still poised.

I looked across the body at Edward and Olaf. Edward and I made eye contact; his face moved so that even behind the dark sunglasses I knew he'd raised eyebrows at me in that *go ahead* gesture.

"Okay, I'm hoping she died before the major damage happened," I said.

"I think we all are," Edward said.

"She would have been dead before he was finished," Olaf said, "but she could have been alive when he began to . . . harvest them." His voice was even, unemotional, which was almost a first for him at this kind of crime scene, at least in my experience. Because his voice wasn't creepy I let myself look at his face. His eyes were hidden behind wraparound black sunglasses, but what I could see of his face with its edge of black mustache and beard seemed normal enough, as in *normal* normal, not Olaf normal around a messy murder scene. I looked for the excitement, the near sexual buzz that he usually seemed to feel, but he looked cold and clinical; almost . . . bored, or let down, like he was disappointed somehow.

"What?" he asked, and I realized that I'd been staring at him.

I shook my head. "Nothing. Sorry, I'm having more trouble than I expected because I saw her alive just a day ago."

"That makes it harder for most of us," Edward said, and he looked past me toward Bernardo. It made me glance back. Tall, dark, and handsome was throwing up at the edge of the parking lot.

"Do you really think the killer harvested the organs?" Lin asked.

"No," Olaf said, "it is the wrong word, but I do not yet have a better one." He squatted down beside the body, balancing easily on the balls of his feet. He took his sunglasses off so he could look at the wounds without the color being changed. He was right; the sunglasses hid things, or could.

"You okay if I check on Bernardo?" Edward asked.

I glanced at Olaf, who seemed to be studying the body in a thoroughly professional way for a change. I nodded. "I think so."

"Yell if you need me," he said and walked wide around the body, moving toward Bernardo, who was now on all fours. Lucky he'd put all that long hair back in a ponytail before we got to the crime scene.

"Does Marshal Forrester always worry about you this much at a crime scene?" Lin asked.

"No," I said, "but he's not usually having to take care of Marshal Spotted-Horse either."

"I heard that Spotted-Horse was the girl's boyfriend. Is that true?"

"*Boyfriend* is too strong a word, I think."

"Were they lovers?" Lin asked.

Olaf said, "Captain Tyburn knows that answer. If he wants to share it with you, he will."

Olaf was right—we shouldn't share information with anyone about the personal stuff. We were in a weird position as part of the investigation and potential suspects. I appreciated Olaf making the save and reminding me that we shouldn't get chatty about anything but the murder scene.

"There are no tool marks that I recognize," Olaf said.

That made me squat down on my side of the body and balance on the balls of my feet; we had plastic booties over our shoes, but the rest of us could still pick up evidence or otherwise contaminate the scene. I was missing the overalls I wore at home, but I hadn't packed for a murder; I'd packed for a wedding. I stared down at the body and wasn't sure there was going to be a wedding. Where was Denny? I pushed the thought away as hard as I could and tried to concentrate on business. If I did my job as if I hadn't known the body lying here, then maybe I could help solve this crime and then we could find Denny. My continuing to freak out because she was missing didn't help her a damn bit. It was an emotional indulgence that neither I nor Denny could afford.

"What do you mean by no tool marks you recognize?" Lin asked.

"I mean that whatever was used on the body wasn't a cutting tool that I am familiar with, and until this moment I thought I knew them all."

I forced myself to take off my sunglasses and look at the gaping cavity that had once been most of the important interior bits of a person. I had to let my eyes adjust to the insane brightness of the sunlight so close to the ocean, but they adjusted like they were designed to and then the bloody parts were too bright, the color contrasts like some garish special effect. I'd been right about seeing some of her spine; it glistened in the sunlight like a pale jewel set in bloody metal. Fuck. I tried to look at it as just meat, just something that was cut. How was it cut up? What did they use? Could I tell?

I rested my wrists on my knees and leaned closer to the opening, trying to see if Olaf was right. Were there no tool marks? Had this really all been done without a blade? It took me a second to realize that the eerie cleanness of the cavity had made me think it was all that neat and tidy, but it wasn't. The edges of the skin were ragged. It looked more like the skin had been torn at, not cut, or not neatly cut. Had it been claws? Or had someone tried to neaten things with the un-known cutting tool?

I leaned in so close my nose was almost touching the body. I didn't see the neatness of a blade or any kind of claw marks I'd ever seen before. I'd held my breath automatically but real-ized if I was going to get that close, I might need a mask to go with my gloves and booties. I leaned back up to just squatting beside the body and took a deep breath. A second later I real-ized it was a bad idea, because this close, there'd be a smell. I waited to be nauseated, or at least bothered, but strangely there was no bad odor. There should have been, because with this much damage her bowels should have been perforated, so the outhouse smell should have been there, but it wasn't. Weird. I mean, I wasn't complaining, but everyone's shit stinks. Betti-na's wouldn't be different, and the moment I thought her name, I couldn't have my face that close to the body. I was suddenly warm and it had nothing to do with the heat. I stood up a little fast, had a moment of my vision swimming. I took a few slow, deep breaths and got myself under control. I hadn't thrown up on a body in years; I wasn't going to start now. I'd done it once at one of my first bad crime scenes, and the police back home hadn't let me forget it for years.

I swallowed hard and looked off into the distance, not just so I wasn't looking at the body, but so I could fixate on some-thing else like that stop sign. I stared at the sign as if I'd memo-rize the feel of it with my eyeballs. It was sort of the same theory as being seasick and staring out at the horizon.

"You okay, Marshal Blake?" Lin asked.

I managed to say, "Yes. Why doesn't the body smell worse? The bowels had to be perforated. We should be able to smell it." I wasn't sure I was actually looking for an answer, more sharing the puzzle.

"The bowels are gone, along with everything else in the lower section of the body," Olaf said.

I looked at him then, where he was still squatting beside

the body. "But even if he, it, they, tore the bowels out of the body, they should have spilled inside the cavity."

"Perhaps the salt water washed it clean," Lin offered.

"Maybe," I said.

"Or perhaps he was just that skilled at removing the internal organs, like a hunter that does not wish to contaminate the meat," Olaf said.

"You think they ate her like meat?" Lin asked.

"I do not know for certain, but they did not eat her as they did it, because it is too neat for that."

I said, "This doesn't look like claws or teeth to me either. Otto is right. I don't see any tool marks that I recognize."

"Wait," Lin said, "if it's not claws, teeth, or tools, what is it? What did the killer use to do that to her?"

"There are teeth marks," Olaf said.

"Where?" I asked.

"You will either have to touch the body more, or come to my side and then perhaps you can see it."

I glanced back down at the body. I didn't want to touch it more; I really didn't. It was freaking me out far more than I'd thought it would that I knew what this body had looked like up and running, talking, living. I'd seen people I knew dead before. Had it bothered me this much? I couldn't remember; maybe I didn't want to remember. You have to get a certain amnesia about how horrible parts of the job are, or you can't keep doing it. It's like my friends who tell me that you forget how awful pregnancy and childbirth are; otherwise you would never have a second child.

I went around the body to squat down beside Olaf. He pointed with one big gloved hand toward the edge of the rib cage. The skin was a little pulled back from this angle. "Do you see the rib bone just there?"

"Yeah, it's been bitten, or I think it's tooth marks on the rib. We'll need forensics to tell us for sure. I mean, there may be some exotic tool that I've never heard of that could do shit like this."

"It is teeth. See the way it marked the bone here"—he pointed with his gloved finger—"and here."

"Damn, I think you're right."

"So it's fangs, like a wereanimal?" Lin asked.

We both looked up at him, as if we'd almost forgotten he was there. "No, not fangs like a wereanimal. Whatever did this is no type of shapeshifter that I'm familiar with," I said.

"It is closer to human teeth marks," Olaf said.

"Are you saying a human being did that?"

"No," we said together, then looked at each other. I motioned for him to elaborate. He was doing great and not being all serial-killer creepy at all. I wanted to encourage him.

"No human could bite through bone in this manner, and it looks as if they plunged their hands into her flesh to tear her open. Again, most humans would neither be strong enough to do this nor have the knowledge to do it."

"Knowledge; what do you mean *knowledge*?" Lin asked.

"You may have the desire to do this to a woman, but you will not know how. For something so potentially savage, it is disappointingly not."

"What?" Lin asked.

I translated. "It's too clean and neat for what was done to the body. I don't think this was done by a human being, but if it was, then this is not their first rodeo."

"If this killer has struck before, it wasn't here, because we haven't had anything remotely like this since I've been on the job."

"How long have you been on the job here?" I asked.

"Five years."

Olaf shook his head. "He has been practicing this somewhere."

"Agreed," I said.

"Well, the perp hasn't been practicing anywhere in the Keys," Lin said.

Edward spoke as he walked up to us. "If he's been practicing, we need to find out where. It could give us a clue to what, or who, it is."

I glanced past him and saw Bernardo leaning against the light pole at the edge of the parking lot. I didn't bother asking how he was, because he looked pale from here. Also, he hadn't come back to do his job, or help us do our jobs. That meant he wasn't doing well at all.

Olaf and I stood up at the same time, though he kept standing up like he found extra inches from somewhere. I knew he was either seven feet tall or damn near, but I was suddenly more aware of it than normal.

"Tell me what you found out," Edward said.

We told him.

"I was hoping one of you would have seen a creature like this before," Edward said.

"Creature?" Lin made it a question with the uptilt of the word.

"*Monster* is considered impolitic for our preternatural citizens," Edward said.

"*Creature* is better?" Lin asked.

Edward shrugged. "It's supposed to be according to the list of approved words the Marshals Service issued recently."

"Are you all certain that this wasn't a human-on-human killing?" Lin asked.

"Yes," Edward said.

"Yes," Olaf said.

"Pretty sure," I said.

"Okay, if our bad guy, or girl, isn't human, then what are they?"

The three of us looked at one another. I shrugged and shook my head. "I've never seen anything remotely like this. I can tell you what it isn't, but not what it is."

"Same here," Edward said.

"It doesn't even have a familiar scent," Olaf said.

"That's right. You're a shifter now. Does that give you a better smeller?" Lin asked.

"Not in human form, but I am more aware of scent than I was before."

"And you say it doesn't smell like human, or a shapeshifter?" Lin said.

"That is correct."

"What does it smell like, then?"

"A mystery."

And that was the best we could do. It wasn't human, or a shapeshifter, or any supernatural creature the three of us had ever run across. It was a mystery. Which didn't help Denny one fucking bit.

51

LIN ASKED US if we were done with the body, and when we said yes, he shooed us back so the next round of people could take the body away. I hoped the medical examiner could come up with more than our guesswork. It was informed guesswork, but none of it seemed to get us closer to the killer or to finding Denny. The three of us stripped off our gloves and booties and went to join Bernardo, who was well out of the way, as the next round of personnel came to collect the body. Sometimes a crime scene is like a relay race, each person handing the body and evidence off to the next leg and the next runner. This time it really was a race against time, because we were all going on the assumption that Denny had been abducted by the same "creature" that had done that to Bettina. Even though none of the other cops knew Denny at all, they would still be racing to find her, to save her, because most people go into this line of work because at heart they want to save the world, to help people, to be that white knight. White knights want to save the maiden and slay the dragon, not just find the body and clean up the mess.

Bernardo was standing up straight and tall beside the light pole at the edge of the parking lot. He'd retied his ponytail so it was even tighter, giving the illusion that his hair was short and close to his head. His sunglasses were firmly in place, and his color was back to normal. Evidently he wanted to ignore what had just happened and move forward. Fine with me.

"Why would he take all the internal organs like that?" I asked of no one in particular.

"He wanted them," Olaf said.

"Wanted them how, or for what?" I asked.

"Trophies," Edward said. "A lot of these guys take trophies—you know that."

"A heart, a liver, some of the other organs that travel well, but some of what he took is messy and hard to transport. How would you keep, say, intestines as a trophy?"

"Freeze them," Olaf said.

"Put them in a preservative, like some kind of specimen in a jar," Edward said.

"God," Bernardo said softly.

"I'm sorry if this upsets you," I said, because neither of the men would say it. I was sort of breaking the guy code even acknowledging that there was an issue.

He nodded. "Thanks, I'm fine." It was such an obvious lie that we all pretended it wasn't one.

"He could have eaten them," Edward said.

Bernardo swallowed hard enough that I could hear it, the strong lines of his throat working convulsively as if he was trying not to be sick again. "I don't think the killer did that. I don't want to think it."

Olaf said, "You know that it is possible."

"But I don't want to hear it out loud. I really don't want to talk calmly about someone, or something, eating parts of . . . her."

"You know the truth of hunting monsters, Bernardo. Why does saying it aloud bother you?" Olaf asked.

"Goddamn it, Otto!" He shouted that and then lowered his voice for the rest. "She was in my bed yesterday. I don't want to hear someone ripped her open and ate parts of her."

Olaf's voice was still calm, dispassionate, as he said, "You know that I don't understand why that matters to you, but if you tell me that it does, I will believe you."

"And I don't understand why it doesn't matter to you, but I know that it doesn't."

They looked at each other, both tall and handsome in their ways, though it had taken me a long time to see that Olaf was attractive. "It would have been better if I had fucked her instead of you, Bernardo. We would both have enjoyed this crime scene much more."

"Enjoyed it, no. Even if I hadn't slept with her, I wouldn't enjoy seeing someone I'd watched at the pool dead like this."

"I would have enjoyed it more."

The question in my head was so loud: *Why? Why would you have enjoyed it more if you had fucked the dead girl instead of Bernardo?* I wanted to ask, but I was almost certain that I would hate the answer. He and I were getting along better than we ever had. I didn't want to give him the opportunity to say something creepy and disturbing. If he said it, that was fine, that was on him, but I didn't want to chum for it.

Normally, if I didn't ask, the men we worked with wouldn't dream of asking, but Bernardo was shaken. It made him ask, because this time he wanted to know, or maybe he always wanted to know, and today he was upset enough to act on it.

"Why? Why would you have enjoyed this more if you slept with her?"

"Bernardo, don't ask him that," Edward said.

"No, Edward, Ted, I want to know. You tell me he's big and bad, and he is, but the rest is stories. He's never done any of that shit around me."

"You will not like his answers."

"Today I want answers, even if they're bad ones," Bernardo said.

Edward just nodded and made a small *go ahead* gesture at both of them. I just stood there like a witness to an accident.

Bernardo's hands were in loose fists at his sides as he turned to Olaf and repeated his question. "Why would you have enjoyed this more if you had fucked her instead of me?"

"Because then I could have been thinking about her body alive and underneath me while I looked at her dead." He said it so calmly, matter-of-factly.

"That is exactly why I had to walk away, Otto. Don't you get that? I was thinking about how it felt to put me inside her, and now all of that's gone, torn out of her by some maniac. It's a fucking nightmare."

Olaf stepped a little bit closer to the other man and studied his face; the way he was standing was not like he was getting ready to fight him, but as if he wanted to observe Bernardo. "I could have looked down at her dead body and thought about how her skin felt under my hands when she was warm. I would have remembered plunging myself between her legs, how tight it felt, how I had to force my way in, and wondered if the killer took enough of her internal meat so that if I fucked her like this would it be looser? Would it be like fucking an empty bag, or would she still be tight, tighter perhaps from the salt water? I have no interest in fucking the dead, but I would enjoy speculating, remembering her alive and screaming my name, and looking down at the empty thing she has become."

Bernardo made a sound low in his throat, body tensing. I knew he was going to take a swing at Olaf before his body moved. Edward and I both moved between them; he took Olaf and I took Bernardo, and we moved them back from each other.

Bernardo yelled at him, "You sick son of a bitch!" He tried to move forward again, and I put hands on his chest and just kept him from getting closer, not shoving him, but acting like a wall. It was just a touch to remind him not to do it.

"I told you that you wouldn't like the answer, Bernardo," Edward said. Olaf wasn't trying to close the distance; he was very still on the other side of Edward. Olaf was watching Bernardo, but not like he was afraid of a fight with him; no, he was observing him—that was the only word I had for this intense watching. I could feel the weight of it through the sunglasses.

"This must have really got your rocks off, then, seeing her like this," Bernardo said, voice breaking a little around the edges, as if he might cry. I know that if I get close to fighting someone and then I can't, sometimes it leads to tears. I'd never seen a man affected that way, but we're all human.

"I told you, if I had fucked her, then, yes, but without that memory, this body is neutral for me."

"What do you mean 'neutral'?" Bernardo asked as if he couldn't help himself, or as if he was hoping he could manipulate it into a reason to fight.

"There is almost no blood, and the killer took all the parts he tore away, so there is no . . . jigsaw puzzle of pieces for me to touch, or reconstruct in my head. This kill is too neat for my tastes."

"So if the killer had torn her apart and made more of a mess, that would have excited you?" Bernardo asked, voice low, not calm, but low. I kept my hand pressed against his chest, not pushing on him, but keeping it there so I could feel when he moved. I would have seconds to decide how I wanted to stop him from hitting Olaf, or maybe I'd just step aside. If I hadn't thought Bernardo would get hurt, stepping aside would have sounded better. Before Olaf had become a werelion, I think I'd have just let it happen. I was trying not to think about what Olaf had said in the last few minutes. I was trying very hard not to think about it, and failing.

"Yes, it would have excited me more," Olaf said slowly, deliberately.

In that moment I realized that Olaf was watching Bernardo's pain. He was drinking in the emotional trauma of it, not feeding literally on it the way I could on anger and lust, but Olaf was enjoying Bernardo's pain. Fuck that.

"We're done," I said, stepping so I could see them both better. "Bernardo, you are done asking questions that none of us want the answer to. Olaf, Otto, you're done answering."

"You do not get to dictate to me, Anita. Not even you get to do that."

"Fine, but, Bernardo, he's enjoying watching your reaction to his answers. You're feeding the monster in him by showing your pain. If you want to keep doing that, fine by me, but that's what he's doing and you're helping him."

"I just want to hit him, to hit something."

"I understand that, but Bettina is dead and Denny isn't. We need to brainstorm and figure out anything we've learned that could help find her, because I do not want to be standing over her body in a few hours, or tomorrow, or at all. So if you can't function enough to help find this killer and hunt for Denny, then say so, and we'll work around you, but I need to know if you can do this or if you're too compromised."

He took off his sunglasses and rubbed his eyes, and then looked down at me from all that handsome height. The pain in his eyes was hard to look at it, but if he could feel it, I could at least not turn away from it.

"I don't know, Anita, and that's the truth, but I'll go along. If I get in the way, hurt the investigation, then you, or Ted here, take me out of the game, but until that happens I'll do my job."

I patted him on the arm and smiled, because he was being honest and brave and that deserved something.

I turned to Olaf then, looking past Edward to meet his eyes. He'd taken his own sunglasses off, so I was staring into the deepest eyes, like caves carved in his face with his dark eyes sitting at the bottom of them.

"You told me earlier that you wanted to try to date me for real, like a *date* date."

"I remember," he said.

"Did you understand that talking to Bernardo like this in front of me makes that even less likely than it was?"

"You know what I am, Anita. You've known the truth about me from the moment we met. I do not have to play games with you or lie to you. I can be myself. It is one of the things I value about our relationship."

"We don't have a—"

Edward interrupted. "Stop it, both of you. We are done with the impromptu therapy session. We are United States Marshals and we are going to do our job. More than finding the killer, I want to find Denny alive, and I will do anything it takes to save her from ending up like Bettina Gonzales."

"I couldn't have said it better myself, Forrester," Captain Tyburn said from the sidewalk just behind us. Detective Dalton was with him. "We have a lot to tell you, but none of it will help find your friend, so what I'm asking the Four Horsemen is, what would you do to find your friend if I gave you all the resources of my department?"

I licked my lips and said, "Would you be willing to think outside the box, outside of the resources of your department?"

"To not see another body like that, hell, Blake, I'd throw the fucking box away."

I smiled. "Then I have an idea."

52

MY IDEA WAS to use a wereanimal as a hypersmart, human-aware search-and-rescue "dog." Tyburn asked only two questions: Had I ever done it before, and could I guarantee the public safety?

"Twice before: Both times we got our bad guy and in one case saved a hostage."

"Did you fail to save the hostage the second time?"

"No, there was no hostage to save, just a serial killer to execute, and that was the first time I used a shapeshifter to track a suspect."

"Can you guarantee that your pet shapeshifter won't attack anyone except the suspect?"

"Yes."

"Just like that, an unequivocal yes?"

I nodded. "If it wasn't an unequivocal yes, Captain Tyburn, I wouldn't be suggesting it."

"How does it work?" Dalton asked. She looked sad and a little pale, but she was doing her job and seemed to be tracking everything that was happening around her. Having been on the receiving end of Rankin's power, I was impressed. I wondered how long he'd been messing with her, but I left it for later. One problem at a time, and right now nothing was more important than finding Denny. Every minute that she was missing upped the chances of her ending up like Bettina. A relative stranger dead was one thing; having one of Donna's oldest and closest friends murdered would probably put a serious damper on the wedding, if we were still doing it tomorrow.

There were so many reasons to postpone, or to skip it altogether, but that wasn't my call. Until Edward or Donna called it off, the wedding was still on. Peter wanted them to do it as scheduled even if the doctors wouldn't let him out of the hospital to attend it. We could have done that, but missing the maid of honor? I wasn't sure we could muscle past that, but one problem at a time. First we had to find Denny alive, and as well as possible. We'd worry about everything else after that, including the wedding.

Tyburn turned to Olaf. "So you and Marshal Blake have done this before?"

Olaf glanced at me and then back at Tyburn. "I was not the wereanimal that she used to track her victims down."

I wasn't sure I liked his phrasing about me, tracking my victims down, but since I'd killed the bad guys we tracked down, it was a little awkward to argue. "Marshal Jeffries wasn't a wereanimal at that time, and we weren't working together on the two cases."

"Are you going to use him now?" Dalton asked.

I thought, *No, absolutely no,* but wasn't sure how to say that without possibly offending Olaf. He surprised me by taking care of it for me.

"No, I am new at being a lycanthrope. I would rather trust this task to more experienced noses than mine, and Anita has more experienced shapeshifters with her."

"You mean Wyatt and Nathaniel?" Dalton asked. It was interesting that they were on a first-name basis already.

"And Micah, Morgan, or Nicky, or Bram, yeah," I said.

"They're civilians, Blake. I'm not sure how I feel about putting them in harm's way," Tyburn said.

"I'm not crazy about it either, but Nathaniel has done this for me before, and it worked."

"Nathaniel Graison is your fiancé, right?" Tyburn asked.

"Right," I said.

"You saw what this thing did to the first victim, Blake. Do you really want to risk getting the man in your life close to that . . . monster?"

"No, and I really don't want it to be Nathaniel this time."

"What's different this time?" Tyburn asked.

In my head, I thought, *Ireland, what happened in Ireland,*

but out loud I said, "I don't know what this creature is. I don't want to risk him with this many unknowns."

"Nathaniel will want to help," Edward said.

"I know. They're friends."

I wanted to keep Nathaniel safe, and instead I was about to take him monster hunting. It seemed like the harder I tried to keep him safe, the more risks he had to take. I knew there was a lesson in there somewhere; I just wasn't sure what the lesson was supposed to be, or maybe I didn't want to learn this particular lesson.

53

TYBURN OFFERED US a ride back to the hotel, but with Dalton in the car there wasn't room for all four of us. We started to divide up two and two, but Tyburn said, "We need to talk on the way back to the hotel, Marshals. The drive back to the hotel is probably the only privacy we'll get today."

"All right, who gets to sit in whose lap?" I asked. I'd meant it to be a joke, but the joke was on me, because Tyburn said, "I'm driving and Dalton doesn't know anyone else well enough to not leave the wrong impression, so that leaves you, Marshal Blake."

"Excuse me?"

"Anita, please just do it and don't argue. Tyburn and Dalton want to share information and Denny is running out of time," Edward said.

I looked at Dalton. "If this was you having to sit on one of your coworkers' laps, would the information be worth it?"

She looked startled, as if she hadn't expected me to ask that particular question, or maybe she just startled easy. She blinked at me, and for a second I thought I'd have to repeat the question, but she answered, "Yes, the information would be worth it, as long as sitting in his lap wouldn't enslave you to him for years." That last part was very bitter, and suddenly I was willing to sit in someone's lap if she'd tell us all about Rankin.

It wasn't me who argued; it was Olaf. "You are the groom-to-be. You cannot drive up to the hotel with another woman on your lap without it getting back to your bride. Do you want a second fight with Donna in one day, during a murder investigation?"

"You know I hate to say it, but I agree with the big guy," Bernardo said.

"Her maid of honor and best friend is missing. Surely even Donna would let things slide until we get Denny back?" I said.

The three men looked at me. Edward's and Bernardo's looks were eloquent. Olaf's look was almost blank behind his sunglasses. He rarely showed much emotion around the three of us, because he didn't have to pretend around us. We already knew he lacked a full set of socially acceptable emotions.

"Well, shit," I said.

"I'm hurt," Bernardo said. "There are plenty of women who would love to have an excuse to sit in my lap." He even managed a weak version of his usual panty-dropping smile. I smiled back, partly because I was just happy to see him starting to rebuild himself after the breakdown.

"No," Olaf said.

"What do you mean, no?" I asked.

He looked at me and again I could feel the weight of his gaze even through the glasses that hid his eyes. "It means that I will not let you sit on his lap."

"You don't have the right to tell me who I can and can't sit with."

"That may be true at this time, but I will only concede ground to . . . Ted and the men already in your life. I will not concede ground to Bernardo."

I fought not to look at Tyburn or Dalton, because I had no way to explain what was happening that didn't make us all look like romantic idiots. I said, "Give us a little privacy, please."

They looked confused, but they moved off so I could turn to Olaf and quietly hiss, "I am not sitting on your lap."

"Then you will be the cause of more fighting and more delays after Donna hears about you and her Ted."

"Are you really willing to risk Denny's life just because I sit on Bernardo's lap and not yours?"

"I don't have the attachment to her that the rest of you do, but there's another question you need to ask."

"What?" I said, and as ridiculous as it sounds, I got closer to him, trying to be "up in his face." With the height difference it probably looked even sillier than it felt, but I was too mad to care.

"Ask Bernardo if he is willing to fight me for the privilege of you on his lap in the car."

"You are not going to fight each other here and now," Edward said, like he was certain.

"No, but there will be later," Olaf said.

"Jesus, Otto, you are a fucking piece of work," Bernardo said.

"Does that mean you will fight me later?"

"No, or not over this. Nothing personal, Anita, but just having you sit in my lap isn't worth fighting him for real."

"No offense. I agree that it's not worth it."

"Fuck," Edward said softly.

"It's just a ride in the car, and we get to know all about how bad Rankin has been to Dalton," I said.

Edward lowered his glasses so I could see his baby blues. "It's never just a ride in the car with him and you, Anita."

"Fine, fine, but we're potentially wasting Denny's life by arguing about it."

"Damn it!" Edward said, setting his glasses back in place and going up to Olaf. "You are going to keep pushing on this until I push back."

"I look forward to it," Olaf said.

"Understand that when he pushes back, so do I, so it won't just be one of us; it'll be both," I said.

It was hard to tell behind the glasses, but I think he blinked first. "I'd always planned on killing you separately if it had to be done."

"You fucking psycho," Bernardo said, "you don't tell people you're going to do stuff like that. You just do it. You don't warn people first."

"That's your only objection?" I asked.

Bernardo shrugged, as if to say, *What did you expect?* The answer was, yeah, that was his only objection, but I let it go.

"Well, Otto, I'd always planned on killing you as sort of a group project," I said.

He smiled. "I never expected you to fight me alone, Anita. You are too practical for that."

"If you do anything in the car that is out of line, we will finish this discussion after Denny is safe," Edward said.

"I will be the perfect gentleman."

"Fine, then let's do this." Edward said it in the tone he usually reserved for life-threatening moments, but we had all threatened one another's lives in the last fifteen minutes, so I guess it counted.

54

TYBURN PULLED OUT into the small cross street where police and emergency vehicles had blocked traffic. It took some
maneuvering, but once we were out of the mess, Tyburn picked
up speed, weaving through the small streets. I'd have preferred
fewer stops and starts and less weaving through traffic since I
was perched on Olaf's lap and couldn't fit a seat belt around
both of us. Dalton seemed perfectly good with how he was
driving from the passenger seat, where she rode shotgun, but
then she was buckled into her seat. The four of us filled up the
backseat of the car. We'd all have preferred for Olaf to ride in
the middle so he'd be pinned, but he was too big to sit comfortably there. I wouldn't have given a damn about his physical
comfort, but sitting him directly behind the driver meant that
Tyburn could not see to drive. What I did give a damn about,
what bothered me more than anything, was that I couldn't wear
a seat belt. Since my mother died because she hadn't been
wearing her seat belt and was thrown through a windshield, I
was a serious stickler about wearing one myself. I usually
wouldn't even start driving a car unless everyone had their seat
belts on, and yet here I was sitting in the lap of the last man on
earth I wanted to touch, and not wearing a seat belt. This day
had so much suck on it.

Edward was physically the smallest, next to me, so he was
in the middle—pressed hip to thigh with Olaf and the same
with Bernardo on the other side. I didn't usually think of Edward as small, but wedged between them like that, he seemed
farther away from six feet than usual. I had to sit across Olaf's
lap with my back to the door because his knees were wedged

into the back of the driver's seat. Tyburn was the second-tallest person in the car, so his seat was back accordingly, which meant that Olaf was wedged into place like a long-legged sardine. It also meant that my legs trailed in front of Edward's, because they had to go somewhere. If I'd stretched my legs out like I was on a couch, my legs would have trailed over all three of their laps. You'd think a man as big as Tyburn would have a bigger car. I wondered if he'd ever had to sit in his own backseat.

"Everyone comfortable?" he asked as he put the car in gear.

"You're kidding, right?" I said.

He gave a little chuckle. Maybe he had been in the back-seat. "Forget I asked."

My pulse was trying to push its way out of the side of my neck. I could keep my breath sort of even but couldn't seem to slow my heart rate, which spiked every time Tyburn proved that he had taken and probably taught a few defensive-driving courses. My fear of riding in cars without a seat belt was not an irrational fear; they improved your chances of surviving a crash, damn it. I just didn't have the confidence in Olaf's lap being as safety tested as the car seats. It didn't help that I was perched across his thighs as if there wasn't more secure lap closer to his body.

Olaf whispered, "You are afraid, why? I have done nothing." His hands were very carefully at his sides because I'd glared at him when he'd tried to put them where they'd normally go when someone is sitting on your lap, which is around the person sitting on you. It's not even necessarily for cuddling; it's just a more comfortable place to rest your hands.

I swallowed past my pulse and spoke low, but didn't bother to whisper. "I can't wear my seat belt sitting like this."

"I had forgotten how strongly you feel about wearing them. You are actually afraid simply from not being fastened into the car."

"Yes," I said, and hated that the one word was breathy with the edge of panic I was fighting.

"I had not anticipated how afraid you would be," he said, voice low and careful.

"Yeah, me either."

He whispered, breath warm against the side of my face, "Fear makes it harder to control my lion."

I turned and looked at him from inches away, both of us in sunglasses helping make it a little less intimate than it could have been. "Your fear, or mine?" I didn't whisper.

He frowned. "I am not afraid of you," and he didn't whisper either.

"Your oversight," I said, and didn't fight the little smile that I got sometimes when it was more threat than humor.

"Do you two need some privacy?" Tyburn asked.

"No, but I'd love to know what was so important that I'm risking life and limb without a seat belt in a car, Captain."

Tyburn and Dalton exchanged a long look as he pulled out onto U.S. 1, which I learned was the only main route to pull out onto. Under other circumstances the long look might have been romantic, but I thought it was more *Where the fuck do we start?* than *Hey, baby.*

"It's complicated," Tyburn said with a laugh. He put the pedal to the metal as soon as he could, and suddenly I was worrying about speed and the fact that there wasn't much on either side of the road except water—ocean on one side and the Gulf of Mexico on the other—but either way, I didn't want to go into the water in a car. Did I mention I almost drowned in a diving accident once? So, yeah, I'm phobic of water, too. Today was just turning out to be full of some of my least favorite things. When I'd been safely buckled into a seat on the drive here, I'd been able to admire the view. Water that looked like melted turquoise and sapphires was pretty amazing, but now it was just one more possible disaster waiting to get me. Phobias aren't about logic; they're about fear.

I didn't even care that I sounded cranky as I said, "We figured it was complicated or you wouldn't have packed us into the car for a little cloak-and-dagger."

"Captain Tyburn, Officer Dalton, the drive won't last forever, so whatever you need to say to us, we need to get started," Edward said, and he sounded much more diplomatic than I did. I wondered if he'd sound as even-keeled if he was the one sitting on Olaf's lap.

Tyburn said, "Rankin is one of my best people. He closes more cases and gets more confessions than any interrogator I've ever met."

I started to say something about Rankin's interrogation

techniques, but Edward touched my leg and shook his head. *Let the man talk,* he was saying, so I stayed quiet and let the man talk.

"He had the same sterling reputation in Los Angeles, where he first became a cop. He left there for Arizona, wanted a place with a yard that he could afford in a nice neighborhood, and on a cop's salary that's hard in L.A., so I'm told. He continued to do impeccable work in Phoenix. I was shocked that a detective with his rep wanted to move to a smaller and much less prestigious force like here. Rankin said he wanted his son raised around his family, who are mostly here. It made sense, and I felt damned lucky to have him.

"Two years ago, I got another top-pick detective from a bigger city when Detective Dalton wanted to leave New York and come here."

Dalton chimed in. "All of us that had been hired and promoted faster because we were psychic were being scheduled to move to different cities now that they felt the program had proven itself enough. If I didn't pick, they would assign me somewhere. I was tired of snow and thought a few years of sunshine would be a nice change. I'll be honest and admit that there was an ex-boyfriend on the force, and it was making things awkward. I'm adding that because I now believe that my 'broken heart'"—she made air quotes around the phrase— "opened me up to Rankin's psychic abilities. He seems to specialize in knowing what you want most that's missing in your personal life, and he offers it to you, and I'll even admit that he delivers on the promises, up to a point. After two years of public dating, I'd started to want a husband and family of my own, and he couldn't give me that."

"Because he's already married," I said.

"Yes, but understand that his wife knows. Hell, I come to dinner and family events. I'm on the list to pick up his son at school if there's an emergency."

"Very progressive and polyamorous," I said.

Tyburn added, "I thought it didn't interfere with their jobs, and if Rankin's wife and family were okay with him dating Dalton, I didn't see it was any of my business."

"You don't have to justify it to me, Captain. I'd be the last one to throw stones at a complicated love life," I said.

Dalton turned in her seat to look at me. She'd taken off her sunglasses, so I could see the big brown eyes with their very subtle but well-done liner and mascara. There might even have been pale eye shadow, but I lowered my gaze before I could be certain, because when a psychic takes off her sunglasses in blinding-bright sunlight and stares really hard at you, you don't make eye contact; you just don't. Maybe Dalton was just being sincere, but I'd already been psychically messed with by one of the local cops; I didn't really want to make it two.

"Thank you for letting the men in your life help break me free of Rankin."

"You're more than welcome," I said.

We'd entered a section of road where the water was hidden by bushes and a fence. Tyburn had to be going at least sixty, maybe seventy, and there was a stoplight coming up. He seemed confident that it wouldn't turn red. Well, at least if we wrecked now, we wouldn't drown. I missed the view, though, as if no matter what, today I wasn't going to be satisfied.

"How did you keep him out of your head, Marshal Blake?" she asked.

"I didn't completely."

"But you didn't fall under his power. How? How did you fight him off?"

I opened my mouth to answer but saw a car coming out of the road that was perpendicular to the stoplight. I yelled, "Car!" I wasn't the only one who yelled a warning of some kind.

Tyburn was already slamming on his brakes. I was thrown forward before I could figure out what to hold on to. Olaf did a perfectly natural thing, grabbing me around the waist and upper body, tucking me in tighter to his body, because with his knees wedged into the back of the seat, he wasn't moving. He shared that stability with me, but I was suddenly in his arms, held tight against the front of his body. I felt the muscles in his arms flex as he held me safe, and the car slid sideways as Tyburn stopped trying for the brake and just tried to move our car out of the way of the other one like something out of an action movie. I'd thrown my arms around Olaf's neck, tucking my head into the bend of his neck like a cuddly version of a crash position.

He held me as the car began to spin, and I knew that he would do everything he could to keep me safe. I knew he would shield me with his own body, and the strength that would have scared me under other circumstances now became the ultimate comfort. I knew that all that energy and strength was now aimed at keeping me safe. The difference between prince and beast is often just a matter of how a man uses his strength and rage. Aimed well, it is a shelter that you can hide behind no matter how great the storm. Turned against you, it makes shelter into a trap. I prayed that Tyburn could control the car, and I held on to Olaf, my face pressed into the warmth of his neck so that I was blind to what was actually happening.

The car stopped moving and there was that frozen moment as if reality took a breath, and then sound came back and I raised my face from the bend of Olaf's neck to see the tall bushes that were pressing against the car window, which meant we weren't on the road anymore, but we weren't in the water, so it was good.

"That was some serious defensive driving, Tyburn," Edward said. I glanced his way and had to turn my body enough to see that he had his arm straight out behind Olaf's arm, like an extra iron bar keeping me safe.

I blinked past Olaf's head and realized that we were on the opposite side of the road, pointed back the way we'd come. Jesus. The adrenaline spiked through my body like fine champagne.

"Sorry about that, everyone, but especially you, Blake. Are you okay?" Tyburn asked.

"Yeah, I'm fine." I realized weirdly that it was true. I was still curled in Olaf's lap with his arms around me, but I didn't push away, because I knew that his arms had held me in place, kept me safe. I couldn't be angry about that. I looked at Olaf, our faces so close, kissing close. "Thanks to Ol . . . Otto holding me tight."

"You are not as afraid as you were earlier, why?" Olaf asked.

"One, I'm good when the emergency finally happens. Two, I knew you would keep me safe, even if it meant shielding me with your own body. I knew you would do it."

"You trusted me to keep you safe," he said.

"Yes," I said, still staring into the swimming blackness of his glasses, so that it was like talking to the tiny reflection of myself that I saw in them.

His beast flared in a flash of heat that chased down my skin in goose bumps. It stole my breath away and made my heart-beat jump. I tightened my arms around his neck, my body wriggling closer to his before I could stop myself. I didn't under-stand it for a second, and then I saw, felt, the amber eyes of my lion in my head. My lioness raised her head and took a big breath of all that power—the power that had just finished keeping us safe. I couldn't argue that he was strong enough to do whatever we needed, but after powerful and strong, my li-oness and I had different things on our lists for potential mates. Very different things.

I smelled heat, ground baked under a sun so hot I could feel it beating against my skin. His lion didn't smell of animal, but of grass burned crisp in the sunlight like the world was a giant oven baking everything to death. I drank in the scent of him with my face pressed to the side of his neck, as his skin ran fever hot with the lion inside him. It steadied me to smell his beast, helped my lioness climb into control and chase back my human fears. We were safe; the danger was over. Why hold on to it when we had much better things to do? My lioness was very clear on what, or rather who, she wanted to do next. That helped me climb back into my head before Edward said, "Anita, are you all right?"

"I am now," I said, and I drew back from basically snuffing the side of Olaf's neck, and unwrapped the rest of me from him. I half expected him to fight to keep me close, but he didn't. In fact he said, "I think my control is not as perfect as I had hoped. I think you cannot sit on my lap and me hold hu-man form."

"So I can sit on Bernardo's lap without you threatening him?" I asked.

"Yes." Olaf lowered his dark glasses just enough for me to see that his eyes were a bright, inhuman orange. I stared into the eyes of his beast from inches away, and my lioness liked it. I just started crawling off of his lap, nearly falling, except that Edward caught me, or rather his legs were in the way of me falling.

"The edges of your auras merged for a second," Dalton said from the front seat.

I clambered over Edward's lap to Bernardo's, because we needed as much room between my beast and Olaf's as the car would allow. I moved fast enough and awkwardly enough that Bernardo had to catch me or I'd have fallen into the door.

"Just to be clear between us, Otto. You're okay with Anita finishing the drive with me?" Bernardo asked.

Olaf nodded, his sunglasses safely back in place so that no one else in the car got the glimpse of those burning-bright eyes that he'd shared with me. I hoped they had faded back to his normal human darkness, but my skin was still running with goose bumps, so I doubted it.

"I am."

"Okay," Bernardo said, and suddenly the arms that had been holding me almost gingerly since they saved me from taking a header into the door curled around me. He actually picked me up a little bit and moved me to a more comfortable position on his lap. I didn't fight it like I had before. In fact, I put my arms around his neck and shoulders without being prompted or having to hold on for dear life as the car spun out of control. I held on and let him hold me close, and it wasn't romantic for me. It was just safer.

"If I turn the car around, is everyone ready to keep going?" Tyburn asked.

Everyone said yes. I said, "If you promise that the rest of the drive will be boring as hell, yes."

He chuckled. "I will do my best to bore the hell out of you, Marshal."

"Then, sure, let's go," I said in a voice full of false cheer.

Tyburn wisely just accepted it and pulled carefully back out onto the road. He turned into the road by a high school that proudly proclaimed *Home of the Sugarloaf Sharks* on a big sign by the road.

"Why did your auras merge like that?" Dalton asked.

"I'll just assume you're aware that I carry lycanthropy," I said.

"But you don't shift," she said.

"No, I don't, but one of the strains of lycanthropy I carry is lion."

"And I am a werelion now," Olaf said.

"I still don't understand why that should make your auras merge."

"My lioness reacted to his lion," I said.

"Does your lioness react to every werelion you meet?" she asked.

"No," I said. I looked across the car at Olaf. He looked back at me. I'd admitted to myself that the new facial hair looked good on him, but now I noticed the black shadows on his head, as if he could have a five-o'clock shadow somewhere besides his face. I wondered if he'd started shaving his head after he started going bald, or before.

A hand appeared in my line of vision so that it was all I could see. I blinked and looked down the arm to realize it was Edward's hand. I looked into his face. "Tell me again that you're fine," he said.

"Why would your lioness react to Marshal Jeffries's lion more than to other werelions?" Dalton asked. She was fucking relentless.

"I'm not sure," I said, and I was half lying. I didn't know exactly why, but I had an idea. It just wasn't one I was willing to share with everyone. I had a leopard to call in Nathaniel, and a wolf to call, more tigers to call than you could shake a stick at, but I had three inner beasts without a corresponding *moitié bête*: hyena, rat, and lion.

As I fought the urge to look across the car at Olaf, I was pretty sure that my lioness had found something she liked, a lot. But this she couldn't have. No, nope, just no.

55

WHEN WE GOT up to speed, admittedly it felt like a lower speed than earlier. I think the near wreck had made Tyburn rethink his driving. I know it had made me determined to speak up if I felt he was driving too fast. Sometimes you need to embrace the suck and just go along for the ride, but sometimes you need to tell whoever is making your life suck to stop being a dick and do better. Tyburn was now on my you-almost-killed-me-so-do-better-or-let-me-drive list.

"Why would you both having lions make your auras merge? It's mostly something I see in couples, but with them it's more consistent. It doesn't come and go."

Edward saved us from the awkward psychic moment. "Before all the excitement, hadn't you just asked Anita how she kept Rankin from getting ahold of her mind and heart?"

"We should stick to asking the things we got in the car to ask, Dalton," Tyburn said.

"Yes, sir," she said. She had to twist more in her seat to see me now, because I was almost directly behind her. She finally turned around to peer at me on the window side. "So how did you keep Rankin from getting his hooks in you?"

"You said that a broken heart may have opened you to him. I didn't have anything like that for him to use. He couldn't offer me anything that I didn't already have in my life. I think if you have no needs that Rankin can tap into, then you're safe."

"Everyone has needs or wants, Marshal," Tyburn said.

"I think my biggest need right now is more alone time. I've got so many amazing people in my life right now that Rankin offering himself to me as a lover was a turnoff, not a turn-on."

Dalton laughed. "Oh, that must have hurt his ego. He thinks he is God's gift to womankind."

"Not just womankind," Edward said.

I glanced at him. "Something you haven't told us?" I smiled when I said it, because he was one of the most solidly heterosexual people I'd ever met.

"He rolled Nathaniel's mind, Anita. That means he offered him something he wanted, or needed."

"Oh," I said, and frowned. He was right. I hadn't had time to ask Nathaniel what Rankin had offered him, but it had to be more than just another male lover, because he had those. What else could Rankin have offered him? He'd tried to offer me a type of sex I wasn't getting, but I was completely happy with the variety in my life, which might mean that Nathaniel wasn't. Crap. If I got a breather from crime-busting and monster-hunting, we needed to have a serious talk.

"Sorry I mentioned it," Edward said, and that made me look at him. "We don't have time for you to think that hard about your love life."

"You brought it up."

"I said I was sorry."

"Ladies and gents," Tyburn said, "back to the problem at hand. Which is that I have a senior detective with a career of over twenty years who has probably been using undisclosed psychic abilities to interrogate suspects."

"If you out him as psychic, then every case he's worked on comes into question," Edward said.

"Unfortunately, yes."

"I know that Nathaniel is innocent of this abduction and what we saw just now, but Rankin was doing his best to make him confess to it. Nathaniel is not a lightweight psychically, not like a straight human or even a normal shapeshifter, so if Rankin aimed his mojo at regular people, then they'd confess to anything."

"I don't think it's that bad," Dalton said. "I think the suspect would have to be romantically attracted to men, and like you said, Marshal, Rankin would have to be able to offer something they wanted or needed. I think for a lot of criminals, romance, or even sex, wouldn't be enough."

"Fair point, but you'd still have to do it case by case, and the lawyers would go into a feeding frenzy," I said. Bernardo made a small movement, as if adjusting for my sitting on his lap. It felt weird having a serious work discussion while I was sitting on his lap with my arms around his neck. It was a date position, or at least a friendly visit, not a police-work position. If he would say something, contribute to the conversation, it might have helped ease the awkwardness.

"It would be a mess legally," Tyburn agreed.

"It would also undermine the psychic program with the police, because I'm one of the first officers that came onto the force as a practitioner and got promoted that way. If it's proven that I was compromised this badly, then they'll use it to hurt all of us."

"So it's just our little secret," I said.

"Yes," she said.

"That's fine," Bernardo said, "unless Rankin has something to do with Bettina's death and Denny's abduction."

I turned in his lap so I could look into that handsome face—from way too close. It would have been more natural to kiss him at this distance than just talk.

"Do you really think Rankin is involved?" I asked.

He nodded. "I saw the film on YouTube of him yelling out that Nathaniel, Micah, and your other men were involved in the crime. Why would he do something that stupid if he wasn't invested in getting someone blamed quick?"

"I thought you were just muscle and handsome. I didn't expect smart on top of all that," Dalton said, aiming those big brown eyes of hers in Bernardo's direction.

Bernardo looked past my shoulder to Dalton, but his face never left the deathly serious expression he'd started with, as if he were oblivious to the flirting, which I knew wasn't true. He flirted like he breathed, but his voice was as cold and relentless as Edward's could be as he said, "Are you flirting with me because you're about to be between boyfriends, or because you want to distract us from the idea that your current boyfriend is involved in the murder and abduction of two women?"

I said, "Bernardo," but when he aimed that look at me, I stopped, because the seriousness of him, the reality of his pain and anger, was there in the flexing of his hands and arms, the tension in his body. His face could hide it, but the rest of him gave the game away.

"Are you trying to distract us from Rankin's involvement, Officer Dalton?" Edward asked.

"No! I mean, I don't know he is involved in all this, but no, I'm not defending him, or covering for him either." She looked at Bernardo then, face no longer friendly, but not as hostile as mine would have been under similar circumstances. "I'm sorry I flirted, even a little bit. I was trying to lighten the mood, trying to feel normal again. The last two years of my life have been a lie, and I don't know what to do about that."

"Rankin can't be personally involved in this murder," Tyburn said.

"How can you be sure?" Edward asked, as Bernardo said, "You can't know that."

"Because I've seen bodies like this before, and Rankin would have been about ten years old when the first murders happened."

That made us all look at him, though all most of us could see was the side of his head, at best. Bernardo startled, arms flexing around me so hard and sudden that it was almost too much. If he hadn't relaxed almost immediately I'd have had to say something. Dalton didn't react as badly as we did, so I was pretty certain he'd told her earlier.

"When and where, exactly?" Edward said.

"Twenty years ago and here."

"And you're just now sharing that information?" Bernardo asked. He sounded angry.

"I've shared it with some of my officers, but until I saw the body I had no way to connect the two crimes." Tyburn's voice held just a touch of heat, as if under other circumstances he might have let himself be angry about Bernardo's tone.

"Tell us what happened twenty years ago," Edward said.

"I was brand-new on the force. I found the first body. We didn't even know we had a missing person. She was a tourist, traveling with her boyfriend."

"Why didn't he report her missing?" Bernardo asked. It was weird to hear him being the first to ask the hard questions.

That was usually Edward or me. It was weirder still to watch him be all serious and hard-nosed while I was cuddled in his lap. It was like a mental and physical dissonance.

"They'd had a fight. She stormed off and we found her body before she'd been gone eight hours."

"So the killer doesn't keep the women long before killing them," I said.

"No," Tyburn said, not sounding happy about it, but truth is truth.

"He didn't keep Bettina longer than twenty hours, maybe not even that long," Bernardo said. I heard him swallow hard and breathe out slowly, as if saying her name had been hard. I could smell the breath mints he'd popped after he'd gotten sick back at the crime scene.

"That was quicker than any of the other victims twenty years ago. He kept them at least three days. I think the longest was five days between abduction and finding the body."

"So he didn't keep that victim alive for five days, because your timeline goes from abduction to finding the body," Bernardo said.

"Yes," Tyburn said, and I heard him sigh.

"How long has Denny been missing?" I asked.

"We're not sure," Edward said.

"Are you saying we have between sixteen hours and three days to find her alive?" I asked.

"I'm afraid so," Tyburn said, glancing back at me in the rearview mirror.

"Fuck," I said.

"I've sent an officer to her room to collect some things to help your men track her," Tyburn said.

"How many victims died twenty years ago?" Bernardo asked.

"Three."

"And then it stopped?" I asked.

"Yes, but not because we caught him. It just stopped."

"Until now," Olaf said.

Tyburn nodded and did that glance in the rearview mirror again. "Yes, until now."

"There have been serial killers that took years off between kills," I said.

"If they're in jail and get out," Tyburn said.

"No, there's the BTK killer. He took that long off, and wasn't in jail," I said.

"To raise his family, right?" Tyburn asked.

"And as a compliance officer. Basically if your grass was too tall, he made you cut it," I said.

"One thing that seemed to trigger him was the children becoming teenagers and rebelling against his authority. As a father of one teenager and one preteen, I can say it is high-stress parenting," Edward said.

Tyburn chuckled. "My sons are all grown-up now, but I remember."

"There was also a book that talked about his crimes at the same time that he was losing control of his home life and his compliance job," Edward said.

"And a television show loosely based on him came out."

"So you're saying that it could be a law-abiding family man here in the area that's suddenly gone back to his old hobby?" Tyburn asked.

"Other than BTK, I'm not sure anyone has ever gone inactive for even a decade and then resurfaced, without a jail term in between," I said.

"Not two decades, no, but there are others that have married and started a family and stopped for a while," Edward asked.

"Why would a family make them stop killing?" Olaf asked.

"For some it seems to be about control; they can be responsible for their families and in control of that, so they don't feel the need to control strangers in the ritual of their killing," Edward said.

I took the next part as if it was a conversational ball that he had passed to me. "For others it's almost like they're bored, so they kill. If their lives are full and busy enough in a positive way, not a stressful way, they don't seem to feel the compulsion to kill as often. If their lives become too stressful in a bad way, they seem to use murder as a way to release the stress."

"You make it sound like it's exercise or sex, or even a hobby," Dalton said.

"If it's the only way they can have sex, then they're less likely to take long cooling-off periods," Edward said.

"The ones that take the longest cooling-off periods are the ones that seem able to have regular relationships with a wife, kids, et cetera," I said.

"I thought the sexual serial killers felt a compulsion like an addict," Dalton said.

"Even addicts can go into recovery," Olaf said, "if they want other things in their life badly enough."

It took almost everything I had not to look at him as he said it. If he was looking at me, I didn't want to know. If I looked at him and then he looked at me, I didn't want to see it. I looked out at the sunlight on the ocean that stretched out and out, so that the road was like a pale ribbon running across brilliant blue cloth.

"Most addicts don't rape and kill women," Edward said.

"Does it really matter what someone is addicted to, if they are willing to fight the addiction?" Olaf asked.

"Do you really think a twelve-step program would work for a serial killer?" Dalton asked.

"Perhaps."

Bernardo asked, "You said that the first woman that died twenty years ago had a fight with her boyfriend."

"Yes," Tyburn said.

"Did the other two women have fights with their husbands?"

"None of them were married. The first one was traveling with her longtime boyfriend on vacation. The second was a local girl that had a reputation for sleeping around. The third woman was the oldest of the three victims; she was divorced and just starting to date again."

"Were they all sexually active but unmarried?" Bernardo asked.

"Yes."

"Denny wasn't here with a boyfriend," I said.

"She doesn't even know how to flirt well, because she's cried on Donna's shoulder more than once about how she just doesn't understand anything about dating or relationships. She wants a relationship, but sex puzzled her. There is no way that she fit into a victim profile that needed her to sleep around casually," Edward said.

"It may be my fault," Bernardo said.

I just had to turn my head to look at him. "How could it be your fault?" I asked.

"Denny saw Bettina leaving my room with the other bridesmaids in their wedding. She and I talked in the hallway about how she wished she could enjoy casual sex like Bettina obviously had."

"Was she hitting on you?" I asked.

Bernardo looked up at me, smoothing his hand down the side of my hip. I don't think it was on purpose, more a nervous gesture. "Not exactly. She was more asking why she wasn't more like other women. She was seeing a therapist about her lack of sexual drive."

"I didn't even know that," Edward said, "and she's Donna's best friend. How do you know that and Donna doesn't?"

None of us protested that Donna would have kept Denny's secret. I think we were all pretty sure she'd have shared it with her husband-to-be, if not more people. "I wouldn't normally share any of this, but if it's important later and I don't share it . . . I'd rather apologize to Denny about breaking her confidence than keep it and get her killed because I didn't share it."

"Share what?" I asked.

"She's in her forties; she wants a permanent relationship, a husband or at least a live-in boyfriend. She dates just fine up to a point, but she wants companionship, not a lover, and most men won't settle for that."

"You and Denny never dated each other. How do you know all this?" Edward asked.

"She wanted a weekend with me, just sex, no strings. She just wanted to be with someone that was supposed to be a skilled lover and see if it made a difference. She said if I was half as good as I looked . . . Anyway, I agreed."

Edward was sort of softly glaring at him. "She's a beautiful woman; of course you agreed."

"Her therapist approved the weekend as an experiment."

"Are you honestly telling me that you went to therapy with Denny?" Edward asked.

"Her therapist had diagnosed her as asexual. I didn't even know that was a possibility as a sexual orientation until she asked me to help her."

"Asexual, but Denny dated men—not a lot, but she dated. She was even engaged once."

"But all the relationships broke up over the fact that Denny was just not interested in sex," Bernardo said.

"You mean she was frigid?" Olaf asked.

"No, according to her therapist that's an outdated term. Denny could feel love and was a very caring person, but she had almost no interest at all in sex. She felt it was ruining her chances at a real relationship and didn't want to be alone forever. I understood that part; for very different reasons, I think I'll probably never marry either. I don't mind as much as Denny did, but I'm conflicted about it, a little."

"Why would she pick you of all of our male friends to confide in?" Edward asked.

"Why? Because I'm a womanizer and haven't had a serious relationship ever?"

"Yeah," Edward said, "there are friends of ours that would love to date her with serious intentions."

"That's why me," Bernardo said. "She didn't want to disappoint anyone else. It took a lot of courage for her to come to me like she did. I respected that."

"So you and Denny went to her therapist and got the doctor's blessing on a weekend of sex?" I asked.

"Something like that, yeah."

"You know, that's a new one on me," I said.

"Me, too," Bernardo said.

"How did the weekend go?" Dalton asked.

"She is a lovely person, but she does not enjoy sex, or maybe she just doesn't understand why everyone else does. She's not frigid. She's warm and caring and has this great laugh, but sex just isn't her . . . thing. Her therapist interviewed me afterward by myself and then with both Denny and me. We compared notes and we parted friends. I swore I'd never tell anyone. I hope we find her alive so she can be angry with me about it."

"Me, too," Dalton said, and she looked teary-eyed.

"Me, three," I said.

"When did all this happen?" Edward asked.

"Two years ago."

Edward shook his head and then clapped Bernardo on the shoulder. "I didn't notice a damn thing."

"Nor I," Olaf said, and they both sounded surprised.

"I'd never had a woman trust me with so much of themselves. I know it sounds weird, but I was more flattered that Denny trusted me with her secrets and her pain, than about the sex. I would never have told anyone if she hadn't been taken."

"But how does you sleeping with the missing woman once two years ago get her in trouble with our killer now?" Tyburn asked.

"We went to the hotel bar to have a drink and talk. We talked about how we both thought we'd never marry and what that might mean for us. We talked about the weekend we had together in a public place where we could have been overheard." He looked at Edward. "The killer had to be there; it was the only time Denny could have been mistaken for slutty, because she wasn't like that. If the killer only takes women who sleep around, then I'm the reason that Bettina's dead, and the reason that Denny is missing."

He lowered his head, as if he didn't want them to see whatever was in his eyes, even though he was wearing sunglasses so none of us could see his eyes, not even me. I felt his shoulders tremble, his breath came out shaking, and I knew he was crying. Quietly, controlled, but still tears. I probably should have pretended not to notice, but I already had my arms around his neck with the ponytail of his hair sliding over my skin. He had me wrapped up close and safe in an intimacy that neither of us expected from each other, but then I hadn't expected the man I'd seen at the pool who had chosen Bettina out of the bikini-clad crowd to have been so careful of Denny, or to be crying over both of them now.

I wrapped my arms around his shoulders and put my head beside his and hugged him as close as I could. His arms wrapped around me and pulled me even closer, and then his shoulders began to shake. He made almost no noise as he cried, but the tears spilled around his dark glasses against my skin. Edward put his hand at the back of Bernardo's head, against his hair. Neither of them could have cried in each other's arms like this, but since I was there for it, they could touch each other, around the edges.

Olaf's arm stretched across the seat and touched Bernardo's shoulder. I glanced at him, more surprised by that than almost anything else.

Tyburn was on his phone telling someone on the other end to find out who had been in the hotel bar yesterday when Bernardo and Denny had their talk. He especially wanted to know staff. We might have just narrowed our suspect list down to a manageable number in the time we had left to find Denny alive. I prayed again that we would find her alive. I held Bernardo while his body shook with silent weeping. Edward kept his hand on his hair and finally leaned his forehead against my arm and Bernardo's face, so we both held him. Olaf kept his hand on Bernardo's shoulder through the rest of the drive.

56

WE LEFT TYBURN and Dalton to try to narrow down the list of possible suspects at the hotel yesterday. Edward went off to call Donna so he could find out how Peter was doing, and to double-check on Becca. Bernardo went off to get control of himself. He wasn't crying anymore, but he wasn't okay either. The rest of us went to the suite that Nathaniel, Micah, and I were sharing. The couch actually was big enough for R and R, plus Nathaniel and Micah, to sit in a row. Bram and Nicky found a piece of wall to lean against. I took the desk chair and faced them so I could tell them what I needed. Ru and Rodina volunteered, of course. Nicky said, "If you need me to do it, I will, but as your Brides, all three of us have a less complete connection to you than an animal to call."

"I thought Anita's happiness was your primary concern," Bram said.

"It is."

"Then how can you suggest endangering Nathaniel like this?"

"Because if Denny dies, that will make Anita very unhappy. I've learned to try to stay ahead of her moods and wants, if I can."

Micah already had his arm across Nathaniel's shoulders, and now he hugged him and shook his head. "And the only reason you don't have more animals to call with you is because I asked you not to bring any other lovers besides Nicky. I trusted him not to intrude on our romantic weekend."

"I do my best," Nicky said.

"Of course it's not very romantic right now," Micah said.

"No, no, it's not," I said.

"It has to be me. I've done it once before with her, and our connection allows Anita to understand what I'm seeing and feeling more clearly than with anyone else here, even you, Micah." Nathaniel moved in Micah's arms, until they were entwined and he could kiss his fiancé.

Micah kissed him back fiercely. "I don't want it to be you, but I know that if I tell you no, and Denny dies, then we'll always wonder if it would have made the difference."

I'd expected Micah to argue. He'd been my last defense against doing it. My pulse was suddenly thudding in my throat and my mouth was dry. I did not want to take Nathaniel anywhere near whatever had killed Bettina Gonzales. I did not want to endanger him again, damn it.

"I will do it," Ru said.

Nicky shook his head. "If one of the Brides has to do it, it has to be me."

"Then why didn't you volunteer? Anita is terrified and very unhappy. Even I can barely breathe," Rodina said.

"I've already said why I didn't volunteer—because we all know who's the best wereanimal for the job, and it's not us."

"What if I said no?"

Nathaniel untangled himself from Micah, and came to me where I was still sitting in the chair. He knelt in front of me and took my hands in his. With him on his knees and me sitting, our eyes were almost at the same level. I gazed into those beautiful eyes that always undid me if I looked too long. He leaned in and kissed me gently. My eyes were hot, my throat tight. Was I really going to cry? Surely not, not me. I had been the tough-as-nails vampire hunter once. I'd have liked to think I was crying for Denny, but I wouldn't lie to myself, and that wasn't why I was on the verge of tears. I didn't cry before it was time, and Nathaniel was safe in front of me.

"You can't keep being so afraid you'll lose me that we can't live our lives, Anita."

Rodina spoke from the couch. "Don't steal your victory before it's won, my queen."

I gave her an unfriendly look. "You stay out of this."

"I would give my life in place of Nathaniel's, because I can feel how much you love him and how much it would hurt you if he died, but he is right, my queen. You must be brave and allow Nathaniel to be brave with you."

"But what if it all goes wrong?"

"It won't," Nathaniel said.

I looked deep into his eyes and said, "You can't promise that."

He smiled. "Get them to let us have Nicky with us, to help wrangle me once I'm a big, bad leopard."

"That's a good idea," Nicky said.

I nodded; it was. "I'll talk to Tyburn about it."

"He'll say yes," Rodina said.

"How can you be sure?" I asked.

"He's gone too far out on the limb to quibble at one more inch."

I wanted to poke fun at her wording, or at least make a smart-ass remark, but I couldn't think of anything clever to say. I kissed Nathaniel and Micah good-bye and went to find Tyburn, with Nicky and Rodina trailing behind me. Ru stayed with Bram to watch over my two fiancés. I'd keep them both as safe as I could for as long as I could. I left Nathaniel with two bodyguards and even Micah armed, and went to finalize the plans to take Nathaniel with me into the field, where so much could go wrong.

57

BY THE TIME we finished the discussion, Tyburn's people had a complete list of the restaurant staff and all the customer names they were certain of for that day. Hotel management had also given up a complete list of staff and people staying at the hotel. I got the impression that they would have given up the complete ingredient list to the secret sauce, if it would make this all go away and not give them the reputation for being "that hotel, you know, the one where the bridesmaids were murdered." I honestly didn't care what their motivation was as long as they kept being this cooperative.

Tyburn and his people would follow the names on the lists and see if they could find the killer from their end, and see if he/she/they/it would lead them to Denny. We'd look for Denny, because in that moment I didn't give a rat's ass if we caught the killer but lost her. Part of wisdom is being honest with yourself, and more than justice, I wanted to find Denny alive and well, or as well as possible. I did not want to have to stand over her dead body and imagine what her last minutes of life had been. No, just no.

Nicky, Edward, Olaf, and I had put on all the gear we'd brought with us, or most of it.

I was wearing the body armor vest that was specially made for curves men didn't have, the two wrist sheathes complete with silver-edged blades. I didn't know if this monster gave a shit about silver or steel, but most of the things I hunted didn't like silver. The knives were for emergencies; the guns were the main thing. I'd tried to stop carrying my Browning for work, but I'd missed it too much. So it was back in a thigh holster over the tac pants. The Sig Sauer P238 .380 went in a MOLLE-rigged holster on the front of the vest for a cross draw. I had my AR-15 M4-styled carbine in a tactical sling. The AR was chambered in 6.8 SPC for a bit more bang for my buck. I was also using frangible rounds, which shattered once they entered a target, so if I shot Bad Guy A, the round wouldn't go through him and into Good Guy B. *Frangible* did mean that if I missed my target and hit someone else by accident, it would be bad, but I didn't plan to miss. I'd given up the knife that usually rode on my back, under my hair, so I could put my Mossberg 500 Bantam in a gun sock or a sleeve attached to MOLLE straps on the back of my vest. I carried the sleeve angled across my back for a right-handed cross draw over my shoulder. If I'd been sure we wouldn't be going into underbrush or some of the over-grown places I'd seen, I'd have just put both guns on tactical slings and pushed them back as needed. But they got tangled in thick brush that way, and I didn't want to get hung up in the trees. I had my cross tucked inside my shirt even though I doubted what we were hunting would care about holy objects, but it was like the extra ammo that I had in pouches and pockets on the vest and pants—better to have it and not need it than to die because I didn't have it. The last thing I added were earplugs that let me hear, until the shooting started, and then they'd lower the decibels and save my hearing.

Bernardo wasn't with us yet, but I knew he'd be well equipped. We all preferred different handguns and shotguns, and we all had personalized our ARs.

I stood there, decked out for monster hunting or a small war, in the bathroom of a hotel suite that was almost a twin of our room, with a police videographer about to record Nathaniel changing shape into a huge black panther. Tyburn agreed to Nicky being with me to help me control the wereleopard. I didn't really need help with Nathaniel in any form, but since Olaf was going to be with us, and we were hunting monsters, I wanted at least Nicky with us. I'd tried to include Ru or Rodina, because why not? The worst Tyburn could say was no. No big surprise. But Tyburn was going out on a limb just using a wereleopard to track a missing person. Including just one civilian put him further out on that limb; four would have been too much weight to bear, so I had to be happy with Nicky. I *was* happy, but I'd have been even happier if Nathaniel wasn't with us.

I turned away so I couldn't watch Nathaniel undress, because I didn't trust my face not to show exactly how much it moved me, and I didn't want that very private look captured on video for strange police officers and maybe lawyers to watch later. I was uncomfortable enough having him take off so much on film without sharing any more with strangers. Tyburn wanted to record it in case there were questions later about how we found Denny and how we caught the bad guy. Because if he was still with her, we'd find them both, and we didn't have a warrant of execution for this one, which meant that we'd have to play by normal U.S. Marshal rules, not the preternatural branch rules, and not kill him/her/it on sight. We don't normally get called into a case until there are enough bodies to get us a warrant of execution for some preternatural bad guy. I had started my career as a licensed vampire executioner. Having a badge hadn't really changed my job description much; there was just more paperwork now.

"Why is Murdock coming with us if he's not going to turn into a werelion and help track?" Dunley asked. The big officer who had questioned Micah, Nathaniel, and me earlier when Bettina had just been missing was the local whom Tyburn had assigned to stay with us while we tracked.

"Because whatever we're hunting may be a shapeshifter of some kind, which means it might be contagious to anyone that isn't already carrying lycanthropy," I said.

"So what, Murdock is going to throw his body in the way in case we're attacked by it?"

"Something like that," I said.

"Or I will fight it for you," Olaf said. He'd insisted on being in the room for the filming. I had to trust that he had enough control of his beast that he wouldn't shift just being near someone else doing it. I did trust him that far, especially after he'd admitted to not having enough control in the car. Since Olaf had stayed, so had Edward. Bernardo had gone off to get himself together, but his parting words had been, "Don't leave without me. I want a piece of this hunt." We'd promised him we would call him so he could come with.

"I'm used to fighting my own battles," Dunley said, and

shifted in such a way that his arms flexed a little. He was a big, athletic guy, used to being one of the toughest, if not the toughest, man in the room. He was looking at Nicky and Olaf and doing the physical math in his head and not sure he would win. Like most people who have spent their lives being the biggest and baddest, he didn't like that idea much.

Olaf stood against the wall, just inside the doorway, so he had a line of sight to the room's main door. Dunley was standing near him, so the difference in height was even more noticeable. I couldn't decide if his standing close to the bigger man meant that he was comfortable with the size difference, or if it was a type of posturing, like he was saying, *Look, I'm big, too.* Standing there meant that both of them were very close to the uniformed officer who was going to be videoing Nathaniel. Officer Milford kept glancing back at them as she set up her equipment. I wasn't sure if the only videographer they had was a woman, or if they thought she'd be more comfortable watching Nathaniel strip than a male officer would have been, or if it hadn't occurred to anyone to care either way.

Nicky had moved away from the two other men and closer to me. Either he didn't feel the need to play "mine's bigger than yours" with the other two, or he was posturing over the only thing he cared about: me and Nathaniel. Mostly me.

"The Marshals Service has a precedent for keeping officers that catch lycanthropy on the job, but no other law enforcement entity does yet, so we're just all trying to help you keep your badge, Dunley," Edward said from his chair near the far corner, where he sat with a wall to his back and a good view of the entire room. He was back to his Ted drawl. I'd noticed it calmed people sometimes, or made them underestimate him. I think both were on purpose.

"I appreciate that, Forrester, but if this bastard attacks us, I'm not sure I can stand back and let Murdock put himself in harm's way for me."

Surprisingly it was Nathaniel who answered the concern. "That's because you look at me and see a man that's smaller, softer-looking to you. You look at Nicky and just think civilian. You don't understand what we are yet."

"I know you're a wereleopard and he's a werelion. I Googled both of you. I found pictures of you in animal form and a write-up about him being the leader of your local lions. I looked up pictures of other werelions when I couldn't find ones of Murdock."

"Pictures aren't the same," Nathaniel said.

I'd been behaving myself and not looking at Nathaniel, but looking at Olaf and Dunley meant I was also able to see Officer Milford as she pointed her camera behind me at my sweetie. Her biggest concern had been the two big guys standing almost directly behind her, which no cop would have liked, but suddenly I watched her sort of startle at what she was seeing through her camera lens.

It made me glance behind me at Nathaniel. I expected him to be naked from her reaction, but the only thing he'd taken off was his shirt. I mean, he had a great upper body, from the spread of his shoulders and the swell of his pectorals to the flat plains of his stomach . . . His hands went to the waistband of his shorts and I looked away. One, so the camera didn't accidentally capture my reaction to him pulling the shorts off, and two, so I could watch Officer Milford's reaction. If she'd reacted that strongly to just his shirt coming off, I wanted to see what she'd do when the rest came off.

"Seeing pictures is different from seeing it in person," Nathaniel said, and I realized he was still talking to Dunley. For a second I wondered if I'd missed part of the conversation looking at him and Officer Milford. I hoped not, but Nathaniel could have that effect on me sometimes.

Looking in Milford's direction meant I could also see the men behind her. Dunley had dropped his gaze so he could sort of keep track of what was happening but not exactly watch. Pussy. But my smile at Dunley's discomfort was spoiled by Olaf's reaction. He looked at Nathaniel without any sign of embarrassment, but he was also watching Milford as she started to blush, and then he looked at me, and then back at Nathaniel. He was watching him strip in a dispassionate sort of way, as if he wanted to see how it was done, and he seemed fascinated by the effect on Milford. I'd never seen a brunette blush so red.

It made me steal a glance behind me. Nathaniel was nude, and the rest of him was just as beautiful as his upper body had promised. All the gym work and nutrition showed in the muscled strength of him, but some things weren't about exercise; some things were just genetic luck, and Nathaniel had been very lucky.

I turned away again because I didn't want the camera to capture how much I liked the view. That was personal, and having him nude for a police video was personal enough. I felt the rush of energy like a warm summer wind dancing across my skin and knew he was changing shape. I turned, shivering in reaction to all that energy, in time to watch his human form be engulfed by new flesh, bones glinting white for a second before black fur poured over everything and he folded down into that other form that was as much him as the human man I loved. All that smooth-skinned beauty was covered in fur now, but there are other kinds of beauty. He looked at me with leopard eyes that were a rich, pale gray. Just as I never met another human with eyes like his human eyes, I'd never met another wereleopard with eyes the same color as his. He opened his mouth in a huge kitty-cat yawn, flashing a mouthful of shiny white fangs.

I heard Milford gasp. It made me glance at her. She looked pale as she lowered her camera. I don't know if she was supposed to stop filming at this point, or if she had forgotten everything but staring at the huge cat in front of her.

"Jesus," Dunley said. I wondered if he realized he had his hand on the butt of his gun. If he'd drawn it, I'd have said something, but the first time you see someone who had been human just a few minutes before turn into an animal, it can be a shock.

"Leopards aren't that big," Milford said, voice a little shaky to match how pale she still looked.

"Wereleopards are," Nicky said.

I looked back at Nathaniel and tried to see him the way that Milford and Dunley's faces showed they were seeing him. His fur was perfectly black, like a piece of darkness carved into velvet-furred muscle the size of a pony. He was at least twice the size of an ordinary leopard, and the look in his eyes was too full of intelligence, humanity—something that was both of those things and neither. The eyes and body were as purely leopard as Nathaniel could ever be, but as I gazed into those deep gray eyes, he was still in there. It was still Nathaniel, no matter what shape was wrapped around him.

"Are all wereanimals that much bigger than the real thing?" Dunley asked.

"Some," Nicky said. He walked up to the big cat, and it rubbed itself around his waist and stomach, because that's how high up his body Nathaniel could reach in this form. It was the same movement that your house cat does around your ankles, except that in this form he could reach a lot higher than our ankles.

"Online he's like the leopardman, not"—Milford made a vague gesture toward Nathaniel—"this."

"We have the best sense of smell in this form," Nicky said.

"Do all shapeshifters have three forms like this?" Dunley asked.

"No," I said, "most only have two." I went to stand with Nicky and Nathaniel.

"Be careful," Milford said, and the fear was so clear I could smell it on the air like some harsh perfume.

"Nathaniel won't hurt me," I said, and stroked my hand through the thick sensation of his fur as he rubbed himself between Nicky and me. I did have to brace so he didn't stagger me backward, or even off my feet. I'd learned that the rubbing against us was like petting your human, except with your whole body, and when your body is that big and that strong, well, you need to be ready for it.

"How can you be sure of that?" Dunley asked. He smelled like fear, too. He was just hiding it better than Milford. He could control his breathing and his heart rate, his body posture, his words, his face, but he couldn't keep his body from reacting at the deepest levels to being in a room with a predator that big and that potentially deadly. At his base level, where the lizard brain lives, Dunley was afraid, and the scent of that was on his skin. It tightened my stomach and I realized I was hungry. I also realized that it wasn't me who was hungry.

I looked at Nathaniel, and he looked up at me with those gray eyes so like his human eyes, but not. I cradled that big, furred face in my human hands and rested my face against the top of his head, rubbing my cheek against the unbelievable richness of his fur. I whispered against one of his soft, triangular ears, "Did you eat until you were full at breakfast?"

He shook his head while I was still holding him. "Damn it, Nathaniel, you're beautiful. You don't have to keep watching your weight like this." Dunley's fear spiked through the scent of his aftershave and soap. He smelled . . . thicker, for lack of a better word, than Milford, as if his scent weighed more. I didn't know if it was because he was actually bigger, or if it was some arcane, unexplainable thing. I knew part of it was that he was just more afraid than anyone else in the room.

"Please stop putting your face that close to his . . . mouth, Marshal Blake," Dunley said.

"Can I pet him?" Milford asked.

"No," Dunley said.

"We need the bag of Denny's clothes so he can get her scent," Edward said from his chair.

I drew back from Nathaniel and looked into his now gray eyes. I lowered my psychic shields, not to let him in but to stop keeping him out. With my animals to call and the vampires I was tied to, I actually spent more energy keeping them at a distance. It was like trying to hold a heavy weight overhead all the time, and now I could finally put it down and just let myself go.

He was hungry, but it was more the fear of the humans, especially Dunley, not the lack of real food. Dunley did smell like food, but we wouldn't eat him. Promise.

I dragged myself far enough back to be just me again. That was the danger, to sink so far into the other that you lost yourself.

I got his collar and leash, which he'd laid on the edge of the tub. The heavy leather collar that had been made for his neck in this form had a silver metal plate on it that read *Pussycat*. Our ex-lover and dominant, Asher, had had it made as a gift for Nathaniel. If we were going to work more often with the police like this, I really needed to get a second collar made that just read *Nathaniel*. *Pussycat* lacked a certain manly police attitude as a nickname.

I smelled lion suddenly, like heat and fur. It made me look up to find Olaf standing closer to Milford. He should have towered over her, but he'd lowered his head enough to get closer to the top of her head, and her hair. Hair holds scent better than skin, and he was smelling her fear. She wasn't afraid of him, but it didn't matter; it still smelled good to him. It still smelled like an appetizer or an aphrodisiac, depending on which way you were feeling at the moment.

Milford turned toward him and said, "Excuse me, Marshal Jeffries, is there anything I can help you with?" Good for her; she was confronting him, letting him know she'd noticed the invasion of her personal space.

"Not right now," he said, and his voice was already deeper than normal. Either his inner lion was peeking out or the scent of her fear had excited him enough to flood his body with extra testosterone and deepen his voice.

"Then take a step back," she said, and her voice was solid, steady. She was smelling less like food every second. Good. But now that she'd turned toward Olaf, I could see the back of her head. I'd known her hair was brown, but I hadn't realized her short hair wasn't short; it was just pulled into a tight bun at the back of her head. She was only a few inches taller than me, with long dark hair. Fuck, she fit his victim profile. I guess, come to that, so did Detective Dalton. So had Bettina; so did a hell of a lot of women here.

Olaf smiled at her the way we'd smile at a kitten or puppy that was trying to be fierce, but he took the step back and stopped looming over her like the scary, pale giant.

Nicky and Nathaniel moved a little closer to him, but it looked like they were moving toward Milford. She moved to one side, away from Olaf and them. Nicky petted the gigantic panther at his side.

Dunley shook his head and finally dropped his hand away from actually touching his sidearm. He wiped his hand against the side of his pants as if his palm was sweaty. I wondered if he had what it took to go monster hunting. "You're still shorter than me, which makes you a bad meat shield to hide behind," he said, smiling.

Nicky smiled back. "I get bigger."

"That's what all the men say," Milford added.

Nicky smiled. "Trust me, Milford, I won't disappoint."

She blushed but said, "That's what all the men say, too."

"I guess they do," Nicky said, smile fading. "I'll just have to prove it to you."

"How?" she said and sounded wonderfully suspicious.

"By doing what I said I'd do. If the monsters attack, I'll step between them and you."

She narrowed her eyes at him, not believing him, and who could blame her? They'd just met. Most men who offer to risk their life for you on first meeting either mean it sincerely or are lying bastards.

"All the monsters," Nicky said and looked past her to Olaf. The two men stared at each other. I stepped up beside Nicky and took Nathaniel's leash from him, and also managed to break their staring contest. I appreciated Nicky being all gallant, but honestly the thought of them fighting for real scared me. I trusted Nicky to win against almost anyone, but Olaf wasn't just anyone.

"Let's go bring Denny home," I said, and led the way toward the door.

"You are so certain of that?" Olaf asked as I moved past him with Nathaniel padding at my side.

"No, but I wish I was."

"You have seen too much to be certain of anyone's safety," he said. He didn't look at Nicky, but he didn't really have to.

"I know that death comes to everyone," I said.

Edward came up beside us as if on cue. "What kind of Horseman of the Apocalypse would I be if I didn't?"

"So the nicknames are true?" Milford asked. "You're Death?"

"Yes, ma'am," he said, in a thick drawl.

"I'm War, and"—I pointed a thumb at Olaf—"he's Plague."

"I texted Hunger. He'll meet us in the hallway outside Denny's room. They've got the bag with her scent items waiting for our search-and-rescue leopard to sniff," Edward said.

Nathaniel strained a little at his leash, and I didn't argue. It was time to go.

58

THE LAST TIME I'd used Nathaniel to track a missing person had been in the mountains of Colorado in damn near pristine wilderness. It's gorgeous here in the Keys, but a pristine wilderness it is not. Nathaniel tracked Denny to the parking lot and then stopped. I thought at first that she'd gotten into a car and he didn't know how to track that, but Nathaniel made a low, unhappy sound. It made me look at him more directly, and he stared at me very purposefully. I took off my sunglasses, blinking in the bright light until I could see him clearly. He looked like a regular leopard, not that I'd ever stared into the face of an ordinary leopard from this close, but if I hadn't known his head and body were larger than those of a normal leopard you'd see in a zoo, I wouldn't have known any different. The bright sunlight brought out the black on black of his spots so you could see that he wasn't pure black, like he appeared most of the time. His gray eyes looked paler with the sunglasses off; it was probably the contrast of the black fur around them, like gray ice in velvet, except this ice was looking back at me with a weight of . . . what? Intelligence, humanity, something that I never saw in any animal's eyes. Nathaniel looked like a leopard, but what stared out of this shape was still not completely an animal. The weight and feel of his personality were still in there looking back at me. One second I was staring into that personality trapped in the eyes of a leopard, and the next I was seeing things inside my head that damn near made me fall down. I'd shared thoughts, feelings, and sensory input with him in every form before this, but it was like I was inside his head, or he was inside mine. It was as if every scent he was smelling slapped me in the face, and the difference in our color vision made me almost dizzy. It was incredibly disorienting. The smells were the most confusing, because a human mind doesn't have enough brain to process it. I didn't realize how distracted I was until Edward caught my arm to keep me from falling over.

"Anita, are you okay?"

I managed to say "Yes," but apparently it wasn't very believable, because he asked what was wrong.

I wasn't sure how to put it into human words, because my head was so full of leopard. I heard Nicky saying something and I realized that as my Bride he was probably getting some of what was in my head. I thought I should understand what he was saying, but it wasn't as important as what I was getting from Nathaniel, or maybe I just didn't have enough brainpower left to concentrate on words when there was so much to smell and feel.

I'd never realized that asphalt smelled so awful, or that car exhaust was bitter, and even the rubber from the tires seemed to coat our tongue and make it hard to smell anything but the heat of the cars and the hot blackness underfoot. It was so hot it hurt; it hurt to walk on it, and in there somewhere was a confused resentment that I was wearing boots that protected my feet, and how could I give up the agility and claws of my back feet. It wasn't that clear a human speech, but that was what my human mind translated it to, because I had to translate it into something human, or I might have gone mad. I wondered if part of the problem when someone first turned into a lycanthrope was that the mind they had couldn't cope with being inside the animal body.

I knew he needed to be off the asphalt; it was too hot in the late afternoon sun, so we started by walking into the grass. To the other cops it probably looked like I walked him to the grass, but in my head it felt more like I was following Nathaniel, so it was him leading me at the end of the leash. He stepped onto the grass at the edge of the parking lot with relief. His feet had been almost burning on the asphalt and would have burned if he'd stayed on it. It's one of the reasons they tell you to test the road surface with your hand to find out if it's too hot for your dogs to walk on, before you try to take them out on it. I'd never thought about it in connection to Nathaniel, because I thought he'd tell me if it was too hot or too uncomfortable. I took a deep breath and then let it out, and another, but I was still almost choking on the asphalt and the car exhaust. This was not a highly polluted area—I mean, it wasn't the Rocky Mountains, but it was still seaside and open. How did were-animals survive in the inner city?

I put my hand on Nathaniel's thick fur and tried to focus just on him, just me, just us. I pushed away the fear of the smells around us and just trusted in Nathaniel and me. We could do this. We could find Denny. Thinking her name helped me find my quiet center, and from one deep breath to another I could feel the great leopard beside me under my hand, and me standing beside him. I could feel Nathaniel in there, not just the leopard. I could feel my inner leopard happily close to the surface, as if she thought this might be her day to break free and run beside him. I had a moment of regret that I couldn't, and then I was back in my head and still aware of Nathaniel beside me.

He started padding forward. I wasn't able to keep direct eye contact with Nathaniel while we walked, but I didn't need to; I knew he was following the scent, sorting it out from all the other man-made smells that weren't Denny's scent. My human mind couldn't make sense of the process, but I trusted that his leopard and mine would figure it out. I could put my sunglasses back on and answer Edward's questions. "Nathaniel said that the car fumes and asphalt are making it hard to pick up Denny's scent, but he's got it now."

"Did you take him to the grass so he could circle the parking lot and try to pick up her scent on the edges of it?"

"No, his feet were hot; the grass feels better."

Edward touched my shoulder. "Anita, I need you here and now, not lost in the leopard's head."

"I'm fine now, Edward, we're fine." Nicky came up to me and offered me his arm to touch. He didn't touch me but let it be my choice. I touched his bare skin with the hand that didn't have a leash in it. My AR-15 on its sling strap bumped me, because my arm wasn't helping hold it beside and behind me anymore, but the moment I touched Nicky I felt more solid.

Nathaniel rubbed up against my leg, and the combination of touching them both at the same time helped more.

"Stay near me, Nicky."

"Whatever you need," he said. He kept one hand on my shoulder and the other hand with his own AR-15 held loose but ready, so it looked like we were trying to clear a room instead of trailing after a giant leopard in SWAT gear in Florida heat. Nathaniel picked the scent back up at the edge of the parking lot. He led us to a parked car, and my stomach fell into my shoes. He rubbed up and down the trunk like he was scent marking. He was happy, I could feel it, but my human mind got in my way. The car looked empty, but I couldn't see inside the trunk and I really didn't want to. It was more than ninety degrees Fahrenheit; in the trunk it would be hotter. Summer heat does really bad things to bodies. I didn't want to see those bad things done to Denny's body. I wasn't sure I'd be able to unsee it and I didn't want Nathaniel to have to see it either. Hell, I didn't want any of us to have to see it, but Nathaniel wasn't a cop; it wasn't his job to see nightmares. I was afraid of what seeing Denny stuffed in a trunk would do to Bernardo, too, just for different reasons.

I gave Nathaniel's leash to Nicky and told them to stand back a little.

"I don't smell anything bad in the trunk," Nicky said.

"You're in human form; you might not smell much more than we do," I said.

"Fine, do you smell a body?"

I had to force myself to think about that, and then finally said, "No; do any of you smell it?"

"We'll have the trunk open in a second, Anita. We don't have to guess," Edward said.

He was right, but still it made me feel a little more hopeful that none of us could smell anything horrible. I looked at Nathaniel where he was standing beside Nicky. Okay, none of us humans had smelled anything horrible. Something had led Nathaniel to the car. Normally I would have just thought the question and gotten an answer, but in that moment my surety of his sense of smell was overwhelmed with my very human fears. It made me head-blind and damaged my ability to sense what Nathaniel was feeling.

Bernardo had moved back to stand on the other side of Nicky. He was thinking the same things I was thinking, and he didn't want to see it either. *Please, God, let her be alive.*

One of the men in full SWAT gear despite the heat brought up the tool to pop the trunk. Even though none of us could smell that sickly-sweet scent of decay, my gut clenched tight as the trunk slowly opened on its own, now that there was no more lock to hold it shut. I tensed as the lid opened wide like some giant's mouth about to take another bite out of someone. There was something in the trunk, wrapped in a sheet. I didn't want to think *body*, just *something*, and I sure as hell didn't want to think *Denny wrapped in a sheet.*

It was Edward who used a gloved hand to lift the sheet. I saw Denny's short blond hair and then her face. Her eyes were closed, face slack. The sheet pulled back and I got a confused glimpse of her nude body curled up in a fetal position. I prayed about as hard as I've ever prayed that she was alive. Edward yelled, "I've got a pulse!"

And it was as if we'd all been holding our breaths and now we could move, we could run. The ambulance that had been standing by started emptying out a wheeled gurney, the EMTs running this way. Bernardo pushed forward and put a hand on the side of Denny's face. He wanted to ride in back of the ambulance with her, but Tyburn insisted on sending a female officer with her and keeping Bernardo with us. When Bernardo protested, Tyburn said, "We still need to catch the man who took your friend and killed Bettina Gonzales. You want to help us do that?" Bernardo stopped arguing after that. The ambulance took her away too fast to see much, but she'd had ligature marks on her wrists; I hadn't seen her ankles. Would they match the ones on Bettina's body, and if they did, why did the killer untie Denny and put her in a trunk? Why didn't he kill her? Did we have two abductors and only one killer? We'd found Denny alive—that's what I'd prayed for. I hadn't prayed to catch the killer, or solve the crimes, just to get Denny back. God moves in mysterious ways when He answers prayers, and sometimes He answers exactly what you pray for, no more, no less. We had Denny back—that was the important thing. I could still hear the ambulance sirens when Tyburn came up and told us we had two more missing women. Well, damn it.

59

THE MISSING WOMEN were from the same damn wedding party that Nathaniel and Wyatt had flirted so hard with. Maybe it wasn't about our guys who flirted with everyone; maybe it was the wedding party itself.

I suggested to Captain Tyburn, "You asked if it could be someone that had a vendetta against Bernardo, but maybe it's this wedding party."

"We looked into them and they're just normal kids."

"Did they disappear from the hotel like Denny and Bettina Gonzales?" Edward asked.

"No, they went to a restaurant with the rest of the brides-maids. They went to the bathroom and never came back to the table."

"What restaurant?"

He told us. "Herbie's."

It was the same bar where Andy the belligerent drunk had been a regular. What were the odds that two more girls would go missing from the same bar? "I may have a clue, but I need to call someone for more information first," I said.

"If you have information to share, Blake, share it."

"One phone call, okay?"

"One phone call, but make it quick, because I want to get you and your super-leopard over to the last place the girls were seen."

I nodded, walking just far enough away to have some pri-vacy, and fished my phone out of one of the pockets on the tac pants. Micah picked up on the first ring. "Is there a reason that the local shapeshifter was in the bar where we found him?"

"What? Why?"

I took a breath and backed up, telling him we found Denny and we had two more missing women. "They were abducted from Herbie's, where we found Andy."

"The bathrooms are within sight of the tables; how could anyone abduct them without someone seeing something?"

"I don't know, but can you call your local contacts and ask why Andy was at that restaurant? Are there more of the local shapeshifters or other supernaturals working there?"

"You sound like all the other humans blaming us."

"Micah, you know me better than that. It's why I called you and didn't tell Tyburn yet."

"I'm sorry, Anita. I know you. I'm sorry, but you've already met one of the local clan."

"No game playing. We're about to head over to the restaurant and see if Nathaniel can sniff out a clue."

"I called Andy's family to check on him and his wife and to see if they knew anything about Rankin."

"Come on, Micah, just tell me. We need to get to the next abduction scene."

"He's one of the family."

"Does he shift?"

"Just started. He was almost forty, so he thought he was safe."

"What's with his voice and shit? Because Andy and his wife didn't do that."

"It's a rare gift in the bloodline. They have siren blood in their ancestry."

"You mean like queen-of-mermaids kind of siren, like the wife of the Vampire Master of Cape Cod?"

"None of them turn into mermaids, but they call the family members that have this gift sirens, and it's a hell of a lot more than just being able to lure sailors to sink their ships."

"He can make you want to confess to crimes," I said.

"Or sleep with him, or who knows what he's made people do over the years," Micah said.

"Will the family testify to any of this in court?"

"Not yet, but I'm working on it. Christy had her baby, and it's got a snake lock."

"You mean Medusa for real?" I asked.

"Yes, the entire family is crazed with grief. They haven't had a newborn with a snake on it since Great-Great-Great-Grandma something, and it wasn't a home birth, because of the complications."

"Shit, they couldn't hide it," I said.

"Exactly."

An SUV with *Kirke Police* on the side had pulled up. Tyburn yelled, "Blake, are you coming?"

I took the phone away enough to yell, "Coming!" and then talked to Micah as I went for the car. "Well, fuck, please ask them if there's anyone that would talk to us at the restaurant. We're headed that way now."

"I'll try to get someone to talk to me," he said.

"I love you," I said.

"I love you, too. Give Nathaniel my love, and Nicky, too. All of you, be careful."

"I will and we will be," I said.

Detective Dalton was driving the SUV. Nicky rode shotgun beside her and I got in the backseat with Nathaniel, who stretched across me like the huge cat he was. Everyone else rode with Tyburn. We hit the lights and sirens and away we went. Since Tyburn had almost gotten me killed last time he drove, I was sort of glad that Dalton was driving.

60

HERBIE'S PARKING LOT was just as full as last time, except some half of the cars were police of different flavors from FDLE, Monroe County Sheriff, Florida Highway Patrol, Kirke, and even one that read *Key Colony* on it, which was a new one for me. Tyburn parked blocking in two customer cars, but honestly, we were out of options on the gravel parking lot. He came over to our SUV and Dalton rolled down the window as if he'd asked. "Marshal, you and your friend stay out of sight until I warn people that he's here to help the investigation."

I stroked Nathaniel's head and he rolled on my lap, with his big head going off one side and his shoulders letting me know how heavy he'd be if I could get more of him into my lap. He started to purr. People tell you that leopards can't purr, but that's not true. They can only purr as they breath out, that's true, unlike domestic cats, which can purr breathing in and out, but Nathaniel purred as he writhed all that fur and muscle across my lap. I knew that two people were missing, and Denny was in the hospital still unconscious, but as I ran my hands over Nathaniel's fur and he filled my lap with purring, like a happy cat, I let myself enjoy it. Bad things happen, but good things happen, too, and if you don't let yourself enjoy the good moments, the bad will eat your life. It was like in *Peter Pan*: Think happy thoughts and you can fly.

Nicky turned around in his seat, face so serious it looked grim. "You guys look adorable; if I wasn't guarding your adorable asses, I'd be all smiles."

"If Nathaniel wasn't in animal form and Micah was okay

with it, we could go back to the hotel and be adorable together,"
I said.

"The three of us don't really do adorable," Nicky said.

The leopard in my lap stopped writhing but didn't stop
purring as he raised his head high enough for Nicky to pet
him. Nicky couldn't help but smile as he stroked the huge
black head.

"I knew you loved Anita, but I didn't know you loved Nathaniel, too," Dalton said.

"He's my bro." Nicky rubbed Nathaniel under his furry
chin, while he closed his eyes in happy slits and filled the car
with a deep bass purring that no small cat could equal.

"Nathaniel likes the term *brother-husband*," I said. It was
a term that Nathaniel used for the men in our poly group
whom he shared me with, and shared domestic duties with, but
didn't have actual sex with himself. There were only two
brother-husbands for him. Micah had more.

"He does," Nicky said and rubbed the big cat between
the ears.

"Do you like being Nathaniel's brother-husband?" she asked.

"Yeah, I do."

Before Dalton could work her way up to asking exactly
how we defined *brother-husband*, Tyburn came back and we
were saved from having to explain ourselves, which you spent
a lot of time doing if you were poly.

The remaining bridesmaids, plus bride, and their respective
men friends had been sitting in a second area of Herbie's. It
looked like a covered screened porch with picnic tables and
benches that could seat much larger groups than the small tables in the bar area. To get to the bathrooms from the
screened-in area, you had to walk outside in the parking lot and
go around to the bar section. There was no direct route through
the building itself. According to witness interviews, the two
women had left together and were seen in the parking lot and
in the bathrooms, but somewhere between leaving the bar area
and walking the few yards back to the screened area, they'd
vanished. Witnesses had the usual conflicting reports of them
getting into completely different cars, trucks, vans. Two witnesses said they'd gotten into a car voluntarily. One witness
said that they'd been fighting and calling for help. When the

police asked the woman witness why she hadn't alerted anyone to their abduction, she had no answer. It wasn't that she was lying really, but once she'd heard *abduction, missing person*, her memory had just filled in the blanks with what she expected. It happens a lot more than you'd think. One of my great disappointments when I started working with the police and then became a marshal was how unreliable eyewitness testimony was. It just seemed so wrong that it didn't work like it did on *Perry Mason* or even most *Law & Order* episodes.

The witnesses screamed when they saw the big leopard. Ironically, I recognized a couple of them from the group that had flirted so hard with Nathaniel in human form. Now they were terrified; fair-weather flirts. Tyburn and some of the other officers cleared the witnesses out of the screened porch area so that Nicky and I could bring Nathaniel in without frightening them more. Edward, Bernardo, and Olaf stayed with us. The area was roomy when it was empty; we could have fit most of the police on-site in it if we'd moved the tables out.

Nathaniel hadn't really needed a personal item to get Denny's scent, because he knew her, but we needed one for the two new missing women. Lucky for them, one had left a light jacket behind and the other had left a huge hobo bag that she used as a beach tote and one of her favorite bags for carrying books around campus.

Nathaniel snuffled the jacket and then looked up at me. I stared into the big gray eyes and spoke before my human brain could get in the way: "Can you get a scent from the jacket?"

He shook his head.

"Can one of you ask Tyburn to see if the jacket is new? Nathaniel isn't getting much scent from it."

Bernardo went in search of Tyburn and the rapidly diminishing bridal party. Nathaniel snuffled at the big, loose purse. It slid off the back of the chair it had been hanging on. He rubbed his face on it, almost burying his head in it. He raised his head and gave a small sneeze-like sound, but he started sniffing the ground, and then as we got close to the door he sniffed the air. He followed the scent across the parking lot, threading his way between the end of the parked cars and the building. Only catlike grace got him through the small tables in the bar area without knocking over the stools and chairs.

The bathroom barely gave him room to go in and turn around, and then back out we came. He followed the trail back out to the gravel parking area and then out into the far side of the parking lot, where it brushed up against the empty lot next door. There he stopped, sitting down by the car parked there.

"Is she in the car?" Bernardo asked.

The leopard shook his head.

"Have you lost the scent?" I asked.

He nodded.

"Did they get in a car and drive away?"

He looked at me, and again there was that weight of intelligence and human thinking in the leopard eyes that no ordinary cat had. He nodded.

Tyburn cursed softly. "We'll try to see if any of the witnesses remember the same car parked in this slot, but I wouldn't hold my breath."

"The jacket was new; she'd never worn it before," Bernardo said.

"Lucky we had the purse," I said.

"They got in a car and were driven away by a man—that's the only thing that the few witnesses that saw them can agree on," Tyburn said. Apparently, while we'd been sniffing purses and jackets, he'd been gathering intelligence to share. It was a nice division of labor; too bad it didn't help us find a clue.

My phone buzzed in my pocket. I got it out and saw that it was Micah. "What do you have for me?"

He didn't chastise me, or say I love you; he just told me, which is one of the reasons we worked as a couple. "Two of the extended family work there. One of them is at the hospital with Christy and the baby. The other one, Cleo, was working today." He gave me her name and then texted me a picture of a smiling young woman with hair so white it couldn't be natural.

"She's got a few streaks of color in the white now, her cousin says; the funky hair color helps hide that she's got snake locks."

"Like the new baby," I said.

"Yes, but Cleo didn't get hers until she was three."

"Thanks, Micah."

"I hope it helps. I'm at the hospital with Bram."

"Where are R and R?" I asked.

"I sent them down to try to get an update on Denny."

"She's still unconscious as far as we know," I said.

"If I find out different, I'll text."

"Thanks," I said, and saw a woman with short white hair and streaks of color. "I think I see her. Love you." I hung up to his "I love you, too."

I tried to question Cleo Stavros, but she panicked at the sight of Nathaniel on his leash. We could hunt for missing persons with a leopard on a leash, but questioning witnesses with him seemed to go under the heading of coercion, or undue influence. Basically, if I wanted to talk to Cleo, Nathaniel had to go somewhere else.

Dalton volunteered to drive Nicky and Nathaniel back to the hotel. Nicky would order some rare steaks and pay-per-view and then wait for Nathaniel to change back to human form. I rubbed my face against Nathaniel's furred one, which made a few more of the witnesses and one of the cops scream; then I kissed Nicky good-bye, wrapping the faint scent of lion just below his skin around me. If I was going to be close to Olaf again, I wanted my lioness to remember we already had a lion in our lives.

Tyburn helped us find a spot to question Cleo alone with just him and the Four Horsemen. I learned how he was managing so many different overlapping jurisdictions out of our way so often. He'd been part of the county sheriff's office, but Kirke Key had offered him more money and a promotion. It still seemed like a political miracle, but so far, everyone seemed to know him and like him. Sometimes the good-ol'-boy network can work for you, instead of against you, even if you're not one of the boys.

61

CLEO'S WHITE HAIR was streaked with pale purple and what I thought at first was black, but in the sunlight, it was a blue so dark it was almost the shade of Jean-Claude's eyes. The hair was shorter than I thought it would be since it was trying to hide the big family secret, but it was thick and straight and almost touched her shoulders. Her eye makeup and lipstick were black and purple to match her hair. She also seemed to stay out of the sun, or she was using one of the best white bases I'd ever seen, because it looked invisible on her skin.

I tried to be friendly, the good cop—I mean, I had Edward and Olaf to play bad cop—but to every question I asked she had only one reply: "I told the other cops everything I know." She worded it slightly differently, but the meaning was the same.

"She's better at avoiding answering the questions than I am at asking them," I said when the four of us took a huddle to regroup. Tyburn was talking to Cleo, his deep voice rumbling in reassuring tones.

"Whatever she is hiding must be important or she would not be working this hard to hide it," Olaf said.

"Maybe we're overcomplicating this," Bernardo said.

We all looked at him. "What do you mean?" I asked.

"What if all she's hiding is the family secret?"

"Go on," Edward said.

"Maybe that's why she's good at keeping secrets; she's had to keep one all her life."

We all thought about it, and I finally said, "You really aren't just another pretty face, Bernardo."

"The compliment would mean more to me normally. Right now, I just don't want to see another girl butchered the way Bettina was."

"Let's lie," I said.

"What do you have in mind?" Edward asked.

"Tyburn will need to be in on it," I said.

"In on what?" he asked.

"We're the Four Horsemen, the scourge of bad little super-naturals everywhere."

"We don't have a warrant of execution for this crime," Olaf said.

"She doesn't know that."

Bernardo nodded. "Nice."

"Simple," Edward said.

"Frightening," Olaf said.

"Yes," I said.

"So we're all bad cops," Bernardo said.

"Exactly."

"I like it," he said.

"As do I," Olaf said.

"Let's do it," Edward said.

62

WE SAT CLEO Stavros down at one of the picnic bench seats and crowded her, though I made sure that Olaf and I were the ones closest to her. I knew she had at least one snake hidden in her hair somewhere. We had to consider the snake potentially venomous, just like you considered suspects armed until you patted them down.

"We don't want to hurt you, Cleo," I said.

She frowned at me, unsure for the first time. "What are you talking about?"

"We know that there's a supernatural element to Bettina Gonzales's murder and the disappearances of the other women."

"I don't know what you're talking about," she said.

"If you tell us what you know before the warrant arrives, then we won't use the warrant against you."

"What kind of warrant?"

I looked at the other men and we bounced our glances around like it was a game of catch. "You know who we are, right?"

"You know what we are," Bernardo said.

She frowned at us all. "You're marshals."

"We're marshals with the preternatural branch," Edward said.

She frowned harder, and then the first flicker of unease went through her eyes. "The preternatural branch. You kill monsters."

"We kill supernatural citizens that break the law," I said.

"We kill monsters that prey on humans," Olaf said.

"I know what the preternatural branch does," she said, and

she still sounded angry, but she also sounded nervous. We were making progress.

"Once the warrant of execution gets here, Cleo, we can't help you anymore. We will be duty bound to execute the order as written," I said.

"There are no monsters for you to kill here."

"Now, Cleo, you know that's not true."

"I don't know what you're talking about, but I want a lawyer."

"Normally, Ms. Stavros, that would be the end of this interview and we'd get you a lawyer," Tyburn said from farther back in the room, "but supernatural Americans that commit murder don't have the same rights as ordinary American citizens."

"I want a lawyer," she said.

Tyburn should have called it, because we didn't have a warrant of execution. We couldn't actually prove supernatural involvement in the first murder or the abductions yet, but we had two missing women and less than a day to find them alive. We'd all agreed to push enough boundaries that Cleo would never be able to be successfully tried for anything, but we didn't want her; we wanted what she knew.

"Talk to us before the judge signs off on the warrant and it gets delivered here, Cleo," I said.

"Once we have the warrant in hand, Ms. Stavros, we will have to consider you part of the conspiracy to murder Bettina Gonzales, and if anything happens to the other two women, that will be added to the charges," Edward said.

"The first murder is enough," Olaf said. "We can only kill her once."

"What are you talking about? You're not going to kill me," she said, and she was more angry than nervous. Had we overplayed our hand?

"I'd rather not kill a beautiful young woman like you, but if you're conspiring to kill human beings, I won't have a choice," Bernardo said, sounding sad.

"What are you talking about? You're all crazy. I want a lawyer, now."

"I'm sorry, Ms. Stavros," Tyburn said, and he looked sad about it, "but the judge has already signed the warrant; we're just waiting for it to be delivered to the marshals. The judge signing it means that anyone involved in the murders, human or inhuman, loses their constitutional rights. If you help us find the other two women before they come to harm, then the marshals have enough legal discretion to spare your life, but once the warrant is in hand, then it is literally a warrant of execution. Your life will be in the hands of the Four Horsemen."

"The Four Horsemen? What are you babbling about? This is ridiculous. I want my damn lawyer, and I want him now!" She stood up and Olaf put a hand on her shoulder and forced her to sit back down.

Her hair moved, not like wind blowing, but like something moved it. Olaf removed his hand from her shoulder; he'd seen it, too. "I guess we're not as infamous as we thought," Bernardo said.

"I am Death," Edward said, and there was not a hint of Ted Forrester anywhere in him. His eyes were cold as January skies.

"I am Plague," Olaf said, and he was so close that his leg touched her leg. It made her jump and scoot away from him.

"I'm Hunger," Bernardo said.

"I used to be called the Executioner, but I killed so many people, I got promoted. Now I'm War."

"Wait, I read about you on the Internet, but I haven't done anything to earn a death warrant."

"Warrant of execution," Edward said.

"Whatever you call it, I haven't killed anyone."

"You helped him kidnap the women today. If he hurts them, kills them, then you're just as guilty as he is for the murders," Edward said.

"I didn't help him do anything."

Olaf leaned over her, so close that his chest almost touched her hair. She looked up at him like he was some fairy-tale giant about to devour her. I couldn't see his expression, but from the look on her face it was scary as fuck.

"We don't have time for this," Bernardo said.

"No, we do not," Olaf said, and the next thing I knew he had grabbed the woman and slammed her down on top of one of the tables. The only reason she didn't scream was that he'd probably knocked the breath out of her. He pinned both her wrists above her head against the table with one big hand. She started to try to kick, but Bernardo caught her ankles and held them on the table.

She got her breath back enough to say, "You're crazy. Let me go!"

Olaf drew a knife longer than my forearm. He held it above her face so she could see herself reflected in the flat of it. "Oh God," she whispered, "you're police. Police don't do things like this."

I came up on one side of the table and Edward on the other. We leaned over her and I said, "We're not the police."

"We're executioners," Edward said.

Olaf caressed the flat of the blade down the side of her face. She screamed and a snake appeared in her hair, mouth wide, fangs bared. If Olaf had been human, she'd have bitten him, but he wasn't human. He moved in a blur of speed, too fast for the snake to bite him. It hissed at him, and she struggled like she knew she was stronger than a plain human. She'd counted on the snake to either kill one of us or startle some of us into letting go. Cleo was playing for the wrong audience. Edward and I were both pointing guns at her. I was looking at a point just above her eyes. Edward was aiming at her heart.

"Attack us again and I will put a bullet in your head," I said. My voice was soft, careful, because I was pointing a loaded gun at her forehead. What had started out as pretend had suddenly become real.

The serpent in her hair was joined by a second. They rose through white and striped hair like deadly hair accessories. Olaf said, "Stupid bitch, we don't have to wait for the warrant now; you tried to kill a U.S. Marshal."

"You scared me," she said.

"We have not begun to scare you," Olaf said, and with that he turned the blade in a silver-edged blur and cut off the head of the snake that had tried to bite him. Blood gushed out and the snake body flopped and sprayed blood over her face, over Olaf, over me and the whole fucking room. She was screaming bloody murder, but the last snake head hid back in her hair, trying to save itself.

When she calmed down enough to talk, she told us about her uncle Terry and how he'd overheard the early dinner plans for the bridal party and how he wanted two of them. "He has this voice, this voice, and people will do anything he wants. I saw him come up to them in the parking lot; he just talked to them and they smiled and they took his hands and they went with him."

"Where has he taken them?" Edward asked.

"I don't know."

Olaf cleaned the blood off his knife over the front of her shirt, across her breasts.

"I swear I don't know."

Olaf twirled the still bloody knife in his hand and said, "You still have one more snake in your hair."

"It hurts, but they'll grow back; we can't get rid of them."

"Do your fingers grow back?" he asked, and he stared down into her blood-covered face with his deep, dark eyes.

I wasn't sure if he was serious, but just in case he was, I said, "Not fingers again. I told you not to start with fingers."

He smiled up at me with her pinned and bloody under his hands. "What do you want me to cut off of her first, then, dearest?" He caressed the flat of his blade down the front of her body, slowly, sensuously.

Fine, I could play. "We talked about this, Holmes. Leave her all the parts that let her do her job and earn money."

"For you, Adler. She is a waitress, so she does need her fingers, but her uniform will cover scars on her torso."

He slipped the tip of the blade underneath her T-shirt so that the naked blade touched naked flesh. I said, "Hold very still, Cleo. If you move, you'll cut yourself on his blade and he'll enjoy that. Won't you, honey?"

"Very much, dearest, very much," he whispered, voice so deep it rumbled.

I saw his hand move minutely and blood blossomed through the cloth of her shirt. She screamed. He cut her again.

I pulled her shirt up so I could see how bad the cuts were. They were surprisingly shallow. I was relieved. She struggled and I watched her movements cause her to cut herself on the razor-sharp blade again.

"Stop moving, Cleo, and he won't cut you again."

Cleo didn't just stop moving; I think she held her breath while the big blade slid farther under her clothes. I came in close to her face, out of snake-striking range but close enough that she could move her eyes and see my face, as I said, "He's going to take the blade away from your skin and then you're going to tell us everything you know, because if you don't, he's going to make you bleed again, and you don't want him to do that again, do you, Cleo?"

She made a small, whimpering, "Hmm-mm."

"Move the knife away, dear, so she can talk to us."

"Only for you, dearest," he said, and he slid the blade slowly out from under her shirt. When she could see the blade and know it wasn't touching her she started to shake, and then to cry, but she told us everything she knew and confessed that she had been willing to sacrifice two more girls the same way Bettina had been sacrificed, because it was supposed to lift the family curse. Cleo even knew where the girls were being held and readied for sacrifice. She also knew it was an accelerated time schedule. They were going to kill them at sundown tonight, something about an astrological event that would make it work better than it had twenty years ago. Cleo even knew about the victims back when Tyburn was a new cop.

"I've told you everything I know. Please, please, don't hurt me anymore."

"You're begging us not to hurt you, when you helped send two other women about your own age to certain death. He guts them, Cleo. He butchers them like a hog or a deer," I said.

"Please," she said.

Bernardo said, "Did Bettina Gonzales say please? Did Bettina beg for mercy? Did she, Cleo? *Did she?* Did she beg for her life, Cleo? *Did she?*" Bernardo let go of her legs and just walked away from her. I think he didn't trust what he'd do if he didn't put some distance between himself and Cleo Stavros.

There was an ambulance waiting outside for Cleo, though once we explained exactly all the parts of her that were bleeding, the EMTs were a touch less eager to put her in their vehicle. I think they were still under the impression that the snakes were pets and might crawl off of her and hide somewhere. If they'd been that easy to get rid of, Bettina Gonzales wouldn't be dead.

Tyburn came to us and took us to one side. "Her uncle Terry is Terry Rankin."

"We figured that," I said.

"I know her grandfather's place. I use to go fishing with her uncles. Hell, I dated her mother before she married."

"Did you know what they were?" Edward asked.

"Murderers, no."

"Did you know about the family curse?" I asked.

He took in a deep breath, let it out, and said, "I knew about some of it, but I thought it was like lycanthropy, just something they couldn't help."

"Can you give us the lay of the land where they're keeping the women?" Edward asked.

"Hell, I can draw you a map, as long as you don't want it too pretty."

"We don't need pretty. We need accurate."

"I can give you that."

"Find a man to keep with Cleo so that she doesn't phone home and warn everyone," Edward said.

Tyburn nodded and went off to find someone to babysit our murdering Medusa, and something to draw us a rough map so that we could plan an assault on an isolated camp of venomous snake lycanthropes. It sounded like a bad B movie.

"I wonder if other body parts grow back like the serpents do," Olaf said.

"If you get a chance to find out, let me know," Bernardo said, and there was a look on his face that I'd never seen before. For the first time I thought not only would Bernardo not stop Olaf from torturing Rankin and his family of killers, but he might help him do it.

I wasn't sure how I felt about that; hell, I wasn't sure how I felt about the little game Olaf and I had played with Cleo.

"You okay?" Edward asked me.

"I'm not sure."

"Did you call him Holmes and he called you Adler?"

I nodded.

"Since when did you and Otto have pet names for each other?"

"It was his idea."

"And you're okay with being his dearest?"

"No, not really."

Edward leaned in even closer and whispered, "Eventually

he's going to ask you to do something you won't do and then you're going to have to kill him."

"I know, but that's not right now. Right now we have women that are going to die at sundown if we don't save them, and Otto is going to help us save them."

"Yeah," Edward said, "he will. Now, let's go coordinate with the other local PD and see how many men and women we have to work with and what kind of equipment they have. I wonder if anyone has a flamethrower I could borrow. You still can't fly with them."

On one hand, fire kills everything; on the other hand, Edward had burned a house down around us once using a flamethrower inside a vampire's lair. I wasn't sure if I hoped he found one, or if I would feel safer if he didn't.

63

EDWARD FOUND A flamethrower to borrow, and an hour later we were standing on a narrow side road. It was mostly white gravel and seashells, not like the shells had washed up on the road, but like they'd been scooped from somewhere else to be used to help fill out the gravel. I'd lived landlocked all my life, so the thought that seashells were that common seemed weird. The vegetation that lined the road was just as alien as the thought that we were walking on seashells. We had almost every flavor of police that existed in the Florida Keys and could be mobilized in an hour's time. It wasn't much more than what we'd had at the restaurant where the girls had gone missing. Tyburn, as the person who knew the place best, had helped plan where each group would enter the overgrown grounds of the hunting camp. There was a house and several outbuildings. He was pretty sure that the girls would be held in the house, so he was going to take us to the house. Other groups had different buildings as their targets to clear, but the four of us, plus Tyburn, got the house.

Once we got into the thick, tropical underbrush, I was glad that I had the shotgun tight to my vest and could snug the AR closer to my body without getting tangled in all of it.

I kept waiting to hear gunfire from one of the other groups, but the five of us moved in a well of silence except for the constant buzz of insects that made me glad we'd used bug spray; only Olaf had turned it down. He said it would ruin his sense of smell and he'd want that in the woods.

We came to the edge of the underbrush and the big clearing that was the main camp. There was only one other group visible; it was at the far end of the clearing, moving toward what looked like a big smokehouse. We nodded at one another, but that was it; they had their objective and we had ours. We put Tyburn at the point of our group, and the rest of us took a two-by-two on either side of him, with the ones at the back also covering our asses. We moved in that awkward bent-knee group walk that I'd learned serving warrants with SWAT. It helped you have a steadier platform from which to shoot, and we all knew how to do it, even Tyburn, though he complained that the last time he'd done it his knees hadn't minded so much.

The house was an original Florida Shaker house, with a tin roof and a small front porch, all of it covered in weathered boards that had aged gray, but it seemed in good repair, which puzzled me. I associated that level of discoloration on houses with decay, but it seemed snug. The windows were open, white lace curtains fluttering in a breeze that came up from the sea. The breeze was what let me know we were close to the ocean, even though the trees hid it from view. The trees also kept most of the wind trapped, but the house and the outbuildings weren't made to withstand a storm by the sea; they had to be built farther back in the shelter of the trees. Tyburn had told us that modern building materials and engineering had enabled houses to sit right on the ocean, but before that, one good storm and your house was wiped out, and you with it.

The door was propped open like an invitation or a trap, or maybe they just didn't have air-conditioning and were trying to catch a breeze. Olaf and Bernardo took the outside to the right, Edward and I took the left, and Tyburn stayed put in hard cover by the covered porch. We'd do the outside of the house and see if we could see into any of the rooms, then meet back at the front—or that was the plan, but like all plans, it didn't survive the battleground.

Terry Rankin called out, "Captain Tyburn, I see you out there, and I can feel Anita Blake's energy. I've got one of the women with me. You come inside and she'll be safer for a little while longer."

I hadn't planned on his having drunk so deep of my metaphysics that he could sense me outside the house; fuck. "If the two of you don't come in and visit, I'll hurt her."

"Terry, it doesn't have to be this way."

"Yes, it does, Captain, and if you and Anita come inside, I'll answer all your questions. I'll even answer some questions you don't know to ask yet."

Tyburn craned up enough to see inside and say, "One of the girls is in there."

"Fuck," I said. I motioned at Edward and the others to do their perimeter check and I'd go inside. Edward didn't like it, but he gave the slightest of nods and vanished around the side of the house like water. The other two were already out of sight on the other side. Tyburn went in first, and I admit I used him as a human shield, just in case. I had my AR snug against my shoulder and ready to shoot anything hostile. If Rankin tried to mind-fuck me, I'd consider it a hostile act and kill him. He hadn't told us to lay down our weapons, so I was using mine until told otherwise.

Of course, as if he'd read my mind, he said, "You can keep your weapons, but if you come through the door with them pointed at me, I'll shoot Stephanie here."

I should have known it was too good to be true. I lowered my AR from my shoulder to my side, though I knew I could shoot from the hip if I had to and still hit most of what I aimed at.

Rankin slumped on the old-fashioned couch with a small end table next to his arm. There was a handgun on the table flanked by two iced teas. Stephanie was curled on the couch beside Rankin, her head on his shoulder and one arm across his stomach, around his waist. Her long legs were drawn up on the empty side of the couch. Her shoes were placed neatly beside it. She looked half asleep and hadn't reacted to our entering the room. She seemed drugged but otherwise un-harmed. The drinks had been there long enough to sweat all over the coasters that were protecting the dark wood of the table. Both the couch and the table looked like antiques—a little worse for wear, but still nice. If the gun hadn't been sit-ting in plain sight, it would have looked like a nice way to spend a lazy afternoon.

"I've got War, but where are Death, Hunger, and Plague? They have to be nearby; they wouldn't let you fly solo. I bet you even have your other bodyguards out here somewhere." He put his head to one side and seemed to be thinking hard. "I don't feel Nathaniel or Micah close by. You didn't bring them. Interesting."

Since he didn't ask about the other horsemen a second time I ignored the question. I did a quick search of what parts of the house I could see from the living room, but I mainly had to keep my attention on the siren and soon-to-be ex-cop on the couch. If there was something dangerous in another room, it would have to wait until Rankin was neutralized.

"How did you know where to find us?"

"Once I realized that you might be involved I remembered your family's hunting camp. It's isolated and you've got room to hold prisoners and do ritualistic murder."

"Some of us think our family is cursed and if we kill the right amount of people in just the right way, it'll be over."

Tyburn managed to look blank-faced, good cop face, but I think I failed to keep a straight face, because Rankin laughed. Stephanie shifted in her sleep, snuggling against him. He petted her hair, soothing her back to sleep. His voice was low as he said, "Your face, Blake. It does sound ridiculous, but we really are cursed; you know that. You saw my cousin Andy in all his glory. If that's not a curse, I don't know what you'd call it."

"I don't know what you're talking about, Terry," Tyburn said. "Andy needs to get a handle on his drinking."

"Their baby, it's a girl."

"That's wonderful," Tyburn said.

"She was born with a snake lock. Someone in the hospital snapped a picture of the baby. It's already on the Internet: 'Medusa Baby Born in Florida Hospital.'"

"Micah told me about the baby. I'm sorry that everyone is so upset about it. How are Christy and Andy doing?" I asked.

"You don't really care about them, about my family."

"Micah Callahan, my fiancé, has spent a lot of time here, trying to help your family. He cares," I said.

"Perhaps Callahan does care."

He glanced down at the sleeping woman, rubbing his hand against her shoulder. "I didn't hurt Bettina Gonzales, and I sure as hell didn't decide to dump her where other police would find her like that. I did help destroy evidence after the fact, though."

"But you never touched the first victim?" Tyburn asked.

"I swear to you that I didn't know what had happened until she was already dead. Then they called me in to help clean up the mess."

"Who's 'they'?" Tyburn asked.

Rankin shook his head, still leaning against the back of the couch so that it looked like he was rubbing his head against the worn upholstery. "Some of the family arrived early for the ceremony, but he got out and he sort of ate all the other cursed ones in the family but me. He still thinks he can cure us, but what he's become, there's no cure for that and there's no saving what he did to the others. You'll see soon enough."

"We can't let you kill these women, Terry."

"I don't think you're going to let me do anything. I think we're just going to do it."

"I know you're a siren, and a powerful psychic, Terry," I said.

"Not psychic, Anita, magic. I don't know where the snakes came from, but we used to be sirens and sometimes one of us will get thrown back and have the voice again, but that's not my only gift. I know what people want, their deepest desire. Take Stephanie here and her friend." He stroked her hair again. "She wants to feel safe the way her father made her feel before he divorced her mother. Valerie wants to sow some wild oats before she settles down with her boring boyfriend. She let us tie her up with a smile on her face, because bondage and sex with multiple men are on her bucket list. She'll have a great time until he starts to cut her up, and then even my magic can't keep her from screaming."

"Tell us where she is, Terry," Tyburn said.

"Anita's partners will find her."

"Is Stephanie drugged?"

"No."

"You're not a vampire, and that's the only other thing I know that can wipe memories and make people do things they wouldn't normally do," I said.

"My family is cursed, goes all the way back to ancient Greece. One of my ancestors pissed off a god—at least that's the story—and they were forced to turn into monsters. We were lucky, because we could be human part of the time, but the monster part craved killing and eating fresh meat."

"Doesn't sound that different from being a shapeshifter," I said.

"You think that now; wait until you see it."

"Like you said, Terry, I've already seen your cousin."

"Oh, it gets much more interesting than that."

"Let's go get Valerie and make sure she's safe," Tyburn said.

"Sorry, Captain, but I'm going to finally tell the whole truth, and then you'll have to rescue her from him."

"What is the truth, Terry?" he asked.

"My mother wanted to make sure her children wouldn't be cursed, so she went to Europe to find a supernatural father that she thought would help end the curse. Do you know what a love-talker is, Anita?"

"It's a solitary type of Fey that seduces women and children with music and charm and then drowns them."

"I love that you know that."

"It's my job to know."

"I suppose it is, but it's a rare Fey."

"It's also considered Unseelie court, which means they can't immigrate to the United States, and even with your mother being a U.S. citizen, if they'd known what your father was, they'd have made her leave the country."

"And that's why I could never tell anyone what I was, or what dear old Dad was."

"I've felt your power inside my own head, and I'm seeing what you're doing to Stephanie now; that's not right, and sure as hell not legal."

"No, it isn't; it goes under the magical malfeasance laws. I'd be lucky to be deported; I'd probably just be executed under the supernatural endangerment acts."

"Maybe," I said. "Honestly, Fey are harder to fit into our laws here, which is one of the reasons that we don't let them in the country much."

He petted the brunette's long hair where it lay across his lap. "It is evil, what I can do. Tell Angela I'm sorry for everything I did to her. I couldn't risk her using her abilities to figure out what I was, what we all are. I didn't want to kill her, so this was the compromise with my relatives."

"Using mind control on her is rape by magical means," Tyburn said.

"I know, I know. I don't have any excuse for it. I was saving her life, but there had to be other ways I could have done that. But I have the ability to see into the deepest desires of people. It's so easy to manipulate them if you can offer them their secret wants. And, God, I am so sorry about what happened with Forrester's son and the other bridesmaid."

"What are you talking about?" I asked.

"I just meant to distract you all, but I pushed at the woman's deepest, darkest desires and didn't understand that she has a . . . crush on Peter Parnell."

"What? Dixie has known him from birth; she babysat him."

"Yes, but something in the boy's background came to light about him liking rough sex is what I got from her memory, and that's her dark, secret desire, to have a man throw her over his shoulder and have his rough way with her. How was I to know that the kid would actually throw her over his shoulder? But I did not mean to almost get him killed. I just didn't understand how deep her emotions were running."

"Even if you know their secrets, you're not supposed to use that against them," I said.

"You think your fiancés are monsters, but you don't know what monster means yet, Anita. I looked online on the website for the club and the Coalition, and both of them are still handsome in whatever form they take. Nathaniel is still beautiful as a big cat. He's always been beautiful, even as a child."

It took me a second to realize what he'd said. "That's the second time you've hinted about Nathaniel. How do you know what he looked like as a child?"

He looked past me to Tyburn. "This is part of what I don't want anyone to know. Love-talkers drown women and children; we seduce both; it's in my genes."

"Are you saying . . ." Tyburn couldn't finish the sentence.

"I swear to you that I have never touched a child inappropriately. I had convinced myself that I found a safe way to get the urge out by watching videos."

"God, Terry." Tyburn sounded ill. I didn't feel much better.

"You know how images and video on the Internet never really go away; they just float out there forever?"

"Is that a rhetorical question?" I asked.

"Maybe, but I found a few older videos that were my favorites. I thought they were my dirty little secret and I could just pretend it wasn't real. Then suddenly I'm meeting my favorite fantasy in person, except he's all grown-up. Those eyes—you can't change those eyes. I thought they must have colored his eyes for the film, because no one has violet-colored eyes, not in real life."

I was suddenly cold. The room was still over ninety degrees, and the breeze wasn't helping that much, but I still felt cold.

"They didn't use his real name, or even the name he uses onstage at the club, so I didn't connect your Nathaniel with that little boy. It was when he showed up with his hair cut short that I realized it was the same . . . person. I had convinced myself that those videos didn't hurt anybody. I think I thought of them as movies, made up, not real children like my son. I love him and I would never hurt him. I don't look at him with lust in my heart, thank God. It's like a normal father having a daughter. You don't lust after your own kids. I've never touched a child in real life, never. I would never."

"But you watched the videos," I said, and my voice didn't sound like me.

He nodded. "I could lie to myself that no one got hurt, that somehow it was special effects or a trick, until I met your fiancé face-to-face. I thought it was just a coincidence until I ran his name and got his background; then I realized it was him all grown-up, and for the first time I wanted something I couldn't have. I wanted him to be evil. I wanted him to be a monster that preyed on children and women and whored them out, abused them, the way he'd been abused, but he wasn't like that. He isn't like that. He's remarkable for his background, so healthy, so happy, so real."

"That's why you tried to frame him for the crimes."

"I needed a fall guy, and what better way to get rid of my pathological crush than by making him the bad guy. I'm sorry for that, sorry that I was one of the adults that watched his films and helped exploit him. *Exploit*, such a clean word, a nice word for what it actually means."

"God, Terry, you've sat through the lectures about child pornography and what happens to those children. You've helped us find pedophiles and put them on trial, and the whole time you were one of them," Tyburn said.

"I am not one of them. I have never, ever touched a child in real life."

"Did you pay for the films you watched?" I asked.

He glanced at me and then away, staring down at the woman in his arms. "Yes, the films are still popular enough that they cost."

"Then you know that the person you paid money to used it to make more films, to abuse more children. You know that, right? You're a cop; you know how it works."

"I do," he said and reached for his gun.

"Don't do it," I said.

"Terry, don't do this," Tyburn said.

His hand was just resting on it; he hadn't even picked it up. My AR was back at my shoulder and aimed at him. "Ease down, Marshal," Tyburn said.

"Captain, either she shoots me or I eat my gun. Remember all those old stories about dragons and monsters terrorizing the countryside back in medieval times and earlier, Anita?"

"Yeah," I said, voice soft and careful so that I could keep my aim on his face.

"When one of us becomes our monster half and stays there, we go after our victim of choice. Most of them go after young women, the legend of the maiden sacrifice, but it's like we chase what we're attracted to."

"Vampires kill their nearest and dearest first, sometimes," I said. I raised my gun barrel toward the ceiling, because he still wanted to talk and I couldn't keep a rifle pointed at him steady forever. I didn't point it at the floor, because I didn't want to cross the woman in his lap with the gun barrel.

"If I change into my monster and don't come back to myself, I'll hunt children, Captain. I can't let that happen."

"Come with us, Terry. We'll take you in, lock you up; you won't hurt anyone."

"You still don't understand what's happening—but you do, don't you, Anita?"

I didn't actually, not all of it, but I asked what I wanted to know, while I watched the center of his body, waiting for him to tense, which would let me know he was moving his gun into play. "Why do your people kill women every few decades?" I asked.

"The reason that he wants to kill these two is that the auguries were good when he gutted the first girl."

"Auguries, what are you talking about?" Tyburn asked.

"It was an old method of divination to read the entrails of a sacrifice. He thinks he has the gift of prophecy with reading animals' death throes and then what their internal organs look like after death. Like I said, he's crazy. But some of the others believe that he can read what the gods want, so he needed another woman that was tied to Bettina. He overheard Bernardo talking to Denny and thought a shared lover would be enough of a connection, but I knew we couldn't take one of the people from a U.S. Marshal's wedding party. I knew Forrester wouldn't rest until he found her, so I persuaded them that she was too high risk a target. They let me put her somewhere she'd be found, but on the condition that I use my powers to get two suitable victims to replace Denny. I did it, but you know they tried this twenty years ago and it didn't work. He's convinced that it wasn't the right connection between victims, and there's some astrological event tonight that will make it perfect. Helping clean up after a murder is one thing, but I can't live with myself bringing them like lambs to slaughter. I can't live knowing that just watching the videos of your fiancé hurt him and hurt every child who's used like that. I can't pretend anymore. My son is almost the same age that your Nathaniel was in those first films. I think what I would do to anyone who touched him like that, that stole his childhood away like that, and I thought I'd kill them. I'd shoot them. I'd look them in the eyes and shoot them dead."

His chest moved, his hand closing on the gun but not raising it much. It didn't matter; he had the gun in his hand. I aimed at his face. I'd normally go for a center-mass shot first, but with the woman draped across him I couldn't risk it. It would have to be a head shot.

"I don't have a warrant of execution for you."

"Captain Tyburn will testify that I gave you no choice."

"You won't shoot us, Terry."

I wondered where Edward and the other two horsemen were. Were they listening in to the confession? I pushed it out of my mind and just concentrated on the man in front of me. Yeah, he wanted suicide by cop, but that didn't mean he wouldn't shoot us to make us shoot back.

"When I die, my magic dies with me; Stephanie and Valerie will both know that they aren't safe. I'm sorry for all the harm I've caused. The rest of us aren't bulletproof, or bladeproof, but if you don't set fire to the wounds, they heal. I know that if anyone can kill him, it's the horsemen. Don't let him get to the water, or he'll swim away and you'll lose him." He raised his gun toward us.

I let out my last breath and the world closed down to that quiet center. There was no doubt, no fear, no anxiety, no questions of right and wrong, just his face at the end of my gun barrel, his eyes so big and dark. I'd hit just above them. He could have tried to use his gaze on me, but he didn't. He didn't want to win. He wanted to lose. He brought his gun up and started moving his hand to aim it at me, but he knew he'd never make it. He didn't want to make it.

I pulled the trigger and the gun jumped in my hand. His head rocked back against the couch, spraying blood all over the upholstery. Stephanie woke screaming, falling off the couch, looking at the blood, at his face. Tyburn and I both went toward the couch, Tyburn to help our victim up off the floor and get her out of there, me to look Rankin in the eyes one more time and pull the trigger again with my barrel almost touching his skin. His brains blew out the back of his skull to add thicker things to the blood that was already on the couch and wall. Once the brains come out, even vampires and shapeshifters are dead. I'd had to kill him, but the thought that he'd sat in the dark in private and watched Nathaniel as a little boy being hurt, that he was a cop and he'd tried to use that authority to pin crimes on Nathaniel, that it hadn't been enough to be part of his abuse, he'd tried to take his life, our life, away . . . If I could have killed him more than once, I would have. But as I'd told Peter once, if they're dead, that's as good as vengeance gets. Once their brains are plastered all over the wall, you're done.

The only thing that saved my hearing was the high-tech earplugs. I heard yelling, and some kind of animal sound like a bull roaring, or maybe a lion, or something I had no word for, but it was loud enough to reach through my ringing ears.

We had more monsters to kill. I left the body on the couch to finish bleeding out and ran for the door and the sounds of fighting, but before I got outside I heard wood splintering inside the house, a woman who wasn't Stephanie screaming, and that bellowing sound again, except this time it was behind me inside the house. I turned with my rifle to my shoulder, putting a wall to my back, and looked down the hallway to find Edward at the end of it with a broken back door behind him, and Bernardo with the redhead from the pool in his arms. She was screaming one long, loud scream after another, but we'd found Valerie Miller. Olaf and Edward were both looking into the room that I thought they'd gotten her out of. I thought the door was closed and then realized that it wasn't a door unless it was painted black. No, it wasn't a door. There was something filling the doorway. I had a moment of Edward, Olaf, and all of us seeing one another, and then the blackness filling the doorway moved into the light of the hallway and I knew why Valerie Miller wouldn't stop screaming.

64

IT WAS A mass of black tentacles that had to be more than ten feet tall and wide enough to fill most of the hallway, so that it seemed to flow toward both Edward and me at the same time. The tentacles had snake heads, or maybe the entire mass of the thing was made up of hundreds of individual snakes. There were faces, or things that looked like faces, here and there, but I wasn't sure if there was a human face in the writhing mass, or if my mind just so desperately needed something human in it that I was seeing things.

I think I heard Edward yell at Bernardo to get the girl out. I yelled something similar to Captain Tyburn about Stephanie and knew that he got her out, even as I took an angle to shoot into the mass of snakes that wouldn't overpenetrate and hit Edward or Olaf on the other side of the house. The thing screamed and seemed undecided whether it wanted Edward and Olaf or me more. Then one of the faces in the mass opened its eyes and looked at me. For one horrible second I recognized Andy Stavros, the drunken husband and new father. Another head higher up opened its eyes and screamed at me. Was it one of the men from the pictures that Micah had shown me? Was this thing made up of more than one of the family? What the fuck was going on?

Andy Stavros's head screamed at me again, and this time I shot it, instead of the mass of snakes. The head bled from the hole in its forehead just like Rankin had. I yelled, "Shoot the heads!" For all I knew, Edward and Olaf were already doing it, but it didn't hurt to try to share intel. The monster seemed to be retreating toward the back door. I didn't know where the others were in relation to it, so I didn't want to shoot into the mass while it was moving that way. I heard Edward yell, "Fire in the hole!"

Shit! I had time to start backpedaling for the front door before I heard the whoosh of fire and heard the monster's mouths scream for real. You didn't have to understand anything to know that those were pain sounds. Fire kills everything, even Lovecraftian horrors like the thing that was now trying to crawl toward me. I ran out the front door as much to get away from the fire as to flee from the monster. The old house went up fast: Either the wood was ripe for burning or Edward had used an accelerant. Either way, the house started to collapse with the monster still inside it, or I thought that was what was happening, and then the black tentacles burst out of the burning house. I had a second to guard my face from flying fire and debris, and then I was firing up into a mix of snakes, tentacles, human heads like some kind of trophy stuck into the nest, and things my mind couldn't see, didn't want to remember. I was shooting as I moved backward, and didn't watch where I was going. One minute I was shooting fine and the next I was flat on my back with a huge tree branch tangling my feet.

I didn't scream as the moving nest of burning snakes reached out toward me. I just kept firing, trying to find its heart or brain, or something. I kept firing as it blotted out the sunlight, and I thought, *I wonder if I'll die from venom, fire, or just be crushed.* I was weirdly calm as a hand yanked me to my feet and Bernardo was rushing us both backward out of reach of the snapping snake mouths. We got the big tree that the limb had fallen from between us and the beast, and then we put our shoulders together, snugged our AR-15s against our shoulders, and started shooting the burning beast.

Edward and Olaf joined us. Olaf put his shoulder beside mine and he joined Bernardo and me shooting into the creature. Edward stayed on the outside and used the flamethrower again. I felt the backwash of heat from it, and the next thing we knew, the big tree that had slowed it down and helped give Bernardo time to find a safe shooting distance started to burn. I had to step wide to Edward's right to make sure that my bullets weren't in danger of hitting him. Bernardo was safe on his side. The three of us kept shooting into the center mass of it, as Edward sent another sheet of flame whooshing toward it. We had to back up from the tree as it started raining burning debris down on us like the house had. Fuck flamethrowers.

The creature turned away from us and started trying to move past Bernardo, since he was on the end of our defense and farthest away from the flamethrower. Behind me were trees and plants that would burn if it made the tree line, but beyond that was the Gulf of Mexico, and I remembered what Rankin had said, that it could swim away and heal.

I aimed at one of the heads nestled tight to the center of the body and pulled the trigger. The flames hid most of the damage from me, but the beast staggered. Something about the heads clustered in the middle hurt it more. I yelled, "Shoot the heads in the center!" I wasn't sure Olaf or Bernardo would hear me over the whooshing of flames, gunfire, and the beast's screams, but then one of the heads seemed to partially explode. Bernardo had heard me. I emptied my AR into the creature and yelled, "Reloading!"

Olaf and Bernardo took a step forward and fired faster into the creature, while I popped out the empty magazine, got one of the extras to slip in place, and did one last hit to make sure it seated right. And then I moved back up with them and we fired shoulder to shoulder again, or as close as we could get with the height difference.

Olaf yelled, "Reloading!" He stepped back to get his new magazine and I stepped forward to fire into the heads. The smell of burning flesh and hair burned my throat and eyes. The wind had changed, and the smoke was blowing toward us now. Crap!

Bernardo yelled, "Reloading!" and we covered for him.

Edward kept hitting it with fire, and it was hurt, but it didn't die. I knew he was out of fuel to burn it with when he stepped up on the other side of Olaf with his AR to his shoulder and started shooting with us. There was movement behind us, and it was the other police; reinforcements had arrived. They cursed and yelled about what the fuck was that, but they put their shoulders to ours and started shooting it. They'd have done the same thing if it had been a bunch of bank robbers shooting at us.

Two mags later and I was out of ammo for the AR. I

switched to the shotgun. It rocked a little more than the AR, and pieces of monster fell away where it hit.

Olaf yelled, "Empty!" and had to step back from the line, because he'd actually run through all his ammo in all his guns. Edward, Bernardo, and I closed the gap where he'd been standing and fired into the still-burning, smoking, screaming creature. The cops had formed a line on either side of us like some sort of impromptu firing squad.

I pulled the trigger and came up empty. I felt for more ammo, but there wasn't any more for the Mossberg. I dropped it and pulled the Browning, knowing I didn't have the stopping power I needed, not for this monster. I used it anyway, until I was empty again. "I'm out!" I yelled and stepped back from the line; Edward was the last of us standing with the police when the monster stumbled and then slowly collapsed to the ground. It was still burning and they were still shooting into it, but it had stopped bellowing.

Edward hesitated, lowering his rifle. The rest of the police kept shooting until they ran out of ammo, too. We shot it long after it had stopped moving, or screaming. Normally, I might have encouraged people to conserve their ammo, but I didn't know how to be certain that it was well and truly dead. It had three heads and seemed mostly made of tentacles. I had no idea where its heart might be, or if those were all really heads, or if there was only one real head and the others were sort of decoys, like the tip of a lizard's tail that looks like a worm to predators so they won't attack the lizard's head. The creature smoldering on the ground by the still-burning shed was so alien that we couldn't even decide when it died, or if it had.

I don't think I was the only one flashing back to all those old monster movies from my childhood where the big monster was never really dead; it only seemed dead until the next movie. The fire department got there, alerted by the smoke, but they were just as puzzled by what to do as we were. The only thing we all agreed on was that we weren't going to try to save it.

Epilogue

THE LOCAL AUTHORITIES have the monster carcass, and several museums and zoos have sent experts down to look at it. So far no one knows what it is, but they also can't prove that it was ever human.

Edward using his crime-busting superpowers to save one of Donna's oldest and dearest friends made her take another look at her views about his job. She decided that being jealous of his work and especially his closeness with me was just another way of repackaging her old jealousy issue about our "affair." She owned it, she apologized to all of us, and when Denny got out of the hospital with a clean bill of health, the wedding went forward, with plans for serious couples therapy. Donna and Edward both want to make this work badly enough to work at it, which is more than I can say for most of the couples I know.

The hotel and all the rest of the wedding business agreed to Nathaniel's request that they delay everything until Denny and Peter could be with us. There were no extra charges and they felt badly that a relative had caused so much harm.

I was standing beside Edward when he looked down that flower-petal-strewn beach at his bride-to-be. His face showed everything that you could ever want to see on your groom's face. The love, the faith, the hope—all of it was there in Edward, the most cynical person I'd ever met. In Donna he'd found all the naïve, impossible things that he'd wanted when he was younger, before he became Edward. For that look on his face, it was all worth it. I didn't have to understand it. I didn't have to be in love with Donna. I just had to stand there and see that my best friend adored her above all other women on the fucking planet, and that was good enough for me. The second-best face at the altar was Peter's. He damn near glowed with happiness as he watched his mother walk up the aisle and take Edward's arm. I don't know if Donna would have kicked Dixie out of the wedding or not, because Dixie took the choice out of her hands. She went home early, too ashamed of what she'd done to Peter to face everyone. I'd like to think that she would be getting therapy, too, but I'm not holding my breath.

Since I didn't have a warrant of execution for Rankin, the shooting had to be reviewed, but Tyburn backed me up and it was eventually declared a clean shoot. He's pretty sure that the "us" Rankin kept talking about was his extended family, but we have no proof. Rankin chose to die rather than betray them, and the ones who showed up to slaughter the women were absorbed into the monster we killed. The murderers are all dead. Cleo might have seen jail, or even been executed for real, but we'd violated her civil rights so badly, it gave her a get-out-of-jail-free card.

Nathaniel, Micah, and I talked about what Rankin told me. Nathaniel took it better than we did. Rankin wasn't the first person to see the films that his abuser made of him as a child and then seek him out. He'd never told either of us that. Strangely, he had told Jean-Claude, as owner of Guilty Pleasures.

Nathaniel admitted that what Rankin offered him that kept getting through his shields was the illusion that he would be Micah for him. That this version of Micah would want him completely and utterly, in every way physically. Micah wants to try to meet more of Nathaniel's physical needs, but he doesn't think he'll ever be able to meet them all. There are men in our poly group who can and will, but if Micah and Nathaniel are going to be the ones marrying each other, then is it okay that they don't meet every need? We're talking about couples therapy for us, too.

Olaf went back home, wherever that is, and I answered his question. I preferred Adler to Irene. He preferred Holmes to Sherlock. I suggested Moriarty for him, but he said it didn't match the naming convention. He was right, so there you go. We had pet names for each other. I don't have pet names for most of the people I'm living with, so having them with Olaf seemed even weirder. I need to find a lion to call before my lioness forces the choice, and it cannot be Olaf, damn it.

Peter is healing more than human-fast. He comes up inconclusive for lycanthropy, but inconclusive isn't testing as human normal either. He may still be able to join the armed forces because he doesn't change form; he still doesn't test positive for a contagious disease yet. It's still made Peter even more eager to join the other half of the family business, because world-class assassin and monster slayer will be all that's left of things he wanted to be when he grew up if he does go from inconclusive to testing positive. I'd promised years ago that I would go with Edward on Peter's first hunt, and I will go, but I'm still wishing a different life for the boy I met all those years ago. Something gentler and kinder than hunting monsters.

Melanie saw the Internet story about Christy and Andy's baby and the monster that we killed. She talked to Nathaniel when we got home, and he brought it to us. Melanie's original name was Echidna, the mother of monsters. She'd been afraid I'd use the knowledge to get a warrant of execution and kill her. I guess I wasn't the only one still disturbed by our first meeting, years ago. She thinks the family in Florida are her descendants and that maybe, just maybe, she might have enough power left to help them lift the curse, or maybe get them closer to her own transformation. Something that they could control and that perhaps could be directed, so that they could choose how the change comes out. She used her own venom to change human men into pseudo-lamia mates for her once, so she wants to talk to the family about trying to modify their shape-changing. There are no promises, but there is hope, and that was what Micah really wanted for Christy and her new daughter and the rest of their family. Maybe it wasn't a happily-ever-after ending yet, especially for Christy, who had lost her husband, but sometimes when you fight monsters and are trying hard not to become one of them, hopefully-ever-after is a good place to start.